CONQUEST OF THE REALMS

TIMOTHY HEATH

Original version copyright © 2013 by Timothy Heath
This version Copyright © 2025 by Timothy Heath
All rights reserved.

ISBN: 978-0-9897966-0-6
E-book ISBN: 978-0-9897966-1-3

Conquest of the Realms is the first book in "The Conquest" series.

For Xavier, Chance, and Serenity

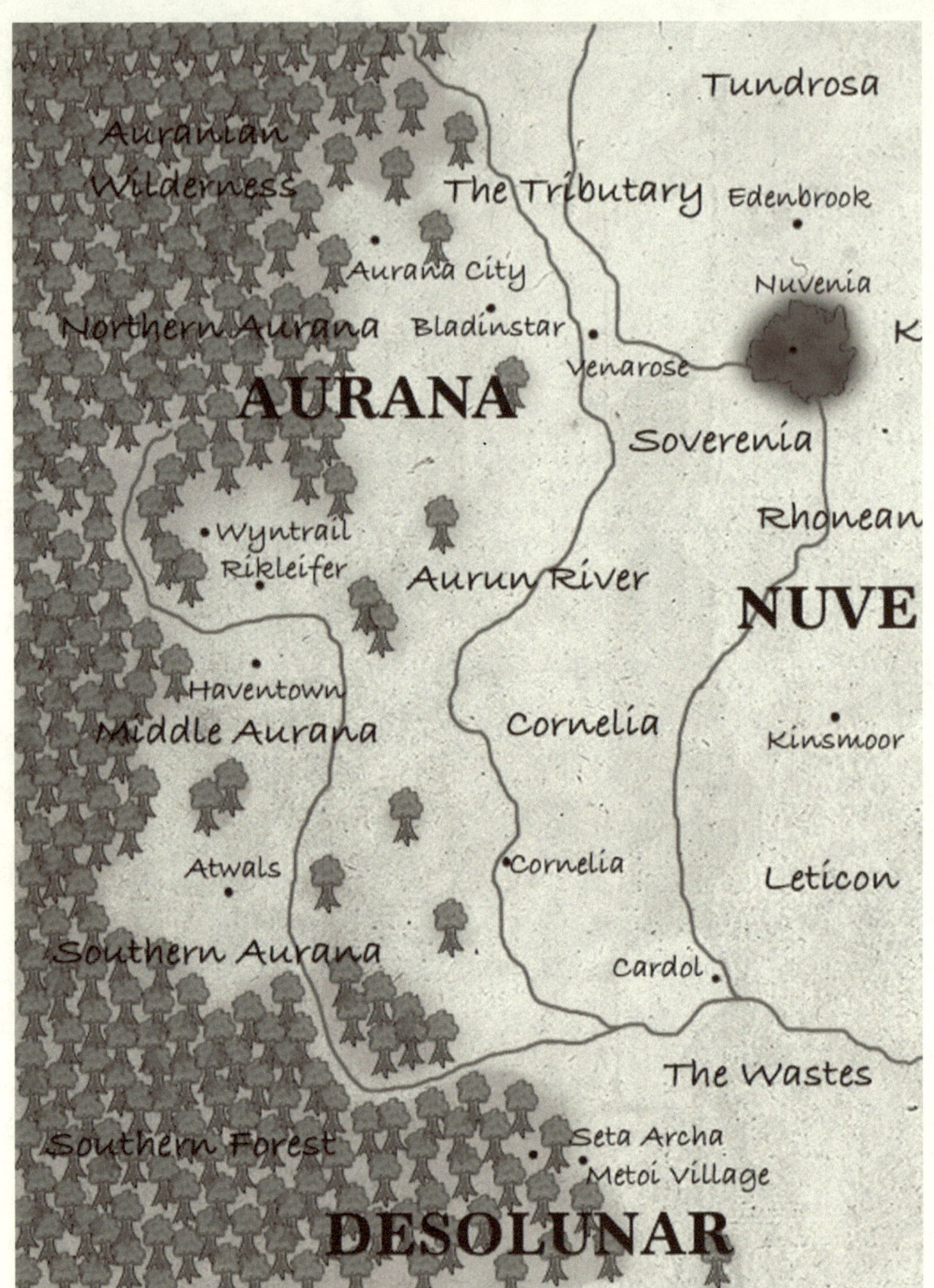
Tundrosa
Auranian
Wilderness
The Tributary
Edenbrook
Aurana City
Nuvenia
Northern Aurana
Bladinstar
Venarose
AURANA
Soverenia
Rhonean
Wyntrail
Rikleifer
Aurun River
NUVE
Haventown
Middle Aurana
Cornelia
Kinsmoor
Atwals
Cornelia
Leticon
Southern Aurana
Cardol
The Wastes
Southern Forest
Seta Archa
Metoi Village
DESOLUNAR

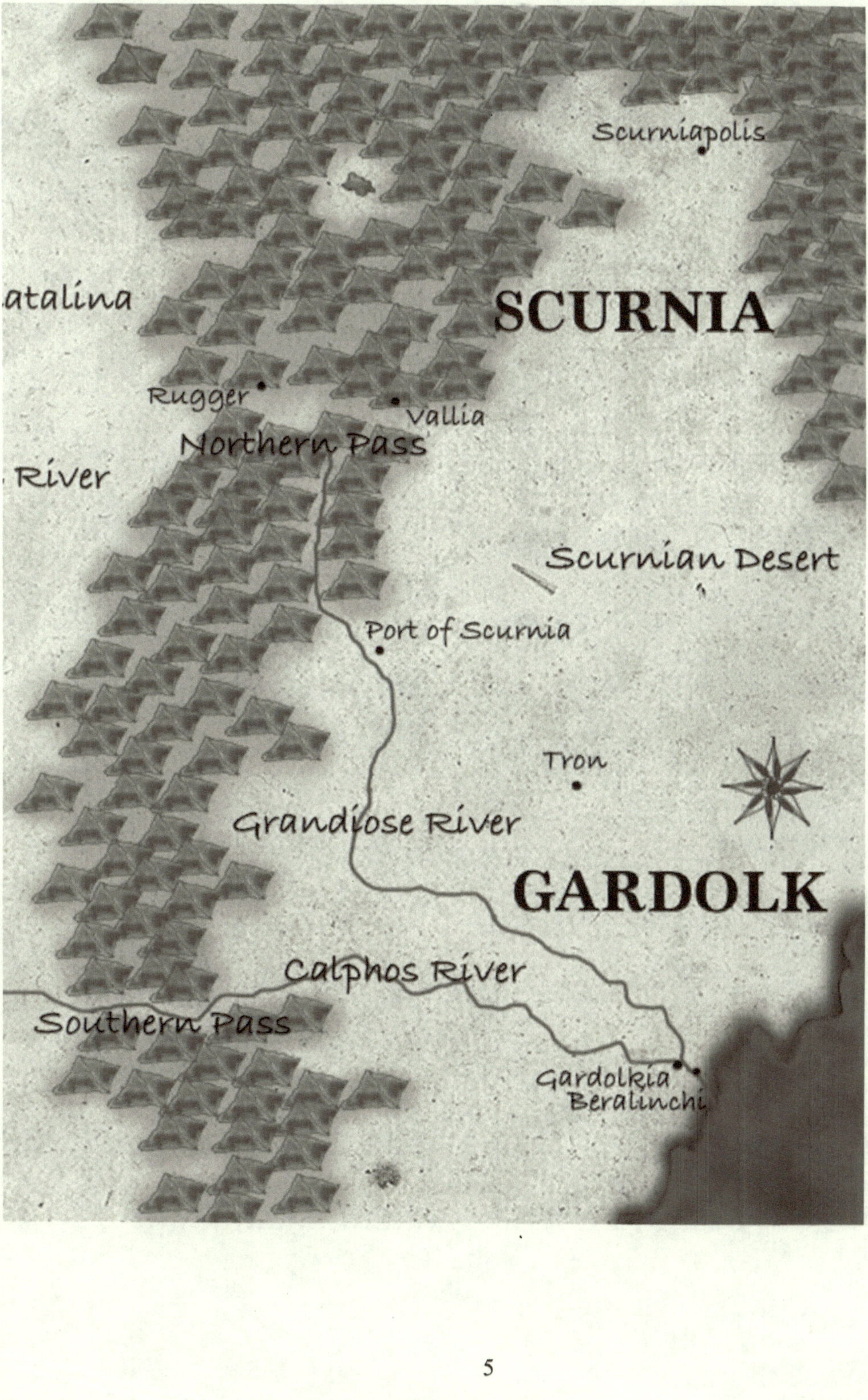

Scurniapolis

atalina

SCURNIA

Rugger

Vallia

Northern Pass

River

Scurnian Desert

Port of Scurnia

Tron

Grandiose River

GARDOLK

Calphos River

Southern Pass

Gardolkia

Beralinchi

Chapters

Prologue

A lone pathway through the trees at the border of the kingdoms of Aurana and Desolunar was about to be the site of chaos.

For twenty years, the kingdom of Desolunar had risen and quickly expanded. Its military force was gigantic, and its troops were as well trained as they come. It had never lost a battle in its few short years, conquering territory at its whim.

And it was hellbent on destroying everyone in its way.

Along the current border, which was quite a distance north from where it had originally been, the troops of Aurana had been rushing to hold the line. To the route between Aurana and Desolunar, they had sent War Commander "Ironman" Eukert to command its defense. A distinguished warrior and a veteran of the "savage war"—more formally known as the Alliance-Daritel War—the commander was an excellent strategist and leader.

Oddly enough, Eukert was not given any specific strategies to use in battle, and was also denied extra troops to help him hold the border. This had frustrated Eukert, since it was the decision of the king of Aurana, and not a military decision, to refuse the reinforcements. Eukert did not understand why he was being declined this, but he could not argue with it.

Improvisation was one of Eukert's skills, however, and he had managed to set up an ambush with his inferior number of troops. Using the trees as cover, he placed ambush units on both sides of the pathway. Knowing that the Desolunar troops would have to funnel in through the pathway, at only a few men across, Eukert hoped to take advantage of the thinning of enemy troops and attack them from the flank, using the trees as camouflage. Wearing green uniforms in the springtime, they would be well difficult to see.

Quietly, he and his men waited in silence. Next to him was his second-in-command.

"Has everything been put into place?" asked Eukert.

“Indeed,” nodded the second-in-command. “All is in place. The troops on both sides are ready to deploy as soon as the signal is given. No one is remaining on the pathway, and every troop is in position.”

Eukert nodded. “Excellent,” he said. Then he paused for a moment, as he and his troops waited for the Desolunar forces to arrive. He let out a sigh, reached down and pushed on the crossguard of his sword, and took a few deep breaths.

“Something on your mind, War Commander?” asked the second-in-command.

There was another pause. “Negative, Commander Tetel,” Eukert finally responded. He sighed again and said, “Simply that it’s hard to imagine that twenty years after one huge war, another one has consumed our land.”

Commander Tetel chuckled, in an awkward sort of way. “Still thinking of old times, I presume?”

“Precisely,” said Eukert. “It was a different time, maybe a better one. Of course, something like that is hard to say when one talks about a time of war.” The war commander began to reminisce, pausing to take a breath. “In that war, the kingdoms were led by sensible individuals, and there was a much greater sense of camaraderie. Nowadays, though, none of that is in place.”

Shaking his head, the much younger Commander Tetel responded, “Sure seems that way. I can only say I’ve heard the stories you’ve experienced, Eukert. You and your retired friend John Bryant, Commander Sayo, and the legendary Vincent the Pure One. Now those are real war stories.”

Eukert nodded in the affirmative. As he stood looking out upon the dark wilderness to the south, a scout from down the road approached him. He appeared to be out of breath and desperate to deliver a message. As soon as the scout was within a few steps of him, Eukert ordered to the scout, “State your name and your reason for being here, soldier.”

The scout stopped when he was within an arm’s length of Eukert, stopped to catch his breath, and responded, “I come with news for you, Commander.” He paused to try and catch more breath, before continuing. "The Desolunar forces are advancing now, with a very strong force."

Accepting the news with a silent and unwavering countenance, Eukert had expected this move would happen, and he knew that his troops were well placed for it. "Very well, then," he said, as he nodded to the scout and instructed him to fall into rank in the unit. Then, Eukert raised his voice. "Units to the ready!" he exclaimed.

The sound of swords unsheathing, of archers arming their bows, of men with all different types of weapons taking hold of them for battle, rang through the air. Within a moment, all was silent yet again, as the troops were setting back into position, trying to be as quiet as possible. All were on the ground, taking advantage of the natural cover of the coniferous forest to hide.

Silently, Eukert listened to every sound he could hear. In the distance were the sounds of marching footsteps and war drums.

Showtime.

As Eukert and his troops listened closer, the footsteps became very loud. He pulled his sword up front as he saw the black uniforms of Desolunar marching closer and closer.

Still, he and his men had to be patient, or they would risk ruining the ambush. And yet, the sounds of marching men were becoming louder and louder.

Carefully, Eukert looked toward the sounds of footsteps. What he saw was exactly what he expected: troops. Hundreds of men, marching in rank and file, were approaching them. All of them were wearing black uniforms of military jackets and pants, with the leaders wearing gold trim against the black. All of them already had their weapons drawn. Then, Eukert spotted the leader of the opposing forces: the only man on horseback in the formation. He sat patiently, his eyes wide open and shifting between the trees in the forest.

Though they may not have necessarily known about the ambush, Eukert suspected they knew his unit was present and they were hunting for it. His Auranian troops, clothed in the green military uniforms of Aurana, had some camouflage against the forest background in which they were hiding, but Eukert knew it was not like being invisible. Desolunar soldiers were taught to be aggressive, and the second he and his men were spotted, they would be attacked. Now was the time for a decision. Should Eukert have his men attack now, or should he wait and hope the Desolunar troops do not notice his men so he can use the double-sided ambush?

While pondering this, Eukert managed to get a good look at the leader. He was someone Eukert recognized: a former Auranian commander by the name of Sayo, who was a friend turned traitor. Now General Sayo of the Desolunar forces, the general said very little when it came to battle. He was a man of few words, except for the orders that meant the most. Negotiation with him was impossible. Trying to discuss a compromise would be futile. General Sayo often operated under the principle of not bending until he was broken.

Suddenly, Eukert saw General Sayo raise his hand, and all of his men behind him stopped, as did he and his horse. Silence filled the air. Nervously, Eukert awaited his opponent's move. What happened next would make his decision for him.

For a second, Eukert observed Sayo nod. Then, surprisingly, a Desolunar soldier stepped forward, a couple of steps ahead of General Sayo. He began to recite, in an announcing fashion, "Hear me, soldiers of Aurana!"

General Sayo knew the Auranian troops were there! He had seen through the ambush!

The announcer continued, "By order of Lord Demonicus, ruler of Desolunar, you are to be terminated immediately, and your border defense is to be removed. How will you respond?"

That was a taunt. It was very blatant to Eukert.

"Flank to the south!" commanded Eukert, essentially giving away his own position. By this point, however, with the Desolunar forces knowing where his troops were already, it was pointless to maintain the ambush positions that would be vulnerable now. His men were up and formed their lines. Then, Eukert turned and glared at Sayo. Their eyes met, and locked on for a brief moment. Since Sayo had joined Desolunar, there was bad blood between Eukert and Sayo.

There was a moment of pause. Eukert would not respond, and Sayo would say nothing.

After this moment, Sayo lowered his right arm, and said three words. "Cut them down."

Hearing this, Eukert commanded to his men, "Charge!"

Hundreds of Auranian soldiers, upon hearing their commander's order, started charging toward the Desolunar forces. Eukert joined them, and led the running charge himself.

As the Auranian forces lunged at the army of Desolunar, chaos erupted. The battle instantly started with soldiers from both sides fighting viciously, whether for victory or just their own survival. Eukert himself lunged into battle alongside his forces, managing to defeat several soldiers on his own within the first couple of minutes. For an older man such as himself, especially as a commander to fight alongside his forces was rare, yet there was no man more experienced and better at it than War Commander Eukert.

Left, right, left, left, duck. Eukert wielded a sword with power and grace. For such an older man as he was, reaching into his fifties, Eukert was quick and agile.

Sword swings coming from all sides. Eukert was ducking and weaving to avoid all of them.

After about a minute, Eukert's eyes fixed on Sayo. So much fury, so much anger ran through his soul, when he though of his treasonous friend. Conquering his homeland was not a crime that Eukert took lightly.

Sayo's eyes locked on Eukert's as well. Now was the time. Instantly, Eukert started rushing toward Sayo, sword drawn. The pathway to Sayo was almost clear as the Auranian forces were pushing hard forward. With all the speed he had left in his aging legs, Eukert ran as fast as he could toward Sayo.

Justice was in his head. Justice against an individual and a nation. Justice had to be done. No one needed to tell Eukert what was wrong and what was right.

General Sayo, however, made the oddest move in response. Instead of turning to face Eukert, he turned away.

Eukert was puzzled at this move. It caused him to lower his defenses for just a brief second.

Enough time for Sayo's horse to kick Eukert square in the head.

The shot of force threw Eukert back. Still caught in a daze,

Eukert started stumbling backwards, knowing he was injured and he had to get out of the way.

As Eukert stumbled back, all he could hear was Sayo yelling, "Lord Demonicus has spoken!"

Continuously, Eukert kept stumbling backwards, ending up off the road a short distance into the forest. There, unable to keep himself steady any longer, he fell to the ground. As much as he tried, he could not regain the balance to stand. Trying to figure out what happened, Eukert stroked his left hand over where he had been kicked. There was blood gushing in a massive amount from the wound. It was serious blunt force trauma, and Eukert was horrified to see the blood in his hand.

Then, unable to regain himself, Eukert fell unconscious.

Several minutes later, all was quiet on the road, as the battle ended almost as soon as it had begun. A great number of Auranian troops lay dead on the road, compared to only a few Desolunar troops. The surviving Auranians were fleeing back into Aurana. All of the men who were still there were dead, yet Desolunar had also pulled back after the battle. It was simply a show of force.

Though Eukert was able to regain his consciousness, he still could not stand. He felt very weak, almost unable to move entirely. As he lay face down in the dirt a short distance from the road, he was certain that the wound he had suffered to his head would eventually be fatal. He was unable to stand up or crawl anywhere due to exhaustion and the injury. Eukert was barely able to see, but the little bit that he saw indicated that the result he had feared had indeed become what had happened.

Everything was coming to an end for Eukert. As he realized this, his mind drifted to the other sword on his belt. It was a legendary sword, belonging to a close personal friend of Eukert: Vincent Stryker, also known as Vincent the Pure One. Eukert knew he was no great hero like his friend had been, but after acquiring the sword, he kept the sword with him at all times to remind him of his friend and the great victory they had achieved twenty years before. It had been a war to defend against conquest, and the brilliance of his friend had led to victory.

Now, fate had led the world and Eukert into an even deadlier situation. It was one that was taking innocent lives day after day. It was one that was against an unbeatable foe. It was one that seemed almost destined to be devastating to the great nations of the world, a conquest beyond any told in history. Yet today, Desolunar had won. And history seemed bound to repeat itself in a new form.

Using the last bits of energy he had as he lay face-down on the ground, Eukert pulled this sword and yanked it quickly out of its scabbard, almost throwing it. It hurt badly to hold the sword because of a magical effect, one that Eukert did not fully understand, and he gripped it as long as he could. As he looked upon it with his head tilted up, Eukert said, with the last effort he had, "Please, dear gods, I beg of you, let this sword find its true master once again. We need you, Vincent."

As he finished his sentence, Eukert fell unconscious again.

Chapter 1

A Day in the Life

Somewhere in between the extremes of phantasmal space lie the realms of existence, where the seven magical energies collide and form what might be known as a world. To the mortal, it is simply "the world", but to the immortal, it is referred to as "the mortal realm".

On one of these planes of existence is this realm. It is home to the mortal beings, most being of a civilized nature. Mortals are known to be able to manipulate some amount of magic with enough study, but oftentimes steel is their strongest weapon. The mortal realm is a place where light and darkness are in balance, and elemental magic is the dominant controller of the realm. Many had turned to worshipping the "nameless ones", the terms they had for the images in their head of immortals. Ultimately, however, what they really saw was their own creation and not a reality.

Though the political landscape had changed much over the course of history, through eras of nomads, of tribes and feudalistic small kingdoms, five large kingdoms remained to this day. These superstates were Aurana to the northwest, Nuve in the north-central, Scurnia in the northeast, Gardolk in the southeast, and Desolunar in the south; the last being in existence for less than twenty years.

Prior to the rising of Desolunar, the walled city-state of Seta Archa stood independent of any other nation, as it had done through the feudal centuries and into the superstate kingdom years. Then began an uprising by a nomadic tribe known as the Daritel, from an area known as The Wastes, east of the city-state. Driven by unperceived forces that made this tribe strong and power-thirsty, the Daritel sacked Seta Archa, took control of the city, and used its people to build an army to conquer the north.

In response, Aurana, Nuve, Scurnia formed the Triple Alliance as an attempt to defend from this new threat. However, the alliance began to fail almost immediately as the Daritel began to invade and seize victory after victory, threatening to conquer both Aurana and Nuve, while Scurnia awaited its fate behind the protection of the Peaked Mountains and dealt with a territory dispute with its neighbor, Gardolk. Battle after battle took place in Aurana and Nuve, and the Daritel continued to make advance after advance against the alliance. To some, it seemed like an inhuman power gave the Daritel such strength that every tactic seemed to be outdone by raw power rather than strategy. Every battle was bloody as the Daritel cared not for the rules of war; they fought viciously, dirty, and violently. There were no answers as the alliance quickly exhausted their forces trying to defend their homelands. It would only be a matter of time until the defensive lines broke and the alliance would have no troops left to reinforce it, and the Daritel would simply overrun the alliance.

All of that changed thanks to a Auranian-born, Scurnian general named Vincent Stryker. Bringing with him an iconic sword that glowed blue when he wielded it, Stryker pooled his troops with some from Aurana, leaving only a skeleton crew behind at the war fronts and using the forces he had left to punch through and execute a strike on Seta Archa, isolated from their supplies and behind enemy lines. Although it was a desperate attack, it worked to great success. The Daritel were soundly caught unaware and defeated, causing the whole of their efforts to collapse. The fall of Seta Archa was the end of the Alliance-Daritel War.

After the battle, Vincent Stryker disappeared without a trace as he retreated from public life, and eventually, disappeared entirely. The Triple Alliance disbanded, as each nation had its own internal and external conflicts that needed to be resolved. All three nations, with the lack of interest in maintaining their alliance, abandoned Seta Archa, leaving a power vacuum with the removal of the Daritel. Many of the leaders of the alliance nations simply assumed that the Seta Archans would form a new government without assistance, and everything would return to how it had been.

They were wrong. In the absence of leadership, a cult by the name of the Enlighteners from the Shadows seized control. Their powerful wizards and sorcerers, a rarity in the modern world, made easy work of killing anyone who would oppose them. The cultist Demonicus, whom the cult claimed to be the "chosen one", became the leader, and he proclaimed his new nation the "Kingdom of Desolunar", although he never claimed himself to be a king and ran the country more as a dictator. He also kept his Enlighteners close to him, never introducing them as the force behind his newfound power.

Within only a handful of years, war was breaking out again, tearing Aurana and Nuve apart. Without Vincent Stryker and the ties that bound the Triple Alliance together, it seemed, nothing could stop Desolunar's endless rampage. Nuve's capital city of Cardol fell rapidly at the start of hostilities, as did the major Auranian city of Atwals. Over the years, Desolunar absorbed The Wastes to the east and was absorbing large pieces of both Aurana and Nuve to the north, immediately threatening whole provinces of those kingdoms and potentially the entire kingdoms within a couple of years.

Still, those who were fortunate enough to live in areas still in peace were making the best of their lives. From the city of Rikleifer, Aurana, about a three-day walk from the current front lines between Aurana and Desolunar, a young man by the name of Kevin Trent watched the sky above. He was lying on the grass in front of his home, staring upward. It was a perfect spring day, he thought. Nothing could go wrong on this day. A day in the beautiful city of Rikleifer—translated meaning "The City of Dreams" according to the ancient language—was like heaven. Though Kevin had had some rough days as of late, the warm weather today seemed to indicate that today would be a good day.

His house was on a dirt street in the outskirts of Rikleifer, a plain little home with only a couple of rooms fashioned from wood, cheap stone, and clay. It was a rather common setting across the land to see a town or city with a great deal of homes made from such materials, although usually in different amounts of each depending on where one traveled. Such was relatively common of the lower classes, which constituted the majority of the population across the world.

There was a window without glass in Kevin's bedroom that allowed him to see out into the center of Rikleifer and view the castle in the center. It was a minor castle designed to hold the local city council, be the home of the Duke of Rikleifer—a member of the royal family of Aurana—and aid in defense of the city. However, as Rikleifer had not been under attack for at least three centuries, the last aspect was unimportant.

The city of Rikleifer was designed in a series of concentric circles. Streets either looped through the city in a circle or split the city in half across the diameter, except for the roundabout. The castle was in the center of the city, which had the roundabout, the innermost circle, surrounding it. Like many cities, Rikleifer was very close-knit; there was not much space between houses, and the city did not have areas of fewer houses before reaching the city limit. Everyone lived inside the city, as close as they could to one another. This was usually for protection, a concept from the original founders of Aurana hundreds of years ago, and the idea stayed with the people through many generations.

Kevin's home in Rikleifer was situated in the kingdom of Aurana. Among the five kingdoms of the world, Aurana had the leanest laws, the most freedoms and least hassles allotted to the people, yet also the most legal documentation and procedure. In terms of geography, Aurana was a land of mostly forests and meadows, a setting full of natural resources. A large bit of farming supported the people, as did forest products and trade. Mining and other industries were mostly few and far between. Of the known world, Aurana was to the northwest and central-west, with most of the territory further west and north of the country being unexplored due to the expansiveness of the large Auranian Wilderness, of which an end had not been discovered.

As for Kevin himself, he was not an athlete, but rather average for someone of his age. He was sixteen years old, trying hard to live on his own and make something of himself. Legally an adult at that age by all standards across all of the kingdoms, Kevin was now on his own to figure out what he would do with his life.

What that was, Kevin was not sure yet. Still, he did know some things about what he was and was not interested in doing. He was a lover of fantasy stories and plays, and daydreamed that he might someday get to travel the world. Though he was not an athlete, he enjoyed playing games with his friends, as well as taking his classes at the Rikleifer Academy for Youth, his school which met from fall to spring and was provided by the government of Aurana free of charge. As was normal for Kevin, he wore a red shirt and brown pants, in a fairly normal style for someone in his class of living. His clothes were made of durable, cheap materials, and the colors seemed to complement his short brown hair and hazel eyes just a little bit.

One of Kevin's favorite activities at the school was swordplay, for which he took a basic skills class. But, that was just a hobby. As someone who was not athletic and had heard of deadly war raging in the south of his country, Kevin had no desire to join Aurana's army. More than likely, Kevin knew, his best shot at success in life would be to complete his education and find a trade to adopt. He had no idea what he really wanted to do with his life at the moment, and he would soon need to make that decision.

Kevin looked to his side and saw Arthur Falchor, his lifelong best friend, walking down the dirt street. Arthur's short blond hair and blue eyes were something that his drunken mother took pride in, but to Arthur, that was all that she saw as good in him. Arthur wore a blue shirt and black pants all of the time, his only actual full set of clothing. Compared to Kevin, Arthur was a bit more passive, and was willing to let the world take him to where he would go. Arthur was the best friend to Kevin that he could be, albeit while retaining his sarcastic, different perspective on life.

Walking along the street and catching Kevin's attention, he stopped in front of Kevin and said, "Kevin, are you daydreaming again?"

Kevin, without turning his head, replied, "I guess I am, Arthur." He gave a long sigh. Though it was a perfect day, and fantastic for relaxing, his mind had wandered to the thought of his future shortly before Arthur had walked up. He wanted so badly to leave Rikleifer and become a traveler. He wanted to have adventures, somewhat like the characters in the books he used to read.

Arthur shrugged and said, "You dream too much. I know what you're dreaming about."

Kevin thought briefly about what Arthur said, still without turning his head. He and Arthur were only sixteen years old, and despite the fact that they were legally adults, neither of them were headed anywhere soon.

Noticing Kevin's lack of a response for a moment, Arthur then said in a slightly more irate tone while raising his arms, "You *do* dream too much. I can't believe you just lost it in another daydream."

Kevin finally turned his head, stood up, and replied in his normal voice, "Not exactly. I was actually thinking about what you said. I guess you're right. What could happen to us?"

Arthur let his arms fall and replied, "Exactly my point. I mean, look at us, Kevin. Some guys we are. You and I have a lot in common in that the world's left us so far in the dust that we have to build our own futures, and let me tell you, daydreaming won't get you anywhere."

"I get the message," responded Kevin as he rolled his eyes. He disliked it when Arthur made him feel bad about dreaming.

Neither Kevin nor Arthur were particularly wealthy, and their families were not, either. In fact, both of them were missing parents. Kevin had never known his father or who his father was. Until about three years ago, he was raised by his mother, a scribe by the name of Lavinia Trent. However, nowadays he lived alone, as Lavinia had passed away three years before by a mysterious illness that had also made Kevin very sick as well. For the moment, Kevin was living off of a small amount of savings left behind by his mother, as well as some emergency compensation from Aurana that amounted to a couple of pieces of copper a month, barely enough to stay fed. Now at sixteen, Kevin did not have much silver or copper left to keep himself sustained. Pretty soon, he would have to find out how to acquire more, and he hoped not to have to leave school just yet.

Likewise, Arthur had never known his father, but he did have a living mother by the name of Rita Falchor. An alcoholic and abusive by nature, Arthur's mother cared very little about how things worked in Arthur's life, to the point where Arthur questioned at times how, or even if, Rita Falchor could be his mother. This left Arthur in a situation that led him to Kevin's house all of the time, since Kevin lived just down the street from Arthur and the two had been friends for the longest time. In many ways, they were each other's only support.

“Well, I’m glad to see you do,” said Arthur, with a little bit of point in his voice. Then, he relaxed it. “I thought we were headed to the castle today to listen to the Duke of Rikleifer speak about the war. It’s about all there is to do today, anyway.”

“We still are, as far as I know,” replied Kevin, slightly confused.

“Not as long as you keep daydreaming,” responded Arthur, chuckling.

Kevin had to laugh at himself for that one. “All right, all right. We’re going, then.” He then gestured to Arthur, pointing down the nearby diameter road. As Kevin’s house was at the corner of one of the circles and the diameter road due west of the castle, it was a straight path down to where the duke would be speaking.

Taking the gesture, Arthur started down the road, and Kevin caught up with him quickly. The castle was just a couple of minutes away. “So, Kevin,” began Arthur, trying to stir up some conversation, “did you hear about the dangerball game last night?” He was referring to a popular sport played in Aurana, and to the Rikleifer Rangers, the city’s professional team.

“No, I didn’t hear about it at all,” responded Kevin. “Did we win?”

Arthur nodded. “We sure did,” he said. “The Rangers are the best team, after all. It was the last night of their series against Aurana City, though, so there won’t be any more games for a while.”

“Yeah,” nodded Kevin. “Kind of a shame that there’s a lot of war south of here, or else there might be more games and more teams.”

“And more to talk about,” added Arthur. He shrugged, “Oh well, that’s the world we live in, I suppose.”

Kevin shrugged back. “I don’t know about that,” he said. “Surely we live in better times than that. They can’t be that bad.” Starting to ramble about his thoughts, Kevin continued, “We live in a world of honor and pride for our homelands, don’t we?”

Arthur just shook his head. “You’re way too much of a dreamer, Kevin. But that’s okay, and that’s you: always the optimist and always in some reality other than the actual one.”

“I’m surprised I haven’t scared you off with it yet,” Kevin retorted.

Laughing, Arthur joked, "There's no way you're getting rid of me that easily. Not like how you got rid of Rachel, at least."

Instead of getting a good-spirited response, Kevin merely turned his head away.

Knowing exactly why, Arthur continued, "Too much? Sorry, Kevin, I didn't know that it still bothered you so badly."

Kevin tried to shake it off. "Don't worry about it, Arthur. I know it shouldn't get to me so much. She wanted to be friends, at least."

"Ah, it happens to the best of us, Kevin," said Arthur. "Girls like Rachel Reinhart come to all of us as friends, but they're not actually interested in us. Most of the girls our age, and even those just a little older like Rachel, are all into these richer guys or the good-looking ones. It's just the way it is."

"You really take a negative view on it, don't you, Arthur?" interrupted Kevin.

Arthur chuckled. "Always you and being a hopeless romantic, again?" he said.

"I wouldn't say that," shrugged Kevin. "I just don't think it's that general. It's pretty wrong to say all girls are like that."

Seemingly unbothered by Kevin's comment, Arthur replied, "Well, maybe not all, or even most. But in Rachel's case, I think you dodged a crossbow bolt. I think it'd be rough actually being with someone who's such a cynic."

Exhaling a small sigh, Kevin put his face in the palm of his hand. "You know, I don't think that word means what you think it means." He paused for a second.

Immediately, Arthur stopped and turned to look directly at Kevin. "Oh, whatever. You don't have to get all noble and defend her. That's not your job."

At this, Kevin merely gestured and let the subject go. Arthur Falchor was always a very sarcastic, joking person. It was just the way he was, and Kevin had grown to accept the fact that Arthur was going to sound like a jerk sometimes, but he never meant to insult. Plus, the less Kevin thought about Rachel and not forming a relationship with her, the better. But, those mental escapes were not to be. At the next crossing, he noticed someone. So did Arthur.

It was the aforementioned Rachel Reinhart.

Rachel was two years older than Kevin, but the two were good friends despite Kevin's unspoken past crush. They had met in the Academy. Rachel was a few inches shorter than Kevin, with long, flowing dirty blonde hair and blue eyes, wearing a dark green and brown dress made of sturdy fabrics for traveling and a shiny locket she kept around her neck. She had few friends, as she had only moved to Rikleifer about a year and a half before, from Aurana City. Still living with her parents at the moment, Rachel was very adept at writing. She was brilliant at writing short stories and was currently searching for inspiration for a full-length novel. Another skill Rachel was acquiring was using a longbow; encouraged by her family to learn some form of self-defense with the war going on. She happened to be carrying it and her quiver of arrows at this moment.

"Oh, hey Rachel!" Kevin called out, getting Rachel's attention.

Rachel turned and saw Kevin and Arthur, as she was tucking her locket into her dress. "Oh, hey guys," she said. "Heading to hear the Duke speak?"

"We sure are," smiled Kevin. "Not like there's much to do around here today."

"Speak for yourself," Rachel smirked. "I'm getting ready to go on a trip."

Kevin's interest was piqued. "Oh really? Anywhere exciting?"

"Probably to hell," mumbled Arthur.

Typical Arthur, Kevin thought to himself.

Rachel picked up on this, too. "Maybe you could say that," she laughed, brushing Arthur off. "Actually, my book club is headed on a trip to Cardol. It'll be a couple of weeks there and a couple of weeks back, but we're going to get to spend a week checking out books at the Library of Cardol, still the largest and one of the oldest libraries in the world."

Immediately, Kevin and Arthur were both surprised. "You really are going to hell," commented Arthur.

"Are you sure it's safe?" asked Kevin. "I mean, we've all heard about what Cardol is like since Desolunar took it over. Plus, it's pretty close to the front."

There was a second's pause, after which Rachel said, "I'm not worried about it. There's no one in Cardol, and the book club head has a safe route planned for us."

Kevin took a step closer to Rachel. "I'm still going to be worried about you," he said.

"Relax, Kevin, I'll be all right," Rachel answered. "I wouldn't be doing it if I didn't think it was safe." She paused for a second. "And you know me, I'm a realist."

Arthur rolled his eyes. "You mean a cynic," he smirked.

Suddenly, Rachel's countenance dropped to being slightly upset. "I'm not a cynic," she said, seriously. To both Kevin and Arthur, it was clear that Arthur had gotten the better of Rachel in this exchange. It was a long-running gag, dating back to their days in the Rikleifer Academy, that Rachel would occasionally refer to herself as a realist and Arthur would call her a cynic.

Despite his concerns, Kevin decided to be a good friend and give his support to Rachel. "I trust your decision," he said with sincerity. "I hope you have a blast down there at the library."

"Yeah, me too," added Arthur. He did not sound quite as sincere as Kevin. Kevin picked up that Arthur had reservations about Rachel's safety that made it difficult for him to be supportive, but he was clearly not being sarcastic in this moment.

With that, Rachel had to part ways with Kevin and Arthur. She still had plenty to do to get ready for this trip. The abandoned city of Cardol would be a couple of weeks away, in the kingdom of Nuve and across potentially dangerous territory to the southeast. The whole idea just seemed like a bad one to the boys, but it was hard for Kevin, ever the curious himself, to deny what an opportunity such a trip was. Cardol's library was legendary, like a source of all of the knowledge and stories of the world. Especially for someone like Rachel, who loved to write, who would want to pass up the opportunity?

After Rachel walked away, Arthur rolled his eyes. "Hope she likes getting caught in the war," he said, starting to walk. He then paused; Kevin was about to scowl at him, but then Arthur continued, "I do hope she manages to stay safe."

Trying to brush off his thoughts, Kevin said, "I'm sure she'll be just fine. It sounds a little bit like she's going on a quest." His eyes glossed over a bit. "In that way, she's getting to do something exciting."

Arthur laughed, seeing Kevin was getting dreamy again. "What is it with you and questing? Daydreaming again?"

"Well, maybe so," chuckled Kevin.

As the boys walked, they approached the city center where the castle stood. A crowd was forming up around the entrance on the west side, and several people were standing on the garrison above the west gate. Among these people was Edmund Cleary, Duke of Rikleifer. A relative of the royal family of Aurana, it was the Duke of Rikleifer's right to control his city. The Duke was very devoted to his work, and made sure to lead his city well. Given Rikleifer's level of success as a city, many thought of him as a good leader.

Kevin and Arthur managed to get to the back of the crowd just as Edmund Cleary started speaking. Today itself was not a particularly special day, but in a couple of days it would be, as the crown prince of Aurana would be turning eighteen years old. It was a bit of optimism considering the war happening in the south, of which the Duke had information to share of a recent operation on the front lines.

For Kevin and Arthur, the speech was merely an excuse to do something on another slow day in Rikleifer.

Minutes passed as the duke read his speech to his people, detailing that although the Auranians fought with valor, they had to fall back and the front line would be moving north again. Even so, the Duke reassured his people of Rikleifer's safety.

Amongst the crowd, however, Kevin and Arthur seemed more interested in the people they were seeing around them. As Rikleifer's population was fairly large, being that it was currently the second largest city in Aurana at the time, there were a great number of people in the crowd that neither Kevin nor Arthur had seen before.

It was a little bit of a game to Kevin and Arthur to point out to each other some of the more odd people they could find. Here and there, they saw older people to whom time had not been so kind, people in a class just above Kevin and Arthur that for some reason decided to dress as nicely as they could to hear the speech, and all sorts of other oddities. There were people from the great amount of the poor and lower classes of Rikleifer, of which Kevin and Arthur were part, and a few people from upper classes.

As the duke continued to speak, Kevin and Arthur started listening with more intent, having grown slightly bored. Still, there was not that much to the speech that interested them. They started fading back and forth between listening to the speech and looking around at the people.

Suddenly, one person in the crowd caught Kevin's eye, and Kevin pointed him out to Arthur. There was a man standing a short distance away from them in the crowd, who also appeared to be less focused on the actual speech and more on the people attending. While it may not have been too unusual by itself, there was something very unusual about the person doing it.

"Hey, check that guy out," pointed out Kevin. "What's with him?"

Arthur took a close look, on Kevin's direction. This man was quite unusual, indeed. He was pretty tall and appeared to be middle-aged. The man's dark hair was somewhat long, although not terribly long, and he had a distinguishing mustache and slight beard, about as thick as his mustache but not any longer than his chin. From his very clean look, it was safe to say that he must have been a very well to do man; however, the clothes he was wearing were not exactly typical. He wore robes of white, with gold trim and accents of green and blue streaked across in bands of varying width. Though it was not uncommon for such robes to be associated with a scholar or a wizard well versed in magic, something about the particular style of these robes seemed very unusual, almost antique in nature.

Then, as the man turned, something fell from him.

Without thinking and only wanting to be polite, Kevin bent down to pick up the object for the man. To his surprise, it appeared to be a shard of steel, almost like it was a tiny piece of a blade. As he grabbed it, he tried to get the man's attention. "Excuse me, sir, I think you…"

He stopped as the man looked at him, face to face. Something about his presence felt very odd, very strange.

Then, the man gave Kevin a nod, and gestured to his pocket, to have Kevin return the object there. It was quite an unusual response, but Kevin did as he was suggested.

The man then simply stood and walked away.

Kevin was weirded out, but something gave him the feeling that something was wrong. He pulled Arthur by the shoulder and said, "Come on, let's get out of here."

"Agreed," responded Arthur nervously, as they both turned and started walking away toward the road back to Kevin's house.

Chapter 2

The Stranger

As Kevin and Arthur approached Kevin's house again, the two started to talk a little bit about what had just happened. "That was pretty creepy," said Kevin, shaking his head as he thought about the man that had stared at him.

"Tell me about it," responded Arthur as he shook his head as well. "Oh well, at least he's out of our sight now. And it's good we're gone from there anyway; that speech was terrible."

"Says you," laughed Kevin, still awkwardly trying to shake off the incident. "I thought it was intriguing, although I wish it were better news."

Arthur shook his head. "Yeah, whatever," he said. "Rikleifer is safe; nothing will happen up here as far as the war is concerned. Your house is right here, so can we just go inside and try to forget about the whole thing?"

"Are you really that nervous about that weird man?" asked Kevin. "Why are we talking about this so much anyway? He dropped a shard of a blade, and I gave it back to him." He paused for a moment. "I mean, what more was there to it?"

"Kevin, who carries metal shards in their pocket?" Arthur rolled his eyes. "Great logic. Way to put the pieces together."

Placing his hands at his sides, Kevin glared at his best friend. "Very funny, Arthur," he responded. "It is what it is; I'm not saying there's a reason for it."

"Yeah, yeah, yeah." For another second, Arthur paused, trying to get slowed down. "Oh well," he said, "the image still just kind of sticks out in my head."

Again, Kevin rolled his eyes because the image was invading his thoughts as well. Something was not right about that man, but at the same time Kevin had also convinced himself that the incident was of no real importance. "Let's just try to forget the whole thing, shall we?"

Asking himself the question, Arthur considered what Kevin said and then he replied confidently, "I suppose you've got a point. What harm could that guy do?"

"Exactly," replied Kevin quickly and with an awkward smile. He then took a quick observation of the sun, noting its position in the sky as it was setting quickly. Then he continued, "It might be best if we head inside now. It's going to be nighttime soon. Are you coming along?"

"Sure," answered Arthur. "Just let me go home and grab something really fast."

Nodding, Kevin let Arthur go a separate direction while he entered his own home. Kevin's house was a mere three-room house that he and his mother had shared when his mother was alive. A cheap and very tiny home made of stone and wood, it was a typical small and narrow home for a commoner. In Kevin's house were his bedroom, his mother's old room, and a kitchen of sorts with a pantry. All of the accommodations were modest at best, and the rooms were very small, usually only a couple of steps long. He did not want to have to live in this small house, although it was quaint and gave Kevin that deep feeling of home.

Sitting around his house often gave Kevin some sense of chills, especially when he walked into his mother's room. Every now and then, Kevin still had nightmares about his mother and the days before her death. For now, knowing that it was becoming night and getting colder outside, Kevin proceeded to light a fire in the kitchen fireplace.

Walking inside the house, Arthur decided to lie down on Kevin's bed while Kevin went to the pantry to find some food for him and his friend. As Kevin returned and sat down on the edge of the bed next to him, he found that Arthur had a sword with him.

"Is that the sword your dad left you?" Kevin asked. "And why is it here?"

"Hey, it's not like my mother uses it," Arthur answered. "Besides, if that guy shows up here, we can't be too prepared."

After a short pause to think, Kevin shrugged and let it go at that. It seemed ridiculous, but Arthur had a point. They were both clearly fazed by the stranger in the castle courtyard, and to have some defense was oddly comforting right now. This sword was supposedly left by Arthur's father before he was out of the picture, with specific instructions written in a letter that the sword was for Arthur. It had always been in Arthur's house for as long as Arthur had grown up there, and Arthur's mother had always refused to speak about his father.

Kevin took a look outside the window for a moment as the boys relaxed. The sun was almost fully set by this point as dusk was getting ready to shift to night. As the evening set in, he and Arthur would probably do as they did often; chat about stories, sports, and their lives, while sharing a bit of bread. He took a candle out to the fireplace to light it.

Just at the very instant that the candle was lit, there was a knock at the door. That was quite curious indeed. Hardly anyone ever knocked at Kevin's door.

Kevin waited a moment, unsure that there was really a knock at the door and not just the wind blowing around the shutters. Then, there was another knock. It definitely came from the door, and was not the wind.

"Who is it?" called out Kevin.

There was no response.

Again, Kevin called out, "Who is it?"

Still, no response. Yet the knocking persisted.

A little paranoid because of the day's events, Kevin leaned out and looked over at Arthur, who looked a little nervous himself. Arthur grabbed the sword but left it in its scabbard. He walked out to join Kevin, to back him up.

Silently, Kevin motioned to Arthur. Then, he opened the door.

It was him!

Immediately, Kevin and Arthur froze in fear.

In the doorframe was the mystery man from the speech.

He was still dressed in his white robes with blue and green streaks, and his hair was a dark color, a contrast to his blue eyes. His overall appearance looked to be middle-aged, just as he was in the crowd.

"Excuse me," began the man in a very stately and formal voice, "may I speak with you inside?"

Kevin was surprised. All his and Arthur's fears about this man might have been true after all. He stood there vacantly for a moment, dumbfounded. Then, he looked at Arthur before looking back at the man.

After a moment, Kevin's senses were coming back to him.

This was not what Kevin expected, but the man was being polite. Even so, this was his home. "Not until you explain who you are and why you are here," he said boldly.

"I would be more than glad to explain to you who I am in private," answered the man calmly. "I am willing to tell you here that I want to talk about the metal shard that you placed in my pocket."

Giving the man an odd glance, Kevin asked, "Didn't you drop it? That's why I gave it back."

Silently, the man nodded. "There is more to discuss about it," he said.

Kevin looked back at Arthur for a moment, who still looked nervous. Arthur was still clutching the sword ready to draw it if needed, but so far, Kevin was actually finding this visit more unusual than threatening. He took a step back and said, "Please come in and sit down."

The man nodded again as he entered. "Thank you," he said. As he entered, he walked into Kevin's kitchen and sat down at his table. The small table only had two chairs, so Kevin closed the door and sat at the other one. Arthur stepped alongside the table.

Catching a glimpse of Arthur, the man said, "I do not think you will find your weapon necessary." He pulled his robes out to show what was inside. "I am unarmed and I mean neither of you any harm."

Still paranoid, Arthur said, "We'll see about that."

Wanting to be welcoming to his guest, Kevin said to the man, "Please do excuse my friend. We weren't exactly expecting a visit this late."

"Did you follow us?" asked Arthur suddenly. Kevin gave him a glance for such a reaction, but it was a legitimate question.

There was a short pause. "If you must know, then the answer is yes," he said. He looked to Kevin to address him. "What I have to discuss could not be risked by me being unable to find you again."

Kevin looked puzzled. "Find me? For what?"

The man reached below the pocket in his robe with both hands. With one hand, he undid a button that released the contents of the pocket. His second hand was there to catch it.

Or so it appeared at first.

As Kevin looked closely, he realized that the contents were the metal shard that he had picked up earlier, and that the man was not holding it. Instead, it was levitating above his hand. Carefully, the man kept his palm flat as his hand ascended and gently moved the levitating shard over the table. Then, he moved his hand out of the way, allowing the shard to fall to the table.

Kevin examined the metal shard in awe. It still appeared to be a fragment off of the blade of a sword. The man said, "Please pick it up for a closer look. I think you will find that it is safe for you to touch."

Doing as he was instructed, Kevin picked up the shard. He took a close look at the steel. The edge of the blade was intact as part of this shard and felt very sharp. It was very shiny and surprisingly lightweight for the size of the shard. Where the blade had been chipped off was an irregular edge, but was relatively smooth compared to many metal breaks.

Arthur became impatient. "Oh come on," he began as he reached for the shard, "what's so special about a piece of…"

"Wait!" exclaimed the man, standing up quickly, trying to stop Arthur.

"Aaargh!…"

It was too late. Arthur snatched the shard out of Kevin's hand and instantly screamed in pain. His hand instinctively released the shard and dropped it on the table. Immediately, Arthur was clutching his hand.

With his eyes wide open, Kevin exclaimed, "What was that?"

The man quickly gave a gesture to Kevin to tell him not to stand up. He too started sitting down and said, "He will be all right," referencing Arthur. "What we saw there is simply that the sword this shard is from is not his."

Kevin picked up the shard again, anticipating and observing that he was not being shocked in pain. "Am I to presume that it's mine, then?" he asked.

There was a moment of pause. "In a manner of speaking, yes," acknowledged the man. "But, if I may be honest, I do not know why."

Fascinated, Kevin stared at this magical shard of a blade.

No longer clutching his hand, Arthur looked directly at the man. "Who are you?" he asked.

Reaching a hand out to Arthur and offering to shake hands, he said, "You may call me Kron Kalavere." He shook Arthur's hand, and then Kevin's. The two boys then introduced themselves to Kron.

A brief howl of the wind passed by the windows of the house before Kron continued. "I have been carrying this shard for nearly two decades. As you have noticed, it comes from a 'locked sword', one that is magically keyed to a specific wielder. I cannot touch it myself; this is why I had to have you put it in my pocket when it fell out earlier, and why I had to use a bit of wind magic to levitate the shard to the table. Only carrying the sword in its scabbard, by the scabbard, allows others who are not the owner to handle the blade."

"So you're a wizard, then," commented Arthur.

"Well, not exactly," responded Kron. "Magic is a large part of what I do, but I am no wizard. You could say that I am more of a… messenger." He paused for a moment, as he looked at Kevin. "If I may be honest for a moment, our meeting was by chance, but I am hoping that you can help me, and that is why I came to see you."

Confused, Kevin lifted the shard in his hand. "You want me to help you because for some reason I can hold this?"

"Not for the shard alone," answered Kron, "but if you can hold that shard, you can also hold that of which it is part."

"Which is?" asked Kevin.

Kron leaned in. "A blade called the Sword of Purity." He paused as he sat straight. "It is a sword that was created by the sacrifice of a god. And I do not mean one of your 'nameless ones' that people worship nowadays; I speak of someone real, an immortal, one of those who dare call themselves gods."

Arthur rolled his eyes. "Oh great, just what I needed at night. More religious propaganda." Aside, Kevin chuckled a bit at Arthur's response, but he was trying to listen with intent to Kron.

"I speak not of religion, Arthur," Kron answered. "Please, I understand that what I speak of may seem unbelievable, but I ask that you hear me out before you judge."

Looking at Kevin, Arthur asked, "Are you buying this?"

Kevin thought about it for a moment. "I would at least be interested in hearing about it, Arthur," he answered. He picked up the shard again, examining it another time. "This does have me curious."

Although Arthur still seemed a bit stiff for a moment, he relented. "Okay," he said. "If you're willing to listen, then I will, too." This was a sign that he was willing to drop the combativeness and lower his guard.

Seeming a bit anxious, Kron rolled his neck and took a breath. With Arthur now calmed down and listening, and with Kevin still seated across from him interested in what he had to say, Kron said, "I suppose I owe you both an explanation of who I am and what I want of you. As I mentioned, my name is Kron Kalavere, and that was the name I was born with." He paused for a moment, looking a bit hesitant himself, as though he were struggling to find the words he needed. "I am a member of an ancient society of immortal humans who live on another plane of existence. We refer to ourselves as 'gods', though we are not anyone that anyone worships, at least as far as I am aware. To them, I am known by the immortal name I was given, Kronius, and I am a messenger god for them."

Kevin and Arthur both seemed fascinated. At this point, Kron was at least explaining things that could oddly make sense. They both knew magic was a thing, a dying art in their world but one that existed nonetheless. Curious, Kevin asked, "How old are you, then?"

Kron racked his brain for a second. "I have lost exact count by this point, but it has been a few hundred years. I am actually one of the youngest gods in comparison to my peers, for our society was founded over five thousand years ago by the power zealot Setaeus Demota. It happened during an age of chaos, when kingdoms were much smaller and more numerous."

Arthur raised an eyebrow. "A power zealot?" he asked, curious what that even meant.

“Yes,” answered Kron, “Setaeus Demota was one of the most powerful men to ever live, a true believer in the power of magic and the divine. He was so determined for more power that his efforts led to the discoveries of immortality and the passage to our realm, the ‘Realm of the Angels’, as we call it. Setaeus Demota then took the name of Setadev, a name which he called ‘a god’s name’. It was the dream of Setaeus Demota to create a community of immortals who would watch from above and help the mortal.”

“And that’s you guys, right?” asked Arthur, curious. “You’re still the same group?”

“Much so, but not exactly,” responded Kron. “Setadev is no longer a god, nor has he been alive for five thousand years. I am not sure why this was, but I do know that just a short time later, the gods named a new leader: Vinz Larinion. He brought lifetimes of study, and very minimal intervention in the mortal realm so as not to exert power over societies. A large part of this was due to his philosophies, which we still live by today. The mantle of command was not one to be given to one who would conquer the realms and rule everyone. One man should not ever rule the populace.”

Kevin nodded. “Sounds pretty noble,” he said. “Though isn’t that what every kingdom does today?”

Kron pondered for a minute. “More or less throughout history, yes,” he finally answered. “The best listen to the honest advice of others and rule accordingly, so less ‘one man’ and more ‘by committee’, whether officially or not. Those who have ruled with an iron fist have tended to fail, in due time. And, there has never been only one kingdom in the world. There have always been many, with different ways to rule.”

A slightly frustrated Arthur spoke up. “Okay, enough with the philosophy discussion.” He looked directly Kevin, who shot him a brief glare for being impolite, and then at Kron. “Why are you here?”

Closing his eyes for a second and recognizing that he should get to the point, Kron stated, “I have come for your help because I have been isolated in the mortal realm for the past twenty years. Since the wars around that time, there has been a seal placed on the connection between this realm and the Realm of the Angels. It is one I cannot pass, and I presume the other gods cannot cross it, either, as I have not seen one in that long."

Isolation, kept away from home for twenty years. It seemed so sad to Kevin.

Kron continued. "It is a long story why that is, but I will try to give you the shortest version I can." He thought for a second, trying to be deliberate with his words as he prepared to tell his story. "All had been peaceful in the Realm of the Angels for thousands of years, until about one hundred and fifty years ago. On that day, peace was broken by the god Tyrinion. The god of darkness, Tyrinion had always been a highly intelligent and active god, which made it a great shock when he decided to attack. Almost all of the gods tried to subdue him, and all fell before him; he was more powerful than we ever imagined, stronger than all of us combined. As far as I am aware, we never did identify how he became so powerful, but we worried on how we could have been so blind to it."

"Yeah, kinda seems like something you should know," commented Arthur.

"Quite," answered Kron, "but those who have power and do not wish it visible will find ways to hide it." He paused for a second. "But I digress. After Tyrinion had gravely injured many gods, he nearly destroyed the tower in which we live with a blast of magic, causing a great deal of damage. Then, he simply left. He disappeared, almost into thin air, until twenty years ago."

"You mean during the savage war?" asked Kevin.

Frowning a bit, Kron answered, "The Alliance-Daritel War," using the war's formal name. "I suppose that the 'savage war' is the common name used here, although I do not like the idea of calling people of tribes 'savages'. Vinz Larinion was of a tribal people, and I consider him the greatest person I have ever known."

Kevin had never thought of that; there were no tribal peoples in Aurana and he did not have experience with them. He felt a bit sheepish, and the reaction was visible on his face.

"In any regard," continued Kron, "we the gods were able to figure out that Tyrinion was the driving force behind the uprising against the kingdoms and why it was so effective and deadly. To that end, Vinz Larinion made the decision to sacrifice his own life, to concentrate his energy in a more pure form that could destroy the unbelievably powerful Tyrinion. What he did created the Sword of Purity, the divine weapon we have already discussed. And the person chosen to wield it, and be locked to it, was not an immortal. It was a mortal man, a general from the kingdom of Scurnia by the name of Vincent Stryker."

Eyes wide, Kevin and Arthur looked at each other for a moment. Vincent Stryker was a famous name in Aurana for being the person who planned and led a strike on the city of Seta Archa that ended the war Long known as "Vincent the Pure One", he had for many years since been absent from both Aurana and Scurnia, and there were many who believed he chose to retire to a quiet life. This was a significant historical figure to both of them, and here he was being mentioned in connection to gods and to this sword.

"As the war reached its final battle in Seta Archa, Vincent Stryker went to confront Tyrinion, alone. I know not exactly what happened, but the Daritel collapsed after that, and the war came to an end almost as quickly as it began. It was easy for me to presume we had won. Little did I, who happened to be monitoring what was going on in Seta Archa, know what was really happening."

Kevin was curious. What did he mean?

"As a messenger god, one role of mine is to observe key events in the world and report them back to my society. But just after the battle in Seta Archa ended, and Vincent Stryker and his troops departed the city, a seal was placed on the Realm of the Angels. When I tried to go to my realm to report, I found I was unable to return. Twenty years I have tried and failed to return to my home. Equally as long, I have waited for the gods to find me, yet that has not happened."

No wonder Kron was so desperate for help returning home, Kevin realized in that moment.

"I have long thought that the seal was a dying curse, a last-second act of vengeance against the gods, but what I do know for certain is that I was the only god in the mortal realm at the time because of my role as a messenger. No one else was on assignment at the time, and as a result, I was trapped on the wrong side of the seal, alone."

Kron was not showing sadness as he explained, but he seemed a little somber. He continued, "If there was one bit of optimism I did get, as Vincent Stryker left from that battle, I found this shard near the city's central temple. Once I realized I could not touch it, I knew what it was, and I have kept it since that day."

Quite a sad but amazing story, Kevin thought to himself. It was awful what had happened to Kron, but simultaneously in his hand was a piece of the sword of the legendary Vincent Stryker. A thought came to mind.

"Hold on," he asked after a brief second, as he held up the shard, "so if this sword belonged to Vincent Stryker, why can I handle it?"

Arthur looked on, intent on listening closely.

Kron sighed. "To be honest, Kevin, I do not know."

A little disappointed, Kevin put the shard down and leaned back in his chair. That was helpful, he thought to himself with a bit of the trademark sarcasm of his best friend.

Continuing on, Kron said, "It was not my intent for the shard to drop out of the bottom of my pocket in public like that, but when you picked it up from the ground and gave it to me, I knew that finally I found someone who could help me."

"But why Kevin?" inquired Arthur. "Surely there are more experienced, more talented people out there who could help."

Kevin looked up at Arthur and lifted the shard again. He had the answer already. "It's because I can hold this," he said. "Kron believes I can therefore hold the Sword of Purity, wherever it is, and that it is what can get him home."

Nodding, Kron acknowledged, "Very good, Kevin. You have a sharp mind. I have only known you the length of this encounter, but already I believe you to be someone of talent."

"Oh, don't embellish him with such language," laughed Arthur, poking a little fun at his friend.

Chuckling a little awkwardly, Kevin agreed. "Yeah, I'm with Arthur on this one. I work hard and I study, but being 'talented', I don't think so."

For a moment, there was silence as Kron considered his

response. Then, he crossed his arms. "Well then, perhaps I can give you, and Arthur as well, the chance to prove yourselves as young men of talent." He gestured around. "This shard, as far as I am aware, is the only piece that became separated from the Sword of Purity, meaning the whole sword is otherwise intact. And, I have it on good authority that it is in Aurana, with a soldier who served with Vincent Stryker twenty years ago. With a little knowledge, Kevin, you can make that shard lead you to the sword and allow you to reunite them as a whole."

Kevin looked at Arthur for a moment, as if asking what to do without using words. "Don't look at me," Arthur said. "This is your call, not mine."

Looking back at Kron, Kevin then said, "Okay, so before I decide if I want to help you or not, show me how this works." He waved the shard around a bit.

"Certainly," nodded Kron. "The Sword of Purity has a number of unique features about it that set it aside from a normal sword. If you could hold the shard over the table, I would like to show you how to use them."

An unsure Kevin reluctantly agreed, "Okay." He held the shard out over the table, in his palm with his hand open so that Arthur and Kron could see.

"Now, I would like you to close your eyes."

Still reluctant, Kevin closed his eyes. What was this about and why did he need to close his eyes?

"Okay," continued Kron, "Kevin, now I need you to empty your mind. Find your inner peace, your inner serenity. The Sword of Purity is a tool of peace and it will respond to you when you think about your actions, not simply reacting; when you are acting out of a tranquil position of justice, not of anger."

Doing his best to follow the instruction, Kevin tried to clear his mind for a moment. He was looking for the peace within him that Kron asked him to find. He sat silent for nearly a minute; Arthur and Kron also sat silently while watching with intent, and any second Arthur looked like he was about to object to such nonsense, Kron gestured to him to hold on for a moment.

Suddenly, a slight burning sensation. Kevin immediately

opened his eyes and let go of the shard. He was surprised to see, for just a moment before it fully fell from his hand, that the piece of the blade turned a light blue color.

"Well, that settles it," commented Arthur, his eyes wide. "I'm sold."

As Kevin looked up, Kron said, "Your inner serenity will turn the blade blue and ignite it with divine energy, where its real power is held."

Leaning back in a bit of surprise from what he just witnessed, Kevin said, "That's amazing." He looked at the shard. "What do you mean, though, that it's a tool of peace? Isn't a sword by nature a tool of war?"

"I believe it is a saying as old as time that if you want peace, prepare for war," answered Kron. "But in all seriousness, the sword is not made for vengeance. Methodically, well thought-out decisions are critical to properly carrying out justice." He paused for a second, as he focused on Kevin again. "You can even take it a step further, I understand, and unleash the energy in the blade in a bright flash of divine light. That, however, I do not know how it is done and cannot teach you. It is something you will have to discover on your own."

"Uhm, provided he ever finds this sword," interjected Arthur, throwing his hands up a bit.

That comment brought Kevin to his senses a bit and out of his wonder. "He does have a point, Kron. Clearly you don't have the whole sword."

"Very true," acknowledged Kron. "However, the last power of the sword will help with this. If you reach out with your eyes closed, and from your position of serenity call the sword to you, it will dissolve into energy, flow to you, and reform in your hand, whole. It is a good trick if you lose your sword and it is out of reach, although you do have to be close enough to see the blade for this power to work."

Kevin nodded. "It sounds like a very good power. Am I to guess, then, that using this ability with the shard will make it pull toward the whole sword?"

"Exactly," said Kron, "the energy reforms at the blade's hilt." Then, having finished explaining, he stood up. "And now, I have told you all that you need to know. Now, though, I must ask you formally." He paused and looked at both Kevin and Arthur. "Would the two of you be willing to help me get home?"

At this point, Kevin was still skeptical. Kron had explained a lot in this visit, and so much of it was fascinating. A society of immortals, a powerful sword that for some reason only he could wield, and the chance to help this man by doing an adventure of sorts. But, at the same time, this was still a complete stranger who he had bumped into by random chance. How much could he be trusted? Was anything even worth extorting out of Kevin to begin with? How long, or short, would this take? Though Kevin had plenty of reason to be skeptical of Kron and not trust this odd man who had come to his door, something was nagging at Kevin that made him interested in coming along. Something told Kevin that this might be the opportunity to learn more about himself, and maybe to live out a dream for a day, if only for a day. With this in mind, Kevin took one look at Arthur, and said to him, "We really don't have anything to lose. Are you in?"

For a moment, Arthur just stared at Kevin. Then he managed to say something. Only it was not really saying, but rather exclaiming. "Are you insane? We don't know who the hell this guy is! For all we know, we could be putting ourselves in a lot of danger here."

Kron did not respond.

"Trust me, Arthur," Kevin started to reassure Arthur. "Although we don't know what he's here for, if there was something he wanted out of us, he would have taken it already. But there's nothing he could get out of us anyway; we don't really have anything to our names. And maybe there really is something he knows that we don't."

Arthur thought for a second. "I still think you're crazy," he said. "Why should we trust a complete stranger who found us and came to our door? Have you really forgotten that already?"

"Absolutely not," responded Kevin. He then turned to Kron, curious about the thought of what Arthur said, regardless of his interest.

Silently, Kron lowered his head a bit. "I am sorry that I do not have a reward to offer you, so that I may earn your trust," he said. "I can only express the gratitude I would have for both of you if you can help me."

To Kevin, the absence of a reward actually made him more trusting of Kron, not less. It made Kron seem more genuine, asking only as a personal favor rather than making a possibly false promise of a reward. Adventurers in his stories only pursued rewards sometimes; at others, they turned rewards down to do what was noble.

He looked up to Arthur again. "I'm still interested. Are you in?"

"Seriously?" questioned Arthur, rolling his eyes and giving a disturbed look.

Kevin nodded.

Arthur sighed and clutched his own sword left by his father. "If you're going, then I won't let you go alone. You can't have adventures without me."

Kron smiled. He was going to get the help he asked for, that for which he had searched for decades.

Chapter 3

Emotionless

Kevin and Arthur each took the time to pack overnight for the trip. After some more practice with Kron, Kevin used the shard's power to see which way it would go to reunite with the sword, and it pulled to the south. It was in the direction of the road before the front line in the war between Aurana and Desolunar. Where exactly that front line was was anyone's guess, as it seemed like the border changed daily and the news that reached Rikleifer's public could be slow to arrive.

The next morning, Arthur, Kevin, and Kron set off for the south road out of Rikleifer. They walked all day, but the first day and night were uneventful as they passed through meadows and a bit of forest. Close to nightfall, they reached the outskirts of Haventown, a village. Knowing that there was no inn in Haventown, and they needed to save the money they had, they camped for the night off the road outside the town.

As the sun rose on the next day, Arthur and Kevin packed up and the trio continued down the road. Kron spent a large part of the journey interacting with both Kevin and Arthur, making sure he learned as much about them as he could, and he told them some facts from his mortal life, as well. He shared with Kevin and Arthur about how he had been married, and was selected to be an immortal by the gods while a prisoner of war in an era of many more kingdoms. Such timing, coinciding with his likely death at the hands of his captors, meant that he never had the chance to see his wife again before her death, and that affected him deeply for a time. Before becoming a god, Kron revealed, he had been an academic and a political dissident taking action to make change for peace and a better life for his fellow countrymen in his homeland. He knew a bit of magic as well, as it was more commonplace centuries ago, but stressed that most of what he did know

now came from his years in the Realm of the Angels, studying. As a messenger, it was his job to carry messages to the mortal and share ideas from his fellow gods, as well as observe and communicate back to his society. As such, he spent quite a bit of time in the mortal realm, and did not mind being effectively a runner.

Over the course of the day, the meadows transitioned to a forest of coniferous trees, as they entered the Southern Forest, the unofficial divide between the provinces of Middle Aurana and Southern Aurana. It was a mostly coniferous forest, with large trees everywhere. A lone dirt road carved between the trees, connecting the two Auranian provinces. Somewhere further south was the current war front. Still, at this point having seen no signs of it yet, they pressed forward until dusk. It was around this time that Arthur was talking to Kevin and Kron, sharing his theories on his parentage.

"I just have to believe I'm adopted or something," he told them, holding his sword, "and the more I've looked at this the last two days, the more I believe it."

Kron, unlike Kevin having never heard this story before, stated, "Interesting. What is it about this sword makes you certain that it means you are adopted?"

Kevin rolled his eyes. Arthur was more than likely going to make something up again.

"Well," hesitated Arthur for a moment, as he looked for something to say, "this looks like a good sword, plain but in very good shape. It was left by my father, who I've never met, for me. I just look at it and think it wasn't cheap, and therefore the person who bought this would be far too good for the woman that is my mother."

"Or that says she's your mother," pointed out Kevin. "Or raised you as her son."

Arthur shook his head. "You give her far too much credit, Kevin. 'Raised' is a strong word in this context."

"What do you mean?" inquired Kron.

"He means his mother's a drunk," Kevin interrupted, pre-empting Arthur's ability to speak. "Let's just say she doesn't spend much time with her son."

"Uh, much? I think you mean *any*, Kevin," scoffed Arthur.

Kron nodded and said to Arthur, "I see. I think I understand. You wish her not to be your mother, then?"

That was a harsh question, Kevin thought to himself. Kevin understood it himself; he had met Rita Falchor, Arthur's mother, before, and sure enough she was in a drunken stupor at the time. She tended to be angry when she was intoxicated as well, and it seemed a wonder that she was able to support herself and her son and her drinking habit, if only barely. Clearly to Kevin, she needed help, which would be very hard to find. Even so, Arthur was being quite harsh himself. Kevin really hoped that Arthur would not answer yes to that question; at least he had a parent in his life, and with that he had the opportunity to make things right with her.

Arthur never had the opportunity to answer that question. As the trio walked deeper into the forest, the more that a terrible stench started to permeate the air.

"Ugh," commented Kevin, as the smell hit hard, forcing him to plug his nose.

"What is that awful smell?" yelled Arthur.

Surprising the boys, Kron reached out and extended his arm in front of them, stopping everyone in their tracks. With his other arm, he held it out, as if arming to potentially cast a magic spell. "It is death," he said. "It is a smell I have smelled many times before." Slowly, after looking all around and listening closely, he motioned to the boys to continue on.

And as the trio moved along, it was evident that something very bad had happened here very recently.

They were situated on a small forest path as the skies were darkening while the sun was now fully set over the horizon. Blood and dead bodies of armed soldiers littered the road, stretching a moderate length of the path in both directions from Kevin and Arthur's viewpoint. The bodies were not rotten, suggesting that a battle had occurred here only a short time ago. Torches were still lit around the area, mostly burning as they lay flat on the ground. It was an overwhelming feeling to both Kevin and Arthur, who felt remorse for those who had died here on the field of battle.

Kevin examined the uniforms of the dead, with a sense of awe, and said, "We must be on the Aurana-Desolunar front line right now."

Arthur only nodded somberly in acknowledgement as the two began to toll up the bodies and estimate how many there were. Making his estimate, Arthur stated, "There's maybe about fifty Desolunar troops here, but a couple hundred Auranian troops. We must be in Desolunar territory now, given that kind of difference."

Kevin, still examining, responded, "I doubt it. We didn't see any soldiers from Desolunar on our way here."

Kron nodded, appreciative of Kevin's evaluation. "This looks like it happened today, maybe even in the last few hours. It's almost as if they came up, started the fight, won, and then fell back, satisfied with just the destruction."

As he said this, Kevin was flipping over a dead body. Checking out the name on the uniform and recognizing him as a man whose name he had heard once in Rikleifer, Kevin took out a handkerchief and covered the soldier's face with it, out of respect for the man. Looking around at all of the bodies around him, Kevin only wished that he could show respect for every single one of the dead men. However, he knew he did not the time to do so.

In his pocket, the shard started to vibrate. Kevin pulled the shard out, looking at it closely. It was as if the shard wanted to be somewhere, and it felt like it was pulling on his hand as he held it. He looked over to show it to Arthur and Kron, only to notice that they had wandered away, as if to survey the battlefield further. Not thinking to catch up with the other two and wondering what the shard wanted, Kevin held the shard up and let it guide him where to go.

Kron had seen Kevin wander off separately, thinking he was looking around for clues just as he and Arthur were. After searching through a few more bodies, Kron called out to Kevin, "Nothing here so far."

Kevin heard the callout, but by this point he was far enough away in the forest that he did not clearly hear Kron. He was captivated by the shard, feeling that it was leading him to the Sword of Purity, and that the sooner this was accomplished, the sooner they could leave before trouble could start.

His curiosity was overtaking his nerves.

A few more steps into the wilderness, Kevin stopped at another body. Oddly enough, his was a distance from the roadside. His body was dressed with golden stars and decoration on his green uniform's shoulders, as well as a piece of iron and several medals on his uniform's chest.

After a brief moment of having his head bent, Kevin knelt down and read the name on the man's uniform, saying it out loud. "Eukert. The decorations on his uniform identify him as a War Commander, if I remember the military decorations correctly." Kevin then took a second and knelt down even further, listening closely. After a moment's pause, he said to himself. "He's still breathing, but only barely." He hoped that maybe if Kron were so talented in magic, perhaps he could heal this man. Kevin examined his injury and the way the man was laid out, and noticed a sword near him. The sword, which looked to be of good quality but not ornately decorated in any way, had a small chunk missing from one side of the blade.

Thinking this could be what he was looking for, Kevin held the shard up to the sword. It was a perfect match. As he held the two pieces close, he saw the edges glow in a bright blue magic. The two pieces adhered together and the blue magic flashed and dissipated, as the sword appeared to be whole again as if it had never been chipped at all.

This was it. The Sword of Purity, of which Kron spoke.

It was absolutely fascinating, Kevin thought to himself.

He decided to flirt around a bit with the sword and give it a couple of swings. As he swung it, he felt the perfect balance the sword had in the sword's weight balance, and how it was not difficult to wield. A venation inside it glowed ever so slightly.

It was definitely the Sword of Purity.

As he swung the sword around a little bit, Kevin spotted the scabbard for the sword, situated next to Eukert's body. When he finished his swing, Kevin brought the sword to a stop as he kneeled down to pick up the scabbard. He then strapped the scabbard to his belt and looked to the man from whom he was taking it, hoping he would not mind, if he would survive this night.

With the sword now in his possession, Kevin turned to look for

Arthur and Kron. He did not immediately see them as he looked though the trees. He turned again, and this time he saw a flash. Kevin stared at it for a moment, not sure what it was until the last moment.

Fire. A flying ball of fire.

A shot of adrenaline hit Kevin like a bolt of lightning. Frightened, he tried to turn and run away, only to stumble and fall to the ground. The fireball flew over his back, into a tree behind him before it dissipated.

More fireballs started flying, this time aiming lower. Instinctively and fearfully, Kevin grabbed his sword and held it in front of him to block the fireballs. He was not swinging the sword, only holding it with its flat side out to try and cover himself with it as much as possible. He tried to yell for help, only to find the sound escape his capabilities as he was fighting for his life, grounded and trying to protect himself from fireballs.

A shadowy figure was approaching, throwing the fireballs. Three more fireballs blocked; all were direct hits to the sword. Kevin was able to make it up to one knee, but the figure was closing in, and its assault was relentless.

As Kevin held the sword up, he saw that this figure was a human in a black cloak. It was a hooded cloak made of silk. The hood was set low enough that it covered the figure's eyes.

Another three fireballs. Kevin was slowly trying to get to his feet as he blocked fireballs.

He was not quite fast enough.

Closing in and being frustrated with the ineffectiveness of the fireball volley, the figure jumped out and tackled Kevin, knocking him back to the ground. The figure kneeled on top of Kevin and held a fireball to the left side of his head.

A shiver of fear ran down Kevin's neck. He was in serious trouble.

Still with the sword in his grip, and in his right hand, he saw an opportunity that the figure did not. Kevin lifted the Sword of Purity to the neck of the figure, on the opposite side of the fireball, where the figure had no defense. Now, each one had the other pinned in a killing move.

In a cold and emotionless voice, the figure began to speak. "Go ahead and try to kill me. It will be the last move you ever make."

"You're not in any position to be making threats," said Kevin, pressing the sword closer to the figure's neck. "I want to know what right you think you have to try and kill me."

"Kevin! What's going on?"

That voice was not the figure. It was Arthur. He and Kron had finally made it to where Kevin was. Arthur saw the figure that had Kevin pinned; it was human.

Arthur reached for the sword on his belt, but before he could grab it, Kron reached over and held him back for a moment. "He has the sword, I see," he said to Arthur. "I want to see how this plays out."

Silently, Arthur nodded. Worried as he was, he did not exactly know what to do. He would put his trust into Kron, that Kron knew what he was doing. As for Kron, he had seen already how Kevin was observant, and wanted to see what he would do in a dangerous situation.

Responding to Kevin, the figure said in its same cold and calculating voice, "I warn you not to challenge what I can accomplish. You are trespassing on a battlefield, and I will not allow you to get away with what you are doing here."

Kevin felt his hand tighten on the hilt of the sword. As he listened to the cold, emotionless voice of the figure, he realized something. This voice, as emotionless as it was, was not a male voice. Nonetheless, Kevin continued, "You are not a law enforcer. If you were, you wouldn't be wearing that black robe."

"That does not excuse you," responded the figure in black. "I will destroy you for what you have done or what you were intending to do."

Starting to get angry, Kevin pushed even harder on the sword and grabbed the hilt even tighter. Before he could say anything, though, Kevin looked at his sword, and remembered what he had been told. This was a sword of peace, not one of anger. While he kept his sword held high, he closed his eyes and took a couple of deep breaths, calming himself. He sought to do as Kron advised and find his inner serenity. It was more difficult than he thought.

From aside, though, a smile came to Kron's face. Kevin had been angry, but clearly he had also been listening.

Another breath, and Kevin felt something strange at that moment, as if he had stumbled across a source of light. He opened his eyes. The sword was glowing a bright blue color with the venation in the blade glowing even brighter. He also noticed that the figure was also staring at the sword.

The sword's energy gave Kevin a slight scare, which made him lower the sword. The figure, still staring at the sword for a moment, stood up and knelt down to the ground, allowing Kevin to stand. It said in its emotionless voice, "Please pardon my intrusion." The figure then stood up again and said to Kevin. "I offer you my deepest apologies. I did not realize that I was in the presence of the pure one."

Kevin was stunned as the words "pure one" rang through his ears. That was the nickname of the person who held the sword before him. He stood before the figure. "I am sorry, but I am not who you think I am," he said.

The cold and emotionless voice of the figure responded, "But you are. It is knowledge that has been passed down. Someone has foreseen your arrival." The voice paused for a second. "I am not here to look for you, but I have found you nonetheless."

"Wait a minute," Kevin interrupted, frustrated that the figure was not making sense. "Enough of this. I want to know what's going on here, starting with who you are." As he said this final part of his sentence, Kevin reached for the figure's hood and pulled it down.

And what was under that hood was not what Kevin expected.

Chapter 4

The Peculiar Sorceress

It was a girl. One that was about his age, as well.

She had long, straight red hair, and eyes the color of sapphires. Something about her face by itself gave Kevin a unique feeling, as if there was something special about this girl. Rationally, though, Kevin thought she was quite strange in her behavior, from what he had seen so far.

After about a moment where both of them looked at each other, staring, the girl folded her arms and closed her eyes. "Very well, then," she said, without emotion. "If this is the way you want to play this, then we will." She then opened her eyes and looked directly at Kevin. "I am Caitlin, a freelance sorceress. My home is near here."

There was another fact that Kevin did not expect to hear. A freelance sorceress, at her age. Although Kevin did not know much about magic, he did know that it normally took years to learn. She must be a prodigy at spellcasting, Kevin thought to himself. Noticeably, her voice and her face seemed to lack emotion of any kind. She was perhaps the most peculiar person Kevin had ever met.

"I'm Kevin Trent, from Rikleifer," Kevin quickly introduced himself. "But I promise you, I'm not the 'pure one' that you speak of."

Caitlin sighed. "You are if you are holding that sword," she responded, still with an emotionless tone. "I know what that is in your hand. It's the Sword of Purity."

"How do you know of the Sword of Purity?" interjected Kron, surprised.

"From my father, a powerful wizard," Caitlin responded. "How do you know of it?"

As Kron responded to Caitlin, explaining only how he had carried a shard of it for some time and why they were there now, and not his history, Kevin thought about who this peculiar sorceress was in front of him. For as few magic users as there were remaining in the world, to meet one so young seemed exceptionally rare. There was one small school left in the world teaching magic, in the Auranian town of Bladinstar, and those students had to be adults before enrolling. To be out in the world already and considered "freelance", legally not in the contracted employ of the military but licensed to practice magic in Aurana, seemed almost an impossibility.

Then again, if her father were a wizard as she had just stated, surely she could have learned much of this at home from him. But what explained the emotionlessness? She did not necessarily seem impolite, only cold, as if she felt nothing and expressed nothing. He was so curious to ask her, but he did not want to be rude about it.

"So, he is not a pure one?" inquired Caitlin to Kron, the next line that caught Kevin's attention.

"Not as far as I am aware," Kron answered. "He just happened to be someone who could safely touch the sword."

Caitlin nodded. "I see," she said. She looked across the battlefield. "If you were here to retrieve the sword, then I would suppose its sword bearer was here. As I understand the story, after the original pure one desired to put down his sword, he gave it for safekeeping to a friend of his, a commander by the name of Eukert."

Eukert. That was the name of the person holding the sword from whom Kevin retrieved it.

Gasp! Eukert was still alive, slowly dying in the forest. Kevin just remembered!

Quickly, Kevin raise his hands in front of Caitlin and Kron, and interjected. "Hey! Eukert's alive, but he needs medical attention! Can one of you help him?"

Kron was about to answer, but Caitlin beat him to it. "Show me," she said as she gestured to Kevin to lead the way.

Kevin did not have to go far. He took Caitlin just a few steps away, and gestured down to Eukert's body.

Immediately, Caitlin knelt down next to the dying man and put her fingers on his neck. After a tense moment, she let out a deep breath. "It's a good thing you spoke when you did," she told Kevin. "He's still alive."

Nodding, Kevin took a step back toward Kron and Arthur. He did not know what was going to happen next, but he was hopeful that Caitlin knew what she was doing.

Silently, Caitlin rubbed her hands together, then placed them over Eukert's body. Then, with a sound of unleashing power, a glowing yellow magic emanated from her hands. It was bright and broad, and seemed to glow out from her hands down toward the fallen soldier.

Quietly, Arthur asked, "What's she doing?"

"It's a form of healing magic," answered Kron. "It only works if the person it is used on is still alive; once they are dead, it does not work. Those less skilled in magic can heal small wounds and cuts with this power, but only the most powerful can spare people from life-threatening injuries. Caitlin is clearly one of the latter; the brightness of her magic that we can see is an indicator that she can use a lot of power in this spell."

Again, Kevin was amazed. He, Arthur, and Kron stared on for a couple of minutes, before Caitlin's spell faded out as she stood up. She turned and said, "He is going to make it, but it may take a couple of days before he wakes up again. It looks like he took significant damage, and he will need to rest for quite some time."

Kevin breathed a sigh of relief.

"Could anyone else around here be alive, too?" inquired Arthur.

Kron took a good look around. "I hate to say 'never say never'," he began, "but I only sense death." He picked up Eukert and threw him over his shoulder, and though Kron was clearly quite strong, he did visibly appear encumbered by carrying the man. "Desolunar troops do not leave survivors unless their enemy retreats."

Caitlin lowered her head. "I think it's miraculous that we found even one alive," she said. She then looked at Kevin. "You saved his life."

Frowning a bit, Kevin responded, "I think that was more about you. I wouldn't have had the ability to save his life if I had been alone and found him."

Reluctantly, Caitlin gave a slight nod in acknowledgment. Then, she said, "We should get him to somewhere he can safely rest and recover. My house is just off the road a short distance away. I recommend that we take him there."

Without a second's pause or thought, Kevin took charge and replied, "Lead the way." Though there was much to be curious about, such as who this girl was or why she was acting this way, the darkening sky did make Kevin realize that shelter needed to be the group's immediate concern.

Caitlin said nothing and expressed nothing, but turned and started walking to the north down the road. The group followed, acknowledging that Caitlin was leading them to her house. Kron walked close to the front, keeping up with Caitlin. Kevin stayed a few steps behind, not wanting to encroach on the space of someone like Caitlin and risk his safety. Although he did not fear talking to her, she let off an image of toughness, but not arrogance. It was strength, but it was silent.

After a couple of moments of walking down the road, Arthur stepped up next to Kevin while they were walking and started talking to him quietly. "Kevin, what is with her? There's something very strange about that girl."

"I know," responded Kevin in the same type of quiet voice, "but right now she's the one guiding us."

Taking a breath, Arthur said, "Something scares me about her, though. She seems psychotic, or at the very least heartless on both the outside and the in."

"Whether or not that is her personality inside of herself, I don't know," said Kevin. "But I have a feeling that she has a softer side."

Arthur's mouth dropped. "Kevin, what is wrong with you? You've known her for a couple of minutes, she tried to kill you with a magic fireball, and you think there's a heart inside that empty shell that looks like a girl?"

Kevin brushed his left hand across his face. "I don't know, Arthur. Something about her seems different, though. I can't help but feel that she might."

Arthur shook his head. "Whatever, Kevin. I don't want to think about it anymore. In fact, I would rather just drop the subject altogether."

It was at that moment that Caitlin stopped and turned around.

Kevin and Arthur also stopped: Kevin out of confidence and respect, Arthur out of fear of Caitlin. Without any expression, Caitlin addressed them, pointing to her left. "We have arrived."

Kevin and Arthur looked in the direction Caitlin was pointing, realizing that somehow they were too distracted to notice the house as they had approached it. It was a very small, quaint little wooden shack, but it seemed to have been built well with no visible structural flaws.

For a moment, Kevin and Arthur hung back as Caitlin opened the door and showed Kron to a bed in which for him to place the fallen commander. After a couple of moments, they reemerged, and Caitlin said, "All of you are welcome to stay the night here, if you wish."

Without much thought, Arthur said as they stared at the house, "Great. You guys head inside, while I will stand guard outside."

"That's not necessary," responded Caitlin, quickly. "I assure you that my house is quite safe from any creatures or troops. There should not be any need for you or anybody else here to stand guard, even with the recent battle."

Kevin responded, having taken a moment to think, "Still, it may be a good idea to have someone stand guard. Arthur, how long do you want to stay outside?"

"For a while," said Arthur, quickly, trying to avoid Caitlin. "I don't feel very tired right now, and I think I can watch for a few hours."

After another moment of thought, Caitlin said, "All right. You can stand guard if you wish. I cannot prevent you from doing it."

Sensing that Arthur may not be entirely doing this to be a guard, Kron added, "I will do the same and stay with Arthur for the moment."

Reluctantly, Caitlin nodded. "Your choice," she said. "Kevin, please come with me."

As the door opened and Caitlin walked in, Kevin walked past Arthur and gave him a quick two-finger salute, wishing him well with that short gesture. After the door closed, Arthur took a seat on the ground, against the house. He leaned back and started to watch the stars above, while Kron walked around a bit.

The interior of the house was just as simple as the exterior. Very little was present in this small two-room house. Kevin wondered how anyone could live in such a simple house without any slight pleasantries whatsoever. There were a number of cabinets in the living space for storage, but not really much of a "kitchen" although there was an iron stove. The main room was sort of a mixed living space, while the second room was a bedroom. It was larger than Kevin's bedroom at his house, but still not a large room by any means, and all it contained was a bed.

Caitlin directed Kevin to the small bedroom, where Eukert was resting. "This is where you and Arthur will stay," Caitlin said. "As this man will be resting on the bed, I only have the space on the floor, but I should have spare blankets available."

Kevin nodded. "Thank you," he said. "Your kindness is very much appreciated."

"You are quite welcome," nodded Caitlin. Kevin then expected her to walk away, but she did not. Instead, she removed her black robe, under which she was wearing a black dress that fully covered her arms up to her hands. It was a sorceress dress, one that was designed to be dignified for a professional in the magical arts; one solid color with a few lace elements in the same shade of black around the neck and the arms. The sleeves were tight to her wrists and forearms. After a short hesitation, she said, "If I may note an observation to you, I find the company that you keep to be quite odd, indeed."

"Oh, yeah," Kevin responded, "I know Arthur's kind of out there, but he's a good guy once you get to know him."

"I did not mean Arthur," answered Caitlin, "although I think he's not exactly my cup of tea. I heard him talking to you on the way here; he is crass and a bit judgmental." She paused for a second. "Who I meant was Kron. Am I to guess that he led you here?"

Kevin nodded. "He did."

"I see," acknowledged Caitlin. "I presume, then, that he told you about the Sword of Purity. If you are not the pure one, or even 'a pure one', and just someone who can hold the sword for some reason, why does he want you to have this sword?"

Taking a breath, Kevin was trying to figure out how to explain this without sounding like a crazy person for calling Kron a god or an immortal. "Well, after we found out by accident that I could hold the sword, he told me that I could use it to help get him home."

"Is this man a god?" inquired Caitlin.

Suddenly, Kevin became very nervous. "No, and what do you mean by that?"

Caitlin looked directly into Kevin's eyes for a second. "You're a terrible liar," she pointed out, emotionlessly, "but I understand why you tried."

"How do you know about gods?" Kevin asked, still surprised.

"From my father," answered Caitlin. "He knows much about the immortal society you and I, and Kron, call 'gods'. He also knows of the Sword of Purity; therefore, I know as much as he does about it." She paused for a second. "That is why I asked if you are the pure one; I know you are too young to be Vincent Stryker, but I wondered if you were another one."

And right there, Caitlin also revealed she knew that Vincent Stryker was the pure one before, exactly as Kron had told him. But, at this point, Kevin lost his surprise. Caitlin had already shown that she was pretty clearly one step ahead.

"Oh, nope, not me," Kevin answered. "I don't know why I can hold this, but I'm just someone who was willing to help Kron get home. That's all."

Stepping closer to Kevin, Caitlin put a hand on his shoulder. "You seem to be a good person, Kevin Trent. I hope your innocence and naïveté don't get the best of you." She then turned to grab a blanket and handed it to Kevin.

That was an odd last statement, Kevin thought to himself. What did that mean?

"Anyway, I think we should call it a night for now," began Caitlin. "It's a long journey back to safety in Aurana, so I recommend that you get some rest tonight. Please rest comfortably." She abruptly guided Kevin into the bedroom, and immediately left the room afterward, saying nothing else.

Closing the door between the two rooms, Kevin thought that last action was somewhat rude of Caitlin. Still, he was not willing to argue with her. Deciding that rest was the best thing he could do at the moment, Kevin rolled the blanket in his hands into a pillow and rested his head on it, unwilling to let the Sword of Purity off his side.

He began to think about his friends and his enemies, and where he was right now. He was overwhelmed by what had just happened, and seeing the battlefield where those who represented his kingdom had given their lives for nothing. He looked up at Eukert, the fallen commander laying on the bed, motionless. That man was left for dead, and lucky to be alive thanks to Kevin and Caitlin both. Kron and Arthur were outside, ostensibly standing guard, even if Arthur was only doing it to avoid Caitlin and her emotionless personality and seemingly threatening behavior.

Still, it was nice to run into Caitlin, who seemed more than willing to help him despite her emotions, or lack thereof. Kevin did not see her as a threat. It did make Kevin curious, however, as to how Caitlin knew about gods and the Sword of Purity. She claimed was a strong wizard and was the one who told her about them. That still did not answer his question, however, since it only redirected it to her father and how he knew about it. Perhaps he would come up at a later time.

Also pressing on Kevin's mind was how Caitlin had come to be emotionless. Other than that, she certainly seemed to be a normal person with a surprising talent for magic. He had not seen what kind of power that she had, but she did warn him not to challenge her power, and he was sure that he had no seen the full extent of her powers. Whether it was because she underestimated them when she attacked or because she was bluffing, he was not sure.

After a while of thinking, Kevin dozed off. He was simply too tired to stay awake much longer. It was not a very deep sleep for him, however, given the thoughts that were running through his head. Still, it was able to last for a couple of hours.

The night, however, refused to remain quiet.

Kevin was awakened when he heard growls from outside the house. Getting up and worrying about Arthur, who was standing guard, he ran out of the bedroom and then out the front door. Whatever this was, Kevin wanted to find out because he was worried that it might be something dangerous.

Chapter 5

From the Shadows

Kevin straightened up his red shirt and ensured his sword was strapped to his brown pants. Though he had felt as though what he did know about swordplay could help keep him safe, he was aware that he was by no means skilled and did not want to feel overconfident about it since he knew to do so might be a fatal mistake until he knew exactly of what he was capable.

Ready to go, Kevin walked out the room door and out the door of the house, feeling like he was as prepared as he could be. One look at what was on the road, however, and Kevin was not prepared for what he was seeing at all.

A creature was standing on the road, covered in fur. Caitlin was next to him in a battle pose, still wearing her black dress. Kevin asked her, "What is going on out here?"

Caitlin responded, in her same unwavering tone, "A chimera. Pull out your sword, or go in the house. It is safe in there."

Kevin, not wanting Caitlin to handle this alone, pulled out the Sword of Purity and prepared for battle. Whether or not he was afraid, if Caitlin was going to stand up to it, then so would he.

Chimeras are the top predator of the forests. Attacking in packs and having a strong body with sharp claws, a parted-back mane, and a fierce bark, they strike fear into travelers passing by. Two kinds of chimeras exist: normal brown chimeras and powerful black chimeras. These black chimeras are rare and are more common in the area of Desolunar, but are sometimes in the southern area of Aurana and Nuve.

As Kevin drew his sword, he realized that Arthur was nowhere to be seen. Worried that chimeras may be threatening him, he gripped the sword tight and braced himself as the dark red eyes showed through the forest.

"Black chimera. This just turned out to be a lot worse than I had expected," said Caitlin, preparing a fireball in her hand. The black chimera began to show itself by heading out of the forest, its dark red eyes glowing and glaring at the two defenders ready to fight.

Kevin raised his sword vertically in a defensive stance, preparing for the fight ahead. He was nervous, visibly shaking. This was real danger in front of him, staring him down and terrorizing him, almost more so than when Caitlin had thrown fireballs at him.

Caitlin noticed. "Don't freak out!" she yelled. "Deal with what's in front of you!"

As she said this, the black chimeras lunged toward Kevin.

Its fangs became visible. It was looking for a meal.

A human meal.

Deal with what's in front of you! Almost as if the voice was sounding in Kevin's head.

In a quick flash, Kevin swiped his sword once horizontally and hit the chimera in the jaw and sent it backwards, whimpering audibly. The chimera backed down, but did not retreat.

Caitlin was not going to let it regain the initiative. She shot a fireball at the chimera, spooking it. The scared chimera, usually the apex predator of the forest, ran away.

The threat was gone. Kevin's heart was racing. He was coming down from all the adrenaline that had built up. He had chosen to fight instead of flee, and he was successful. It was an overwhelming sensation.

Calm and collected as ever, Caitlin looked over at Kevin. "Nicely done," she said, as if she were a mentor advising her trainee. "That took a lot of courage for you to stand your ground."

Kevin tried to catch his breath. As he did this, he asked Caitlin a question. "What is a chimera doing here attacking us?"

"Chimeras are native to this environment," said Caitlin in response, "but the black chimera is far more rare and only lives in this forest. Normally, though, humans are not their prey, and they normally don't go attacking people."

"Yeah... tell them that," responded Kevin with a little bit of dark humor. "From what you're telling me, it seems like this chimera is behaving abnormally."

“I’ve never seen chimeras behave like this,” said Caitlin. “It is a little unusual…”

“Wait a second,” interrupted Kevin. He had realized something, and it was something that was definitely not right. Although the chimeras were gone now, Arthur was still nowhere to be seen, even though he supposedly had been sitting outside. “Where's Arthur? Or Kron? They were supposed to be standing guard out here, but I don’t see them at all.”

Caitlin turned to Kevin and said in her normal voice, “I don't know. If they’re not here, then I’m not sure where they could have gone.”

Suddenly, the sound of a loud wail echoed through the forest, away from the battlefield.

Almost immediately, Kevin and Caitlin looked at each other. Then, they both looked in the direction of the wail. Caitlin gave a nod to Kevin, and the two took off together in the direction of the sound.

The direction of the sound took the pair off the road and into the forest, over fallen trees and through the darkness. The light of the moon gave only the faintest illumination.

Two minutes into their trek, as they approached a small clearing, the light of the moon revealed a flash of a white robe with color streaks, lying on the ground. It was Kron Kalavere.

Kevin and Caitlin stopped when they found him. “Kron!” Kevin yelled in surprise.

Kron was lying face down in the ground, bleeding from a wound on the back of his head. It was white blood, which Caitlin immediately recognized as the color of the element of life. She knelt down by his head and started releasing healing light magic. “He’s been attacked,” she told Kevin calmly. “Fortunately, I think his story about being an immortal is true. He should pull through this.”

“How can you tell?” asked Kevin.

“White blood,” answered Caitlin. “Humans bleed red as a representation of the element of fire in the body. White is life. It’s an educated guess, but to bleed white is to have a body so full of life energy as to defy mortality.” She paused. “Still, I don’t know what the long-term effects are.”

Another few seconds, and Kron's body began to stir. Caitlin backed off.

The sounds of grunts came from Kron, followed by, "Ke…vin… is that you?"

Kevin ran over and proceeded to turn Kron over onto his back. "It's me," he said. "What happened to you?"

"Watch… out… it… is… a magic sword…"

"Huh?" asked Kevin. "Watch out for a magic sword?"

It was then that Kevin heard the dark voice behind him say, "Now, then, what do we have here? Might that be the Sword of Purity you hold?"

It was frightening beyond all belief.

It was perhaps the scariest thing that Kevin had ever heard.

Kevin flipped around to see a sword pointed at him. When Kevin looked upon his face, he saw the most horrific of sights. "Arthur? What the hell are you doing?"

There was a slight pause.

"Heh," laughed the voice of Arthur. His voice seemed somewhat dark, as if a second, deeper voice were speaking along with his. "My, what luck we seem to have found," he began, as a second person stepped into view with him. "My compatriot came to reclaim my heir, and what do I find? First, a god, and now a new pure one. How desperate must the gods be!"

A scary realization was coming to Kevin in that moment. "I'm not a pure one," he began, almost hesitant to say what he had to say next, "and you're not Arthur!"

"I am afraid that Arthur does not have any impact on this battle." Arthur's eyes glowed red. "Tonight, pure one, you shall fall." The sword was raised as Arthur jumped high into the air. Arthur sliced downward aimed at Kevin, but Kevin, acting fast ran out of the way.

"Kevin, he's possessed!" yelled Caitlin, as she saw the red eyes. "It's Arthur's body, but he's not in control!"

Shocked, Kevin gathered himself. He noticed Arthur's red eyes. "You are skillful in the ways of the sword," said Kevin, as he backed up a couple of steps and held his sword into a ready stance, "but you are not my friend. Who or what are you?"

"Well, pardon my impoliteness," said Arthur, in a cocky tone of the dark voice, "but tonight your death shall be caused by Demonicus!"

Kevin gasped. Stunned, he stepped back, standing next to Caitlin. This possessor was claiming to be Demonicus, the dictator of Desolunar?! He raised his sword vertically in a defensive stance. He screamed, "What have you done with my friend?"

"What friend?" asked Demonicus. "You mean my son is your friend?" He paused for a second. "Then he has disgraced the family. But it is of no matter."

In that moment, all was revealed.

"No…" stammered Kevin, "that can't be…"

"But it is," answered Demonicus coldly.

With wide eyes, Kevin stood surprised. Could this really be true? Could the dictator of Desolunar really be Arthur's father?

The second figure caught Caitlin's attention. It was someone dressed in a red robe with a hood pulled over their eyes, wearing a gold necklace with a small golden pendant. "I find it interesting that you're aligned with the Enlighteners from the Shadows, Demonicus. Surprising that you, the leader of a kingdom, would be associated with a cult."

Demonicus did not answer, nor flinch at the comment.

"The who?" asked Kevin, maintaining his defensive stance with his sword.

"An ancient cult who worship a being called the 'conqueror'," Caitlin answered. "No time to explain; I'll tell you later."

"If you get to later," interrupted Demonicus. He raised Arthur's sword and pointed it at Kevin. Suddenly, Arthur's sword began to glow a dark red color.

Almost like how the Sword of Purity glowed bright blue.

That was how Kron was injured! But what kind of sword was this?

"You seem confused," commented Demonicus. "I knew all along that Arthur was my son, and I left him this sword to guide me to him when he came of age. It is a gift from my father that I have passed to him, the antithesis of your pathetic Sword of Purity, pure one. It is the Sword of Corruption." He paused for a second. "I knew this day would come, when I would face the pure one in battle and execute him."

Kevin shrugged off all the 'pure one' talk. It was clear Demonicus was going to call him that just because he could hold the Sword of Purity. Thoughts were racing through his head. How could he fight his best friend? What could he do? He could not risk fighting Demonicus without causing damage to Arthur. Then again, could he even beat Demonicus? Could he risk Arthur's life?

"Kevin, fight him," said Caitlin from a few steps away. "If you don't, then Demonicus will kill us both."

Arthur-Demonicus glared over at Caitlin and said, "You stay out of this." Then he took the Sword of Corruption and pointed it at her. A magical blast of lightning emitted from the sword, and blasted Caitlin backwards quite a distance. She slid along the ground, grinding to a stop.

Kevin saw this and became enraged. His instincts kicked in; he had to protect Caitlin. Now he had no choice. He grasped his sword tighter and braced himself for battle.

"Prepare to die!" yelled the thundering voice of Arthur-Demonicus. He then lunged forward with his sword pointing at Kevin. He blocked the attack with his sword, but had trouble holding Demonicus's power as Demonicus pushed hard continuously and Kevin tried to push back in resistance. As Kevin tried to defend himself from the attack, the Sword of Corruption lit up in its dark red color and the force from it pushed Kevin back hard into a tree. The force from the hit was intense and it caused Kevin to black out briefly.

Slowly, his eyes reopened. As Kevin regained consciousness after a few seconds, he saw a sword pointing at his neck. "All too easy," remarked Demonicus. "Now, if you will just hold still, this will be over in a minute." He then pushed his sword to stab Kevin in the neck, lining it up on the side of his neck first.

A mistake that left Kevin with an escape route, if he could make himself go for it.

At the last second, Kevin managed to roll away from the attack. As he rolled away, he regained his balance and stood up again. Quickly trying to make up for his careless mistake, Demonicus swung his sword horizontally, but he could not quite get the distance he needed to reach Kevin. Instead, Kevin was able to evade it and attempt to catch Arthur-Demonicus by the back with his sword with a parry move.

Before Kevin could make the attempt, Demonicus saw what was coming and kicked Kevin in the chest. Kevin fell backward, rolling across the ground a couple of times until he stopped at the feet of the Enlightener.

Kevin landed on his back. He looked up at the Enlightener, feeling helpless. Was this how everything was to end for him?

Suddenly, the Enlightener stepped back, running a few steps backward toward an animal.

A beam of light energy shot past. It looked extremely powerful, for all Kevin could tell.

He looked up to see Caitlin was standing up again, and had her arms extended. She had fired the beam. Then, looking a bit scuffed up, she looked directly at Demonicus and extended her hands. "Enough of this," she commanded. "Stand down, or I will destroy your heir."

Sitting up, Kevin looked on in awe of what Caitlin was doing. She clearly had the situation in hand, even if he did not. Her approach was measured and emotionless, not like the rage Kevin had just displayed in a losing effort to Demonicus. At this point he was afraid for his life again, and also that of Arthur.

Without turning around, Arthur-Demonicus laughed an evil laugh. "It appears I have underestimated you," echoed the deep voice of Demonicus, to Caitlin. "You have left me with no option but to retreat for the moment, as I will not risk injury to my heir." He then turned to Kevin. "But heed these words: I shall continue to challenge you, whether it be from my minions or myself. I will never allow you to interfere with my destiny or that of my immortal father." As he said this, the Enlightener walked up, holding onto a harness attached to a gryphon—a four-legged, two-winged bird-lion that had been tied up in the woods. "And with every fight, I will cause you pain, starting right now." Arthur grabbed the harness and hopped onto the gryphon, as did the Enlightener. Within a matter of seconds, the gryphon was in the air, heading south.

Frantically, Kevin stood and ran toward Arthur, trying to save him. It was too late, however. The gryphon, and Arthur, were gone.

He had failed. And his best friend was paying the price.

Despite the sight of the gryphon flying away, Kevin kept reaching out for Arthur, calling for him in desperation. Once the failure had finally set in a few moments later, Kevin lowered his hand. He took his sword, which was still in his other hand, and spiked it toward the ground, sticking it in the dirt. Kevin took a couple more steps forward to a large tree and fell to his knees, kneeling against the tree. The boy, at only sixteen years of age, was not able to fully overcome the loss of his best friend. His eyes were tearing, but he kept silent, keeping his sadness from the rest of the world.

Caitlin walked up to Kevin and knew that he was feeling extreme sadness, failure, and despair. Still, she decided to treat him like she normally treated everyone else, and said, "Kevin, we must get going. It's not safe for us to be out here in the middle of the forest at night."

Kevin, without lifting his head, said in an emotional tone, "I don't want to go. I couldn't save Arthur…"

Caitlin responded, not wavering in her tone, "Kevin, those red glowing eyes on Arthur were a sign of something called tracer magic. It may have been tested on that chimera that we saw; it would explain why it attacked us. That sword Arthur had must have some magical link to Demonicus, and the Enlightener, who was here as well, must have activated the tracer. Arthur being this far south would have been the perfect opportunity for him to use it if he wanted to kidnap him."

Kevin remained silent. He was not going to say anything.

It was then that Caitlin realized that she was rushing Kevin. All of that information was not going to help him in this moment. She crouched down to where he was and tried to be a little more reassuring, although her tone and emotion did not change, "Kevin, it is true that both our meeting and Arthur's disappearance are unexpected events, but now there is only one path to take."

Reaching to dry a tear from his eye, Kevin looked at Caitlin. "There is?" he asked.

"Of course there is," responded Caitlin. "We can't let this go unanswered. However, there is little we can do for now." She looked over to Kron, who was barely moving, but did have some motion. "Let's gather Kron up and we will rest in my house for the night. In the morning, let's regroup."

Not saying anything, Kevin nodded. While he was still very sad, it sounded like the most reasonable plan for now.

"Things will be difficult, I know," acknowledged Caitlin, as she approached closer to Kevin, hoping to make her words have meaning. "The path forward will be difficult, I know. But you have to stand up, to keep going down that path no matter where it takes you." She paused for a second. "And Kevin, whatever you need from me, I will give you. I will help you, guide you, travel with you… I will walk that path with you. All you need to do is take my hand, and I will do all of that for you." She offered him her hand as she stood up.

Despite still being upset, Kevin knew she was right. He had to stand up, fight on. Caitlin was willing to help him so he would not have to do it alone. Still saddened and in despair, Kevin grabbed for Caitlin's hand anyway, knowing what he had to do.

As he grabbed her hand, Caitlin pulled up, helping to lift Kevin to his feet again. He managed to get up without too much help. "I know you still feel horrible," Caitlin said after lifting Kevin, "but I will let you have the night to yourself to help recover."

Kevin only nodded, still saddened. He needed some time to fully comprehend what had just happened. He picked up his sword, placed it back in his scabbard, and started walking toward Kron. He and Caitlin would have to support him to help walk him back to the house. At the very least, Caitlin was sympathetic, even if she was not emotional.

It would be a very long night for Kevin.

Chapter 6

The Path to the City of Dreams

During the night, Kevin had many dreams circulating through his head. Most of them were nightmares, the horrid memories of what had happened to Arthur passing throughout his subconscious. There were also fears of what could have become of Caitlin had he not decided to fight Arthur-Demonicus. Having seen this vision, Kevin's subconscious was telling him a message. Never allow it to happen. Nobody should suffer that fate again, especially not Caitlin for all of the help that she has promised to provide.

Among these various dreams was one that was comforting. Home. It was the scene of Rikleifer, the city of dreams.

The name Rikleifer translates from the ancient language of *rengan* into "the town of many dreams." Rikleifer had a growth spurt a century before, giving it the status of a city according to Aurana's standards. It was currently the second largest city in Aurana, and was given the moniker "The City of Dreams" by Aurana based on its name translation and its current status. Rikleifer sat a little short of two days away from Caitlin's home, in the province of Middle Aurana, one of Aurana's three provinces. It sat at a large crossroads, making the concentric circle design of the city perfect for the traffic going through it. Roads led to all sorts of places from Rikleifer: north to Aurana City, northwest to Wyntrail, east to the kingdom of Nuve, and south to Atwals and the Calphos River. It was along this latter roadway that Caitlin's home was situated and where Kevin found the Sword of Purity.

This city was almost ideal by a common man's standards and exempt from many of the problems of the world, despite its relatively humble architecture. Residents mostly had available work and usually were able to survive reasonably well. It truly was a city of dreams to many, one that could exist peacefully and successfully without massive amounts of wealth or fancy buildings. The city was also the home of the Rikleifer Rangers, a team in the sport of dangerball, a very rough sport.

Most of this success was brought upon by the Duke of Rikleifer, younger brother of King Arnold IX—head of the Royal Family of Aurana. Much unlike his brother, the duke was a kind, generous man who was not motivated by personal wealth since he had plenty already. While the Duke was the direct ruler of the city of Rikleifer, serving only the King himself, he also held a council of advisors to aid him in making decisions. These advisors were among the smartest men and women in Aurana, and the duke paid much attention to their words and their opinions.

As he was dreaming of his hometown, Kevin woke up, much to his dismay since it was the only pleasant dream he had all night. Therefore, he decided that before he arrived in Wyntrail, as Caitlin had told him they were going to, he would return to Rikleifer and stay a night there. After all, it was on the way.

It was early in the morning when Caitlin decided to leave. She woke up Kevin and had to try several times to succeed, since Kevin was one who would sleep in and was very groggy. After she had succeeded in waking him, she stepped outside to allow Kevin to get ready on his own. Within a reasonably short amount of time, Kevin was ready to go, wearing his normal red shirt and brown pants, the same clothing as always. Caitlin was wearing the same simple black dress that nearly fully covered her body with few decorative features.

Surprisingly, when Kevin stepped out of the house, he saw Caitlin speaking with Kron, who appeared to be okay. Over the course of the night, he had regained all of his faculties. Although it seemed a bit unusual, Kevin recalled that Caitlin had told him Kron would pull through. He clearly was not down and out for long.

"And you think he can help us?" Kron inquired.

"I know he can," responded Caitlin, in an emotionless tone. She stopped there, however, as Kevin emerged from the house.

Kron turned to Kevin as the boy approached him. "Kevin, I have heard about what happened to Arthur," he began. "I offer you my deepest apologies. When I asked you if you could help me, I would have not considered doing so if I thought this would happen."

Kevin looked quite downtrodden, but he tried to shrug it off. "It'll be okay, I hope," he answered. "I had no idea that Arthur was the son of Demonicus."

Nodding, Kron said, "I would have never guessed, either." He looked to the south. "Nor do I know what Demonicus intends to do with him."

"I was confused by that too," shrugged Kevin. "Even if his son were my friend, why would the leader of another country attack us like that?"

Caitlin gave a sharp look at Kevin. She glanced at Kron briefly, and then looked back. "Make no mistake, Kevin," she began, "that Demonicus isn't just the ruler of Desolunar. He's a very dangerous individual, the likes of which poses a threat to the world." She waved an arm around to the south. "All of the destruction from that battlefield where we met? That's all ultimately his doing as he moves his troops north."

"He is out to conquer the world," added Kron, pausing for a second. "And, based on last night's events, he seems to fear the Sword of Purity. He undoubtedly knows what Vincent Stryker did with that sword to the uprising from his home city twenty years ago." For a second he paused again, and glanced at Caitlin. He reasoned to himself, carefully considering his next words, that if Caitlin knew about the Sword of Purity already, then she probably knew the next part as well. "That sword brought an end to the war and to Tyrinion."

Immediately, Caitlin caught Kron's use of the fallen deity's name. "You invoke the name of an immortal," she said.

"I have," acknowledged Kron. "You have already shown you know of them as well."

There was a slight moment of pause. Neither Kron nor Caitlin reacted to that.

"So what happened last night?" inquired Kevin to Kron, breaking the silence. "How did all of this happen?"

With a sigh, Kron took a breath before beginning. "Arthur wanted to 'stand guard', as you know, and I stayed outside with him. We heard a noise, which turned out to be a gryphon landing in a clearing, but we had no idea someone was actually riding it. He pulled out his sword, and immediately after that was the moment his eyes became red and he turned on me."

Caitlin breathed. "I've heard of Desolunar soldiers experimenting with captive gryphons to use them as flying mounts," she said. "It looks like they've managed to do so successfully now." She took a breath. "And they're now allied with the Enlighteners from the Shadows cult, so now they have magic support as well."

"Terrific," commented Kron, sarcastically. He looked up for a moment, wishing he could contact his fellow gods in this moment. This was above his abilities on his own.

Then, Caitlin turned to Kevin. "All the more reason we should go and find my father," she continued. "He's a powerful wizard and teacher, and he will listen to what we have to tell him. I am sure we will need his help if we're to rescue Arthur."

Kevin could not help but crack a smile. "Thanks, Caitlin," he said. It meant a lot to Kevin that Caitlin was willing to help.

Without ideas himself, Kron nodded. "I agree," he said. "But, I think it best if the two of you left without me and let me catch up." He looked toward Caitlin's house. "We still have the matter of the man in there. I do not think we should abandon him, but for the moment he cannot be moved or we risk injuring or killing him."

Looking to the house as well, Kevin realized that he had almost forgotten about Eukert. He knew someone had to make sure that man made it home as well, but he was a bit nervous to leave here without Kron. It was Kron who had brought him here, after all, and he had just met Caitlin the night before. Then again, Kevin thought, he had only known Kron for a couple of days.

Just a few days had passed now since Kevin was relaxing in Rikleifer wondering what to do with his life, with his best friend by his side and all the naivety of being young. Now, thanks to his willingness to help a god get home, he was without his friend and away from everything he knew, in a dangerous place. Furthermore, he had to place his safety in the hands of an emotionless sorceress his age, and trust she really would help as she offered.

No time to think about if he was making the right decisions. This was the road he was on, for better or worse. He looked at Kron. "I hope you catch up with us soon," he said. "Don't forget, I told you I'd help get you home. I still have to do that, too."

Kron shook his head. "We can wait on that a little while longer," he answered, "at least until we have Arthur back. However, I appreciate your thoughtfulness. I will catch up as quickly as I can move the commander."

Kevin nodded in acknowledgment. He reached down to make sure the Sword of Purity was attached to his waist and ready to go.

After a few more minutes of preparations and making sure they had some emergency provisions, Kevin and Caitlin said goodbye to Kron. Soon enough, they were heading north, in the direction toward Rikleifer. It was still the morning as they set off, a nice summer day that was not too warm just yet. A light breeze blew through the air. For the first while that they traveled, taking about an hour and a half, Kevin and Caitlin were both silent. Neither one really had much to say to the other; Caitlin was her normal emotionless self and Kevin was a little nervous about asking her any questions. Kevin knew he would have to talk to her at some point. Fear of what may become, he thought to himself. Irrational, but still paralyzing to the core. Still, he did not want to be unfriendly, but Caitlin seemed a bit unapproachable, even after all the help she had given to this point. To Kevin, she was pretty as well, which just made him more nervous, him being a teenage boy who was a bit socially awkward.

As they walked on, the forest had turned into a meadow, which seemed endless except for the path they were on and the occasional animals they would see. The meadow seemed to stretch to all horizons. It was a majestic sight to Kevin to see such beauty in nature. There were small animals occasionally that Kevin saw. All sorts of animals showed up, such as smaller rodents, squirrels, and other creatures of the meadow. At one point, Kevin even saw a wild horse, a rare sight in the world. In fact, Kevin could not be completely sure that the horse was wild and not a runaway from a stable, but he was fairly sure it was a wild horse.

The more Kevin walked on, the more he felt nervous about talking with Caitlin. Part of this was because he was curious about her and whom she was leading him to. He knew that Caitlin was leading him to her father, but that really did not tell Kevin any information about the man himself. It was just one of the many curiosities running through Kevin's head at the moment.

Fortunately for Kevin, and much to his surprise as well, Caitlin decided to break the ice and started talking to Kevin first. "Are you nervous, pure one?"

"Pardon me?" asked Kevin, not quite hearing what Caitlin said and a little surprised that Caitlin decided to break her silence.

"I asked if you were nervous," Caitlin said in response. "You seem to be a bit stiff in your mannerisms. I was wondering if you're feeling scared about what you have to do. Or, what you don't know to do."

Kevin thought for a second. "Caitlin, I'm really not sure what I can feel anymore. After agreeing to help Kron get home, seeing the battlefield, and then this incident with Arthur… I'm too overwhelmed to feel fear."

Caitlin pondered what Kevin said for a second. "I see," she finally said in response. "I suppose that it was probably inappropriate for me to ask you such a question at this time given the circumstances."

"Then again," Kevin said quickly, without thinking, "I would've expected such a cruel question from someone with your personality." Kevin stopped after he said that, almost dropping his jaw at the fact that that just came out of his mouth. That was certainly not the right thing for him to say, and he could not believe that he just said that out loud. It was something he would have expected out of Arthur, not himself.

"Oh? And what's that supposed to mean?" Caitlin said in response, in her normal tone. She sounded unfazed by Kevin's comment, just like she did from anything else. Kevin could not tell if she was irritated, curious, or anything else.

Kevin started to sound apologetic, worried that he may have irritated Caitlin and still regretting that comment. "Forget I said anything, Caitlin. I apologize for that comment."

Caitlin could tell Kevin was being sincere with the apology, so she replied, in her normal tone, "Apology accepted. I do realize that my personality can appear to be cold, but it is not in the intent to offend you. It is how I am in all affairs, both personal and business."

Not really sure why anyone would have this type of emotionless personality, but not wanting to ask Caitlin any more questions about it, Kevin acknowledged Caitlin's comment with a lie. "I understand," he said. "I think that maybe this whole situation and everything that's taken place lately is starting to get to me. Maybe I just need to take my mind off of everything that has happened."

"Perhaps it may help your mind if we learned a few things about each other on this trip," Caitlin said in response. "If we are to be traveling together, it may be helpful for both of us to know a little bit about each other, if only for a little bit of reassuring confidence in the other person and satisfying some curiosity."

Kevin thought for a moment. That might help take his mind off of a few things and make the trip seem faster. "Sure," he said. "I guess you're right; it might help."

"So, then," Caitlin said with little hesitation, "why don't you start first?"

Kevin gave his mind a second to think. He was a bit surprised, thinking Caitlin would have offered to go first based on it being her idea, but it mattered little. Thinking this, Kevin began to talk a little bit about himself. "I'm from Rikleifer, here in Aurana. I was born there, raised there, and I've lived there all sixteen years of my life. I lived on the west side of the city. Arthur was just down the street from me; we've been friends for years. I don't have parents at this point and he only has a mother who doesn't really care for him, so we've relied on each other for the most part."

"I see," nodded Caitlin. "It is why you care for Arthur so much. Do you have other friends?"

Kevin shrugged. "Not really," he said. "I'm a bit…" Kevin knew he was a socially awkward person, and he acknowledged that personally, but was not sure how to properly express that to someone else. "Let's just say I'm not good at meeting new people and interacting with them."

"Really?" inquired Caitlin. "You seem to be doing fine with me."

Aside, Kevin tried to hide a small laugh. "I didn't have a choice but to meet you. You threw fireballs at me, remember?"

Caitlin only nodded. Just a small reminder she was who she was. Kevin did not take offense, knowing her well enough by now to know that.

"Anyway, why don't you continue?" said Caitlin. "What about your mother and father? Why are you alone?"

Alone. No, Kevin pushed that thought out of his head.

"As far as I'm aware, my father has been dead for some time," he answered. "My mother never really told me who he was, but that it was someone she loved and that he had fought in the war twenty years ago. She said he was gone shortly after I was born, and it was something neither she nor he could control." He paused, knowing he was about to touch on a painful memory, but nonetheless he prepared to talk about his mother without dipping into any despair. "My mother passed away about three years ago from illness. She raised me and took care of me for most of my life, and since then I've taken care of myself."

There was a second's pause after Kevin said this. "I see," responded Caitlin, continuing not to waver. "I'm sorry that your life has gone like this."

Kevin nodded his head. He felt a little more reassured from talking to Caitlin, somehow. He was not sure how, but he was. Deciding to satisfy his curiosity about her, he said, "It'll be all right. Now that you know some about me, why don't you tell me about yourself?"

Taking a breath, Caitlin started to speak. "I suppose it's only fair," she said. "Although I think my history is more dull than your own, I'll tell you about it if you're still interested."

Kevin thought for a second. How could the history of a young sorceress prodigy be duller than his? After all, Kevin did not think his history was all too interesting with the exception of what had only happened over the course of the past few days. Nonetheless, Kevin was still very interested in Caitlin's history. Whether or not her history is interesting, he thought to himself, there was something special about this girl whose emotions were at least never visible, if not non-existent. But who was she? While Kevin was fairly certain that he would not receive all of the answers that he wanted from Caitlin, he still wanted to hear what he could. "Please go ahead," he said to Caitlin. "I am still interested in what is in your history."

"Very well," said Caitlin in her normal tone. "I've spent the past year at my home studying magic, and before that I lived in Wyntrail with my father. He has honed my skills at magic over the years. That's about it."

Kevin was a little stunned at how short Caitlin had made her history. Surely there was more to it than that. Curious about one fact, he bluntly asked, without making any consideration in his mind beforehand, "How old are you?"

Despite this, Caitlin did not even take a second to think. "Fifteen," she said in her normal voice. "I'll be a legalized adult in a few months. I was granted the right to live by myself for the purpose of studying magic."

Kevin was a little surprised. Sure enough, Caitlin was about his age, but legally she was not an adult. Yet she was a magical prodigy with a firm personality and no emotion. What could bring all of this together? After a moment's more thought, Kevin decided not to ask Caitlin about her parents, in contrast to her questions of him. After all, he was going to meet her father soon enough.

"Just how long have you studied magic?" he then asked. "You seem to be very good at it."

"For as long as I can remember," answered Caitlin. "My father is not only a wizard, but a professor at the Bladinstar School, the last place in the world that teaches magic. I've sort of been his apprentice since I could walk and speak."

That was a surprise, Kevin thought to himself. Certainly it was not surprising that she had trained for so much of her life to have the level of talent she has already shown, but it was surprising that she would have been taught magic from such a young age, even with a parent who taught magic to others.

"Amazing," Kevin said to himself. "I've always wondered how

magic worked."

Caitlin shrugged. "It's all about channeling energy through you," she said. "Some have a greater natural talent than others, sure, but through the calling and effort anyone can learn at least the basics." She paused for a second. "Anyone could learn a little bit of elemental magic, I would reason. Fire, air, ice, and earth are all elements that can't really be manipulated too much, anyway, other than how much power is put into it, like a spark, a blast, or a beam."

Kevin was curious. "Then what can you manipulate?"

"Light and darkness," Caitlin answered. "You can do all sorts of things with light and darkness magic if you learn them. You can heal or damage. You can shape elemental magic by using light and darkness with it. You can use it precisely to enter someone's mind, or communicate with them. They say you could even bend reality slightly with the right combination of both." She paused again. "Only my father has been known to manipulate the magic of life, and even then, he can only do so barely."

"It's like you're a pro at this already," commented Kevin. "No wonder you're so disciplined."

"You wish to know why I'm disciplined?" asked Caitlin.

Immediately, Kevin became nervous. He had not intended on trying to get that out of Caitlin.

After a few seconds of awkward silence, Caitlin said, "Please don't worry. I'm not ashamed of the way I am, and I'm willing to share with you."

Kevin breathed a sigh of relief. He nodded, ready to listen.

Caitlin continued, "Magic is my life's work. As such, I have to be extremely focused on it if I want to be good. My father drives me to be better each day, and I wish not to disappoint him. He expects much of me and my training."

Suddenly, Kevin felt a wave of sympathy for Caitlin, something he had not felt for the emotionless sorceress before. It was one thing to be so driven on one's own, but to do so under pressure from a parent seemed cruel. Such harshness would certainly explain a lot, that Caitlin was a young person placed under high expectations that were unrealistic to average people.

What Kevin did not know, though, was that Caitlin was not telling him the whole story.

They walked a few more steps in silence, as Kevin was unsure how to respond. He was pretty sure that Caitlin did not see it as something to feel bad about, although he did. It was a matter of two different minds on the subject, even if he felt Caitlin's mind might be influenced by the way she was brought up.

Then, Caitlin broke the ice by changing the subject. "Do you do anything for fun?"

"Huh?" asked Kevin, slightly taken aback.

"You know, fun," said Caitlin.

Kevin looked at Caitlin. "I'm surprised you're interested in that," he said.

Caitlin shrugged. "It's a good indicator of what kind of person you are."

"Oh," let out Kevin. He still was not sure why this would be relevant to someone he was sure did not know the definition of 'fun', but if she was interested, he did not have a reason not to answer. "I don't have money to spend on fun things, but I do like doing a little swordplay in school. I'll sometimes go to check out a dangerball game if I can afford it, or I'll visit the library and read an adventure book."

Caitlin raised an eyebrow. "You read adventure books?" She sounded slightly interested.

Nodding, Kevin said, "I do." For a moment, he forgot it was Caitlin talking to him, interested in the subject. "I think my favorite I've ever read was *Tale of the Valkyrie*."

That made Caitlin's eyes widen for a second. "That is quite the coincidence," she said. "It's my favorite, too."

Suddenly, Kevin stopped walking, surprised. "You read adventure books, too?"

"Absolutely," answered Caitlin, having stopped as well. "When I'm not practicing magic, it's my one guilty pleasure. And, as expensive as books are, I actually have a copy of *Tale of the Valkyrie* at my house."

"That's amazing!" exclaimed Kevin. "I heard there weren't that many copies of the book written. So awesome that you got a hold of one."

"You can thank my father for that," Caitlin explained. "I think it's such a shame there are so few copies of that book. It's such a great story."

"Agreed," Kevin acknowledged. "The small library in Rikleifer Castle only has one copy. I'm very fortunate it's still in good shape whenever I want to return to reread it."

Caitlin nodded. "Indeed it is," she said. "You know, Kevin, I'm surprised to find I have something in common with you."

There was a slight pause. Then, Kevin smiled as he thought about what Caitlin just said. Even as emotionless as she came off to be, she and he still had common ground, and it was clear that she was not completely cold and unfeeling. It did make him feel much better about walking with her. He was starting to like her.

As Kevin and Caitlin shared a few more facts with each other, they traversed much ground on the road, and the distance just seemed to tick by. The sun began to travel higher into the sky as the day went on. During the whole trip, Kevin and Caitlin were still trading facts, although Caitlin had still not shed her persona. For Kevin, this was a little uncomfortable to be talking to someone who was not exactly being friendly with him, but he knew she was trying in the way that she could..

By the midday hour a short time later, Kevin and Caitlin had reached the town of Haventown, a small town with only about 100 citizens. The town was nothing but a village, mostly home to some of the poorest citizens of Aurana, who could not afford to leave due to their poverty. They supported themselves by subsistence farming and as a travel stop between Rikleifer and the southern Auranian city of Atwals, the latter of which was currently under Desolunar occupation. There was little time to stop, but Kevin and Caitlin did so briefly to pick up some provisions and take a short break. They had to set off again if they wanted to make it to Rikleifer in a timely manner, and Kevin had not forgotten his friend Arthur needed rescue.

At dusk, Kevin and Caitlin had reached the Calphos River, a river nearly half a day's walk north of Haventown. Sourced from further northwest, it traversed Aurana as a small river that flowed southeast. In Aurana, it was only a minor river, but once it intersected with the Aurun River forming Aurana's eastern border, it gained a massive amount of water flow and became a major avenue for transport across the world's south.

Standing at the edge of the river and breathing heavily, Kevin felt his body tiring from the full day of walking. The surroundings had turned from meadow to a light forest A short suspension bridge connected the south part of the road to the northern part. Nearby was an underground burrow, dug out for military usage. A sign outside of it served as a marker, indicating its position as "Aurana Protection Forces Post 3", a common stopping point and rest station for military units. It was fairly common for military units on the move to camp out along the Calphos River while marching down the road to the Desolunar border. It was also fairly common practice to dig a burrow at these sites to provide a more permanent, yet cheap, structure to house the highest-ranking officers of these marches. It would be a safe place where they could spend the night.

Approaching the river, Kevin bent down at the end of the bridge and said to Caitlin, exhausted, "Can't we call it a day? We've traveled for quite a distance. This is the Calphos River, which means we should be more than halfway to Rikleifer by now."

Saying nothing, Caitlin studied her location quickly. Examining the river, the forest, and the burrow, she finally came to a conclusion. "This will be an okay stopping point. We should be in Rikleifer by the midday tomorrow."

A smile came to Kevin's face. Rikleifer. Sure enough, he would be going home. And despite the fact that he knew he could not stay in the city for long, there was still something satisfying to Kevin about having the opportunity to be in his hometown one more time.

Caitlin noticed Kevin's smile, and said, "I take it you're looking forward to going home?"

"Indeed," he said, not turning. He was thinking, daydreaming again, deep in thought. It was like the day when Arthur ran across Kevin daydreaming, the exact day that Kron had found him and asked for help. It was a comfortable place in Kevin's mind for him to be.

Able to see that Kevin was thinking hard about something, she decided to leave him be. Caitlin said to Kevin, as she headed for the military burrow, "Come inside when you are finished with whatever you are doing." She then descended into the burrow.

Kevin was still looking out, just wondering about various things. He worried about Arthur and all about Demonicus. The ruler of Desolunar was indeed powerful and he furthermore ran a kingdom; how could Kevin possibly free Arthur from him? What kind of answer to that question could Caitlin's father provide? And why was Demonicus so incensed by the Sword of Purity?

All of this was brought about simply because Kevin offered to help a god get back home, which he did not know how to do, and Kron had not told him yet. What does the Sword of Purity have to do with this? And why was the price to complete this task so high? This task has already claimed Arthur. Who else will this task claim? Would it be Caitlin?

As Kevin thought about this final question, he began to feel some kind of emotion. It was indeed sadness, but to Kevin this was very odd, seeing as how he had only met Caitlin recently. Kevin was sure there was something very special about the girl. Although she was so isolated, Kevin was fairly certain that there was more to her than what was on the outside. He was already internally defending what he saw in Caitlin, not even knowing if it really was there or not. He was finding that there was something about her that made him like her. Kevin laughed at himself at the intriguing situation that he had put himself in with this, and told himself he was being ridiculous. Still, the socially awkward boy could not help but think of the girl with no emotions, and it brought a slight smile to his face.

Suddenly, Caitlin appeared outside the burrow, in a rush. "Kevin! Get in the burrow now! If you don't, we could be in trouble!"

Reacting quickly, Kevin ditched his thinking, broke into a run, and slid into the hole. After he had slid in, Caitlin immediately started casting a magic spell of light with a continuing stream of energy, shaping it into a shield.

"What's going on?" Kevin asked in a rush, still puzzled as to what happened for Caitlin to call him back.

Caitlin had merely to point to the tunnel entrance with her free hand as the other one powered the shield. As Kevin looked out the entrance in the direction Caitlin was pointing, he saw something standing on top of the spell shield. It was a black chimera.

"If you wouldn't have hurried," Caitlin continued, "you would have been food for that thing. Fortunately, we are safe in the burrow and we won't have to fight it."

Kevin caught his breath and asked, "Why would one be this far north?"

"That's a good question," Caitlin said in response. "I can't believe that there is one this far north. Maybe the battles in the south have driven it this far. I'm really hoping this one isn't being controlled by tracer magic as well."

That was exactly what Kevin was afraid of, as well.

As luck would have it, however, the next few moments were full of silence. Caitlin stopped powering the magic shield of light, satisfied that it was not a possessed chimera and was no longer a danger. The sun was quickly setting, however, and both Kevin and Caitlin quickly decided that it would be better to take shifts guarding the entrance just in case. Kevin agreed to take the first watch.

The burrow had about five feather beds, four in one room for high-ranking officers, and a separate bed in a separate room for the commanding officer. A third room had a table and a few chairs. It was this room that connected to the entrance of the burrow. Caitlin slept in the commanding officer's room, while Kevin volunteered to take the room with the other beds.

Around the middle of the night, Kevin and Caitlin traded shifts. But as Kevin lay down, all he could think about was Caitlin and her safety in doing this task. Even though she had volunteered to take this journey with him, bringing her along meant putting her into danger. Caitlin was still very much a stranger to Kevin, and it was nerve-wracking to Kevin to have her life placed in his hands, even if Caitlin was stronger than him and she was more likely to protect him instead. She had just protected him from what could have been a threat in the black chimera, but Kevin was aware that this type of circumstance would not be the case every time along this journey. It made him a bit nervous, knowing he was weaker but that at some point, she may have to rely on him the same way he had relied on her, and he was afraid he would not be up to the task.

Chapter 7

A Dictator's Kingdom

In the bowels of the kingdom of Desolunar lies the city of Seta Archa, an ancient city of temples everywhere. It is not an easy city to enter, as it is surrounded by a very thick wall with battlements on the top, and no visible gate. Surrounding such a well-guarded city is a very thick forest. Those walls and natural defenses had served Seta Archa well for centuries.

Founded by Setaeus Demota nearly five thousand years before, the city was created as an isolated sanctuary for his last group of followers. Over the years, it became a large independent city-state, separated from the rest of the known world by the southern forest and the Wastes. It became by all means a more normal city as time went by, and traded with other kingdoms during the feudal eras of many small lands.

Change for the worse came over two decades ago, when the Alliance-Daritel War began, and a tribe from the Wastes known as the Daritel sacked Seta Archa while influenced by a god. That same influence, under Daritel threats, then weaponized the people of Seta Archa and began invading the kingdoms to the north. The Triple Alliance of Aurana, Nuve, and Scurnia lost battle after battle and more and more territory, capturing the Nuve capital of Cardol in the process. In a last act of desperation, the legendary Vincent Stryker led forces past the front lines and onto Seta Archa and sacked the city again, ending the war.

The end of the war, though, created a power vacuum as no one was left in charge of Seta Archa and it was too isolated for any of the Triple Alliance kingdoms to control. This allowed Demonicus to rise to power by the use of powerful magic and his association with the Enlighteners from the Shadows, a group who worship a being called the "conqueror". Demonicus took his name from this association, claiming himself to be “the conqueror’s chosen demon” for the work he had done, which he later simplified to “chosen one”.

Slowly, over the next twenty years, Demonicus outfitted Seta Archa society to become a war machine, creating a gigantic and well-trained army. He called his new country a “kingdom” only to establish its legitimacy, but he did not claim the title of king. Desolunar was a dictator’s kingdom.

As time passed, and more ground was taken, people who lived in the areas of the new Kingdom of Desolunar were conditioned to be Desolunarian and started filling the army themselves, although plenty of resistance still occurred as well. Demonicus also struck deals with the tribes of the Wastes to add them officially to Desolunar and offer them protection, in return that they would protect his east flank and promise not to start war with the city of Seta Archa.

Of course, Demonicus did have ulterior motives other than simply establishing a kingdom. But the people of Desolunar were not told this. In fact, the popular reasoning behind the current war was simply that the other four kingdoms impeded their way of life and needed to be overthrown. This was mostly spread by propaganda, as Demonicus exerted sole control of all media in his country and unauthorized spreading of information was punishable by death. In uniforms of black, they struck hard and powerfully upon the southern lands of Aurana and Nuve.

At the center of Seta Archa are two buildings that represent the power of the Desolunar state. One is the Temple of Setaeus, a tiered square pyramid that served as the original gathering site of Setaeus Demota’s followers millennia before. The second is the Pyramid of Desolunar, a tall stone structure in the shape of a triangular pyramid that is the home of Demonicus near the top. At the very top, surrounded by glass, is Demonicus's throne room, and at the bottom, in the ground, is the prison block. The Pyramid of Desolunar stands several stories tall.

From his office, Demonicus sat and considered his kingdom, of which he was not a king. He was the leader, and as far as he was concerned that was all the title he needed. The sun was setting in Seta Archa, as the leader, wearing a red cloak with the hood up as always did his Enlighteners from the Shadows, sat behind a desk and looked out the windows. He was, after all, a man of business who had no time for a throne in his throne room. At the moment, however, thoughts of there being a new "pure one" preoccupied him. He was very concerned about this development and what it meant for his plans.

A thumping sound came from the floor. The access to his throne room was through a floor panel that opened akin to a trap door. Only his most trusted were allowed to get his attention.

"Enter," commanded Demonicus.

As instructed, the Enlightener on the staircase below the floor opened the trap door and ascended the stairs. Coincidentally, it was the same Enlightener who had been with him when he had taken possession of Arthur via the Sword of Corruption. "Lord Demonicus, I have news from our men and women operating in Cornelia." He was referring to a province in the country of Nuve, southeast of Rikleifer across the Aurun River. "We have found the Light."

That seemed to grab Demonicus's attention. "Very good," he said. "How was it located?"

"One of our transit units out of our base in the region ran across a group headed on the road to Cardol," he said. "They claimed to be some kind of book club from Rikleifer. One of them, a young woman, was carrying a locket that held the Light. She and the rest of the group seemed unaware that the Light was there. Although she was armed with a bow and arrows, the rest of her group was not armed at all, and we quickly subdued them. We brought the young woman here in case you would like to interrogate her."

Demonicus was not one to interrogate, and he was fairly certain a good number of his Enlighteners knew this by now, including the one talking to him. He threw a hand in the air and said, "I will dispose of her later, I suppose." He paused for a moment. "Do you have this locket for me?"

Without speaking, the Enlightener took it out of his cloak pocket and put it on Demonicus's desk.

Turning and reaching over, Demonicus grabbed the shiny locket and clutched it tightly. He was channeling energy from it into his own body. In a solid minute he was done, and threw the now dull locket back onto his desk. He pulled up the sleeve on his right arm, revealing two stripes across his forearm, which wrapped up his arm. One was colored purple, and the new one was colored yellow.

"Excellent," he remarked, turning toward a window facing north. "I now have the Light and the Darkness." He paused, and turned his head. "And our man in the north still has the Fire?"

"He does," nodded the Enlightener. "He still has it to use for the task you have given him. It has been a while since word of his progress has reached the relay station, however."

Demonicus shrugged. "It is of no matter," he said. "That is one of our most trusted; he is fully loyal to our cause and to me."

The Enlightener bowed. "As we all are." He then put a fist to his chest. "Loyalty to the chosen one."

Returning the fist to the chest gesture, Demonicus said, "Dismissed."

As instructed, the Enlightener turned and left. On his way to the stairs, he passed a female Enlightener entering the chamber. This was also one of Demonicus's most trusted, but she chose not to knock solely because the door was left open. She was also expected, as she oversaw the prison unit in the pyramid for Demonicus's most personal prisoners, and Demonicus requested regular reports from her.

Recognizing her presence, Demonicus looked to her to ask a question. "Has my son softened up in prison and become ready to accept his role?"

The second Enlightener shook her head. "He has not," she said. "He continues to be defiant."

There was a slight pause. It was clear Demonicus was angry, but at least for the moment, he did not place the blame on his team. "Much like his father; there is clearly potential. He is strong-willed, a trait he should have as my heir, but he should also desire power." He turned back to the second Enlightener. "Dismissed," he said.

With that, the Enlightener put a fist to her chest and turned to descend the stairs.

Demonicus turned back to look out the window. Sometime soon he would have to deal with his son, but he could not focus on that at the moment, so he left his son to sit in prison for a while. At this moment, although he had affairs to attend, the one focus on his mind was the emergence of a new pure one. He did not believe this notion that this "Kevin" was not a pure one. He held the Sword of Purity, Vincent the Pure One's weapon, the sword of the champion defending the gods. If he could hold it, then of course he must be a new pure one.

This was not a roadblock that could be allowed to stand, regardless of how weak he was. The gods could not be permitted to influence his campaign as they did the war twenty years ago, and it was clear that somehow they were. Why else would he have found a god to ambush when his son came into his sphere of influence? They had a plan, and he knew it. No matter how insignificant the threat, he had to stamp it out before it had even the slightest chance.

There was just one problem. That wizard girl. She was protecting him and proved to be something for which he had not planned. And now, surely the new pure one and she were retreating into Aurana, past his sphere of influence. Although Desolunar was quickly conquering more and more territory of Aurana and Nuve, the north was not somewhere he had forces as of yet. He could not track the pure one there. The longer he stayed north, the more time he and the gods had to try and ruin his conquest. Something had to be done.

He needed help.

Seeing he was alone, he looked up through the triangular pyramid's windows into the sky. "Father," he said, "please grant me my assistant you promised. Let him remind me of my enemy and the obstacle I must overcome." He said it as though praying.

Silence filled the room for over a minute.

"Yes, Father, I hear your voice," continued Demonicus. "I thank you for the power you have invested to grant me the tools I need. I shall await his arrival."

Another few seconds of silence pervaded the air.

The sound of the trap door pounding then rang though the chamber. "Enter," commanded Demonicus, turning back toward the center.

As the door opened, in walked a Desolunar army messenger. He walked onto the floor and knelt before Demonicus. "My lord, I bring word from Atwals."

Demonicus let out a breath. Atwals had been the second-largest city in Aurana prior to his conquest of it. The city still held a portion of the population that it did before, and while it was occupied it was also in constant chaos, as the occupying forces had been dealing with a stubborn underground resistance that used hit-and-run tactics to pester his forces. It was a thorn in his side that while the city was in his control, it was not truly subjugated and was proving difficult to use to his advantage.

"The assassination of the resistance leader has been carried out," stated the messenger.

Suddenly, Demonicus cracked a smile. It was not often that the dictator did that. "Good," he said. He knew who he had assigned to that task. "Lieutenant Kirkwood's daughters certainly do not disappoint." He paused. "Does General Sayo believe we will have rid ourselves of the resistance soon?"

The messenger shook his head. "He does not," he answered. "General Sayo stated that while his forces had the most important resistance members cornered, they escaped and Lieutenant Kirkwood failed to pursue them."

Anger suddenly pulsed through Demonicus's veins. He clenched his fists. Although his daughters were certainly no disappointment, Lieutenant Kirkwood certainly was. Surely the resistance would now have a new leader soon enough.

"The general wishes to inform you that he is disciplining Lieutenant Kirkwood for his failure," continued the messenger.

"No," commanded Demonicus, turning with force to the messenger. "Go back to Atwals, and have the general send Lieutenant Kirkwood to me personally. Have him bring his daughters with him."

"As you wish," answered the messenger. "I have more information for you, however." He pulled a letter out from his uniform.

Demonicus was interested. As the messenger passed the letter to Demonicus, he put his fist to his chest and gave a small bow. "Dismissed," commanded Demonicus, giving the messenger the official dismissal he was expecting in that moment. He turned and walked down the stairs, closing the trap door behind him.

With that, Demonicus went to his desk and proceeded to open

the letter. It was marked as strictly confidential from General Sayo, who was handling the situation in Atwals and all invasions north into Aurana. The general was from the province of Southern Aurana, and as such had great familiarity with the region and the city.

As Demonicus read the letter, he came to find out this letter was confidential because it contained information from the resistance in Atwals. Someone there knew something, had met someone before, knew approximately where that someone was.

Immediately as he finished reading, Demonicus folded up the letter and placed it in his desk drawer. Suddenly he now had a new focus to worry about, an issue that in his mind had to take priority over all others, even over the issue of this new person holding the Sword of Purity. It quickly became his new focus.

Taking out a clean sheet of paper and some ink and a feather pen, Demonicus began to write. He had plans to create and critical decisions to make. Briefly, he looked down at the yellow and purple stripes wrapped from his right wrist up his arm, knowing that they would be the key to his seizure of the realm.

Chapter 8

Hometown

The next day, Kevin and Caitlin had set off from the Calphos River to the north, in the direction of Rikleifer, the "City of Dreams" as it was sometimes translated. Once again, Caitlin had to wake up Kevin, who seemed to have a habit of sleeping in every day. Nonetheless, Kevin was ready to leave shortly after waking up, desiring to see his hometown and sleep in his own bed in his own house the next night.

As they continued to travel northward across the meadows of Middle Aurana, Kevin continued to have recollections of the special feeling he had experienced for Caitlin the night before while resting alongside the Calphos River. Kevin himself thought it was ridiculous logically, but something was telling him that something was different about the emotionless Caitlin, something more than what could be seen from an outer perspective.

Still, Kevin knew he was being a normal teenage boy, almost desperate for the girlfriend every boy his age desires. He had already felt mildly heartbroken before, knowing that getting one's hopes up for feelings unreturned only ever ended that way. Of course he was still young, but never had he found someone who had similar feelings for him over any length of time, much to his dismay. What, of all things, would make a girl with no emotions whatsoever any different? In this case, the answer would be nothing. He resolved to put the entire matter out of his head and keep his mind clear of any obstructions he possibly could avoid.

Still, Caitlin had more questions, and Kevin was willing to answer. Kevin even started to come up with more of his own that did not involve Caitlin's status as a sorceress. While this may have been Caitlin's tactic to ease things over with Kevin and make them less awkward, it was working and Kevin was quite appreciative of that. If nothing else, Kevin thought to himself, he was slowly but surely making a friend.

And even to Caitlin, she was surprised to find that as well. Kevin was a relatively normal person to most, but what Caitlin knew of a normal life was somewhat foreign to her as well given her focuses in life. She was curious about him, finding a lot of his life intriguing, even if it were dull to him. That they shared mutual interests, such as a love of adventure stories, was even more intriguing as well. Caitlin was especially astonished that Kevin, a boy, said that his favorite adventure story was *Tale of the Valkyrie*, a rarity in the world as a story focused on a female hero. That was part of what drew Caitlin to the story herself, but as she understood it usually boys liked stories where men were the heroes. Kevin was different in that way.

The sun was just setting on their third day, as Kevin became a little sad. Even with thoughts of rescuing Arthur on his mind, and the budding friendship he was building with Caitlin, he had been quite hopeful to reach Rikleifer this night and sleep in his own bed. All around were meadows and open space, nowhere to take shelter if they did not reach Rikleifer tonight.

Caitlin could sense Kevin's disappointment. "We must not be far from Rikleifer," she told him, as if to reassure. "I believe we'll make it before the sun goes down."

Kevin shrugged. He then sighed and said, "I really hope so."

Still little excitement from Kevin, despite this optimism. Then, a thought occurred to Caitlin. "If it makes you feel better, I realize that I may have forgotten something." She thought for another moment. "I did," she then realized. "I had forgotten what day it would be when we arrived. My father actually has a guest lecture in Rikleifer tomorrow. He told me he would be here tomorrow, so we can actually catch him in town and not have to leave immediately."

That did make Kevin feel better. His body language changed; he looked like he was lightening up a bit. "That would be great," he said. "I hope he can help."

"He can, I'm sure of it," said Caitlin. "My father is the greatest wizard in the world. If anyone can help you free Arthur and get Kron back home, he can."

At this point, Kevin was not really sure how a wizard could

help, but he was trying to trust Caitlin. He then asked, "So is there some kind of magic your father specializes in, or does he just do one or two kinds, or something?"

"Oh, he's talented at all known kinds of modern magic," Caitlin answered. "Elemental, light and darkness, magic theory, mind magic..."

"Mind magic?" Kevin's attention was caught.

"Have you ever heard of mind magic?" Caitlin then asked Kevin.

Looking a bit confused, Kevin asked, "You mean like a psychic?"

"Sort of," answered Caitlin. "But not to be confused with those scam artists who pretend to talk to the dead or predict the future. The real mind magics can do many things, but only the most powerful can learn it, and it must always be done with permission. It's very dangerous in the hands of the wrong person who behaves unethically with it."

"I'm guessing that's not a problem with you," stated Kevin.

"No, of course not," said Caitlin, "but even with my talents I can only do so much with it. I could read your mind if I placed my hands beside your head, but that is extremely unethical and about the worst offense someone with mind magic could do."

Kevin's eyes widened. "That is absolutely terrifying," he said.

"It is," acknowledged Caitlin, "and that is exactly why studying magic users are required to stick to an ethical code."

"I see," said Kevin awkwardly, turning his head. Now, he was quite scared of what Caitlin could do, but thus far he had no reason not to trust her. He believed that for as much as she was talking about ethics, surely she was sworn to the same ethical code. "Is there anything less invasive you can do with it?"

"Aside from that, I could send you messages, but that's about it."

Kevin raised an eyebrow. "Show me," he said.

I see you are curious.

That voice was in Kevin's head. It was Caitlin's. She had not moved her lips this time.

I would not do this had you not told me to show you. But, you may find this useful if we're a short distance apart.

But how would I respond? Kevin thought to himself.

Like that.

Kevin was surprised.

If we're communicating like this, all you have to do is think and I'll be able to understand you. When you project your thoughts, it works along the same connection.

"Okay," said Kevin, aloud. He was still curious. "Does this mean you can manipulate the thoughts of others?"

Caitlin shook her head. "Oh, no," she answered. "There's no messing with the free will of others, no matter how strong-minded or weak-minded they may be. About the most one could do, I suppose, would be very subtle influence, and even then it's never focused enough to really change someone's mind like their political stance or their likes or dislikes."

Kevin frowned a little bit. "I think I get some of it. I'm not sure what a 'very subtle influence' is, though."

For a second, Caitlin paused. She had to think on whether or not she could explain this to Kevin; the best explanation she had was one of her biggest secrets. Having traveled with Kevin for several days now, she decided it would be okay. "Like my discipline," she said.

Raising an eyebrow, Kevin turned his head toward Caitlin as they kept walking. "So what does this have to do with your discipline?"

Caitlin took a breath. "I asked my father, years ago, to place an emotional block in my mind."

That made Kevin's eyes widen. He tried to look away, and Caitlin did not catch it. She was true and honest to her word that she was not going to be invasive.

"I understand this probably comes across as a surprise," continued Caitlin, as she looked at Kevin, "but as I've grown older I've come to find it was the best way to avoid distractions of feelings, and the best way to do so is to suppress my emotions. It has helped to make sure I can truly delve into my studies. I share this with you so that you won't think of me as cruel while we travel."

So much was cycling through Kevin's mind at this point, and it was tainting the opinion Kevin was forming of Caitlin's father before he had even met the man. Whether or not Caitlin had asked for this, what parent does this to a child? Was Caitlin effectively denied a childhood by losing her ability to feel things from a young age? Now he felt prejudiced toward Caitlin's father before even meeting him, that he was wrong for allowing this even if it was Caitlin's request.

Still, Kevin would not judge Caitlin the same way. Because it was an unreasonable request to him did not mean it was one to her. "I don't think I would think of you as cruel," he said. "You're just a little different, that's all."

Quietly, Caitlin gave a little nod. "As are you, Kevin Trent."

And even that, Kevin had to agree. Although they were two quite different people, they did have some similarities, and being different people in society was one such similarity.

As the sun reached halfway across the horizon, Kevin saw what he was waiting so long to see. It was the castle in the center of Rikleifer, standing out against the buildings of the city. As Kevin saw his hometown, he broke into a run to the city limits. It did not matter to Kevin how tired it made him or how much his lack of stamina made it more difficult for him to keep running. He was going to keep running until he made it home. Caitlin struggled to keep up, but did manage to catch up to Kevin by walking, a few minutes after Kevin had reached the city limits.

Kevin was still catching his breath, but it was worth every breath for him to reach the city limits. He was home. This was Rikleifer, the one true place he could call home. Knowing that he probably would not be able to return to Rikleifer for a very long time, Kevin wanted to savor every moment in the city that he could.

The great city was a wonderful sight to Caitlin, who had never seen the city before. While the city itself did not appear wealthy, lavish, or in any other way a "city of dreams" from the exterior, it was still a large city that was well-kept. To Kevin, however, it was the only true place he could call home.

As Caitlin finally walked up to Kevin, who had just finished catching his breath from running to the city limits, Kevin said, "Welcome to my hometown."

"I've been through here a few times," Caitlin answered, "but I can't say I've ever stayed here too long."

A smile came to Kevin's face. "This is a neat city," he said, very excited. "The city is designed in concentric circles, with a few roads running through the city's diameter. At the center of the city lies the city castle, where all of the government offices are. Just to the north is Ranger Arena, home of the local professional dangerball team, the Rikleifer Rangers. My home is on the fifth circle from the end just north of the West Road at the corner, which is where we can stay tonight."

"All right," responded Caitlin, taking note of all of the things Kevin had said. Then she asked, "Kevin, is there anything that you need to do here before we leave?"

"Leave?' inquired Kevin, puzzled. "I thought you said your father would be here?"

"I meant 'leave' only in the sense of if you have other obligations you should fulfill before we turn in for the night."

"Oh." Kevin thought for a moment. "The only thing that I can think of is that I should probably speak with Arthur's mother about what happened to him. She is a drunk, though, so I am not sure if she would really care too much about Arthur's whereabouts," he said. "Nonetheless, I think it's important that I give it a shot, at least."

"Then perhaps we should hurry," said Caitlin, pointing toward the sun. "We won't have long before dark."

Kevin agreed, and he led Caitlin around one of the ring roads to the west. Minutes passed by, as the sun continued to set even further. When Kevin and Caitlin had reached Arthur's house, Kevin knocked on the door and received no answer. He then opened the door and peered inside. Arthur's mother was already gone. Kevin reasoned that perhaps she had gone out drinking again.

So, having given up for now, Kevin returned with Caitlin to his own house. During the walk there, he could not help but think of Arthur's mother's reaction to her son's kidnapping by his father. There was always a good chance that Arthur's mother actually did not care about her son, but neither Kevin nor Arthur actually knew about what Arthur's mother really thought about him.

Once Kevin and Caitlin were at Kevin's house, Kevin allowed Caitlin through the door first, and then followed her inside. Caitlin sat down at Kevin's small kitchen table, while Kevin grabbed some available preserved food and offered it to her. He then began to rummage through his few possessions for something. Having not found what he was looking for, Kevin began to dig under his bed, still searching for something.

"Kevin, what are you looking for?" asked Caitlin, curious, after she finished a bite of the food. "You're tossing everything in the house everywhere."

Kevin felt no need to respond, for within five seconds of Caitlin's comment, he found what he wanted. It was a small bag filled with pieces of copper and some silver. Then he showed it to Caitlin and said, "This. It's all the money I have left."

Caitlin merely nodded, acknowledging its importance for Kevin to have, and changed the subject. "Anyway, what do you plan to do with Arthur's mother? Her son was kidnapped, after all. It is something that she should know about personally."

"It is," responded Kevin, sadly, "but how much it matters to her, really, I don't know."

"Nonsense," replied Caitlin, maintaining her usual tone. "Whether or not she is a person with demons as you have described, she is still a mother. It will affect her."

Reluctantly, Kevin nodded. It was cruel not to tell her, true, but he knew Rita Falchor and the way she treated Arthur. It was difficult for him to put it past his mind that anyone with such a connection to Arthur deserved that level of respect, but Caitlin was right. He had to let her know, somehow.

It was getting to be too dark to pursue this any further tonight, though. Politely, Kevin showed Caitlin to his mother's room, a small bed with a small strip of available floor to walk in and out. His was no bigger, but the separate chamber would allow Caitlin to get some privacy while she slept. Caitlin thanked him, and proceeded to close herself in the room just as the sun had completely set.

With the night sky in full bloom, Kevin decided to do the same in his own room, and closed the door. His room had a window without glass, and he looked out to see the stars and the moon. He then let out a sigh, with so much weighing on his mind.

Arthur was still kidnapped and needed rescue. When he caught up, Kron would still need help getting home, a task Kevin felt he had to see through. And Caitlin was proving to be such an unusual person; initially he had just thought of her discipline as just part of her training and her initiative, but what kind of person actually *asks another to block their emotions for them*? And who was this father of hers who would be powerful enough to do it and willing to go through with it on his own daughter?

And why did he feel like she might be a special person to him?

Chapter 9

A Plan for Rescue

The next morning, Kevin woke up a bit late. He left his bedroom to find that Caitlin was gone. On his table was a note:

Went to get my father after he is done with his lecture at the castle. Will be back with him. Caitlin.

Kevin studied the note, realizing that this meant he had a little while before Caitlin would be back. He took to getting himself together for the day, including strapping the Sword of Purity to his waist as usual. It had now been a week and he was getting used to wearing it. Knowing he had some time, he decided to take Caitlin's advice and make another effort to reach out to Rita Falchor, Arthur's mother, to let her know of the bad news. Fearing the worst, that Rita would not be home again, Kevin decided to sit at his table for a bit and pen a message for her.

Then, Kevin set out for the short walk to Arthur's house. Sure enough, Kevin was right: Rita was not home again. He took his message and pinned it on the door, informing Rita that Arthur's father had come to claim him. Then, feeling a little sad thinking about the circumstances, he headed back for the house.

As he returned, he saw Caitlin outside the front of his house. She was with a man wearing long red robes over black ones. He appeared to be over middle-aged, but with blonde hair that was slicked back into points. A feature he did have was piercing blue eyes, almost like Caitlin's eyes. This had to be her father, Kevin reasoned.

Kevin could hear that the two were talking. "I had heard of the battle to the south," said Caitlin's father. "I am glad that you are safe."

Despite the fact that her father was there, Caitlin was still as emotionless as she always was. "Of course I am safe, father. Did you expect any less of me?"

Her father started to chuckle and smile. "Of course not, my

daughter," he said as he chuckled. "But a father will always be concerned for the safety of his daughter. It is only natural."

Completely unlike his daughter, Caitlin's father seemed to have normal reactions to everything. Unlike Caitlin, he did not appear to be without emotions. This made Kevin curious as to what would make Caitlin want to be emotionless. He stood there, thinking, having not yet said a word.

"Naturally," Caitlin responded to her father's comment. Then, her and her father realizing that Kevin was approaching, she turned to direct her arm toward Kevin. "Allow me to introduce Kevin Trent, who I have brought to see you."

"Indeed," responded her father. He turned to Kevin and offered a small bow. "It is a pleasure to make your acquaintance."

Kevin extended a bow. "It is an honor to meet you too."

The professor rose as Kevin did. "I am Professor James Magnon, instructor and freelance wizard. What do you call yourself, pure one?"

"My name is Kevin Trent…" answered Kevin, before stopping. "Wait a moment. I'm not a 'pure one'."

The professor pointed at Kevin's belt. "You are carrying the Sword of Purity, are you not?"

Surprised, Kevin glanced at Caitlin before he glanced at his sword. The Sword of Purity did not exactly look distinct.

"Don't worry," said Caitlin. "I told him."

"But I would have recognized it regardless," stated Professor Magnon. "I have seen that weapon personally, twenty years ago during the Alliance-Daritel War. It was on the belt of Vincent Stryker, Vincent the Pure One."

Kevin looked down at the sword. "So I've heard," he said. He then looked up. "You must be quite strong if you fought in the war and saw this sword."

Professor Magnon began to laugh. "Well, you could say that," he said, still chuckling. "Several of my fellow accomplices in the field of magic would say that my magic prowess is acclaimed to be greater than that of anyone else in this world. Only the gods themselves have more power." The professor started to chuckle again at his own words.

"Of course, I still do not believe it myself, but I have never met a man who I could not best."

"I'd rather not test that theory," responded Kevin awkwardly.

The professor realized he had overstepped. "I meant not to challenge you, Kevin. Allow me to inform you that I did not fight in the war. When it comes to affairs of country, I am a pacifist and refuse to fight in wars. I do not like to fight others."

Kevin nodded. He understood the professor's position.

Then, a shadow crossed the ground as the sunlight faded. Kevin looked up to see that rain clouds were moving over Rikleifer. They were dark; it would surely rain soon. As a slight breeze blew past the house, Kevin then invited Professor Magnon and Caitlin into his house.

The two agreed, and Kevin opened the door to let them inside. He asked Professor Magnon and Caitlin if they would like the two chairs in the kitchen while he served them water. As he was serving them, the rain started to fall outside, making a faint rattling sound. Kevin adjusted his shutters, pulling them closed so they would not let the rain in.

"So, Kevin," continued the professor after taking a sip of his water, "Caitlin has informed me of your situation. I am very sorry about your friend. For me to help you, it's important that I know what happened."

Wiping his hand across his forehead as he knelt on the floor beside the table, Kevin responded, "It has been a rough week, let me tell you." Before beginning, a thought came to mind. He turned to Caitlin. "Does he know about Kron?"

"Yes, I told him about the god," Caitlin answered.

"I have heard about Kron Kalavere," added the professor, addressing Kevin. "I believe he is also known as the god Kronius."

"That's what he told me," acknowledged Kevin. "Do you know him?"

"I know *of* him," answered the professor, "but that is all."

Kevin wondered how that could be. However, these were questions for another time; Professor Magnon was not here to answer questions about himself. "Well, this whole thing started about a week ago when I bumped into Kron at the castle. A shard of metal fell out of his pocket, and I picked it up and gave it back to him. Later that night, he came to my house and told me it was a shard of the Sword of Purity that I had picked up. He told me that since I picked it up, I was the only person who could help him get home."

Briefly, the professor considered this. "So, Kronius is trapped in this realm," he mumbled to himself. "Did he tell you why he is trapped here?"

"Just that it had to do with the war, and that a seal on his home was established when Vincent Stryker fought Tyrinion, and he was on the wrong side. For a while, he believed it to be Tyrinion's dying curse."

"Excuse me?" exclaimed the professor, almost jumping up a bit.

This surprised Kevin greatly. Caitlin reached over and grabbed her father's arm, trying to tell him to calm down. "Is there a problem?" asked Kevin, a little scared.

Settling back down into his seat, the professor took a breath. "No, there is no problem, Kevin," he answered. "I simply find the notion that a god would believe in a 'dying curse' to be absurd, as there is really no such thing. One cannot establish a magic to activate on their death."

"Could it have been set shortly before dying?" asked Caitlin, ever inquisitive to increase her magic knowledge.

The professor shook his head. "I would highly doubt it, not something that elaborate in the middle of a fight."

Kevin could see this was getting a bit off-topic. "Anyway, my friend Arthur and I agreed to go with him to find the rest of the sword, using the shard to guide us where to go. It led us to a battlefield right by Caitlin's house, where we found the sword and Caitlin then attacked us."

Before the professor could look at her, Caitlin clarified, "I thought he might be a thief or a desecrator. I didn't realize he was a pure… I mean, someone who could hold the Sword of Purity."

Professor Magnon looked up at Kevin. "Kronius did not explain to you why you could hold that sword, did he?"

It was striking Kevin as odd that the professor was continuing to use Kron's god name, but he proceeded to answer. "No. He didn't know."

There was a pause. Professor Magnon was clearly thinking more. "I see," he said. He then considered, aloud, "I think I may know why, but before you ask, I will have to do some research. I will not speculate."

Fair enough, Kevin thought to himself. The last thing he needed was to believe something that turned out to be false. He continued, "After we met Caitlin, Kron and Arthur stood guard over the house while Caitlin and I rested, and…" He was struggling to figure out how to explain this part.

Fortunately, Caitlin had a solid grip on the explanation. "Arthur was possessed via his sword, which apparently belongs to Demonicus. It turns out that Kevin's friend Arthur was Demonicus's son all along, and Arthur's unsheathing of the sword gave Demonicus, who had tracked him to where we were, the ability to take control of Arthur and attack. His eyes glowed red, and he had an Enlightener from the Shadows with him." She looked at Kevin for a moment, and felt she could not take full credit. "We fought him off, but he retreated with Arthur by using a gryphon."

The professor's eyes slowly widened as he heard this account. "Tracer magic for the possession, I suppose," he muttered. "And what of Kronius?"

"He was injured, but okay," answered Caitlin. "He stayed behind to watch over an APF officer named Eukert, who we found on the battlefield. He was still alive but gravely injured. I healed him, and Kron stayed to make sure he recovered and could be directed back to Aurana's held territory."

The professor acknowledged the explanation. Kronius was okay; he would simply be delayed. Kevin's friend, however, was not, and that was Kevin's worry. "Okay, and now I understand," he said.

Kevin looked at the professor intently. He was waiting to hear what the professor had to say.

He looked directly at Kevin. "I need you to understand that I am not a miracle worker. Even with my help, I cannot help you fight your way into Desolunar to free Arthur like some kind of heist. If Arthur is truly the son of Demonicus, he will not simply be in a prison cell and ignored. He will likely be close to Demonicus, in Seta Archa. No matter how hard we would fight, how well we would plan, how many others we manage to gather to help, we could not simply blast in there and free him."

"I understand," nodded Kevin. "I wasn't sure how you could help."

"Now, I do not mean I cannot help," the professor shot back. "Caitlin was right to bring me to you, because I do think I can help." He glanced again at the Sword of Purity. "We must simply use a different approach to the problem."

Visibly frustrated, Kevin's voice raised unintentionally. "And what are you suggesting that we do, then? You've already told me we can't go take Arthur back. The way you make it sound, we'd need a whole army to rescue him!"

Professor Magnon smiled. "And that is exactly what I plan to give you."

Kevin's eyes widened.

Caitlin looked over at her father. "I'm curious what you mean by that."

The professor reached into his robes and pulled out a map of the known world. He unrolled it on the table and motioned to Kevin to come closer. Caitlin leaned over her end of the table to observe, as the professor placed his finger on the map and began pointing.

He then began to explain the premise of Kevin's next actions. "Kevin, if you are going to rescue your friend, then you must have the nations of the world united for a purpose. At the very minimum, Nuve and your home kingdom of Aurana are already fighting Desolunar, but they fail because they are not united."

Kevin was slightly confused as to what the professor meant, not understanding politics. "How so?" he asked.

"There are conflicts with every nation, and no land is exempt," answered the professor. "Aurana is slowly spinning out of control under a weak, self-important leader. As you may imagine for a wizard like myself who is registered in Aurana through the country's Department of Magic Affairs, I have some political connections in the capital of Aurana City. I know much of King Arnold IX, and unfortunately he is the reason Aurana cannot adequately defend itself."

Kevin frowned a bit, but continued to listen.

"Nuve's corruption runs through the core of a war-torn nation that cannot keep itself together. Two separate groups have already declared independence and are fracturing the kingdom, and while the Nuve government has its own issues of corruption and ineffective leadership, it is also fighting a civil war while trying to defend its own territory from invasion."

Then, the professor dragged his finger further across the map. "Scurnia is too far away from Desolunar to be under invasion, but has little reason to supply aid to the war due to border problems with Gardolk, to its south, and seeing Aurana and Nuve flounder. Fix the two former members of the Triple Alliance," he said as he pointed to Aurana and Nuve, "and reach out to them, and Scurnia will surely aid its former allies again, regardless of its border issues."

Kevin crossed his arms and let his head down. He was in thought for a short moment. "I can see your point," he finally responded. "United we stand, divided we fall. It's a simple principle. But what does this have to do with me? Why would I be able to fix two kingdoms and reunite the Triple Alliance? I'm a commoner, not some kind of hero. A week ago I was worrying about what kind of work I'd have to find to keep myself alive, not the problems of the world."

"Correct me if I am wrong," responded the professor, "but that sword you hold used to be the sword of Vincent Stryker, is it not?"

"It is. What's your point?"

"That it carries the clout that you need," the professor answered. "Everyone knows and respects Vincent Stryker. Stories of his sword that glowed a bright blue, that no one else could hold, are legendary. If you truly can hold it, and can energize it, then you will carry that same clout with society whether or not you are a 'pure one' like he was."

Quietly, Kevin took a deep breath. He was trying to calm down. After a short pause where he did calm down, he drew his sword, closed his eyes, and tried to cool down further, finding the inner serenity within himself and the ability to make calm, rational decisions. When he opened his eyes again, he saw the sword glowing blue, exactly as it had done for him before.

Seeing this, the professor rose to his feet. "As it did for Vincent Stryker, so the sword responds for you," he said. "This will certainly draw the respect of the leaders of nations."

Kevin stood puzzled. "Okay…" he stammered, as he unlit the sword and put it away, "but that still doesn't really help me to know what to do."

Caitlin looked at her father. "What are we doing, anyway?"

The professor smiled. "Patience, to both of you," he said as he sat back down. "All will be revealed in due time. I do not have specific plans as of the moment," he continued as he looked to Kevin, "because your arrival has prompted these plans. Although you may not see it yet, I believe you are capable of many things that I am not, just as I am sure my daughter is. Allow me to develop these plans fully and make contact with my connections in Aurana City, and I will discuss it with you when we meet again in Aurana City."

"So, you're asking me to go to Aurana City and trust you?" inquired Kevin.

"I am asking *both* of you," answered the professor. He then turned to Caitlin. "Please, my daughter, take good care of this young man. He will need your help."

With a nod, Caitlin agreed. "I have already told Kevin that I would walk his path with him, to help him save Arthur. Even if you had not asked," she then turned to Kevin, "I would have chosen to continue to walk that path with him."

Aside, Kevin could not help but feel touched. Even if it were some sense of duty, Caitlin still wanted to be with him, to be his traveling companion, when she did not have to be. "Thank you," was all Kevin could muster to say to her in this moment.

"Anytime," answered Caitlin. She said it without emotion as usual, but her word choice was almost pleasantly surprising to Kevin. It was almost as if something of an emotion slipped through the cracks.

The professor sat back down. "I must ask, Kevin, does this satisfy you as we form a plan for rescue? Essentially, to distill down the plan into a basic form, I would ask that you help me to fix the political situations in Aurana and Nuve, while encouraging them to reform the Triple Alliance. We can then inform Scurnia of the news, and, provided the three countries united can fight back, take an army into Desolunar and liberate Arthur while Demonicus is overthrown."

Kevin gave a quick nod. "As little as I know how we'd get it done, it's the best we have and I understand why it is the best choice. There is one thing I don't understand, however."

"And that is?" asked the professor.

"What's in it for you?" Kevin asked. "It feels like you've been thinking on this for some time. How do I know I can trust you, and that you're not just manipulating me to gain your own ends?"

Caitlin's eyes widened. She had never heard someone challenge her father like that. Reluctantly, though, she acknowledged that Kevin made a very good point. She turned to her father and said, "It is a lot you seem willing to do for Kevin. Turning whole nations around is not something one does just to save someone's friend."

There was a short pause. Then, the professor looked at his daughter. "You are quite right." He then turned to Kevin. "And I must say, Kevin, that if that is your method of thinking, I think you will be quite safe in the world. Considering one's motivation is perhaps the most important thing you can do." He then paused briefly again. "To answer your question, yes, I do have something in this for me, if you must know." The professor looked to one of the window shutters, which had cracked open a bit, revealing the pouring rain outdoors. "As you have been taught, I am sure, Demonicus is very much a dangerous person with bad ideas of conquering this realm. The matter is further complicated with involvement by the gods against the one that fell. Regardless of whether he is 'evil' or not, a simple philosophy that history has borne out should be followed: One man should not ever rule the populace."

"I get that." Kevin was listening intently, observing with the last statement that Professor Magnon was referencing both Demonicus and Tyrinion. His bit about philosophy sounded like something Kron had said once, too. So far, however, the professor was meandering a bit, and Kevin was trying not to get distracted.

"As it comes to myself…" the professor continued, pausing for a second, "while I do have concerns about the world's political situation and what may be going on involving the gods, the truth of the matter is that I have a personal issue with Demonicus." He glanced at his daughter, who seemed slightly confused, before turning back to Kevin. "It is quite a long story, but the short version is that before Caitlin was born, Demonicus was responsible for the death of a member of my family."

A small tear came to the professor's eye, and Kevin saw it. Whoever this family member was, that person was clearly near and dear to him.

"The truth be told, I had thought of intervening for quite some time. When I am ready to do so, I will tell you why, but you are my opportunity to do so, and in turn I can help you to get your best chance to rescue your friend."

Silently, Kevin nodded. The professor's explanation was very open and honest; explaining that he had a personal issue with Demonicus did not make him look the best, but he was willing to say it, anyway. That Demonicus was threatening to conquer Aurana and the rest of the kingdoms was frightening enough as it was to sound like a noble quest to overthrow him, but the professor still admitted his feelings. Kevin felt as though he could trust the professor, for now, at least.

"What do you say, Kevin?" asked Caitlin. "Are you in?"

"What do you think?" Kevin asked back.

"Ultimately, it doesn't matter what I think," Caitlin answered. "If I told you we should go, I might sound biased because my father proposed this idea. But I will tell you that I don't have any other ideas on how I can help you save Arthur."

"Then it's decided," said Kevin. He turned to the professor. "I suppose we're traveling to Aurana City, then?"

The professor nodded. "Indeed, but I will have the two of you go on ahead of me. I must wait here a couple of days; I have business to which I must attend. As important as what we will do to unify the kingdoms again is, this business is equally important."

A little surprised, Kevin was about to question the professor as to what could be so important, but Caitlin stood up, unintentionally interrupting him. "We'll head out tomorrow morning, then, after the rain has stopped. I trust you'll catch up with us?"

“I will,” acknowledged the professor. He then rose and extended a hand to Kevin. “It was my pleasure meeting you today, Kevin Trent. Trust me when I tell you that in you, I see a young man with great potential.”

Kevin returned the handshake. “Thank you,” he said. “I appreciate what you’re willing to do for me, whatever that turns out to be.”

“And you for me as well,” acknowledged the professor. He then glanced at his daughter before turning back to Kevin. “I have asked Caitlin to take care of you on this trip. Please do the same and take care of her as well. She is my only child and I care very much about her.”

Looking directly at Caitlin for a second, Kevin said firmly, “I will.”

Caitlin caught that Kevin looked at her as he said that. It was his promise to keep her safe the same way she said she would for him.

With that, the professor dismissed himself and headed for the door. Kevin and Caitlin waited in the house, staying dry while they waved him goodbye. They saw the professor, as he exited, raise one arm and create a shield of light, essentially functioning to keep the water from falling on him. He headed out and toward the center of the city.

“Well, what did you think?” asked Caitlin.

“About what?” inquired Kevin.

“About my father and his plan,” answered Caitlin.

“Oh, well, your father seems like a kind man,” Kevin said. “On the plan, though, we really don’t even know what that is yet. We’re just told to trust him.”

Caitlin nodded. “He can be trusted, I assure you,” she said. “If he says he has a plan, I believe him. It’s on us, then, to execute it.” She paused for a second, as she and Kevin looked out the door at the rain. “You know, he sees something in you that you don’t see in yourself,” she continued.

“So it seems,” acknowledged Kevin. “I just wish I knew what that was…” Kevin paused to look down at the sword in its scabbard on his belt. “And I hope it’s not because of this thing.”

“If it were that alone, I still don’t think he would place his trust in you," answered Caitlin.

And the two of them stood there and watched the rain for a while.

Chapter 10

A Night in the Wilderness

The next day, Kevin and Caitlin were ready to set out for Aurana City. It was a relatively safe walk for the moment, as nothing north of Rikleifer was in any danger from Desolunar as long as the city remained in Aurana's control. They quickly split in the damp morning for Caitlin to say goodbye to her father and for Kevin to see if he could catch Arthur's mother one more time. Again, Rita Falchor was not home, but Kevin did see that the note he left on her door had been removed. Hopefully this meant that she had received the message, Kevin thought to himself.

A long day ahead, Kevin and Caitlin reunited and set out on the north road to Aurana City. The capital city of Aurana and also the seat of power for the province of Northern Aurana, Aurana City was quite a distance away, wrapped around on three sides by the Auranian Wilderness, a large and dense forest that for many was impenetrable. Plenty of wildlife lived there, and in extensions such as those that reached into towns, there were also logging operations. Because of the Auranian Wilderness and the southern forest, Aurana had the largest supply of wood in the known world, and frequently traded it for other resources.

With a full day of walking ahead, Kevin and Caitlin spent the whole day talking to each other. Although Caitlin did not waver from her emotionless tone, he almost felt like he and Caitlin were becoming friends. They spent time discussing adventure stories they both enjoyed and those that inspired them, as well as how they viewed the world and their personal philosophies. It was on this trip that Caitlin learned that Kevin had been facing a decision on needing to pick up a trade if he wanted to continue to survive, being that he had no family left and his only friend was Arthur. Kevin in turn learned that Caitlin had always looked up to her father and his talents, but was strongly encouraged by him to learn and practice magic from a young age, making her as talented as she was. When Kevin asked her if she ever wanted to do anything else, she shared a few ideas she had had for a living but never seriously pursued. Magic education was her sole focus since she was young, and she was motivated to become the best in the world at the magic arts.

A few thoughts of the previous day's events also went through Kevin's head. Professor James Magnon was a great person to meet, of course, but Kevin wondered what this plan of his could be. He felt as though he had a better understanding, although not a full one, of why this person would place an emotional block on his daughter's mind on her request. Very much he seemed to be someone about the business, although he himself expressed some emotions. Still, to Kevin, being focused on business was no excuse to artificially enforce the same on his daughter. Kevin also picked up on a couple of smaller things. Namely, unlike his daughter, the professor always spoke without contractions and in a vocal tone that sounded very lightly like a foreign accent. He almost sounded a bit like Kron in that way, but Kron's accent was not a match with the professor's, either. Perhaps it was simply that the professor was very formal with his language, as a person in high stature.

As the sun set, after many hours of walking, something became visible.

"Well, this could be a problem," stated Kevin. "Which way do we go?"

They were at the edge of the wilderness, where a projection of the forest was in the way between Rikleifer and Aurana City. One very old path through the forest was never traveled; another that went around the forest and to Aurana City was well maintained. The former was much shorter, but often considered dangerous.

Caitlin nodded. "I think the sooner we get to Aurana City, the better." She paused. "Regardless, we're out of time for today. We need to spend a night in the wilderness. It'll be dark shortly."

Looking at the sky, Kevin agreed. Nightfall was setting in. Caitlin was right as well that they should head into the wilderness a short distance. Because the road around was much heavier traveled, camping on the side of that road could make them targets for bandits traversing the road. It would actually be safer to camp in the woods than out of them, he reasoned.

Within a half hour and a short distance into the forest, Caitlin packed a bundle of sticks together and set them on fire with a bit of magic. Kevin took his sword and scraped from the ground a pair of flat spaces for he and Caitlin to sleep without having to rest on any rocks or plants. The forest would be their shelter tonight; Kevin and Caitlin would have to take turns keeping watch in case something dangerous happened.

With the sun beyond the horizon and the site put together, Kevin decided to sit down on a log from a fallen tree next to the campfire. Caitlin was off establishing a perimeter, making sure they had not hastily placed their campsite near a dangerous animal or any other hazard. As night quickly fell, Kevin had a lot to consider. If they were going to take the faster route, it was going to be much more dangerous. Even though he had agreed it was a good idea to camp here and not out on the encircling road, he was starting to second-guess that decision.

Then, while Kevin was sitting and pondering this, Caitlin sat down next to him. "The site should be safe," she acknowledged, "though I wouldn't say safe enough that we can let down our guard. We'll have to take turns sleeping."

Kevin nodded. It was a reality of which he agreed.

As Caitlin sat next to Kevin and warmed her hands by the fire for a moment, she said, "You seem a little quiet tonight since we set up the camp."

"Oh, I'm just frustrated, Caitlin," Kevin responded. "I'm worried. I feel like I'm in an unsafe position, and I'm a little concerned I can't afford to feed us when we get to Aurana City."

"If money's your concern, how come you didn't ask me?"

Looking directly at Caitlin, Kevin answered, "All of this with Arthur isn't your problem. You're traveling with me out of the kindness of your heart. How could I ask you for money on top of that?"

Caitlin considered this for a moment. "I suppose you have a point," she said. *But if your pride is keeping you from asking, you don't need to worry about speaking the words.*

It was projected into Kevin's head. Thoughtspeech, again.

Thinking it out to you doesn't make me feel better, Caitlin.

Nonsense, Kevin. You shouldn't feel bad about it at all.

Kevin looked up at Caitlin.

"You're getting better at recognizing when I project thoughtspeech to you," said Caitlin. "That's good. We may need that to communicate silently someday."

Sighing, Kevin looked down. "I suppose," he said, reluctantly."

What's wrong, Kevin?

"Could you not do that?" asked Kevin, as he sat up. "It's weirding me out."

"Oh, I'm sorry," answered Caitlin. She actually sounded like she had just the slightest bit of remorse in her voice this time. Then, she adjusted her tone back to normal. "You seem like you have a lot on your mind tonight."

Silently, Kevin lowered his head again.

Caitlin turned her head to face forward toward the fire. "I understand," she said. "When you're ready to talk, I'll be right here."

"Can I ask you something?" Kevin suddenly said.

This quick question caught Caitlin a little off guard. "What is it?"

He reached down and pulled his sword out a couple of inches. "Is this why you're staying with me?"

Shaking her head, Caitlin said, "Of course not. Why would you say that?"

Kevin sighed. "You didn't kill me a week ago because I was holding this sword and you recognized it. You even called me a 'pure one', the same that Demonicus did later that night. What aren't you or your father telling me about this sword?"

Shrugging her shoulders, Caitlin said, "I don't know much about it myself. It's pretty well known among veterans of the Alliance-Daritel War, I understand, that it belonged to Vincent Stryker, also known as Vincent the Pure One, and that it was a magic sword that no one else could touch. The most I could otherwise tell you is that my father told me a new 'pure one' would someday come to reclaim the sword, but I didn't expect you to be able to touch it."

Sliding the Sword of Purity all the way back into its scabbard, Kevin then said, "So the sword did have something to do with it."

Caitlin frowned. "I'm not sure I would've actually followed through with killing you. I threatened it, yes, but only when I didn't know who you were." She paused for a second. "I live in what's become a pretty dangerous area, and those who hang around are often up to no good. That said, usually a good scare gets rid of them."

Kevin shook his head. "That still doesn't really answer my question," he said. "I guess if I must be straightforward, are you accompanying me for me, or for the sword?"

"For you," answered Caitlin. There was no hesitation in her answer.

"Do you always follow people you meet?"

"What kind of question is that?" asked Caitlin.

"I mean, you decided to help me after Arthur was kidnapped," Kevin answered, "but you had no reason to tell your father that you would have chosen to stay with me without his request. I know he's helping because of the sword; he's even said as much."

Caitlin looked directly at Kevin. She reached out and put a hand on his shoulder. "Think about what you just said for a second. You know my father offered up a plan to rescue Arthur because you have that sword, but I told him I'd stay and help you even if he didn't ask me to. Doesn't that prove to you that I'm not in this for the same reason he is?"

Kevin's eyes widened a bit. Caitlin had a sound logical point. He looked up at Caitlin. "I suppose you may be right," he said, his tone lightening a bit. "So, what is your reason, then?"

There was a long pause, as Caitlin took her hand off of Kevin's shoulder. She was not saying anything.

Remembering what had just happened a couple of moments before, Kevin asked, "If you can't say it, maybe you can think it to me?"

Turning her head back, Caitlin looked at Kevin and nodded.

There was a second that she appeared to be thinking, before Kevin heard anything in his head.

I'm sure you can understand that I don't have friends. I keep to myself, focus on my studies, and suppress my emotions. But then I met you, and we spent time talking the whole way from my house to Rikleifer, and then to here. I think... as much as we've only known each other for several days at this point, that you might be my friend. You don't treat me like the rest of society does; even when you're interacting with me, you don't treat me as an outsider when I'm not showing you any emotion. You talk to me and find common ground and don't think of me as alien... and I appreciate that.

Caitlin… I'm sorry for questioning you so much tonight. Maybe I'm not so unique when I didn't even consider that you might think of me as a friend.

It's okay, Kevin. I know I don't make these things easy to discern. I've never had a friend before, so it's new for me, too.

There was a momentary pause. "So, I guess we're friends now?" asked Kevin.

Caitlin looked at Kevin. "If you want to be," she began, "I want to be."

Kevin smiled at Caitlin. "Sure, Caitlin," he said, "I'm honored to have a good friend like you."

Their eyes were fixed on one another for several seconds.

Then, Caitlin turned back toward the fire to warm her hands more.

Seeing this, Kevin did the same. But so many thoughts were now traveling through his head. He hoped Caitlin could not or would not read his thoughts if he was not thinking them out as he did when he was messaging with her. That Caitlin wanted to be friends was surprising enough, albeit pleasantly so. What was more surprising, though, was that Kevin was almost certain Caitlin had put some emotion into her thoughtspeech, even if it was unintentional. Maybe she was not truly emotionless at all, emotional block be damned. Was she hiding emotions that she was actually feeling?

And that long look into each other's eyes… was she feeling the same attraction to him that he did to her? Maybe this was not such a ridiculous idea after all. Maybe… in the right time, this could be…

No, Kevin thought to himself. Not now, at least. He would be a good friend and be satisfied with that. Caitlin clearly needed a friend, and he happened to come along at the right time, in that odd sort of way.

Suddenly, the sound of twigs snapping rang through the air.

"What was that?" asked Kevin.

Immediately, Caitlin sat up and channeled wind magic through her hands to blow out the fire. She then reached over and pulled Kevin, signaling to him to come off the log and get down. She then shushed him and pointed to her ear, telling him in less time than it would take to thoughtspeak that he needed to listen closely.

Kevin understood and did as he was instructed. A few more twigs audibly snapped.

He tapped Caitlin's shoulder and pointed north, deeper into the forest.

The sound of cracking twigs sounded like it was getting closer.

Hearing the sound getting louder, Kevin climbed over the log, tugging at Caitlin to follow him, which she did. They then used the log as cover and peeked over the top.

A bright full moon was in the air. As Kevin and Caitlin looked in the direction of the sound, a large silhouette rose from the forest floor into the trees, illuminated by the moon.

Tapping Caitlin's shoulder again and pointing to his head, Kevin thought outwardly.

What is that?

I don't know.

A loud screech rang through he air as the silhouette approached at high speed. It was not human.

In fact, it was nothing the likes of which Kevin or Caitlin had ever seen.

It appeared to be a very large bird that could walk on its two feet, and taller than Kevin. It had red feathers all around the head and down the torso. At the abdomen, the feathers became orange, and the down and surrounding area were in yellow feathers. Some of the down feathers were dark green. Under the red to yellow wings, following the same color pattern as the body, was a plume of color, with dark green tips at the innermost surrounded by yellow feathers, surrounded by orange, surrounded by red.

Before Kevin knew it, the bird swooped in and grabbed Kevin and Caitlin each with one talon. Kevin was stunned; he looked over to see Caitlin serious but not surprised.

The bird creature extended its wings. "You are trespassing. Why are you here? Answer me, creature of the night!"

"Creature of the night?" asked Kevin. "You've never seen a human before?"

At this, the bird swung its legs up with a slight ascent, grappling Kevin and Caitlin by their shoulders and lifting them into the air. It was too quick for either to try and fight it off or react.

Kevin was trapped now, unable to reach for his blade and unable to move period as the bird held him up in the air. He looked again over at Caitlin, who seemed to be trying to think of a way out. Then, however, they went higher and higher above the trees. Now, if Caitlin attacked the bird, she and Kevin would probably fall to their deaths. That was no longer a strategy.

"Now then, humans," continued the bird, "you are being taken into custody for trespassing on this sacred land of Avalon."

Kevin was confused. Avalon? Was this not Aurana? Had just a short distance into the Auranian Wilderness put him in this mysterious land of Avalon that he had never heard of? Kevin was not sure exactly what to think about this one.

Caitlin noticed Kevin's confused reaction. She thoughtspoke, *I have no idea what he's talking about, either.*

As they tried to figure this out, the bird began traveling to the west. The bird ascended, and suddenly Kevin and Caitlin were high above the Auranian Wilderness, unable to safely get down.

And the bird was carrying them in its talons, heading to the west, beyond the reach of humans.

Chapter 11

Trespassers

Two hours later, after a long flight in the warm night, the bird dropped Kevin and Caitlin into an opening in a stone building. They felt the impact of hitting the ground, but safely landed on a cushion. Having reached the ground, Kevin slowly pulled himself up. He looked over to see Caitlin doing the same; she looked like she was okay as well.

They were in an iron cage, with its cushioned floor a short distance above the ground. The cage was mounted to its opening in the roof. Other than a fire pit with a burning fire behind him, there was not much to the building. It looked to be a very old building, definitely ancient. In front of him were a couple of tables with papers, but nothing else. There was nothing to help escape from the cage.

Worse yet, Kevin checked his belt, only to find that his sword was not with him. It was gone. Kevin started to flip out. Had the bird taken it? Had it fallen while in flight? What had happened to it?

Slowly, Kevin pulled himself up on the cushioned floor. He looked over to Caitlin. "Are you okay?"

Caitlin was also picking herself up. "I'm fine," she said. "I'll give some credit to this floor; clearly it was designed to drop in prisoners without killing them on impact."

Kevin shook his head. "I don't get it though," he said. He then paced around a bit, taking care not to trip on the big cushion. "What did we do wrong? We were clearly in Aurana. I'm not even sure what this 'Avalon' is that the bird was referring to. Any ideas?"

Shaking her head as well, Caitlin answered, "None. Sorry, Kevin, but this goes beyond what I know about the world. That bird, though…" She was thinking hard.

"You recognized it?" asked Kevin.

There was a pause. "Not exactly," said Caitlin, "but I feel like

I've heard of such a creature before, as if it were in a legend. I can't put my finger on it, though."

Frustrating, Kevin thought to himself. "I think he has my sword, too."

Caitlin sighed. "That's not good," she said. She was looking around the cage. "That was my only idea on how to get out of here, to see if you could light it up and cut through these bars when it's illuminated in magic."

"Wait, you can't just blast a bunch of fire on this thing?" asked Kevin.

"If I wanted to incinerate us, then yes," answered Caitlin. "Metal needs to be extremely hot to melt, so much so that we'd be dead from the heat first. I could always blast ice and then fire to make water and try to rust them away, but that would take too long. As in, years."

Aside, Kevin smirked. She said it emotionlessly, but he was almost sure that was a small flare of sarcasm that Caitlin showed. In all seriousness, however, this was a huge problem. Forget for now they were probably lost somewhere where there were no humans. If they were simply left in this cage for any period of time, they would not live long. Escaping through the hole in the top seemed impossible; although the cage had horizontal and vertical bars, it narrowed toward the top and was not a straight ascent out. Kevin was not so talented a climber that he could hang from the angled bars to get to the roof, and he figured Caitlin was not, given that she was not an athlete, either. At this point, he did not know if having his sword would help, but Caitlin's idea was about as sound as any he heard.

Would they be trapped forever if Kevin did not get the Sword of Purity back?

Just as Kevin was thinking that, the bird that had captured him walked in the front opening of the building, with the scabbard and Sword of Purity slung around his neck on a strap. It was visible enough that Kevin fixated on it for a moment, already thinking about his next move.

The bird spoke to Kevin and Caitlin, "So, human male and human female, now you will not flee nor fight. You will answer why you are trespassing in Avalon."

"We didn't try to flee or fight," answered a confused Kevin. Having had two hours in the air with nothing to do but think, and the additional time in the cage, he did feel as though the bird had jumped to conclusions and that he had the moral high ground. "I don't understand why you brought us here. Surely we could've talked about this?"

The bird scoffed, as it flung down the Sword of Purity onto the table. "Then talk, human," it said.

Kevin was about to respond, but Caitlin extended her arm in front of him and took the response. "Our apologies, of course," she said. "We're from Aurana and we only meant to stay a night in the Auranian Wilderness because we couldn't get past it before nightfall. We didn't mean to trespass."

Caitlin was clearly showing her diplomacy here, Kevin thought to himself.

For a moment, the bird paced. "All of the forest," he began, "belongs to Avalon. We stay clear of humans during the day, but at night it is our hunting ground. Your presence there, and that you have seen me, jeopardizes the whole of our society. Now that you have seen me," he paused for a moment, "you cannot be allowed to leave."

"If you intend to leave us here as prisoners," answered Caitlin, calmly, "know that people will know we are missing. They will come looking for us."

The bird turned and looked at Caitlin, and scoffed. "Not out here, they will not," he said. "No human has ever set foot on the lands of sacred Avalon."

"Until we do," commented Kevin. He looked at Caitlin, who looked back at him and gave a nod. Kevin continued, "Once Caitlin and I are out of this cage, we'll be the first." He winked over at Caitlin, and pointed to the sword. He recalled that Kron told him he could call that sword to him, and while he had never done it yet, he had seen that power when the shard reintegrated into the sword when he first found it.

Then, the bird shrugged. "No, you will not be," he said. Then, he gave an explanation. "Please try to understand that we cannot allow any human to see us and know of our existence. Humans are not understanding of other intelligent races, and will not permit us to keep a peaceful existence. Even if you are good humans, we cannot risk our existence becoming known to those who would harm us." He then bent over and slid the Sword of Purity off his neck and placed it on the table, before turning for the entrance. "I will see to it that our society feeds you and cares for your basic needs. I would rather not that we kill you simply for a mistake you made."

"A mistake *we* made? Kevin asked pointedly. "We were within the legal boundaries of our country. It's not like you had a sign somewhere that said it's your territory at night. Seems more like *your* mistake for veering too close to human lands."

For a brief second, the bird appeared frustrated. Then, it answered with a calmer demeanor, "If that is your position, then so be it. However, it is and will not be the position of the phoenixes. Our lands are our lands, whether they have since been claimed by humans or not."

Caitlin's eyes widened.

Then, the bird turned for the entrance. "I will return soon with some rations for you. I am sure our leader will want to speak with you within the next few days. You may plead your case to him. In the mean time, please try to remain calm and come to terms with your situation. The easier you make this on us, the easier we will make it on you."

With that, he then exited the building.

Kevin just shook his head, as the bird exited. After he was sure the bird was far enough away, Kevin turned to Caitlin and said, "Who the hell does he think he is, that bird? Trying to keep us calm and understanding when he's unjustly taken us prisoner."

"He's a phoenix," answered Caitlin.

That caught Kevin's attention. "So you do know what he is?"

Caitlin nodded. "He said it once. I've heard of them and their history from my father."

Kevin wasn't surprised by that. "I've only heard of them as a mythical creature. Know anything about them?"

"A little," acknowledged Caitlin. "They were thought to be an extinct species that existed from at least the Second Era to about a thousand years ago, and their culture and behavior patterns had not changed much over their period of existence. That's why most people think they're mythical, because they've been gone so long. We do know that they carried the powers of fire and air, but to what extent is unknown. No one knows why the phoenix disappeared, but the accepted hypothesis among those who know of them is that the phoenix went extinct as humans forced them out of their lands."

Shrugging, Kevin said, "So much for them being extinct." He paused for a second. "We don't have 'a few days' to wait and plead our case, and hope someone's willing to help us."

"Agreed," acknowledged Caitlin. "Especially if we do have to go around the Wilderness as well." She pointed to the Sword of Purity on the table, having seen it placed there. "If we could only get a hold of that sword."

Kevin had an idea for that. He reached his arm out, with his palm facing forward. He just kept pressing forward, looking increasingly frustrated as time went by.

"What are you doing?" asked Caitlin.

"Kron told me that I could call the sword to me," he answered. "It's a power he told me that the sword has. I can call it to me and it will reform in my hand." He then lowered his hand. "I've never done it before, though. I'm not really sure how this works."

"Oh, I bet it's like a few other magical items," Caitlin said. Promptly, she put her hand under Kevin's arm and held it up, in the position Kevin had it in before. This caught Kevin by surprise. She put her other arm on his shoulder and said, "Close your eyes. Focus only on the object in front of you. Don't pull hard and aggressively; just envision it appearing in your hand."

Doing as he was told, Kevin closed his eyes. As he did, he was a little distracted. Caitlin was helping by holding his arm up while comforting and easing him. That was a nice feeling.

No, no time for that now. Focus on the sword.

The Sword of Purity would be the key to this cage.

Kevin stood silently for a moment. He tried to find his inner serenity, that which would light the blade up in magic as well. Maybe it would help with calling the blade to him. He worried about if this would work or not, what the stakes would be if he failed. What if they were trapped forever?

No, they could not be. He still had Arthur to rescue. Memories of the battlefield and the death he saw still ran through his mind frequently. He still had a promise to keep to Kron. His newest friend was stuck with him and he could not let her stay here forever, either. He had to do this, for them…

"Kevin! Kevin, open your eyes! You got it!"

Hearing Caitlin's voice, Kevin opened his eyes. Then, they widened, as he realized he was holding the Sword of Purity. It was lit up in its bright blue magic.

With that, Caitlin took a step back. "Would you care to do the honors?" she asked.

Kevin nodded at her, confidently. Then, he looked forward and stabbed the sword into a space between the cage bars in the floor. Almost effortlessly, the blade began cutting as Kevin moved it horizontally, slicing the floor out. He then continued around the edge of the whole floor of the cage, while Caitlin climbed up one cage bar and clung on to let Kevin cut the floor out.

When it was sliced out, the floor of the cage fell straight down onto the ground, taking Kevin with it. Kevin was not injured, since he was prepared for it to fall a short distance.

Just in time for the bird to return.

"Unbelievable!" exclaimed the phoenix. "I did all I could to keep from having to kill you, and this is how you repay me?"

Ignoring the phoenix, Kevin ducked under the cage side. After he reached the ground, the cage's lowest edge was at the height of his waist. He turned to Caitlin before standing up and offered his hand. "Do you need a hand getting down?"

Gently, Caitlin let go of the edge of the cage and took Kevin's hand as she climbed down. She then let go, brushed herself off, and said, "You know, I appreciate it but you don't have to be chivalrous to me just because we are friends."

"I didn't mean for it to seem chivalrous," Kevin said. "You helped me figure out how to call the sword to me. I thought I should help you if you needed it."

"Oh," answered Caitlin. "I thank you anyway." Then, she looked toward the phoenix.

"Excuse me!" the phoenix exclaimed. "You will climb back in

this cage and I will lower it to the ground, or I will have no choice but to kill you!"

Caitlin glanced over at Kevin, who nodded. She then turned back toward the phoenix. "I think not," she said. She then raised her arms and fired a shot of ice magic.

The phoenix tried to fly away to avoid the attack, but forgot he was in a closed building. He was struck by the ice shot and fell hard to the ground.

As he landed on his belly, with his head on the ground and his neck out, Kevin walked up to him and pointed the Sword of Purity at his neck. It was a common display in sword fighting as a way of asking your grounded opponent to surrender.

The phoenix sounded hurt, as if the combination of the ice shot and the fall had injured him. Sounding beat and reluctant, he said, "You win, human. If you must end my life, I only ask that you do so quickly."

Over to the side, Caitlin was charging another ice blast in her hands. Kevin waved at her, suggesting he had an idea instead. Seeing this gesture, she stopped charging magic and lowered her hands.

Kevin then looked at the phoenix. "I don't want to kill you," he told him. "You seem like a noble and loyal person to your society, yet one who shows unusual compassion while handling your duties. I'm no person of great importance, but I would like to think I'm the same as you in that regard."

"You and I are not the same," said the phoenix.

"That's only what you think," Kevin said back. "If you took the time to get to know myself and my friend over there, and were willing to look beyond the differences in our societies, you might see that. Instead, you put us in a cage."

"Human, you do not understand the dangers of your race, that your ancestors taught us."

Caitlin stepped forward. "And is every human like that?" she asked. "I'll ask it another way; would every phoenix try to spare our lives and not kill us instantly?"

The phoenix scoffed. "No, of course not," he said.

"Exactly," Caitlin answered. "We're giving you the same

courtesy you showed us, except we're not throwing you in a cage."

Then, Kevin stepped back, withdrawing his sword. "Please stand up, if you can," he said to the phoenix. "Maybe we would be best if we started over."

Silently, the phoenix struggled to stand up. He looked Kevin in the eye.

"My name is Kevin Trent," he said, then gestured toward Caitlin. "This is Caitlin Magnon. We are human beings of the Kingdom of Aurana, but we're just people. We're traveling to try and rescue another friend of mine who was kidnapped several days ago, far south of here, by the Kingdom of Desolunar."

Kevin and Caitlin briefly awaited the phoenix's response, wondering if he would answer them honestly or not.

He did.

"I am Wheldon," he said. "I am the second-in-command of the City of Phoenixes, subservient to our leader, the Red Phoenix."

Kevin smiled. "It's my pleasure to meet you, Wheldon," he said.

Taking a breath, the phoenix then nodded. "My pleasure to meet you too, Kevin and Catie."

"What did you call me?" questioned Caitlin, suddenly.

"Oh, my apologies," Wheldon said, as he gave a short bow to Caitlin. "I had a sister named Catie, who we lost to illness when I was but a fledgling. I will make sure not to do that again."

Caitlin thought about it for a moment, then shrugged. "It doesn't bother me," she said. If it makes you more comfortable, then you may call me Catie."

Wheldon bowed. "Thank you, Catie," he said.

She offered Wheldon a small curtsey.

"I hope that someday we can be friends," acknowledged Kevin.

"Perhaps one day we will," nodded Wheldon. "In the meantime, I have seen it is getting late outside. May I offer you some more proper lodging for the night?"

Kevin looked at Caitlin, and then back at Wheldon. "I think we'd like that," he said.

"Very well," said Wheldon. "For me to do so, however, will

require me to take you to the Red Phoenix."

Without skipping a beat, Caitlin answered, "Then take us. I am sure we would like to speak with them." Only then did she look over to Kevin, to see him give her a nod in full agreement.

"As you wish," said Wheldon, raising a wingtip toward the entrance. "Please follow me outside."

Rushing over to the table, Kevin grabbed the scabbard to his sword and fastened it to his belt. He kept his sword out as he rejoined Caitlin, unsure of what they would see outside. Kevin took a breath, and accompanied Caitlin and Wheldon as they exited the old ancient building.

Outside was still mostly forest, but they were on a small summit. Ahead was the most fascinating of sights.

Chapter 12

Seven Powers

It was an ancient city, with a number of buildings organized around one large, long promenade with a gigantic temple at the end. All of the structures were carved in beautiful white stone and appeared to be very sturdy. The structures each showed their age, however, in their wear along the building faces. Fires burned in large torches at the top of the larger buildings, as well as large ones up and down the main thoroughfare through the city. A natural clearing made up the landscape of the city, while the forest stood all around. It was a very plain landscape in the clearing, lacking any trees whatsoever.

"Whoa," Kevin said. "What is this place?"

"Wheldon referred to this land as Avalon," answered Caitlin, "but as for this specific city, I have no idea. Certainly appears to be quite old."

"Indeed it is," acknowledged Wheldon. "This is the City of Phoenixes. This city has stood for millennia." He then leaned down, laying on his stomach with his wings out. "If the two of you would please climb on my back, I will take you to the Red Phoenix."

Kevin's eyes widened. Now they would get to take flight, something other humans could only dream of. He climbed onto Wheldon up by his neck, while Caitlin sat on the phoenix's back behind Kevin.

With a few heavy wingbeats, Wheldon took off, taking care to keep Kevin and Caitlin on his back. It was a short flight for Wheldon to reach the temple, but it was exhilarating for Kevin nonetheless. How many humans got to fly? Even the night wind in his face did not bother him, as he was enjoying the trip. He turned once to check on Caitlin, to see that she was struggling a bit to keep her hair out of her face. Still, she was keeping her discipline, calmly maintaining her mounted position.

Wheldon flew up to the top of a flight of stairs in the front of the temple, near an archway that led inside. He set down very gently and allowed Kevin and Caitlin to hop off. "Please follow me, but do so quietly," he instructed. "Even at this time of night, the Red Phoenix may be quite busy."

Doing as instructed, Kevin and Caitlin stayed silent and followed Wheldon through the archway and into an unlit hallway. They stopped to wait at the entrance to a chamber, which was lit by torches. Kevin and Caitlin looked closely to see two phoenixes.

As Kevin started listening, he heard the words, "Are you sure?"

This was the question of the Red Phoenix, the leader of all phoenixes who resided in his throne room in the temple. The Red Phoenix's feathers were all bright red, in direct contrast to other males of his race, who had the color variation from the bright red through orange and yellow to the dark green tips on some feather tips. The other phoenix was covered in orange feathers from head to the middle torso and the outer wings and had lower bodies and inner wings in yellow feathers. Caitlin was fairly certain she could identify this phoenix as a female.

"Yes, great Red Phoenix," answered the female phoenix in the room. "Two humans were captured by Wheldon at the edge of our hunting grounds. He has placed them in the cage."

"Humans in Avalon," considered the Red Phoenix, glumly. "That is all that we needed right now." He paused as he paced a bit. "Our flight from human-controlled areas a thousand years ago into this sacred land was in hopes of avoiding humans ever again." The Red Phoenix paused and took a brief look around his throne room, whose plain stone walls had etchings of the story of the phoenixes.

"So, which should we prioritize?" asked the female phoenix. "The humans or the ravens?"

The Red Phoenix considered this for a moment. "We cannot afford to ignore the ravens. The Grand Raven will come to attack us again soon. Although humans are here, they are only two, while there are many of the Grand Raven's children."

Kevin, Caitlin, and Wheldon tucked around the corner, no longer to listen down the hallway and to be out of sight. "It looks like we will have to wait a short while," Wheldon instructed. "The Red Phoenix is speaking to Carrigan on very important business. I would not interrupt him."

Leaning back a bit from being weary, Kevin asked to Wheldon. "Who are these ravens he's talking about?"

"They are a group of phoenixes, allegedly," Wheldon answered. "The Grand Raven was the first, supposedly a phoenix who was discolored black and gray from birth as a result of a disease that killed many of our kind. Sometime after he became of age, he violently attacked and killed the previous Red Phoenix. Then, he ran off, but continues to violently attack phoenixes."

Caitlin nodded, intrigued. "How are there so many of them, then?" she asked.

For a moment, Wheldon appeared to be thinking. "They are all his children, and they all look like him with the black feathers," he answered. "A phoenix named Ravena met the Grand Raven, and became his bride. That is actually how they received the name 'ravens', from Ravena's name."

Also intrigued, Kevin nodded. He tried to stifle a yawn for a moment.

Suddenly, there was a loud sound.

Boom! An explosion!

Immediately, a loud horn sounded, as phoenixes were alerted and started coming out of their homes.

Kevin and Caitlin were unnerved. What was happening?

"Hurry, run and hide!" exclaimed Wheldon to the two humans, as he started to take off. "They are here!"

"Who's here?" asked Kevin.

Before Wheldon could answer, he had already taken off.

More sounds echoed through the air, with the sound of screeches. Above, Kevin and Caitlin could see the moon. The silhouettes of many birds were visible as they passed.

While Kevin was stunned, Caitlin grabbed him and started running. "Come on!" she yelled to Kevin.

Immediately, Kevin snapped out of it and followed Caitlin. He was not sure where they were going, and neither was Caitlin, for that matter. Instead of descending the stairs of the temple, Caitlin took Kevin around the outside.

Behind them, the Red Phoenix and Carrigan emerged from the temple. The Red Phoenix was issuing orders. Kevin had no time to stop and listen; he was hustling to keep up with Caitlin.

Where could they go to hide?

Loud sounds were echoing through the air. They needed shelter now.

The landing on which Caitlin was leading Kevin turned a corner around the side of the temple. An opening into the building was visible ahead, appearing to point downward at an angle. Without hesitation, knowing they needed to take shelter, Caitlin slid down into the tunnel. Kevin followed immediately.

There was a short slide down into the stone temple. It was dark, pitch black inside. Some moon light emanated into the slide entrance, revealing from where they had come. Whatever area of the temple this was, it was not one that was in use. Kevin hit with a small thud as he reached the bottom.

For the moment, now they were hidden.

"Kevin, are you okay?" Caitlin asked in the pitch black.

"Yeah, I'm fine," Kevin answered, brushing himself off as he stood. "You?"

"I'm okay," Caitlin answered. She then lit a bit of light magic on the tip of her fingers to see where they were. She could now at least see Kevin standing in front of her, appearing a little dirty but generally okay.

Kevin took a second to catch his breath. Outside, Kevin could hear faint sounds of what could be battle. It sounded absolutely chaotic. "Whatever is going on out there, I sure hope that Wheldon is okay."

Caitlin turned to survey her immediate surroundings. "Think you may have found another new friend?" she asked.

A smirk came to Kevin's face. Kevin connected that he had sort of met Caitlin the same way that he and her had met Wheldon. "I would hope to say that maybe *we* have one," he said. He looked up the shaft they slid down. "Then again, wherever in the world we are, I think we could really use one right about now."

Facing toward the moonlight, Caitlin saw a pair of torches mounted up against the wall. She removed the light magic to prepare something else. "Agreed," Caitlin said. "It's doubtful we'll be able to escape the City of Phoenixes without one." She thought for a moment. "Is this supposed to be the way to make friends, Kevin?"

Kevin's eyes widened. "Oh no!" he exclaimed. "Normal people don't make friends with those who try to attack, kill, or imprison them. That's really strange and probably very unsafe."

As she lit fire magic on the tip of her fingers, Caitlin asked, "But then again, you and I are not exactly normal people, are we?" She then cast the fire at each of the torches, lighting them up and dimly illuminating the whole room.

After a moment of thought, Kevin answered, "No, I suppose not."

As they turned around with the room now lit, they saw that this was an isolated chamber, not connected to any other part of the temple other than through the slide to the outside. Against the wall on the far side of the chamber was a shrine with a small phoenix statue on it. The walls all around were composed of tan stone bricks, as were the ceiling and the floor. It was a relatively small chamber, but large enough that Kevin and Caitlin could take several steps in any direction before reaching a wall.

Briefly, Kevin looked around. "I guess this will work as a shelter for the time being," he said.

Caitlin's eyes were fixated on the shrine.

Kevin took notice. "What's up?" he asked her.

She kept staring. "There's something about that shrine," she finally said. "It's hard to explain, but I've never felt anything like it." She paused for a moment as she approached, with Kevin keeping pace a couple of steps behind her. "It's almost like… a powerful wind is blowing, even though there's no wind in this chamber. And, it feels like it's coming from this shrine."

Kevin was intrigued. "Does it seem dangerous?" he asked Caitlin.

Caitlin continued to stare. "I don't know," she said. "You don't feel that?"

Shaking his head, Kevin said, "No, not at all. The air just feels stagnant in here to me. I certainly don't feel a pull or a gust."

For a moment, Caitlin considered this. She then looked at the wall behind the shrine, which had numerous words carved into it. "I'm not even really sure what this chamber is for."

Baffled, Kevin's attention had turned to the writing as well. None of it looked like any word he had ever read. "If any of that gibberish on the wall made sense, I would hope it would tell us."

"It's not gibberish," answered Caitlin. "It's *rengan.*"

"It's what?" asked a confused Kevin.

"*Rengan*," Caitlin said. "It used to be the main language for millennia, but it hasn't been in quite some time." She paused for a moment. "It speaks to how old this temple is." She squinted at the words even longer. "I'm not entirely sure I can make this out. I know a little bit of *rengan*, but I'm not sure I've seen all of these words before or know what they mean."

Kevin nodded. He had heard of there being an ancient language in school, but did not know it had a name. In this moment, Kevin was realizing just how brilliant Caitlin was. She was clearly highly intelligent.

He took a couple of steps closer to the shrine, where he found a paper sitting on it, folded up. Turning quickly to see Caitlin visibly and audibly trying to work out the *rengan* words she saw, Kevin unfolded the paper. He was surprised to find that written on the paper were not *rengan* words, but ones in the common language that both he and the phoenixes spoke.

It appeared to be a poem:

Take thy sword and raise it high,
For tonight you will spread your wings and fly.
A journey starts to stop the bad
Who walks around in darkness clad.
The hidden angel will be your guide
And you will find others in your stride.
Along the way you will find tools,

But remember there are certain rules
Such as how you must protect
Energies so they will not defect,
For should he claim any one part,
The end of the world will break everyone's heart.
Seven powers, yes they are
Of stronger powers than the stars
That watch from above, overhead
As you lay down in your bed.
The powers of light, and earth and sky
And fire and ice and darkness and life;
Collect all seven, and there will be
Your weapon of choice in the fight to see.
The amazon shall hold the first,
But her fate shall not be the worst.
The phoenix guides you to another
And the centaur protects the power's brother.
An evil beast of existence
Holds another as he will prance
While he slowly begins his kill
Unless a secret is revealed.
One is kept by a man of magic;
Another by a god so tragic,
Made so by a vicious lie.
Several times it has made him cry.
The last is held by the darkened heir
Whose evil is seen everywhere.
This power, though, is not the end;
There are two more things to get to defend
The world from complete collapse.
The Key of Hearts, which might lapse
Out of your memory, but remember it so
Because it is needed to reverse evil's flow.
But when all is said and done,
You must merge them into one;
And should you survive all blasphemy,

You have a small chance at victory.

On the back of the folded paper were some hand-scribbled notes that read "LTTA 1, CLSD". Kevin had no idea what that meant, or why this common language poem was here when the writing on the wall was in r*engan*.

Before he could ask Caitlin if she had an idea, however, Caitlin started speaking, reading her interpretation of the wall. "That which rests here… sacred treasure of the phoenixes…" She was omitting the words she could not translate. After a short pause, she continued, "energy contained in a statue… the weapon of the Great One… a piece entrusted to us… one of seven… united, the ultimate power…". She paused again. "That's all I can make out from the wall."

Kevin took a breath. "That doesn't sound good," he said. "Is whatever it is dangerous?"

"Seems like it could be," acknowledged Caitlin. "Did you find something?"

With a nod, Kevin passed Caitlin the poem on a paper. She read it over briefly. "It's very odd that this is in the common language while the writing on the wall is in *rengan*," she said as as she was reading. "It suggests that this isn't original to the shrine, that it came by later. It looks a lot like human writing as well; I don't know if phoenixes can write or what that would look like, but it looks like normal ink and pen." She kept reading.

Then, she stopped.

For a moment, Kevin looked at her, waiting for an explanation.

"Oh dear," she said. "I fear I know what this is."

Kevin put his arms out from his sides. "Then what is it?"

"I'm not exactly sure," Caitlin continued, "but it seems like something of which my father has told me before. I don't remember what it's called, but if the *rengan* on the wall is accurate and this poem is referring to it, it's some kind of energy that I think is in the statue. And whatever it is, it could be very dangerous in the wrong hands."

Whoa. That was a lot to process, Kevin though to himself. The main idea, however, was clear. This was something dangerous. And given the careful hiding of this shrine where they kept it, the phoenixes valued it. Maybe the ravens did as well.

Whether or not that was what the battle outside was about, Kevin had an idea on how he could put an end to it.

"I have a thought," he said to Caitlin. "You say this power is an energy?"

"I think so," acknowledged Caitlin. "I don't know why, but I'm apparently also sensitive to feeling it. Based on the feeling of a powerful wind I get from it, I think it might be of the element of air."

Kevin nodded. Then, he walked up to the shrine. "It's something they find valuable," he continued, moving his hand around the statue, tempted to touch it. "If we could take this to them and show to them that we have it, maybe we can get them to stop fighting and talk with us."

Caitlin seemingly understood. "You're suggesting that something valuable being in the hands of a third party would allow that party to demand they come to negotiate for it, with that party awarding it to the successful group."

"That's a bit technical," commented Kevin, "but yeah. Maybe I can get them to let me mediate their disagreement by forcing their hands… er, wings."

Turning to look directly at Kevin, Caitlin said, "For what it's worth, I can appreciate a diplomatic solution, but there's a lot of danger in attempting this stunt, Kevin. You would have to interrupt their whole battle and get their attention, and hope no one just attacks you and they just listen. Even before that, who knows what touching that statue will do?"

"There's one way to find out." Kevin reached out to touch to statue.

"Wait, Kevin! Don't!"

Too late. Kevin touched the statue.

Suddenly, there was a brilliant flash of orange. Kevin felt the force of great winds trying to push him back, as he held his hand to the statue. Caitlin watched on as a surge of orange-colored energy flashed through the statue and into Kevin's hand.

Then, the winds felt like they were dying down. Having had his eyes closed in fear, Kevin opened them and looked at his right hand. Everything looked normal, except for his wrist. There was a mark of orange across his wrist encircling his entire arm and wrapping around it helically. Kevin could not see where it ended, but he did not see this marking anywhere else on his body.

For a solid minute, Kevin stared at his arm.

"That's exactly what I was afraid it was," Caitlin commented. "I think my father referred to them as the 'Seven Stripes'. This must be one of them."

Kevin kept looking at his arm. "That's interesting," he said. "I didn't expect it to be absorbed by my body. It's freaking me out a little bit."

"How do you feel?" asked Caitlin.

"To be honest, kind of queasy," Kevin answered, "but I think that's subsiding."

Caitlin breathed a sigh of relief. At least he was okay. Then, she walked up to him. "I'm glad you're all right. If I may be honest, that was pretty stupid of you to just touch that statue knowing it was dangerous."

Silently, Kevin nodded. He then said, "I know. But it was a risk that I felt I had to take. We don't have a better solution."

"I get that, but I'd rather not have to tell people I lost the only friend I have because he touched a statue," answered Caitlin.

That made Kevin chuckle a bit. "You have a point. I'll be more cautious in the future."

The sound of an explosion sounded outside the chamber, close to the building they were in.

Kevin and Caitlin both looked toward the exit shaft after that sound. "I suppose I should lead the way," Caitlin told Kevin. "Hopefully I can shield us before an errant burst of fire incinerates us."

Gesturing toward the shaft, Kevin said, "Ladies first, of course."

Chapter 13

Of Ravens and Phoenixes

As Caitlin and Kevin slowly made their way up the shaft back to the outside, the sounds of fighting became louder. Kevin was still not entirely sure at the moment how he was going to stop this fight, or how he or Caitlin would survive it.

It was a bit more difficult climb up the shaft, but the slope was not so steep as to prevent Kevin and Caitlin from climbing it. Caitlin led the way up to the top, intent on casting a shield if something came down at them. Fortunately, however, nothing did. She and Kevin made it to the outside without much hassle.

At the top of the shaft, Caitlin reached down to help Kevin make it up the last little bit to the ledge on the temple. They stood up together, and looked overhead at the war in the night skies.

Above, several phoenixes charged in a V formation toward the ravens, organized in a line. Kevin noticed that many of the phoenixes had color patterns similar to Wheldon, with feathers cascading from a deep red through oranges and yellows, down to a dark green in some places. Others had solid orange feathers along the top and back, and yellow feathers on the bottom. Although he did not know what this meant, Caitlin next to him knew these phoenixes were female, simply in line with the biology of birds and males possessing flashier color patterns to attract females. Such could be extrapolated to these large birds as well.

Across the sky, the ravens were much more difficult to see in the night, even with the number of torch lights from below. When one became visible, it was evident that many of them were covered in black feathers, while some had feathers in a dark gray shade. Kevin looked back to see a phoenix behind the lines of the ravens. While he could not be sure, he assumed it was Ravena, the phoenix who traveled into raven territory and became one of them. If she was back there, he figured, then maybe the raven leader was present, too.

Neither he nor Caitlin could pick out Wheldon, however. They hoped for his safety.

Carefully, Caitlin led Kevin around the side of the temple to its entrance. They were still quite high on the building. From there, the battle was looking more grim than Kevin had initially thought. The phoenixes were being driven back by the attack, but the Red Phoenix refused to yield. He made sure his phoenixes fought on against the attackers. The ravens, however, were blasting fire that pushed back many phoenixes, and several fell to the ground in pain. Kevin knew that if he and Caitlin did nothing, the phoenixes would be crushed. However, being human had its limits, and as far as Kevin knew, his Sword of Purity could not attack in the air at his will. He pulled it out and lit it up anyway, as he tried to think of something to do.

"Would you like me to get their attention?" asked Caitlin.

Of course Caitlin would have an idea, Kevin realized. "Be my guest," he told her.

With a nod, Caitlin raised her arms. She hoped Kevin's plan would be sound, as she prepared a brilliant flash of light. As she did, Kevin withdrew his sword and lit it up in its bright blue magic. Then, Caitlin let the magic loose.

The bright flash sustained for just a second, illuminating everything in a white light. Phoenixes and ravens all stopped and looked at the source of the light, coming from the temple. After briefly pulling up his sleeve to reveal the stripe visible on his body, Kevin waved his sword in the air. "Hey! Phoenixes and ravens! See this?" he yelled as loud as he could, watching as the eyes of every avian were fixed on him. He moved the sword close to his arm to put some light on the stripe, not knowing that holding the sword that close actually made the stripe glow. "If you want it, you'll have to negotiate with me!"

Almost the second that Kevin finished vocalizing his demand, a nearby raven started flying straight at him. Kevin reacted and held his sword up, not sure what he could do to defend himself. He trusted that Caitlin had the answer, in the three seconds he had before being hit and knocked off the temple.

He was right to trust Caitlin.

With a fast reaction, Caitlin lit up a shield of light and the raven flew right into it. Caitlin held strong as the raven fell to the landing in front of her, as if he had flown smack into a a wall. As quickly as he could, Kevin then ran toward the raven and pointed the lit sword at his neck, while the phoenixes and ravens continued to watch. Kevin then yelled aloud to the avians, "I will negotiate with the leadership of both phoenix and raven. You will meet here in a few minutes. Attack again, and I will slay this raven and anyone who approaches." This last line, Kevin was bluffing; he had no desire nor intention to kill anyone, nor was he sure he was capable of doing so.

For a moment, no one seemed to move. Every phoenix and every raven appeared to try and maintain their positions, beating their wings to hover where they were and waiting for the other side to make a move. Kevin clearly had their attention.

Then, a phoenix came down toward Kevin and Caitlin, slowly, not rushing in for an attack. Kevin could see this was Wheldon. He came down to land by Kevin and extended his wingtip. Quietly, he said, "I hope you know what you are doing. You are playing a dangerous game with what phoenixes and ravens value most in their struggle for power."

"I don't know," answered Kevin, "but I have to try."

Wheldon nodded. "I respect that," he said. He then spoke in a more normal volume, not enunciating but not speaking quietly. "I will invite the Red Phoenix."

At the same time, the ravens appeared to be falling back and regrouping. To Kevin, this was a sign they were going to discuss this. He then looked over to see Caitlin now had her hands over the raven that had fallen and was casting a glowing magic upon it, a healing magic. After a bit, that raven then took off and flew away, back toward its own kind.

Caitlin looked out across the City of Phoenixes, as the lines retreated. "You go inside and negotiate, Kevin. I have to stay out here."

Kevin looked at Caitlin, with a bit of fear in his eyes. "I don't think I can negotiate this without you," he said. "I think you understand more about how to do this than I do. You're much more of a worldly person than I am."

She turned to Kevin. "Much as you admire my talents frequently, I can't walk on water," she said. "I've never negotiated anything politically in my life. But do you know what I can do?" She gestured toward the city. "There are a lot of injured out there, maybe even many killed. I can't fix death, but I can heal the injured."

Still with a worried look on his face, Kevin nodded.

Caitlin stepped over to Kevin and touched him on the shoulder. "Don't worry. You'll be fine." She paused for a second. "What you've shown me in the last week is that you're a trustworthy person, Kevin. I can trust that you will find a way to do what needs to be done here, while I do what needs to be done out there."

While he still felt unnerved by what he was about to do, Kevin did feel better knowing Caitlin had confidence in him. He said to her, "Go do what you need to do."

With that, Caitlin turned and headed down the stairs toward the city. At the same time, Wheldon indicated to Kevin that he was taking off to get the Red Phoenix.

For just a moment, Kevin smiled a bit. Caitlin was truly someone he admired, and she had just shown that she knew the limits of her strengths and was going to use them where she could. Of course, this meant she could not cover for his weaknesses in this situation, but she did make it clear to him that she had no experience in this, either. He would have to solve this problem on his own, and he would have to find the confidence to do so.

At least it seemed like Wheldon was willing to help.

From the temple stairs, Kevin looked out for a moment. Parts of the City of Phoenixes were in flames, but at least the stone structures would not be susceptible to burning down. There were some injured that were visible; Kevin hoped that none were dead, but he could not discern that from here. He sadly assumed that some were, remembering the battlefield near Caitlin's house that he had seen with his own two eyes.

That reminded him to hope for Arthur's safety, and to hope that he could catch up with Kron after he had taken care of the War Commander, Eukert. Being here in Avalon was merely an unintentional detour.

With that thought in mind, Kevin turned and walked down the hallway into the temple. Inside was a fairly large chamber, big enough that a few avians could meet in here, lit by torches in the room's corners. It would do for a room to negotiate. This was likely the place that the Red Phoenix did his official duties, Kevin reasoned to himself. Now, all he had to do was wait for the negotiating parties to arrive.

He did not have to wait long. From the hallway before the throne room echoed a voice, "Excuse me, Sairon, but may I explain?"

The Red Phoenix looked into the hallway. "Wheldon, please proceed into the chamber. You can explain yourself later."

Wheldon did as he was instructed. Kevin felt quite a bit nervous at this point, as Wheldon and the Red Phoenix entered the chamber. Unlike most of the other phoenixes who had the two color patterns that differentiated them between male and female, the Red Phoenix's feathers were solid red all across his body. His title was quite appropriate in this case.

Seeing Kevin before him, the Red Phoenix, being unwilling to cower in front of anyone, advanced to Kevin and stood in front of him. Still, as daunting as the figure was, the Red Phoenix extended it the same courtesy as he did to all. "Greetings, stranger," he said, extending a wingtip. "Sacred Avalon has graced us with your presence today. I am the Red Phoenix, the flame of life and protector of all that is sacred. I am the ruler of all phoenixes."

Kevin reached out and extended his hand to shake the wingtip. "A pleasure to meet you as well. My name is Kevin Trent."

Immediately, the Red Phoenix let go and turned to Wheldon. "I presume something went wrong in the cage?"

Lowering his head, Wheldon said, "The humans cut through the cage with magic. I tried to stop them, but they overpowered me."

"I see," answered the Red Phoenix, then looking at Kevin. "Did you hold him hostage, then lose him when the battle started?"

"No, not at all!" Wheldon snapped, quickly. "They actually took mercy on me, and only wanted to talk. They are not here to start something."

The Red Phoenix thought for a second. "Quite," he said. "I would say, Wheldon, that theft of our most prized treasure counts as 'starting something'."

"I don't want your treasure," said Kevin, boldly.

"Hold your tongue!" commanded the Red Phoenix loudly to Kevin. Immediately, Kevin felt a shiver down his spine. He backed off a bit.

"Sairon, look at them and do not let your prejudice cloud your judgment," Wheldon then said. "These humans did not know they were in our lands, and they spotted me. Yet although they refused to be prisoners, they have demonstrated that they are just and noble humans, who wished that someday we may be friends, not foes. They had me in a position where they could have killed me, or taken me hostage, or who knows what. Instead, they chose not to do that and to try to make peace by parlaying our treasure." He paused as he looked at Kevin for a second. "I think that makes them worth a few moments to speak and explain himself."

Kevin and Caitlin looked at the Red Phoenix, who looked extremely tense. Then, he let out a sigh and put a wingtip on Wheldon's shoulder. "You would not be my second-in-command if you were not capable of speaking your mind, and for that, I will take your advice." The Red Phoenix considered for a moment. "Indeed, perhaps we have been wrong. However, let us determine just what kind of man this is. Allow the Great One to show us his guidance once again."

"My deepest apologies," said Kevin, puzzled, "but who is the Great One?"

"Why, how uneducated you are! I did not expect a human to be so uneducated as to not know of the Great One!" exclaimed the Red Phoenix. Kevin did not flinch or fidget, he just stood next to Caitlin, displaying an intent to listen. "The Great One," the Red Phoenix continued, "is the single deity that created and governs all: the earth, the sky, the sea, and so on. He is the one who sets prophecy to his will and watches over all. We, the phoenixes, try to stay in his best interest."

In human religion, which was relatively universal, the "nameless ones" were the protectors. The gods were real, too, and had essentially assumed that role as far as he knew. "Very well, then," he responded. "I will keep that in mind. Now, I do have a question. What is this place?"

Seeing a logical, honest question, the Red Phoenix responded, "This is the land of Avalon, a sacred land blessed by the Great One, and this building is our temple to the Great One. It has lasted for thousands of years, beyond the reach and knowledge of humans. None have charted the regions of this sacred land, but it is said that the once and future king came here to die and someday be reborn. It is this tradition on which our society is built."

Interesting mythology, Kevin though to himself. Then again, having heard of phoenixes as a mythological creature themselves, and how they are supposedly reborn from the ashes of their own deaths, Kevin could see a parallel. "I see," Kevin said, not thinking about that what he knew of phoenixes was just mythology and not based in fact, nor from what he had just seen in the battle outside, "much as members of your society are reborn."

"Err…" Wheldon stammered for a second, trying to keep the Red Phoenix from giving a thundering response, "that actually has not been the case for generations. We do not know why, but we have not undergone a cycle of rebirth for a very long time. It is… a sensitive issue in Avalon, and one we consider taboo of which to speak."

Almost instinctively, Kevin took a step back and bowed. "My apologies," he said. "I didn't mean to offend."

Then, in a bit of a surprise to both Wheldon and Kevin, the Red Phoenix stepped forward. "Please, do not apologize," he said, placing a wingtip by Kevin. "You did not, nor could not, have known. I cannot be angry with you for that."

Silently, Kevin nodded as he lifted his head.

"I must ask, however," the Red Phoenix continued as he withdrew the wingtip, "what are your intentions with our treasure?"

Kevin looked down at his right arm. "You mean this stripe?" he asked. "It is as I told everyone from the temple stairs. I intend to have you and the ravens negotiate for it."

"And what are your demands?"

"Peace. That is all I demand."

"Peace is all we dream," commented the Red Phoenix, "but I do not believe the ravens will go for it. They, I am sure, will want the stripe for themselves, and I cannot simply allow it to be given to them in exchange for peace."

A little frustrated, Kevin frowned. Was all this warring really over this magic energy? Or was it something else, and the Red Phoenix was afraid this magic would be used against them?

Kevin asked the Red Phoenix a direct question, pulling up his sleeve to reveal the stripe coloring his arm. "Why is this so important to you? And to the ravens, for that matter?"

The Red Phoenix said nothing for a moment. He looked at Wheldon, who then gave Kevin the answer. "We know little of it, other than it is called the Stripe of Air. It is one of seven, and the combination of all seven forms the ultimate power of the realms. Such is said in prophecy, written into our temple in the ancient language. No one knows how to use it on its own, but should the ravens find it and figure it out…"

"It would be very bad for all of us," interrupted the Red Phoenix. "They would destroy the City of Phoenixes and annihilate us all."

"And why would they want to do that?" asked Kevin.

Before he could get an answer, Kevin heard a thunderous sound at the entrance to the chamber. Down the hallway, he could see a very large raven with black feathers transitioning to gray under the wings and at the tail. The raven was berating what appeared to be a smaller phoenix trying to guard the entrance. "Out of my way!" yelled the booming voice of the raven.

Taking a step back and clutching his sword, Kevin braced for an unpleasant negotiation.

The raven rapidly made his way into the temple chamber, alone. Behind him, however, it was clear that ravens were forming up down the hallway. Any threat to this raven would likely lead to another attack.

Quickly, the raven arrived in the chamber, and looked directly at Kevin. "I will make this negotiation simple, human," he said, leaning his beak in toward Kevin. "Give me the stripe and I will give you an opportunity to escape. Choose to resist, and the talons of my ravens will tear you to shreds."

Kevin held his sword up to the raven. He had seen the raven's entrance long enough to realize he would likely be a subject of intimidation and he would not allow that as a negotiator, no matter how frightening it might be to stand up to him. "That is not how this will work," he said, as he lit the sword in its bright blue magic again. His inner serenity and determination for peace drove the power of his sword. "You will calm down and negotiate in good faith."

"Human, you know not to whom you speak. I am the Grand Raven. Who do you think you are to make threats to me?"

"I have not threatened you," responded Kevin, "but I'll do what I must to enforce the rules of this negotiation. You won't dictate them; I will."

The Grand Raven scoffed. "What makes a pathetic human like you think I will not destroy you?"

Wheldon spoke up. "I will not allow that." He moved next to Kevin. "This negotiation is between the Red Phoenix and yourself, not me nor Kevin Trent, the negotiator. I am his personal bodyguard. Spill my blood, and the whole of the phoenixes will make tearing you apart our personal mission."

For a second, the Grand Raven glared at Wheldon.

"Please, Grand Raven, negotiate in good faith," spoke the calm words of the Red Phoenix. "I am here to do the same, and you do not see me threatening our negotiator."

"Pathetic," commented the Grand Raven, as he turned toward the Red Phoenix. "How dare you trust a human? Have you no respect for the society set forth by our elders? We do not allow humans in our lands. We must never risk them threatening our society again, as they have time and time again in our history."

Our elders? Our society? The words of the Grand Raven were reminding Kevin that the founding raven was a discolored phoenix. Wheldon had even said, before this battle broke out, that that raven had killed the previous Red Phoenix.

As Kevin considered this, Wheldon was speaking in his defense. "This human has shown me kindness, courage, and mercy that I have never before seen in their race. The one out there in the city now, healing your wounded, has also shown these traits. We have kept humans away from us for millennia. I think for such extraordinary humans as those here, we can make an exception."

Kind words, Kevin thought to himself. He would have to acknowledge them later. "Let's begin, then," he said to the Red Phoenix and Grand Raven. "My goal is to forge a peace between phoenixes and ravens for as long as possible, so that battles like the one tonight don't happen again. I'll award the stripe accordingly as a bargaining chip to the offer that makes the best promise for peace."

"What interest do you have in peace?" asked the Grand Raven.

"Only that there be no more bloodshed," answered Kevin. "This quarrel of ravens and phoenixes cannot go on without much suffering. Why must that happen, when your races are one and the same?"

The Grand Raven scoffed again. "We are not like them. They are the discriminators, and we are the assaulted. They would not allow us to live like them, and so we fight them."

"Lies!" shouted the Red Phoenix in response. "You are the assaulters! We have not done anything to your race, and yet you attack us!"

"We will do what we must to gain our rightful place in the world, Red Phoenix. I do not think you will ever understand the pain you inflicted on us."

"Pain?" asked the Red Phoenix. "My phoenixes and I have only ever fought in defense since I have been their leader. How much pain have you and your family inflicted on my people in these countless battles?"

At this, Kevin raised his sword. "Stop the squabbling, both of you." He then looked at the Red Phoenix. "If you're really fighting only in defense, I'd presume you would welcome peace pretty easily as it's in your interest as well."

"It is in the best interest of my people," acknowledged the Red

Phoenix. "For millennia we lived peaceful lives in Avalon. We wish only to continue to have that peace."

Kevin nodded, as he turned to the Grand Raven. "What's your issue with the phoenixes, then? You're clearly one of them."

There was a slight pause.

"Am I, negotiator?" inquired the Grand Raven. "Because I sure do not appear to be one, do I?"

"You have a different color pattern," Kevin answered, "but you otherwise look the same to me. Why should your color pattern matter?"

"Why should it matter? Why should it matter!" exclaimed the Grand Raven loudly, his thundering voice booming through the chamber. He was clearly very angry. "You try being branded by the color of your skin, human. You try explaining to others that you are discolored from an infection and that you are not contagious, and see if they believe you! Only then can you speak to me about the color pattern of my feathers!"

"It was a mistake, Grand Raven," interjected the Red Phoenix, his eyes open. He appeared to be realizing something. "Yes, my predecessor made a mistake to judge you that way, to tie your feather discoloration to carrying the disease that was ravaging our society at the time. It was wrong that you were treated that way."

The Grand Raven appeared frustrated and confused for a second. "Of what madness and nonsense do you speak, old bastard?"

At this, the Red Phoenix's eyes lit up. He knew now for sure that he recognized the voice. "Uruson, my brother, is that you?"

"Your brother?" asked the Grand Raven in a strong tone. "What do you mean, Red Phoenix, you old bastard? You never showed me any care in the world! Why even bother adopting me? All your attention was always toward your real son, Sairon."

"Uruson," said the Red Phoenix, "I am Sairon."

The Grand Raven just stared at the Red Phoenix. "Sairon? How long have you been the Red Phoenix?" he said with a brightening tone.

"Since the day you left," said the Red Phoenix, with a more grave tone.

That was when it hit the Grand Raven that he had killed his

father, not merely attacked him. In shame, the Grand Raven turned his head and closed his eyes.

Kevin put his palm over his face in a sort of embarrassment. All of this war, Kevin thought to himself, and it all comes down to a family matter and a misunderstanding. Realizing then that that would not be helpful, he decided to sheathe his sword and walk up to the Grand Raven. He spoke quietly, "Take all the time that you need."

The Red Phoenix walked on his claws up to the Grand Raven and extended a wing around him. "For what it is worth, I am sorry," he said. "I had no knowing that you were the Grand Raven and not another affected phoenix who fled. I was told you were dead."

"No, no, I am sorry, Sairon," the Grand Raven said in response. "You were always good to me even when our father was not. I had no idea he was dead by my talons." He paused for a moment. "But you need to know it was self-defense, Sairon. He was going to end my life to 'eliminate a spreader of the infection', as he put it."

"I never believed you were spreading the infection," the Red Phoenix answered. "We played together for years before he came up with that hypothesis, yet I was never affected. Why he thought you affected so much of our society, I will never know."

Stepping back, Kevin stood next to Wheldon as he let Uruson and Sairon bond. Wheldon had a tear in his eyes as he watched.

The room felt full of tears at the moment.

Wheldon leaned in to Kevin and spoke quietly. "You did quite the job here, Kevin."

"If I may be honest, I don't feel like I did much."

"And yet you have the end result we all wanted to see," answered Wheldon. "I do not think anyone ever asked the Grand Raven if he was a phoenix or called him one. That it provoked the response that allowed the two adopted brothers to reunite was the perfect move, whether you knew it at the time or not."

Kevin looked up at Wheldon. "Did you know?"

Wheldon shook his head. "Many phoenixes died during the infection. A few had their feathers turn black, and Uruson hatched from his egg that way, but none survived except the Grand Raven. Those that did knew our Red Phoenix at the time, five years after the infection had started and was still killing phoenixes year after year, had ordered their deaths in what we know now was a misguided attempt to stop the spread. All had the opportunity, as that Red Phoenix felt it important for everyone's safety to do that job personally." He paused. "No, I had no idea that Uruson was the survivor. We were all told he had died."

Taking a deep breath, Kevin shook his head. "So much bloodshed in the battle, all because of a misunderstanding. It's no wonder the ravens would constantly attack the phoenixes when they were outcast from that society unjustly."

"An injustice that you have resolved, my friend," said Wheldon.

"Yes, well, I…" Kevin stopped for a moment. "Wheldon, did you just call me your friend?"

Wheldon nodded and looked directly at Kevin. "Indeed, I did," he said. He offered a bow. "May we always be friends, in this life and our next."

Kevin smiled. So much for "someday" being friends; that day was today. "May we always be friends," he acknowledged. "And I hope that Caitlin is your friend, too."

"She is," acknowledged Wheldon. "Catie will always be my friend."

Everything seemed as it should be, Kevin thought to himself. He leaned in toward Wheldon. "Should we exit the chamber and give them a moment?"

Wheldon responded in the affirmative. He then led Kevin out of the chamber to the temple entrance.

Outside, Kevin and Wheldon stood for several minutes, looking over the battlefield. The fires that had been there were now extinguished. It looked as though on both sides, everyone had fallen back into their own groups to tend to their wounded and families. It was a painful process of healing, but one that would be important. Although no one knew yet that there would be peace, that the factors that led to attempts at vengeance were now gone, the atmosphere was certainly more peaceful. No more raven or phoenix guards were attempting to guard the temple entrance; they had each retreated to care for their people. Something simply seemed different, as though war was clearly over even when it had not been declared yet.

Yawning, Kevin was tired. It was very late, and he and Caitlin had set up camp hours ago. Now it was very late into the night, and neither had the opportunity to rest. Now that all of the adrenaline of the last few hours had finally settled, all Kevin could think about was getting a good night of sleep.

At the bottom of the stairs, Kevin could see that Caitlin was making the climb toward him. Though she looked to be trying to maintain her usual disciplined self, it was becoming clear that she was very tired as well. The night was wearing on her. Simultaneously, behind Kevin, a phoenix and a raven flew in. Wheldon appeared to recognize one of them and waved them in. Kevin did not see who went by, nor did it seem to bother him at the moment.

As Caitlin reached the top, Kevin said to her, "I don't know how we did it, but we have peace."

"Oh, good," answered an exhausted Caitlin. "I think I healed a good number of avians. I don't think there will be very many casualties when this is all said and done."

Wheldon stepped in. "Most excellent. Thank you, Catie, for all you have done for us. I must get lodging for you and Kevin very quickly."

Caitlin only gave a wave, as if to signal it was not a big deal. She then asked to Kevin, "So who'd you give the stripe to?"

Immediately, Kevin's eyes widened. "Uhm…"

Now, Caitlin's eyes widened a bit, breaking her discipline slightly. "You still have it?"

"Yeah. Imagine that."

"You can't keep that," Caitlin answered firmly. "If you do, you'll only provoke more war; if not between them, it'll be between them and humans."

Wheldon looked at Kevin, as the sound of steps came from down the hall. "I agree with Catie. You need to put that back in the temple."

"No, I disagree, Wheldon," came a voice from down the hall.

Everyone turned. It was the Red Phoenix, emerging at the temple entrance.

The Red Phoenix spoke to Kevin, "Uruson's family is with him now, caring for him. This is an affair we can handle from here on out." He paused for a second. "Thank you for all of your help with us, Kevin Trent. Perhaps true strength, sometimes, is not all from fighting power. Because of you, it is possible that our peoples can live as one from here on, thanks to your help."

"No problem," said Kevin, tiredly. He looked over at Caitlin, before looking back. "Please don't forget Caitlin, though. She did a lot to provide medical healing to your people."

Inside, Caitlin felt a little warm, even if she would not show it. Kevin certainly wanted to share credit where it was due.

The Red Phoenix looked at Caitlin and offered a bow. "I thank you for everything you have done for my people."

A little awkwardly, Caitlin offered a small curtsey in return. To have a leader bow to you was the utmost sign of respect, and one that Caitlin knew. She was indeed being acknowledged.

Then, the Red Phoenix extended a wingtip to Kevin. "As thanks for your work, I want you to be the caretaker of our treasure, the Stripe of Air. I have given it thought, and I acknowledge that the healing of our societies and unification will take some time. It will not be as simple as my reconciliation with Uruson. While we work on this process together, I have decided that it would be best if the treasure were far away from here for a time. We do not need a temptation of power that can be seized to reignite any wars between factions."

This very much surprised Kevin, to be entrusted with such a responsibility. "I… well, I…I'm honored."

"Sairon, if I may have a word," interrupted Wheldon. "Kevin and Catie are friends of mine, but there will be a great upheaval in our society if it is found out that you gifted our treasure to humans. Only a phoenix will do as a bearer of the Stripe of Air, in their eyes."

For a moment, the Red Phoenix looked hard at Wheldon. "Right, indeed," he acknowledged. "That should be rectified." He then looked back at Kevin, and motioned down with his wingtip, signaling to Kevin to kneel down.

Tired, Kevin did not question it, but did as he was instructed.

The Red Phoenix then put the wingtip on Kevin's shoulder and said, "Be it known now, throughout all of our lands, that sacred Avalon bestows its grace upon Kevin Trent. Forevermore, he shall be an honorary member of our society, entitled to all of the rights, privileges, and responsibilities of the phoenixes. Kevin Trent is an honorary phoenix."

As Kevin opened his eyes, he saw the Red Phoenix and Wheldon bowing to him. A few phoenixes had been gathered near the stairs; they began to caw in approval. This was the most amount of glory Kevin had ever felt, and it was in this moment with being who he had never known until a short while ago.

Caitlin stepped back and clapped a couple of times. She was proud of Kevin tonight; most of the plans were his and he showed tremendous courage. She hoped this would serve as a confidence booster to him, to make him realize that he could be great himself and not have to lean on her so much. Deciding to cement this, she thoughtspoke to him: *Don't bother asking them if I should be an honorary phoenix as well. You did an amazing job tonight, Kevin. I want you to have this honor alone.*

As Kevin stood up, the Red Phoenix then said to Wheldon, "Would you take them to our guest quarters in the temple? I am sure they are very tired. We do not have human beds, but we can offer them the most comfortable bedding we have."

Wheldon nodded in acknowledgment, and told Kevin and Caitlin to start heading down the stairs. They would have to walk around to the back of the temple to get to some comfy lodging for the night, and the well-earned rest they deserved.

As they walked down the stairs, Kevin asked Caitlin, "How come you don't want the same honors I have?"

"I don't need it," Caitlin said in response. "Not that I wouldn't be honored to have it, but I got my recognition when the Red Phoenix bowed to me. Besides, you were responsible for a lot of the ideas tonight, and you pulled off the peace."

Kevin put his hands behind his head and stretched his arms, flaring his elbows. "Yeah, but I sort of backed into it accidentally," he said.

"Whether or not that's the case, you got the results," Caitlin answered. "You should enjoy the credit that follows." She paused for a second. “How do you feel?”

For a moment, Kevin thought about it. “Tired,” he answered. “Very tired.”

“Understandable. I am, too,” Caitlin said. “But what about if you were rested, like you will be tomorrow morning. How will you feel then?”

There was another moment’s pause. He thought of Arthur.

“Honestly,” answered Kevin, as he continued to stretch his arms and he finally felt a senes of pride in his accomplishment, “I’ll feel so good, like I could fly into Seta Archa and storm Demonicus’s palace myself.”

Chapter 14

The Heir of Desolunar

"Arthur? Hey Arthur, wake up!"

Arthur Falchor felt his eyelids start to open. He felt like he had been asleep for so long, longer than he ever had been. His cognizance was just starting to function after what felt like an eternity. Consciousness was coming to him very slowly, and he was not being snapped awake even as someone was yelling at him to wake up.

He had no idea how he had been out so long or what had happened. The last thing Arthur could remember was patrolling around the house of a sorceress named Caitlin, while his best friend Kevin Trent slept inside, and he was accompanied by Kron Kalavere. While his brain was slowly stirring, he could not recall how he had fallen unconscious.

"Come on, Arthur, wake up! I have to get you out of here!"

Slowly, Arthur's eyes were opening. His vision was blurry, but slowly coming into focus. He could see that he was in a dungeon cell of some kind, surrounded by stone walls and bars on the door. There were no windows allowing in any outside light, but there was a bit of light from a torch in the hallway shining in between the bars.

Still disoriented and not sure where he was, Arthur finally said groggily, "Huh? What?"

"Come on! We've got to go!" He felt the person drag him toward the door.

Arthur was still coming out of his daze. "Wha… who are you?"

"Don't you recognize me, Arthur? It's me, your best friend Kevin!"

Kevin?! He was there to rescue him?

As quickly as he could, Arthur tried to shake off his sleepiness. He squinted his eyes to try and bring them into focus. It sure looked like Kevin towing him out into the hallway, wearing his red shirt and everything.

Although he had been taken by surprise a little bit, Arthur's legs were starting to catch up and he began working harder to keep up with Kevin. He had no idea how or why, but Kevin was leading him down hallways and around corners. Were they trapped somewhere and needing to get out? How did Kevin know where to go?

Three or four corners later —Arthur had lost count—Kevin suddenly stopped. "Wait here, Arthur," he said. "You're still out of it. I'll make sure the way ahead is clear, and I'll come back to get you and take you home." Then, Kevin ran off down the hallway.

At this point, Arthur was finally regaining full control of his senses. Why was Kevin rushing him out of here so quickly? What was happening? Kevin had moved so quickly that he did not even make sure his best friend could give him a coherent response. Looking around, Arthur tried to get a better idea of where he was. There were torches on the walls illuminating what was otherwise a dark dungeon. Gray stone lined the walls and floors, while periodic wooden doors were entrances to prison cells.

While he was waiting on Kevin to return, Arthur walked over to the nearest door and peeked through the bars. The room inside was not illuminated, but Arthur noticed someone moving on the floor. Grabbing a nearby torch from the wall, Arthur held it up to the bars to try and look inside. When this did not work so effectively, he squeezed the torch in between the bars and dropped it onto the stone floor below, illuminating the room.

He gasped. Lying on the floor, face up in the clothes in which he had last seen her, was Rachel Reinhart. Suddenly it occurred to Arthur that he was nowhere good.

Arthur tried to open the door, hoping it may open from the outside. He was wrong; it was locked. He tried calling Rachel's name; he could see she was still breathing, but she was not responding to his calls.

Then, from down the hall, he heard Kevin yell, "Arthur, hurry this way! Let's get you out of here so we can go home!"

"Rachel's in here!" Arthur yelled back. "We can't leave her!"

"We have to!" Kevin yelled as he ran up to Arthur and pushed him forward, making him take the lead. He was pushing Arthur toward an open iron door.

Without a second to think, Arthur was shoved forward through the door. Immediately, the door then shut.

Arthur then turned around, catching himself from the shove. He was now face to face with an iron door without bars. So much was wrong with what just happened.

What did just happen, anyway? And where was Kevin?

If Kevin was okay, and Arthur presumed he was the one to shut the door and had some kind of plan, then all Arthur could think of was Rachel. Kevin could not be so cruel as to leave her behind. He started to sob, as he pounded the door with his fist. "Rachel, I'm sorry…"

"Leave the girl, Arthur. She is of no importance right now."

Arthur turned around to see this room was a little different. It was well illuminated by torches and larger than any room he had seen yet in this dungeon. A table and chairs sat in front of him. It was a small table with two large chairs on opposite sides of the table. Arthur took a seat in the one closest to the door, figuring that he was intended by someone to sit down.

From another large metal door on the other side of the table entered a man who appeared to be in his late thirties, dressed in a large robe that was dark red and wearing a gold necklace with a tag hanging from it. He was followed by four guards of the Desolunar armed forces, dressed in their black military uniforms. Strangely enough, the man bore a striking resemblance to Arthur, with the facial features and blonde hair color. Arthur ventured a guess at who was in front of him. "Well, well, well," started Arthur, "I presume you are Demonicus?"

The man took his seat. In a calm but deep voice, he responded, "You have my identity correct, my son."

"Son?" asked Arthur. "Is that some kind of sick cultist joke where you're the 'father' to everyone? Because you're sure dressed like a cultist."

Demonicus appeared to be angered. He kept his composure, however, and said, "I am no 'father' to a cult, but I am a father to you. Who do you think left you that sword?"

Suddenly, Arthur's eyes widened. Demonicus knew about the

sword he had been left by his father. Could he really be Arthur's father?

Why? And how? Arthur kept asking himself that. Somehow, between the similar appearances and that Demonicus knew about the sword, Arthur feared it was true, that Demonicus was his father. Suddenly it was all starting to make sense. This was why Arthur's mother, Rita Falchor, had never told him about his father. If she knew his father was Demonicus, she was clearly keeping him far away from Desolunar. He would likely need a sword someday when he came of age, so maybe she hoped he would never connect the sword to his father. Even so, how could his mother never tell him that?

Nearly a full minute passed as Arthur slouched in his chair. The thought resounded in Arthur's mind. "I believe you," he responded, without emotion. "Somehow, I feel like I know it to be true."

"Ah, so I see you have chosen to acknowledge your heritage rather than suppress it," answered Demonicus. "You are the heir of Desolunar, the son of the chosen one, he who our father has selected as his own son. In that way you are the grandson of our father."

Arthur gave a shrug, snapping out of his funk. "It isn't one's birth that makes them who they are. It's their choices." Arthur paused to take a breath. "I mean, look at Vincent Stryker. As I understand it, had he not chosen to accept the Sword of Purity, he would not have kicked your father's ass the first time around." Referencing what Kron had told him about the Alliance-Daritel War and Tyrinion, Arthur was being more cocky with this last statement.

"My son," started Demonicus, "if I were you, I would not say such things about him. He is my father and your grandfather, albeit indirectly, and he would not like it much if you taunted him and spread lies."

Arthur suddenly became confused. "Indirectly your father? What the hell does that mean, first of all?"

"Well, I see no harm in explaining it to you," said Demonicus. "Our father chose me to be his successor, to rule this land of Desolunar and to carry out his ambitions. I may not be his child, but I am his heir. You are mine by blood."

Shrugging, Arthur looked away. He was not wanting to hear

any of that.

"And that is why I have brought you here today," Demonicus then continued. "I have brought you back to Desolunar to take your rightful place as my heir. I am building a kingdom greater than any the world has ever seen, and it will only be a matter of time before I conquer every realm." He stood up from his chair. "And I am sure you have already seen that the conquest of the realms has already begun…"

"And I want no part of it," interrupted Arthur.

Demonicus rolled his eyes. "You will once you receive your first taste of power, my son. It will become a thirst that you will only quench when everything is yours."

"You say that, but I'm not willing to have any of it," said Arthur. "I don't want to be a ruler. I'm not interested in bossing others around or bearing responsibility on that level. I've only ever wanted a normal life, and I stand by that now even with you trying to offer me the world."

Demonicus decided to change the subject and interrogate. "The new pure one, he is your friend, is he not?"

"What 'new pure one'?" Arthur was very confused.

"Do not play stupid," Demonicus demanded as he slammed his fist. "Your friend, the one who can hold the Sword of Purity. Only the pure one can hold that sword, so clearly he is the new pure one. He is your friend, isn't he?"

Arthur looked up at Demonicus. "What does any of that have to do with you?"

"By holding that sword, he is my enemy," answered Demonicus, "and by virtue, he is now your enemy as well."

With a cross look on his face, Arthur responded, "Except you are my enemy, so that's all the more reason for him to be my friend."

"Why am I your enemy, son?"

"Oh, I don't know, maybe by the way that you chose not to be a part of my life in any way until this moment?"

Demonicus grimaced for a minute, pulling his fist back and off the table. "I did so for a reason," he said. He then regained his composure. "I allowed your mother to raise you as she willed. I have a kingdom to run, but I left you that sword, the Sword of Corruption, so that when you became of age and could wield it, it would guide me to you."

Arthur looked at Demonicus scornfully. "And in doing so, you sentenced me to growing up with an abusive alcoholic. Whatever your reasons are, your absence was the worst thing you could do to me."

"Would you rather I have locked you and your mother in a prison cell?" growled an angry Demonicus.

"No! I would rather that you'd have been a father!" yelled Arthur. The years of trauma and being raised by Rita Falchor were clearly visible all over his face as he screamed in anger. Everything else about his situation was slowly being forgotten in the moment.

Furious, Demonicus stood from his seat. He leaned in to one of his guards, and gave a direction which caused the guard to leave the room. He then reached into his belt and pulled out a small knife, one that was quite short. "Be that as it may," Demonicus then said to Arthur, "I am offering you now the opportunity of a lifetime, and one that I only offer you because you are my son. Join me, and I will give you ultimate power. The only ones to whom you will answer are me, and to my immortal father, he who chose me for this power. You can correct the things that are wrong in your life, all with a simple agreement."

Arthur gave no reaction.

Demonicus then showed his hand, took the short knife, and sliced across his palm. He made sure that Arthur saw the blood coming from his hand, as well as the fact that the knife was now stained with it. "This is my commitment to our agreement," he said. "I agree to keep my promises with my own blood." He then threw the knife across the table, sliding it down to where it stopped in front of Arthur.

As the knife arrived, Arthur stared down at it for a moment. The blade on the knife could not be any longer than his index finger. It was a double-sided blade, now with the red stain of his father's blood on it.

Whatever had happened in the last few days, he was clearly in Seta Archa, the capital city of Desolunar. Demonicus would likely not be here otherwise. He was in a dungeon somewhere, with Rachel Reinhart, of all people. That was a question for another moment. What options did he have at the moment? Arthur felt put on the spot and trapped. If he did not take the deal, would he be imprisoned forever?

Then, the door behind Demonicus opened. Accompanied by the guard that Demonicus had sent out, was Kevin. They walked in together, as Kevin started walking around the table to Arthur.

"What the hell, Kevin?" Arthur asked, upset. "You said we were going home!"

"We are home, Arthur," Kevin said. "This is your home now, where you belong. You have your father at last. Doesn't that mean something to you?"

Suddenly, it was adding up to Arthur. Demonicus made a blunder in his anger. What Demonicus had said about Kevin, and how this person was behaving now, and how nonchalant his father seemed to be about him walking in like this…

Arthur reached down and picked up the knife.

He knew now what his decision would be.

Kevin walked up to Arthur and put an arm around his shoulder. "It's the best way, Arthur. We won't have to worry about our livelihoods anymore."

Arthur clutched the knife. He placed his left hand over the blade while his right hand clutched the hilt.

"What's wrong, Arthur? Why are you hesitating? Just slice your hand and get it done. For us."

"For us?" asked Arthur.

"Yeah, for us," Kevin answered. "We're friends, aren't we?"

Swish!

Immediately, Kevin screamed and leapt backwards in pain. He was clutching his face, covering his left eye.

Arthur had taken the knife and sliced him across the eye. His face was full of anger and rage. "You're not Kevin!" he yelled.

The guards in the room ran over to grab the lookalike and escort him away. One pointed a short sword at Arthur, but Demonicus waved that guard off. "Very well spotted," Demonicus observed. He then continued, "Well, in light of your continued resistance, I can see we will be getting nowhere today."

"Or any day," commented Arthur. He was still clutching the knife.

As the door closed behind Demonicus with the guards escorting the false Kevin out of the room, Demonicus sat back down. "Then allow me to make you a deal, one that will allow you to earn what you really want."

Arthur held onto the knife tightly. He would not sit down, but he glared into the eyes of his father. "You have my attention," he said.

There was a momentary pause. Demonicus took a deep breath. "I do not understand why you would refuse me, but if such is your choice, then I will do without an heir. However, you are still bound to me by blood. I will not release your bind unless you do a favor for me first."

"And that is?" asked Arthur.

"As you can imagine, my forces are quickly advancing into Aurana, but deep in Aurana, I have no influence as of yet. That makes someone like you, a citizen of Aurana, quite useful to me for what I want you to do."

Arthur raised an eyebrow.

Demonicus became firm in his speaking. "I want you to kill the pure one. Spill the blood of your best friend and bring me the Sword of Purity."

A shocked look came to Arthur's face. He regained his composure and asked, "Why would I want to do that?"

"Because if you don't, I will keep you imprisoned here forever," Demonicus answered, "and if you run from me, I will capture you and have you tortured daily. There is nowhere in the world that you are safe from me. But if you do as I have offered, and after that you are still adamant that you want no part of the power you could have here, then I will release you from this bond and give you my assurance that I will not pursue you again. Should you change your mind, however, I will welcome you back with open arms… but only if you kill the pure one first."

Arthur thought hard about this for a moment. He remembered seeing Rachel in the prison cell. "One condition," Arthur retorted, as he pointed out the door. "Send Rachel with me. Her fate will be the same as mine."

Demonicus looked puzzled. "You mean the young woman in

the cell down the hall?" He thought for a moment, recalling that he had already obtained what he wanted from her and did not have any use in keeping her here—he had simply not had her disposed yet. "That can be arranged. I understand that she kept a bow and arrows around for self-defense when she was captured, so I will do you the favor of providing her one of my highest quality bows manufactured in Seta Archa. I am sure you could use the extra set of hands with your assignment."

"Done deal," Arthur answered.

There was a brief moment of silence. Demonicus raised a hand.

"Then the deal is made," he said.

Immediately, Arthur blacked out from the magic coming from Demonicus' hand. An orb appeared briefly in it before disappearing.

All fell silent for the moment. After a short pause, Demonicus then stood up and exited through the door.

Briefly, Demonicus gave instructions to his guards to have Arthur and Rachel removed from the city, and that the Sword of Corruption, a new bow with small quiver of arrows, and provisions for a few days were to be left with them. He then proceeded for the dungeon exit, which led directly up into his capital building. This was the dungeon under the pyramid in Seta Archa.

As Demonicus proceeded upward back to his office, he felt furious. This was not what he wanted to do with Arthur, but he had bigger issues at the moment than his succession. Anyone who could be a carrier of the Sword of Purity was a threat to be dealt with, lest the end of the Alliance-Daritel War twenty years ago repeat itself. The immortal father could never be placed in danger again, or the guts bestowed to Demonicus would be revoked and he would be punished severely. Arthur could at least be a tool for that, if he would play along. If he did not, then Demonicus could be rid of him and pretend he never existed. No sense in taking aboard an heir without any ambition, after all.

Upstairs in his office, he had an important meeting planned to rectify that situation once and for all. He would also follow up with the progression of his forces and how his invasions were proceeding. The advancement of his Desolunar forces was still unabated at this point, and Demonicus was intent on keeping things that way.

It took nearly fifteen minutes for Demonicus to make his way from the basement to the tip of the pyramid, where his office was located. Upon arriving, he sat at his desk and contemplated his fury at his son for a few moments. No matter the bigger issues, he was still incredibly angry that his son would simultaneously accept his parentage and deny his place in power. Demonicus did not understand anything about being a parent, nor about young adults. In truth, what he was hoping for in giving Arthur such a task was to rid himself of the pure one regardless, and that accomplishing this task would drive him to return and take his place of power. If he did not do that, and he ran, then he would be a coward and unworthy of being the heir to begin with, and Demonicus would seek pleasure in executing him personally.

The sound of a knock on the trap door of his office signaled to Demonicus that his meeting party was assembled and ready to meet with him. With his authorization, they entered his office and took positions for the meeting.

Assembled together were five individuals, gathered around the desk of Demonicus. Standing in Desolunar military uniforms were two men. One was General Sayo, the usually silent general who had leadership over the complete invasion of Aurana. His second-in-command, Lieutenant Detaqh Kirkwood, stood next to him, also in a military stance. Behind Lieutenant Kirkwood were two young women. One of them had a deep tan complexion with dark brown hair tied up at each side of her head, wearing a very short pair of shorts and a tank top cut off above the abdomen, colored yellow and appearing to have been stained repeatedly with dirt. She appeared to be in excellent physical shape and was quite tall for a young woman. The other, who was more pale complected and shorter than her sister, had long, straight brown hair and wore a spellcaster's dress with yellow and green stripes on the skirt, which was cut off at the knees. Her dress looked like it was very worn. These were Lieutenant Kirkwood's daughters, who were the two most skilled assassins Demonicus had in his forces, but neither was an official member of his army as he forbade females from serving directly.

The fifth individual, the fake who looked like Kevin Trent, was seated in a chair. He appeared more casual and not as respectful to his leader. Now wearing a Desolunar military uniform designating a high rank, even more elaborate than that of General Sayo across the room from him, he looked like Kevin minus the fact that his left eye had clearly taken significant trauma and there was a massive scar diagonally across his face, through the eye socket. He was now blind in that eye.

As Demonicus welcomed his guests, with his hood up, he began by addressing the fake from his desk. "I see that the wizards have taken to healing your injury, and that you are back in service so quickly."

"We will speak of it later," said the fake, sounding as though he were furious in his voice. His voice did sound almost exactly like that of Kevin Trent, although only Demonicus knew that.

"Lord Pseudo," said Demonicus to the fake, "you may speak of it now, if you would rather. If you have something to say, you may say it to the group."

Pseudo sighed. "Very well," he said. "Do you realize that I, a creation of your immortal father whom you asked to bring here to assist in leading your kingdom, am now ruined? I know why you assembled us here; you are concerned there is a new pure one, and I was created to share his image as a reminder of who to destroy. I could have been used for more, to replace the pure one and ruin him. But instead you decided to use me to taunt your son, and he took out his wrath on me such that now I am permanently disfigured. I hope you are happy with yourself."

"Quite," nodded Demonicus, who then turned toward the group. He made it clear he was ignoring this complaint. This was his kingdom and no one would go against him; Pseudo only had the leeway to vocalize such a complaint because he was a gift from the immortal father.

Demonicus then sighed. "I received a letter several days ago. Some news has come in from the Enlighteners from the Shadows' furthest reaches. It appears that one of the members of the organization has discovered that Vincent Stryker, Vincent the Pure One, is still alive. While we have allowed his continued existence up until this point, the emergence of a new pure one who is wielding the Sword of Purity means that we cannot allow this any further. He is far beyond our reaches at the moment, but I have no qualms about sending a group to kill him no matter how far into another country we must go."

"And you have taken the time to wait for us to assemble here to send someone to kill him," interjected Pseudo.

"I have," acknowledged Demonicus, "because among this group is the person, or persons, who will make this task happen." He then stood from his desk, and looked at Pseudo. "Certainly you are on that list, Pseudo. Being a creation of my immortal father's, you have all the tools you would need to lead a strike force for several months to do the job. You are also my second-in-command, so you would be setting an example for our men that no one is above such a dangerous assignment."

"In other words, even after you went through the trouble to request for my creation and await the completion, I am still expendable," said Pseudo.

"No one is not expendable," answered Demonicus, coldly. He then stepped over to the two soldiers. "General Sayo, you are perhaps my most trusted soldier. Once a son of Aurana yourself, you now lead our forces against Aurana, and to this point, you have yet to be denied your objectives."

Sayo offered a salute by placing a fist to his chest and bowing.

"I understand that you have moved back and forth between removing defensive units at the border and crushing resistance in Atwals," Demonicus continued. "Lieutenant Kirkwood has been a rising star in your forces, and largely responsible for keeping Atwals under control."

Lieutenant Kirkwood saluted. "Aye, sir," he said.

"And yet," continued Demonicus, getting in Lieutenant Kirkwood's face, "what is this I hear that you allowed a group of resistance leaders in Atwals to escape?"

There was a slight pause, as it became apparent that Demonicus was expecting an answer. Lieutenant Kirkwood finally said, "We were needing all the forces we had to secure the northeast sector of the city. I did not have enough forces to send a detachment to pursue, or else I would have risked the resistance gaining a foothold."

"I see," acknowledged Demonicus, not reacting emotionally at the moment. He then turned his attention to the two women. "Rouge and Resa Kirkwood, two of our finest assassins. You have fine daughters, Lieutenant Kirkwood."

Lieutenant Kirkwood nodded. "Thank you, sir."

Demonicus took a closer inspection to the girls, who were expected to stay stood at attention. He then said to Rouge, the taller girl with the more athletic build, "I understand the two of you are quite well traveled. Sixteen successful eliminations within the past four years, with the most recent being the top resistance leader in Atwals." He then stepped closer to Resa, the shorter girl in a dress. "The two of you would be undertaking your biggest assignment yet, if I gave it to you. But, you would not need a strike team of our forces." He looked back at Rouge. "Are you capable of such a task?"

"Yes, my lord," Rouge answered, looking at her sister quickly.

Resa also nodded.

Demonicus appeared pleased. "Very good," he said, as he walked back to his desk. He did not sit behind it, but instead stood. "So, now, who do I select for such an important assignment?" He looked around the room briefly again. "Lieutenant Kirkwood, please step forward."

Doing as he was instructed, the lieutenant took a step forward.

Demonicus then addressed him, "With this assignment, you could prove that you are worthy of a generalship. You are pragmatic, high achieving, and talented, as I understand. I would need General Sayo to remain committed to subduing Atwals and advancing our borders further into Aurana. As such, you are the one with the skills to lead a team discretely into foreign lands and do what must be done."

Lieutenant Kirkwood smiled.

"Except for one thing," commented Demonicus. "I do not tolerate failure." He raised his hand and said, "Die."

A black wave of magic came from his hand. Immediately, Lieutenant Kirkwood fell over, dead.

Rouge and Resa rushed to their father's side.

General Sayo did not flinch.

Demonicus then looked over at Pseudo. "I will give you the information, and you will lead a team to Vincent Stryker's location to kill him. I want you to have a team assembled with adequate provisions gathered and a plan in place to leave by the end of the week. I have given my heir the assignment to kill the new pure one whom you were designed to resemble; if he has not done so after you take out Stryker, I want you to kill the pure one, and kill the heir as well."

Pseudo rose to his feet, his arms crossed. "As you wish," he answered.

Then, Demonicus turned. Rouge and Resa were crying over their father's body. He addressed General Sayo, "I will command you to return to Atwals in the morning. Finish Lieutenant Kirkwood's job and hunt down the resistance leaders that escaped. After that, I will send plans for the next major advance. We will march on Rikleifer soon."

Sayo gave a salute and walked away.

Demonicus then looked at Rouge and Resa. "Ladies, your attention, please."

On command, Rouge and Resa stood up. Their eyes were clearly wet with tears, but if they did not do what Demonicus told them, they feared their fate would be the same.

"At the moment, I will not hold you accountable for the failure of your father. However, any indiscretion from the two of you and I will do so. As such, I have an assignment for you. Lord Pseudo will kill Vincent Stryker, and either he or my heir will kill the pure one. I will give both of you that opportunity as well, but I do not want either of you leaving Desolunar until you prove your loyalty to me supersedes that of your father. As such, I know of at least one location where the pure one has been in territory we recently took from Aurana." He paused for a second. "I will have you wait there, for as long as it takes. Take a good look at Lord Pseudo, and imagine him with two functioning eyes, and that is for whom you will be waiting. If you fail, I will execute one of you in front of the other. If you run, I will kill you both."

Tearfully, but trying to maintain some discipline, the young women stood tall and each nodded.

Demonicus took one last look around the room. "Dismissed, all of you," he commanded.

It took moments for everyone to leave the room. Again, Demonicus looked down at the two stripes on his wrist, one yellow and one purple. These were the basis of his ultimate plan: to plunge the world into darkness. Just as his father would want him to do.

Chapter 15

Beware, All Who Know

It had been a trying few days for the god Kronius, living in the mortal realm as Kron Kalavere. He felt deeply responsible for both Kevin Trent and Arthur Falchor, and in a fight against Demonicus and one of the Enlighteners from the Shadows, he had failed. Now, Arthur was gone and Kevin was traveling alone with a sorceress, all because he had to stay behind to care for a fallen soldier.

At least that had only taken a couple of extra days. Kron had since walked all the way back to Rikleifer with the fallen soldier, War Commander Eukert, with him. Eukert was very appreciative that Kron had cared for him and made sure he could get back safely into Aurana's territory it still firmly controlled. From there, he would report about what had happened in the southern forest and the immediate need for defense of Rikleifer.

As Rikleifer came into view while Kron and Eukert walked along the road into town, Kron said, "It looks like we are finally here."

"Indeed," acknowledged the war commander. "Mr. Kalavere, I must again thank you for what you've done for me. I will make sure to mention you in my report to APF command."

"Oh, that is not necessary," responded Kron. "I did what I did only because it was the right thing to do. I do not need special commendation."

Eukert looked at Kron for a second, then nodded. "If that is what you wish," he said. "Still, I want you to have my personal appreciation."

"That," Kron smiled, "I would be willing to accept."

In front of Kron and Eukert on the path, standing before the first buildings of the city, was a man in red robes with blonde hair slicked back into points. He looked to be middle aged or perhaps a bit older.

And he was staring a hole into Kron.

Seeing who it was, Eukert approached the man. "Professor Magnon," he began, "this is quite a surprise."

Professor Magnon nodded. "It is, although I foresaw this may happen. How are you doing, Milton?"

"I'm all right, all things considered," Eukert said in response. "I have Kron, my traveling companion for the last few days, to thank for that."

The professor contemplated this for a second. "Kron is your traveling companion…" he mumbled a bit. Then, he straightened up and extended his hand to shake. "A pleasure, Kron. I am Professor James Magnon."

"Indeed it is," said Kron, trying to keep his cool as he shook the professor's hand. "I am Kron Kalavere. It is a pleasure to meet you too, professor."

The professor paused for a second, apparently contemplating the name. "Such an interesting name, Kron. Is it a *rengan* name?"

Keeping control, Kronius responded, "Yes, it is. A name my parents picked for me."

"Interesting," said the professor, "considering that the word *kron* is one of several words that means messenger in *rengan*. Though that is not its most common usage. More or less, it was just a simple name."

"Well, my parents were never really the normal type," chuckled Kronius, uncomfortably. For some reason, Kronius did not like the situation he was put in with the professor. Something was not right to him. "Speaking of *rengan* names, Professor," said Kronius, having just realized something, "is your last name not *rengan* as well?"

"It is," responded the professor. He paused for a second. "I am sure you are wanting a rest, so I will not keep you any longer," he continued to Eukert. "As I was told you would be along, I have already informed the castle of your impending arrival, so the Duke will be waiting for you."

"Thank you," acknowledged Eukert, not questioning what the professor had said or how he had heard. He was simply tired and ready to report on what had happened. He then looked at both the professor and Kron. "I will take my leave of both of you now. Hopefully we will all meet again soon."

The professor and Kron each extended a goodbye to Eukert, and the war commander headed off into the city, bound for the castle.

Then, the professor said nothing but just looked into Kron's eyes. No words were spoken. To Kron, it was clear. The message was in his mind, sent directly into his head. And it read:

You know, it is really not necessary to hide your identity in front of me, Kronius. I know you well enough. You are best not to make assumptions right now, as it will be your undoing.

It was stunning to Kronius. How did the professor know?

"You impress me, Professor Magnon. May I suggest we have a walk together and discuss this more thoroughly?"

You mean about what you are doing with the new pure one and my daughter?

How do you know about the new pure one?

That does not matter right now. Let us go somewhere safe where we can discuss this in words. Mind communication is not always safer if the wrong person is listening.

Kron thought for a second. *Kevin's house?*

That would do.

The pair walked on in silence for another ten minutes along a side street. They were headed for Kevin's house, which was currently empty. At the very least, it would be a quiet place for them to interact. And the professor had a point, Kron reasoned—verbal arguments could be heard within earshot, but someone listening for a mind communication, albeit a far fewer number, could probably intercept those messages in an area as large as the castle grounds of Rikleifer. Who knew if Demonicus had Enlighteners hiding in town, listening for what they could hear with magic?

The walk to Kevin's house had been awkward. Professor Magnon opened the door, and allowed Kron inside first, before following him in and closing the door. He then walked around the small house to make sure every shutter was tightly closed and that there was no risk of sound getting out.

"I want to know what this is about," started Kronius, once the pair was inside and the shutters were verified to be latched. "I presume that you must be Caitlin's father, and she brought Kevin to you. I want to know what your role in this whole incident is, and how you know my real name and position."

The professor paused for a second and then responded, "Fine. You shall have your answers, in due time. But I want to know what you are doing here. What are you leading the pure one to?"

"Excuse me," replied Kronius, sounding more irate, "*but what right do you have to ask me what I am doing here?*" Kronius finished his sentence speaking *rengan*, the ancient tongue, as his frustration, expressed in his tone of his voice, came out stronger in the ancient tongue.

Professor Magnon picked up where Kronius left off in speaking *rengan. "Do you not think that it is unusual for a god to be here in the mortal realm when there is a seal on the Realm of the Angels?"*

"How do you know that?" asked Kronius in a more surprised tone. *"And I must say, it is very interesting that you can speak rengan as well. Very few modern mortals know how to speak it fluently."*

"I have my ways of knowing, Kronius. Of knowing everything, and yet nothing at all." The professor paused for a second. *"You do know, however, that it is not in my best interest, and neither is it in yours, for me to reveal how this is so."*

"Not in my best interest!" exclaimed Kronius, letting the rengan words echo around the room. *"It is in the best interest of myself and of the pure one to know what you are capable of and how this is so."*

Professor Magnon took a breath, and began to explain to Kronius. *"If you knew what was involved with this, I think you would see things my way."*

"Then tell me."

"I cannot. Not now, at least. Please, just trust me that I will reveal all when the time is right. I will tell you why I know what I know, but for now it is not safe for me to do so."

"*Do you presume me to be Tyrinion?*"

"What?" The professor exclaimed in the common language, extremely surprised. "Why would I assume that?"

Kron continued in *rengan*. *"If you know me to be a god, then who else would you presume me to be? It is evident now that he is still alive and driving Desolunar and its ruler Demonicus forward; I bore witness to this power a few days ago. Who else is bound outside of the Realm of the Angels at this time?*"

The professor shook his head. "*No, Kronius, I know who you are, and that you are who you say you are. I know you are trapped here, and that you asked Kevin to help you get home.*"

Allowing himself a moment to consider how to respond, Kron took a breath. "*Indeed I have,*" he said.

"*What is your plan?*" asked the professor.

Kron shrugged. "*I do not have a fully developed plan,*" he said. "*I know enough to know the Sword of Purity is the only thing in the mortal realm that could possibly damage or destroy the seal. Putting it in the hands of the pure one was the most logical step to do this, and then I would have to figure out how to get it open.*"

The professor considered this. "*I see, and you stumbled upon Kevin. Why did you not tell him that he was a pure one? He is convinced that he is not.*"

"*Because I did not consider him one,*" Kron answered. "*Of course he is if you consider one who can hold the Sword of Purity as one, but he was not chosen to be a hero by the gods. It is not right to treat him as one and fill his head with those thoughts when he is not that person. He is simply someone who could hold the sword and wants to help.*"

Silently, the professor shook his head. "*You did not tell him of the conquest prophecy, did you?*"

"*No, and why would I? How do you even know about it?*"

"*As I mentioned, I have my ways,*" the professor answered. He then began to recite: "*A hero will arise and end the conqueror's rampage, but his wrath will only be delayed. The conqueror's evil shall seep through the realms and his influence will spread. He will cause great pain and suffering, unless the purest of heroes can stop him. The reign of evil can be defeated, but victory will be difficult. The first one will fail no matter what, but the second might succeed, should he be able to stand out against the evil flow and survive. The odds are against the light, and darkness will expand. Beware, all who know this prophecy, for the conquest of the realms has already begun.*"

Beware, all who know this prophecy, for the conquest of the realms has already begun. Words that had as much impact in *rengan* as they did in the common language. It was a prophecy that Kron knew all too well. "*You are suggesting this is a true prophecy, and Kevin is the second,*" Kron said.

"*No, I think the whole thing is bunk,*" said the professor, "*as are all prophecies. No one can see the future, and even if they could, it could change in a heartbeat.*"

"*Yet you bring up one of the most feared ones known to the gods*," said Kron. *"Why?"*

At this, the professor reached into his robes and pulled out a paper folder. He then set it on the table in front of Kron. "*Merely to point out coincidence, that even a wild stab in the dark can be correct from time to time, and I am sure it is something you do believe,*" he said. *"I think this speaks for itself. It took me quite a while, even with my political access, to find this. I was rather surprised something like this was sealed as well as it was.*"

Reluctantly, Kron picked up the folder and looked through it. Suddenly, his eyes widened. He looked up at the professor. "*You are serious*."

"I am," the professor picked back up in the common language. "I sent Kevin with my daughter to Aurana City with the intent on causing major change in Aurana to help him be able to rescue his friend that Demonicus kidnapped. This, though, means there is far more at stake for him than simply a rescue operation." He paused for a second. "And you are going to tell him the truth about it all."

Kron looked up from the folder. He could not be mad at the professor at this point. Reading what was in front of him, he simply agreed.

With that, the professor briefly checked the shutters again. Then, in the middle of the kitchen, he built light magic in one hand and darkness magic in another, spinning them around to form a teleportation gate. "Come, let us head for Aurana City," he told Kron.

For a moment, Kron stared vacantly at the gate. This was an extremely rare and ancient magical tactic that required decades of practice and was virtually unknown; he had seen it but did not know how to execute it properly. There was much more to Professor James Magnon than met the eye.

And that terrified Kron.

Chapter 16

When in the Capital

The skies were lit up in apocalyptic thunder, spreading light across a darkened sky. The world was tearing itself apart in the wake of the chaos that had just ensued… an aftermath foreshadowing the end of a long journey that would change the world forever. The end was coming.

In front of a tall white temple, larger than any building around within the ruined city, the sorceress Caitlin Magnon stood watching the temple. It was an ominous sight among the skies of lightning and the ruined city surrounding, but it was a sign of the final battle to come. Fires burned all around, some from the burning buildings of the city and some from the troops, relaxing in victory.

But the final battle was not over yet.

Several steps ahead of Caitlin was Kevin Trent. Sword drawn, he was walking into the pyramid. Caitlin could only stand and watch as he walked in, prepared to follow his destiny.

Something was not right. And Caitlin realized it.

"Kevin! It's a trap!" she screamed hysterically.

All at once, the white step pyramid went up in flames in an explosion. The shock waves were so powerful that Caitlin was knocked off of her feet. As she tried to lift herself up, she saw the rubble that remained. There was no more temple. It was destroyed.

She sat up and nearly screamed. The force of her reaction had thrown the covers off of her.

Caitlin started to catch her breath and realize where she was. It was her quarters in the City of Phoenixes, where she had been for a week.

It was all a nightmare. One very vicious nightmare. And yet, it had seemed so real. She felt strong feelings of fear coursing through her veins.

Fear was a feeling that Caitlin could not escape. She had felt fear before despite her emotional suppression, but to feel fear as she was now was almost traumatizing, and she was not so well equipped to handle it. Caitlin had to spend a couple of minutes regaining her composure and realizing that all of it was just a nightmare. Nevertheless, the feeling of a nightmare was very odd to her, because she had not had any dreams, any subconscious whatsoever, in years. It was a part of her purging herself of any emotion whatsoever and having a block placed around her emotional state.

Deep inside, though, Caitlin felt like she was falling apart. She could not keep herself together. She was afraid to change, and was trying desperately to maintain herself the way she was – never showing any emotion, maintaining her strength in her persona. This nightmare, though, had really shaken her. The fear was very strong, especially for if she lost Kevin.

What is wrong with me? Caitlin kept thinking to herself. This was completely unlike her. She had spent several days with Kevin at this point, and yes, it was the first time she had interacted with anyone except her father on an extended basis. Already she found in interacting with him that he was her only friend.

As she sat up in her dark room in the middle of the night, Caitlin lit up a spark of light magic in her fingers and looked around. She was in a small stone room with a pile of hay for a bed, exactly where her quarters had been for the past week while she and Kevin interacted with the phoenixes. Slowly, she stood up and walked around the room for a minute, regaining her composure. She also looked outside the room to see if anyone had heard her. Fortunately, it appeared in the quiet of the night that no one had. She looked to the temple to see it was still standing, and furthermore did not look like the temple in her nightmare.

After taking a few minutes to pace and calm herself down, Caitlin set herself back down in the hay. It was no use going outside to another small building to find Kevin's quarters and check on him; clearly, nothing had happened. Still, Caitlin kept contemplating what was going on with her.

She had spent a lot of time with Kevin in the last two weeks. During that time she had kept her discipline as it normally was, even if she would admit to herself that she had some sentiment for him. She did consider him her only friend, after all, something that she had never really had for anyone else. To her, he was someone special.

Now, she was showing signs of being afraid to lose him. That was the source of her fear. But at least for now, he was okay.

Caitlin curled up to herself in her pile of hay, closing her eyes and keeping her hands together. She decided to meditate in this position for a while, thinking that doing so would help her overcome this interruption and allow her to focus on her discipline. She could not have this fear in her life.

The thoughts kept going through Caitlin's mind. What was that nightmare all about? Am I actually afraid? How can I be that scared to lose someone who I only met a few days ago? Is it a bad thing that I care about him so much? How can I discipline myself to make this fear go away?

Soon after, she fell asleep again.

A few hours passed before the morning arrived. Much to Caitlin's surprise, as she awoke and readied herself for the day, she noticed that Kevin was out walking in the street. He was already up, not sleeping in. But was he up early, or was she awake late?

After getting herself ready, Caitlin met up with Kevin. This was the day they would be returning to the human lands, and at their request, Wheldon had agreed to take them to Aurana City, which had been their next destination. That way they would be close to schedule for their arrival in comparison to having to walk around the Auranian Wilderness.

Within the morning, Kevin and Caitlin said their goodbyes to the Red Phoenix and Grand Raven, as well as their families. The two societies appeared to be closer than ever before with a full week of healing so far, and now Kevin was an honorary part of that society as well. Sure, Kevin had done little actual negotiating and was more successful just by bringing these two parties together for the first time, but it was a success nonetheless.

During the week spent in the City of Phoenixes, Kevin and Caitlin had become fast friends with Wheldon the phoenix as they got to know each other better. Wheldon was their guide during the week of peace, and he spent plenty of time interacting with his new friends, learning about their culture and sharing his with them. Today, that had to come to an end, but at least he would be the one to take them to Aurana City. Kevin and Caitlin boarded Wheldon together, and they took off for the capital of Aurana.

The flight to Aurana City took a few hours, but Wheldon did his best to make sure the flight was stable for his new friends and that they did not risk falling off. He reasoned with this new job of carrying humans that carrying two caused him to need to be extra careful, but he may be able to fly more aggressively if only carrying one. He did not think he could carry more than two safely.

After those few hours, Aurana City came into view. Kevin and Caitlin had the rare opportunity to look at it from above. Aurana City, at least on the outside, was relatively average in citywide beauty, though the national palace was absolutely astounding. Kevin still considered Rikleifer a much more beautiful city, but he saw a bit of the real world in Aurana City as he looked around the buildings. Arranged in a grid pattern with additional crossing streets in all sorts of shapes and angles, Aurana City was a bit more urban sprawled that the plotted-out concentric circle design of Rikleifer. Also unlike Rikleifer, it was evident from above which neighborhoods were more affluent and which were slums. Aurana City served as a cross-section of Auranian society that way—Aurana's largest city, with all walks of life represented there.

Wheldon brought Kevin and Caitlin down near the edge of the forest, just a short walk from the city. He did so within the forest itself and a little away from the trail, to make sure that his bright feathers were not spotted by any other humans. After a quick set of goodbyes, Wheldon the phoenix started his trip back to the City of Phoenixes alone. Kevin and Caitlin then headed for Aurana City, a fifteen minute walk away.

Once he entered, Kevin and Caitlin saw the glories and the struggles that were the capital city of their home nation. The city streets were dirty and a number of houses were run down, much more so than Kevin's modest home in Rikleifer. In the distance, however, the green glow of the Emerald Palace, Aurana's capital building and residence of the royal family, shone like a beacon even in the daylight. Clearly in that direction was a more affluent area of the city.

The more that Kevin walked through Aurana City, however, the more he felt the Sword of Purity tug at him. It was as if it wanted to be drawn, like it had a consciousness of its own. Thinking a little bit, Kevin reasoned that this was why the sword had to be stored in its special scabbard: to resist the magical tug. However, the tug was not dissipated completely.

"That's odd," Kevin noted, drawing Caitlin's attention. He turned to his side to show Caitlin the blade in its scabbard, not wanting to draw the sword.

Caitlin looked closely. "I don't see anything unusual," she said.

"It feels like it's wanting to be taken out," Kevin answered. "It's never done that for me before."

For a second, Caitlin thought about it. "Maybe then you should draw it? You need to know what your sword wants to do."

Sound advice, Kevin thought, especially while they were not facing down an enemy. Deciding that Caitlin was right and maybe it would be best to follow the sword instead of ignoring it, Kevin drew the Sword of Purity.

At once, the Sword of Purity tugged him so hard that he nearly flew off his feet. Immediately, Caitlin gave chase and yelled, "Wait up, Kevin!"

"I would if I could!" Kevin yelled back.

Kevin had never seen the Sword of Purity do something like this before. This tug pulled him toward the south down a side street. Kevin was lucky that it was down a street that was not used much, because the Sword of Purity's tug became so great that Kevin actually tripped over and the sword kept dragging him, with Kevin trying to regain control of the sword. Caitlin was running as fast as she could to keep up. Eventually, Kevin managed to catch his footing and pull back on the sword. As he pushed hard to place the sword back into its scabbard, Kevin started to wonder what had made the Sword of Purity tug so hard.

Kevin heaved, out of breath from the running. Caitlin finally caught up to him. "That was wild," Caitlin said to Kevin, having watched the whole ordeal from the chase.

Breathing heavily and trying to catch his breath, Kevin said, "You're telling me!" He stopped and took a few more breaths. "At least I know," he took another breath, "it wants me to go this way."

Caitlin nodded, herself breathing a little heavily. She then said, "It would be reasonable to follow the direction of the sword's tug anyway, just to see if anything is in that direction."

Still catching his breath, Kevin agreed. He and Caitlin started walking further down the street, past houses in the poor neighborhood they were in. What in here could the sword have been targeting? The further Kevin and Caitlin walked, the closer to the edge of the city that they were heading. It became clear after a bit that this side street led to a road that swept around the west part of the city, and a city gate.

And Kron was waiting there.

Though he was tired from being dragged around, Kevin broke into a full run when he saw Kron at the gate. "Kron!" he exclaimed. Caitlin once again ran to follow along. It was a run of less than thirty seconds before Kevin made it to him.

At the city gate, Kron appeared a bit surprised, but also relieved. "Oh thank goodness," he said as Kevin and Caitlin approached him. "I was worried about you."

As Kevin and Caitlin slowed up approaching Kron, Caitlin said, "We were never in any real danger, I don't think. How did you get here so quick?"

"I had a little help," nodded Kron. "I am here with your father, Caitlin."

"Ah, perfect," acknowledged Caitlin. If he was here, surely he had his plan ready.

Kron nodded. He then noticed the orange ribbon marking along Kevin's right arm; Kevin was wearing short sleeves, so the mark was visible from the back of his hand all the way up his arm and into his shirt. "Did you get tattooed, Kevin?

Kevin looked at his arm. "Oh, this?" He awkwardly laughed it off. "I'll have to explain that one later."

Awkwardly, Kron chuckled. He then changed the subject. "May I ask how you got here so quick?"

"We found an express way to get here," Kevin answered. "Let's just say it was a fast method of travel." Although Kron was an immortal, Kevin was adamant, for now, that he would keep his promise to the phoenixes not to reveal them, and he did not know if Kron knew of them or not.

"Speaking of which," Caitlin thought aloud, "I should go check in with my father." She then turned to Kron. "Do you know where I can find him?"

"I do," said Kron. "He is at the Rider's Tavern. It is an inn just south of the Royal District where the palace is. I think he is making arrangements for his plans there, as he has had meetings in the last couple of days there with some very influential people in Aurana."

"Oh?" asked Kevin. "Like who?" Kevin knew he likely would not recognize names, but might know positions.

"I know he has met with the Head Commander of the APF," Kron answered. "He has not met with any of the king's advisors other than the Head Commander, but he has also met with a number of people in the crown prince's advisory group. I think he may be trying to arrange a direct meeting with the prince." He paused for a second. "Although, I do believe that may be difficult. As I understand from Professor Magnon, the prince tends to sneak out of the palace. How receptive he will be concerns the professor."

"Hmmm, that seems unusual," commented Caitlin. "My father has more political connections to the king's advisors. I wonder why he has selected the ones he has…" She seemed intrigued.

Kevin caught onto her tone. "You have a guess why?"

"Perhaps," answered Caitlin, "but I don't want to speculate too much."

Kron nodded. "I think I know why as well, based on that selection. I hope he knows what he is doing, as I fear the ramifications if he is wrong."

Surprised, Kevin threw his hands up. "Someone want to tell me what I'm missing here?"

Caitlin looked at Kron. "You may as well tell him, when you have a private place," she said. She then gestured into town. "For now, we need to catch up with my father. Kron, can you lead us to this tavern?"

Kron said nothing, but gestured for Kevin and Caitlin to follow him.

It was a long walk into town. Aurana City was quite a bit larger than Rikleifer, which was by no means a small city itself. Kron navigated Kevin and Caitlin across a number of city blocks, some of which were wider streets and others were narrow alleys. Mostly they were traveling through poorer neighborhoods and slums, which depressed Kevin to see. Such was the reality of life, though. He too was poor, although he felt it fortunate that he still had his mother's house and that it was still structurally sound. Some of these homes looked very dilapidated.

Eventually, they reached the Rider's Tavern, an altogether modest building of two stories sitting along a street near the Royal District. As it was not in the district, though, this was very much a tavern for normal citizens and not an affluent place. As Kevin and company entered the bar, the faint odor of beer was all around, though none was out. As it was midday, the bar was closed.

The tavern was completely made of wood, both exterior and interior. Inside, the bar looked like it had just been cleaned up. Everything appeared like it was in order for now. Behind the bar stood a middle-aged woman, who had a little bit of excess weight on her. She was cleaning up some of the glasses that were dirtied.

Kron and Caitlin started looking around, while Kevin walked up to the woman and asked, "Excuse me, are you the innkeeper?"

The woman responded, "I am. I am also the bartender and I do just about everything else around here," she continued in a slight bit of frustration. "What is it that you want?"

"I would like to stay here overnight," said Kevin. "What rooms do you have available?"

"Well," said the woman, trying to recount what was open, "many of our rooms are already reserved for guests tonight, but I believe we have a few rooms open. They are all single room with two single-person beds. It will cost you five silver pieces to rent for the night."

Kevin pulled out a small bag of coins and looked through what was left of the money his mother left him. There was not much there.

Kevin pulled out five silver pieces and held them in his hand as he put the rest of the bag away. "Five silver? That seems rather expensive."

"Includes a breakfast," responded the woman quickly.

From down the hallway, someone overheard the conversation and walked quickly into the bar area. "No need to worry about that," he said, catching the attention of both Kevin and the innkeeper. "I have him covered."

Kevin turned. It was Professor Magnon.

He walked into the bar area. "I already have made arrangements for you, and paid for them." He then turned to the innkeeper. "He is with me. So are the gentleman and the young lady over there. They are my guests under my reservation."

"Ah, yes," nodded the innkeeper, "very good." She then reached behind a desk and passed Kevin a key. "Room 104," she said. "Straight down the first floor hall."

Then, a grizzled old man's voice yelled out, "Hey woman! Y' got dat bar cleaned up yet?"

The woman sighed in frustration and screamed out, "No, you lazy bastard, I'm not done yet!"

Silently, the professor, who had the attention of Kevin, Caitlin, and Kron, waved them down the hall into the inn. No one wanted to be involved in this argument.

Down the hall, the professor stopped in front of Room 104. "Kevin and Kron, this room is for you to share." He then pointed next door, to Room 106. "Caitlin, that room is for you. I have a room upstairs, so I will not be on the same floor as you, but I will stay in the same inn. We will be here a couple of days, and we will have a group meeting tomorrow to discuss the plan in detail."

Kevin raised his hand. "Can I ask what is the plan?"

At this, Professor Magnon noticed the mark on Kevin's arm that was different from the last time they had met. He chose not to say anything about it. "All will be revealed in the coming days," answered the professor. "Please have a little patience." He then looked at Kron. "Unless you want to tell him."

Kron said nothing.

"Now, if you do not mind," continued the professor, "I would like to speak with my daughter for a while. Caitlin, would you follow me upstairs?"

Caitlin nodded, and proceeded with the professor.

After a moment, when the professor and Caitlin had disappeared from view, Kevin asked Kron, "What was that all about?"

"Truthfully, Kevin, I have no idea," Kron answered. "Professor Magnon is rather strange."

Kevin nodded. "He's magically inclined and politically connected. Odd things must happen in his presence all of the time."

"I would agree," added Kron. "And I think I may know why he is so inclined."

This caught Kevin's attention. "Continue," he said, as he opened the door to the room and invited Kron to step inside.

Kron led the way in, and Kevin followed and closed the door behind him, giving them a room where they were unlikely to be overheard. "Well," began Kronius, "since I first met him, something scared me. Something familiar. It felt like a presence, a presence that I have felt millions of times but not in years."

"So, did you tell him who you were, if you felt like you knew him?" asked Kevin.

"No," answered Kron, " I told him my name was Kron Kalavere, which it was during my mortal life and the name I use while bound to this realm, as you know. He told me he knew who I was, and called me by my holy name, Kronius. Now, by this point, I was very afraid, because being a god stranded where I am has serious complications, but I was too afraid for my own safety and yours to say anything." Then, Kronius paused for a second. "Professor Magnon seems like a kind and helpful person, Kevin, and he seems like he wants to help you. But if I were you, I would be cautious around him."

"I understand," said Kevin, somewhat quickly. He was already aware that he needed to be careful around Professor Magnon, having met him before and feeling the same thing. "I definitely don't want to be a pawn of his."

"I think you should keep that in mind," acknowledged Kron. "Do you want to know what I believe his selection of advisors tells me?"

"Oh right, I almost forgot about that," said Kevin. "What does it mean?"

Suddenly, Kron leaned in to Kevin. He was going to say this quietly, to assure that no one overheard it. "It means he wants to overthrow the king of Aurana."

Just as Kevin was about to exclaim, he threw a hand over his mouth.

What was the professor thinking?

Why would he stoop to such an extreme?

"Professor Magnon is speaking with the head of the APF so he can have the army on his side for his proposals. The other advisors he has asked for are those of Prince Andrew, the son of King Arnold IX. Professor Magnon says he does have connections with the king's advisors, and if that is the case, then he is deliberately not talking to them in order to circumvent the king and place his son on the throne."

Kevin was stunned. "Why would he do that?"

"He wants to fix this situation where Aurana's military is losing battle after battle to Desolunar," continued Kron. "I have not heard this from the professor, but I know from years of living in Aurana among the mortal that King Arnold IX is often blamed for the frequent losses, and not without good reason. As a matter of fact, I have heard it firsthand."

"From who?"

"From War Commander Eukert," answered Kron. "He is fully recovered, as we thought he would be, and has returned to Rikleifer to regroup with the APF."

Kevin let out a sigh of relief. "That's good," he said. "I'm very relieved to hear that he's okay."

"Indeed," acknowledged Kron. "I escorted him back to Rikleifer from Caitlin's house. On the walk, he told me about how he felt he was set up for failure, how he had requested multiple times for more troops. His boss, the head of the APF, was more than willing to send him reinforcements, but those orders were countermanded by the king, interfering with those who defend his country. Supposedly, according to Eukert, the king is a believer in the superiority of Auranians and thinks that his forces should be able to be outnumbered and still fend off their attackers. It is a dated view that gambles the lives of his soldiers and his civilians, and it is evident so far that he is losing that bet. He also does not tend to spend much time on his duties, choosing instead to make decisions on a whim and spend much of his time enjoying his life."

Considering this for the moment, Kevin then asked, "And of the young prince?"

"Eukert has met him," said Kron. "He said that the young Prince Andrew is very bright and not a fan of his father's dated beliefs and lack of action. Supposedly, Eukert has said that is why he disappears often; he is a responsible person but disillusioned with palace life with his father."

"I see," nodded Kevin. He then laid down on one of the two single beds and stretched out over the covers. "This is just a lot to think about," he said. "I wonder what Professor Magnon has in mind for me, if that's his plan."

At this point, Kron said nothing. He was not ready to tell Kevin everything just yet. He just kept thinking about what was coming, concerned about his association with Professor Magnon and wondering what he had done to Kevin.

Chapter 17

The Life You Take

Later that day, Caitlin was returning to her room. Her father did not say much to her about his plans, only that he had one. He did, however, confirm her suspicions were true but would not give details just yet. For the most part, Professor Magnon had only wanted to spend a little time with his daughter and talk about their recent travels. Caitlin rarely had a chance to talk with her father, so she was willing to take the time to do so.

She did not tell him about her nightmare from that morning. Although her father could surely provide some guidance or help reinforce her emotion block, Caitlin did not want to talk about it. She wanted to keep it secret and hide it, bury it, and hope it never reared its ugly head ever again. She did not want her father to know she felt fear. She did not want anyone to know that.

Even so, she could not shake the feeling that she was afraid of losing Kevin.

Turning the doorknob to Room 106, Caitlin entered the room. There was nothing really extravagant about the room; it was very plain with only a single bed and an end table next to the window. Like every other room in the building, it was the same style: solid wood with some slight furnishings. The wood was a fairly dark shade, as if it had weathered some.

Seeing no need to rest, Caitlin decided to walk back out into the hall. She thought she might check in with Kevin. Then, she looked down the hall. She had a clear view of the tavern, which had opened a short while ago. In the tavern, a drunken man appeared to be picking a fight with someone, standing up and shouting. However, she did not have a good view of the second man.

Walking down the hall, she had a better view of the tavern. And then she saw the second man. It was a young man in plain brown clothing, probably a little older than her or Kevin. He had just entered the tavern and walked up to the bar when the drunken man stood up and confronted him. There appeared to be a dispute between the young man and the older drunken man over the younger man simply sitting at the bar. It seemed a petty dispute, and the young man appeared to be backing down, not interested in fighting, but the drunken man would not let it go. He was harassing the younger man.

Then someone else walked into view as well. It was Kevin.

Caitlin observed that Kevin did have the Sword of Purity strapped to his belt and that while he was talking to the drunken man, he was using his left thumb to push up the sword from its scabbard by the crossguard, showing that he was aware that he might have to use it.

As Caitlin approached the tavern, she started to hear the argument Kevin and the drunken man were having. "You better get out of here, boy, if you don't want me to rip yer head off," said the drunken man.

Kevin refused to back down. "No," he said. "You're not going to sit here and intimidate him. He has just as much a right to be here as you do."

Good for Kevin, Caitlin thought to himself. He was standing up for what he thought was right, protecting someone from being harassed. This was a rare bit of confidence he was showing. She stood back and admired him for a minute, seeing this new side of him that he must have had all along but never would reveal before.

"I'll do whatever the hell I want!" yelled the drunken man.

The younger man grabbed Kevin's shoulder. "Hey man, I appreciate the assist, but it is not worth all of this. I will just leave. I do not want to be trouble."

Kevin shook his head. "No, this isn't right," he told the young man. "You shouldn't have to leave because some big bully wants to push you out." He then turned toward the drunken man. "What's your problem with him, anyway?"

The drunken man seemed to become even more enraged. He grabbed Kevin's left shoulder and gripped it tight. "You and you young people are always takin' me booze at this joint! Now you get out of here before I rip yer head off!"

Kevin stood unnerved by the man. "I'm sorry others have taken your drink before, but I refuse to leave. I have a right to be here, and I will stay."

At this point, the drunken man let go of Kevin's shoulder and turned around. "Fine…" he started to say. Then, he continued, "Then you will die for this!" He pulled a short sword and spun around, swinging it at the same time.

Kevin had a split second to pull out his sword and block the attack. Nonetheless, he was able to pull this maneuver off, the sloppy drunken swing being somewhat easy to catch. His block was backhanded, as he had just pulled out his sword in time to block the attack.

The drunken man continued to press his attack. Needless to say, his swings were not very accurate because of his inebriation. Not a single strike came close to Kevin, as he just took two steps back and watched as the drunken man continued to swing his short sword aimlessly.

Kevin was trying to think how he could safely take care of the drunken man. He was not really a bad person, Kevin thought to himself, just drunk.

Taking a quick look around, Kevin did not see anyone else in the tavern. The barkeep was not at the bar at the moment. He did not see Caitlin in the hallway. Using care, Kevin pointed his sword at the drunken man. He turned it vertically, with the sharp edges pointing up and down. Then, on the next missed swing, he pummeled the drunken man in the side of the head.

Down the hall, Caitlin gasped.

The drunken man fell over to the ground. Kevin was breathing heavily, the anxiety of the moment getting to him. He was trying to knock the man out, hoping just to incapacitate the drunken man.

Something seemed wrong, the more Kevin looked at him. Kevin sheathed his sword. The flat side of the blade did not leave a mark on the man, so Kevin did not think he hit him that hard. However, the man did not seem to be breathing.

Reaching in the man's shirt pocket, Kevin found a key. It was his room key. On the back of it was stamped the number 124. He put the key back and called for the barkeep to help him take the man back to his room.

As the barkeep came from the back of the bar, Kevin realized that he had forgotten something. The drunken man was still holding the short sword in his frozen hands. Seeing the barkeep coming around the corner of the bar, Kevin quickly pulled the sword out of the drunken man's hands and threw it to the ground, not wanting to let the barkeep know there had been a fight. The younger man helped without asking, picking up the short sword and taking it outside as he left, not wanting to be involved with what just happened.

At the next moment, the barkeep grabbed one arm of the drunken man, whose arms had gone limp. Kevin grabbed the other arm, and the two escorted him down the hall to Room 124.

Caitlin had ducked back into her room before Kevin could see her. She closed the door behind her but listened closely at the door.

Upon reaching Room 124, the barkeep opened the door and helped Kevin move the drunken man onto the bed in the room. Kevin stood back and said to the barkeep, "Hmmm, I wonder how much beer he ingested." He was trying to play it cool, not implicating himself for anything.

The barkeep answered, "He's been drinking for a while now. Poor guy, he got ditched by his wife today and started drinking at all the bars as soon as they opened. He came in right after you left. I think he had about fifteen drinks today."

Kevin turned toward the barkeep. "Good guy?"

The barkeep replied, "No, I wouldn't say so. He's an ex-convict who really didn't do much to turn his life around. Today he still does the things he used to that got him into trouble in the first place. Regular here, he is. Also, he's a mean drunk with an uncontrollable rage, but he's good enough as a drunk to maintain a slight sense of balance. Guess he doesn't have a good tolerance of alcohol, but good enough for him. I don't really know more about him than that."

"Oh", Kevin replied lightly. He continued to stare at the man's body. But something kept plaguing him. Something was not right.

On a hunch, Kevin walked up to the man's neck and checked his pulse. The barkeep did not ask any questions as Kevin did so. Over the course of two minutes, Kevin was moving his fingers on the man's neck and listening closely.

Then he returned to the barkeep's side, and spoke somberly. "No pulse. No breathing."

The barkeep lowered her head out of respect for the man. Kevin did the same. However, as he did, a sickening though crossed his mind: What have I done to him?

It was a thought that would plague Kevin's mind for a long time. He had taken a human life, and one that had posed a minimal danger to him. Despite the fact that this man attacked him, Kevin could not help but feel guilty for him.

Somberly, Kevin left the barkeep walked back to his room. The barkeep let him go without a word said to him. Kron was out walking around Aurana City, so Kevin knew he would be alone when he returned to Room 104. He opened the door to his room, entered, and closed the door. In the next room, Caitlin heard the sound of the door closing.

Caitlin knew something bad had happened. She thought Kevin could use time alone to process, but that ultimately he would want help. Little did she know, however, that Professor Magnon had also witnessed the events in the tavern from the upstairs balcony above the bar. He came down to speak to Kevin himself.

As he lay on his bed, Kevin could not rest. The thoughts of the drunken man were still plaguing his mind, more so than anything ever had before. The man was an alcoholic, and it was possible that he had died of alcohol poisoning. Still, it was impossible to shake the feeling that he had killed the man.

As he continued to think, Professor James Magnon knocked on the door. Kevin told him to enter, having left the door unlocked. As the professor entered his room, he sensed something was wrong with Kevin. He began, "Kevin, are you all right?"

Kevin sat up and turned on the bed away from Professor Magnon. "Close the door," he said to Professor Magnon. He wanted to talk to someone about this, hoping that it would help him. And who else would know better than Professor Magnon? The professor was a knowledgeable person, someone who may be able to relate.

Professor Magnon did as he was instructed and then sat down next to Kevin. He did not make eye contact with Kevin, however. "What seems to be the problem? You certainly do not seem to be yourself."

Kevin let out a sigh, with his face in his hands. "Professor Magnon… what would you do if you might have accidentally killed someone?"

"Killed someone?" replied the professor. "Well, I have probably killed my fair share of men within my hundred and fifty years. It is just how some things are in this world, that sometimes you must kill to survive."

"No," said Kevin in a slight whisper. "You don't understand. This man didn't deserve to die. It shouldn't have happened."

"Oh," responded the professor in a state of realization. He thought for a moment about what he could do, and came up with a slightly extreme idea. "In that case, would you allow me to read your mind and search your feelings so I may understand what happened as you saw it?"

Kevin only nodded, still too distraught to say much. He wanted to get his thoughts out, however, and was willing to let Professor Magnon find out any way possible.

Preparing for the mind read, Professor Magnon stretched his hands out, extending each finger. Then he curved them slightly and placed them on Kevin's head. Upon contacting his head, the power activated.

All at once, he saw a jumble of thoughts that belonged to Kevin. Ignoring all of these and looking deeper, he began to search for the thoughts that plagued Kevin. As Professor Magnon was very skilled at reading minds, he knew how to search through the many various thoughts for one in particular.

Suddenly, he found it. The thought that haunted Kevin was heavily pressing on his mind. He saw the fight all over again. He felt Kevin's sympathy for the drunken man after hearing his story, and the events of his death. Seeing all that he needed to see, Professor Magnon started to back out of Kevin's mind, not wanting to invade the more private thoughts of Kevin's mind. There were ethical standards to uphold here, after all.

At that point, the professor let go of the mind reading and began to talk to Kevin. “Well, Kevin, the first thing I can tell you is that it is not your fault for what happened to that man.”

Kevin began to straighten up. “How do you figure that?” he asked in a skeptical voice.

“Well,” said the professor, “the result of his death was a combination of alcohol and his drunken attack. If you did not hit him hard enough to leave a mark, I cannot credit you with the kill.” The professor then turned further toward Kevin. “But I cannot lie to you, Kevin. I believe that it may have been a factor.”

Kevin let his head sink. “That's what I was afraid of,” he said somberly.

The professor changed his tone to be more uplifting. “Brighten up and let me give you some advice. Though you may bring life to those you save, it is the life you take that can create the most impact on you. Sometimes you can feel somber after saving a thousand lives and one of them dies because of you. However, sometimes it is necessary to take some lives in order to save many more.” The professor put his arm around Kevin in an attempt to reassure him. “I have a feeling that killing others will happen many times in your quest, as the dangers of this world are very numerous and Demonicus will not pull any punches with you. I know it will be hard for you, but perhaps it is for the best that this has happened to you today. It will give you the chance to get the sorrow out of your system. Granted, it is likely to happen several more times, but the first one is always the hardest.”

Kevin lifted his head, still feeling down. He paused for a moment, and then responded, “Thanks, Professor Magnon. I appreciate your advice, and I think... I think I’d like to spend some time alone right now.”

The professor moved his arm. “All right, I can give you that. The time will do you some good.”

As the professor stood up, Kevin began to turn and lay down on the bed. He did not feel like giving a goodbye in his depressed state. He did tell Kevin, “If you ever need some help or some advice, I will always leave my door open for you. It is my honor.” The professor turned his head to walk out to look at Kevin desperately trying to find peace, let out a sigh, and exited the room, closing the door behind him.

Kevin relaxed his body, hoping to take a nap. He wanted the sleep to take away his pain and the pain of the memories of the drunken man.

About an hour later, Kron returned to the Rider's Tavern. He bumped into Professor Magnon on the way in, who had told him that he had a talk with Kevin a while ago and that he was resting now. Upon arriving at the door to Room 104, he checked his robe, only to realize that he had left his key in the room. It was a mistake, the first in a while for him. He looked around for a second on the floor to make sure he did not drop it accidentally, and then he looked around to see if anyone else was watching him. Instinctively, Kron grabbed the knob, only to realize the door was unlocked. And inside the room, Kevin was laying down on his bed, stirring awake from a nap.

Kron, having noticed that Kevin was relaxed for a moment, made the first comment. "Kevin, how are you feeling right now?"

Kevin wiped his right hand across his eyes. "I'm okay. I just needed some time to relax, that's all."

"Oh, I see," responded Kron. "Is that why Professor Magnon was in here earlier?"

"Um, well, kind of," replied Kevin. "Actually, that's not quite true. You see, I'm afraid I might have accidentally killed someone today."

Kron was a little stunned. "You killed someone?"

"There's more to it than that," said Kevin. "It was an alcoholic who tried to attack me. I tried to incapacitate him with the flat side of the Sword of Purity, but I guess his system was just too damaged by the alcohol over all of those years that it claimed his life."

"Hmmm…" Kron said as he started thinking. "Well, I suppose that may be."

Kevin just stared at Kron in disbelief. With a more firm tone, he asked, "And the fact that this is the first time I've ever taken somebody's life, whether accidental or intentional, has nothing to do with it?"

Kron was caught off guard by this comment. Realizing his

ignorance, he said, "Oh, dear, I am sorry, Kevin, I forgot. That must have played havoc with your emotions. I remember the first time I killed somebody, and it is not a memory I like to have. And it was an intentional kill, too, not an accidental one."

After hearing this, Kevin relaxed again. "You couldn't be any more correct, Kron. I couldn't get over it by myself, but then Professor Magnon walked in and was able to give me some advice. Then I spent some time to myself, and thought about what he said and what had happened. I'm still not completely fine, but I don't feel as bad as I did."

"That is excellent, Kevin," assured Kronius. "It is going to be important that you learn not to fear taking the lives of others if it means saving the lives of the innocent." He paused for a moment. "May I share some words with you?"

Kevin looked a little puzzled. "What's up?"

Kron sat next to Kevin. "Oh, I just wanted to share with you some advice I was told by Vinz Larinion, the former king of gods. He said, 'If you truly believe in something, then you will give up everything you have for it. All of your worldly possessions: your wealth, your memories, your friendships, and even your love, must be forsaken for your cause. You must even be willing to give up your existence for what you fight for. Do not fear it, for if the cause is good, others will follow your example and fight for your cause. So be willing to forsake everything and follow your heart to a better future.'"

Having listened carefully, Kevin still felt lost.

Kron continued, no longer quoting, "Today, you sacrificed your innocence. However, you have a greater cause, and that is to rescue your best friend. It is but one sacrifice you will make, but you have to be willing to do what is necessary to carry your cause forward."

Silently, Kevin nodded. "You forgot, I still have to get you home as well."

Shrugging Kron said, "Do not worry about that right now."

"But I will," Kevin responded. "It's important to me that I get you home, too. I made a promise to you, and I intend to keep it when this is all said and done."

Kron smiled. "Thank you, Kevin Trent," he said, as he patted Kevin's shoulder. "You are a good person."

Then, there was another knock at the door. Caitlin then pushed it open slightly and asked, "May I see Kevin for a moment?"

Standing up, Kron nodded. He looked down at Kevin and said, "I will let her visit with you for a few moments. Let me give you kids some space." He then proceeded to exit the room, allowing Caitlin to enter behind him.

As she walked in, Caitlin said, "I saw everything." She walked in and sat down by Kevin. Checking quickly to make sure the door was closed, she then turned and gave Kevin a big surprise.

She hugged him.

Kevin was sure she was just trying to be sympathetic, but her hug was the best thing he had felt all day. Those thoughts he had of liking her, of wanting to be with her, that had been nagging at him since the night they took shelter in the military burrow at the Calphos River were creating a warm feeling in this moment.

Caitlin wanted to show her friend that she cared and wanted to give him all the support he needed, and this was what he needed right now. But she could not deny the warm feeling it gave her to hug him.

In that moment, both of them felt something special in their embrace, even if they could not show that to each other.

Chapter 18

A Greater Sin

The next day, after a tough night of rest for Kevin, he awoke and went out to the bar to eat his breakfast. As he sat out and ate alone, he pondered why the authorities had not at least come to speak with him about the drunken man. Surely, even if he were not in trouble over it, someone would at least want to ask him about it in relation to the death. He expected they would have by last night or this morning.

So much was running through his mind right now. Regardless of the drunken man's attack yesterday, Kevin still could not help but feel bad for what he had done. Kron had told him that the Sword of Purity was a sword of peace, and instead, Kevin acted rashly. He may have thought out the attack to try and make it not fatal, but he still chose a violent solution when a nonviolent one could have been found. Whether it was directly his fault or not, someone paid with their life for that. Even if he was a jerk in that moment, he had a family as everyone does. Surely someone out there cared about him.

As he sat there eating his breakfast, Kevin turned his head down the hall. He saw Caitlin walking out to approach him. She sat at the bar next to him and asked the barkeep for a cup of water. Then, she told Kevin, "Good morning."

"Good morning," Kevin said back to Caitlin. "I hope you slept well."

"Probably better than you did, I imagine," Caitlin retorted. There was a brief pause, before she continued, "Are you feeling okay?"

Kevin took a sip of his water, which was sitting next to his breakfast at the bar. "I think so," he said. "Have you ever done something like that?"

"Oh, no," Caitlin answered, "not like that. My father has been a pacifist since I was born, and I've learned the same from him. I would only fight in defense, never in attack, and I've never had to fight in defense. I probably can't relate like my father or, maybe, Kron could."

"I talked with both of them last night," Kevin acknowledged. "They both were pretty helpful. But not as helpful as you were."

For just a quick second, it looked like Caitlin was holding back cracking a smile, before her discipline returned. "I'm glad I could help," she acknowledged. "I just felt like that was what you really needed in that moment, and you're my friend, so I wanted to help any way I could."

Kevin smiled at Caitlin. "In fairness, it probably was what I needed," he said. "Thank you."

"You're very welcome," answered Caitlin. She took another sip of her water.

There was a pause of a few seconds before Kevin asked, "Are you going to have any breakfast yourself?"

"I already did," Caitlin said. "I've been up longer than you have."

"Okay," acknowledged Kevin. He then had an idea. "Then, after I finish up, do you want to go check out Aurana City with me?"

Caitlin appeared a bit surprised. "Huh?" she asked.

"Well, we won't be busy until this evening," Kevin began, a little nervous. "Your father slid a note under my door this morning telling me it'll be this afternoon before he has a meeting for us to attend. So we have all day, and I don't think you, nor I, want to just sit in an inn all day."

Caitlin considered this for a moment. "You have a point," she said. "That does sound like something to do, and something that could be useful."

"And time spent with a friend," added Kevin. "That's always enjoyable."

For just a second, Caitlin looked away. She then looked back. "It is," she said.

As Kevin observed what Caitlin had just done, he noticed that it seemed like Caitlin was trying not to show something. He wondered what that was all about, but he did find it nice that Caitlin was willing to spend time with him for something more leisurely than functional.

It took a few more minutes for Kevin to finish his breakfast, but

Caitlin sat next to him the whole time and sipped at her water. After he had finished, Kevin made sure he had his room key and told Kron where he would be and when he and Caitlin would be back. Then, he made a quick plan with Caitlin for all the things he knew in Aurana City that they should see, that he had never seen but of which he had heard, and together they set off.

For the next couple of hours, Kevin and Caitlin explored Aurana City together. Being near the Royal District, they were relatively close to most of the things that would appeal to outside visitors. At the city center was the Royal District and the Emerald Palace, which Kevin wanted to walk around and see it from multiple sides. The Emerald Palace was a large, three-story building, as wide as three city blocks and as long as four. Beautiful plants and vegetation surrounded the Royal District, accenting the bright emerald green walls of the palace itself. Each wall was ornately decorated with various arches and false columns that were actually part of the wall itself. An upper balcony wrapped around the third story, serving as a walkway around the entire palace that was only accessible from the inside.

Nearby the Royal District was a stadium, belonging to the Aurana City Force dangerball team. Kevin, being a fan of his hometown Rikleifer Rangers, knew that the Force were the rival team of the Rangers and chuckled a bit at seeing the place where his team had gone in as visitors and won many games before. The stadium was relatively large, but from the outside it was simply decorated. Game days tended to be uncommon since teams would visit other teams for long stretches of time due to the length of time it took to travel to other cities, so today was not a day to see a game here.

Another building on the periphery of the Royal District was the Aurana Museum of War and Science, a place where various artifacts were on display and where the few scholarly people of Aurana tended to work, exploring new finds. Caitlin expressed interest in entering the two-story building, so Kevin took her inside to see. Some things they found included ancient weaponry, magic staves, ancient animal teeth, and textiles from kingdoms of old that had survived to this day.

A couple of hours had passed and it was nearing midday, so Kevin and Caitlin decided to return to the tavern to catch up with

Professor Magnon. "You know, I didn't know you would be into museums," Kevin said to Caitlin. "Maybe I shouldn't be surprised."

"Don't be," Caitlin answered. "Especially when it comes to old magic implements, I always find artifacts of history fascinating." She paused for a second. "I am a bit surprised, however, that you do as well."

"Oh, absolutely," commented Kevin, "but I don't get to go very often. Rikleifer has a small museum, but it's nothing in comparison to Aurana City's." He paused for a second. "I was psyched to see that old suit of armor, like people in the day used to fight with. They had it on loan for a short time in Rikleifer but I didn't get to see it then. I was really hoping I'd get to, someday."

"Well, now you have," answered Caitlin. "I'm not sure anyone except a king could afford one of those nowadays."

"I guess so," smiled Kevin. He thought for a second. "That's another thing we have in common now. We both like going to museums together."

Briefly, Caitlin looked at Kevin before looking forward again. "You're right," she said. "I am surprised just how much we do have in common. A love for fantasy novels, an enjoyment of museums, we're both sort of social outcasts… and when we talk, you may be the most understanding human when it comes to interacting with me."

Kevin smiled as they rounded a corner. "If I felt like it was a talent, I'd tell you."

Around that corner along a street in the Royal District on the way back, they happened upon a jewelry store with a large glass window. Many small gems were on display; Kevin knew enough to know that larger gems would be secured in the building, and that such a store could only be because it was targeted toward those in the circles of the king's court, whether it be royal family members or those with political influence. That which was on display was relatively inexpensive, made of smaller rocks, chips of gems, or just basic metal.

In front of the store, Caitlin stopped. A strange reaction from her, Kevin thought to himself. "What's up, Caitlin?"

"It's just…" she began, trying to express herself properly while keeping herself together, "it's so beautiful."

Kevin could understand most young women being enamored with jewelry, but for Caitlin, who was supposedly emotionless, it seemed a strange fixation. Taking a step back, Kevin looked to see where Caitlin was looking. Interestingly, her eyes were fixed on an inexpensive piece of jewelry that did not have a gemstone. It was a key, probably made of brass or steel, attached to a thin leather tie to function as a necklace. The key was painted a light pink color, with a bit of red accents painted below the head. The shaft of the key was cylindrical and straight, and the head was also cylindrical but bent into the shape of a heart. Although it was not expensive as far as jewelry was concerned, Kevin still knew it was not something he could afford.

Did she want it, though?

"It's the Key of Hearts," Caitlin said, "like from the poem."

Seeing the captivated look on her face, Kevin said, "Someday when I can afford it, I would like to get that for you."

Caitlin's head snapped over to look at Kevin. "Really?" she asked. Her eyes looked surprisingly innocent. A couple of seconds later, she looked like the comment may have been making her tear up in a corner of her eye. Almost as immediately as this happened, however, Caitlin turned her head back, as she caught herself. "That would be very kind of you, but it's not necessary. We have other things to worry about."

"I know," acknowledged Kevin, himself not being the most forward with Caitlin about how he felt about her for fear of a bad reaction. He took a small chance with what she said next. "But when I can afford it, I want you to have it."

There was a momentary pause. Kevin noticed that Caitlin was hesitating. She stood staring at the key, not reacting. That was very unlike her, to stutter and not have a very logical response. Was she feeling emotion?

Caitlin reached over and dried her eyes on her sleeve. She turned away from Kevin and said, "Thank you. It's a kind gesture." She started walking in the direction of the tavern, without even looking back at Kevin.

What was that all about? Kevin thought to himself. He followed Caitlin anyway, choosing not to walk directly beside her. For the first time he had noticed, she seemed exceptionally restrained, like she was actively trying to keep herself from reacting. Something about that interaction was making her behave differently.

Maybe that was the bad reaction he was fearing, and she acknowledged with a "thank you" so as not to be rude. Or maybe it was her being touched by his remark, and actively trying to maintain her discipline. Unfortunately, Kevin had no idea for certain, and was not sure how he could find out without talking with her more, which she seemed disinterested in doing at the moment.

A couple of minutes later, Kevin did start walking next to Caitlin as they went. She did not appear bothered, nor excited; she gave no reaction that he could discern. When they arrived at the tavern, however, a sign was posted stating the tavern was closed for a special event.

"That's odd," noted Kevin.

Caitlin nodded. "I don't recall my father mentioning something about this."

As they stood there pondering, however, Professor Magnon opened the door in front of them. "Please do come in," he told Kevin and his daughter.

Kevin and Caitlin did as they were told and stepped into the tavern. Kevin noticed that the bar was completely empty, save for the professor and Kron. "What's going on?" he asked.

"I have made arrangements with the tavern for a private meeting," the professor answered. "It is past checkout time for the rooms, and check in time will not be for a few hours, so the only difference from normal is that the bar is closed."

"Who are we meeting with?" asked Caitlin.

"It is our future king, Prince Andrew II," answered Professor Magnon.

As both Caitlin and Kron had anticipated, Kevin realized.

Suddenly, the door opened. In walked a tall man, who appeared to be a military man. He wore a uniform decorated in many ribbons, medals, and trim. After walking in, the man stood at attention and gave a salute to the entire group.

Professor Magnon instantly recognized him. "Ah, Head

Commander Forkman, I am glad to see you have made it." At this moment, Commander Forkman stood at ease. The professor continued, "Is the prince with you?"

"Yes, he is," responded Commander Forkman. Then he turned, opened the door, and said, out to the hallway, "All clear, my lord."

As Commander Forkman held the door open, in walked an elegantly dressed man wearing clothing in green, with blue and red accents. He wore a golden necklace and golden bracelets, as well as white gloves.

Everyone else in the room kneeled at the sight of their prince. Kevin, however, recognized him. He had met the prince before.

"Rise," commanded the prince. Everybody stood up.

Professor Magnon was the first to greet the prince. "Welcome, Prince Andrew. It is an honor to make your acquaintance again."

With a slight smile, the prince responded. "The pleasure is all mine, Professor Magnon."

"Indeed," replied the professor. "I am sorry that you had to come here without bodyguards or a royal introduction."

The prince shrugged. "It is of no importance to me, Professor Magnon. A royal introduction is merely a formality, the way I see it. I feel no shame or disrespect to greet people without a red carpet or a chorus of trumpets. As for the bodyguards, I trust Commander Forkman enough with my security when I do not have the luxury to have additional protection." Observing the number of people in the room, Prince Andrew continued with a question. "This seems like quite a few people here to discuss what we are planning. Can you trust all of these people?"

Without a second's pause, the professor replied, "I can trust them as much as you can trust Commander Forkman." Pointing to his daughter, the professor continued, "This is my daughter, Caitlin." Then he changed direction and pointed to Kron. "And this is Kron Kalavere, my faithful assistant in my duties as a wizard and instructor."

From this introduction, Kron was both angry and confused. He knew that being Professor Magnon's "assistant" was just a disguise of his real identity, but it felt like he was being talked down to and seen as inferior in the eyes of the professor. Still, Kronius did not raise any comment nor change the expression on his face.

"I see," continued Prince Andrew. "Trust can sometimes be misplaced, but I do have faith in who you place trust in as well, Professor Magnon. So where is this 'great hero' that you have told me of?"

Immediately, Kevin looked aside for a moment. He could not believe Professor Magnon would have told the prince something like that, especially when Kevin considered himself far from a "great hero".

The professor gestured toward Kevin. "This is him," he said.

Prince Andrew nodded. He then reached out to shake Kevin's hand. "I see we have met before."

"Indeed we have," acknowledged Kevin as he shook the prince's hand. "Although, your highness, I believe you were dressed quite differently then."

"Oh, well, you must forgive my impropriety," answered the prince. "Sometimes I find royal life tiresome, so I dress as a normal person and mingle with the city folk. I did not, however, mean to cause you trouble here yesterday with the man at the bar." He paused for a moment. "That being said, I appreciate that you stood up for the right thing. It speaks volumes to me about your character."

Kevin had no response for a moment, but gave a little nod of acknowledgment so as not to be rude. The death of the drunken man still weighed heavily on his mind. It suddenly occurred to Kevin that this was why the authorities had not come to question him; Andrew was the one who had removed the drunken man's short sword from the tavern and probably ensured there would be no investigation and had the situation treated as a simple death.

He took a few steps back, which allowed for Professor Magnon to speak. "Indeed, let us begin immediately," said the professor, as he pulled out a seat at the head of the table for the prince to sit down.

Kevin walked over to the drapes on the two windows in the room and closed them, and Caitlin lit a fire in the fireplace using her magic. Then, everyone took his or her seat at the table in the tavern. Professor Magnon sat at one end of the rectangular table, while Prince Andrew sat at the other. Kevin sat next to Caitlin on one side of the table, while Kronius sat next to Commander Forkman on the other side.

Commander Forkman began the conversation. "Professor Magnon, would you begin please by giving us the basics of what we will be doing, and a rationale for it?"

"Certainly," replied the professor, "and I do not think I will be saying anything in opposition to what anybody else here believes. As we all know, King Arnold IX has ruled Aurana for approximately three years, and in his three-year reign, Aurana has lost countless battles and decreased in its quality of life for its citizens. This is due to the king's lack of effort in properly running his country and his belief in fighting for glory, an overly idealistic belief that, despite countless urgings to abandon it, continues to poison the mind of the king and thus endanger all of Aurana. Despite this, however, nothing that the king has done constitutes the punishment of taking his life. What King Arnold IX has done for Aurana, while it has severely hurt the nation, can only be assumed to be in good faith for the desire to help Aurana and not hurt it. Therefore, we have come to the conclusion that the king should not be assassinated or killed by any other means."

The professor then paused briefly and looked over to Andrew, as if to verify that Andrew was not going to stop him from speaking. Andrew had been briefed on this idea already by his advisors, and would not have been here had he not been aware this was how the conversation was going to go. Professor Magnon had been smart enough to speak with advisors sympathetic to his idea and willing to persuade the prince that it was the best thing for Aurana. That the prince was already disdainful of his father and was a more responsible individual himself who cared about how the country was ran, gave him a reason to consider participating.

"In order to protect Aurana from further harm, King Arnold IX must be forced to abandon his throne. To accomplish this, we will force him to sign a document renouncing his throne and leaving his son, Prince Andrew II, in charge of Aurana. After this is done, he shall be escorted by military guards to a private retreat, where he shall spend the rest of his days living his life of splendor that he would rather do anyway."

Everyone else in the room was a little stunned. This was the first time that any of them had heard of the plan, and for something so complex, that would have such a great impact upon the world, Professor Magnon dictated it as though it was just a simple battle tactic. For Prince Andrew II, this plan reached his nerves the most, because even though the prince had denounced his father, disowned him, and knew this plan was what had to happen, King Arnold IX was still his father. With that sense of feeling, the prince knew that this plan would be difficult for him to execute.

Kevin then raised the question, "How are we going to force him to sign the document, though? I seriously doubt we can just walk right up to King Arnold IX and ask him to forfeit the throne."

"I have another plan for that," replied Professor Magnon, with a sound of confidence in his voice. "In order to force the king to sign the document, I have scheduled an appointment with the king for Kevin. Prince Andrew, I must thank you for arranging this."

Kevin was stunned. Absolutely stunned. "How did that happen? And what the hell am I supposed to do then? I can't just simply ask for him to abandon the throne."

"Patience," replied the professor calmly. "I wish to advise you not to jump to conclusions or become so frustrated so easily, because there is a way that you can do so, and I will explain it to you if you will allow me to speak it."

Kevin settled back down. "By all means, please continue. I apologize for stepping out of line."

Then, the professor looked over at Kron. "Did you tell him, like I asked?"

"Not yet," answered Kron. "I did not feel the time was right."

Kevin was confused. What were they talking about?

Suddenly, the professor looked enraged. He pointed down the hall and told Kronius firmly, "Go and get the file."

Reluctantly, and upset with the professor, Kron stood up and went to get the file. This was neither the time nor the place to start an argument.

The professor calmed down before he continued. "While he grabs that, Kevin, I can give you the second part of your answer." He looked over at the prince, who nodded briefly, before he continued. "Prince Andrew will accompany you in to see the king."

Prince Andrew then took the lead to Kevin. "Unfortunately, my father is so distant and self-absorbed that he will not meet with me or listen to me unless I have official business, and even then, he usually does not truly listen to what I have to say. So, I have made some official business to intrigue him. I have told my father that I have found the ideal person to be named our new Vanguard of Aurana." He paused for a second. "As you may know or have been taught in school, Aurana has not had a Vanguard in fifty years. We are long overdue to have one."

Kevin put his face in the palm of his hands. He could see where this was going. The only question was, why?

Vanguard was a special rank not only in Aurana, but in every country of the world. Only one was allowed per country, usually, and in most of the world the Vanguard of a nation was allowed open access between countries for diplomatic reasons. It was usually treated as a military rank within each kingdom's designated armed forces, but was not by itself necessarily a military position with responsibilities to lead. Vanguards all used the same insignia to designate they were the vanguard of their nation, as well—a black triangle inside a red triangle outline.

At this moment, Kron returned and sat down with the file. As he sat, Kron noticed that everyone remained silent, giving him room to talk. It looked as though the professor expected it. Reluctantly, Kron sat next to Kevin and placed the file in front of him. "Kevin, I am so sorry for this," he began. "When I met you, I did not know what I know now."

Confused, Kevin asked, "What do you mean?"

Before Kron could continue, the professor then asked, "Kevin, did you know that your birth records in Rikleifer were sealed? They were very difficult to obtain because of that."

"No," said Kevin as he shook his head. "I also don't really know what that means, but I do know they had a harder time than normal when I had to register for adulthood on my sixteenth birthday." Kevin was referring to a legal process in Aurana, where turning sixteen, being the legal adult age in the country, had to coincide with a visit to the local records office near where one was born on their sixteenth birthday exactly to verify they had made it to adulthood.

Next to him, Prince Andrew smiled. He knew what the professor was about to tell Kevin, but did not realize Kevin's trepidation. He leaned over a bit to verify what he was about to see.

Kron then continued where he left off. "I think it would be best if you opened this file and read it yourself."

Kevin looked at Kron for a moment, almost as if he did not want to do this. This did not excite him; he felt as though he was going to learn something he did not want to know. Knowing he had to do what he did, Kevin opened the file in front of him.

Inside the file was Kevin's record of his birth, dated sixteen years before. It certified that he was born on what day he knew as his birthday, and it had signatures from both of his parents. The signature of his mother, Lavinia Trent, was easily recognizable as Kevin had seen her sign her name many times before. Then, Kevin saw there was a signature on the line for the father, in his father's handwriting.

It read "Vincent Stryker".

Looking higher on the page, Kevin noticed that his name was not registered as what he thought it was. Always believing himself to be Kevin Trent, sharing the same last name as his mother and only that name, he found that his parents had registered him as "Kevin Trent Stryker". Trent was only his middle name, and his actual last name was Stryker."

Silently, Kevin closed the file, nearly speechless. "That explains a lot," he said, thinking about the Sword of Purity strapped to his waist. He was deeply conflicted about how to feel. Most would likely be enthralled with such a discovery, but this was never something he wanted.

"More than I realized at the time," Kron said to Kevin. "Again, I am so very sorry. I did not mean for you to have to find out this way."

Next to Kevin, Prince Andrew had just seen the document himself, proving what he had been told. He was surprised to see that Kevin was so glum, but did figure that this may be quite a bit to process. Trying to lighten up the situation, Andrew put a hand on Kevin's shoulder and spoke. "When I was first told about you, and who you were based on this file, I understood that it would be easy to convince my father that the son of Vincent Stryker would be the perfect person to name as a Vanguard, and thus allow us private access to him that even I do not have on my own. But then I met you yesterday and saw what you did for me presuming I was a commoner and not the prince, and I knew then that that was the type of man I would want to be my Vanguard. I did not know that was you at the time, either, but I am grateful that it turned out to be."

Quietly, Kevin nodded, not wanting to make a fuss about the upsetting situation. "Thank you, your highness," he said.

After a second's pause, Caitlin then asked, "So, what exactly is the plan for getting the king to abdicate his throne?"

"It is a simple plan," answered the professor. "Andrew will escort Kevin personally to the throne room and introduce him as his new Vanguard of Aurana, and the king will complete the naming. All Kevin needs to do is follow Andrew's lead. Once that is done, Andrew will order Kevin to arrest the king and to take control of the throne room on behalf of the citizens of Aurana. Andrew will order the guards to stand down, but any who choose to listen to the king may have to be dealt with. We will join you after you have the king secured."

"Wait a second," Kevin interrupted, a little frustrated from what he was hearing. "Wouldn't it be easier if Prince Andrew dismissed the guards before we enter the throne room, including the ones inside? That would make taking the king into custody quite a bit easier, and a needless difficulty would be avoided."

Professor Magnon thought for only a second. "While your logic does make sense, Kevin, dismissing the throne room guards inside the room would raise suspicion, especially as they are also rotated only on order by the king. We will try to have the rest of the guards around the throne room dismissed before then, but we should be able to have all of the remaining guards dismissed by the time you have the king in custody."

Kevin sighed a little bit in depression, since this assignment of his was going to be tricky to implement, and might mean more bloodshed in the throne room should the guards not agree with him on arresting the king. And, more than likely, they would not. Kevin was not really a warrior, so he would have to hope he could spook them with the magic of the Sword of Purity.

Prince Andrew then picked up the conversation. "I understand the plan and my duties associated with it. The plan is to be executed at high noon tomorrow, so we will have time to discuss this in the morning should that be necessary. Now, if I may make a suggestion," the prince continued, "I think that all of us should dismiss for lunch, with the exception of Kevin and myself. I wish to speak with him personally."

Everyone else was slightly puzzled, but everyone rose and bowed to the prince nonetheless, obeying the prince's mandate.

Kevin remained in the room while Professor Magnon, Kronius, and Caitlin walked out of the room in a line down the hall. Commander Forkman walked over to the prince instead of leaving, however. He leaned his ear in to listen to the prince, as the prince whispered a command. "Fetch him for me." With that command, Commander Forkman also walked out of the room, leaving only the prince and Kevin in the room.

Kevin then approached the prince, bowed, and asked, "Your highness, I am slightly confused. What, may I ask, is your reason for speaking to me personally?"

The prince turned toward Kevin, with a smile. "If you are really a hero to Aurana as the professor suggests, and I am to become the king, then I believe it only makes sense for me to get to know you a little bit better. I live a very publicized life as the prince of Aurana, as you know, but there is no possible way for me to know anything about you prior to now."

"Interesting idea," Kevin replied. "But despite your public life, I had no idea that you like to be so personal with people."

Prince Andrew gave a little snicker. "Yes, well, not everything can be heard about me through Aurana's newsletters, of course." He started walking towards the window, as Kevin walked with him. "You see, while being such a public personality can be a thrilling experience at times, I despise living my life in the light of the media scribes. However, I have accepted this as a reality that cannot be changed." At this point, the two had reached the window. The prince began to lean on the window ledge and continued to speak. "Sometimes I do wish I could just lead a normal life, but to do so would be to endanger my homeland, this beautiful land of Aurana. This is why I have chosen to take the professor's suggestion and take my father's place at the throne, because it is what I honestly believe is best for this land." He paused for a second. "It would be a greater sin, I believe, to do nothing at all than to continue to allow us to plummet into oblivion for the sake of following authority."

Kevin placed his left arm on the windowsill and leaned against it. "An honorable cause, indeed, Prince Andrew. I think, just from what you've told me, that I have a greater purpose and reason for this task I'll be doing tomorrow. Thank you for restoring my confidence."

Prince Andrew started to smile a bit. "Certainly, although I have done nothing more than state the truth to you today. You seem to be a good man, Kevin. I would very much like to see you succeed, whether or not you are the son of Vincent Stryker."

Kevin took a step back. It was still not a thought he had.

The prince noticed this. "Is something the matter?"

"It's just… I'm not really a hero, or whatever Professor Magnon made me out to be," Kevin answered. "I know the professor because his daughter has been accompanying me. I didn't even know I was related to Vincent Stryker until now."

For a second, the prince thought, but then he smiled. "Then, if you do not want that to define you, do not let it," he said. "Clearly the professor saw an opportunity just because of your name, but that does not need to be how you are going forward. You changed my opinion yesterday, Kevin. You showed me you have the sense of right that a Vanguard should have, and I also noticed that you tried to knock him out without killing him."

"Yeah, about that…"

"I know," the prince answered. "I made sure it was not investigated, but from what I have been told by the professor last night, it may not have actually been your fault. Regardless, if that is what happened, it was absolutely self-defense, and defense of a member of the royal family, at that."

"Removing his short sword didn't help that argument, though," said Kevin.

“And it did not need to help,” Andrew answered. “You did not need to deal with accusations of a fight. Even if the authorities would disagree, I would not allow it to be judged that way.”

Kevin nodded. “I'm simply glad I could help,” he said.

Then, there was a knock at the door. Four hits, a short pause, and then three more hits. “Enter,” ordered the prince.

The door swung open and Commander Forkman walked through the door with another man behind him. Kevin and Prince Andrew both noted the presence of the two men, and then Prince Andrew turned to Kevin and said, “I have arranged for a small gift for you. It shall be ready for you tomorrow, but for the moment, I have brought a tailor to take your measurements.”

Kevin was surprised. “You’re presenting me with a gift of clothing? Well, I suppose anything is better than these tattered old rags,” he said, pulling his faded red shirt a little bit. Then he turned to the prince, bowed, and thanked him.

As Kevin was being measured for a new set of clothes, the prince then asked, “So, Kevin, while you are being measured, please tell me about yourself. I would love to know more about the actual person, not just the name, who I will be selecting for our new Vanguard.”

Meanwhile, as Kevin talked with the prince, Caitlin, Kronius, and Professor Magnon were invited back in by Commander Foreman and began enjoying a hot lunch at the bar, as the barkeep had kept to herself in the kitchen and knew lunch was part of the meeting. Within a half hour or so, Kevin, Prince Andrew, and Commander Forkman had joined them at lunch, and the six enjoyed a meal together, fully aware of the duties that would befall them the next day.

It was to be an event that would change the world as they knew it. And all six of them prayed that this change would be for the best for the world.

Chapter 19

The Bloodline

All around Seta Archa, visible from the throne room, was a lush forest with no roads even coming near to the walls of the city. Beyond the forest and to the east were The Wastes, a very large area of wastelands where few lived and supplies were scarce. It was not as arid as a desert, but barely any visible life was present there.

Mostly devoid of water, only a handful of tribes thrived in The Wastes. Those that did manage to survive there, however, were very hardy people, strong and sturdy. They were also very territorial people, and since The Wastes stretched from east of Seta Archa all the way to the Peaked Mountains, each tribe of The Wastes held large areas of land. In terms of the five civilized states, however, Desolunar held claim to The Wastes. It was from The Wastes that the Daritel tribe, which had caused the war twenty years before, had come.

Arthur woke up and realized that he was outside of the city, lying on the ground in an apparent wasteland. Upon waking up and seeing where he was, he looked to see Rachel Reinhart lying next to him, stirring.

Rachel was still groggy from all of the sleep, but she stood up and took a look around. She had been unconscious the whole time from her capture until just this moment. "Where am I?" She then looked over to see Arthur. "Arthur Falchor? What are you doing here?"

Arthur slowly rose up. "Rachel, I'm just glad you're safe," he said. "I think we were both captured separately and released together."

Looking puzzled, Rachel asked, "By whom?"

Slowly, Arthur looked at her. "By Demonicus."

Rachel looked confused at Arthur. "Why?"

Arthur shrugged. "I don't know about you," he began. "As for me… he's my father."

Rachel's face turned serious. "No…" she said.

"Yes," acknowledged Arthur. "I believe him when he tells me."

Eyes widening, Rachel looked around. "Okay…" she said, stretching out the sound of her word. The moment felt awkward, and she felt very puzzled. "That doesn't explain why we're out here together, wherever this is."

There was a long pause. "I know why we were released," Arthur then answered calmly, looking directly at Rachel. "I agreed in exchange for our freedom to kill Kevin Trent."

"What?" exclaimed Rachel. "Why would you do that? Why would Demonicus even want him dead to begin with? He's a friend of ours in Aurana, not some existential threat to his kingdom!"

"Well, apparently not," Arthur answered. "Remember how we met up in Rikleifer before you left on your book club trip?"

Rachel nodded. "I do. We never made it to Cardol, by the way."

Arthur acknowledged the response. He decided for the moment to explain the next part without the "immortal" explanation, just to keep things simpler. "Well, later that day Kevin and I ran into someone who showed us a piece of Vincent Stryker's sword. A couple of days later, Kevin, this person, and I found it, and Kevin can hold it when no one else can."

"And that's enough for him to want Kevin, our friend Kevin, dead?"

Arthur nodded. "Yeah," he said, "it is. He wanted me to join him at his side as his heir, and I refused. Demonicus told me he'd choose not to pursue me further if I killed Kevin instead."

Rachel was shocked. "Don't tell me you're actually going to go through with that!" she yelled at Arthur.

"Of course not!" Arthur yelled back. "I wouldn't have asked for your release as well if that's what I was going to do." He paused, allowing Rachel to calm as well, before he continued. "We're going to run, Rachel. As far away as we can go." He paused again. "I don't think we can go back to Aurana; he threatened me with torture and death if I ran away."

It was taking Rachel a moment to process all of this. So many things were different since a few days ago for her. She had been traveling with her book club to Cardol when they were ambushed outside of the city. Now, her entire situation had completely changed, and here she was in the middle of nowhere with someone she would consider a friend of a friend, not really a friend of hers. "Okay," she acknowledged after a moment, considering her best move. "It sounds like I owe my life to you, so I'll go with you."

Arthur looked at Rachel again. "I couldn't ask you to do that. I don't know where I'll go or what I'll do. I just need to run away, and I can't put you through that."

"Doesn't matter. You asked for my release, so you have me, regardless. I'm not going back to Aurana to leave you here to die, so I guess I'm going with you."

There was a moment's pause as Arthur thought. Then, he said. "Thanks, Rachel. I guess you're a better friend than I gave you credit for."

"I try," nodded Rachel. She would not tell Arthur that he was not really her friend. She figured he already knew that, but in this circumstance there was no reason to make a point of it.

As Arthur looked around, he remembered that Demonicus had promised to leave weapons and provisions. Pretty soon, he spotted them and signaled to Rachel that he saw something a few steps away. Then, he walked over and picked up a sword in its scabbard.

Rachel asked, "What is it?"

Arthur responded, "This is the Sword of Corruption. It's the sword Demonicus left with my mother for me to have when I became older." He put the sword into the scabbard and strapped it to his belt, on his right side. Arthur was left-handed, so this made it easier for him to draw his sword. Then, he picked up the bow and quiver full of arrows he saw behind him. "Apparently, they also left us these, too." He handed the bow and quiver with arrows to Rachel.

Rachel examined the bow. Unlike a typical bow, this one was painted black and was fairly large. It was definitely a longbow, no doubt. She pulled the string to check the tension and found the string was set to a perfect tension for a bow of its size, not too loose but not too tight. Examining the arrows in the quiver, she found that about half of them had some black splotches on the arrowheads. A sealed bottle of poison was also in the bottom.

It was a Desolunar prototype bow, ones used by only the highest-ranking archers in Desolunar currently.

Rachel was impressed with its quality.

“This is a prototype bow,” Rachel said to Arthur. “Also referred to as the 'death longbow' in Aurana. Very powerful and amazing accuracy, I hear. I must say I'm very impressed.”

Arthur was stunned. “Rachel, how do you know all this? Why do you even know all this?”

“What can I say? I'm a girl into archery,” responded Rachel with a little lift in her voice.

“As much as you are into writing?” asked Arthur.

Rachel responded, “Well, just about. I love to write, but archery is another favorite hobby of mine. In fact, there’s a little piece shaped like an arrow in my…” She reached at her neck, and became confused. “That's odd,” she said. “My locket is missing.”

Arthur was curious. “Locket?”

“Yeah, my locket. I’ve pretty much had it since the day I was born.”

Arthur started thinking what significance this had to the reason Rachel had been captured, or if it was merely coincidental. “I wonder what’s up with that,” Arthur said. “He kidnapped you, threw you in a cell, and stole your one piece of jewelry?”

“Apparently,” shrugged Rachel. “At this point I’m just glad to be alive, so I’m not too worried about it being missing.”

“I guess that’s good,” acknowledged Arthur. He then looked around, with the morning sun beating down on them. “Any idea which way we should go?”

Also looking around, Rachel then looked at Arthur. “I don’t see any pathways or landmarks to guide us,” she said, “but if we’re in Desolunar somewhere, the first thing we’ll want to do is get out. Easiest way to do that is to go north.” She pointed to the sun. “If it is the morning like we think it is, then that’s roughly east.” She then turned to her left. “So I’m not sure exactly, but that’s roughly north, I think.”

“You can lead the way,” Arthur told Rachel. “I’ll trust what you tell me."

And with that, they set off. The hot sun was beating down on them, and although Demonicus did leave some provisions, it was maybe enough for a day or two, and no water. Without any clear signs of where to find water, heading north was their best bet. Hopefully Rachel's idea would lead them to water and an escape out of Desolunar. Arthur had no idea where to go from there, but hopefully Rachel could help him come up with some ideas as they went along.

About two hours later, Arthur and Rachel were pushing their way through The Wastes. Neither of them knew much of anything of the geography of Desolunar, which meant that they did not know of the large size of The Wastes. There still had been no sign of water as of yet.

Frustrated with herself a little bit, Rachel stopped to adjust her clothing, a forest green and brown jacket over a skirt made of padded fabric, typical clothing for a traveling woman to protect her from the elements. Arthur stopped as well, so as not to let Rachel fall too far behind.

"Are you about set?" asked Arthur.

"I think so," answered Rachel. "Where the hell are we, Arthur? So help me, if you got us lost..."

"Me get us lost?" Arthur argued back. "What happened to you leading the way?"

Rachel finished adjusting her clothing. She sighed in frustration. "I guess there's no reason to fight about this now. In this wasteland, we want to make sure we keep moving. We can't stay too long in one place without water."

Reluctantly, Arthur nodded. She was right.

Then, Rachel paused for a second and said, "Something doesn't feel right. It feels like we're being watched."

Arthur put the palm of his hand over his face in a bit of frustration. "That or you're just delusional. There's no way anyone could be out here in this place."

Rachel became even more frustrated at Arthur. "Delusional? Wow, Arthur, I didn't think you could ever stoop so low as to throw an insult like that. I should just turn back and leave you here for the vultures to pick at."

"Whoa, hey, slow down!" responded Arthur. "Look, I didn't mean anything like that. I'm just a little frustrated with this, being here in the wastelands without any idea where we are."

Rachel backed down. "I'm sorry, Arthur. This is not what I was hoping to do either, but we didn't have a choice. Think about it for a second. Why else would we be left with weapons with nobody following us? You were right, something was up. We couldn't stay, and without a doubt, every possible route we could take has probably been planned for, although this one would seem to be pretty unusual considering where we are."

Turning away in frustration, Arthur said, "Let's go. The more we dawdle around out here, the larger risks we take by being here in the wastelands. We can keep talking as we keep moving, but it's best not to stay here."

Rachel said nothing.

Arthur turned back around toward Rachel. "Hey, can't you hear me? We need to…"

Too late.

About ten tribesmen were lined up with bows drawn at Rachel and Arthur. Rachel already had her arms up to surrender. Upon seeing the tribesmen and being caught off guard by their presence, Arthur followed suit.

The tribesmen wore no clothing except for a short skirt-like piece of clothing around their waists. Tattoo markings of various colors were everywhere all across their skin, which was of a darker color than that of Arthur, Rachel, or any other person that either of the two of them had ever seen. Their skin was rough and dirty, a complement of life in The Wastes, given the scarcity of water.

Without turning or moving any, Arthur whispered over to Rachel, "Remind me to trust your premonitions in the future."

"Your fault for not listening," Rachel replied, also whispering.

Arthur rolled his eyes in frustration. He certainly was not amused by some of her traits.

Along the line of tribesmen, one of them towards the middle pushed the string of his bow back in to loosen the tension of the string, and then let the arrow simply fall out of the bow. He then stepped forward, and said, in a somewhat deep, but commanding, voice, "You are trespassing on the lands of the Metoi tribe of The Wastes. Unless you have authority to be here, strangers, you will be slaughtered."

It was over. Arthur and Rachel were pinned. There was nowhere that either of them could go to without being killed, and no way to escape. Also, neither of them had the authority to be there.

Or maybe Arthur did.

He had an idea. Perhaps the Sword of Corruption could be his proof of authority. As much as he did not want to acknowledge it, he was Demonicus's son, after all. If the people of The Wastes were submissive to Demonicus, as he had learned in his history lessons in school at the Rikleifer Academy, then perhaps they would recognize the Sword of Corruption as a symbol of Arthur's heritage and a right to pass through these lands. On the other hand, however, drawing his sword could mean that the tribesmen would fire their arrows on him for pulling out a weapon. This made the decision very difficult for Arthur.

Very slowly, Arthur raised his right hand. He then slowly moved his left hand across his body to the hilt of the Sword of Corruption, sitting in its scabbard. Arthur saw the bowstrings on the archers' bows tighten even further, but with confidence, he grabbed the hilt of his sword, and pulled it hard and quickly.

Out came the sword across Arthur's body, with a flash of a red-purple color that surprised Arthur as he had never seen it do that before. It surprised Rachel and every one of the tribesmen, who stared in amazement. In amazement from the sight of the Sword of Corruption, the tribesmen lowered their bows and knelt down in respect. The one who had spoken earlier also knelt down, and addressed Arthur. "My deepest apologies, your highness. I did not realize that I was in the presence of the son of our overlord!"

Arthur lowered his sword, but still held it in his left hand, which was the hand Arthur used to wield his sword. He had an idea, and saw some possibilities to get some answers. "Spare me the pleasantries," he replied. "This is my first time in the Wastes, so I would appreciate it if you would share some knowledge with me."

The same tribesman gave a bow. "Certainly. We will bring both you and your guest here to the village, and then we shall give you all the answers that you desire. Hail to the heir of Desolunar."

Arthur was a little confused. "Village? Where is this village?"

The tribesman signaled to his left. "Over there."

Arthur looked in that direction. Sure enough, there was a village in that direction, a short distance away, clearly visible in the wasteland. How had he and Rachel missed it? Arthur felt like the biggest idiot in the Wastes for missing something like that. Had he seen it, he would have headed in that direction for supplies, whether or not the villagers would have been hostile toward him.

Nonetheless, Arthur and Rachel decided to follow the tribesmen back to the village. The walk was a short one, but during that walk, Arthur and Rachel saw exactly what life was like in the Wastes. The buildings were small and few in number, made of dead, crude wood and other materials from the wastelands. Arthur wondered how anybody could live in a place like this for very long, especially in the conditions of the Wastes where the sun would beat down on the dry clay earth and water was scarce. It was not exactly a desert climate, but given that it lacked life even more so than a desert, the Wastes seemed like an even more hostile environment than a desert.

As Arthur started to put the pieces together, he began to realize why the peoples of the Wastes had a darker skin tone than people from the rest of the world. Their skin was better adapted to deal with the harsh sunlight of the Wastes. Arthur had to make sure that he could find some shade in the village so he and Rachel would not burn from the intense sunlight. Expanding on this notion, Arthur was also certain that there were other adaptations that the men and women of the Wastes had.

As they entered the middle of the village, the native people of the Metoi tribe stared at Arthur and Rachel, having never seen them before. Arthur and Rachel tried to ignore this, however, as the men they were traveling with led them into one of the larger buildings of the village.

Once inside the building, the tribesman who spoke the same language as Arthur and Rachel dismissed the other members of his archery unit. As soon as all of them left, the tribesman began to speak.

"I do hope you will forgive the intolerance of my men and people, but it is uncommon for them to see any men of your skin complexion, much less the heir himself. I am Aspectra, chief of the Metoi tribe of the Wastes."

Arthur approached the chief, and although he was not sure if the gesture of a handshake meant the same thing to the Metoi as it did to the majority of the world, he shook the hand of the Metoi chief and said, "It is a pleasure to make your acquaintance. My name is Arthur Falchor, successor of Desolunar. And this young woman I am traveling with is Rachel Reinhart, faithful archer and my bodyguard." Arthur was somewhat lying about this part, but he felt that he needed to come up with some reason for Rachel to be dragged along with him.

"Odd," said the Metoi chief in response. "I do find it strange that you are traveling with a woman, especially considering Desolunar's policies and customs restricting the rights of most women. However, given that you are the heir, I will not question what you see as the most apt way to travel."

Rachel started to become angry, but Arthur was motioning to her to calm down. It was not the practice in Aurana, especially in Rikleifer, for women to have restricted rights. Rikleifer itself was especially lenient on these restrictions, allowing women almost all of the rights that men held, with the major exception of joining the military. Despite this, women still filled defensive ranks within Rikleifer as a type of civilian defense system. This was not the practice across the world, however, and it appeared that Desolunar had some of the most restrictive standards on women.

Arthur decided to play into this situation, and winked at Rachel to let her know he was up to something. "She is a reliable archer, which is why I travel with her." This statement by Arthur made Rachel relax a little bit, giving her a sense that Arthur did value her somewhat, at least.

The Metoi chief Aspectra continued, "You have stated that you have never been in the Wastes before, so I think it would be helpful if you understood how the politics of the Wastes work. We are the Metoi, the farthest west tribe of the Wastes. To the north of us lie the Toronaga, with whom we trade for water. There are about thirty-five separate tribes that occupy territory in the Wastes."

Deep in thought, Arthur stopped the Metoi chief to ask a question. "Thirty-five tribes of the Wastes, and all of them have submitted to become part of Desolunar?"

Aspectra bowed. "Of course. Demonicus promised us peace and prosperity through a confederacy. We would become a part of his new nation he was establishing in the city of Seta Archa, and his strict authority would keep every tribe in check and allow us to reside in peace with one another. While Demonicus does not allow the most amount of freedoms to our people, he does keep us at peace with his rule."

Peace through strong, tight leadership. While dictatorship of a country similar to the way Demonicus ran Desolunar certainly had many drawbacks to its people's rights and powers, peace within the nation was the one benefit. Under such a tight rule, people were held back from fighting one another by force, which was an effective way of maintaining the peace. This by no means justifies dictatorship, Arthur thought to himself, but it does provide a reason as to why the people of Desolunar did not fight with Demonicus for control of the country. He was able to maintain peace among his people, despite the many restrictions of his rule and his attempt to conquer the world.

Rachel was not saying anything. Figuring that restrictions on the rights of women in Desolunar might also mean it was inappropriate to speak to the chief, she decided not to say anything. Of course, she could not be sure if that was the policy or not, but she decided not to take any more risks than were necessary.

After considering what the chief said for a moment, Arthur finally spoke. "Quite interesting, Chief Aspectra. I can see where my father's rule has brought stability to your region. For certain, he has won your heart."

"Anyone who could bring the Wastes, a land that had been torn by war for thousands of years, to peace will always be loved by the people of the Wastes," responded the Metoi Chief. "I do hope as well that after the death of Lord Demonicus, you would be willing to continue from his position. Your sword is your proof; the fact that you were able to draw it without staggering in pain, without flinching for a moment means that you are the heir to Desolunar."

Arthur dropped his head for a second. "Desolunar is not exactly a monarchy. It is more of a dictatorship, which guarantees me nothing." He drew the Sword of Corruption again, and a flash of red-purple lit up again. "This sword… it brings me nothing. No proof, no justification, nothing. I am my own man, and that is all I can be." Arthur was speaking from his heart with this statement.

"Now, now," started the chief. "While it is true that Desolunar does run as a dictatorship at the moment, its citizens have believed in an heir to continue to maintain the peace of the land. You are that man. Do not let anything tell you otherwise, for you are that man for certain."

Puzzled, Arthur asked, "How do you know?"

"We, the Metoi tribe, are the protectors of knowledge of Seta Archa," answered Chief Aspectra. "Lord Demonicus has entrusted us, not the people of Seta Archa, with his knowledge of everything. It is better protected in our care among the people of our small village rather than among the people of the gigantic city that is Seta Archa." He paused for a second. "That you possess that Sword of Corruption, locked only to your bloodline, and can withdraw it freely, shows that you are the heir."

Huh. Interesting, Arthur thought to himself. It made perfect sense to Arthur for Demonicus to hide his information here, out of the sight of most others. Demonicus was quite a bit craftier than he had first anticipated. By doing this, he had given himself a need for the Metoi. The Metoi had a need for him as well to maintain peace by force. In essence, Demonicus had tied his Desolunar state, centered around Seta Archa, to the Metoi tribe in this way. Given this theory, Arthur was fairly certain that Demonicus had probably done something similar with all of the tribes of the Wastes, making the entire area a stronghold given the knowledge the tribes had of the land. United together, and given a purpose to fight for Desolunar, the Wastes were a virtually impenetrable area of the land. The Wastes made up almost the entire eastern half of Desolunar, which would prevent efficient attacks from the nations of Scurnia and Gardolk.

A thought came to Arthur's head. If the Metoi were the keepers of knowledge for Demonicus, then maybe they knew where Arthur and

Rachel should head next. It was a bit of a longshot, but Arthur thought it was worth it."Perhaps you would be able to help us then, Chief Aspectra," Arthur started to say. "We are seeking a direction where to go."

The Metoi chief thought for a moment, but came up short. "I do not understand, where do you wish to head? Perhaps it is possible that Lord Demonicus knows, since there is much that he does not share with anybody, not even us. You might want to go back and ask him about it."

Arthur rolled his eyes at himself. How was he going to get out of this one? The last thing he wanted was to go back to Seta Archa and see the dark lord himself face to face. He needed something first, before he even thought about going after Demonicus. He needed more power than his sword had. He needed a stronger ally.

What he needed was Kevin Trent, his best friend.

"I will not be returning to Seta Archa anytime soon," Arthur said confidently. "It is my desire to find more of my knowledge from the rest of the world. I appreciate what you have told me today, but what if I wanted to find more knowledge about broader subjects?"

Rachel stood back, puzzled about what Arthur was thinking.

Chief Aspectra thought for a moment. "It is good to know that you are seeking knowledge from the world, your highness. Lord Demonicus must be very pleased with your spirit." Arthur rolled his eyes again as the Metoi chief continued, "If what you seek is knowledge greater than what you can find here, then I recommend that you and your companion travel to the city of Cardol. Once the capital of Nuve and one of the most beautiful and ancient cities of the world, Demonicus has kept the city empty and left everything intact there, almost as if the city were frozen in time. One of the largest libraries of the world is still there, untouched in years. Travel north from here through the territory of our allies the Toronaga to the Calphos River, a trip of several days. After you make it to the river, follow it to the east. It will take a few more days once you make it to the river, but the lands around the river are much more lush than those around here and will be able to support you. Once you reach Cardol, you should find much more information than we are able to provide you. We will grant you enough provisions to survive the trip to the river, as well as passage through our lands. Other than this, however, you will be on your own."

Arthur stepped up to shake Chief Aspectra's hand again. "Thank you," he said to the chief. "We will leave tomorrow morning for Cardol, then."

"Very well, then," responded the chief. "Your highness, we will allow you and your archer to have this building for the night. Do not worry about your provisions for your trip, since we will stock them for you. Everything will be ready for you by sunrise tomorrow."

"Excellent," said Arthur in reply. "Please extend my gratitude to your people. They, along with you, deserve it for all the help you have granted me today."

The Metoi chief smiled. "I will do so, your highness. For now, I must begin collecting your provisions and organizing my people. Therefore, I must be going now. Please do enjoy the rest of your day." With this, Chief Aspectra bowed to Arthur and walked out of the building.

Almost as soon as the chief had left, Rachel approached Arthur and said, "Why are we going to Cardol? What are you expecting to find there?"

Arthur turned toward Rachel. "I have no idea. But it gets us out of Desolunar, so I'm going with it."

That made sense. "Got it," Rachel acknowledged. She then paused. "Way to play up the heir of Desolunar angle, by the way. It probably saved our lives this time."

Arthur turned his head away. "Don't remind me," he said.

Chapter 20

Responsibility

As the next morning came around, Kron was reading a book in the tavern before dawn. Professor Magnon was up early and out of his room. As he walked into the tavern and saw Kron reading his book, he noticed that Kron was reading a book that he, the professor, had written. It was called *The Rise of Dictators, The Fall of Kings*. More than simply political theory, it also contained information on magic's influence in politics. "I see you are finding knowledge in what I have written, Kronius," said the professor. "It makes me proud to know that a god such as yourself knows the value of knowledge."

Deciding not to be rude, Kron respected the words of the professor. "Indeed, Professor Magnon. Knowledge is power, after all."

"It is the rule that I have lived by," responded Professor Magnon. "Can you see why I have been a teacher for so long? Our future rests in the next generation, continuously, and to preserve knowledge is to preserve power to the next ones to come to this world."

"Absolutely," said Kronius in agreement. "Still, I find it surprising that you have amassed such great amounts of knowledge. There is more here than I think any mortal has previously amassed. This book may, perhaps, contain much that even the gods themselves do not know of."

"I believe it does," responded the professor. "Knowledge is power, and power in the wrong hands can be abused all too easily."

Kron was a little confused. "Then why even write the book?"

"Because," responded the professor quickly, "in the right hands, power can save a world."

"True," acknowledged Kron. He thought about starting a long-overdue discussion with the professor about Kevin, but before he could say more, he heard footsteps down the hall approaching the bar where he and the professor were. As the footsteps approached, he and

Professor Magnon recognized the person as she approached. It was Caitlin, who was by now awake as well.

Deciding to give Caitlin time with her father, and that his conversation with Professor Magnon was little more than small talk, Kron returned to his room that he was sharing with Kevin. He walked down the hallway and heard no conversation until he made it to the room's door.

Out in the lounge, Caitlin stood in front of her seated father and started the conversation with her father directly. "I want you to reinforce my emotional block."

Professor Magnon raised an eyebrow. "That is quite the unusual request, my daughter. Did something happen to you?"

"No," stated Caitlin. "I just have felt as though it might be failing, and wish to have you strengthen it. It is my responsibility to the world to be as logical as possible as I hone my skills, after all."

There was a short pause, as Professor Magnon pulled up a bar stool. He sighed. "Caitlin, I am not sure I fully agree with this procedure."

"Yes, I know. You objected before, but were still willing to do it."

"That is because I believe you can learn to be disciplined without being completely without emotion," Professor Magnon said. "You can achieve your goals in your field and still be a normal person."

"No. I do not agree." Caitlin stepped next to her father. "I am best off as I am. It's the only way I can focus on my studies."

"Caitlin, you are by no means a remedial student in magic," the professor responded. "I think, at this point, that you would be better learning to harness your emotions rather than burying them deep."

"If you won't do it, then I will find someone who will," Caitlin said back.

Professor Magnon sighed. "Very well. Step closer."

Doing as she was told, Caitlin stood in front of her father, who stood up from his bar stool. He then placed his hands on the side of his daughter's head while his hands glowed with light and darkness magic, the two keys to any successful mind magic.

"While we do this," the professor began, "I must ask. What

really made you want this sudden reinforcement? Tell me about your recent episode."

Naturally, her father had figured out there was a reason for this request, Caitlin thought to herself. Still, she was hesitant to tell her father the whole situation. "I almost had a breakdown," she said. "I've felt the block start to loosen recently."

"Has it?" asked the professor, intrigued. "These blocks do not expire. The only thing that would loosen the block is a powerful emotional feeling, enough that the mental magic is unable to hold it back."

Caitlin said nothing, but her mind was rushing in multiple directions. She did not know that that was the cause. If she were hiding feelings for Kevin, and those were bubbling to the surface like they did when she saw that key and then Kevin promised to buy it for her, could those feelings be undoing her block?

It would explain the nightmare, and all of the feelings of fear that came with it. She had never felt such a connection to any human being as she did to Kevin. By no means was Caitlin any kind of social person, but never before did she feel like she related to someone like Kevin. He was also relatively socially isolated and, despite their significant differences, also shared a lot in common with her such as their love of fantasy stories and a desire to travel the world. Now they had been traveling together for several days, and already she felt special when he interacted with her.

That had to stop. She had her dedication and her craft, and she was growing fearful of what such changes she was feeling would do to her personality and her future. It could not be allowed to happen. She could not risk being hurt. "I suppose," she finally told her father, after quite a bit of thinking.

"You suppose?" asked her father. "Did the boy with whom you are traveling do this to you? Did he hurt you?"

A bit of her thought may have slipped out into an area of her mind that her father was working, Caitlin realized. "No, nothing like that," she said. "I would have abandoned him by now if that were the case."

The professor nodded. "Good. We have placed much stock in

Kevin, and I would hate to scrap everything because he turned out to be a horrible person." He continued to work on Caitlin for another moment, before de-powering his hands. "There we go, all finished. Your block is reinforced for the time being."

"Excellent," commented Caitlin.

"However," began the professor, "I must warn you that the block may not be permanent if you have had emotions loosen them. A strong enough emotion may be so powerful that it breaks the spell entirely. Should that happen, you will be at the mercy of your emotions, and as you have never fully experienced them…"

"I will be fine," interrupted Caitlin.

Down the hall, while the professor and his daughter were interacting, Kron reached the room to which he was assigned to share with Kevin. He entered as quietly as he could and closed the door behind him, but the sound of the door was still enough to disturb Kevin in his bed. Kevin flipped over but remained in the bed.

"Sorry," Kron apologized to Kevin, "I did not mean to disturb you."

Kevin grumbled a bit. "It is what it is," he said as he stirred. He sat up on the edge of his bed, trying to get himself together.

Kron nodded. He sat down on the edge of his bed with the book.

"Hey Kron, can I ask you something?" Kevin asked.

"You can ask me anything," Kron answered.

"How come you didn't tell me about my father?"

Putting the book down, Kron turned to Kevin. "Truthfully, Kevin, when we met I really did not know."

"But you suspected," Kevin retorted.

There was a pause. "When you picked up the shard of the Sword of Purity, yes, I suspected it was possible. I knew you were what we as gods called a 'pure one', simply because you could hold the sword. I had thought that a relationship to Vincent Stryker, who was the pure one, was possible but I could not prove it."

Kevin sat up a bit taller. "That's what I don't get," he said. "Why not tell me? I've gone this whole time telling people like Demonicus I'm not a 'pure one', and now allegedly I am? Apparently it's now confirmed because of who my father is in the records."

There was another pause. Kron had to gather his thoughts. "Kevin, I hope you understand that I did not lie to you to harm you. I wanted to protect you from what that meant, to be the next pure one. You have already lost so much because of me with Arthur's kidnapping, and still you have shown kindness to me and told me you would take me home." He paused briefly. "To tell you the truth, I do not know how to get home. I knew only that the sword you hold is the key to do it, but I know little else."

"I understand that, but don't lie to me again," acknowledged Kevin. "We may not still be allies if you do."

"Duly noted. I will not," said Kron.

Kevin then asked, "Anyway, what were you protecting me from?"

"From Demonicus," said Kron. "Actually, not from him. From Tyrinion."

"Tyrinion?" asked Kevin.

"Yes," acknowledged Kron. "Tyrinion is certainly the benefactor for Demonicus. The cult faction of which Demonicus is part, the Enlighteners from the Shadows, they are worshippers of a 'conqueror' who is immortal. What is happening now in the south is almost identical to the Alliance-Daritel War, except with Demonicus and his Enlighteners as the driving force. Tyrinion continues to pull the strings, like a puppeteer with his marionettes. Even with a power vacuum, it is difficult to imagine that Demonicus would grow to be so powerful without help from the immortal he considers his father."

Kevin frowned at Kron. "How are you so sure?"

"Remember our fight with Demonicus?," said Kron. "That kind of tracer magic he used to control Arthur's body is not something that is taught today. It is lost to ancient history, such that not even the gods know it. It can only have come from someone old enough to know the spell, then set up for Demonicus to operate it."

Listening intently, Kevin was a bit surprised.

"I had hoped that if you could get me home, I could regroup with the gods and try to find some other way so I did not have to involve you. But if you are a new pure one, which we now know,"

Kron said, "I have to tell you that you are the only one who can stop Tyrinion. That Sword of Purity was designed specifically for that purpose, and it contains the sacrifice of a god." He paused. "It means that I have, regretfully, drawn you into a conflict between immortals that threatens your realm and mine, in an event prophesied as the 'conquest of the realms'. Preventing it should never have been your responsibility, but now I must ask that it be."

Suddenly it all made sense. That was what Kron was keeping secret. Kevin understood why Kron felt guilty about all of this, but it was not as though Kron picked who could hold the sword. Now, Kron was telling him he had to save not one, but two worlds.

Overwhelming as all of this was, Kevin had one thought in mind. He wanted to focus on what was directly ahead of him, and simply go from there. So far, he had more and more placed at his feet since Arthur's kidnapping, and with each additional task he simply dealt with it as it came. What this meant for his future, he did not know, but he was already treading new ground every day and facing new dangers regularly. What did this change now, at least?

"Kron, I've got to tell you, you've sure put me up for a lot," he said.

"I know, and I apologize profusely. It was never my intention to get you in this deep."

Kevin shrugged. "It is what it is," he said. "All I know now is that I have to deal with it one step at a time." He then lied back down to rest more.

Kron did not say anything else to Kevin as he eventually went back to sleep. Kevin clearly was not impressed, but he did not seem angry, either. More or less, Kron felt as though he had disappointed Kevin more than made him angry, and that upset him.

Within the hour, as the sun rose, Prince Andrew II and Head Commander Travis Forkman arrived at the tavern. By the end of the hour, though, Kevin was still asleep, which led to Professor Magnon waking him up. Although Professor Magnon wanted to let Kevin have more sleep, it was not a day to sleep in. Today was a day for action.

Together, all of them joined up in the bar and were treated to breakfast by the owner of the Rider's Tavern. Everyone enjoyed the breakfast as quickly as they could before gathering their things and heading for the palace. It was finally time to end the rule of King Arnold IX and bring a chance for Aurana. Kevin was going to confront King Arnold IX himself and, with Prince Andrew II, force him to abdicate his throne. The prince would help Kevin get through the defenses of the palace interior. Then, he would walk to a meeting room in the palace to pay witness to the king's abdication and verify the prince as the new king of Aurana.

It was not guaranteed to work, however. In order for Kevin to force the king into abdication, there was a good chance that he would have to overcome the guards inside the throne room on his own, which is why he needed his sword. He had to be confident and sure in his actions, and be mindful of his defense. Kevin had practiced a bit of swordplay in school, but he had never really tried it before in a real situation. He hoped not to need to try.

As they walked to the palace as a group, Kevin started to second-guess the actions he was about to perform. Kron's words from before had stuck in his head about allowing Professor Magnon to use him as a political tool. He was about to aid in overthrowing the king of his homeland because an old man with more magical power than anyone had ever seen before had told him that it would be what had to happen in order for lives to be saved, for a turn in the war with Desolunar, and to rescue Arthur. But why was he trusting Professor Magnon almost blindly? And was this really the right thing to do?

Kevin had to reassure himself that what he was doing was right. Having met Prince Andrew II, Kevin had grown to trust him in a very short amount of time. Andrew was a spark of light in the ever-dimming landscape of the world. He was honored to be in the service of the young prince this day. As for Professor Magnon, Kevin reminded himself that he was listening to a man who knew more than he did about how the world worked.

Approaching the palace, the group split apart. Commander Forkman took Caitlin and the professor through the main gate at the front of the palace. As the Head Commander of the Army of Aurana, Forkman was an advisor to the king and was thus permitted within the palace. It was important for him to be present at the inevitable meeting in the great hall of the palace should the king decide to step down, as it would be his task to oversee the passing of the crown. Certain that the presence of Professor Magnon and his daughter would not be problematic to this, he decided to bring both of them in with him to the great hall. They would have to be cleared by security at the palace, but it would not be too difficult to do so considering that an advisor of the king was escorting them inside.

Meanwhile, Prince Andrew II led Kevin around to the rear of the palace to take him through the courtyard and into the palace. There was less security in that direction, which meant that there was less of a chance that the armed guards would ask the prince about what he was doing. Andrew had insisted on this, desiring not to take any more chances than he had to.

It was not too difficult for Andrew to get Kevin past the first security checkpoint at the rear of the palace, at the entrance to the palace courtyard. Entering the courtyard, Kevin was amazed at the natural beauty of the various small trees and flowers growing in the relatively large courtyard. There were colors of every shade imaginable in the growing flowerbeds, and the trees were equally beautiful. A white stone fountain sat in the center of the courtyard, with water constantly flowing through it. Beyond the courtyard itself, the emerald-colored walls of the palace almost blended in with the color of the leaves. In fact, every wall of the palace was painted in emerald green. This was to be expected, however, as green was a color commonly associated with Aurana, much like how blue was associated with Nuve, red was associated with Scurnia, purple was associated with Gardolk, and black was usually associated with Desolunar. These "color identities" could be seen well within the flags of each nation and the colors in which their armies dressed.

As Kevin walked through the courtyard, continually staring at the natural beauty of the courtyard, Prince Andrew started a discussion with him. "Enjoying the courtyard?" he asked to Kevin, to break the ice.

"It's magnificent," Kevin said as he was still looking around. "I must imagine that you spend quite a bit of your time here. I certainly would, if I had the chance."

"Whenever I have the time, I do," responded the prince. "I do not have quite as much free time as I would really like to have, however. It is one aspect of being a future ruler: every day, you spend most of your time learning the facts about your country. Despite this, I do not think I could ever imagine having your life, Kevin."

Kevin started to laugh a little bit. "Had you said that two weeks ago, I would've argued with you, but today? I don't think you could. Even I can't imagine it most of the time."

Andrew started to laugh some too as the two of them approached the fountain in the middle of the courtyard. As they walked up, however, a voice started to sound from a short distance in front of them. "Prince Andrew! Prince Andrew!" the voice called as a man approached. He was relatively short, but fully adult, and dressed in modest clothes that were perfectly cleaned.

Prince Andrew greeted the man, recognizing him as one of the paid servants that worked in the palace. "What can I do for you?"

After having stopped to bow to Prince Andrew, the man extended his left arm, with which he was carrying a folder. "Here are the documents that you requested. I hope that I have managed to get them to you in a timely fashion like you had asked for."

Prince Andrew smiled. "It is timely enough. Thank you, I appreciate this. You are dismissed."

"No need to thank me, your highness," said the servant as he bowed again. Then, acknowledging his dismissal, he walked back into the palace to continue with his duties.

As soon as he had left, Prince Andrew opened the folder and began to read the files within it. Curious about what the folder contained, Kevin asked, "What is in that folder, Prince Andrew?"

Andrew looked up from his reading and over to Kevin. "These are the abdication documents. I had them written up by an advisor close to me, the kind who I knew would not snitch to my father. Needless to say, getting caught with these probably means game over for both of us and life sentences or executions, so we must proceed carefully."

That sent a shiver down Kevin's spine. Treason was punishable by death in Aurana. If this did not work, the consequences were very severe. He was risking his life in this moment to try and do something to help save Arthur's.

If he did not, though, Arthur was all but gone. Kevin's mind was made up. He could not let the worst happen to his best friend.

As they continued to head toward the palace side, Kevin decided to change the topic a little bit. "You know, your highness, that with you taking the throne here shortly, there will be those who demand that you have an heir. Have you thought about that?"

"Oh, I do not think it will be a major issue," responded the prince. "Let me let you in on a little secret, Kevin. I do have a lover."

"Oh?" asked Kevin, very curious. "I would have expected to know if you did since the royal family is so publicized across Aurana. You do live your life in the eye of the public, after all."

"That is true," responded the prince, "but that does not mean that everything becomes public." After saying this, he stopped in his place. Kevin stopped as well as Prince Andrew approached him closer and said quietly, "To be honest, not even my father knows about it. The one I am in love with is a peasant girl."

Kevin leaned back a little bit. "Well, I suppose you can find love in any place if you look for it. I have often thought that if you can see something special in someone, no matter who they are, then you have found the person that you are looking for."

Prince Andrew pondered this for a moment. "That is deeply philosophical, Kevin. It sounds like you know what that means. Do you have someone like that already, Kevin?"

A little uncertain what to say, Kevin leaned in toward Prince Andrew and said quietly, "She doesn't know I see that in her, though."

"Oh, I see," responded Prince Andrew. "Nervous to tell her?"

"It goes deeper than that," Kevin continued. "It's a little hard to describe, but she's not exactly full of heart, if you know what I mean. She doesn't have any emotion, any feelings, any type of personality whatsoever. She seems so cold all of the time, and yet I can see something special within her."

Prince Andrew II started to become perplexed at this description Kevin was giving him. "And you really see something special in that? To use your own words, 'I suppose you can find love in any place if you look for it.' But I must ask, just where did you find such a person?"

Kevin leaned in toward Prince Andrew. "Professor Magnon's daughter," he simply said.

"Really?" asked Prince Andrew, stunned. "Very interesting, indeed."

As Prince Andrew finished saying this, the two passed the security checkpoint and into the palace's backside. A short distance down the hall was the throne room's central entrance. It was only a few minutes through the second checkpoint and the two crossing halls in front of the throne room.

At the throne room door, Prince Andrew looked at Kevin. "And here, Kevin, is the point of no return. If we go, I want you to follow my lead and let me do most of the talking. Are you still in?"

Kevin nodded in the affirmative. It was time for him to do what must be done.

Chapter 21

The Point of No Return

Here at the entrance to the throne room, two guards were manning the doors. Prince Andrew approached them with Kevin beside him, and said, "I have an appointment with my father, to name the new Vanguard of Aurana. This is him, with me."

The lead guard, standing on the left of the door, responded, "Certainly, Prince Andrew. I will admit him immediately, but he must not carry in any weapons. Why does he have one with him right now, and why did security at the front not take it?"

Kevin responded, thinking quickly, "This is no ordinary sword; it is proof that I am who I say I am, and why I am to be named. I asked if I could leave it with the guards inside the throne room so the king could see it." He was lying.

Prince Andrew II added to this spontaneously. "I can vouch for all of this. I gave him the permission to leave it with the inner guards." Andrew, too, was lying.

The guard sighed, not exactly sure what to do at this point. It was his job to enforce the laws and rules of the palace, but the prince had granted permission for a weapon to be carried into the throne room, provided it be left with the guards. "Very well, then," he finally said. "You are to leave your weapon with the guards as soon as you walk in the door. Understand?"

"I understand," responded Kevin firmly as he unstrapped the scabbard of the Sword of Purity from his belt.

After that acknowledgment, the guard opened the door to allow Kevin and the prince inside. Kevin walked in and was instantly overcome by the sights of the throne room. Mostly colored in a lighter green than the walls of the palace, the throne room was decorated in marbled stone. It was one of the most majestic sights that Kevin had ever seen. The throne room's ceiling was very high, almost two floors tall, and very broad otherwise in all dimensions. Truly, this room was fit for a king.

Kevin turned to the guards inside the door as he entered and gave his sword, in its scabbard, to one of them. As he did, Kevin began to look at the room from a strategic point of view. There were three doors in the throne room: one to his left, one to his right, and one behind him where he had entered. Two guards stood at each door, meaning there were six total. There was nowhere to hide in this large room, meaning that Kevin had to be on his guard if something bad happened.

At the far end of the throne room, King Arnold IX sat in his throne, patiently waiting. He had known of this appointment, much like the many daily appointments he took most days every week. His throne, a golden throne, was upholstered in fine red fabric, in the most elegant materials Aurana could create. A man in his forties, Arnold IX appeared to be stately and professional.

When Kevin reached the center of the large room, he knelt down and looked to the ground, in respect. Prince Andrew offered a bow to his father, but did not need to kneel.

"Rise," commanded the king, in his bold, stately voice. Kevin did as he was commanded, while Andrew straightened up. The king then looked toward his son. "Andrew, I understand you have brought someone you believe should be our new Vanguard."

"Indeed, father," acknowledged Prince Andrew. "May I present Kevin Trent Stryker, the son of Vincent Stryker, the Scurnian general originally from Aurana who led the battle that ended the Alliance-Daritel War twenty years ago."

Kevin offered a small bow, playing his role but also in awe of being in the presence of the king. "It is my honor, your majesty."

The king appeared to consider this. "Interesting find, Andrew," he commented. "And how can you be sure of this?"

"I have seen his birth record, father," Andrew answered. "It was kept sealed in Rikleifer. Its contents have since been revealed to me, showing this man is indeed the son of Vincent Stryker. Surely you would find this selection to be one rooted in the glory of our nation, as we have long considered Vincent Stryker a son of Aurana, being that he was born here and lived here for a time."

"I do find it an interesting idea," the king answered. "Vincent Stryker was indeed a hero to Aurana, one whom we celebrate in Aurana."

Next to Kevin, Andrew looked intrigued, like this might work.

"However," the king then said, "Vincent Stryker was not of noble birth, and thus neither is this Kevin Trent Stryker that you have brought to me. Our Vanguards have always been of noble birth, related to our family, and it is a tradition I wish to uphold. Being the descendant of a national hero is, while respectable, not worthy enough to assume the title and responsibilities of the position. Only one of noble birth can be worthy of filling the role."

Andrew scoffed. "You have got to be joking, father. We have not had a Vanguard in fifty years. I offer you someone who fits your vision, and instead you decline it simply on the basis of whether or not his blood is royal in some way? He stomped off to the guard behind him, who was holding the Sword of Purity.

"It is our tradition, Andrew, and you will respect it," answered the king.

"Is it our tradition to send our people to be slaughtered at the hands of Desolunar?" Andrew grabbed the sword by the scabbard. Not one of the guards was willing to tell the crown prince not to do that.

"Andrew, you misunderstand. Our men are glorious in their strength. They will overcome our invaders and turn the tide of war soon enough."

"What do you know about that?" said Andrew as he turned back to his father, with the Sword of Purity in his hands and started walking back to where Kevin was standing. "You do not speak with Commander Forkman. He comes to me to talk about the military situation because you do not listen to him. And he tells me the truth, while you tell everyone that the war is going well."

Suddenly, the king appeared cross. "The truth is what I dictate it to be, Andrew. Do not go behind my back to get your beliefs."

As Kevin heard this, he understood now why King Arnold IX had to be removed. Any ruler who believed the truth was whatever words came out of their mouth was unfit to rule. How could someone in his position not accept reality? To hear the world was different than they believed and to shape their nation to their reality and not the real world? It was not simply dangerous; it was reckless, and indicative of someone to whom only the power they held mattered to them. Kron had told him before, "one man should not ever rule the populace", and Professor Magnon had said the same as well. This was proof as to why.

"No, father, that is not how this will work," Andrew stated firmly. He handed the scabbard to Kevin, with the sword inside. The guards around the room prepared their weapons, after hearing the prince make such a provocative statement, but still they did not act otherwise, as they were also dedicated to protecting the prince.

The king asked, "What do you mean?"

"You cannot speak the truth into existence," Andrew answered. "It is always there, no matter how many lies are spoken to obfuscate the truth. Aurana needs a bit of honesty and a good look in the mirror. How can we give it that when you demand the truth is what you say, while you care not to learn the actual truth?"

"Andrew, silence!" commanded the king. "If you continue to speak up to me like this in official session, I will have no choice but to have you taken to your chambers and secured."

"Yeah, that is not going to happen, either," Andrew said. Then, he turned to Kevin. "Arrest him for treason."

"What?!" exclaimed the king, leaping to his feet. "Guards!"

Quickly, Kevin pulled out the Sword of Purity. As the guards started to approach, Kevin took a second to find his inner serenity, enough so that Andrew was slightly confused why he was not moving. Then, the Sword of Purity illuminated in its bright blue magic.

The guards stammered backward at the sight of the illuminated sword. It was, to everyone who had heard of it, clearly Vincent Stryker's sword.

Kevin had thought how to make this as official-sounding as possible as he approached the throne with the lit Sword of Purity. "In the name of Aurana and its continued existence, I hereby place you,

King Arnold IX, under arrest for failure to act in the best interest of the kingdom." It was not truly a crime, but that was the best Kevin could improvise.

Arnold IX failed to act, surprised to have a sword in his face. His guards all stood back watching, as Kevin slowly made his way up to the king's throne. He was serious. Even so, as Kevin approached, he was very scared the guards would make a move for him. He would be dead on the floor very quickly if something did not happen soon.

"Andrew, how could you?" demanded the king. "You would commit treason for 'the best interest of the kingdom'?" asked the king. "How paradoxical, indeed."

"There is no paradox to it," stated Andrew, firmly. He then ordered. "All guards stand down, immediately. You will take no action for the next couple of minutes."

Now, the guards were caught in a tough predicament. Their oaths were to the royal family, but this was very much a conflict between two members of that family.

Kevin stopped short of the throne. As he did, sword pointed at the king, Andrew handed him the papers. Kevin then took a deep breath, knowing he was doing, and handed the papers to Arnold IX, sword still pointed at him. "You will sign these."

Arnold was stunned as he looked at the documents. The headline on them boldly stated them to be a declaration of abdication, that the king was voluntarily agreeing to give up the throne. "My son," he began, addressing Andrew, "who is this young man you have sent to arrest me?"

"Why, father, do you not know?" began Andrew, somewhat cocky as he stepped up next to Kevin, "I was honest when I told you he is the son of Vincent Stryker. He will be my Vanguard as I begin my rule."

"This commoner?" interrupted Arnold IX. "What are you thinking, Andrew, my son? You have demanded I step down from the throne of Aurana! Today, you have committed treason against the very country that you would someday rule!"

Andrew looked aside, with the answer to this question already in mind. "It would be a greater treason…" he paused for a moment, struggling to say the words because of his emotions, "to do nothing at all. It would be a greater treason to Aurana," he said, regaining confidence, "to let you continue to rule this land and drive it into oblivion before I am ever given the opportunity to rule. I have done what is right, and considered it carefully before taking any action."

It was a realization that Andrew had had, one that had finally truly sunk in not just through words and actions, but through feeling and intuition. Seeing Andrew's emotion King Arnold IX asked in fury, "My son, why have you done this? Why must you force this from me?"

Andrew looked down for a moment, almost afraid to make the response that he knew he had to. "Because, father," he began nervously, "you never listened. Whether or not you thought what you were doing was right, you would not listen to those who were trying to help you. You were not listening to your advisors, you were not listening to your commanders, and you would not…" Prince Andrew could not say it, although he knew he had to force the words through. "You would not listen to me, father. We cannot make our country great if we continue to obfuscate the truth with falsehoods and proclaim it to be so. And now, Aurana is suffering." Everything seemed to open up all at that point. There was definitely more than just politics behind the breakdown in relations between Andrew and his father, and both of them realized it at this point. Andrew continued through this, "Being royal is not a right. It is a responsibility to our people to determine what is right for them, listen to them, and help them see their dreams as we find ours in making Aurana prosperous. If one of us cannot do that anymore, then it is time for that person to step down."

Arnold IX said nothing. No more words were needed.

Seeing his life in danger if he did not comply, that the guards had not moved at the doors and that Kevin had a sword nearly to his neck, Arnold signed the abdication documents and left his son in charge of the war-torn nation of Aurana. As he set the pen down, Arnold IX said little. He was both angered and ashamed, not only to lose his kingdom but to have his son effectively put him in his place. Then he rose, abdication papers in hand, and passed them to Andrew. Arnold set down his crown, scepter, and cape on the throne.

Prince Andrew II accepted the papers and watched as his father walked toward the door of the throne room. Knowing that Commander Forkman was working on dismissing the guards outside the throne room, he ordered the guards to throw the doors open. Since he was now the new king, and the guards had seen him sign the papers, they did as they were ordered without hesitation. Outside the room near the courtyard entrance, Commander Forkman and two soldiers were there to escort the deposed king.

Andrew knew it would likely not be until the next day when the high priest of Aurana would come to coronate him, so he took his father's former standing position near the throne, but did not don the crown. Then, Andrew took up the scepter and said, "Kevin, would you please kneel?"

Kevin stepped one step forward and knelt, as he was requested to do. Everyone including the soldiers in the room watched intently, as there would be many witnesses to what was about to come.

"I do hate to make this so informal and rushed," continued Andrew, "but as I understand, you do have a job to do, as Professor Magnon has let me know. Tomorrow will be a busy day in the capital, and you will not want to be here for too long, for Aurana City will likely be swamped with crowds before too long because of what has happened here today. Therefore, I am going to make this as short as possible, and just do this here and now."

Kevin looked up. "The coup is done. You still want to go through with this?" In this moment he had forgotten about being measured for clothes yesterday.

Prince Andrew nodded. "When I told you that I wanted you to be my Vanguard, I meant it, whether it was necessary for this or not. You have shown me the kind of person you are. I believe someone who is willing to help and do what is right, even when it is not to your personal benefit, is the kind of person who should represent Aurana."

Feeling very honored by Andrew's kind words, Kevin lowered his head in respect as Andrew extended his arm with scepter in hand.

"Kevin Trent Stryker, today you have done much for Aurana, your homeland. As a reward for what you have done, I hereby award you the title of Vanguard of Aurana, for you will be the forward guard, the one who keeps Aurana safe through your works. You may rise."

Andrew withdrew his scepter as Kevin stood up. "Now," continued Andrew to Kevin, "Aurana relies on its vanguard to bring peace to the nation. I am certain, though, that you can handle this burden. You possess more heart than my best men. From this day on, I proclaim that it may be said of you, 'the heart of the dragon, the spirit of the phoenix, the strength of a warrior together united.'"

Kevin was not really sure what that meant, but it sounded nice. He reached for Andrew's hand to shake it. "Thank you, Andrew. This is a great honor, indeed."

"No, Kevin," interrupted Andrew, "it is I who should be thanking you. You have given Aurana a chance, and you have at the same time given me a second chance with my father for us to see each other as people. I am sure that in due time, he will come around. For that, I owe you the world. However, I can only give you so much at the moment." He paused and looked to Professor Magnon. "Professor?"

Hearing this cue, Professor Magnon pulled out a set of clothing and set them in Kevin's hands. Kevin examined these pieces of clothing and realized what they were. They were a military uniform jacket and pants. It was a full military uniform in green, the color of Aurana. On the arms were patches, the largest of which was a red triangle with a black triangle inside of it. Kevin did not visually recognize this symbol, but Andrew knew Kevin was not going to, so he explained it to Kevin. "That patch is the marking of the Vanguard. It is symbolic of your title."

Examining the jacket, Kevin was amazed with it in general, much less the fact that it was his to wear. As he examined it, he flipped it to look at the front, and there, on the right side, stitched above the chest pocket, were the words "K.T. STRYKER" in bold capital letters.

Wanting to try it on, Kevin flipped the jacket around his shoulders. He left the jacket unbuttoned, however, leaving his red shirt exposed in the front. It was very comfortable like this, and Kevin was unsure that he ever wanted to button it up. He would put on the matching pants, in the same green color as the jacket, later when he had a little more privacy to change pants.

Andrew continued, "I have also arranged for transportation for you and Caitlin to the Nuve border. You will be escorted by some troops and horses past Bladinstar. We will take you as far as the Aurun River, right across the border from the Nuve town of Venarose. It will shorten the time you need to get there, and it will be waiting for you just outside the palace right away."

"Right away?" asked Kevin. "Really, that fast?"

"Of course," answered Prince Andrew. "If you wait too long, Aurana City will be overcrowded with people coming to see the new king, not to mention the skeptics that will be looking for those involved. For your own safety and sanity, you have to leave now, before you end up stuck here."

Kevin nodded, knowing that the prince was right. "Then I guess it's time to say goodbye, Andrew." Kevin then turned to address everyone. "Where is everyone here headed next?"

"To put Aurana on the right path," answered Andrew. "Hopefully everything will work out well from now on for Aurana. I will see to that myself."

After the prince finished his sentence, Professor Magnon stepped in with Kron next to him. He said to Kevin and Caitlin, "I will be taking Kron with me, and we will catch up with you two later." The professor raised a finger to Kron, silencing him for a bit. "We have something that we must do. Caitlin, please take good care of Kevin, and Kevin, take care of my daughter."

Frustrated, Kron said nothing. What was the professor up to this time?

"And so it has come time for us to part," said Andrew as Kevin was straightening out his new jacket. Despite having taken several minutes already, Andrew knew he could not keep Kevin for very long. "It is a shame that you cannot stay one more night and enjoy a day in the palace, but I think it is for the best."

"Unfortunately, I think you're right," said Kevin as he shook Andrew's hand one last time, disappointed in not being able to remain longer in the company of the prince. "I need to start moving quickly if I'm going to keep up with everything. But I am sure that your coronation will go well without me, and I look forward to an Aurana under your rule."

Andrew smiled. "As do I look forward to seeing what the

Vanguard can do for Aurana. Kevin, had I never met you, I do not think I would be the same ruler as that which I will be now."

"I recommend you stop this," interrupted Caitlin, approaching Kevin and the prince. "If we're going to make it out of town before the ruckus, then we have to leave now."

Kevin was surprised. Although Caitlin had always been ignorant of emotions to him, he had never seen her be so blunt about it. Kevin was not sure if this was the first he had ever seen of this and it was just a regular quality of Caitlin, or if it was something new to even her.

"Indeed, let us go," said Andrew as he pointed to the door. He was indicating for Kevin and Caitlin to follow him out the door, which they did. Andrew was leading Kevin and Caitlin to the courtyard, from which they could exit the palace. Through the emerald-colored halls they walked, down the long hallways of the palace. Kevin was not exactly sure of the way out himself from the throne room he was just in, so he was grateful to have the prince leading him out.

"I have orders for you, Kevin," continued the prince, as they walked down the hall. "I have heard from Professor Magnon that you are seeking to reunite the Triple Alliance?"

Kevin's eyes widened. "I mean, that's sort of the idea," he said. "I don't really know how to do that."

"So I understand," Andrew said. "Having a friend kidnapped by Desolunar does not give you many options, I can believe. At the very least, I can give you the next piece. I can rekindle Aurora's alliance with Nuve and Scurnia, but in Nuve there is a civil war happening. The most I can ask for, as my new Vanguard, is for you to go to Nuvenia, the capital city of Nuve, and see if you can get them to put down the war for a while and commit to fending off the Desolunar threat first."

Kevin looked confused. "How am I supposed to do that?"

"That is for you to figure out," Andrew answered, "but you now represent Aurana in a formal sense as the Vanguard. You have all the tools I can give you."

"I think you can do it," said Caitlin, grabbing Kevin's attention. "And I'm still coming along."

Looking over at Caitlin, Kevin smiled at her. It did make him feel better to know that Caitlin was still supportive of him.

As Caitlin finished this statement, she and Kevin had made it to the courtyard with Andrew leading them. At the far end of the courtyard, to Kevin's surprise, there were horses and a military escort waiting at the final checkpoint. This escort would cut the travel time to Nuve almost in half if they moved at a reasonably fast pace.

Unsurprisingly, Kevin and Andrew took several minutes to divide from one another as they said their final goodbyes. Within a day, they had become friends. For Kevin, this would be a strong alliance to be friends with the king of Aurana, and from the other side of the coin, Kevin was willing to do anything for the new king. Likewise, as Andrew pointed out, he would be willing to provide Kevin with anything he needed, although Kevin declined any monetary compensation. After all, Kevin was the Vanguard of Aurana now. He was the forward guard, constantly putting all of his efforts into helping his homeland. This was not a job to be doing for money. It was one to be doing for the love of his home country.

"And remember," added Andrew as Kevin mounted his steed, "any work that you do in Nuve is on the authority of Aurana, and you represent us there. If they will unify, we will support them, too."

Kevin nodded confidently in acknowledgment to this comment.

As Kevin said his final goodbyes, Andrew ordered the escort to proceed. At the head of the escort were two military officials, followed by Kevin and Caitlin, then two more military soldiers. They accompanied Kevin and Caitlin to a covered carriage, waiting at the courtyard gates.

Chapter 22

The Poisoned Rose

Nuve extends from the Aurun River to the middle of the Peaked Mountains, along the tallest peaks in the center. To the south, it formerly ran into much of what is currently Desolunar territory, at the border of a wasteland simply known as The Wastes. That land to the south is where ancient Nuve stood before its expansion, centered around the former capital of Cardol on the Calphos River.

Nuve is made up of five provinces: Soverenia, Tundrosa, Katalina, Cornelia, and Leticon. Desolunar has already invaded southern Nuve. Their acquisitions include the city of Cardol, which lost its status as the capital city of Nuve because it was conquered. Currently, the capital of Nuve is the city of Nuvenia, possibly the most impregnable city in existence. Large bridges connect to the city from the west and north, where the city lies on an island in the very deep Abyss of the Royal Sovereign. It is one of the most fortified cities, both naturally and man-made, that exists. All around Nuve, from the Aurun River to the foothills of the Peaked Mountains, a barren plain with limited resources across the entire countryside spaces out Nuve. Much of the land is infertile or is only barely so.

Kevin had never left Aurana before. This would be a whole new experience. As the escort left Aurana City, with Kevin and Caitlin riding in a carriage toward the east, Kevin considered the adventure in front of him. Somehow he had to end a civil war… or at least bring it to peace long enough to ally with Aurana and resist Desolunar. Maybe Caitlin had some ideas.

Caitlin. Kevin could not deny what he felt for her. Though it had seemed like folly at first, a simple oddity, Kevin had come to realize that his feelings for Caitlin were real. He still had not changed in believing that there was more to Caitlin than she showed. Perhaps in Nuve he would find the truth behind the girl's discipline, but he still did not want to force anything. He wondered, though, if behind her hard exterior she felt anything for him beyond friendship.

Arthur also nagged on Kevin's mind. Kevin knew this nagging would be present until the day he found Arthur, or what had become of his best friend. Arthur was Kevin's closest friend, after all. Until Arthur was safe, or his fate was known, Kevin could not have any peace of mind whatsoever. Even if every other issue in his life and on his quest was put to rest, Kevin was sure of this.

After the high noon and into the mid-afternoon, the escort reached the outer limits of Bladinstar, currently the third largest city in Aurana and a popular site of tourism, as Nuve was only a day's walk away. On horseback, like this escort was, it would be much less.

The military escort routed Kevin and Caitlin through Bladinstar, not stopping. Nonetheless, Kevin was impressed with Bladinstar as his horse continued through the city. Down the main thoroughfare of the city, Kevin managed to see the splendor of the touring industry. As Caitlin pointed out, however, the tourism industry was down at the moment due to the wars with Desolunar.

About halfway through the city, Caitlin pointed out to Kevin the Bladinstar School, where her father, Professor Magnon, taught classes every day for years. It was one of the simpler and less elegant structures in Bladinstar, but Kevin was still glad to see and learn something about Caitlin and Professor Magnon from this.

"My father teaches magic control and ability here," she said. "It's the only school for magic left in the world, as far as I know, and there aren't many students."

Kevin was curious. "Why not?"

"Well, anymore not everyone develops a knack for magic," Caitlin answered. "You can have natural talent, but even if you don't, you can develop skill in magic if you train hard at it. Not only does this take a while, but it's not easy to make the time commitment to come here unless someone else is supporting you financially."

"Fair enough," nodded Kevin. "Is that why magic is sort of a dying art form?"

"I think that's part of it," acknowledged Caitlin, but it's not like talented individuals are easy to come by, either. At least, that's what my father says. He does his best to teach everything he can, but even he will say it's getting harder and harder to find people to teach."

Kevin shook his head. "That's a shame," he said. "Imagine what more wizards, sorcerers, and every other recognized magic ranking could do for Aurana."

"Quite a lot," acknowledged Caitlin. "Wizards are valued, and that's why my father has so many political connections as he does. If you're certified by the Aurana Department of Magic Affairs, you're a desired commodity in many ways."

"I bet," acknowledged Kevin.

There was a long pause.

Kevin then asked Caitlin, "I know you're much more worldly than I am. Do you know anything about the civil war in Nuve?"

"A bit," acknowledged Caitlin. "What do you want to know?"

"Why they're warring," he answered.

Caitlin thought about this for a minute. "In short, because there is distrust of the king of Nuve and the Collective Council, its elected leaders. They serve as a check on each other, but when all they do is bicker with each other, it leads to hostility."

"I can see that," interjected Kevin. "I think I'd be annoyed if it were my country, too."

"As would I," Caitlin said. "Three major factions are dividing Nuve up into multiple pieces. The strongest of these factions is the Demonstrative Organization of Northern Nuve, or Demons, which control much of the northern tundra and some plains to the west of the capital of Nuvenia. They are not to be confused with Demonicus or Desolunar, who has no relation to them that I know of. The second faction controls much of southwestern Nuve, above the border of Desolunar. This group is known as the Cornelia Chimeras, and they are in open rebellion with Nuve. The Cornelia Chimeras are so named for the province of Nuve that they control, Cornelia. Cornelia remains untouched by Desolunar due to the presence of the Cornelia Chimeras actively being in rebellion. The last faction isn't so much of a faction as it is a group, known as the Knights of the Dragon, a small yet powerful collection of warriors. It may be hard to consider them a faction since they are more or less just a few warriors, but Nuve has considered them a threat since they reside mostly in the mountains between Rugger and Vallia, cities in eastern Nuve and western Scurnia, respectively. Not much more is known in general about the Knights of the Dragon, other than that they are led by the vicious Lord Dragon."

Almost as soon as Caitlin had finished her explanation, the carriage stopped and there was a knock on the carriage door before it opened. "Excuse me, Vanguard, but we've arrived at our overnight stop," said an Auranian soldier.

Here, Kevin and Caitlin both disembarked and were escorted to a hotel for the night. Each were given their own separate rooms. They shared dinner and more conversation in the hotel's pub before turning in for the night. The next day started early when the same Auranian soldier woke them up to continue the escort. They barely had time to grab breakfast at the pub before the carriage was ready to set off again.

As the lights and glamour of Bladinstar disappeared into the distance, Kevin thought of life in such a city, where tourism was the industry. Surely, Kevin was certain, it was not such a glamorous life for everyone who lived in Bladinstar; although he was also certain that the wealth of the city had helped somewhat.

Directly across the Aurun River, about a day's travel east of Bladinstar, lies the city of Venarose, a dark town known in Nuve for its crime rates. The town itself is a center of contention between the government of Nuve and the Demons faction, although the city's crime and slum issues have made it difficult for either to have a strong grasp. The government of Nuve is the only recognized government in Nuve, however, and is recognized as the controller of Venarose.

Soon enough after a long day of travel, the sun began to set, and Kevin started to grow worried as he sat on his horse that he would not be making it to Venarose in time. Though he was not looking forward to arriving in the town during the night, Kevin had spent his entire day already, since leaving Aurana City and helping Andrew out in the morning by ousting King Arnold IX, traveling to make it to Venarose by nightfall. It was getting to be very late, and the darkening sky seemed to be growing ever more ominous as Kevin traveled on.

As the sky began to turn black and the sun had disappeared over the horizon, a call came from the escorting troops at the front of the line. "The Aurun River is ahead," called out one of the troops to the rest of the escort.

Kevin looked out, trying hard to see the river in the darkness. At last, however, he was able to see it. Dirty, brown, and cloudy, the Aurun River ran full of sediment from the soil below it. It was both a wide and deep river, the lifeblood of several communities around it.

Across the river, torches burned, providing some illumination. It was Venarose, the poisoned rose itself. A dim glow formed around the city because of the torches, just a faint indicator of where the town was in the nighttime. As for what the city looked like itself, Kevin could not tell from this distance. He would have to do so when he got into the town.

Kevin could see that he was approaching a bridge on his horse as his vision became clearer upon nearing the Aurun River. It was a simple wooden bridge, built with sturdy supports bracing it from the river below. It was not a suspension bridge, but instead a solid one. As wide as it was, there were no rails on the bridge at all.

"This is where we leave you," said the leader of the escort from the front, as he pulled up on his horse to stop it from crossing the bridge. "We are going to need both of you to dismount your horses right away. They cannot travel with you past the border."

Acknowledging this, both Kevin and Caitlin dismounted their horses and walked toward the bridge. Standing on the edge of the bridge, the escort leader wished luck to the Vanguard and his accomplice, then commanded his escort and horses to begin heading back to Aurana City.

Once they had finally disappeared from sight, Kevin turned to Caitlin and said, "Well, I guess we had better start going. There's no safety in waiting here for the night."

"Indeed," responded Caitlin in her normal tone. "Let us go, then."

Following this, Kevin began to walk down the bridge to Venarose, with Caitlin right behind him. The bridge was dark, as no torches illuminated it. Venarose was just off to the left of the bridge. As they started to reach the halfway point of the bridge, Kevin began to see just how rundown Venarose was. The entire town, at least from what Kevin could see, was very poorly kept. It was a moderately sized town, probably holding a few hundred people. From the little that Kevin could see from the bridge, it looked like a place that the gods had forsaken. The image of this could not escape Kevin's head.

"Venarose," Kevin pondered aloud. "Sounds appropriate for the town, based on how it looks. The name almost sounds like a combination of the words 'venom' and 'rose'."

"It is," answered Caitlin. "That is the root behind the name of Venarose. That is also why many people have given the town the nickname 'The Poisoned Rose'. It is tainted and withering, just like a dying flower."

"Well, that's pretty appalling," responded Kevin. "Why would anyone name a town after a bad reputation that it is known for?"

Before Caitlin could answer, Kevin heard something snap. He immediately stopped in his tracks, and extended his right arm to stop Caitlin as well. Closely, Kevin was listening for any more sounds, his suspicions aroused from the cracking sound.

As Caitlin stopped as well, she asked, "What's wrong, Kevin?"

"Did you hear that?" responded Kevin.

Caitlin was confused. "Hear what?" she asked.

"That sound," Kevin answered. "Someone's nearby."

As he said this, a whistling noise went through the air. It stopped very suddenly, almost as soon as it had begun. Caitlin was not sure what that noise was, until she turned to Kevin.

There was a dart sticking in his neck.

Kevin realized there was something in his neck, and pulled it out to take a look. He saw the dart and realized exactly what it was; in a town like Venarose and its surrounding area, with the large amount of crime in the city, it almost had to be a sleeper dart.

As this thought crossed his mind, though, Kevin fell unconscious, toppling to the floor of the bridge. He was right, and the sleeper dart had caused him to pass out. Caitlin turned, trying to find the assailant so she could defend herself and Kevin. As she tried to seek out the assailant, though, another whistling sound penetrated the air, and another dart hit Caitlin in the side of the neck. She fell over and collapsed face first, unconscious on the bridge floor.

Chapter 23

The Syndicate

When he finally regained consciousness, Kevin could tell he was in a chair with his hands tied behind his back. His sword was gone, though, and so was his military jacket. A faint smell of stale air was present, and so was a dim light that Kevin could barely see through his recovering eyes. His hearing was working well, however, and he could hear two men talking in front of him. Still struggling to overcome the effects of the drug in the sleeper dart, he tried to focus all that he could on listening to the conversation they were having.

"Hast thou administered the antidote yet?" asked the first individual.

"Yes, sir," answered the second person. Both of them sounded like men, very scruffy and with very odd accents. Perhaps, Kevin thought to himself, this was a Nuve accent. The voice of the second individual sounded much deeper than the first.

"Excellent," responded the first person. "Thou hast done well. Now, what kind of objects have thou retrieved off these individuals?"

Kevin's vision started to come back at this point, and he was able to see both men walk over to a wooden table next to him. The room was lit only by a couple of torches, and appeared to have walls made of whitewashed wood. Little else was in the room.

"Let us see," responded the second person, as he stood over the table. "There are some preserved provisions and a small pouch containing some silver and copper. This jacket, however, is odd. It appears to be Auranian military, but the patches on the arms do not match any known rankings in the forces of Aurana's army."

"Let mine own eyes have a look at it," interrupted the first man, curious as to the decorations on the jacket. He began to examine it with much scrutiny. "Well, the name inscribed on the jacket is not one we know. It is marked, 'K.T. STRYKER'." Then, the first man looked closer at the patches on the side, and began to laugh in a bit of an evil tone.

"What hast thou discovered?" asked the second man.

"See this?" the first man said, indicating the red and black triangle patch. "This patch identifies a Vanguard, one named by the king to be the forward guard of a country. There has not been one of these from Aurana in a while, but it appears there is a new one at last, and he is in our custody. Now, grunt, if thou wouldst not be willing to continue?"

"As thou requests," responded the second man. "This sword, in its scabbard, was also in his possession."

"Interesting," responded the first man as he picked up the sword by the scabbard to examine it. "This design is one I hath not seen before. Now, let us see if the blade is equally amusing."

The first man grabbed the hilt of the sword, and screamed before letting go. Like it had done with every person other than Kevin who had grabbed it, the sword sent a painful shock up the first man's arm. He dropped the sword as soon as he felt the pain, clutching his right arm. As he did so, he started to laugh in a somewhat evil tone, as if he had come to a realization that he was glad to know.

"What hast thou discovered?" asked the second man, curious.

The first man looked to the second. "This is a locked sword," he said. "It used to be in the old days, when many wizards and spellcasters were also wielders of the sword, or what we might call a paladin today, they would lock their swords with a magic spell that made their swords unable to be wielded by anyone other than themselves. It would appear that we have located one."

"How much does thou think we can sell it for?" interjected the second man.

Sell it. The words just rang through Kevin's slowly awakening mind and he finally realized who he was listening to: black marketeers. A common problem around the nations of the world, members of the black market were often searching for items to sell by robbery, pick pocketing, and in rare cases, kidnapping. They were not just valuing Kevin's items like his sword; from the discussions of his jacket, Kevin was sure they were valuing him as a hostage.

"Depends," responded the first man. "But let us wait on this discussion. Someone has awakened." He was indicating to Kevin, who was trying to see using his eyes as the drug wore off. "Hello, sleepy one," he said to Kevin. "Canst thou hear me?"

Kevin was shaking his head, trying hard to get as much of his sight and other senses back and fully coherent before he responded. "Yeah," he finally said. "I can, but it's pretty hard to see you right now."

The first man turned to the second. "Auranian lower or middle class. Thou canst tell from his accent." Then he turned back to Kevin. "It is normal for thou to have such symptoms as the sleeping drug wears off. Does thou know where thyself is currently?"

Still trying to see, Kevin shook his head. "No," he answered. "Who are you, and why am I here?"

"Thou art in the presence of The Syndicate," responded the first man. "The Syndicate is the largest sector of organized crime in Nuve. We openly support no faction of government, nor do we support anyone who interferes with our actions."

"Oh?" responded Kevin. "Then who do you support behind closed doors?"

The first man just stared at Kevin. "Thou hast a smart mouth for one who holds the title of Vanguard, Mr. K.T. Stryker. Normally, it would not matter if thou were a smartass or not, but since thou does not hold more than pocket change in terms of the coins we found on thy person, thou art of little use to us so far."

Kevin's vision was beginning to return to normal, so he began to take note of who exactly he was up against. The first man was very well dressed and well kept, of about average height. The second was a larger man, with a very muscular build, wearing cheap clothing that was torn. "If I am of so little use to you, then why do you keep me here? Why do you neither let me free nor end my life?"

At this, the first man became angry and lashed out, smacking Kevin across the face. "Because I choose to!" he exclaimed. "And you will do as I say, or be punished!"

Kevin coughed, trying to breathe the stale air as best as he could despite not being accustomed to it. "You must be the leader of The

Syndicate, I presume. Your clothing, your demeanor, everything suggests it."

"Thy logic is solid," responded the first man, "and close to the truth. I am the regional leader of the Venarose region of The Syndicate. Perhaps thou art not as thickheaded and cocky as I had originally thought. Nonetheless, I would not presume thou to be a Vanguard upon first glance."

Seeing no need to continue, but instead needing to find Caitlin, Kevin asked strongly, "Where's the girl who was brought in with me?"

This time, the regional leader did not snap at Kevin for asking a question. He instead responded coolly, "That is something that is none of thy concern anymore. Nor shall it ever be again, for as long as thou are in our custody."

As the regional leader said this, the door shot open, and in rushed an armed man, short of breath. He held a spear in his arms that was broken in half at its midpoint. "Sir!" he exclaimed as he rushed into the room. "We have an escape in progress! Bottom floor! Someone is using magic to fight!"

Magic. Maybe it was Caitlin, Kevin realized.

"Get my halberd and gauntlets!" barked the regional leader, running to the door. "And get more men down there! Do not let the prisoner escape!" Out the door flew the regional leader, with the man who ran in to get him. The door slammed behind them, and only silence filled the air after the slam.

Now it was just Kevin and the second man standing guard in the room. Kevin was not sure what he could do next. If it was Caitlin rampaging through the bottom floor of this building, then Kevin had to break himself loose and escape with her. But how could he overcome the guard? Calling his sword to him could work, but then he would be spotted for sure and possibly killed for attempting to escape before he broke himself loose.

Several seconds after the door slam, the large second man drew a knife from his belt, approaching Kevin slowly then circling around the chair to his backside. Kevin felt an icy fear shiver down his spine as he felt the man breathing down his neck.

Suddenly, Kevin felt the ropes that bound his hands snap and fall off his wrists. He was surprised to find that his arms were free now. "Art thou all right?" asked the second man.

Kevin was still stunned that he was free. "Who are you?" he asked.

The large man answered, "I am an undercover operative investigating The Syndicate, under the order of the Demons."

"The Demons?" asked Kevin. "The faction of the north?"

"Apparently thou hast not been in Nuve for long," answered the operative, crossing his arms. "But this discussion must wait until we are out of here. The magic attack on the bottom floor, is it thy friend?"

A little puzzled, Kevin asked, "It's not yours?"

"Negative," answered the operative. "The Demons have not been planning any attack here for any reason. Our policy is never to give up a cover unless it is absolutely necessary."

Kevin thought for a second. "It would make sense that it is a friend of mine, then: a girl named Caitlin who was captured alongside me. But why would you blow your cover here to set free two Auranians?"

The large operative glared at Kevin. "It is also the policy of the Demons not to directly, or through inaction, allow any nation's Vanguard to come to harm, even if it is that of Nuve's official government. Thou art the actual Vanguard of Aurana, correct?"

Kevin gave the operative a nod. "Yes," he answered. "Kevin Trent Stryker, Vanguard of Aurana."

"Very well, then," answered the operative as Kevin walked over to the table to put on his jacket and sword, as well as grab his other possessions. "If thou walks out the door," the operative continued as Kevin did this, "thou will find a flight of stairs. Follow that down to the bottom floor and get thyself and thy friend out of here. I will meet up with thou outside of Venarose on the road to the north."

"Okay. But where are you headed?" asked Kevin.

"To protect my cover to The Syndicate," the operative answered. "This way, hopefully my entire operation will not be shot because of thy presence here."

This made Kevin feel a little bad for his timing in arriving to Venarose and being captured, but he had no time to waste. He had to get moving. Without so much as a thought, he nodded and rushed for the door, then out to the left and down the stairs.

There were two flights of stairs Kevin had to run down. At the bottom of the stairs, though, many areas of the floor were on fire, although the building had not turned into an inferno yet here. Had Caitlin been shooting fireballs in defense to escape? It seemed likely to Kevin by this point.

Also at the bottom of the stairs was a guard, dead. It looked like the fire had roasted him. This made Kevin worried. How violent was Caitlin, really? What were her limits? It was something Kevin did not have time to consider at the moment.

As Kevin hit the first hallway at the bottom of the stairs, he saw one of the most frightening sights he had ever seen. The building had become an inferno on the bottom floor, and the hallways were lit up in fire. Smoke was starting to build at the very top of the hallway.

Looking down further, Kevin saw a door. It was large, thick, not yet in flames, and had a window placed in it. Kevin was sure it was a door to the outside, and he was willing to risk a trip through the heat for escape.

Cautiously, Kevin took a couple of steps into the hallway. The heat was nearly unbearable, but he knew that he had to keep pressing on. The door was a good distance away, however, and the flames were getting higher. The more Kevin looked down the hall, the more he felt like the trip down the hall would take an eternity.

As he made it to about a quarter of the way down the hall, a beam snapped directly in front of Kevin and started to fall. Kevin only had a couple of seconds to step back and avoid getting hit. He was unscathed, but now the beam was wedged diagonally between the burning walls of the hallway, impeding his progress. There was no exit the other way, and Kevin had to escape the burning Syndicate building.

Trying not to burn himself, Kevin reached for the Sword of Purity, hoping that the metal was not too hot yet to make it untouchable. If he could use it, he could cut through the beam and open his pathway forward.

Kevin began to touch the Sword of Purity, hoping it would not burn his fingers. Surprisingly, though, the sword had not changed temperature even in the heat of the burning building. He was unsure as to why this was, but given the powers he had already learned about with the Sword of Purity since he began to wield it, he was not surprised. Concentrating, Kevin lit the sword up in its bright blue magic, and sliced at the beam on both sides. Using the sword's energy, he made two clean cuts, which dropped the beam to the ground. He then hopped over the beam and continued to proceed down the hallway, this time with a running pace.

At the halfway point down the hallway, about the same distance between the thick door and the stairs, another hallway crossed with the one Kevin was in. Kevin stopped to see if anyone was down either hallway before he continued on. Nothing appeared to be an exit more so than the door in front of him.

But as Kevin tried to continue past the intersection, something pulled him backwards. It was not throwing Kevin backwards, but it was strong enough to be noticeable. As he felt it, Kevin knew exactly what it was. The tugging was familiar. It was the Sword of Purity pulling him, just like it had done in Aurana City the day before. But what did it want now? This building was on fire, and Kevin had to escape it. Kevin kept telling himself that, even going so far as to say it out loud to "convince" the sword of that.

Still, the tugging persisted. Coming to the realization that no matter what he did, the sword would not quit tugging at him until he went in the direction it wanted to go, Kevin decided to follow the Sword of Purity, maintaining a firm grip and a slow pace to make sure the sword did not drag him along the ground again like it had done in Aurana City. In a burning building where even the floors were beginning to catch fire, this was unsafe, not to mention unpleasant in any place that was not on fire.

After returning to the intersection, the sword tugged Kevin to the right, down another hallway that was on fire. Kevin was nervous to follow the sword down the hallway. It would take him further from the exit, and Kevin was not sure how much time the building had left before it collapsed due to fire damage.

What would Kron tell him to do? What would Professor Magnon tell him to do? Kevin kept asking himself these questions, hoping that maybe he would find the right decision somewhere. Kevin knew he had been reckless before with the lives of his friends, and these decisions had resulted in their imprisonments. Now, with his own life in his hands, could he trust the Sword of Purity?

With faith in himself and his decision-making, Kevin let the sword guide him down the hallway. The sword guided Kevin down the hallway until about three doors had passed on his right side. At the fourth, the sword stopped and tugged Kevin in the direction of the fourth door. It looked just like any of the rest of the doors around the building.

This confused Kevin. What could be behind that door? The only answer was to find out.

With the hallways burning, Kevin decided that the door would be too hot to open by the knob. He would most likely burn his hand trying to open the door. Instead, Kevin had an alternative ready. He stepped back, concentrated with his sword, and took a broad, almost vertical slash at the door. The door fell apart as Kevin finished his slash. The end without the hinges flew off and onto the ground, and the end with the hinges stayed hinged and swung open. Beyond the threshold of the door, Kevin saw something he never expected. It hit him like a thunderbolt, for this was why the sword took him here.

In a chair in the middle of the room, Caitlin sat unconscious, still tied to her chair. Kevin had been completely wrong about who set the fire. Caitlin did not start it; instead, she had been trapped here the whole time. By this point, a bunch of questions were racing through Kevin's head, although he did not have time to answer them all. He had to rescue Caitlin and escape the burning building himself as well.

Circling around to the back of the chair, Kevin used his sword to cut the ropes that bound Caitlin's hands. Then, he tried to wake Caitlin. He called her name, shook her gently, and even yelled in her ear as a last resort. Still, she did not awaken.

Desperate to save Caitlin's life, Kevin sheathed his sword and picked up Caitlin lengthwise. He was able to lift her frame in this way, but he was struggling to do so. The fires were quickly becoming hotter, the smoke was building up more, and the building was approaching ever closer to collapse.

Yet Kevin continued to press on. By shear willpower, he was able to carry Caitlin out of the room, back to the intersection, and down the hall to the thick door. At the end of the hall, Kevin leaned in and managed to grab the door handle. He opened the door as quick as he could, and rushed through it with Caitlin in his arms.

A cool breeze fluttered in the air as the dark, peaceful night sky loomed overhead. Sure enough, Kevin was right about the door leading to the outside. Taking no chances, Kevin continued to run off with Caitlin to the north side of town, per the instructions of the Demons operative. He had to stop and take several breaks on his run, setting Caitlin down at every stop. As he rushed through Venarose, Kevin took note of the buildings and city as he ran past. Much of the town was in distinct disrepair, including the building that he had just escaped. It was one of the town's larger buildings, and was still on fire as Kevin fled to the north.

Venarose was a relatively large town, possibly a borderline small city. Some ports sat alongside the Aurun River on the western edge, and as dirty as they were, they may have been the nicest places in the town given the dismal state of the urban areas. Everything appeared to be in extreme disrepair, and many buildings looked as though they had been standing for ages. Torches lit the city's main four streets, but the other smaller streets in the town were not lit at all. This made the side streets a dangerous place for travelers at night.

Close to the town limits, Kevin heard a loud thud as he continued running. Although he had neither the time nor the strength to stop and look back, he presumed that the burning building of The Syndicate had finally collapsed. Still, without hesitation, Kevin continued to run, exerting all of his energy running the short distance.

As he passed the final buildings, Kevin hurried on until the town seemed to be a reasonable distance away. This was where the forest tree line was as well, where the forest began. Here, Kevin set Caitlin down and stopped to catch his breath. He was exhausted from the fire and running. Kevin knew he did not have the most stamina of anyone in the world, but he was surprised to see just how far he had gone as the embers of the burning building glowed in the distance. Venarose's fire brigade was out there now, attempting to battle the blaze with water from the Aurun River.

A few moments later, Kevin was still breathing heavily when the large Demons operative showed up. He appeared to be in good spirits, and completely unscathed. "It is fortunate to see thou hast escaped," he began. "My job here in Venarose is done anyway. Without the building, The Syndicate has likely scattered, and my term with them does not need to last any longer."

"Excellent," responded Kevin. "On the downside, though, we were wrong about who set the fire." He stepped a couple of steps out of the way to reveal Caitlin down on the ground, unconscious.

The large operative took a good look. "Is she still alive?" he asked Kevin.

Kevin nodded. "Still breathing," he responded. "When I found her, she was still tied to her chair in a room downstairs. By the time I got there, the whole lower floor was on fire, but there was little smoke in the room. My only guess is that the sleeper drug hasn't worn off yet."

Considering this, the large operative responded, "We gave you an antidote to rouse you; she may not have received the same. She should be fine within an hour or so. Thou did well to carry her as far out as thou did. However, I presume this is the friend that thou thought might have set the fire, since thou did say we were wrong about it. This leads me to believe that there are two possibilities about it."

"Oh?" asked Kevin, curious about who nearly killed him and Caitlin in the fire. "What do you think?"

"It is not something I can discuss until I file a report, per our policy."

Kevin was thinking. "I understand," he said. "But, to be honest, I understand little about the factions of Nuve and their motives, their territory… well, anything. This is my first time in the country."

"Speaking of which," interrupted the Demons operative, "I have been meaning to ask thou about that. Why is it that the Vanguard of Aurana is here in Nuve?"

Unsure exactly how to answer this question, Kevin tried his best to fabricate a response. "Well, how can I describe this?" he began, still figuring out what to say. "I'm here to unite Nuve, at least temporarily so the fight against Desolunar can prove successful."

After a moment's pause, the Demons operative began to laugh. "Good luck accomplishing that," he said, still laughing. "I have serious doubts thou will even come close to getting the groups of Nuve to work together even once."

"Still, I have to try," responded Kevin, seriously. "There is more to Desolunar than meets the eye. Their forces are led by Demonicus, a man intent on conquering the world. But there is more to it than that. The powers that he and his forces possess will mean the inevitable death of everyone if we do not work together against him. It is beyond what anyone believes, and soon the territory losses will be much greater."

The Demons operative considered this. "So you fight not just for Aurana," he responded. "Very noble, indeed."

"Aurana is my homeland," responded Kevin, "but there are more serious problems than just that in my homeland. Earlier this week, some of those homeland problems were resolved."

"Oh?" questioned the Demons operative. "I seriously doubt that. The only way Aurana will do better is if King Arnold IX steps down over there."

Kevin glared into the eyes of the Demons operative. It was a message of body language, one that resonated very deeply within the operative.

"I see," he answered. "So now Aurana has a new king, and a vanguard. That would make sense."

This confused Kevin. "What do you mean by that?" he asked.

"Honorable Vanguard," began the operative with the answer in mind, "Aurana has not had anyone holding the title of Vanguard in over fifty years. You are the first in a long time to represent Aurana in this way. No doubt Aurana would be embarrassed if their first new Vanguard in that long were captured, and they would pay a heavy ransom."

"No wonder The Syndicate regional leader thought I was a valuable person," answered Kevin.

"Exactly," responded the operative quickly. "Now, if I may ask thou a question, where do thou intend to head next? I intend to lead thou to Edenbrook, if thou are willing to follow. The Demons can offer thou protection while thou are here in Nuve."

Despite his already-formed opinion on the matter, Kevin gave it a moment's thought anyway before answering the operative. "Thanks, but no thanks," he answered. "I have a job while I am here, and I must follow through on it. In order to do that, I need to head to Nuvenia, to the capital city. My next move is clear."

The operative crossed his arms. "Very well, then," he answered. "Nonetheless, thou shall receive my help anyway. I am still headed to Edenbrook, but when I arrive, I will have a message sent to Nuvenia alerting the Demons headquarters branch in the city of your incoming arrival. They will provide thou a shelter in Nuvenia should thou need it."

"Excellent!" exclaimed Kevin, glad to have some support behind him already. "I'm sure I can make use of that. Thank you very much, Mr…"

"It is best that you do not know my name," interrupted the operative, stopping Kevin from asking about his name. "For thy own safety, mine, and that of the Demons, it is best that things remain this way."

Kevin saw no reason to question the wishes of the operative. He was probably right: less information spread meant less information that could be taken by an enemy. "As you wish," answered Kevin. "I will be setting out for Nuvenia tomorrow."

"Do thou know the route to Nuvenia?" asked the operative. "You will need to return to Venarose to head down the road, but there is a faster way that you can get to Nuvenia than that. If thou walk along the road, thou will find the tributary that feeds into the deep Abyss of the Royal Sovereign, in which Nuvenia sits on an island. At the point where the road meets the tributary waterway, there is a small boating shop which charges some absurd fees to borrow a boat and return it in Nuvenia. However, if thou tell the man operating the desk the passphrase 'the nobles of Tundrosa', then he will allow you to borrow a boat for free."

Even faster travel, Kevin thought to himself. The less of this traveling that he could accomplish, the faster he could try to unify Nuve and add their forces to those engaging Desolunar. Though it seemed like a longshot to fix years of damage, Kevin knew he had to give it a shot, and take every opportunity he could.

"Now," continued the operative without skipping a beat, "the time has come for us to part. I must be heading back to Edenbrook as soon as possible." The operative reached out to shake Kevin's hand. "Good luck, vanguard."

"And I wish the best of luck for you," responded Kevin. "May your trip go well."

The operative let go of Kevin's hand. "As for yours as well," he said. Then, with no further comment, he turned and walked toward the east. He was a man of strength, one who had no need for the word 'goodbye'. Kevin could see that in the operative's eyes. It was a trait shared by those who had committed themselves to something.

As he finished this thought, Kevin heard some odd sounds behind him. He turned around to see Caitlin slowly starting to regain consciousness as the drug wore off. Reacting to this, Kevin walked over to where Caitlin was and knelt down to talk to her. "Stay down," he said to her, "you're safe now."

With little strength in her voice, Caitlin replied, in a short and to the point question, "Where are we?" Her reply sounded like she was mostly still asleep.

Kevin was just happy to see that Caitlin was all right. "North of Venarose," he said. "This should be a safe spot for us to rest for the night."

For a moment, Caitlin did not respond, and Kevin was slightly worried. Then, Caitlin had a response. "Good. Wake me up when we're leaving tomorrow morning, okay?" Then she rolled over and fell asleep again.

Chuckling, Kevin found amusement in that remark. Wake her up? He was the one who always needed to be woken up early. Still, wanting to be kind, Kevin took off his jacket and spread it out over Caitlin's body, in the fashion of a blanket. Then, he walked several steps to the west, closer to the Aurun River, and set himself down, hoping to have a peaceful night sleeping.

Of course, the usual things pressed on Kevin's mind. But by

this point, Kevin was so used to the feeling of asking himself the same questions over and over that it did not bother him from getting to sleep. Only the future could answer those questions that continually pressed on his mind, and Kevin knew it.

Chapter 24

Coronation

As night fell, sounds of horns and celebrations were breaking out all around Aurana City, as the authorities of Aurana passed the crown down to King Andrew II. People were gathered around the front entrance of the palace even though security was tight all around the entrance stairs and columns surrounding the doors that opened to the inside of the emerald palace. Instead of the normal private ceremony of coronation inside the throne room when a new king took his seat for the first time, the newly crowned king had decided to have this ceremony take place outside, in front of the people of Aurana City.

Thousands of people, nearly the whole population of Aurana City, had gathered around the palace entrance, waiting to hear the new king's first speech, one that King Andrew II had planned following the coronation ceremony. In his speech, King Andrew planned to outline what he wanted to bring to Aurana, although he wanted to avoid making it all about politics.

Nearing the end of the public ceremony, the crown was placed on Andrew's head and the scepter placed in his hands, and a great cheer echoed throughout the crowd. Today was a day for celebration, indeed.

After the crown was placed, Andrew stepped up to the podium placed in front of the palace entrance to speak. "My friends," he began, to a cheer of the crowd. Humbly, he stepped back to take a bow as the cheer grew louder. As it settled, he stepped back up to the podium. "My friends," he began again, "it is a great privilege to be serving Aurana as your king. This country is all about you and what I can do for you. Gone now are the days of fighting only for glory without actually fighting for victory. Gone now are the days when politicians looking to push their own agendas and earn money will influence the leadership of Aurana. Together, we stand united for ourselves!"

As he yelled this, the crowd flew into another cheer. Andrew paused to allow this to occur before he continued. "As you all know," he finally continued, "those of us from Aurana who live in the south have lived in the face of death as the nation of Desolunar continues to encroach and push back our borders. As a new king, one who looked from the outside might think that a new king, at such a young age, might be a weak leader who cannot protect his country. But I will not allow this to happen. I will begin to bring in and listen to military advisors, and I will heed the advice of all of them. We will regroup the forces of Aurana, unite with those who also have been victimized by Desolunar, and begin to retake the land!"

Another cheer went through the audience before Andrew continued. "As my first act as your king, I have appointed to Aurana its first vanguard in fifty years. He is a symbol of the valiant people of Aurana: a young adult, but even at his age, he stares at the face of death every day. It is not by choice that he does so, but because it is what has to be done." He paused for a second. "Over the course of the next few days and months, you may find that my actions are going to be drastically different than those that my father, King Arnold IX, had used. To start things off, I am going to listen to your voices, people. I will consider every opinion, listen to every story if I have to, and become the power of the voices of this nation! Together, we will make our home nation the best in the world!"

As King Andrew II shouted his closing line, the crowd erupted in cheers. Horns blew, streamers flew up into the air, and people were starting to enjoy themselves as the king walked back into the palace. Then, the crowd slowly began to disperse.

Toward the back of the crowd, Professor James Magnon and Kron Kalavere stood. They had been listening to the speech together, not making their presence known in the crowd. As the crowd began to disperse, they did as well, heading off to the west side of the city toward the city limits.

"A good speech, indeed," said Kron to the professor, continuing to walk with him toward the west. "King Andrew certainly seems to be promising much hope for Aurana. He certainly sounds honest and trustworthy at least."

Professor Magnon crossed his arms. "And yet, I cannot place

my complete faith in King Andrew. I know I have been a supporter of him, and I know his intent to be a good ruler for his people and not someone's agenda, but sometimes the best intentions can end with the worst results. Only time will tell if King Andrew's rule is a good one or not."

"I fully realize that," responded Kron. "I am sure, that since you know who I am, that you know I am older than you. I know this already. I have seen leaders rise and fall over the years, and observed many rulers in my years."

Giving a look of scowl, Professor Magnon responded, "Are you sure you are right about everything that you just said, Kron? I believe you are assuming too much."

It took Kron only a second of thought to come to the realization. If Professor Magnon was implying what he thought, Kron would feel very afraid. He instantly became nervous, worried about the danger of the person standing next to him.

Chuckling, Professor Magnon responded, "There are some things you are not ready to know yet. Perhaps I can explain more to you on our way to where we are going."

Kron raised an eyebrow. "And where are we going?" he asked. "You never really did explain too well what we are going to be doing away from Kevin."

"Well," began the professor, "immediately, we are headed far enough outside of Aurana City to where we can open up a teleportation gate without being seen. I have a lead we should follow concerning Vincent Stryker."

Trying to maintain a calm demeanor, but somewhat excited by the news, Kron said, "You do?"

The professor nodded. "I do. I know not whether Vincent Stryker is still alive, but I have my contacts in Scurnia as well. I have heard from some of his last known location."

"I see," acknowledged Kron. "How do you know these contacts so far away, anyway?"

"They are people with whom I have worked," answered the professor. "I spent some time in the Scurnian city of Tron helping to mediate the disputes between Gardolk and Scurnia and trying to battles that later happened there. As a matter of fact," he paused, "I met Vincent Stryker there."

"Wait, you *know* him?"

"I do," acknowledged the professor. He looked around for a second, before continuing in *rengan* to protect what he was about to say. "*I was looking for the pure one, and I found him.*"

Kron was confused. "*Surely you would have known the Alliance-Daritel War was long over by then. Why would you need the pure one?*"

"*That I cannot tell you now.*"

Frustrated, Kron threw his hands up in the air. This felt like typical Professor Magnon behavior at this point.

"*But I will tell you,*" the professor then continued, "*that he was far from the same man than his reputation was. He was there to help prevent the war that followed, as I was, but when I met him, he was clearly a man who was a shell of himself.*"

A bit sad to hear that, Kron lowered his head. Aside, he had been hoping that an alive Vincent Stryker might be a great help. Now, those hopes were fading. He walked silently alongside the professor.

Then, the professor turned his head toward Kron as they walked on. "*Tell me, Kron, because I wish to know. How much do you know of Setaeus Demota?*"

Baffled, Kron asked, "*Why do you want to know?*"

"*Surely a loyal adherent such as yourself would like to tell the story of your founder.*"

"*Well, I do not know all that much,*" Kron answered. "*Setaeus Demota was a power zealot who eventually became a very powerful god by the name of Setadev. He was the one who gathered together the gods and brought them to the Realm of the Angels. The city of Seta Archa in Desolunar was founded by him, and it is said that he retired to that city after he was stripped of his immortality and banished for his domineering style of rule.*"

"*Great man, indeed,*" acknowledged the professor, "*but I think lesser of him. Powerful as he was to establish the gods as we know them, the crimes he committed were unforgivable. History spreads, you know, even across realms from person to person, and I heard how*

Setaeus Demota ruled. He wanted to be an overlord, with every god as his personal force and the mortal realm as his domain. To control the world, against the will of everyone else, is of the highest crimes."

Kronius let out a sigh. "*Still, had it not been for this man, I would not be the same person that I am today. Does what Demonicus is doing seem to be the same case today?*"

"*I would say so,*" responded the professor, with no doubts. "*It was a crime then, it is now, and it should always be morally reprehensible to perform such a horrific act. Why do you ask?*"

"*Because,*" answered Kronius, "*by that principle, then the highest punishment should be handed out to Tyrinion for the conquest of the realms that he is currently spurring on through the use of his son Demonicus's kingdom.*"

"*Tyrinion, Kron Kalavere?*" asked the professor. "*What makes you believe that the true evil behind this act is Tyrinion? Do not hold back any details, tell me everything that leads you to believe so.*"

Kronius stopped to think for a second. "*Very well, then,*" he began. "*Tyrinion, real name Tyrin Amtensen, was one of the original gods who came to the Realm of the Angels in the first place. He ruled as the god of darkness, and was a rather docile individual. I remember him vividly. He always had a nice teaching lesson for everyone, much like yourself, Professor Magnon. That was until a day I lived through, a day that the gods have since labeled as Day X, Tyrinion attacked the Realm of the Angels with all his might. Angel Tower, the building in the Realm of the Angels, suffered severe damage, and many gods were badly injured. A vivid glow of red was in his eyes as he attacked. Then, Tyrinion fled to a realm below, and since then, his son Demonicus has sprung up and several other peculiar things have happened. And you know the story from there; he inspires the Daritel to rise up and war with the world, Vincent Stryker conducts a strike on Seta Archa, fights Tyrinion, and the war ends.*"

"*I see,*" considered the professor. "*And yet, Kronius, I ask you this. What proof do you have that it is Tyrinion, then? From what you have told me, all that you know is Tyrinion left in an attacking storm, and then someone attacked the mortal realm later where Demonicus has since sprung up. In fact, have you ever even heard Demonicus claim that Tyrinion was his father?*"

"*Not directly,*" answered Kronius. "*None of that is direct, of course, but there is only one immortal not in the Realm of the Angels aside from myself, so who else could it be? It is the only possibility. When every scenario is considered, it must be the truth.*"

Professor Magnon stared into the eyes of Kronius. Then he began, "*It is wise to consider absolutely every aspect of every detail if you are going to make a judgment on the basis of eliminating everything else. Understand, please, that I am not trying to judge you, Kronius, nor am I trying to defend anybody. All I want to do is be sure, and be sure that you are sure. So, I will ask you now, are you certain?*"

Kronius nodded with a brazen confidence. "More certain than you," he said, in the common language.

Crossing his arms, the professor responded, "Very well, then. At least you are certain, and that is the most important part." He then turned and led Kron into an abandoned house on the city's fringe, and quickly checked to see if anyone was inside before entering. "This should be far enough," he answered. He then conjured light magic in one hand and darkness magic in the other. He spun them together and formed a spiral. Spinning magic colored purple and yellow glowed in a circle, and the teleportation gate was open.

"Interesting technique," Kronius said to this. "Creating a teleportation gate by using light and darkness in such a way to cause a rift in the space of the realm. Very old technique, one that is all but extinct today."

"Old but effective nonetheless," replied the professor. He then signaled toward the gate to Kronius. "After you," he said.

Seeing no need to question why he was going first, Kronius said nothing but walked through the gate silently. Professor Magnon followed through the gate a few seconds later.

Chapter 25

Under Pressure

Kevin was not happy. In fact, he was very frustrated.

It had been three full days since he had set sail down the tributary that led to the Abyss of the Royal Sovereign. Despite having no trouble acquiring the small boat and spending every moment of the past three days traveling down the waterway the entire day and night, he had not arrived in Nuvenia, much less seen any town or person other than his traveling companion, Caitlin. The slow, shallow tributary had by this point carried Kevin deep into Nuve, with no sight of the city or any other landmark.

By this point, the lands all around the tributary had become barren plains. Some dry grasses were growing around the water and deeper into the land, but none of the usual green color of the landscapes that Kevin had seen were in sight. To top it all off, Kevin was frustrated at himself. Three days earlier, after he and the Demons operative had escaped the building run by The Syndicate crime organization, Caitlin had never realized what Kevin had done for her in carrying her out of the burning building. This was because Kevin never told her. All that he had said was that after being knocked out, he simply woke up next to Caitlin where they were, and that his memory was shaky as to what happened just before and just after then.

Why had he not told Caitlin the actual truth? Kevin continuously beat himself up for it. True, he was trying to be humble and not play up his role in what had occurred, but there was not a reason for him to hide it. Thinking about what it meant, he could not help but laugh at himself a bit, randomly, at his folly that may have earned him some credit with Caitlin.

Noticing Kevin laughing, Caitlin interrupted him. "What do you find so funny?" she asked directly.

Kevin tried to calm his laughing. "Oh, it's nothing," he said.

"I'm getting pretty sick of this trip, and being as bored as I am right now, I suppose that it's not difficult to find humor in anything."

As Kevin still chuckled, Caitlin rolled her eyes. "If I had a sense of humor," she began, "then I might say the same. However, as I do not, I have to think that perhaps this long boat ride is starting to affect your mental clarity."

"Mental clarity?" asked Kevin. "I don't have any problems with mental clarity."

Caitlin shrugged. "Kevin, you have been bored, sickened, and otherwise unhappy for the past three days. All that I have seen you do is look around the boat, lean over the side, and mope around. And now, you begin to laugh. I think you might be becoming delusional from the long boat trip."

"Heh," responded Kevin. "Well, believe what you want to believe."`

"Indeed," Caitlin said. "The observations I make are my own, and your defense of yourself does not change anything."

Kevin sat up. "I never said I was defending myself," he said. "Maybe it's better to be a little crazy sometimes. It's a good way to relieve some tension and stress, to take life lightly for a time. Sometimes," Kevin chuckled, "life is better when you're insane."

Suddenly, it happened. For a second after Kevin said that, a laugh came from Caitlin. She caught herself immediately after doing it, but Kevin heard it anyway. Whatever Kevin had said, it had made Caitlin slip up for just a second. As soon as Caitlin straightened herself up, she responded, "If that is what you believe, then so be it."

Now, Kevin was at the point where he was most suspicious and certain that Caitlin was masking her true self. If only he could find out what she was thinking, he could discover the truth. But alas, by what seemed to be a cruel twist of fate to Kevin, she possessed that power but he did not. Of course, doing so would also be deeply unethical, as Kevin had been taught by Caitlin.

A reflection of light in the distance distracted Kevin for a second. He stood up in the boat as carefully as he could as to keep himself from tipping the boat over. In the distance, Kevin could make out a massive spreading of the water, as though it was emptying into a larger body such as a lake. Finally, he had arrived. Kevin was almost certain that what he saw was the Abyss of the Royal Sovereign, the large body of water in which the city of Nuvenia sat on an island. He called Caitlin's attention to it, upon which she carefully stood up as well to observe the reflection.

"That's the delta," said Kevin, pointing to the reflection. A hint of excitement was in his voice. "I'm sure of it."

"Let us hope so," responded Caitlin. "I do believe that you are correct, but I suppose we will see for sure as soon as the boat arrives. Perhaps it would be best if we took our seats for the moment."

Kevin agreed, and carefully sat back down in the boat. Caitlin followed suit as soon as he had sat down. Perhaps the tributary was just slower than he thought. Within a few minutes, Kevin's observation was confirmed, and the boat entered the Abyss of the Royal Sovereign. Water went on for long distances in each direction except for backwards. The island of Nuvenia, and its respective city, were still nowhere in sight.

After sitting down again, Kevin looked down at the water, trying to find a bottom. Failing to do so, he looked back up at Caitlin and said, "I can't see the bottom. How deep is this lake?"

"Nobody knows for sure," answered Caitlin, thinking. "I've never seen it myself, but supposedly that is why it is called the Abyss. No one has ever found the bottom of the Abyss of the Royal Sovereign."

Kevin rolled his eyes. "I see," he said, disappointed a little bit that he did not have a real answer. Still, it was the best answer he would be able to get, and he knew it.

Off in the distance, Kevin could spot dark clouds and a storm brewing in the distance. To him, it seemed like a smart idea to stay clear of the storm, and he proceeded to direct the boat away from the direction of the dark clouds as he continued to search for Nuvenia.

That was only to last a few minutes, however, when suddenly Caitlin had a revelation. Her eyes widened as she felt something, and began looking in the direction of the storm. "Kevin," she began, a little softer in tone than she normally was, "I sense something. It seems almost oddly familiar, but I don't know what it is."

"Oddly familiar?" asked Kevin. "How so?"

"Well," began Caitlin, "for some reason it seems like an energy that I have felt before. It feels somewhat like the presence of something very cold, but not quite. It is not a very steady energy, though, and it feels as though it has been moving around but has stopped for the time being."

Kevin did not even need a second of thought. "So you have no clue what it is, basically?"

"To put it short, yes," answered Caitlin.

Kevin chuckled, finding humor in what Caitlin had said. "Then what's the big deal?" he asked. "Chances are it's not something important if we don't know what it is. I can't sense anything."

Then it hit Kevin. The feel of cold, as Caitlin had described it. It sounded somewhat familiar. Caitlin had described a feeling of moving wind in front of that statue inside the temple in the City of Phoenixes. It contained the Stripe of Air.

Was it a stripe that Caitlin had inadvertently found? Here, in the Abyss of the Royal Sovereign? How would she even know of it as a "familiar feel" if it really was a stripe? Maybe, was she able to feel the stripe from contacting Kevin's skin when she grabbed his arm that night? Maybe it happened some other time? Kevin could not be sure.

Still, Kevin had to be sure he was right in the first place. "I have an idea," he began, extending his arm and pulling back his sleeve a little bit. "I want you to grab my hand."

"Why?" asked Caitlin. "What purpose would that serve?"

"I want you to feel the Stripe of Air again," answered Kevin. "And then, I want you to tell me if the energy you sense feels like a stripe."

Caitlin responded only with a nod, and then grabbed Kevin's hand sideways. She then closed her eyes, apparently focusing to sense the energy. Within a few minutes, Caitlin opened her eyes again, with an answer. "That's exactly it," she said. "It feels so similar, but instead of air, it feels like ice."

"Well, then, I suppose we have a detour to take before we reach Nuvenia," Kevin responded to this. He looked at the back of his hand, where he could barely see the marking from the Stripe of Air that curled up his arm, hidden by his jacket sleeve. "If this is a powerful weapon, I think we should pursue it if we can. It may be helpful if someday we take this fight to Demonicus."

"I would suppose so," answered Caitlin. She pointed toward the storm. "If that's what we're doing, it feels like it's over there, but not quite. It feels more like it's below us than it is over there."

"Below us?" Kevin exclaimed. Then, he leaned back again, and continued, "Just great. A stripe that's impossible to reach in the deepest body of water possible. This couldn't get any worse if Demonicus were to attack now."

"Oh well," responded Caitlin. "It is important for you to have some optimism right now. We'll get the stripe. Nothing is impossible. For all we know, a tornado could spawn from that storm and open up a hole or something that lets us get to the bottom."

As they floated into the storm, it was apparent this was a very small but powerful microburst of energy. Lightning was coming down everywhere around them in a matter of seconds, along with heavy rain and rougher water, almost as if they were on the sea and not a large lake.

"I think this was a bad idea!" yelled Kevin as the first strikes of lightning came very near the boat.

A few more strikes came closer and closer. Caitlin, to defend them, cast a shield of light above them and focused on putting energy into it to keep it up. Some of the strikes started hitting Caitlin's shield. To Kevin's surprise, Caitlin appeared to be having difficulty trying to hold the lightning strikes back.

"I don't think this is a natural event!" Caitlin called out to Kevin.

In response, Kevin drew his sword. He took a moment under the shield to light it up, just in case something bad were to happen.

Suddenly, from above and below, the air and water around the small boat began to spin around. Slowly, it became faster and faster until eventually it reached its maximum speed. Kevin looked around him to see the whirling winds were circled all around the boat, almost as if he was trapped. Above him, Kevin was surprised to find that the sky had no clouds in it at all; a stark contrast to the overcast skies that had dominated the day so far. Below him, though, was a much bigger surprise.

The water was all gone, formed into a whirlpool in which they were stuck. The bottom was not visible, but no more water remained covering it. The boat was stuck coasting along the walls of a whirlpool with a cyclone around.

"We're sinking!" yelled Caitlin, as water started to become visible above the edges of the boat.

The air currents began to push up more, causing Kevin and Caitlin to look down and try to find the cause of the changing currents. What they both saw, though, caught both of them off guard. It was not the bottom of the Abyss.

It was black, something steaming with energy, almost tearing through the ground.

"What is that?" yelled Kevin.

"No idea!" asked Caitlin. "Whatever it is, the stripe feels as though it is through there!"

Kevin nodded in response. "Hang on to your dress," he yelled to Caitlin, "because this could get a little hairy!"

Caitlin was very confused. "What do you mean?" she asked.

Too late.

Within a second as the boat approached the bottom, Kevin took his sword and plunged it into the blackness. He was going to find out what was through there.

Then, all went black.

Kevin and Caitlin felt a weird sensation, as if both of them passed through the a hole, one that made both of them very uncomfortable.

In the next instant, Kevin and Caitlin were standing in a room with rock walls. They had not landed from falling, or anything of the sort. Instead, they were just standing in the middle of the room. There was no door, no window, nothing. All around them was rock. The room was shaped in a cylinder, with a dirt floor and rock covering the ceiling. The walls were rigid and craggy, although not so much as to be an eyesore. It was approximately fifteen steps wide across its diameter, meaning it was reasonably small although not as small as any room in a house.

Kevin was still looking around the room in amazement, as he sheathed his sword. "Where are we?" he asked. "This place is pretty small. It doesn't seem at all like a normal cave, though."

"I'm fairly sure it's not an underwater cavern," responded Caitlin. "What we went through was something similar to a supernatural phenomenon my father described to me once. He called it 'corrosion' in the realm, although he was uncertain as to what would cause it. The fact that we just fell through one and ended up here standing, and not falling, makes me think that we fell through a hole into another realm, somehow."

"So bizarre," said Kevin, bewildered. "Still, how would a hole end up at the bottom of the Abyss of the Royal Sovereign, and even more so, how would a stripe end up here?"

Caitlin paused for a moment before responding. "I don't know," she began, "but I can feel it now. It's definitely here. Only question is, where is it here? It feels like it's all around this room."

Then, there was a loud sound of thunder.

Before he had any time to react, Kevin was hit by a large black tentacle and slammed against the wall of the room and held him there. It hurt badly to be hit against the wall, but Kevin did not let out a sound other than one of surprise. The tentacle was not something like flesh, but something different. Kevin felt this as he tried to escape the tentacle's grip, to no avail.

A second later, Caitlin was also hit in a similar fashion, also caught by surprise by a similar tentacle. She did let out a scream of pain as she was hit.

Kevin and Caitlin could only look on as more of the same material that had pinned them against the wall began to seep through the wall on the other side. It started to mass on the other side, growing larger and larger. Then, its shape began to become more defined, and start to take a form. Most distinctly, a face started to come out of the dark matter, shaped as the face of an older man. It began to move; then, it began to speak.

"What is your business here?" asked the dark matter. "How dare you trespass in this space?"

Kevin tried to breathe, still in pain from being slammed against the wall. "We mean you no harm," he said, trying to fabricate a response. "We were searching for something, and we found ourselves here, or wherever this place is."

"This is my territory, and you are trespassing on it.," responded the dark matter quickly.

Despite his interest in where he was, Kevin's mind was focused on another subject. How was he going to get out of this one? Kevin had no control of his arms, as they were held in place by the tentacle. Right now, he figured, his only way out was to talk this out.

Caitlin, however, appeared to have the same idea and was the first to start. "A space between realms," she observed. "Interesting place you have here," she said to the dark matter's face. "So, who are you and how did you come to be here in this space between realms? Your presence and powers intrigue me."

After a slight pause, the dark matter seemed intrigued by Caitlin's curiosity. "I am the Existence, that which does not live but only exists."

Existence. Why did that word give Kevin a chill? He was not sure for a while, until the poem came back to him, especially these lines:

An evil beast of existence
Holds another as he will prance
While he slowly begins his kill
Unless a secret is revealed.

It fit the poem perfectly, although the lines were a little haunting. Worse yet, what was "a secret" that needed to be revealed?

"I see," acknowledged Caitlin, trying to keep the Existence talking. "How did you get here?"

"Why should I tell you?" demanded the Existence, forcefully.

"You don't need to," Caitlin answered, "but I want to understand who is holding me and my friend captive at the moment."

After a pause to consider, the Existence gave Caitlin her answer. "I know not why I should answer to trespassers, but since you must know; thousands of years ago, my life was as a mortal man. My lifelong rival found the unthinkable: the secret to immortality. With that, he was intent on killing me with his newfound powers, once and for all. Unfortunately for him, I found his secret and stole it. When we fought next, our fight took us across the ends of the earth. Eventually, we fought our way here, where he pulled his most powerful move. He made my body explode. The pieces of my body disintegrated, and what was left was the Existence."

Kevin had an interesting thought based on what the Existence had just said. "So you were forced to live on because you were immortal? Though your body had exploded, you could not die because of the life energy you still held."

"Your intuition serves you well, trespasser," responded the Existence, still not loosening its grip. "I have made this place my territory. I control everything that happens in this space."

Taking another look around, Kevin commented, "Rather small space you have here. Is it really so big to be the controller of a place like this?"

Unfortunately for Kevin, his comment was not taken well by the Existence. It shot a force of energy down the tentacle, blasting Kevin harder against the wall and gripping him tighter there. The pressure was nearly unbearable as Kevin felt his chest compressed hard against the wall. "Your comments will only serve to anger me," said the Existence.

"Be careful, Kevin," said Caitlin, still pinned up on the other side. "What about your rival?" she then asked the Existence.

"He was a despicable man by the name of Setaeus Demota," responded the Existence. "He claimed himself to be a 'god' and thought he was superior to most. I will admit that as a mortal my intentions were not pure, but compared to Setaeus Demota, they were saintlike."

Setaeus Demota. That was whom Kron had identified as the founder of the gods, and later the god Setadev. That might mean the Existence was an enemy of the gods; at the very least, he was one of their short-lived founder.

There was then a long pause. "Now then, enough of this small talk," the Existence continued. "Answer why you have trespassed here. Why did you come to my dominion?"

Still struggling under the pressure of the tentacle, Kevin mustered up words to say. "We floated on a boat into a storm, looking for a powerful magic energy."

The face of the Existence glared deeply at Kevin. A flash of blue came across its forehead. "Do you happen to mean this energy?" asked the Existence.

Kevin could only respond with, "Yes. That is it." He was hoping that the Existence would take it kindly, and be willing to part with the stripe peacefully. Or, at the very least, he might be willing to negotiate.

It was not to be, however. With this comment, the Existence grabbed Kevin with his tentacle and started whipping him against the back wall. "You distracted me!" screamed the Existence. "Did you honestly think that there was any way you could convince me to part with my greatest treasure? How dare you attempt to part me from *my* treasure! You will die for this!"

Flailing around, Kevin had little option on what he could do to get himself out of this situation. Obviously, the situation had not gone as smoothly as he had hoped. The Sword of Purity was still on his belt, but he could not reach it and could not wield it even if he called it to him. In fact, Kevin still had no control of his arms, as they were restrained by the tentacle's grip.

An idea came to Kevin, and though it put him into danger, he had to try it anyway. Focusing hard with his mind, he tried to call the Sword of Purity to his right hand, whether or not it was pinned down. The sword formed in his hand, and Kevin waved it around, trying to strike the energy.

It was enough of a disruption that the force clinching Kevin tight was gone. He slid out of the grip of the Existence and lit up his sword.

The Existence struck down with its tentacle, but Kevin sliced through it with the Sword of Purity first. He then ran over to Caitlin and sliced through the tentacle that held her there, freeing her too.

"Astounding," said the Existence to this feat. "No magic that I have can do that. Congratulations, you have a bit of respect from me."

Kevin, not in any mood to hear any "praise" from the Existence, walked up to the middle of the room and pointed it at the face of the Existence. Caitlin took her place next to him, as he was breathing heavily and bleeding from several cuts that he had suffered from being slammed against the rock. "You can throw me around a room," began Kevin, enraged. "You can attempt to suffocate me by the chest. You can even try to kill me. But you won't keep me down!"

"Interesting," said the Existence, as it began to laugh. "I am enjoying this challenge, the first in a long time."

Suddenly, from the other side of the room, two tentacles of dark matter came from the backside out of the rock. Kevin managed to catch one tentacle just in time, splitting it down the middle. Caitlin did not see the other tentacle in time, however, and ended up thrown against the wall again, pinned up back where she was.

Instinctively, Kevin began running toward Caitlin to free her again. But as Kevin raced over to Caitlin to help her, a tentacle came up from the floor, snagging Kevin, slamming him to the ceiling with a great amount of force, and pinching him tight around the chest. Kevin could barely breathe, and lost consciousness. His head fell slack as his lack of air forced his body to start shutting down.

No more words came from Kevin. No sounds, no motions, nothing. The Sword of Purity hung loose in his hand's grip. Every body part of Kevin's went limp, and blood flowed out of the many cuts Kevin had from the injuries he had sustained. He had been beaten around the rocks more than enough times to be fatal.

For all Caitlin knew, he was dead.

Caitlin saw this and let out a scream.

She had snapped from her emotional block in sadness. She saw what she presumed was a dead Kevin. Tears began to fall from her eyes as she saw this. It was a nightmare, turned reality. She started to cry, the emotions so powerful and overcoming that she could not hold it back any longer.

Kevin was her only friend. Her charge to keep safe. And now he was gone.

The Existence took both of its tentacles carrying an unconscious

Kevin and a fully conscious Caitlin and brought them up to its face. First, it addressed Kevin. "I control everything in this realm," it said. "You never had a chance." As the Existence finished his words, the tentacle dropped Kevin to the ground, where he still did not move or make any sound.

Then the Existence turned to Caitlin, whom it saw crying. "Now what is wrong, little girl?" it said, insultingly.

Caitlin only continued to cry, very upset. She could not lift her head, struggling to hide her tears. Everything had fallen apart for her all at once. Every emotion hidden, every reaction held back, all came out at the same time.

"Oh, I see how it is," continued the Existence after seeing this. "You mortals, always so easy to read your thoughts, even if I did not use magic to do so. I find this true with the hearts of women and men alike. As much as some like to keep it hidden, the truths of their hearts are never fully shrouded." He paused for a second. "You were keeping a secret from this boy, were you not?" asked the Existence in a heartless tone, pointing to Kevin with a tentacle from the wall. "Your thoughts make you vulnerable. But you have known this, have you not? You have tried to mask your emotions, to appear to be strong. Still, as much as you tried to make it work, something got in the way of that. This boy, was it?"

Still crying, Caitlin rushed over to where Kevin had fallen, since by now the Existence had withdrawn its tentacle. Whether or not the Existence could read her mind was irrelevant right now. She kept crying, this time kneeling over Kevin's body.

"So it is," continued the Existence, not caring what Caitlin was doing. "You were never strong. You are weak. It is such a shame that your affections are worthless now."

Kneeling by Kevin's body, Caitlin was becoming more and more angry at the Existence. Her sadness had pent up into anger, and more and more she wanted to destroy the Existence by any means necessary.

But what would Kevin say? The thought entered Caitlin's mind, especially what Kevin had done before and would have done if it were he in her situation. Certainly, Caitlin was sure that Kevin would fight for something more than simply revenge. He would not fight out of sheer anger. However, would he fight for love? He would. At least, Caitlin was sure he would.

Love. Now, she finally felt it. It was the emotion hidden deep beneath all of the walls she had built up, beneath all of the strength she possessed, beneath every little bit of herself. It was love. For Kevin. It was undeniable.

Caitlin began to feel her heart start to race. Almost every body part of hers began to shake. Her senses became more aware, her instincts much more keen. She had something to do in order to protect the one she loved most.

Kevin was not actually dead. She could feel it in her heart. And now, he needed her help.

As the emotion coursed through her body, the energy of the raw emotion charged through her, giving her more and more power. Caitlin began to feel herself begin to float upwards into the air, and a burst of light came from all around her. She was not sure what it was, unable to look at herself, but whatever it was, it had given her more power, more energy, more desire. Now was the time to act.

Not paying any attention, the Existence was staring at Kevin, particularly his right arm, which lay slack with the Sword of Purity barely in his grip in his hand. "What do we have here?" began the Existence. "Another treasure. I suppose that whatever was his is mine for the taking!" A tentacle reached out, pointed toward Kevin.

"Stop!" screamed Caitlin, surging with energy. "You shall not harm him!" Caitlin was charging energy up as she said this, preparing for a blast of light energy to unleash on the Existence.

The interruption and building energy caught the attention of the Existence, who turned to see Caitlin, floating in the air, charging energy intensely. But something else was different about her as well, and the Existence saw it instantly. In surprise, it screamed, "You? What are you?"

In its own defense, the Existence shot a tentacle out of the back to grab Caitlin. Sensing it coming in advance, however, Caitlin turned around in midair, grabbed it, and blasted it with powerful light energy, splitting it apart instantly. The tentacle of dark matter then disintegrated as the remnants tried to retreat into the rock wall.

Caitlin then turned back toward the face of the Existence. Scared, the Existence screamed hysterically, "It is you! What are you doing?"

Charged up and ready, Caitlin extended her arms in front of her, and blasted every bit of energy she had into the face of the Existence, letting out a loud scream as she did.

Every bit of power shot in a beam into the Existence, continuing for almost a minute.

When it was done, Caitlin let down her arms to see the Existence's face still sat in front of her

For a moment, silence. There was nothing.

Then, the energy of the Existence began to dissipate.

She had done it. The Existence was starting to break apart.

In a serious tone, the Existence spoke as its face continued to disintegrate. "Very well done, little girl, very well done. Such a power, one that has never seen the light of day before; it is only fitting that it should be what finally ends me. So, Setaeus Demota was right after all when he said that immortals could be killed. Somehow, someway, this is the power that can." The disintegration became very severe by now, leaving only a bit of one of the eyes of the Existence still visible, as he said, "This is the most divine power… the… pow… er… of… the… a…"

It was gone. Finally, the Existence had disappeared for good. Its voice, its face, everything was gone. The Stripe of Ice was loose in the room too. Deciding to make sure that she left with it, Caitlin raised her right arm and took the stripe into her own body and secured it within herself.

Hesitating not for a second more, Caitlin rushed over to Kevin and said, "Kevin, are you all right?"

There was no response.

Taking this as a cue, Caitlin extended her arms toward Kevin, and let a gentle burst of light flow from them, in the form of a healing spell. Slowly, the cuts on Kevin's body began to seal up, and the blood stopped flowing out of his body. His internal injuries were fixing themselves with the help of this magic.

It would not have worked had Kevin not clung to life and lived through his injuries to this point. As Caitlin saw her magic work, she was very happy to see this, knowing what it meant. She then knelt closer to Kevin and said again, "Kevin, are you all right?"

Still, though, there was no response from Kevin. Caitlin asked again, also to no response. Tears began to well up in her eyes a little bit.

A minute had passed, and Kevin was still not conscious. Seeing this, Caitlin leaned all the way down and held Kevin closely for a moment. "I promise I'll get you some help, Kevin. I swear it!" she said, as a couple more tears rolled down her eyes, although this time with a bit more hope.

Looking up, Caitlin was searching for the exit to this "space between realms", as the Existence had described it. Surely there had to be one, if there was an entrance. Caitlin was looking for something similar to the hole that Kevin and she had seen that led them to this space in the first place. After a couple of minutes, she found it almost directly above her and Kevin.

Picking up Kevin almost with no effort as her newfound power coursed through her, Caitlin floated with him up to the exit. Caitlin clutched Kevin's body tighter, whispering, "I promise, Kevin. I promise."

Through the hole they went together, pushing up until Caitlin saw the Abyss of the Royal Sovereign once again. They continued to float upward through the depths of the abyss. Then, with the surface in sight, Caitlin's power flickered and faded out. She stopped floating upward

As the powers faded, Caitlin became worried instantly. She looked down at Kevin. Holding her breath, she angled one of her hands downward and forced wind magic out of them, pushing herself and Kevin upward to the surface as fast as she could.

Then, they broke through the surface.

Caitlin took a deep breath as she reached the top, and made sure Kevin reached the surface as well so he could breathe. She wiped her eyes, looking around for any land. None was in sight amidst the slightly choppy, yet otherwise calm, Abyss of the Royal Sovereign.

Then, Caitlin turned around to see the fortress city of Nuvenia sitting on its island a very short distance away. Immediately, she started swimming toward the island with Kevin in one arm, using wind magic with the other to propel herself and keep her and Kevin up. The trip to the island, although not taking very long, seemed to take an eternity to Caitlin. Still, it was worth every effort to Caitlin, because she had promised to find Kevin some help, and she would do whatever it took to fulfill that promise.

Finally, Caitlin reached the land, but found difficulty in trying to carry Kevin up the rocky surface of the island toward the open entrance through the city's tall fortress wall. The best she could do was to sling Kevin's arms over her shoulders and drag his body, but because Kevin was much heavier than Caitlin was capable of carrying comfortably, she had to walk slowly to maintain her balance and carry Kevin's body to somewhere where he could get help. She tried to use wind magic to help push upward and lighten the weight.

Fortunately, Caitlin was lucky. The first building she saw after entering the fortress walls with Kevin was a large building with crimson red and black flags flying across it. Caitlin was not exactly sure what these meant, especially since the color that Nuve itself most associated with was blue, sometimes with gold or white trim on their military's uniforms. However, also posted on the side of a building was a flag with a red cross on a white background. This was the international sign for a site that provided medical care. This gave Caitlin a reason to trust the building anyway, and enter it with Kevin.

Upon entering the first room in the building, the two people in the room immediately turned toward Caitlin. It seemed apparent to Caitlin that these people did not usually have too many visitors, but she could not be sure. "This young man needs medical attention," she said to the two people. One was behind a receptionist's desk; the other was in front of it.

Both the older woman behind the receptionist's desk and the younger man standing in front of it rushed over to Caitlin and helped lift Kevin off of her shoulders. They both took Kevin onto their shoulders, with the woman on the left and the man on the right.

"Take him to the second floor, room 204," ordered the older

woman receptionist to the young man. “I shall help thou carry him up. Then, I will need thou to fetch a first aid kit.”

The younger man nodded in response and proceeded to help the receptionist carry Kevin up the narrow flight of stairs on the opposite side of the room as the door. Caitlin followed closely behind, concerned deeply for Kevin’s health.

Despite the fact that Caitlin did all that she could do, Kevin was still unconscious. He had suffered some severe injuries, had been healed by Caitlin’s magic, and yet he was barely clinging onto his life.

Chapter 26

Truly Heartless

"Thou were right to bring him here," said the female receptionist. "From a first appearance, at least, it would appear that he is in a coma. Whatever injury he suffered, it was serious enough to shut down his body."

Kevin was unconscious on a bed in the medical ward, little more than the second floor of an inn in a three-story building. The receptionist was there as well, along with Caitlin, while the young man was running errands at the command of the receptionist. To Caitlin, the receptionist definitely appeared to be the person in charge at the moment.

"I don't know how," responded Caitlin. "He was thrown around a bunch of rocks and was knocked out. His physical wounds were easy enough to heal with magic, but for some reason he hasn't regained consciousness."

"Oh, so thou art a spellcaster?" asked the receptionist.

Caitlin nodded. "Indeed," she said. "More so, I hold the rank of sorceress by the Aurana Department of Magic Affairs. Probably very close to wizardess by now."

"I see," responded the receptionist. "Magic is not capable of healing everything, though. It can do great things, indeed, but there is also very much that magic cannot do. For future reference, I recommend that thou keep this in mind."

"I know that," said Caitlin. "Still, I have never seen anything like this when using magic to heal. Never have I found a limit to its capabilities unless the person the spell is being cast upon is dead or has lost a large amount of blood, as in a cut to the neck, and is bleeding rapidly. Those who can master magic have never found any limitations to healing any wound caused in this…" Caitlin stumbled on her last word, realizing a distinct possibility as to why Kevin had not regained conscious.

"This what?" asked the receptionist.

"World," answered Caitlin. It had just hit her: could the fact that it was an otherworldly being, the Existence, that had injured Kevin that made him unable to wake up?

A slight pause came before the receptionist responded, "Well, perhaps the world is more complex than we all think. Anyway, as for the medical treatment, it appears the boy does not have any other injuries, and only the coma is hampering him at the moment. To treat this, I will have herbal remedies administered that will try to bring him out of his coma. They may take anywhere from a few minutes to a few days to work; however, it is about all we can do for him at this moment."

Acknowledging the treatment, Caitlin said, "Very well, then. What day is it today?"

"Let us see," considered the receptionist. "I believe tonight the moon will be at its full stage, if I remember right."

A full moon? Caitlin was stunned, because that night in Venarose was the night of the moon being half full. The gap on the lunar calendar meant that about a week had passed since that night in Venarose. Somehow, about three or four days were lost that could not be attributed to traveling.

Had time moved faster in the space between realms? It was the only conclusion Caitlin could come up with. It was the only possibility that made any sense at all.

Noting that there was a moment's pause, the receptionist continued with her own comment. "Interesting uniform that this young man is wearing. Auranian military?" she asked.

"Yes," responded Caitlin without much thought. "The uniform itself was a personal gift from His Majesty, King Andrew II of Aurana."

"Must be very special," responded the receptionist, as she stepped closer to the bed where Kevin was unconscious. "He must be a commander, then. He is awfully far from Aurana right now." She reached down, picked up Kevin's arm, and turned it to see the patch embroidered on the side indicating Kevin's rank. To her surprise, however, the patch was not that of the Auranian commander rank.

Instead, the patch was a black triangle inside of a red one.

The receptionist dropped Kevin's arm immediately as she saw this, and addressed Caitlin in a strong voice, "Why did thou not tell me this man was a Vanguard? We have been expecting the Vanguard of Aurana here for several days. We were told to."

"Told to?" asked Caitlin, curious. "By who? I'm not even sure really what this place is."

By this point, the receptionist was at her desk again, where she started shuffling through her files as she answered Caitlin's question. "This is the local headquarters of the Demonstrative Organization of Northern Nuve, usually referred to as 'Demons' for short."

Caitlin took a look around the room again, noting the desk and small "lounge area" filled with wooden chairs and tables. She had also seen the second floor earlier by now as well. "Rather small place for a headquarters of a faction as large as the Demons," she said. "It is little more than an inn, really."

"It used to be an inn," responded the receptionist. "After the Demons acquired the property rights to this inn on the north side of Nuvenia, it became clear that Nuvenia was not a very safe place for the Demons to operate in a public setting with the influence of the official government of Nuve being very strong here in the capital. For this reason, the Demons decided to keep this building as an inn, although there is much more to it. The crimson red and black flags fly in support of the faction, but nothing else is left to chance in appearance. A medical ward is here on the second floor, as you have seen, but it is still in the guise of an inn floor. The third floor is left directly as an inn for visitors in order to maintain our image, although Demons faction members and supporters do stay here as well. This first floor has just the lounge and my files here, but the lower level is an entirely different story. For reasons of safety, however, I would like to leave it at that."

"Understandable," responded Caitlin. "But why have you been anticipating the Vanguard of Aurana's arrival? That part still doesn't make sense to me."

The receptionist took a breath, and continued, "About a week ago, an operative of our faction came into contact with the Vanguard of Aurana, and sent us an advanced warning of his arrival. A couple of days later, we received a copy of the incident report he filed, outlining everything that happened. We have a copy of both here, if I can just find them." The receptionist was still digging through her files.

Caitlin was lost. How did Kevin communicate with an operative of the Demons? She was with him the whole time. Curious, she asked, "Would you mind if I see the incident report? I'm curious as to what it says."

The receptionist pulled out a couple of pages from her files, having finally founded what she was looking for. "Here thou art," she said, passing a couple of papers off the top of the stack to Caitlin.

Carefully, Caitlin started to read over the incident report. She walked over to the other side of the room as the desk, where there were a couple of empty tables and a fireplace. Then, she began to read the report aloud, but quietly to herself.

"Incident report, filed on identifying date 2047926, night of the half moon. Report filed by Demons operative #443. Filed in Venarose, Soverenia, Nuve; copied to Edenbrook, Tundrosa, Nuve and Nuvenia, Soverenia, Nuve. Confidential report, please do not spread to personnel who are not associated with the Demons organization."

Confidential? Caitlin became very curious about this, especially since the receptionist more than willingly passed the report over. Nonetheless, she continued to read on.

"Reported location of incident was Venarose, Soverenia, Nuve, approximately five days before the filing date of this report, or identifying date 2047921. Parties involved: filing operative, The Syndicate crime organization, K.T. Stryker the Vanguard of Aurana, young anonymous female friend of K.T. Stryker. Unconfirmed parties possibly involved: Cornelia Chimeras operative or force. Damages sustained in incident: building in flames, likely under compromised structure and may not currently be standing. Lives lost: none known directly of.

"Incident, as described by reporting operative: On the declared date, I was working undercover with The Syndicate, following my current mission assignment to study for information that would lead to the future collapse of the crime organization should action need to be taken.

“On said night, I was ordered by The Syndicate regional leader of the Venarose region to investigate a captured hostage. Upon inspecting the hostage’s personal effects, however, I realized that the hostage was the Vanguard of Aurana, Mr. K.T. Stryker. He had been knocked out by sleeper dart, just like all victims taken in by The Syndicate. Per Demons policy statute 46.15.2, I freed the Vanguard and asked him to leave, when the building caught fire. The Vanguard specified that he had a suspicion that a friend of his might have lit the fire with magic as a means of escape.

“I sent Mr. K.T. Stryker out through the downstairs as I escaped out the side window from the second floor and began to try and locate where the members of The Syndicate were fleeing. In general, their direction was, from the site of the building, at a heading of three-eighths turns from due north, or more simply, to the southeast.

“After I had located the direction, I turned back toward the building to see that the entire building had become an inferno. Taking account of this, I proceeded to the edge of the forest just north of Venarose, where I met with Mr. K.T. Stryker. He was there, along with an unconscious young woman, who he had claimed was the friend of his he had thought started the fire. He had carried her out of the burning building by herself. It was apparent by now that she had not actually started the fire. Her unconsciousness was caused by the ‘purple powder’ sleeper drug, which is known by both the Demons and most other governments to cause greater effects on women than men. According to Mr. K.T. Stryker, there was little to no smoke in the flaming building on the lower level, suggesting a magic-induced fire.

“I invited the Vanguard to join me in returning to Edenbrook, but he declined, claiming that he had something to do in Nuvenia. Then, I left him and his friend and returned to Edenbrook to file this report.

“Because of the complexity and events of the situation, I believe the Cornelia Chimeras may have been the ones to set fire to the building. The fact that the Vanguard was there might be completely coincidental, although this cannot be confirmed. For this, a corresponding form A-91 Suspected Operation Interference form will also be filed about this situation.

"I hereby affirm this incident report is true to the best of my knowledge, and that I have reported only the facts and personal opinions relevant to the situation that may shed light on the occurrences listed in this report. Signed in affirmation, Demons Operative #443.

"Additional note from the administrator: Actions listed in this report appear to have severely compromised the operation of which Operative #443 played a part in. Operations involving The Syndicate will need to be re-evaluated, and another operative deployed after sufficient intelligence has been gathered. Although further evaluation may be necessary on The Syndicate, such actions are preceded by the presence of the Vanguard of Aurana. Per the request of the head of administration, future action is to provide aid to the Vanguard while he is in Nuve. For insurance of this aid, a copy of this report shall be sent to the Demons Headquarters on the north side of Nuvenia, as the Vanguard is headed in that direction with his female friend, with direction to aid as necessary."

Caitlin stopped reading at this point. She started looking back through and rereading parts of the report, and realized that she had missed something. Every time the word "vanguard" was used in the report, it was referring to Kevin. This meant that Caitlin herself was the "female friend", and this incident had never happened according to her memory. She remembered being hit by the sleeper dart that night, but nothing more than that.

Kevin had lied to her about nothing more happening that night. More had happened, and from what she could tell in the report, Kevin had saved her life from a burning building. Almost like how she had just saved him from death underneath the Abyss. Or at least, she was hoping she had saved him. Kevin was still unconscious at this point.

Still, this gave Caitlin reason to question why Kevin would have hidden this. True, Kevin was relatively humble, or at least from what Caitlin had seen. That did not explain, however, why Kevin would not tell Caitlin about the incident and meeting with the Demons operative. Kevin did not have anything to hide, so why would he shy away from the truth?

That was it, Caitlin realized. Kevin was shying away because he was shy about something. He was nervous. But why? Was he in love with her the same way she was with him?

That thought struck fear into Caitlin's heart. True, she had to come to terms with the fact of the matter of her own feelings down in the Abyss, but now that event was passed. The idea of having emotions, and the fracturing of the emotional block around her, frightened her. She was determined to maintain herself and purge herself of the emotion she had felt before. She was scared, afraid of change.

Three core fears Caitlin was familiar with. Her father had taught her them a long time ago, and called them the three irrational fears: the fear of rejection, the fear of injury or death, and the fear of what may become. However, Caitlin, in her unfamiliarity with emotion, struggled with fear. It was the effect of being the same emotionless person that she had been for years.

Having finished with the report, Caitlin took it back to the desk and handed it to the receptionist. "Thank you," she said. "It was nice to read that report. Very interesting information."

"I thought it might be," responded the receptionist as she filed away the report. "Now, wouldst thou be willing to come with me? I am going to check on the Vanguard again, as the anti-coma remedy will work at different rates depending on the situation, and it is important that we take regular observations during this time."

Caitlin nodded in acknowledgment. "Very well, then. Lead the way."

The receptionist stepped up closer to Caitlin, antagonized by that statement. "That is my line," she said. Then, she began walking toward the stairs, indicating for Caitlin to go first. Seeing no need to debate, wondering if the reason for this was for the receptionist to feel more secure with a stranger in her building and a faction to protect, Caitlin started up the narrow staircase just in front of the receptionist.

Seeking to stir up a discussion, the receptionist began, as she climbed the stairs, "So, young lady, are thou like this all the time, or only when responding to distress?"

"What do you mean?" asked Caitlin, unsure of the question's intent.

"Your emotions," answered the receptionist "Since thou has

arrived here, thou has shown no emotion to anything, including the Vanguard who is in a coma. Art thou truly that heartless?"

Caitlin scowled. "You don't have to call it that," she responded, as she stepped onto the second floor. "Besides, what right do you have to ask me something like that?"

The receptionist raised her hand as she reached the second floor and stepped off of the staircase. "I did not mean to impose or hurt thy feelings," she said, in an apologetic tone. "Forgive me for implying so. I meant only to start a little discussion, and to note that I have seen little to no emotion out of thou, while I would also presume that thou know the Vanguard because thou brought him here. I thought the situation was curious."

"Oh," responded Caitlin. "That is how I always am. To show no emotion is to be focused, and such is the way that I choose to live my life."

The receptionist stopped in the hallway, and Caitlin stopped as well. "I see," said the receptionist. "It is a shame too, thou poor, poor girl, that thou choose to live that way."

"I'm sorry you feel that way," Caitlin responded. She was more or less ignoring the comment.

A little miffed, the receptionist said, "Feel? Well, if thou must know the truth, I know what that is like. What thou art now is what I was a couple of decades ago."

This sparked Caitlin's interest. Never before had she heard of someone who had chosen the same path she did when it came to emotions and self-control. More so, just because of this spark of interest, she also believed the receptionist was not lying, even though she had not heard anything about what had happened yet. "Go on," she said to the receptionist. "I'd like to hear more."

The receptionist put her hand against her face and wiped her eyes, appearing to be slightly distressed. "Thou will have to pardon me," she said. "It is not a time of my life that I like to remember." Still, the receptionist continued, "It began years ago under a heat of frustration. As much as this world is becoming fairer on women, this world was, and still is to this day, very much a man's world and I did not feel I fit into it. Seeing no need to have emotion anymore, I purged myself of all emotion and left my memories behind. I wanted to be fearless, not to let my feelings or perceptions of me determine my actions in the eyes of others. Unfortunately, however, all I found down that path was fear and sadness. I had become nothing more than an automated machine made of body tissues and bones. I had lost all that made me human, and no matter how much I tried, I could not purge the sadness. It took a long time for me to fix the damage I had caused to myself."

Caitlin crossed her arms. "Amusing," she said. "My reasons have been far different, however. I am…" Caitlin's voice began to shake as she struggled to finish her sentence, "that which I choose to be."

Chuckling, the receptionist responded, "Thou does not sound as confident as thou did earlier about the issue. Art thou hiding something from thyself? Has thy fear paralyzed thee?"

Caitlin turned her back. "No, I am not hiding something from myself."

"Yes, thou art," responded the receptionist confidently. "Look, if thou does not want to talk more about the subject, that is fine with me. But I do ask thou, please, do not lie to thyself. That is the worst thing thou can do."

Suddenly, as the receptionist finished what she was saying, a noise was heard from down the hall. It came from Kevin's room.

Immediately, Caitlin and the receptionist began rushing toward Kevin's room in the medical ward. When they arrived there and looked into the doorway, they both saw Kevin rolling around a bit, making some sound as he did.

"The coma is beginning to wear off," commented the receptionist as she and Caitlin observed this. "The herbs are starting to take effect. It should not be too long until he is out of the coma, although depending on how many hits he took to the head, he may not behave the same as he did before."

Caitlin let out a sigh of relief. At least Kevin would be fine. He was a survivor after all.

The receptionist knelt down beside Kevin and held him down with slight pressure. "Careful, careful," she said. "There is no need to panic. Thou will be fine."

Kevin stopped rolling, and cracked open his eyes, trying his best to see with them. Slowly, they began to come into focus, when he saw the receptionist. "Where am I?" he asked, in a very weak voice.

"Thou art in safety," responded the receptionist. "This is the medical ward of the Demons Headquarters in Nuvenia. Thou have been out for quite a while, Mr. K.T. Stryker."

"Please," interrupted Kevin, "call me Kevin."

"Very well," acknowledged the receptionist. "Do thou know thy full name?"

There was a slight pause as Kevin tried to focus. "My name… is Kevin Trent."

The receptionist stood up and shrugged. "Kevin Trent? His name matches neither the reports nor the name on his jacket." Then, she turned to Caitlin. "Do thou know the reason?"

"His full name is Kevin Trent Stryker," responded Caitlin. "It is abbreviated 'K.T. Stryker' on his jacket. It's only been a week since he has known his full name, and he's just been Kevin Trent all his life until then."

Kevin was confused as he was still trying to shake off the condition. "A week?" he asked, his voice still weak. "It has been more like three or four days," he said.

"I see," responded the receptionist, slightly confused. "Well, then, Mr. Trent, please try not to use up your strength just yet. I will have my assistant bring up some medical supplies to help you regain your strength, but until you feel strong enough to get out of this bed and walk around, please stay in bed."

Carefully, Kevin nodded lightly to acknowledge the request.

"Anyway, I shall leave you two alone for a while, then," continued the receptionist. "By nightfall, he should have his strength fully back. In the mean time, Caitlin, would you mind catching him up on what he has missed in the coma?" The receptionist then turned for the door and left, closing the door behind her. She did not even wait for any response from Caitlin, who was not sure if the receptionist was making a pointed statement or not with that remark.

After the door closed, Kevin turned his head over to the side of the bed where Caitlin was. "Did we win?" he asked.

Caitlin nodded. "We did." She lifted her right arm to reveal the Stripe of Ice on her forearm, wrapped around in a ribbon as Kevin's Stripe of Air was around his arm.

Kevin turned his head back, still very tired. "Keep it for now," he said. "I'm too tired to take it."

"As you wish," responded Caitlin as she lowered her arm. "We wasted four days down below, Kevin. For some reason, time must have moved faster while we were in the space between realms. It's now been a week since we left Venarose."

Letting out a sigh, Kevin did not move his head. "Great," he said with sarcasm. "I guess I should count my blessings I'm alive at all. I wish I would have stood a chance against the Existence, though."

"Now, now," responded Caitlin, "everyone has their limits. Besides, you can't expect to win every fight, though together we won this one."

Carefully, Kevin rolled his head over in the direction of Caitlin. "That's true," he said weakly, still struggling to make the words come out in his weakened condition. "You saved my life back there, Caitlin. I owe you a million favors for that."

"Oh, don't say that, Kevin," said Caitlin. "If you must think of it as something, think of us as being even after what you did for me in Venarose."

Kevin's eyes widened a bit, although not much. He rolled his head back to a neutral position. "You found out about that?" he asked.

"Yeah," responded Caitlin. "The Demons operative you met in Venarose filed a report about the whole situation, and I was permitted to read it. Also, the fact that these people thought you were important because you have that red and black triangle patch on your jacket made that report detailed about everything."

Kevin let out another sigh. "The treatment has been nice from having it, although I am curious as to what all does come with the title."

"I suppose we'll find out," said Caitlin. "Every day brings something new. By now, it's been two weeks since we've started this together. You have saved my life once by now, and I have saved yours. We certainly make a good team, don't you think?"

"Sure," responded Kevin, still tired and struggling to talk. "Have you ever thought, though, that sometimes being a team is not enough?"

"What do you mean by that?" asked Caitlin.

There was another pause. "Nothing," responded Kevin. "Listen. You don't need to be by my side right now if you don't want to be. It's all right with me if you'd like to go someplace else right now and do something else."

"There's nowhere else I need to be," answered Caitlin. "Nor is there anywhere else that I would like to be at the moment."

"All right," acknowledged Kevin. "So tell me, Caitlin, what does Nuvenia look like? What's it like out there?"

Caitlin was confused. "Odd question," she said. "I thought you would ask how we arrived here, or what happened after you blacked out, or something like that."

"It's not important right now," said Kevin. "But I do want to know something about where we are, while I'm stuck in this bed."

Reluctantly, Caitlin began, "The city is kind of dreary. The skies are covered in clouds blanketing everything above in white, the city is practically encased in high fortress-type thick walls, and not a plant can be seen growing anywhere in the city. Most of the buildings are in decent shape, but some buildings do have some damage, just from what I saw on my way in to the city. The roads are all the same gray brick as the walls, as well."

There was another pause. "I see," Kevin finally responded. "I can picture it now."

And as Kevin continued to talk with Caitlin, he eventually drifted to sleep again, this time not in a coma. He was still very tired. For several hours, Caitlin sat next to him, keeping him company and making sure he was not struggling to breathe or anything of that sort as he slept.

Chapter 27

Revelations

Eventually, nightfall fell upon Nuvenia, and a strange silence filled the air. Kevin was still fast asleep for the moment. Thoughts of him filled Caitlin's mind.

Once again, she was thinking about him, and about the feelings that she had experienced just a short while ago. No matter how hard she tried to suppress them, they kept surfacing, touching her heart and bringing tears to her eyes.

Now, she had to walk away from him, for at least a short while. She had to get away from Kevin so she would not think of him. She needed somewhere peaceful to think and clear her mind. Without hesitation, she stood up, walked downstairs, informed the receptionist as to where she was going, and left the headquarters.

Several minutes later, Kevin finally woke up. He pulled himself out of bed, although not without some effort, and started to get a hold onto his balance again. He stretched to loosen up his muscles, and then pulled his jacket to straighten it out. Seeing Caitlin was gone, he let out a sigh, certain that Caitlin would not have had the extraordinary amount of patience it would take to sit for that long. Kevin left his sword in the room as he fastened his belt, tied his shoes, and walked out of the room and down the stairs.

At the bottom of the stairs, the receptionist was waiting for him behind her desk. As he reached the bottom, the receptionist stood up from her chair and saluted Kevin. "Oh, please, that's not necessary," responded Kevin upon seeing this. "I'm not really one for military conduct and such."

The receptionist dropped her salute. "Thou art noble and kind for a Vanguard," she said as she sat back down. "It is good to see thou moving around again and doing well."

"Thank you," responded Kevin as he approached the

receptionist's desk. He had been thinking on what he wanted to do about the unification of Nuve situation all week while drifting in the boat toward the Abyss of the Royal Sovereign. Now seemed to be a good opportunity to put that plan into action. "Now, then, I have a few requests for you, presuming you're the one in charge here. Are you a leader?"

"Thou would be correct," responded the receptionist. "I am the one in charge here, the Nuvenia Operations Administrator of the Demons. You have excellent logic, Mr. Trent, and you would make an excellent operative if you ever wanted to be."

Kevin shook his head. "Spare me all of that," he laughed a little awkwardly. "Would you be willing to help me with my requests?"

The receptionist nodded. "The message we received here said thou would be requesting our help soon, so thy requests are anticipated and will be dealt with."

"Excellent," said Kevin. "You may want to write this down, as this could get to be a little long."

Fortunately for both of them, though, the receptionist had already grabbed a feather pen and paper earlier in the day, and as such had them handy next to her. She unfurled the paper, dipped her pen in ink, and prepared to take the request.

Kevin began, "I am assigned by the King of Aurana to request an alliance with Nuve to help defend against the invasions of Desolunar. Unifying Nuve, at least temporarily, is my priority for now, and to ask for the alliance from all of the sides represented. For this to happen, I need to have a meeting arranged with the leaders of the Demons and the Cornelia Chimeras, together with the king of Nuve." He deliberately left out the Knights of the Dragon for now, remembering that Caitlin said it was not truly a faction and just a small group of warriors, and the last thing Kevin needed were more complications. "Call it an armistice negotiation, if you must, but nothing more. I, Kevin Trent Stryker, Vanguard of Aurana, will make the pitch to their representatives personally. If we can make arrangements for all three parties to be comfortable with this, then let us do so."

The receptionist chuckled, as she wrote the message down. "I doubt they will ever be comfortable, no matter what arrangements thou make. Nonetheless, the Demons I am sure will authorize these expenses because of your title and because what thou speak of, this armistice, is a desire of our group, even though the leader of the Demons, Steffen Robert, does not at all get along with the king of Nuve, Raijin Lester."

"Raijin Lester?" asked Kevin. He seemed confused by the name.

Taking a breath, the receptionist put her face in her hand, and then lifted it out. "Of course, thou art Auranian. In Nuve, and not in anywhere else in the world, the family name comes before the given name. It is part of the culture, the dialect, everything here."

"I understand," responded Kevin. He then continued, "I want every attempt to be taken. The sooner we can get everyone together, the better. How long would it take to get this meeting underway?"

The receptionist began to calculate. "Let us see. Given that the farthest leader is the leader of the Cornelia Chimeras in the southwest of Nuve, the time it would take to send messages by trained falcon, and the amount of time it would take for the leaders to arrive in Nuvenia by horseback, if we ordered them here immediately, I would say two weeks would be reasonable."

Kevin was stunned. "Two weeks?" he exclaimed. "I don't know if I can wait that long. Too long for me to make any progress, too short for me to continue on and return to the city."

"I can have the time lengthened if thou would like," interrupted the receptionist.

"No," responded Kevin. "As I said, the sooner the better. The more we wait, the more likely Desolunar invades further north. Rush the job as quickly as you can."

"Very well," said the receptionist. "While thou are at it, is there anyone else you would like to have brought here to meet?"

Considering this proposition, Kevin said, "Depends. How far away is the Vanguard of Nuve?"

Thinking, the receptionist said, "I believe he is in the city of Cornelia helping to settle the dispute between the Chimeras and Nuve's government. I would be careful around him, though, as he is King

Lester's younger brother, Raijin Shane. Still, if thou would like, I can have him come up here with the Cornelia Chimeras and arrive here at about the same time as they do."

"That works," responded Kevin. "Just get him here. I would like to meet him."

"As thou wish," responded the receptionist. "Shall I book a room for thou here for the next two weeks, then?"

Kevin was very hesitant. "No thanks," he said. "I don't have enough money to afford an inn for two weeks." Kevin knew his small bag of silver and copper would not cover two weeks of room and board at an inn.

"Oh, please," insisted the receptionist, "consider it free of charge. For a Vanguard, the Demons will grant thou whatever thou need. Thou will have to share a room with thy traveling companion, but it is still free for both of thou."

This changed Kevin's mind, and although he did not want to be a burden, he was glad to have the service of the Demons behind him. "All right," he said. "That would be great."

The receptionist nodded. "Thy room will be in 301 on the third floor. Anything else thou needs?"

"Just one thing," said Kevin. "Where's Caitlin?"

"The girl?" asked the receptionist. "She said she was heading to the north bridge outside the city. Said she wanted a bit of peace and quiet for a little while."

That did not make sense to Kevin at all. Did she not say there was no place else she needed to be? Caitlin was not one to change her mind often. There had to be another reason. And Kevin was going to find out. He would go to the ends of the earth and back, just to know Caitlin more. That feeling of something special in Caitlin had never faded from Kevin's mind.

With no further comment, Kevin rushed out the door and headed for the gate in the wall to the north. As he hit the opening, however, he stopped dead in his tracks.

On the solid wood bridge in front of him, Caitlin was leaning with both arms on the west side rail, looking out upon the water. The waters of the Abyss of the Royal Sovereign were moving slowly and calmly this night, making the setting much more peaceful than it had been. The sky was also completely clear of clouds, and the stars were out, as well as the full moon. Though Nuvenia had been a dreary city in the daytime, or at least it was according to Caitlin, the scene around the bridge at night under a clear sky and above a peaceful lake was one that stood in contrast to Caitlin's description of the sights and city itself. Perhaps the daylight would illuminate these flaws. However, for now, the scene was lovely in the darkness.

Out on the bridge, Caitlin had been thinking, alone. She kept thinking about her father's words about strong emotions and what that would do to her emotional block. More and more, she worried about her ability to keep them suppressed. She was afraid of what she would feel if they were not. Then, she noticed Kevin, and immediately felt a feeling: that of nervousness. She tried to suppress it, as she did all others.

Kevin started walking up to Caitlin, slowly. "Caitlin," he began, "what are you doing out here by yourself? It's a bit chilly out tonight."

"I know," responded Caitlin without turning. "It's good to see you out here walking around, Kevin. You must be feeling much better."

"Very much so," responded Kevin. "I still feel a little beat up, but I only suppose that's natural. Hopefully something like that never happens again, because it honestly feels horrible."

"I'm sure it does," said Caitlin. "I was very worried for your safety after that. Believe it or not, magic alone was not enough to heal you after that."

Kevin raised an eyebrow. "I was wondering about that," he said. "It did seem odd to me that I woke up in the inn and not earlier."

"Yeah, real surprise, isn't it?" asked Caitlin. "The receptionist at the inn had anti-coma remedies that she was willing to administer to you. I would guess that her medication was why you woke up."

Sighing, Kevin said, "Well, as long as it worked, I guess. Still, though, you haven't answered my first question. What are you doing out here by yourself?"

Caitlin took a breath. She felt more fragile than she ever had been. "I just needed some time to think, and it's peaceful out here. That's all, Kevin. You don't need to worry about me."

"I may not need to, but that doesn't mean I won't," said Kevin. "I want you to be safe, both physically and mentally." Kevin leaned up on the railing next to Caitlin. "And recently, I've become a little worried about you."

"How so?" asked Caitlin, suddenly a little paranoid. Had she accidentally revealed more of herself than she intended? "I see no reason why you would need to be worried about me or the way I think."

"But I do," interrupted Kevin. "You haven't been yourself lately, Caitlin."

Caitlin turned her head away. "I have not cracked," she said. "In fact, I have no idea what you're talking about."

That was almost an admission. Kevin did not even bring up Caitlin "cracking". "Yes you do," responded Kevin firmly. "Please stop lying about it."

Shaking a bit, Caitlin responded, "I'm not lying."

Caitlin's voice in her response had given Kevin more than reason to believe that Caitlin was insecure about what she had just said. She was shaking, not confident, or anything. This was not typical Caitlin behavior. Surely, Kevin was getting closer to the answers about Caitlin that he had been looking for.

Still, Kevin wanted to be delicate with this. He did have feelings for his traveling companion after all, and he was starting to have trouble holding them in. There was also the fact that Kevin knew something that Caitlin did not want him to know. Kevin's head was guiding him, but his heart was leading the way. "You're doing it again," said Kevin. "You're lying to yourself more than you are me. I can see the conflict going on within you."

Getting off of the rail, Caitlin left one hand on it as she turned to face away from Kevin and the city. "Is that what this is about?" she said in her normal tone. "Are you really going to accuse me of sheltering emotion behind my discipline? I have none, end of story."

Speechless, Kevin tried to come up with something to respond with, something that would not upset Caitlin, but he was unable to do so.

"How dare you!" began Caitlin, her rage starting to build as she yelled at Kevin. "How dare you accuse me of lying? How dare you tell me that I have something that I do not? How dare you!"

Kevin wanted to speak, but Caitlin was starting to change, and Kevin saw it. She could not maintain her posture. Her tone started to become sadder as emotion began to leak through her shell. Her voice became louder and more involuntary, as well as higher pitched. "Why do you do this to me?" she asked as her head dropped and tears began to fall from her eyes. "Why do you have to break me like this? Why? Why?"

"Caitlin, I…"

Then, Caitlin put her hands against her face, and started to run to the other side of the bridge, crying. Never before had Kevin seen Caitlin react like this. She was fully emotional and breaking down. He had to act quickly if he was going to stop Caitlin from running away. He had to get this right, somehow, someway.

"Caitlin, wait!" he called, trying to stop Caitlin from running.

It did not work. Caitlin continued to run, crying.

Then, Kevin said it. It came straight out of his heart, not from his head. "I know how you feel about me," he said.

I know how you feel about me.

The words stopped Caitlin in her tracks. Her hands fell over her heart as her eyes stopped tearing. The sensation in her heart was powerful, overtaking her bit by bit. She did not turn around, but she asked, in a voice more innocent, "How?"

Kevin started to approach Caitlin, "I was conscious while I was on the ground when you fought the Existence, for a little bit. I could not move or see, but I could hear and I could feel. What you said and what you did then… well, it led me to figure it out."

Caitlin said nothing. Her hands remained over her heart, and she still did not turn to face Kevin.

Taking a deep breath, Kevin knew what had to happen now. He had to tell her the truth. She needed to hear it now more than ever.

Kevin continued, pushing the words from his heart as he stepped up behind Caitlin, "The fact is, though, that even if you don't care, if you want to try to push all of the emotion from your body, my emotions won't change. And the truth of the matter is, I've felt there was something special about you for a long time. Like any person out there, of course I've had my fears about saying anything, but if there's going to be any time that I tell you the truth, it should be now, when you need to hear it most." Kevin took a deep breath, preparing to push through his own shyness and speak stronger from his heart than he ever had before. "So here it goes. I love you, Caitlin."

I love you, Caitlin.

More tears began falling from Caitlin's eyes as they widened. But these tears were not tears of sadness; they were tears of happiness. A great shattering resonated through Caitlin's heart, tearing down the walls that had been for years and years. The block was completely gone.

A gust of wind blew from the east to the west, in the opposite direction it normally did. This wind gave lift to Caitlin's long reddish hair for a second. It stood as a symbol of the rapid change occurring within Caitlin: just as the wind changed, so had she. The breaking of the emotional block struck like a bolt of lightning, tearing apart all that she had placed around herself. All that was left was her own heart, and that which she had buried away years before.

In that moment, though, the fear disappeared. What she felt, was love.

Quickly, Caitlin turned and pushed herself into Kevin, burying her face up against his body. In her state of chaotic change, instinct had driven her reaction.

Kevin, sensing within himself exactly what was going on within Caitlin, placed his arms around Caitlin's shoulders gently, using very little pressure. "I know you're scared," he said, trying to be delicate. "But you're strong and you'll make it through. And I'll be there to help you any way I can. I promise it to you."

Suddenly, as soon as Kevin had finished what he said, Caitlin wrapped her arms around Kevin, much to Kevin's surprise. "I'm not scared," she said after a second. Something was very different about her voice, though, and Kevin noticed it. Her voice was much lighter and gentler. Then, she looked up at Kevin, some tears still in her eyes. For the first time that Kevin had ever seen, a smile was on Caitlin's face. "I'm happy," she said. She put her head back down and grabbed Kevin tighter as she continued, "You knew it all along, didn't you? You knew I secretly loved you too."

"I think I did," responded Kevin, thinking of how he had always thought of Caitlin as being very special to him.

Caitlin grabbed Kevin tighter, holding him closer. All she wanted in that moment was to be close to Kevin. Energy was surging through her body, and her heart was beating quickly. It was almost beyond anything she had ever felt before. It was such a happy moment. A great spark felt like it was going across Caitlin's heart, illuminating herself with happiness and energy.

Then, Kevin felt Caitlin pushing upwards, almost as if she was trying to stand up on the ball of her foot. "You don't need to try and stand up higher just because you're shorter than I am," he said.

Confused, Caitlin asked back, "Huh? What do you mean, Kevin? I'm not trying to stand up higher."

Now, Kevin was very unsure of what was going on. Carefully, he looked down and around Caitlin's head, and he saw a sight that scared him.

"My gods," interjected Kevin, startled, "Caitlin, look at yourself! You're floating off of the ground!"

Surprised by this, Caitlin let go of Kevin, allowing him to take a step back. Then, Caitlin looked down to see exactly what Kevin had seen.

Caitlin was floating a short distance above the ground. More so, there was a slight glow of white all around her as she did.

"Wow," said Kevin, stunned as he saw more of Caitlin.

"This is amazing," Caitlin said in awe. "This has happened once before, down in the space between realms when we fought the Existence. I just started floating, and felt a surge of power flow through my veins. I wonder why it's happening now, too. What do you think, Kevin?"

Kevin did not respond.

"Kevin?" Caitlin asked as she looked up to see Kevin staring at her, pointing his finger. Something had surprised him.

"Caitlin, you might want to take a look at yourself," he said. "You're not just floating."

Not sure what Kevin meant by that, Caitlin dropped to the

ground and looked over the bridge rail to see her reflection in the Abyss of the Royal Sovereign. And what she saw was a complete surprise.

It was a set of white wings coming from her back, spanning about as far as Caitlin's body was long if they were extended. Caitlin reached her right hand back to try and feel the wing, only to realize that she could not. The wings were not actually there, but they were translucent, almost like what one would imagine a ghost to be like. "This can't be!" said Caitlin, still with a look of extreme surprise on her face. "How is this possible?"

"I don't know," responded Kevin, also surprised, "but what you are is… is…"

"An angel," said Caitlin as she stared at her hands in surprise.

Angels were mythical figures. In stories and lore, they were half-immortals, the children of the immortal and the mortal. With the translucent white wings, Caitlin looked exactly like one.

"Surely your father knows something about this," said Kevin after this moment of thought. "He does know a lot more about a great many things than we do."

Caitlin was still staring at herself. "Maybe," she said, not focusing on what Kevin had just said. Instead, she was starting to break down. "I just…" she stuttered, trying to hold back tears, "I don't know who or what I am anymore."

This made Kevin a bit sadder to hear Caitlin speak of herself that way. "You're you, Caitlin," he said affectionately, as he stepped closer to Caitlin. "You're a wonderful person. In fact, I think you're stronger and more beautiful than anyone I have ever seen before."

Caitlin turned her head to Kevin, not normally taken by comments like these, but in this moment feeling strong emotions. "You really mean it?" she asked with an innocent tone of voice, as if taken by the sweet compliment.

Kevin nodded, with a smile on his face. "Yes," he said. "I mean it from the bottom of my heart."

Before Kevin had the opportunity to say any more, Caitlin jumped toward Kevin with her arms extended and latched herself around him again. "How did I ever get so lucky," she asked delicately, "to find someone like you?"

Kevin smiled at this comment as he held on to Caitlin as well. "I'm not sure," he said, "but I'm happy I found you, too."

The two stayed clung together for about a minute. Then, simultaneously, almost as if their hearts told them the same thing at the same time, their heads rolled back as they still held on to each other, and their eyes contacted each other before they shared their first kiss.

Chapter 28

Where Time Stands Still

"So it's just over there?" asked Rachel.

For several long days, Arthur Falchor and Rachel Reinhart had been traveling north through the lands of the Wastes, on the advice of the chief of the Metoi tribe, Chief Aspectra. As they continued north, the Toronaga tribe, allies of the Metoi, had shown Arthur the same kindness as he had received from the Metoi.

After reaching the Calphos River, Arthur and Rachel had continued alongside it, just as the Metoi had instructed. The Toronaga had given even further detail about the location of their destination, the city of Cardol. The lands around the Calphos River were lush when compared to the Wastes. Life pooled all around the river in this area.

"I believe so," responded Arthur. "Got any ideas how to get across?"

Rachel shook her head. "None," she said. "There's no bridge or anything anywhere I can see.

Arthur turned and snapped his fingers. "Damn," he said. "So close, and yet so far away. I hate it when that happens."

Putting the arrow back in the quiver, Rachel asked, "Is it really that necessary that we make it to Cardol? If we're trying to get out of Desolunar, we could try and find a bridge down the river somewhere."

"I don't know," said Arthur, contemplating his answer for a moment, "but if there's any chance that it will help out Kevin, then I have to take it."

"How so?" asked Rachel. "You've tried to explain this whole thing between you and Kevin several times, and how I got involved in all of this, and I still don't get it. Every day, I hear more of a god this, your father that, and so on, and so forth"

Arthur put his face in his hand. "Jeez, Rachel, you're such a cynic."

"I told you, I'm not a cynic!"

"Fine. A skeptic, then."

"And a skeptic I will be," said Rachel. "I want to know where you're getting these delusions. Why are we out here in what used to be southern Nuve? What good does this do?"

Shaking his head, Arthur said, "Look, Rachel, I don't know what else to do, okay? We've got to run, but I don't just want us to be cowards. If anyone can help us, it's either Kevin if that sword he had makes him have super powers or something, or it might be Kron Kalavere. We can't seek them out if Demonicus wants us to kill them, but maybe after some time and the heat dies down, we can find them and help them."

Rachel looked at Arthur with a confused expression. "Does that plan make sense to you?"

Arthur rolled his eyes. "You don't understand, just like when Kevin had a crush on you some time ago."

"Oh, well you're one to…" Rachel interrupted before stopping, which also repressed her excitement somewhat. "What do you mean that Kevin had a crush on me? When was this?"

"About a year ago," recalled Arthur. "Kevin was really crazy about you during that year in the Rikleifer Academy. He tried to get you to notice, but you never did. After a while, he gave up, a little heartbroken."

"Oh, I see," responded Rachel, sounding a little down. "I never even knew. And yet he has still tried to be my friend after that?"

"Indeed," said Arthur, nodding. "But that's just Kevin for you. Always trying to be everyone's friend, never an enemy despite the situation. I think he's a fool for thinking so, yet it's not as though he cares to hear my advice about that."

Rachel glanced at Arthur for a second. "Well, you know more about him than I do. To be honest, I never had any interest in him anyway although he's been a good friend."

"Rachel, I doubt there's any young woman who has any interest in Kevin, so what you're saying doesn't surprise me," joked Arthur, with a bit of a chuckle. "If he found one between when I last saw him and now, I won't know whether to think that's great, funny, or scary."

Rachel rolled her eyes. "If you say so," she said. "You're lucky that you're Kevin's best friend, or else you probably wouldn't get away with making that kind of comment."

"I'm sure," chuckled Arthur. "But seriously, if you don't want to come with me to Cardol, and just want to head back to Aurana, then go right ahead. I won't stop you."

Rachel shook her head. "No," she said. "You're going to need my help. And, I kind of owe you one for getting me out of the dungeon in Seta Archa. You really stuck your neck out for me back there."

Silently, Arthur nodded. He did not want to talk about it further. He had just felt it was the right thing to do in that moment.

Taking a moment to take stock of their supplies while trying to figure out a solution to this problem, Rachel found something in her quiver. "Hey Arthur, check this out," she said as she showed him the supplies in the quiver. "There's a rope in here."

Arthur stared at the rope for a second. He then looked across the river, and back at the rope. "What do you have in mind?" he asked Rachel, not sure what she was thinking.

"I'm thinking let me tie the end of this rope to an arrow, and shoot it," she said. "This isn't a very wide river, and I think I can get an arrow stuck in one of the trees on the other side. We could then tie the other end of the rope to a tree over here, and then we could use the rope to help us wade across the river without getting swept away."

Arthur just looked at the river, saying nothing.

"No opinion?" Rachel asked.

Shrugging, Arthur said, "You have an idea. That's one more than I have, so let's just go with it."

Reluctantly, Rachel nodded. After tying the rope to her arrow, she placed it on her bowstring, pulled the string back tight, and let loose an arrow straight at a tree on the other side. This would be an interesting test of how effective this bow was.

The sharp tipped arrow flew across the river. Rachel had perfectly calculated in her head how the weight of the rope would affect her shot, and landed it perfectly in a softwood tree on the other side. It was difficult to tell from the side she was on, but it looked to be a good, deep shot.

Impressed, Arthur's jaw dropped a bit. He knew Rachel practiced a lot of archery, but she just demonstrated a ton of talent with that shot. Then, Arthur took it upon himself to grab the other end of the rope and hand the end to Rachel as well.

Rachel tugged on the rope gently. "I think this will do," she said. "We're just going to have to get wet." It was a spring day and warm, but not very, so this concerned her.

Arthur nodded in acknowledgment. Regardless of how wet they would be, they had to cross the river. Even if they were still in Desolunar's held territory, being out of Desolunar proper would be a great relief and an important step in their escape from the kingdom.

Carefully, Arthur and Rachel walked into the Calphos River, keeping their hands on the secured rope. Although it was not a very wide river, it suddenly became deep a short distance in, leading both of them to keep both hands on the rope. Neither one of them were dressed to swim, and Arthur had a heavy sword on his waist, but the rope was holding well. Rachel's shot had been that good.

Fortunately, although the current was flowing, at no point was it so forceful as to make their crossing difficult. Arthur felt heavy as he pulled himself across, but he remained buoyant enough not to sink under his own weight and force his hands off the rope. By the time he reached the other shore, his arms were very tired, but he had made it. Rachel had also made it, worn out and tired.

"Nicely done, Rachel," Arthur said, out of breath, looking back at the river. "We did it."

Rachel was staring at the city. "Uh, Arthur, I know we're soaking wet, but you're going to want to see this."

Curious, Arthur turned around, and saw a sight he never imagined. Through the trees, visible now that they were close enough to see past them, was a path to a distant city. And it was a spot of bright white.

Arthur and Rachel took the next couple of hours to build a fire and dry their clothes. They took turns with the clothing to make sure no one had to see the other without them. Then, after drying out and taking a bite of their provisions, they set off together down the pathway to Cardol. It was a short walk of a few minutes.

Once there, the sight was even more amazing. White stone buildings, white brick roads, fountains, trees, and other decorative plants were everywhere. Among the buildings, flowers bloomed all over the place. It was a place where time stands still. This was the city of Cardol. Ever silent, save for the fountains in the city, nobody walked these streets. It was vacant, preserved, a jewel lost in time. Nothing seemed quite as lovely, yet also quite as strange, as this city.

"Well, you were right," said Arthur. "I'm amazed. It's quite a sight."

"Told you so," said Rachel, as she and Arthur walked down a city street. "Can you imagine that city when it was filled with people just a few years ago? What a city this must have been!"

"Really, it must've," responded Arthur as Rachel reached the top of the ramp. "I can see why Chief Aspectra directed us here. A city this large, this wondrous, surely must have a library here."

"I guess I finally made it even though the book club didn't," Rachel commented. "But you think there's more than just a library, don't you? Otherwise you wouldn't have dragged me here to Cardol."

"Chief Aspectra said that the Metoi were the keepers of knowledge of Desolunar. If he was willing to send me here, knowing that I am 'the heir', or whatever he believes, then the information we can find here in Cardol is particularly strong."

Rachel put her face in her hands, sighing. "So it wasn't too well thought out, then, just like I said. Shoot first and ask questions later, huh? Just for one day, I'd like to live life in your shoes."

Arthur laughed. "I wouldn't do that if I were you. You might find some things that you never wanted to see."

"Oh, is that so?" interjected Rachel, also laughing by this point. "I think maybe I ought to reconsider, then."

"I would if I were you," joked Arthur.

By now, Arthur and Rachel had reached the main thoroughfare through Cardol. The wide brick street, once bustling full of people and small market stands, was devoid of any life whatsoever other than the grasses beginning to grow through the bricks and the occasional tree in front of a building. The largest buildings of Cardol sat along this street, as empty as the thoroughfare they were lined up on. Some of the buildings were newer, while some were old, but all were constructed in the same style nonetheless. As lovely as the city of Cardol was to Arthur and Rachel, especially now that they had seen the main thoroughfare, it was also an eerie sight. A city that was so well kept and also a major city for a surviving superstate such as Nuve should not be sitting vacant like this. It was as though the city was a ghost town.

Almost ten years or so before the present date, deep advances into Nuve by the nation of Desolunar, led by Demonicus, had placed Cardol in severe threat of capture. Seeing a need to protect his people, King Raijin Lester, the Nuve king, ignored the advice of his Collective Council and forced his city's citizens to evacuate. While some left to other parts of Nuve, such as Cornelia or the province of Katalina, most followed an escorted march to the city-fortress of Nuvenia, in the province of Soverenia. Nuvenia was established as the new capital of Nuve.

As the Nuve forces retreated, losing several battles to the Desolunar forces, Nuve surrendered Cardol to Desolunar, electing not to engage their forces. This was a decision made by the Collective Council, to prevent Cardol from being destroyed. Though Cardol could have very well been destroyed by the Desolunar forces anyway after the capture, Demonicus decided to let the city remain untouched, himself an admirer of the city's ancient beauty that had survived the years, wars, and cultural renovations.

A short distance down the main thoroughfare, Arthur pointed out that he saw the city's library, a large building with an elegant front. The library was gigantic, as large as the abandoned buildings that had been a part of the city's administration and homes of the royal family. Appearing several stories tall, it was made of pure white stone with large columns at its front. A staircase adorned its main entrance. Upon pointing this building out to Rachel, Arthur began running to the building's front, with Rachel following closely behind. As they entered the building, however, neither could anticipate the sheer magnitude of what they saw.

The inside of the library was even more grand than its exterior. Bookshelves lined every wall. Bookshelves sat in tight rows across almost every bit of floor space, save for that which allowed people to walk through single file. Bookshelves towered all the way to the ceiling, all completely filled with books from the top to the bottom.

Arthur let out a sigh. "Well, I can see why we were told this would be a good place to come," he said. "We could spend our whole lifetimes here and never find anything useful."

"Or maybe everything useful," countered Rachel, staring at the room in awe. Herself a writer, this was quite the sight. "I could stay in here forever and never, ever get bored."

Snapping his fingers, Arthur said, "Okay, time to snap out of it. If nothing else, this would probably be a safe place to stay the night, and we can look around for anything useful while we're here."

"Oh, right," said Rachel, as if coming out of a trance. She took the quiver she was carrying off her back and set it on a nearby table. "I guess it sure beats sleeping out in the open again." She looked at Arthur. "Maybe I can take one or two of the smaller books if I find something I enjoy reading."

Arthur shrugged. "Suit yourself," he said. He walked off deeper into the library.

A couple of hours had passed, and Rachel had made herself comfortable at one end of the library. Although certainly a formal place of serious business, she was relieved to find a couple of pads designed to bend and sit in chairs. It gave her a comfy place to sit, and she could make a bed out of them for the night. Near where she was, there was a large fireplace for warmth. She lit a fire with the flint she had in her quiver and some dry firewood that had been left by the fireplace. There, she warmed her hands, pulled up a chair, and sat to do some reading.

A few of the books had caught her eye. *The Essence of Nothingness* was one she recognized from school, but she quickly cast it off as nonsense. *The Tale of the Valkyrie* was a great fantasy adventuring story, but she was not a fan of the genre. Finally she stumbled across a book of poetry, and decided to sit and read that for a while. She looked around briefly, noting that Arthur had been elsewhere in the library and was still nowhere nearby, and sat down and opened her book.

She opened up the book and read the first poem she saw when she opened it.

Look at the world and you may find
That world events seem rather benign.
Look at the sky and you might see
The tolls that life doth take on thee.

Mine is full of troubling times
And various thoughts of different crimes.
But I have a secret, I can see
That the best is yet to be.

Shallow peace of a "kind, fair world,"
Yet blood stains all when the flags are unfurled.
Looking at the world may betray thee,
Or maybe 'tis darkness one truly sees.

Wars and crimes, acts and lies,
With every issue, a part of me dies.
But I find my escape when I decree
That the best is yet to be.

A shattered heart may be the cause
When the memory of a lost love gives you pause.
Or maybe fear paralyzes thee
From observing more sociability.

Still I find myself at peace
Even when my hands are stained with grease.
Life and love, through all I still see
The truth; the best is yet to be.

So to you, I share these words

In the hopes that you'll take flight like birds;
You may see black, but can't you see
That the best is yet to be?

And though you see a world of plight
And want so badly to give up the fight:
Surrender not, for the blind can see
That the best is yet to be.

The poem was attributed to "Anonymous". It was a very inspirational, somewhat well known poem, and yet no one had taken credit for it. Rachel was very moved by the work of someone so humble.

And yet, its lesson was relevant as well. Optimism was the way forward in the darkest situations, and to Rachel, where she was and why she was there still seemed very obscure. Still, words were only words, after all, and though some words can be strong, most words mean little.

"Hey, Rachel!" echoed Arthur's voice from the back of the library. "Come back here! I think there's something back here!"

Surprised, Rachel raced to follow Arthur's voice. It was coming from a narrow room in the back of the library. As she stopped at the room's entrance, Arthur pointed to an old book lying on the floor. "Check this out," he said as he picked up the book gently. "I can't read the title of this book; it must be in the ancient language."

That instantly dated the book more than several hundred years. Although Rachel was not sure what drew Arthur to it, he clearly seemed intrigued enough to call for her. "Try checking the card in the front cover of the book," responded Rachel. "If there was a translation going on, a card with the translated title would be in the front of the book. Then we'll know for sure if it's really something or not."

Doing as he was instructed, knowing it was a good idea, Arthur flipped open the front cover of the book and found a translation card. He pulled it out and read the info on the card. "*Immortality is a Truth* by Setaeus Demota. Originally published over five thousand years ago. Translation is in progress, and papers are pressed in the book in various places where translation has occurred. Warning: Book may contain large amounts of either hypothetical or dangerous information. Private collection only, top shelf. Do not permit for checkout or study without special permission."

"Wow," said Rachel, actually surprised. "So maybe we have a hit after all." Then it hit Rachel that she did not know what they were looking for in the first place, so she asked, "By the way, what exactly are you looking for?"

"I'm not exactly sure," responded Arthur, trying to answer the question himself.

"Yeah, you told me that on the way here," interrupted Rachel, rolling her eyes again. "But this is a really intriguing find, I'll agree. I wonder if something like this has advice on ancient powers, or something like that."

"Who knows," answered Arthur. "Maybe we stay here for a couple of days to get good rest before moving on. In the meantime, we'll remove the translation papers pressed into the book and see if any of the translated parts contain anything we can use."

Nodding, Rachel responded, "Sounds good. I suppose I'll just have to get used to how you drag me around anywhere you damn well please."

"I already said you can leave at any time you'd like," frowned Arthur.

"And I said I wasn't leaving," said Rachel. "I'll get used to it, though. Somehow."

Arthur chuckled a bit at this. "Yeah, you'll learn to put up with me at some point," he said.

Chapter 29

The Nightmare Returns

The skies were lit up in apocalyptic thunder, spreading light across a darkened sky. The world was tearing itself apart in the wake of the chaos that had just ensued… an aftermath foreshadowing the end of a long journey that would change the world forever. The end was coming.

It was an ominous sight among the skies of lightning and the ruined city surrounding, but it was a sign of the final battle to come. Fires burned all around, some from the burning buildings of the city and some from the troops, relaxing in victory. In front of a tall white temple, larger than any building around within the ruined city, the angel Caitlin Magnon stood watching the temple.

Wait a moment. This seems familiar, Caitlin realized in her head. Something was not right about this. She started to look around, looking for hints.

In front of Caitlin, Kevin Trent Stryker stood facing the white temple. His sword was drawn and he was charging toward the temple. Now was the time for him to follow his destiny.

Something was very wrong, and though Caitlin could not shake a feeling of familiarity, she could not realize why this was so familiar. Yet she knew Kevin was in danger.

"Kevin! It's a trap!" Caitlin screamed hysterically, unable to control herself.

"Let him go," echoed a voice beside her. "He can't hear you."

Completely taken by surprise, Caitlin turned to see perhaps the most frightening sight. It was the last thing Caitlin expected to see.

It was herself. The Caitlin she was looking at was dressed in her typical black dress, with an emotionless appearance and tone of voice.

Caitlin looked down at herself to notice that she did not look the same as the Caitlin standing next to her. Instead, she was floating off the ground a little bit, ethereal angel wings wrapped around from her backside, and instead of a black dress, a long white cloth wrapped around her as covering. Caitlin then ran her fingers through her long, straight red hair, noticing that it was a little longer than it had been before.

Noting all of this, Caitlin turned toward her double. "What are you talking about?" she exclaimed. "And who are you?"

"Call me Amelia, but I am you," she said. "Only how your sub-conscience chooses to process these images."

Amelia was Caitlin's middle name.

Before Caitlin could get a word in, however, Amelia said, "Don't fear it. Learn from it. You have the power to prevent catastrophe, if you don't let him go it alone."

"But…"

Then, Amelia raised both of her hands to about the level of her eyes, and clapped twice.

After the sound of the clap, Caitlin's eyes popped open in bed. It had all been a dream after all, and Amelia did not exist. Or did she? If she was a part of Caitlin, then Caitlin reasoned that maybe she really did exist after all. The hour was very late, however, so she drifted back off to sleep with the thoughts of Amelia in mind.

It had been two long weeks. The days had passed by slowly as Kevin Trent Stryker waited patiently in Nuvenia for the arrival of the leaders of the Demons and Cornelia Chimeras factions, so that an armistice could be discussed. Fortunately for Kevin, the Demons had shown him great kindness in Nuvenia. For the past two weeks, Kevin and Caitlin had grown closer together than they ever had been before. They spent every day together, explored Nuvenia and the waters of the Abyss of the Royal Sovereign, and shared as much of their life stories with each other as possible. Every day they spent together was another treasure they had.

That led Caitlin to a decision, as well. Although she was a little scared of what was to come without her discipline, the block that protected her from emotion, she was excited by the time she spent with Kevin and the amazing potential she had to explore what being an angel meant. Because the latter had only happened under intense emotion, she decided not to have her father restore the block. Albeit nervous, she was confident that this was the way she wanted to go forward, for now. It helped that Kevin had encouraged her to just be herself, and that if she still had natural discipline and the ability to exude strength from that, there was no reason to force herself to change.

Plus, she really did find that she loved Kevin, and that he loved her, too. That feeling was so good that Caitlin did not want to give it up.

Over the course of the two weeks, Kevin and Caitlin had come to find that cloud cover and a fully overcast sky was very common in Nuvenia, and that the night of clear skies two weeks ago when they were on the bridge together for the first time was actually uncommon for the city. Cold stone lined most of the walls and buildings, though the museums in the city were warm. The city did not have a palace like Aurana City did, but instead used a castle as its capital building, with many defenses placed all around.

Soon, Kevin would be inside that building with King Raijin Lester of Nuve, Demons faction leader Steffen Robert, and the leader of the Cornelia Chimeras. The Demons administrator who ran the inn had kept him informed and told him, much to her surprise, that his request had been successful with each faction. Now, Kevin would do his best to negotiate the temporary peace he needed to bring Nuve into action that would save both it and its neighbors.

Early on the morning of the fourteenth day, before Kevin and Caitlin were awake, there was a knock on their room door. The voice of the receptionist leaked through the door as she knocked and said, "Excuse me, Mr. Trent! The Vanguard of Nuve is here to see thou!"

Caitlin was the first to wake up. She pushed herself up from the bed and started to wipe her eyes. As she heard the knocking, she started to gently press Kevin on his shoulder. "Kevin," she said, "Kevin, you have to wake up. The Vanguard of Nuve is here to see you."

Kevin merely shook around a bit, apparently trying to resist waking up.

Seeing this, Caitlin pressed on Kevin again. "I'm serious, Kevin," she said. "You have to wake up!"

Still, Kevin did not budge.

Caitlin let out a sigh. "All right, then," she said. "We'll play this your way." She put a little ice magic at the tip of her fingers, ready to touch Kevin with them, just enough to make him cold.

A grunt came from Kevin for a second as he acknowledged what Caitlin had said, seeing what Caitlin was doing and not wanting to feel a cold touch. "Are you sure it's not actually playing it *your* way?" he asked tiredly.

"Who cares whose way it is," she laughed. "Just as long as you get up."

Knowing that he had to get up anyway to meet the Vanguard of Nuve like he had wanted to, Kevin struggled to roll his way out of bed. Still tired, he grabbed his Aurana military jacket with the vanguard patch and threw it on. Then, he took his sword and strapped it to his left side, as he always did. He ran his fingers through his hair to straighten it, then rubbed his eyes and straightened his posture.

As Kevin was fixing the collar on his jacket, Caitlin walked up to his front and said, "I'm surprised you actually managed to get out of bed at all."

Kevin let go of his collar with a smile on his face. "Well, now," he said, "I'm not here to disappoint, you know."

Caitlin smiled wide. "I know," she said as she leaned in and gave Kevin a hug. "Try to have a good day with the meeting, okay? We'll do this together."

Kevin nodded, a slight smile coming to his face.

Then, the banging on the door became louder. "Mr. Trent," called the receptionist, "the Vanguard of Nuve cannot wait for thou all day."

"She's right," said Kevin. "Business is business, after all."

"Naturally," responded Caitlin.

Kevin let Caitlin let go of him before he headed to the door, opened it, and proceeded through it. Caitlin followed him through the door and down the stairs.

On the bottom floor, the receptionist was with a middle-aged man, probably in his forties or so, dressed in a blue uniform with some white trim. His face was covered in a thick mustache and beard of black hair matching his head. Several medals were on his military jacket, and a patch was on the side of his arm with a red triangle and a black one inside of it. It was the patch identifying the Vanguard, much like the one Kevin had on his arm.

The receptionist extended her arm toward Kevin, and said to the man in the blue uniform, "That would be him. Kevin Trent Stryker, Vanguard of Aurana. He is the one who requested thy presence here today."

The man in blue turned toward Kevin. "Oh, so thou art the new Vanguard." He extended his hand to Kevin, who reached out as well to shake his hand. Then the man continued, "My name is Raijin Shane, Vanguard of Nuve. It is a pleasure to meet thou."

"The pleasure is mine," responded Kevin. "I would introduce myself, but it appears that the receptionist here has done so for me already."

"Indeed," said Shane. "The Cornelia Chimeras traveled with me to this meeting that thou has asked for. Although they did not seem to like the idea, they decided to come along anyway and listen to thy proposal nonetheless."

Then the receptionist interrupted, "Demons leader Steffen Robert arrived earlier today as well, and the meeting with the king of Nuve is going to be today. Mr. Trent, I hope thou knows what thou art doing, or else the rulers of Nuve may not be so kind to thou as to let thou live. We may allow safety to the Vanguards of the world, but cause torment to any of them and thou wilt find thyself at the bottom of the Abyss of the Royal Sovereign."

Heh, Kevin thought to himself. He had been there already, in an unusual sort of way. "I won't take your words lightly," he said.

"Excellent," responded Raijin Shane. "Thou art wise to heed the words of such a wise woman carefully. In Nuve, many a smart mouth has been killed for saying the wrong thing to the wrong person. It is part of life here." He paused for a second. "Now, if thou would be so kind as to follow me, I shall escort thou to the Castle of Nuvenia, where the royal family resides and where this meeting shall take place.

On the way there, thou can explain to me this whole situation in thy own words."

Kevin responded with a nod. "Sure," he said. "Caitlin and I would be glad to follow along."

"I am afraid not," interrupted Shane. "Thy traveling companion here has not been given authorization to come to this meeting with us. She cannot come along."

Caitlin was very disappointed. She was eager to be there to hear Kevin's developing skills as a negotiator, but instead she would not get the opportunity. Unfortunately, this was Nuve's policy, it seemed. At least Kevin would still be able to tell her about it. Furthermore, the feeling of disappointment felt so new to Caitlin. It was the first time she had felt this emotion in a very long time. Every different emotion was something new to her as she tried to relearn that which she had forgotten so long ago. And despite the fact that Caitlin had only found her emotions again two weeks before, no longer could she imagine herself any other way.

"I'll be fine," Caitlin finally said, trying to retain some optimism. "I'll walk around town by myself today and maybe look into trading for a new dress. Mine is starting to tear since it's not really designed for traveling."

"Perfect," responded Kevin. Except he did not feel perfect. He was very nervous not to have Caitlin with him. She was a sound source of good advice and how to best approach situations like this, where Kevin was completely unfamiliar. Having her there would have made him feel much better about the task ahead.

Picking up on Kevin's nerves, Caitlin walked up to Kevin and gave him a hug. "You'll be fine," she said. "You can do this. I'll catch up later and I'll be glad to hear about what you've accomplished."

Kevin smiled, as he hugged Caitlin. "I'm so grateful for you, Caitlin." Then, as the hug released, Kevin turned to Shane. "Let us be off. Lead the way, Vanguard."

Raijin Shane bowed. "As thou wishes, Vanguard." He then opened the door and proceeded out through it, with Kevin following close behind. Then, he turned southward, toward the center of the city where the Castle of Nuvenia was located. Kevin started walking by his side, preparing for the task ahead.

As they walked into the street, Kevin could not help but feel that Raijin Shane was a little abrupt. He seemed to be focused only on the business, not on trying to be personable. Kevin hoped this was not part of Shane being snobbish, being a member of Nuve's royal family. Even if it was, Kevin had no choice but to cooperate. This would be his only shot at getting Nuve in on helping Aurana and his country to stand any chance against Desolunar. But there was more than just Aurana at stake here, and Kevin had to remind himself that this was the truth.

Beyond the walls of Seta Archa, the capital city of Desolunar, was the conquering dictator Demonicus, who had kidnapped his best friend. Yet, if Kron was to be believed, he was not the ultimate enemy here, and Kevin also knew this.

Kevin found, though, that he did not have much time to think on his way to the castle, as much to his surprise, Raijin Shane was attempting to start a conversation. "So then, Vanguard of Aurana, how long have thou been the Vanguard?" asked Shane.

"It's been about three weeks," answered Kevin. "I was so named by His Majesty King Andrew II, as a special token of thanks from the young king, and in the hopes that what I am doing for Aurana can save it."

Shane let out a chuckle. "Thou art noble, in a good sort of way," he said. "Three weeks as the Vanguard means that you must have been named by King Andrew on the day he took the throne. By now, the news of the resignation of King Arnold IX has reached all around the world. I am glad to see, though, that one way or another, Andrew was willing to think ahead well enough to name a Vanguard for Aurana."

"And I am honored to have the title," responded Kevin. "I understand that I am Aurana's first in fifty years or so."

"That is true," Shane said. "Nuve has kept up, Scurnia has, and Gardolk has. Usually we Vanguards do not speak with each other very often, but I was glad to hear that thou desired to speak with me."

"Yep," Kevin said. "If I may be honest, Mr. Raijin…"

"Call me Shane," the Vanguard of Nuve responded.

Kevin nodded. "And you may call me Kevin," he answered. "I

kind of thought you had no interest in chatting with me other than for business."

"Oh, well, I do apologize to thou," Shane said. "When I am in front of representatives of other factions, whether they are kind to me or not, I try to maintain that demeanor. Nuve's official policy is not to recognize the two factions that control parts of our legally-defined kingdom."

That made sense, Kevin realized. He felt bad for thinking poorly of Shane. He then nodded and said, "I was hoping you would be able to tell me more about the situation between the factions of Nuve and help me negotiate with them. After all, I am from Aurana and I am not an expert on this situation."

"Then why art thou here?" interrupted Shane, a little too snappily. Then he cut back his tone, realizing he had overreacted a bit. "I apologize if I am sounding rude," he continued, "but since thou requested my presence here and asked for the leader and representatives of the Cornelia Chimeras to arrive in Nuvenia, I have been wondering what has been thy plan and thy motives. Would thou be willing to explain?"

Taking a breath, Kevin answered, "Certainly. How much do you know about the nation of Desolunar to the south of both Aurana and Nuve?"

Raijin Shane began to think. "Desolunar is responsible for taking territory from southern Nuve almost effortlessly, including what was our capital city in Cardol. Thousands of people have been forced north, but recent advances on Nuve have been slow while Nuve and its factions fight each other."

"And you don't find that appalling?" asked Kevin.

"It has been a matter long since left behind due to the faction issues," answered Shane. "Though Cardol has been a hard loss for all of us to bear, we decided we had bigger issues here at home."

Kevin sighed. "I wish it weren't so," he said. "The ruler of Desolunar is a very dark man by the name of Demonicus. He will not stop until the entire world is under his control, and the fact that Nuve will not fight only hurts everyone, as his forces are very strong. Aurana is suffering, and I've come to ask Nuve for help. Without the help of

Nuve, both Aurana and Nuve will eventually fall."

"Then why would he slow down his move on Nuve?" asked Raijin Shane. "If his force is as strong as thou claim it is, he would have no need to stop his advances."

"You don't see it, do you?" said Kevin, stressing the point. He was getting aggressive in his frustration, even though he was by far the junior to Raijin Shane. "I speak of the strength and threat of Demonicus, and yet Nuve is fighting itself. I know Demonicus, and I know that he is not backing down. Aurana is continued to be made to suffer at his hands while he waits patiently for Nuve to destroy itself from the inside. And then…"

"Then he makes his move," realized Shane. "We play the fool while he takes our flank in Aurana, then advances on a weakened Nuve. And all the while, all of Nuve is blinded to a force to which it is already losing territory. That is why thou art here."

"Exactly," said Kevin. "I fully realize that it is impossible to unite all of Nuve or divide it up at this moment, and to do so in such a short time would be. But I was hoping that a temporary agreement, such as an armistice, could be reached, and the alliance with Aurana could be restored to unite against Desolunar."

Shane considered this. "Unlikely," he said, "but certainly not impossible. My brother Lester is a reasonable man, and I am sure he will take everything thou have to say close to heart."

"That's great to hear," said Kevin in approval. "By the way, what can you tell me about King Lester? The more I know about him, the better I can try to negotiate once we enter the castle."

Shane took a pause to gather his thoughts. "Lester is a good man," he began. "He is about ten years older than I am, my older brother. He has a wife and a daughter, who will be the future Queen of Nuve. I do not think there are many who have an unkind word for my brother."

"Heh," interrupted Kevin. "Funny you say that when there are two entire factions who apparently do not like his rule or his philosophies."

"Thou misunderstand," said Shane. "The Cornelia Chimeras only seek independence for their own rule and their own region. Ruling philosophy matters not for them. As for the Demons, they take opposition to the statist rule of Nuve in preference of a more libertarian and liberal point of view, but it is not King Lester who promotes such a point of view of statism."

"It isn't?" Kevin asked.

"No," answered Shane. "It is, in fact, the decision of the Collective Council of Nuve. I know it is for this nation and for my brother that I wear the Nuve uniform with the red and black triangle patch, like that on thy Aurana uniform, yet I honestly cannot listen to the Collective Council without becoming sick. It was centuries ago that the Collective Council was formed to offset the king so that one man or woman would not have all of the power of Nuve in his or her grasp. Yet the Collective Council, despite being created for a noble cause, is and has always been, filled with the most corrupt politicians of Nuve, seeking only greed and power despite their consistent denial of it. Pity, too, because Nuve would be different, very much so, without the Collective Council." Shane paused, then resumed, "Thou will not be able to rid Nuve of the Collective Council, however. It is buried into Nuve's system, and to overthrow them would be to throw chaos into Nuve, even under the rule of King Lester."

There was not much Kevin could say in response to this. So much of what had happened seemed to be a lot of finger pointing. Though Shane provided an explanation, no one was assuming the blame for the factionalism, of the direction of Nuve, or of their future downfall. Kevin was not even willing to blame the Collective Council at this point, knowing Shane was the king's brother and would obviously be on his side in this dispute. Uniting these groups and getting Nuve to recognize them might be more difficult than he thought, especially if the king and the Collective Council stood at odds on an armistice.

Letting out a sigh, Kevin said, "It figures as much. It is a shame, too, that I simply do not have the time to completely fix the problems here between the factions and Nuve's interior."

"Nor should thou," responded Shane. "The issues of Nuve can only be permanently solved by its people, not foreigners. I admire thy desire to aid a foreign nation like Nuve, but there are some things that thou simply do not have the capacity to fix."

"Fact of life," said Kevin, acknowledging reality. "I was not expecting to fix anything permanently here, though, so it is only a minor disappointment."

Shane chuckled. "Thou sound like my brother," he said. "Knowledgeable about thy limits, and knows that thou do have limits."

Kevin joined in chuckling. "If you want to call it that," he said, still laughing a bit. "Speaking of which, that does have me intrigued about something. You are the Vanguard of Nuve, and you are also the brother of the king. Doesn't that make you a prince?"

Shane took a breath. "It does," he said. "However, as I said, my brother has a wife and daughter, who would be next in line to the throne should Lester pass on anytime soon, which means I am not in line to inherit the throne. But it does not bother me, for I have never been one to enjoy the sedentary lifestyle of living at the castle and being a part of government, although there is hardly a dull moment when it comes to governing a country so chaotic as Nuve."

"You must enjoy life by the sword," responded Kevin.

"Ah, but the sword is only part of it," said Shane, in a teaching tone of voice. "One must be truly adept at many styles of war, especially in a land such as Nuve. In Nuve, we have weaponry found nowhere else in the world." Shane then began to unstrap something from his left wrist. "Which hand is thy sword hand, Kevin?"

"It's my right," said Kevin, confused, "but why do you ask?"

"For this," responded Shane as he took a plate of metal off of his left arm and placed it on Kevin's, under his jacket sleeve. Deciding to take a close look at it, Kevin examined the metal. It was fashioned into a plate that covered the arm and back of the hand. Lined in silver, it was painted blue with a bright gold capital letter N in the middle of the hand section. Cloth and fasteners were attached to the metal, designed to strap it to the arm.

"This is a Nuve stealth bracer," continued Shane. "It is designed for one-handed swordplay as a way to block attacks with the left arm, if necessary. The metal itself is high-density fortified steel, with the official emblem of Nuve on the hand plate, and lined in silver for decoration. What makes this plate unique, though, is that if thou flip up the end of the hand section at the knuckles, and clench thy fist, thou can activate a trigger that fires a tiny crossbow-type bolt. The bracer holds five bolts, but thou will need to flip up the metal plate and access the space in between to reload the bolt and rewind the firing wire manually, so it is effectively one shot at a time."

Kevin was still staring at the bracer. "Astounding," he said. "It is probably the most unique piece of fighting equipment I have ever seen. But I can't accept this from you. It just seems too valuable."

"Keep it," insisted Shane. "I have about ten or so of these. I want to thank you for doing what you are about to do. I hope it will be for the best for Nuve."

This was a kind gesture from the Vanguard of Nuve. Very grateful and staring at the bracer in awe, Kevin said, "Thanks." He was a little excited as he strapped the bracer to his arm. "I am sure this will be useful on my journey."

"It has been useful to many for years," responded Shane, "and I am sure that its history will prove useful to you as well."

Nodding, Kevin looked up. He and Shane were still a good distance from the castle. "Please, tell me more about its history," Kevin requested. "We have time before we reach the castle."

Shane looked up and saw they still had quite a walk, and thought this might avoid awkward silence to tell the story. "Very well," he began. "Thousands of years ago, as you may know, the most common form of warrior was the armed knight; a man fully wrapped in armor, carrying a shield, and a choice of weapon depending on the knight's preference. Those days are long since gone, however, since steel armor makes movements very difficult, is very expensive, and though it seems like a tradeoff to trade thy speed for the powerful armor, it became all too easy to exploit the weaknesses of armor for those with the agility. These days, military jackets and padded shirts are the way to go, as thick cloth materials will protect moderately well against swords and other bladed weapons without sacrificing any mobility."

Immediately as Shane finished his last sentence, Kevin had to dodge a passerby. He was listening with so much intent that he forgot to watch where he was walking.

Shane continued, "But things in Nuve were not as smooth as the transitions were made from defense to mobility. An entirely new type of warfare developed in this nation where war is the driving force: stealth warfare and sneak attacks. Many stealth weapons were developed, including the stealth bracer that thou wears now. It is basically a stripped-down pistol crossbow firing mechanism, disguised in a metal bracer. Nowadays, however, it is used more as a defensive tool than a pistol crossbow. Just like the days of old, however, the darts in thy stealth bracer are also tipped with a powerful poison, in order to make them deadly. Take extra care with the bracer, and it will take care of thou."

Kevin had not realized the bolts in his bracer were poison-tipped. He had to be extremely careful with it. After completing this realization, Kevin responded with, "And so I will. I appreciate your kindness, Shane. Truly, you are kind."

"Well, I am the Vanguard, after all," Shane began to laugh. Kevin joined in laughing with him, finding humor in it. Both of them were Vanguards of their own nations, standing together.

Today, their nations would be inextricably linked should Kevin be able to succeed in his negotiation with the leaders of Nuve. Kevin had never been a mediator to any discussion before, but today would be his only chance to bring Nuve together with negotiation.

Chapter 30

Self-Destruction

A short walk further down the road, Kevin and Shane were standing in front of the Castle of Nuvenia, the capital building of the nation. Towering high, the castle's turrets seemed to scrape against the sky of the fortress city. The castle's walls were extremely weathered, however, just like the outer walls of the city, which added an ominous feeling to the sight of the castle. Altogether, the castle did not seem too out of place in Nuvenia, where the upkeep of the city was not as high as in other areas of the world.

None of the guards asked any questions as Raijin Shane led Kevin inside the castle walls. Together they walked through one set of doors into a hallway running from left to right, and at the exact opposite side of the hallway, directly in front of them, was a larger set of doors. Shane stopped here. "This is the Great Hall," he said. "Here is where all of the factions of Nuve and Nuve's government have undoubtedly organized this meeting. By now, all of them are here. Thou had better be very careful and watch thy words closely."

Kevin only responded with a nod as Shane pushed open the doors to the Great Hall. Briefly, he had a conversation with a guard and a messenger, before he then proceeded inside, helping guide Kevin to the center of the room.

Below Kevin was a white and black alternating tile floor, sitting under the entire vast Great Hall. The room's height was three stories, serving to resonate sounds made in the room. Only one window sat to light up the space: a large window sitting at the top of the hall at the far end of the room. The walls were entirely made of the same weathered dark gray brick as the castle walls with no additional ornate decoration save for a couple of tapestries.

A table and two chairs sat in the middle, while large wooden benches, almost similar to those of the jury section of a courtroom, sat along the sides. At the far side was another set of benches, along with a judge's chair above. It was clear to Kevin now that this Great Hall was not just for everyday use as a meeting room. It was a courtroom, in some senses.

Over to the left benches, men and women dressed in crimson red and black filled the area. A flag was mounted in a flag post at the corner of the bench. This flag was crimson red from its upper left corner to the rectangle's diagonal, from whereon it was black below that. Kevin recognized this flag as the flag of the Demons faction. At the far corner of the bench was an elderly man dressed in an elegantly decorated military uniform in the red and black colors of the Demons. Though others in the left benches wore these same colors, his was the most decorated. Kevin hypothesized that this man was Steffen Robert, the founder of the Demonstrative Organization of Northern Nuve, or Demons.

On the other side, the right benches were filled with those decorated mostly in light blue and gold trim. A flag sat in the post to the right, displaying the head of a chimera in gold on a light blue field. Certainly this had to be the flag of the Cornelia Chimeras. In the same position that Steffen Robert sat on the left side, a middle-aged man in an elegant light blue military uniform with gold trim sat on the right side. Kevin guessed that this man was the leader of the Cornelia Chimeras.

Directly in front of Kevin were many members dressed in dark blue with white trim, some of which wore dress suits instead of military jackets. They were members of the Collective Council, Kevin thought to himself, along with some Nuve military leaders. At the judge's chair above these benches sat an older man in royal blue robes wearing a crown. This man was His Majesty King Lester of Nuve. The eldest member of the ruling Raijin family, he appeared to be about ten years older than the middle-aged Raijin Shane.

Two flag posts sat at the ends of the forward benches where the Nuve government representatives sat. On each of these posts flew a dark blue flag with white trim and a golden letter N in the middle. It was the flag of Nuve. All of the different flags in this room reminded Kevin a bit of the flag of Aurana: three red triangles lined up horizontally on a green field. These flags were all mostly new to Kevin, however, representing nations with which he was not intricately familiar. And now he would have to find peace for all of these nations.

Raijin Shane indicated for Kevin to sit in one of the two seats at the table. He sat at the other seat. Now, in the middle of the hall, two Vanguards sat with the intention of peace. King Lester was the first to break the silence after the Vanguards took their seats. "Guards, thou art to keep the doors to the Great Hall secured at all times," he ordered in his stately voice. "No one shall get in or out while this session is in order. If there are no other objections, then allow us to begin."

As the king finished his sentence, a messenger came from behind the bench and unfurled a scroll. He began to read from it: "Members of all parties are here today on an armistice negotiation, on this day, identifying date 2047942. Here today to mediate the discussion and spearhead the talks are Raijin Shane, Vanguard of Nuve; and Kevin Trent Stryker, Vanguard of Aurana. Present parties include King Lester, members of the Collective Council, select military leaders of Nuve, select members of the Demonstrative Organization of Northern Nuve, and select members of the Cornelia Chimeras." Then, the messenger rolled his scroll back up and stood at attention.

The announcement surprised Kevin a bit. He did not know Shane had taken an official position to help mediate.

King Lester looked down and made an observation to begin the day's events. He spoke to his brother, "Raijin Shane, Vanguard of Nuve, I see you have not joined us at the benches this morning and have elected to stand next to the Vanguard of Aurana and assist him."

"Indeed," acknowledged Shane, "and I do apologize for the late change. However, this morning I have met with the Vanguard of Aurana and felt swayed enough that I wish to help him present his case for armistice. I notified the messenger at the door as I entered that this would be so."

For a second, Kevin felt honored. He would have help, after all. He felt very lucky that he had convinced Shane in such a quick and informal fashion to the point where Shane was willing to help him.

The king nodded. Then, he turned to Kevin. "Mr. Stryker, this is one large crowd thou have asked for on this day. I will now ask all other parties to please allow Mr. Stryker to answer all questions, provide all points, and make any other comments before judging what he asks for. To put it simply, listen to it before thou judge it." He then focused on Kevin. "Now, Mr. Stryker, allow us to begin. What have you requested us all here for today?"

Kevin stood from his seat, pushing all of the confidence he had into himself. He was nervous, but he knew he could not let that get to him. "Your Majesty, esteemed men and women of Nuve, supporters of the government, the Demons, and the Cornelia Chimeras alike, today I stand before all of you in the hope that together something can be done about a very threatening situation currently brewing. You'll have to pardon me, as I'm not the greatest speaker, but I hope that what I say today will be clear to all of you. It is true that I am Auranian, and I do live in Aurana. However, the situation at hand affects both Aurana and Nuve. None will find themselves exempt from the terror that is to come." Kevin paused to catch himself up and figure out a way to phrase his next statements.

"And of what do you speak?" asked the king. "Please proceed, Mr. Stryker."

Kevin nodded. "South of both Aurana and Nuve lies the kingdom of Desolunar, under the rule of Demonicus, a man with the ambition to rule the world. His forces, centered around the old city of Seta Archa, have already caused great tolls on both the sides of Aurana and Nuve. In Aurana, the great city of Atwals fell years ago. And here in Nuve, I am sure that all of you are familiar with the loss of your capital at Cardol. Now, it is true, as all of you know, that Desolunar has not advanced in recent times on Nuve. However, they continue to advance on Aurana, and it is only a matter of time before they advance on Nuve once again. I have come here on behalf of King Andrew II of Aurana to request that Nuve and its factions set aside their differences for a time, and reforge its alliance with Aurana against this threat." He paused for a second. "For the purpose of this alliance, Aurana will neither support nor oppose any factional group. A united Nuve, even temporarily, is all we are willing to support." Kevin knew he was taking a risk here saying this. If the factions could not put aside their differences temporarily, he was now saying that Aurana would not openly support an alliance with the Nuve government alone. He hoped saying that would give encouragement to the factions that Aurana was not in this just to support the government.

Shane was sitting beside him, and gave no reaction. He understood Kevin's position, whether or not he agreed with it.

Before Kevin could continue, however, a member of the Collective Council rose from the bench in front of Kevin. He interrupted the speech, "And what demand thou, Auranian? Thou will not receive help if thy demand we acknowledge anyone other than the government of Nuve as its rightful rulers."

Then, Raijin Shane stood up. "Your Majesty, if thou and all of those present would be willing to listen to what Mr. Stryker has to say here, I am sure all of thou will find that Mr. Stryker's words bring up an alarming truth that Nuve has neglected to acknowledge under this guise of factional war."

As Shane finished, King Lester announced, "The councilor will abstain. Shane, if thou would be willing to clarify the situation, then I will ask thou to continue."

"Very well," said Shane as Kevin took a seat. "The thought, I will admit, had not occurred to me until I spoke with Mr. Stryker myself, but it makes logical sense. Does it not seem to make sense to all here that Desolunar stopped its advance on Nuve around the time that factions began to develop here? Aurana is a nation directly to our west, and Desolunar has focused on them instead. Should Desolunar continue to go unchallenged and their conquest of Aurana is complete, they will be able to take advantage of our self-destruction and outflank us. Every faction will be in danger unless we are willing to temporarily call a truce and unite together against this menace, before it has the opportunity."

A councilor from the Demons then rose. He raised his hand, and the king nodded at him, allowing him to speak. "Mr. Stryker, if thou would please, can thou tell us how far north the Desolunar forces are in Aurana, and why an Auranian is here in Nuve about it?"

Kevin then stood again, hoping that he had the words for this answer. "Last I heard, the Desolunar forces were just south of Haventown, Aurana, about a day's march from the Calphos River," he said, remembering deeply the battlefield he had seen where he found the Sword of Purity.

The king then rose again and asked, "So, then, what do thou request of us, Mr. Stryker? What specifically have thou brought us here to ask?

Taking a deep breath, Kevin continued. "Ladies and gentlemen, I ask not for you to put aside everything that you have worked for to accomplish this. I ask only for a temporary armistice and for everyone to work together for the good of all, alongside and with the support of Aurana. Only together can we defend ourselves from the threat of Desolunar."

A clamor broke out in the Great Hall as people started to discuss the issue with the people next to them. There was chaos in the room.

"Order! Order!" declared King Lester, causing all to fall silent. "Though I am sure that Mr. Stryker's words are strong, it would be best if we eased up and took this one person at a time." He then pointed down to a member of the Collective Council, who appeared eager to speak. "Thou may be the first," he said.

The bureaucrat stood up. "This whole idea of an armistice is preposterous," he said.

Silently, at the table, Kevin was aghast. Maybe he was not such a convincing man after all.

"Nuve does not recognize any group or government other than its own east of the Aurun River or west of the Peaked Mountains," the bureaucrat continued. "To sign some type of armistice would be to give recognition to rebellious groups in Nuve. That would be giving them what they want," the bureaucrat's eyes slid over to the leader of the Cornelia Chimeras, "would it not, Mr. Arsuf?"

There was a second of silence. That was a personal political statement.

Finally, Mr. Arsuf nodded. "So it would be," he answered. "No worse, however, than what the Demons up north are doing."

A general from the Demons bench next to Steffen Robert appeared to be getting up to challenge Mr. Arsuf, but Steffen Robert raised an arm and pushed him gently back down, not allowing him to blow his top. Mr. Steffen then stood up himself, and said, in a gentle voice, "It is only what is necessary. Recognition may be the last of Nuve's worries should Mr. Stryker's warning go unheeded. We must keep that in mind first and foremost, and in order to protect ourselves from it, we must set aside our differences."

"As what?" asked another member of the Collective Council. "As soldiers of Nuve, or as three separate groups? I will not accept a divided Nuve for war with any other country!"

Now was Kevin's time to step up. He couldn't let this farce continue. "Hang on, hang on for just a minute," he said, interrupting as he stood from his chair. "Let me ask you, what was the Triple Alliance? Was it all under one command?" He asked this, knowing the answer because it was something he had been taught in school.

"No," responded King Lester, as he shook his head. "It was a coalition where all merely worked together and no nation took a lead."

Kevin nodded. "And that is all I ask of for this armistice. Let everyone come together with no leader, and join with Aurana and Scurnia. Let us together unite against Desolunar before they destroy us all. Then, everyone can go back to where they were and continue to assault one another, for all that matters. Just please," Kevin slowed down, "let it be just for now, if it must."

A second of silence was heard. Then, Mr. Arsuf interjected, "I still do not like this. Such an armistice allows for any one group to backstab another while their defenses are down for this attack. We simply cannot afford to give up what we have worked for for some trap, or some seized opportunity."

Getting defensive, Kevin stepped over toward the Cornelia Chimeras' bench. "That is the trust you must place in your fellow man," he responded. "Look at yourselves, all of you. Regardless of who you represent, why you are here, or what your ideals are, all of you are the people of Nuve. Surely my trust must be earned because I am from Aurana, of course, but if you cannot trust your fellow man, then who can you?"

There was yet another moment of silence. "An excellent point," King Lester finally added. "Certainly, if an agreement is made, we should trust our fellow man to honor by the terms they have agreed. Mr. Stryker, I thank thou for thy speech today and thy mediation. I believe we have been sufficiently briefed of the situation by now, and that Nuve military intelligence can answer any more details later. Now, before we take any votes on the matter, I would like to know if any others have any more words."

"I do," said Raijin Shane as he stood up again from his seat. "Ladies and gentlemen, lords of Nuve, for several years I have served as thy Vanguard from within the Army of Nuve. However, today, I stand with all of thee. Demons, Cornelia Chimeras, and nonfactionalist people of Nuve, as this nation's honorary forward guard, I will personally stand for all of thee."

Kevin sat down, listening to the Vanguard of Nuve make his closing argument.

"Have we not suffered enough?" questioned Shane. "Our loss of Cardol was a tragedy that affected everyone here. How many more cities must we lose?" He looked to the leader of the Cornelia Chimeras. "Would Cornelia be next? Maxwell, thy home city is the next largest city in the south of Nuve." He turned to his older brother and the Collective Council. "Can we afford to lose another capital, even if it takes a few years?" Then, he turned to Steffen Robert. "It would only be a matter of time before they make it to Edenbrook." Shane returned to to the table. "The Vanguard of Aurana, Mr. Stryker, was kind enough to journey all the way from Aurana for our sake. We must not let his words go to waste." Then, Shane lightened his voice some after a pause. "The next move is thine," he said as he sat back down.

After another pause, King Lester stood and announced, "If there are none others, then we will begin the voting on the matter. As all have been aware of what the negotiations have been about for the past two weeks, all should be ready to consider the point presented and present their decision. Terms of said armistice proposed would be resolved in discussions after this session, and in private, but today we will vote on a resolution to create an armistice. Nuve remains divided, and it is true that the government, including myself, does not recognize the independence of either group. However, in fairness to their factions and members in such a sensitive matter, I ask for the leaders of each faction to make their voice heard through this courtroom."

This was the moment of truth. Under the table, Kevin placed

his left hand, and crossed his fingers that this would work.

The king then turned in the direction of the Cornelia Chimeras. "Arsuf Maxwell, supreme leader of the Cornelia Chimeras, what say thou of the position held by the Cornelia Chimeras based on the proposal given?"

Kevin held his breath. His wait for two weeks, his trip into the city of Nuvenia, both hinged on what the Cornelia Chimeras leader had to say. Every second that passed seemed like an hour as Kevin sat nervously in his seat.

The Cornelia Chimeras member in the most elegant military uniform, Arsuf Maxwell, stood up from his position at the corner of the right benches. Appearing to be sound of mind, he announced, "After consideration, the Cornelia Chimeras elect to abstain for the moment and listen to what others intend to do first."

Stunned, all Kevin could do was stare. What had happened to make the Chimeras want to abstain? True, this did not mean that it was over yet. The Cornelia Chimeras were doubtful and waiting to hear what the Demons would do, Kevin was sure. Perhaps his words were not as powerful as he had hoped they would be, which did disappoint Kevin some.

"Very well," answered the king. "Understand, however, that by Nuve court doctrine, thou art permitted only one abstain during this session." The king then turned to his right, Kevin's left. "Steffen Robert, what say thou of the position of the Demonstrative Organization of Northern Nuve?"

From the corner of the left bench, Steffen Robert rose. His age was apparent all over his body, as his white hair, bald head, and frail appearance showed. Still, Kevin was sure that this man was wise beyond his years if he was the leader of the Demons.

Prepared, Steffen Robert began his statement. "Ladies and gentlemen, one thing that the Demons pride themselves in is protecting their people. Though it is true that the north is commonly considered our domain, we, as a part of Nuve, consider all of Nuve as our people. We tend to think that we fight for all of them. Now, it is true that we are here not to follow politics, and it is for good reason that we choose not to bring anything political into the discussion today. However, the fact remains that although we remain divided, the logic and truths presented by the Vanguard of Aurana are solid."

Was that a good sign? Kevin hoped it was.

Steffen Robert continued, "We are in danger, and we know it. We have always known it, since Desolunar first advanced on Nuve soil in the south. And yet, we have been ignoring it to pursue our own petty arguments with each other. It is for this reason, for the people of Nuve, that the Demonstrative Organization of Northern Nuve elects to agree to an armistice and take part in the battles against Desolunar that are sure to come." He paused and turned to Kevin. "Furthermore, we would agree to an armistice pursuant to a Nuve alliance with Aurana."

A sigh of relief came from Kevin.

As Steffen Robert took his seat once more, King Lester spoke. "A fine speech," he said. "Truly, no words can put it better than that. And for that same purpose, I, King Lester of Nuve, will sign such an armistice, with or without the support of Nuve's Collective Council, that will allow Nuve and all of its parts to come together and hopefully reclaim that which we have lost. Such fighting between Nuve and its factions can wait until later." He paused for a second, and stared at Kevin. "I, too, endorse an alliance with Aurana for the purpose of defense."

Below the king, though some members scowled, others of the Collective Council nodded. This, to them, was what had to be done. Generally it appeared that more of them were supportive, at least in their expressions, than dissident.

King Lester then eyed over at Arsuf Maxwell. "Have thou come to a decision yet, Maxwell?" he asked.

Arsuf Maxwell then stood up again. "The Cornelia Chimeras will take part in the armistice as well, so long as it is temporary as it was proclaimed to be in this meeting, and that another party be created to ensure that one force does not double cross the other two while an armistice is in effect."

Relieved, Kevin was thanking Steffen Robert under his breath. Kevin had taken a gamble staying in Nuvenia for two weeks knowing he was not really a negotiator and that he had little chance on his own. He was certain that Steffen Robert and Raijin Shane had made this work in a way Kevin could never make it work on his own.

"Very well," answered King Lester. "The support of all three parties shall be enough to justify an armistice. Councilors, thou art to draw up an armistice for the reasons given by Mr. Stryker. Have the initial proposals drawn up by moonrise tonight and prepared to enter negotiation tomorrow morning. I expect for the leaders of the Demonstrative Organization of Northern Nuve and the Cornelia Chimeras to meet again here in the Great Hall to discuss the terms." He paused for a second. "Before this court is dismissed, however, I wish to make some closing comments. As the King of Nuve, I am very disappointed and saddened to see that Nuve is unable to remain together on its own. This conflict has made us vulnerable to outside forces, more than we realize, and it took a visit from Mr. Stryker all the way from Aurana for us to realize this. For this reason, I wish to personally thank Kevin Trent Stryker, Vanguard of Aurana, for what he has presented today. Should someday Nuve find an answer to the chaos within itself, one way or another, the entire nation will be in better shape with this threat eliminated."

There was a small applause from different parts of the room. Kevin smiled at what we was seeing—the potential for a reunited Nuve.

"Court is dismissed," proclaimed King Lester.

As discussions broke out among most of the people in the benches, many of which were about the session that just took place, Kevin and Shane both stood up and Shane shook Kevin's hand. "Congratulations, Mr. Stryker," he said. "It looks as though Nuve will do a lot better because of thou. Thy bravery in calling the leaders of Nuve here was great."

Kevin chuckled a bit. "I wouldn't call it bravery. I'd say it was me having no idea what the hell I was actually doing. I couldn't have done it without you."

"Of nothing," responded Shane, also laughing some. "Thou should really be thanking Steffen Robert, though, because had he not decided to agree and say what he did, it is quite possible that no one would have agreed. Say, how would thou like to head over to the tavern across the street? I would be willing to buy thee a drink."

"Well,"said Kevin,"I don't know about that drink, but why not?"

Chapter 31

The Mediator and the Vanguard

Kevin then proceeded to follow Shane out the doors of the Great Hall and of the castle. It was a walk of several minutes. Outside, rain was beginning to fall hard on Nuvenia, as water washed down the walls of buildings. Kevin looked up, let out a sigh, and proceeded to follow Shane across the street to the tavern, simply called the Pour House. Inside, the tavern looked very similar to the Rider's Tavern back in Aurana City, except the inner woodwork appeared to be in much better condition as it was not nearly as worn down, and appeared to be freshly stained. Twin fireplaces lit up the room in a soft glow.

Several minutes later, Kevin and Shane were sitting at a table relaxing. Shane had a drink in his hand and was enjoying it. Kevin had decided to pass on the drink in favor of a simple glass of water. "Some might call thou a courageous mediator for what thou has done today. The Mediator and the Vanguard," said Shane. "Thou art a collector of titles, it would seem." He began to chuckle.

Kevin did not chuckle, as he took what Shane said seriously. "Yeah, I guess so," he said. "Shame thou passed up on the drink," continued Shane, "because I would have purchased any drink available for thou." He paused for a second, having sat with Kevin for a few minutes at the Pour House now and looking for another topic of conversation. "Have thou decided where thou art headed next? I am certain that thou art headed back to Aurana to report back about what thou have done here."

"Far from it, actually," Kevin said. "I'll send a message for that. I'm on a campaign to restore the Triple Alliance and unite against Desolunar before they destroy us. Aurana is ready, and now Nuve will be as well. I'm racing against time, Shane. For all we know, we could all fall within a matter of days if we don't get this together."

Shane considered this. "I see," he said. "So, I would presume thou art headed to Scurnia next, to the east, to reunite the full Triple Alliance."

"Yes, I am," Kevin answered. "I wonder what I will have to do there to get Scurnia on board with the Triple Alliance again."

"Should not be anything," responded Shane, taking another sip of his drink. "As far as I know, Scurnia has no internal issues, and only has minor conflicts with Gardolk to its south. King Warren is well favored and runs a prosperous country in the highlands of Scurnia. Unlike Nuve's internal division, no such thing occurs there, at least not at such a scale."

Interesting, Kevin thought to himself. This seemed like it might be easy. At least, easier than Aurana and Nuve had been.

As Kevin was thinking, Shane continued to speak. "If thou wish to head to Scurnia, thou will almost have to go through the Northern Pass. From here to Rugger at the mouth of the pass, it is about a nine day trip."

"Nine days?" Kevin nearly leapt out of his seat upon hearing this. "There's no way to make it any faster than that?"

"Sadly, no," said Shane. "From Nuvenia and the Abyss of the Royal Sovereign, thou art headed uphill when headed to the Katalina province, and Rugger in particular is exceptionally high. There is no quicker way of transit leading to Rugger unless you can afford a horse."

Kevin sighed. "Great," he said sarcastically, knowing he could not afford a horse. "I suppose I should've expected a longer walk. I had better head back to the inn and tell Caitlin we're heading out tomorrow morning after we restock our supplies."

"Always in a rush?" began Shane. "Thou should know, it is not good to overexert oneself. Take a break, thou have time. Counting the meeting and our time here in the tavern, it has been a couple of hours since we left."

"And yet the rain continues to fall," responded Kevin, looking outside the window. Then, he turned back. "I've spent the last two weeks here, Shane. As much as I love the time off, all of us must know when it's time to get back to work."

Shane took another sip from his drink. "So I see," he said. "In that case, why not spend a day with thy lady friend? Carmen, Catherine, what is her name?"

"Caitlin," responded Kevin. He thought about this for a moment. "Actually, I probably should spend the rest of the day with her. We travel together so much that, save for this two week vacation before this meeting today, we had never had time to stop and take a break."

"Then what art thou still doing here?" said Shane. "I am kidding, of course. Pick up thy water glass, and share with me one last toast, and then head back to the inn." Shane picked up his drink and raised it over the table. "To the health of Nuve, and to new friends."

Kevin picked up his glass and met Shane's. "To the alliance of Aurana and Nuve," he said as he clanked his glass and took a drink along with Shane.

"I can only hope that we will meet again on the front of battle someday," said Shane. "Perhaps if the action thou asked for against Desolunar works out well, we will meet again on the same side." He reached out to shake Kevin's hand.

Returning the shake, Kevin responded, "And I hope to see you as well." He then stood up, and proceeded to the exit of the tavern. Truthfully, Kevin was very appreciative to Shane for everything he had done. Shane stayed in the tavern, enjoying a few drinks with his fellow countrymen in the pub.

Outside, the rain continued to fall, but Kevin was not bothered by it at all. Instead, he simply headed north, back up to the Demons Headquarters on the north side of Nuvenia. Kevin's clothes were soaking in the rainwater as he headed for the inn. It was a lengthy walk out from the city center to the inn, at the edge of town.

At last, Kevin reached the inn again, glad to be anywhere that was dry. Taking a second to pull off his wet jacket, he noticed the receptionist still sitting at the desk at the inn. She noticed him as well. "Mr. Trent, Vanguard," she said, "congratulations. Steffen Robert stopped by personally, and although he regrets that he is unable to speak with thou in person, he has written a letter for thou to read." She placed the letter on the desk where Kevin could reach it.

Pleasantly surprised, Kevin passed the wet jacket to the receptionist as he reached for the letter. "Excellent," he said to the receptionist. "Can you take my jacket and hang it up somewhere?"

"Certainly," responded the receptionist as she took the wet jacket.

Kevin proceeded to open up the envelope the letter was in and unfold the letter. He read it closely, anxious to see what Steffen Robert, the Demons faction leader, had to say to him:

Dear Mr. Kevin Trent Stryker,

I wish I could thank thou personally for thy help in Nuve today. What thou have done has changed the course of the history of this nation. Perhaps together Nuve will find the solution to its internal problems through dealing with Desolunar alongside our allies.

To be honest, the Demons have been more than willing to combat against Desolunar, even though the territory we control in Nuve is far away from Desolunar. We have known that they have been dangerous for years. Despite our distance, we have felt that to do right was the most important thing to do. Still, we took no action for fear of being overrun. Because we are not independent from Nuve, we could not risk abandoning our territory in the north.

Thanks to thou, however, both Nuve and the Demons have been guaranteed a while longer to last. Since thou first came into contact with our operative in Venarose, #443, we thought that thou might be the type of person we needed here to unify Nuve, even if only temporarily.

As thanks from the Demons, we unfortunately do not have much to offer thou. However, I have also left with the receptionist at the inn that we use as a headquarters in Nuvenia two patches. Each of them is designed in a rectangle shape and colored in the same way as our unofficial flag – crimson red on the top and left, black on the bottom and right, and divided precisely down its diagonal. If thou wish to have them attached to your jacket tonight, the receptionist can take care of that for you. I am sorry we cannot offer more, but resources around the Demons are tight, and we hope thou understand. To carry our standard and not be one of us, though, is a symbol of the greatness thou have and the gratefulness we wish to bestow upon thou.

I wish thou the best of luck in thy future ventures.

Sincerely signed,
STEFFEN ROBERT
Demonstrative Organization of Northern Nuve

"Wow," was all that Kevin could say in response. "I'm glad he was able to leave me a letter. Just knowing he appreciates what I've done is the best feeling I could have."

"Would thou like me to sew on the patches after thy jacket dries?" interrupted the receptionist.

Kevin nodded. "Sure," he said. He thought about it as he said that; having the flag of a different faction of a different country sewn on his Auranian uniform. Odd as that would be, Kevin considered it a badge of honor and recognition, and he was not one for military decorum and culture anyway. About the only way he would see an issue with it were if the king himself told me it was wrong. He continued, "This will be our last night here, so is there anything else that I should know about?"

The receptionist considered this for a moment. "Indeed, there is. Caitlin left me a message. She has a surprise for thou, and she is waiting upstairs."

Kevin nodded, thanked the receptionist, and headed for the stairs. He could not be sure how long Caitlin was waiting for him upstairs, much less what the surprise was anyway. He had completely forgotten Caitlin had said that she was heading out today into the city, but he had no clue Caitlin would have a surprise for him. Had he wasted his time and irritated Caitlin by going with Raijin Shane to the tavern after the meeting? Kevin was not sure.

As soon as he reached the room door, Kevin knocked a couple of times. Soon as he had knocked, however, Caitlin's voice echoed from inside the room, "Just a second."

Patiently waiting, Kevin looked up to the ceiling. Somehow, his rushing up the stairs and worrying had made him the impatient one and not Caitlin. Kevin had to chuckle at himself for the irony he had created inadvertently by doing so.

A moment later, the door opened, and Kevin walked in to find Caitlin standing in front of him. She was wearing a new dress. That was the surprise she had for Kevin, and Kevin realized it as soon as he saw her wearing it. Over the previous course of events, Caitlin had worn nothing different from her plain black dress.

This new dress was a white dress with vivid red trim. An additional piece of fabric sat over the shoulders of the dress and ran down the sides to about a fourth of the way down the skirt. Also like Caitlin's last dress, the arms and abdomen section were very tight around her body, as was common for a traveling dress. A little bit of the red trim like that on the additional piece also streamed across the abdomen section and down the skirt.

"This is a dress made for a wizardess," she said smiling, as she realized Kevin was staring at it. "It's made of a more durable fabric than my black dress. It's also made of a stain resistant fabric and will stay white despite traveling."

"It certainly is beautiful," said Kevin, still staring at the dress. "It suits you well. You must really like dresses if you chose to get another one for traveling. I'm sure that dress is not the most comfortable thing to wear."

"Actually, it is," responded Caitlin. "I think it's very comfortable, just as I did my last one. Plus, as a spellcaster, it's important to wear a flowing garment such as a dress or robes, since tighter clothing can actually restrict capabilities with casting magic."

"Oh," responded Kevin. "I didn't know that."

Caitlin nodded. "It's true, though," she said. "There are some magicians of all levels of magic who practice the art naked to maximize their efficiency. If you're not one of them, though, a robe for men or a dress for women works almost as well." She paused for a second. "I thought you might think this better represented a new side of me I'm learning to embrace. Do you like it?"

All Kevin could do was smile. He almost could not believe just how much Caitlin cared for what he liked on almost everything. She seemed, in her newly emotional state, to be showing her attachment to Kevin. Even now that she was not hiding her emotions behind a shell, she still was something special that Kevin was slowly uncovering every day, while still showing more confidence than most would have in such a situation.

"I love it," he said.

Caitlin smiled.

After a moment, Kevin then continued, "I hope you've got everything else packed up, though, since we're leaving tomorrow. We're headed to Scurnia."

"Exactly as we planned," nodded Caitlin. "Success today?"

"Yes," responded Kevin.

"Great job," said Caitlin, smiling. "You're getting really good at this." She gave Kevin a giant hug as she said this. "It'll be a long walk starting tomorrow. Are you sure you're ready?"

"I think so," responded Kevin, as he thought, "and we have plenty of reason to go. There's a lot there in Scurnia, as far as I understand. The 'third faction', the Knights of the Dragon, are near there." He raised his arm and pointed to the Stripe of Air. "There may be stripes there that we don't know of. There's also…"

"Your father?" interrupted Caitlin. "You know your father lived in Scurnia most of his life and was a Scurnian soldier."

"Is that a ridiculous thing to use our precious time on?" asked Kevin. "To know what became of him?"

Caitlin thought about it a second, but then shrugged. "My father hasn't come to find us yet, so I'm guessing he's not ready with what he's working on. If we're going to Scurnia to codify an alliance anyway, there's nothing wrong with a little side questing as long as we go when my father catches up with us."

Kevin nodded in response, glad to have Caitlin by his side. Sure enough, Caitlin really was willing to accompany him anywhere. And their next destination was Scurnia.

With Aurana and Nuve once again reunited, only Scurnia remained of the Triple Alliance nations. But there was more in Scurnia as well, and Kevin did wonder what he might learn about his father's fate. Though Kevin was not sure whether or not he would be able to find his father, he was glad to have Caitlin with him to help him find his way through life.

Chapter 32

The Pass Between the Mountains

If you truly believe in something, then you will give up everything you have for it. All of your worldly possessions: your wealth, your memories, your friendships, and even your love, must be forsaken for your cause. You must even be willing to give up your existence for what you fight for. Do not fear it, for if the cause is good, others will follow your example and fight for your cause. So be willing to forsake everything and follow your heart to a better future.

As the days passed by, Kevin Trent Stryker started to find more and more to fear in these words that were imparted to him by Kron, who first heard these words from former king of gods Vinz Larinion. Initially, Kevin had taken these words lighter than he should have. He initially took it as needing to push through for those close to him. It was the way he had interpreted what Kron had said at the time, not that he had to forsake them, as the saying seemed to imply more and more. Since then, however, Kevin was starting to grow concerned for Caitlin, and was afraid to lose her as well. Now, Kevin had to make sure that she would be safe too, and he was afraid that he would be unwilling to surrender Caitlin if it meant pursuing what he was fighting for.

As it had turned out, Kevin and Caitlin's trip across Nuve had taken them nine days, just as Raijin Shane had told them. They had crossed through the rest of the Nuve province of Soverenia and through all of Katalina on their way. Naturally, Kevin and Caitlin talked the days away the entire trip, although this time they held hands most of the way and spent time talking about their new relationship.

Over this time, Kevin was piecing together more about what Caitlin's mental state was like. Her new exposure to emotions had been put to the test on this long walk across Katalina, and what Kevin had found is that for the most part, Caitlin was acting like a normal person, although one that still exuded an aura of power in a lot of ways. If there was one area where her emotional suppression was impacting her now that it was no longer in place, it was that she seemed prone to overreaction or underreaction, depending on the situation. Kevin would ask her on a regular basis how she felt, and she assured him she felt all right, that she was still a little afraid, but she was also happy and, in traditional Caitlin fashion, willing to put in the effort to learn.

After nine days, much of which had been an uphill ascent up the plains, the pair had finally reached the Nuve town of Rugger, nestled in at the foot of the Peaked Mountains and at the mouth of the Northern Pass. Not wanting to dawdle too much, Kevin and Caitlin seized the opportunity to restock their supplies in Rugger and take a night off before heading into the pass. Slowly but surely, Kevin was seeing the small amount of coins he had brought on the trip dwindle until almost none were left. However, this did not bother Kevin so much as long as he had enough to get himself and Caitlin through the trip. Kevin was not seeking wealth with his task as an adventurer. All of that with figuring out his finances and what trade he would have to take, could wait for now.

Since the night when Arthur Falchor was possessed and taken over by Demonicus, Kevin's motivation was fueled by this desire to rescue his best friend, and to do his best to save Aurana from being conquered. Maintaining his course and protecting the world from the wrath of Demonicus and the immortal Tyrinion was naturally the best way to do this. Not to do so would seem to leave things incomplete. Even so, Kevin was finding himself feeling off today.

To get to Scurnia, Kevin and Caitlin had to travel through the Northern Pass, a natural formation in the middle of a thin spot in the Peaked Mountains. It was an opening through the dense mountain range that had almost appeared to be carved out of the large formations of rock. The pass was moderately wide, usually wide enough to march a couple of army units through, despite a couple of narrower points. A long day's walk through the pass would take someone traveling through there to the town of Vallia, a small mountain town in Scurnia. The town was a popular lodging site in Scurnia for exactly that reason.

Currently, however, the day was at its high noon point, and the sun was beating down heavily. Although this was a mountainous area and normally being higher meant colder temperatures, a heat wave was affecting the region, making it hotter than it had ever been across the Northern Pass. Often, Kevin found himself sweating in his military jacket and had to wipe his forehead with his sleeve. He kept the jacket open as he normally did to allow airflow, exposing his red shirt that he wore underneath it. Next to Kevin, Caitlin seemed to be rather unaffected by the heat. In her white dress with red trim, she was sweating some as well, but appeared to be sweating less than Kevin. The hot day had made traveling the pass difficult, but the two pushed on through the rough trip anyway.

Walking through this heat, Kevin had a great deal to think about. Noticing Kevin thinking hard about something, Caitlin turned to him and asked, "What's wrong, Kevin? You don't really seem like yourself today."

"It's nothing, Caitlin," said Kevin.

Caitlin rolled her eyes. "When you say it like that, I know it's not 'nothing'. I thought you would have more trust in me by this point."

"That's not what I meant," responded Kevin. "Truth be told, I can't even really explain it to myself, so how can I explain it to you?"

It took a few seconds of thought before Caitlin responded. "I hate it when that happens. I've felt that before. Usually it's self-frustration that's the cause, the feeling that something isn't right."

"You've felt that?"

"In a manner of speaking, I have," Caitlin acknowledged. "You've talked a lot with me about my feelings since we left Nuvenia. What can you tell me about how you're feeling?"

Kevin turned his head. "Something's not right," he said. "That's how I feel."

Mildly frustrated with that response, Caitlin decided to stop and take a breath. She realized in that moment that it would be best to be supportive. "There's not a lot of certainty in our lives right now, I know, and I'm sure a lot doesn't feel right at the moment," Caitlin responded. She then paused. Something was nagging at her as well. She wanted so badly to just encourage Kevin, to be there for him, to show him that she loved him, but it felt like something was pulling her back, something was hesitating, something was resisting. It must be something about her old life conflicting with her new one, she thought. Trying not to let it get to her at the moment, Caitlin gathered herself up and continued, attempting to show the true feeling in her heart.

Looking at her for a second, Kevin was wondering what Caitlin was about to say.

She grabbed Kevin's hand tightly, getting him to turn and look at her as they both stopped. "But wherever you have to go and whatever you have to do, I promise I'll be right there with you to help you. We're still friends, and I made the same promise to you before. I haven't forgotten, and I hope you won't, either."

As Kevin looked at Catilin still clutching his hand, he saw the determination in her eyes. Maybe she was a little clung to him right now, being new to understanding her own emotions and expression, but it was clear she meant what she was saying, from the bottom of her heart. It made him feel better. Kevin smiled and nodded. "Thanks, Caitlin," he said gently. "I really appreciate it."

Caitlin reached out and gave Kevin a peck on the cheek. "I know you do," she said.

As they shared a little bit of time there on the pass, taking pause for a couple of moments, two people were watching Kevin and Caitlin from a cliffside above. Carefully they watched down the halfpipe-like wall of the Northern Pass, observing and studying the little they could see from that height.

On that cliffside, Arthur Falchor stood looking out over the Northern Pass, attempting to observe what he simply saw as two people standing out in the middle of the pass. Next to him, Rachel Reinhart was kneeling with her bow drawn and a sharp, standard non-poisonous arrow armed and ready to shoot. More than three weeks of long travel had brought them across Nuve from Cardol all the way through a mountain road. Around the mountains they had proceeded to the northeast, not stopping to rest for any days at all. They had traveled a large distance in such a short time by continuing to press on despite their doubts about whether or not they were headed in the right direction.

"Mind explaining to me why we're here again?" asked Rachel.

Arthur sighed. "If I've told you once, I've told you a thousand times, Rachel. We didn't find much from the old book, *Immortality is a Truth*, but we did find several references to 'the pass between the mountains in the north', and this is the only one that we know of. If there's something here, we'll find it."

"Hmmph. 'If' is the key word in that sentence," said Rachel. "I still think it just gave you an idea of somewhere you could run away."

Rolling his eyes, Arthur commented, "Whatever." He stopped for a second. "What do you make of those two down there in the middle of the pass?"

"Rough to tell," responded Rachel, looking carefully down the line of her arrow, "but I do have some worries. One of them appears to be in a military uniform of some kind. I can't tell the color, but it doesn't appear to be anything familiar from this distance. The other figure appears to be dressed in white, as far as I can tell. I also can't really see anything about it either. It appears to be traveling with the other one across this vacant pass."

Arthur wiped his eyes, sweating in the hot temperature of the day, and now faced with a difficult decision. After a moment of thought, he was ready with an executive decision. "Rachel," he began, with a bit of hesitation, "I want you to shoot an arrow directly in front of them."

Rachel looked up at Arthur, confused. "And why would you want me to do that?" she asked.

Still hesitating in the heat, Arthur continued, "They could be Desolunar spies. It's bad enough that you and I aren't completely sure yet what we're doing. So, we're going to try and spook them a bit with the arrow, and that way we can make sure we aren't seen somewhere we're not safe."

"I see," said Rachel skeptically, not fully agreeing with Arthur's logic. "It will be difficult to place an arrow from this distance, but I'll give it a shot if you think it's worth it."

Arthur nodded. "I think so," he said. "Just take the shot."

Doing as she was requested, Rachel pulled her bowstring a little tighter, and aimed her black longbow in front of the two figures she saw. Carefully, she aimed her arrow as precisely as she could, knowing that a slight mistake would be magnified at this distance, and released the bowstring.

The arrow flew straight, piercing through the air with only a silent wisp. Unfortunately for Rachel, the arrow did not land in front of the two figures in the pass.

On the ground, Kevin was screaming in pain as the arrow had hit him in his right shoulder. He fell to the ground, wrenching in pain as he reached back to pull the arrow out from his body.

Reacting quickly to the arrow shot, Caitlin turned immediately in the direction the arrow came from, and shot a powerful beam of fire at the cliff top. At the top of the cliffside, Arthur and Rachel had only a second to react and retreat from the cliffside before the blast of fire scraped the top of the cliff.

When Caitlin cut off the beam of the fire, she immediately rushed to Kevin's side, screaming, "Kevin! Kevin! Are you all right?" Her angel wings were becoming visible but translucent, as they had done before when she felt a stronger connection to Kevin than usual.

Getting back up on one knee, but clutching his shoulder, Kevin grimaced in pain, "I'll be fine, Caitlin." Then he took his left arm off of his shoulder, which still had an arrow embedded, and pointed to the top of the cliffside. "Go after them," he said. "You can worry about my injury afterward."

Caitlin nodded in acknowledgment, her eyes full of determination. Looking toward the cliffside, she stood up and let her angelic powers float her to the top of the cliff. While her control over them was only semi-voluntary, she managed to make them work anyway. Up the cliff she went, in pursuit of the attackers, until she disappeared over the top of the cliff.

From the bottom of the pass, Kevin tried to look on and see as much as he could of what was occurring at the top. He could see several flashes of color, signs of different types of magic. Caitlin must have been in a fury and was firing off all sorts of magic in an effort to strike back. How the pursuit was actually going on the top, however, he could not see. Kevin clutched his right shoulder again in pain, still trying to watch as much as he could, but he could not see anybody at the top of the cliff.

Were they attackers of Demonicus? Kevin was unsure, since it had been so long since Demonicus had tried to kill Kevin, and it seemed very unfavorable for Demonicus not to keep the pressure on Kevin. He knew an attack was long overdue, but surely someone with as many resources as the ruler of Desolunar would know to use more than an archer or two from an absurd distance such as that. It seemed shoddily prepared.

Suddenly, though, someone who was definitely not Caitlin took a short leap from the top of the cliff and started sliding down its long, pipe-like side. For a moment, Kevin thought nothing of it, thinking that it was one of the attackers that Caitlin was chasing off. However, as the person kept sliding down the cliff, Kevin saw that the person had a sword drawn. And where he was sliding down, it appeared to Kevin, was in line for an attack on his weakened self.

Kevin drew his Sword of Purity, the first time he had done so in a couple of weeks. As he did, he stayed knelt on the ground, but picked up his sword carefully with his right arm in a defensive stance. Because of the arrow in his shoulder, Kevin used his left hand carefully on the flat side of the blade to help brace for a charge.

When the person sliding down the cliff finally hit the ground, he began running with his blade up, charging toward Kevin. Just as Kevin had predicted. Holding his sword low, Kevin waited until the last second when the person made a leaping move toward Kevin. As the person made his move, Kevin lifted his sword in his defensive, braced stance, and the person's unchecked momentum from the deflection made him stumble and fall over Kevin's head. Kevin had pushed the person over with his sword, until the person landed on his face in the dirt behind Kevin, his sword out of his hands.

Carefully, Kevin stood up, trying not to antagonize the wound in his right shoulder where the arrow was still sticking out. He pointed the Sword of Purity at the attacker's neck and said "Roll over."

Slowly, the person rolled over, appearing to have been badly scuffed up from sliding down the cliffside and being thrown over

Kevin. The person's blue shirt and black pants were torn up a bit, and were now very dirty. A couple of cuts appeared to be the only injury that the person had as he lay on the dirt grounds of the Northern Pass.

Then, the face of the person appeared: a young man with blue eyes and short blonde hair. Stunned at what he was seeing, Kevin's eyes widened as he backed away his sword from the young man's neck. "Arthur?" he asked, very surprised. "Is that really you?"

It took Arthur a second to widen his eyes and observe who was pointing a sword at him. As the sword backed away from him, though, he started to stand up, still staring at the man in the military jacket. "My gosh," Arthur said, "Do my eyes deceive me, or am I really seeing my best friend?"

Kevin started laughing. "Arthur Falchor, I never want to hear you ask if your eyes 'deceive you' again. You sound ridiculous."

"Oh, so I show legitimate concern for you, and all you can do is laugh?" scoffed Arthur sarcastically, with a bit of a chuckle. "I always knew you were crazy, Kevin, but now I know you're really out of your mind."

This made Kevin snicker even harder. "Hey, I was only joking," he said. Kevin was more excited than he had been in weeks. "It's great to see you again, Arthur. I was very worried for your safety."

"You were worried for me?" asked Arthur, still with a sarcastically cocky tone in his voice. "I'll let you decide who was more worried for who."

"We can talk later about it," chuckled Kevin. He then let out a whistle, hoping that Caitlin would recognize it as a signal to stop pursuing whatever she was still following. As he finished his whistle, however, Kevin did not notice another person sliding down the side of the cliff into the pass. Then, Kevin turned back to Arthur. "You're lucky I'm still letting you be my friend," he said, turning to reveal the arrow in his right shoulder. "Are you responsible for this?"

"Uhm," Arthur was dumbfounded by how to answer this to Kevin, "in a way, yes. I was trying to have the person shooting the arrow put it in front of you, and apparently she put it in your shoulder instead." Arthur then turned toward the cliffside, and glared at a sore Rachel who was brushing herself off at the bottom of the cliff. He knew now where to place the blame and not be forced to feel guilty. "Rachel!" he called. "Get over here and apologize to Kevin for shooting him in the shoulder!"

Rushing over because she heard Arthur, Rachel did not quite understand what he had said to her. As she walked over, still brushing herself off, she said, "I didn't understand what you said, Arthur. Are you all right? That cliffside is just an awful place to go sliding down without suffering injury, and..." Rachel stopped mid-breath when she noticed that the other man standing next to Arthur was Kevin, wearing a green military jacket in the style of the Auranian army. She paused, absolutely stunned at what she was seeing. "Kevin Trent!" she exclaimed in her surprise. "What in the world are you doing in a place like this?"

"I should be asking you the same question," said Kevin. "Instead, I'm standing here staring at you in pain with one of your arrows sticking out of my right shoulder." He turned a bit to show Rachel the arrow, and the small pool of blood that was building out of the wound and in his jacket's fabric.

"Oh my gosh, Kevin, I'm so sorry," apologized Rachel. "I really didn't mean to hit you with that arrow. I wouldn't have shot it at all if I had known it was you down here. I'll see if I can find something to get that bandaged up for you."

Kevin shook his head. "Don't bother," he said. "I've got something better." Then, Kevin turned to the cliffside, clutching his shoulder again, and called, "Caitlin! If you can hear me, come back down into the pass. It's all clear."

From behind him, though, Kevin heard Caitlin's voice. "I'm right here," she said.

Kevin, Arthur, and Rachel all turned to find Caitlin standing behind them. Her angel wings were no longer visible. "I heard you whistle earlier," Caitlin said to Kevin. "I just figured that you might want some time to reunite yourself with your two friends here."

"Oh, okay," said Kevin, pleasantly surprised. "Mind healing up the arrow wound in my shoulder now?"

Acknowledging this, Caitlin started working on the back of Kevin's shoulder using her magic. She worked at it carefully, trying to be gentle. While she was working, however, Arthur interrupted, "Friends, huh? Then why were you attacking us with magic up there? I don't think I've ever been that afraid of someone in my lifetime."

Before Caitlin could answer, however, Kevin responded, "That's my fault, Arthur. After the arrow hit my shoulder, I told Caitlin to go after you, thinking we were under attack by someone." As Kevin finished his sentence, however, he yelped in pain as Caitlin pulled out the arrow using her hands. Snappily, Kevin turned his head and remarked to Caitlin, "Hey! You think you could be more careful with that?"

Caitlin showed the removed arrow, now stained in blood, to Kevin. "Well, it had to come out, Kevin. I probably could have warned you, but it would have hurt the same nonetheless."

A little flair of the old Caitlin there, Kevin thought to himself. Tact was clearly something she was still figuring out.

Rachel then raised her hand, getting Caitlin's attention. "Do you think I could have that back?" she asked. "You can't waste good arrows if you have them."

Reaching over Kevin's shoulder, Caitlin passed the arrow to Rachel. "Suit yourself," she said. Then, Caitlin went about finishing the healing process on Kevin's shoulder, including removing as much blood as possible from around the wound.

Kevin placed his hand on his shoulder, feeling no wound there at all. "Thanks," he said. "Almost feels like it never happened."

"That's the idea," remarked Caitlin. She then turned to Arthur, who she realized was staring at her. "Nice to see you again too, Arthur," she said.

"Where have I seen you before?" asked Arthur, still staring at Caitlin. "You look familiar in a weird sort of way, and it's obvious you recognize me."

Kevin started snickering again. "I guess he doesn't recognize you, Caitlin."

Hearing this, Caitlin began to snicker alongside Kevin.

Arthur gasped in realization. "You?" he said, starting to step back. "Whoa, wait a moment, what are you doing here with Kevin?"

Seeing a chance to make the point as well as tease Arthur for his irrational fear of her, she stepped closer to Kevin until she was right next to him. "Well, actually…" Caitlin began as she grabbed Kevin's hand, "Kevin and I are kind of together."

Reacting to this in surprise, Arthur did nothing more than close his eyes and say, "Kevin, may I speak with you for a moment, please?" Acknowledging this, Kevin began walking toward Arthur, when Arthur grabbed him by the sleeve and dragged him over several steps, catching Kevin by surprise.

Watching this happen, Rachel and Caitlin started laughing together. "Isn't that quite a sight to see?" asked Caitlin.

"It certainly is," chuckled Rachel. "You know, if it weren't for the fact that those two are the best of friends, neither of them would be getting away with that kind of move, no matter who was tugging who. Men are weird sometimes, aren't they?"

"We think they're unusual, and they think we're unusual," said Caitlin. "That's the way it works, you know. The best thing men and women can do for each other is to accept that fact and that we're going to do different, unusual things sometimes."

Rachel nodded, still chuckling a bit. "Indeed, that is true," she said. "By the way, I don't believe we've met. I'm Rachel Reinhart." She reached out to shake Caitlin's hand.

Caitlin extended her hand as well, and returned the shake. "Caitlin Amelia Magnon," she said. "Don't mind Arthur, he's just scared of me for no real reason. I bet that's why Arthur pulled aside Kevin to talk."

"I wouldn't be surprised," laughed Rachel. "So what did you do to scare Arthur?"

"Long story," responded Caitlin. "We'll talk about it on our way through the pass, okay?"

"Sure," said Rachel with a smile. "I have a feeling, just from this little meeting, that we're going to become fast friends."

Caitlin nodded with a smile. Maybe it was easier to make friends than she had ever thought before.

All the while, over a few steps away, out of the range of the girls, Arthur had begun to talk to Kevin with an aggressive, yet quiet comment. "Do you mind explaining to me why *she* is here and what the hell you have to do with her? She's psychotic!"

"Relax, Arthur," said Kevin. "Caitlin is not psychotic. She's a little different now, and that's a long story, but she's good."

Thinking for a second, Arthur looked up at the sky and the sun's position in it. "A long story? I've got time," he said.

"Later," said Kevin. "I'm sure that all of us have questions about what has happened over the past month or so that we cannot answer individually. I think that if we all four discuss it, however, we'll have an easier time piecing together the events that each of us has missed."

Contemplating this, Arthur raised his index finger, and pointed it upward, leaning toward Kevin. "Smart thinking," he said. "Which way are you two heading?"

"We're off to Scurnia," responded Kevin. "At the east end of this pass is the town of Vallia. So far, we've been in the process of reuniting countries, which is in itself another longer story. And Scurnia just happens to be the next one that we are headed to." He paused for a second. "Now, I want to know, what in the hell are you and Rachel doing up here?"

Arthur shrugged, then put his hands behind his head as he stretched his elbows. "Honestly, we're running away."

Kevin glared at Arthur. "From Demonicus, I presume?"

"Yes, from him, who else?" Arthur snapped back. "Turns out Rachel got captured by him too when her book club was ambushed before making it to Cardol. Demonicus agreed to let us out on the condition that we seek out and kill you."

Suddenly, Kevin's eyes widened. He had no reason to believe Arthur would actually kill him, but he was stunned for another reason. Demonicus was still pursuing him this far north? "Why would Demonicus want that?" He looked at the Sword of Purity. "Just over this?"

"That's what I understand," Arthur acknowledged. "He sees you as a threat to him and his 'conquest of the realms', as he called it."

Before Kevin could continue to ask questions, however, a call came over from the girls. "Hey, guys!" shouted Caitlin. "Are we just going to stand here in the hot sun all day, or are we actually going to go somewhere?"

Kevin started chuckling. "Sure, we're going to Vallia, if that's okay with everyone."

Adding to this, Arthur yelled out, "I hope that's fine with you, Rachel. I don't have any better ideas."

"Better than where we were going, which is nowhere," said Rachel as she and Caitlin approached Kevin and Arthur, reforming the complete group. As Kevin and Arthur joined them, the entire group began to continue down the pass to the east, in the direction of Vallia. The road was long and the temperature was hot, but four friends, some new and some old, were united together.

"So, tell me," began Rachel, "what's all of this about? Arthur's tried to explain it to me many times, but I still don't quite get why I'm here or why I ended up where I was."

Kevin nodded, acknowledging Rachel's question. "With all due respect, I'm lost as to why you're here as well, so don't expect me to tell you why you're here."

"I wasn't expecting you to," Rachel replied, as if Kevin had answered a question that she meant as rhetorical. "Just curious, that's all. But I suppose that curiosity killed the cat, as the old expression goes."

Caitlin raised a finger. "Curiosity will not cause the cat to die, Rachel. Only the lack of it will. If you're willing to explore new things, you'll always find it's to your advantage to have that knowledge."

"That's an interesting twist on the old adage," interrupted Arthur. "I don't think I've ever heard it put that way before." He then glared at Rachel. "But I bet the cynic over there doesn't believe it."

Immediately, Rachel was frustrated. "I told you I'm not a cynic!" Arthur had managed to get under Rachel's skin, again.

Seeing this, Kevin and Arthur both laughed. Caitlin thought this was odd. She grabbed Kevin's sleeve and asked, "Why are you laughing?"

"It's an inside joke," Kevin told her. "It's something Arthur has been calling Rachel for some time, just to get that reaction out of her."

Caitlin looked at Rachel, confused. "It doesn't look like

Rachel's having too much fun over it, though."

Rachel turned and looked at Caitlin. "Oh, it's fine," she said. "If I really thought Arthur meant to hurt me with that comment, I'd have an arrow in his back already."

That made Arthur's eyes widen. He chuckled a bit awkwardly.

Caitlin had a reasonable suggestion, as she talked to Rachel. "Perhaps it would be easier for you to understand, and for all of us to know what happened to each of us while we were separated, if we started from the beginning and each told our part of the story."

"Sounds good," said Rachel. Kevin and Arthur also nodded in agreement.

And from there, the foursome spent their entire walk along the Northern Pass sharing the stories of their travels. Kevin and Arthur talked about meeting Kron—explaining to Rachel that he was a god, with Caitlin backing them up that they were serious—and heading south to find the Sword of Purity, meeting Caitlin, and Arthur's kidnapping. Rachel recounted that about the same time, she had been traveling with her book club to Cardol when they were ambushed. Then, Kevin and Caitlin talked about meeting with her father and making a plan for rescue, a detour into phoenix territory—Kevin was not so hesitant to tell people he had known for years about them, as opposed to those he had not known so long—the coup d'état in Aurana City, being kidnapped in Venarose, the battle with the Existence leading to their opening up to each other, and the armistice negotiations in Nuvenia. Arthur recounted meeting Demonicus and discovering he was the son of the dictator, and negotiating for his and Rachel's lives. He and Rachel then talked about meeting the Metoi and the Toronaga, heading north into Cardol and finding the *Immortality is a Truth* book they were still carrying, and without knowing where to go next, deciding to go to "the pass between the mountains to the north" as mentioned in the book. They took a long route from Cardol up the Rhonean River in the middle of Nuve, but tried to avoid towns and cities as they traveled so as not to be caught by Demonicus for not trying to hunt Kevin and Caitlin down.

As they walked, Kevin was so grateful to see Arthur again. Now, he did not need to worry about a rescue. That being said, Kevin realized that his work was far from done. He still had a promise to keep to Kron to take him home. And after getting Aurana and Nuve back on track, why not see it through and get Scurnia on board as well?

Memories of the battlefield where he found the Sword of Purity were still vivid in Kevin's mind. The losses there were a sure sign of what would happen to Aurana if he could not get help. And the best way to get that help was to complete the professor's plan and deliver an army of the Triple Alliance.

Up ahead in the Scurnian town of Vallia, he and his friends would have the chance to regroup. Kevin kept looking at Caitlin as they walked together, and saw how much interacting she was doing in a more free manner than she had before, talking much and sharing stories with Arthur and Rachel alike. She had changed much without her emotional block.

A thought sent a shiver down Kevin for a moment. Professor Magnon would catch up with them eventually. How would he react to the changes in his daughter?

Chapter 33

Dragons in Vallia

Nestled at the edge of the Peaked Mountains and at the mouth of the Northern Pass, the Scurnian town of Vallia sat at the gateway to the Scurnian Plateau. Like most of northern and central Scurnia, Vallia sat on raised ground with little vegetation. Prosperity came to Vallia quite easily on the sole basis that it was located at the mouth of the Northern Pass and thus was a quick rest stop before entering the daylong journey through the pass. In total, however, the town's permanent population numbered about five hundred. It was a small town, mostly focused around the town's tavern and inn, called The Old Ball and Chain because the tavern had formerly sat next to a jail. By the current day, however, the jail was long gone, and the tavern stood toward the center of the town. All around the town, little wooden shacks sat in various patterns. They formed "streets" in their arrangement, although most of the time there was no road at all, not even through the center of the city. In the center were the tavern and a town hall where religious events, messages, government, and much more were handled.

The sun was setting quickly over the Vallia horizon as Kevin, Caitlin, Arthur, and Rachel sat at a table inside The Old Ball and Chain enjoying their first sips of water in over a day. There was no water to be found in the Northern Pass, especially in the record heat. Fortunately, Vallia had a supply of water imported from other parts of Scurnia to make up for the town's lack of water in such a high mountainous area. Like it normally was, the tavern was full with over fifty people enjoying themselves and having a good time. Normally travelers would be a part of the tavern crowd, but at this moment only Kevin and company were not from Vallia among the people present there.

Tucked back into a corner of the lively tavern, Kevin raised his glass above the table he and his friends all sat at. "To friends," he began. "Old and new, close and distant, and all other types."

Caitlin, Arthur, and Rachel then raised their glasses, tapped them to Kevin's and took a sip with him out of their respective glasses.

"It sure is good to get a few minutes of break time," said Caitlin. "It's quite a bit cooler here in Vallia than it was in the middle of the pass."

"Certainly nice," added Arthur, putting his hands behind his head and leaning back a bit. "Still, it's a shame we can't really afford some rooms here in the inn. It would really be a nice convenience as opposed to having to find shelter outside again."

Caitlin nodded. "We'll manage," she said. "As nice as it would be to have the inn, we'll do as we have to in order to save some of the remaining money we have left. Remember, most of what we have left belongs to Kevin."

Letting out a sigh, Kevin added, "I'm not sure how much more we can go on it, though. I don't want to do what we're doing for money, but spending so much money on provisions for us to keep traveling might make finances a limitation here soon. I didn't have much to start with, so by now, we're really drained on money."

"Maybe we'll just have to find a sign," said Rachel, trying to perk up the mood. "Who knows. Maybe we'll find a way through it. Whether it's by something happening or someone showing up, maybe we'll get lucky."

"Luck indeed," scoffed Arthur. "There's no such thing as luck."

Rachel scowled at Arthur. "Who's the cynic now?"

Everyone shared a laugh for a moment.

Before anyone else had a chance to respond, however, the tavern door thundered open and in walked a man dressed entirely in brown leather with a metal plate over his chest. All fell silent as the door opened and the man walked in and up to the bar. The silence was eerie as the heavy steps of the man clad in leather sounded throughout the tavern. Everyone in the tavern stared at this man as he walked. Kevin looked on as well, confused as to who this man was.

As the man approached the bar, he stopped and removed his leather headpiece, revealing his dark hair and face, which made him appear to be in his mid thirties. Then, in a commanding yet celebratory voice, he said, "Drinks are on me, everyone! Bartender, a glass of your finest ale for everyone in the tavern!"

With this, a massive amount of celebratory screaming from the patrons of the tavern shook the building's structure. Kevin started chuckling a little bit while he rolled his eyes. Anything for a free drink for these people, he thought to himself.

The bartender began pouring as many of the drinks as he could, straight from the tap, and the patrons of the bar started to pass around drinks to everyone, making sure that all of the people in the tavern received a drink. As the drinks reached the corner of the room, however, Kevin and company passed entirely on the free ale. Thirsty as they were from the long day's travel in the heat, only water would satisfy their thirst.

In a short amount of time, the drinks were all passed out and the bar became even more social. Many people in the tavern seemed to be attempting to make contact with the man in the leather who had bought the drinks.

"Do you see that?" pointed out Arthur. "All of them swarming to him because he bought them something to drink. He must be some kind of big shot around here."

"Must be a local for the reception he's getting up there," commented Rachel. "Who wears leather protective clothing all over their body anyway? It's expensive material that also makes movement more difficult. And I'm not even going to talk about that metal plate over his torso."

"It's definitely different, I see," observed Kevin. "Interesting design on the back of his torso plate, though. Can you guys see it? It's a traced out red dragon printed on a thin layer of silver on the iron plate."

"A silver base with a red dragon…" considered Caitlin, trying to remember if she had seen the logo before. "I can't make heads or tails of what it means."

Before Kevin or anyone else could respond, however, Kevin's eyes accidentally locked with those of the man in leather while Kevin was looking around the tavern. Upon this occurrence, the man in leather began to approach the table where Kevin and company were sitting. The man stepped right up in front of the open chair at Kevin's table, and said, "What do we have here?" in a lighthearted tone of voice. "Some travelers passing through Vallia, I presume?"

Kevin nodded to respond. "Indeed," he said. "We made it through the pass earlier today."

"Ah, so we have some fresh arrivals here," responded the man. "Horrible day for a group like the four of you to be traveling through the pass, though. Very dangerous conditions for the unprepared. Good day to be a vulture, though."

Rachel smirked. "That's just awful, but still funny," she said. "I'm sure a day like this makes plenty of food for the vultures today."

"It sure does," said the man as he kicked out the open chair at the table and took a seat in it. "So, then, who are the four of you, and what brings all of you to Vallia today?"

Kevin started, "I'm Kevin, the Vanguard of Aurana. To my left over here in the white dress is Caitlin. Left of her in the brown and green blouse and skirt is Rachel, and to her left, my best friend in the blue shirt and black pants, Arthur."

"Vanguard, huh?" asked the man. "Interesting to hear, indeed, especially since Aurana is quite a distance from here."

"It certainly is," answered Arthur before Kevin could respond. "We're all from Aurana here. Now that you know a little about us, though, we'd like to know a little about you, if you would be willing."

"Most certainly," nodded the man. "I'm Christoph Dewellus, better known to many around Vallia as the Lord Dragon. Native of Vallia, born and raised."

"You certainly seem to be quite the superstar around here," said Caitlin, taking another sip from her glass of water.

Lord Dragon nodded. "Pride of the town," he said. "Vallia has been very supportive of the Scurnian government, but even more so, they support a group of warriors of the noblest order, the Knights of the Dragon."

"And you are their leader," observed Kevin. "Explains your popularity and the amount of money you hold to be able to purchase a drink for everyone here in the tavern, not to mention the expensive leather."

"I have to be able to afford the leather for everyone," responded the Lord Dragon. "We, the Knights of the Dragon, are so named for the talents we've made use of in taming dragons for use in flight and other uses such as warfare. Protecting oneself from the heat of a dragon's fire, as well as from its rough skin, however, requires more than what padded cloth can offer us for protection." He paused for a second. "Of course, most of my hundred or so members don't wear their leather while off duty."

Caitlin nodded. "Your breastplate carries the standard of your organization on the rear, doesn't it? A silver field with a red dragon printed into it. Identifies your organization wherever you are at if you can't carry a flag with you all of the time."

"Well thought," responded the Lord Dragon. "My organization means more to me than my life itself. So do the people here in Vallia." He paused, as he extended his arm out into the tavern. "Good spirits, humor, and people just enjoying themselves are normally difficult to come by here in Vallia. This is a small mountain town without a great food or water supply, surviving mostly around this tavern."

"So you bring the spirit yourself when you and your men show up in the tavern," realized Kevin.

Lord Dragon nodded. "This town counts on us to make jokes, spend some money, and altogether bring some sparkle to this cloud of dust that is this town. Those of us who have been longtime residents love this town and never want to leave. I still consider it fortunate that the Peaked Mountains provide an excellent place to train our dragons; it allows us to remain close to Vallia."

"King Andrew II of Aurana seems to think your group is a faction in Nuve," said Kevin as he stopped the Lord Dragon for a moment. "However, having interacted with the actual 'factions' of Nuve myself, I don't think that King Andrew would consider a faction to be an organization as small as yours, especially if you're not jockeying for position with the government of Nuve."

"We don't jockey with anyone," answered the Lord Dragon. "Nuve, we have no quarrel with, and we are supported by the government of Scurnia. The latter sees us as caretakers for Vallia as long as we are bringing some prosperity into Vallia to supplement that which the traffic brings in. We've traipsed into Nuve occasionally, but we try not to do that." He then turned toward the bar, and yelled out, "Bartender! Can you send over another glass of ale?"

At the bar, the bartender nodded, and began to tap out another glass of ale for the Lord Dragon.

"Well, I think I can speak for all of us," began Rachel after taking a sip of her water, "that we're all very interested in the Knights of the Dragon. Taming dragons in itself is quite a feat."

"And speaking for myself," observed Caitlin, "I've noticed you've been very open talking to us, as outlanders, about yourself and what you do."

"And what is this world without trust?" responded the Lord Dragon. "Had I not had trust for any of my men, we would not have become what we are now. I worry not about sharing, because if someone wanted to steal our dragons or try to slaughter us, our dragons would tear them apart. Being open with who we are and what we do gains us more trust by the good people of the world."

Kevin nodded. "Which is why you walked over to the table and introduced yourself to us, Mr. Dewellus."

"Please," said the Lord Dragon, "call me Lord Dragon. Like I said, I've had to grow accustomed to the title, and I have. I can presume someone like yourself has had to grow used to being called the Vanguard of Aurana, after all."

"That's true," answered Kevin as he took a sip from his water glass. "Believe me, I've had quite a time trying to get used to people calling me that."

"Well, get used to it," responded the Lord Dragon. "Life's about as predictable as the weather around here."

Kevin and company all got a laugh out of the Lord Dragon's joke, keeping in mind the record-setting weather they had just walked through in a high mountain pass to arrive in Vallia. As he laughed, Kevin had an idea. "That reminds me," he said, "I'd like to ask you something. How would you like to test your dragons in combat?"

Lord Dragon's thoughts were aroused. "What do you mean by that?" he asked. "Naturally, I would certainly like to use my dragons legitimately in combat, but I can't honestly lead my men and my dragons into combat blindly."

"Fair enough," said Kevin. "So here's the facts: Aurana and Nuve are engaged in combat together against Desolunar, a nation led by a dictator called Demonicus."

"Ah," interrupted the Lord Dragon. "I have heard about his atrocities. Scurnia often reminds us of it, well aware of what Desolunar does. But, with the harsh terrain separating us with Desolunar, not to mention battles with Gardolk, Scurnia is simply unable to do anything about it."

Frowning a bit, Kevin asked, "So that's it? I had thought that Scurnia had been helpful in the war twenty years ago, and that action took place in the same area as Desolunar."

"Cheer up," said the Lord Dragon. "Fortunately, there may yet be a chance for Scurnia to participate, as long as Nuve and Aurana are on board as well. Recent news reports suggest that there may be a treaty signed between the two sides here soon, which will end the distraction Scurnia has with our neighbors to the south. It's not so much of a war as it has been an annoying boundary dispute that has had a few meaningless battles."

"That's good news," responded Kevin.

"Indeed, we all are better if it ends," acknowledged the Lord Dragon. "If what you are asking is that we fly the silver and red in action against Desolunar, then naturally we'll be glad to cause some serious damage. We desire a chance to test our mettle. But we won't defy the king of Scurnia, King Warren. It will be his call as to whether or not we are permitted to fight."

Kevin nodded with a smile. "Still glad to have you on board," he said as he reached out to shake the Lord Dragon's hand. "Someday I hope to get to see you and your dragons in action."

"Oh yeah, we're always the lords of the battlefield when we have our dragons," said the Lord Dragon, holding back his excitement while chuckling as he shook Kevin's hand.

As the Lord Dragon finished his sentence, the door to the tavern opened again, and two men in robes walked in, drawing the attention of everyone in the tavern, including Kevin and company. Kevin squinted his eyes, trying to make out what the two people looked like amidst the crowd of people in the tavern.

One appeared to be a reasonably young man wearing white and gold robes, with dark hair and some facial scruff, and blue and green streaks across his robe. The other, however, appeared to be quite a bit older. His hair was blonde, slicked back into points, and his robes were both red and black. Their appearances were deceptive. Kevin immediately recognized them as Professor James Magnon and Kron Kalavere, also known as the god Kronius. As he stared at them to make their identification, however, the Lord Dragon asked Kevin, "Friends of yours?"

Kevin nodded. "Yes," he said. "How did you know that?"

"By the way you're staring," answered the Lord Dragon.

He was right, and Kevin knew it. Body language gave away more than words ever could.

Kevin looked over to Caitlin to see her with her eyes wide open. "Kevin, that's my father," she said quietly in a worried tone of voice. "He's here."

"I know," answered Kevin, a little confused. "What's wrong? I thought you would be glad to see your father."

"I haven't seen him since before that night at the Abyss of the Royal Sovereign," she said, still with a worried tone of voice. "He's going to be shocked to see what I've become. Probably not angry, but maybe unpleasantly surprised."

Truthfully, Kevin was worried about this as well, but he had had the chance to think on it already, and decided that it was what it was. Then he looked over the other person. "Look at the other one with him. Is that…?"

"That's definitely Kron," answered Arthur from across the table, looking over in that direction as well.

"Sure looks like him," said Kevin. "I'm not sure what they're working on, but they must be here for a reason."

Indeed, Kevin, echoed the voice of Professor Magnon in Kevin's head. He was speaking to Kevin through magic and his mind, using the same power that Caitlin had used with him. *You really should learn to control your voice better, though. I can hear you from the other side of the tavern when I sort through who is talking in here.*

Kevin rolled his eyes.

Sure enough, Professor Magnon and Kron both approached the table where Kevin and company were sitting at, and pulled up a couple of chairs. Everyone briefly exchanged greetings for a second. Caitlin sat back, silent. She seemed more than a little nervous.

"It is good to see all of you here," began the professor. "Kron and I had to work together to find you here in Vallia, and I apologize that we could not connect with you sooner." He looked around the table briefly. "I see you've expanded your little group, Kevin."

"Oh, of course," acknowledged Kevin. "Allow me to introduce you to Rachel Reinhart and Arthur Falchor, fresh from escaping Desolunar."

Arthur snapped back at Kevin. "I wouldn't call it 'fresh', Kevin. After a few weeks on the road, I could certainly freshen up, if you get the picture."

Silently, Rachel shook her head, somewhat in disbelief Arthur would make a comment like that. Then, she reached out to shake the professor's hand. "A pleasure to meet you, sir."

"The pleasure is mine. I am Professor James Magnon, Caitlin's father." The professor then sat down at the table. Kron reached over, briefly introduced himself to Rachel and to the Lord Dragon, then sat down at the table as well.

The professor then looked at Kevin, seeing that his daughter appeared to be distracted at the moment. "I would presume that things went well in Nuvenia?"

Kevin nodded. "Better than I'd hoped," he said. "Caitlin and I had some help from Raijin Shane, the Vanguard of Nuve. We managed to get the government and representatives of the Demons and the Cornelia Chimeras to at least resolve to put together a temporary armistice, and the king agreed to resume an alliance with Aurana once the terms are worked out. And now we're here in Scurnia to see the new Triple Alliance through."

"That is quite amazing, Kevin," commented Kron. "I can hardly believe that you and Caitlin managed to make that happen."

The professor looked at Kron. "When they are given the proper opportunity, Kron, I am convinced these young adults can do anything."

"Ah, most certainly!" exclaimed the Lord Dragon. "How the young have so much potential once they see what they have."

Professor Magnon turned all the way to his other side. "Good to see you again, Mr. Dewellus. Still training dragons with your organization, I presume?"

"Indeed," answered the Lord Dragon.

Stunned, Kevin asked, "How do you two know each other? Honestly, I didn't expect that."

"Everyone who has some knowledge of magic knows Professor James Magnon for his brilliant skill," said the Lord Dragon. "My knights are not just warriors, or dragon tamers, or anything of that sort. We're a group with a variety of talents. Because of this, I had Professor Magnon come to our headquarters a couple of years ago and give a lecture on learning advanced magic techniques. His information was very helpful to the couple of spellcasters we have in our ranks."

"Your group was one of the best I have ever taught," added the professor. "They were a very determined set of individuals."

"They still are," the Lord Dragon acknowledged, as he stood up. "I will be headed to the bar to make pay arrangements for all of these drinks, and I'll catch up in a bit." With that, he walked across the tavern to the bar.

Professor Magnon then turned to the other side of the table. "Arthur Falchor, your name is, correct? Kevin has told me much about you, mostly about how dedicated he was to finding you again after your kidnapping."

Arthur started chuckling. "Well, actually, it kind of happened the other way around. I found him by mistake."

"I see," acknowledged the professor. "You escaped?"

"With Rachel," nodded Arthur. "We ran through the Wastes, into Cardol, and through Nuve."

The professor nodded, with a smile. He then looked to Kevin. "I guess you don't need an army to rescue your best friend anymore."

Kevin sighed. He knew that the professor wanted him to finish the job even without that motivation. Plus, Kevin still had motivation; the memory of the battlefield in Aurana made him wish that no one in his homeland would ever have to suffer like that again. "No," he finally answered, "but we're still going to get one, to protect Aurana."

"A good motivation," the professor nodded, "spoken like the nation's Vanguard should." He paused for a second, as he then looked at Arthur. "And you're still with him?"

Without hesitation, Arthur nodded. "He did all this just for me, and if he would've known about Rachel being kidnapped as well, probably for her, too."

"We owe it to Kevin to help him do what he needs to do," added Rachel. Then, a thought occurred to her. "Speaking of which..." she said, as she turned her head toward Arthur, reached down into her quiver, and pulled out some of the translation pages she took from the book in Cardol. "I bet if anyone could help us with this, it's the professor," she said.

Arthur looked confused for a second, but then bent over to help Rachel remove the book. He realized that Rachel was right."

"Well, what do we have here?" asked the professor.

"It's from a book we found in Cardol," answered Rachel. "We weren't sure if anything useful might be in it, but it was a translation in progress from a very old book. It was called *Immortality is a Truth* by someone named Setaeus Demota. We thought maybe it might be useful given how old it was."

Kron's eyes widened. "Well, I will be!" he exclaimed. "I had no idea a copy of that book survived into the modern age."

As Kron reached for the book, the professor snatched it as Rachel pushed the papers onto the table. "Quite a surprise, indeed," said Professor Magnon. "I will have to spend some time with this to tell you what I can discern from it, but it does interest me, indeed."

Kron looked taken aback. Kevin thought this was unusual. Then, he realized something. Discretely, Kevin nudged Arthur. "You should probably tell him about the... you know... Demonicus stuff."

"Oh, okay," Arthur answered awkwardly, not really knowing the professor.

"It's all right, Arthur," the professor said, as he raised his hands. "I know already that Demonicus is your father. My daughter told me about it when we were planning to rescue you."

Shrugging, Arthur said, "It's not that. The way Rachel and I made it out of Desolunar was by agreeing with Demonicus that I would kill Kevin."

"We're worried he will come to collect on that debt, and that he's watching us," added Rachel.

"I see," commented the professor. He then turned to Kron. "When you saw Arthur be possessed by Demonicus, did it happen on its own or did it happen when he grabbed that sword he's carrying?"

Arthur's eyes widened. He looked down at his belt. He knew the "Sword of Corruption", as it was called, was supposedly associated with and locked to his family and his bloodline. Not once did he think this could be how he was being tracked and that he could be possessed.

"He grabbed the sword," affirmed Kron, "and that is how it began. Red glowing eyes and everything."

The professor nodded. "So, a bit of tracer magic, it is, then. It must be embedded in the sword." He looked back at Arthur. "May I see it, please?"

Doing as he was asked, Arthur unfastened the sword and its scabbard from his belt. He passed the sword over, in its scabbard. "I wouldn't touch that, if I were you. I've been told it's not safe to touch unless you're part of Demonicus's bloodline."

The sword went to Kron, who passed it over to the professor. "Whatever you say," chuckled the professor, as he took the sword. Then, he pulled it out of its scabbard, without flinching, and set it on the table. He then closed his eyes and raised his right hand with two fingers up to just below his eyes. In a short moment, he reopened his eyes and lowered his hand. "The tracer inside is now gone, Arthur. Demonicus will no longer be able to control you or use you."

Almost instantly, Arthur became excited. "Awesome!" he said. The thought of being Demonicus's puppet again had been scaring Arthur for a while, and now thanks to Professor Magnon, he would not have to worry about it again.

Immediately, Kevin looked at Kron, and Kron looked back at Kevin. Something about that was not right. How could the professor simply grab that particular locked sword like that?

Before Kevin could think about it further, the professor turned back toward his daughter. When he saw her white dress with red trim, his eyes popped open wide. "My goodness, Caitlin," he began, "when did you get that dress? I thought you swore that you would never wear a white dress, even with other colors, because it did not look as strong as plain black."

All Caitlin could do was look down. In that moment, she was not acting like herself. "I've changed, father," she mumbled, barely audible.

The professor's glance turned into a glare, and there was an awkward pause for a moment. With a serious tone of voice, the professor then said, "Caitlin, Kevin, may I see the two of you outside for a moment, please?"

Kevin rolled his eyes, but he still stood up anyway. Caitlin did so without any complaint, with her head still down, and proceeded to follow the professor with Kevin toward the door of the tavern.

When the door closed again after the three had left, Kron said to Arthur and Rachel. "So, that was awkward. Does anyone have an idea what that was all about?"

"No idea," said Rachel. "Do you know when was the last time Professor Magnon saw his daughter? She mentioned something about her having 'changed' before they walked off."

Arthur slammed his hand against the table. "I know what it is now. Caitlin's father, this Professor Magnon, doesn't know she's 'together' with Kevin. Or at least he didn't know, but it looks like he put two and two together and got four."

Rachel frowned. "What's the big deal about that? They're about the same age, and it's only natural we start to find others we connect with."

"The big deal is, that was not Caitlin until recently." He paused for a second. "I called her 'psychotic' before, but that's not the Caitlin we've talked with all day. When I met her, she pretty much had no emotions, was very focused on just her magical studies while she lived alone. Wore only plain black, as well"

Her eyes widening and her jaw dropping. "That's the same Caitlin?"

Arthur nodded. "Trust me, it's her."

Kron put his face in the palm of his hand. "Professor Magnon is going to be upset," he said. "He is proud of her as a student of magic and her ability to stay disciplined. If Kevin and Caitlin are dating now, as you suggest… I cannot imagine how upset he will be."

And he was right.

Chapter 34

An Emotional Spark

Outside, Professor Magnon made sure that there was no one else around the front of the tavern. Late evening had begun to set in, and while there were plenty of people in The Old Ball and Chain, few were out on the street. The professor pulled Kevin and Caitlin around the side of the building before he began to say with force, "What have the two of you done? I can see it in your eyes; it does not even take mind reading to figure this one out."

Kevin began to try and respond, but Caitlin stopped him. "Let me," she said quietly, still not acting like herself. Then, she turned back to her father. "What are you so angry about, father?"

"Are the two of you out to endanger each other?" he asked. "I do not know how or why this happened, but I can tell your emotional block is gone. Not fractured, not splintered, but gone. How did you manage that, Caitlin?"

"It's hard to explain…" began Caitlin.

"And so what of it?" exclaimed Kevin, becoming frustrated. "Something happened, and now Caitlin has emotions. It's a good thing for her."

"How would you know?" interjected the professor. "This is not what she wants, Kevin. She has made it clear to me before she wants to be able to stay focused on her studies." He glared at Kevin. "What did you do to her?"

"I didn't do anything!" Kevin answered. "Do you really think I'd try to hurt your daughter?" A scowl came to Kevin's face. Professor Magnon had been so helpful and supportive of him, but now he was made to feel like a problem.

"Whether or not you would try to do so is irrelevant," the professor stated. "You did something to her." He raised his voice even more forcefully. "And so help me, if you hurt her…"

"Just stop it!" screamed Caitlin suddenly, catching both Kevin and the professor by surprise. "Stop it, stop it, stop it!"

Kevin and the professor fell silent.

The instability within Caitlin emerged, and it fueled her temper. Still, she took a few seconds to breathe before she continued. She paused, and tried to gather herself. "Father," began Caitlin with a little more confidence but still sounding saddened, "you used to be upset with how I lived my life. You hated how I kept myself free of emotion, purged myself often of it and focused on my discipline. Still, you set up the block for me, encouraged me to focus on my studies, reinforced it when I asked."

The professor was visibly starting to calm down. He was listening closely.

"I'm not that same girl anymore," Caitlin continued as a slight smile started to show on her face as her confidence grew. "Kevin and I traveled together, and we became friends. Then, we became close friends. Then… all of the barriers came crashing down, and…" Caitlin's hands came up until they were clinched together over her heart, "we became more."

"Caitlin, what are you…" stuttered the professor.

"I faced my fears, father," she continued. "Much as I said I was emotionless, I wasn't completely. I was afraid. Afraid of what would happen if I wasn't the best at my skills. Afraid to interact with society in any meaningful way. Then, I was afraid to lose Kevin. That's what loosened the block the first time, and what eventually shattered it."

Kevin's eyes widened. He did not realize what Caitlin had gone through.

"I found that I was better embracing who I am, and what I feel, just as you had always told me before," Caitlin continued. "And now you tell me that I'm doing the wrong thing. Well, I will tell you what I know, father. I know that I am stronger now. And I'm happy, father." A tear came to Caitlin's eye. "For the first time since I was a little girl, I'm actually happy."

Kevin was surprised to hear these words from Caitlin. If what she said was not a true confession of love and happiness, then he did not know what was.

Professor Magnon's eyes widened. He was still a bit skeptical. "Caitlin, I just want to be sure this is what you want." He took a quick glance at Kevin before looking back at his daughter. "You have done so well with your studies, and you are without a doubt the greatest spellcaster at your age. I have no doubt in your abilities, but I must make sure, is this what you want?"

A bit anxious, Kevin looked to Caitlin, wanting to know her answer.

"Kevin always took me for who I am, even before this change, so I wouldn't need to 'throw away' anything." She paused for a moment, like she was bracing herself. "I know now that I'm addicted to the happiness he brings me." She looked at him. "As long as he continues to accept me for me, I've decided I want to embrace this new side of me, and add it to what I was before. It… gives me such a powerful feeling."

There was a momentary pause.

Then, the professor spoke. "If you are certain, my daughter, then I see no reason to tell you what you can and cannot do." He gave his daughter a hug. "I am so sorry for my behavior today," he said as he held her. Then, he looked up and toward Kevin. "And I am sorry to you as well, Kevin. I was wrong to judge you so quickly."

"Don't worry about it," answered Kevin humbly. "Everything will be all right."

Then the professor looked back up at Kevin as he let go of his daughter. "Kevin," he said in a stately yet proud voice, "you have my blessing to stay with my daughter as long as you promise to take care of her. Do you understand?"

Kevin nodded. "I do," he said, "and I promise."

"And I promise to take care of him, too," Caitlin said. She stepped next to Kevin and grabbed his hand to hold it.

"Of course you do," answered the professor, "because you are you. I have seen great things from both of you, and I trust the two of you to take care of each other." He paused for a second. "I am sure the power the two of you hold together is greater than the angels that watch from above." He was citing lore.

Angels. Neither Kevin nor Caitlin had mentioned that yet, and it occurred to both of them at this moment. Both of them looked at the other, realizing this. "Kevin," began Caitlin, "would you be willing to head inside and rejoin Rachel, Arthur, and Kron? I'll explain to father about the you-know-what."

This caught Professor Magnon's attention. He immediately glared at Kevin and asked, "You did not…"

Kevin placed his hands in front of him, shaking them hesitantly. "No, it's nothing like that, I swear," he said. "Really, I've never even thought about doing something like that."

Hearing this, Caitlin laughed at the assumption and Kevin's reaction to it. "Kevin's right," she said, struggling to speak through her laughter. "Nothing like that ever happened."

Professor Magnon let out a sigh of relief. "That would have been quite awkward indeed," he said. "I would have strangled you if that were the case."

Getting an awkward chuckle out of this, Kevin turned and headed for the door into the tavern again. "I'm sure you would," he joked as he entered the tavern to join Arthur, Rachel, and Kron.

As the door slammed behind Kevin, Caitlin began by asking, "Father, what can you tell me about my mother?"

The professor took his arm and placed it around his daughter, pulling her aside gently. "A wonderful woman," he said. "Your mother was very special, for as long as I knew her."

Caitlin looked away from her father. "That's all you ever tell me," she said, "but the fact is that there's more you need to tell me."

"That is all I can ever tell myself, my daughter," answered the professor. "I cannot even bring to terms with myself any more than that."

"But why?" asked Caitlin. "What could possibly be that bad? And how is it any worse than letting a girl grow up without a mother or any hint whatsoever at who was the person who gave birth to her?"

Professor Magnon could not answer this question himself. "Tell me what it is that you have pulled me aside for. Whatever it is that connects your mother to this, I suppose I will find out."

Ashamed to hear Professor Magnon dismissing the subject, but excited about what she was about to say and hopefully find an answer for, Caitlin looked up at her father. "Something wonderful has happened," she said. "Something so unbelievable I still don't understand it myself." Caitlin then took a second to pause, preparing herself for her next sentence. "I'm an angel, father. And I mean that literally, too."

"Caitlin, are you not a little too old to be using such terms? I would not think you would use such a word to describe yourself."

Frustrated, Caitlin grabbed her father by her arm and pulled hard to get his firm attention. "Look into my eyes, father," she said with a serious tone. "I want you to look into them and tell me that I am lying or trying to be cute. I'm being completely serious with you."

For a second, Professor Magnon did as he was asked. He looked into Caitlin's eyes closely, seeing the determination that was there, the absolute truth in her eyes. "My gosh," he gasped, "you mean it literally! How do you know? And when did you find out?"

"About three weeks ago," responded Caitlin, softening her voice. She was actually surprised that her father seemed to believe her so easily. "It was the night that Kevin helped to open up my heart. We found ourselves together for the very first time in love then, and… wait a moment, that's not right. Now that I think about it, I think I might have found out before then. Kevin and I were fighting something called the Existence and Kevin was knocked out. I thought he was dead, and for about five minutes, I found my feelings for Kevin in a strong outburst that led me to float above the ground and feel a strong surge of energy. I didn't know what it was at the time, but it felt very similar to when my angelic powers took over for sure at that first moment I was describing."

"Curious indeed," responded the professor, considering the situation. "Are they voluntary or involuntary powers?"

"Semi-voluntary," answered Caitlin. "I can't control when it happens, when I start to gain the ability to float or the translucent wings become visible, but when they do, I have a moderate amount of control over them and what I can do with them."

"Interesting," said the professor, still considering the situation as more of a case of his own interest than that of the mysteries of his daughter. "Both times, it sounds as though Kevin was at least partially responsible in some way for the transformation taking place and the powers perking up when they do. And from what you have told me, it sounds as though during the two instances you are telling me about, your connection to Kevin was stronger than it normally had been."

This stirred Caitlin's thoughts. "I'm not sure I understand quite what you're talking about, father."

"Well, it is actually rather simple," answered the professor. "You see, the sensation of a strong emotion, such as love, hate, fear, sadness, and so on can trigger an emotional 'spark' within an individual, especially the magically inclined. We in the magic community sometimes call the trigger of such effects the 'Key of Hearts' in lore and such because of what it has done to 'unlock' said powers. It is a very poetic term."

"Lovely words," remarked Caitlin, briefly remembering the key Kevin showed her in Aurana City, "although I'm sure the term doesn't always mean a spark based on love. Any emotion can affect the heart."

Professor Magnon nodded. "That is true. Nonetheless, you should not think of yourself as any less special because of that, because in your case you do know which emotion it is, if it is the 'Key of Hearts' effect that is the trigger."

Caitlin nodded.

"Also, let me make one thing clear, Caitlin," continued the professor. "You are one of a kind, and you know it too. The angel may be a 'mythical figure', but you are one. And despite the lore that an angel is a combination of the immortal and the mortal, let me tell you that if I knew it to be true, I would tell you. The truth is that no one knows since you are the first. I know that is why you asked about your mother, but I ask you to please trust what I tell you. If you want to know more about your mother, I will tell you when the time is right, okay?"

"All right," answered Caitlin meekly, disappointed.

As Caitlin finished up her sentence, the door to The Old Ball and Chain swung open, and out walked Kevin with Rachel, Arthur, and Kron in tow. "Are you guys good? Everyone wanted to talk," said Kevin, approaching Caitlin and the professor. "Lord Dragon will be with us in a moment; he's finishing buying a couple more drinks for his friends in the tavern."

"Fair enough," said the professor. "I suppose you will be wanting to hear where Kron and I have been."

Kevin nodded. "So, then, why are you and Kron here?"

Stepping up, Kron began to answer. "We were lucky to find you guys," he said, "but Professor Magnon has impeccable intuition. After the coup in Aurana City, the professor had a lead for us to follow on the location of Vincent Stryker."

Kevin gasped.

"You mean the war general, Vincent the Pure One?" asked Rachel.

"A little more than that," responded Kron. "Vincent the Pure One was the champion of the gods, twenty years ago." Kron had forgotten to tell Rachel that he was a god himself, but Rachel already knew, since Kevin and Arthur told her on the walk into town when recounting their stories. "He was the one responsible for leading the force that overthrew the Daritel and ended the war. He also took the fight to Tyrinion, the immortal puppeteer, and silenced him."

"He's also my father," interjected Kevin.

Arthur's jaw dropped. Rachel's eyes widened. Neither of them had been told that just yet, and neither had noticed the "K.T. Stryker" on Kevin's jacket, written in fairly small print. It was a minute detail easy to miss if one were not looking for the name on the jacket.

"Kevin, are you sure?" asked Rachel.

"Completely," nodded Kevin. "Professor Magnon dug up my birth records in Rikleifer to prove it. Apparently, they were sealed, so someone tried to protect that secret."

"Someone with a high level of authority," acknowledged the professor. "It may have been the king, or the Duke of Rikleifer, or someone very high up in the military, maybe even Vincent himself. And although he was a Scurnian general, Vincent Stryker is Auranian by birth and highly respected in Aurana for what his actions did for the old Triple Alliance. It very well could have been he himself who was able to have it sealed. We really do not know."

"No wonder you can wield that Sword of Purity," commented Arthur, in realization. "It's your birthright."

Kevin looked a little upset. Arthur realized in that moment that he did not get the reaction that he expected.

Caitlin came to Kevin's defense. "It's not his birthright," she said, "just as the sword you're holding from Demonicus is not yours. Sharing blood with someone isn't enough when that person wasn't in your life, for it to be your 'birthright'. Kevin is no more some kind of hero than you are a conqueror. You two actually have a lot in common that way."

Arthur thought about it for a moment. He looked down at the sword on his belt, which, because he was left-handed, he wore on the opposite side as Kevin. Arthur certainly did not consider himself a conqueror, or a dictator, simply because his father turned out to be the most dangerous conqueror and dictator in the world.

"It is merely happenstance," added the professor. "Locked swords tend to be finicky. Even when designed that way, sharing the same blood does not guarantee someone can use a locked sword. The magic is tricky business."

"And as far as I am aware, because I witnessed its creation, no one shared any thought of inheritance when the Sword of Purity was designed," mentioned Kron.

There was a momentary pause. Kevin seemed to be feeling less awkward.

"Anyway, you were talking about Vincent the Pure One?" asked Rachel to Kron, looking to get the conversation back on track.

"Of course," continued Kron. "One of the first places we headed to search was Gardolk, While there, we decided to try to bring them into the war with us. Unfortunately, after trying to find a way to convince the Gardolkians of the dangers of Desolunar, Queen Mildred of Gardolk decided that her nation was quite safe because of the Peaked Mountains running between the Wastes of Desolunar and western Gardolk. However, we did fortunately find out that Gardolk is planning to pull its forces out of war with Scurnia soon, freeing them up."

"We already knew that," interrupted Arthur. "Lord Dragon mentioned the truce while we were in the tavern."

"Oh," said Kron in realization. "Well, we did get more information about Vincent Stryker while there by following the lead we had. It led us north, into Scurnia as one might expect, but we still needed to know where. We kept following lead to lead as we gained more information, and we eventually found out about a friend of his who has been caring for him."

"Where at?" asked Kevin.

No one noticed as the Lord Dragon opened the tavern door and stepped out to join the group. Kron continued, "It is just south of here, in a place called the 'Cliffs of Vallia'. Maybe half a day's walk at worst."

"Ah, I've been there many a time," interrupted the Lord Dragon, immediately garnering everyone's attention. "Quite a treacherous place, it is."

"You know quite a bit about the cliffs?" asked Rachel, stunned.

"Of course I do," answered the Lord Dragon. "The cliffs are incredibly steep. They go on for a long distance along the mountains to the south, and the only safe route running to the north and south is the cliffside road, which runs next to the edge of a steep drop to the east and a steep climb to the west. It's not very wide, perhaps only wide enough for a horse-drawn carriage at its narrowest points. My dragons and riders train along the cliffs to practice motion commands in three dimensions. The cliffs help the riders to learn how to measure lengths when ascending and descending."

"Anyone live out there?" asked Arthur.

The Lord Dragon shook his head. "Not as far as I'm aware of," he said, "but I suppose I wouldn't put it past someone. There's a few caves along the cliffside road for those who really don't want to be found. I can lead all of you there tomorrow, if you'd like, and we can be back in Vallia before sundown tomorrow."

A general sense of excitement came across the rest of the group. "That's excellent!" said Kevin. "We'll be glad to accept your help, Lord Dragon."

"Of nothing," responded the Lord Dragon passively. "My faction will do a great job without me for a day. Besides, I could use a good day's walk, anyway. And by the way, consider all of your rooms compensated for as a special gift from me."

Amazed, Kevin asked, "Really? That's very kind of you." He

was excited not to have to sleep outside tonight.

"It was kind of you to invite me and my faction into war," responded the Lord Dragon. "For so long, what the Knights of the Dragon would give for a chance to participate in a good fight would be more than what money can buy. And it's not as though you're costing me much. It's only money."

"I don't think I've ever heard it put quite that way before," laughed Rachel. "Only money? I've never heard of such a thing."

"Relax, I've got enough," said the Lord Dragon. "And so do the rest of my troops. What we lack, though, is the chance to flex our muscles and those of our dragons in Vallia and the surrounding areas." He paused for a second. "So, will three rooms be sufficient for the six of you?"

Chapter 35

Suspicions

Kevin, Caitlin, and their party spend the evening in the tavern enjoying dinner and a relaxing evening. It was a rare opportunity for everyone to have the time to do so, especially together as a group. Lord Dragon offered to pay for a good meal as well, but Professor Magnon insisted that he would cover this portion.

Nightfall soon set in, and the soft glow of candles lit up the tavern. By this point, Kevin and company were all seated in front of the large fireplace in the tavern telling stories to one another. The stories were usually funny ones that gave everyone else a good laugh, but occasionally there was a serious one every now and again. It was not long, however, until the night became darker and everyone was heading off to bed. The Lord Dragon returned to his home in Vallia, and Kevin watched as his friends and family headed off. They had three rooms to share; one for Caitlin and Rachel, one for Kevin and Arthur, and one for the professor and Kron.

Quietly, as his friends headed to bed, Kevin told Arthur that he wanted to sit at the fire for a little longer. Arthur was tired and insisted on going to bed, so he told Kevin to be quiet when he returned, and left his best friend in the tavern. The night set in, and only Kevin was left out at the fireplace. Kevin told the bartender, as they closed up the tavern for the night, that he would sit and tend to the fire until it burned out for the night.

Upstairs and down the hall in Room 234, Caitlin and Rachel were both staring toward the ceiling in the dark room, lying in their beds. A single candle burned in their windowsill. Caitlin had been looking forward to this opportunity to talk more with Rachel one-on-one, so she could make a friend. "So, Rachel, how old are you?" she asked, starting a conversation.

"I'm eighteen," answered Rachel. "Two years older than Kevin and Arthur. What about yourself?"

"Fifteen," said Caitlin. "Still not legally an adult yet. But my birthday's in the winter, so I'll be an adult in about half a year."

"I see," said Rachel. "Well, let me tell you from experience that the next three years aren't really that different from the last couple. You get a few more rights, a little more interest in boys, but other than that, it's just three more years of learning the everyday lessons of life."

"I don't know about that," responded Caitlin. "I tend to think that those everyday lessons of life are important."

"Oh, no, you're right," interrupted Rachel. "Little changes do make something big in the end. It's just in those three years your life doesn't change much unless something seismic happens. This is the first time I've been outside of Aurana, so I'm kind of going through one right now."

Caitlin shook her head. "You're not the only one," she said, but she did not say it sarcastically. She said it straightforward.

Rachel raised an eyebrow. "Were you just put off?"

"Put off?" asked Caitlin.

"You know, bothered," Rachel answered.

"Was I supposed to be?" asked Caitlin, shrugging with a little confusion.

"A little," Rachel answered. "I spoke a little soon before realizing that of course you're going through some major changes yourself right now. Did that bother you?"

Caitlin shrugged. "Not really," she said. "I guess I didn't see it that way. Was I supposed to?"

Smiling, Rachel said, "Not if you don't want to, I suppose, but a lot of people would jump to conclusions. It's an emotional reaction, and you didn't react."

"So I didn't. Isn't that a better reaction?"

"Perhaps, but it makes me question if you actually do have emotion."

Caitlin rolled her eyes. "You really are a skeptic, aren't you?"

Rachel laughed. "Thanks for not saying 'cynic'," she blurted. "A skeptic, though, that's what I hear from others that aren't Arthur, at least. I just think of myself as a realist, that's all. I don't really have

Arthur's sarcasm or Kevin's idealism and optimism."

"It could be worse," said Caitlin. "You could have no personality whatsoever."

"I suppose so," chuckled Rachel. "I didn't know Kevin was into girls like that."

Caitlin gasped and instantly became upset. "You take that back!"

Immediately, Rachel backed off. "Sorry, I was only teasing a bit," she said. "I know you have a personality. I sure get it now that you can get emotional."

Sliding backwards a bit from Rachel, Caitlin was wide-eyed in surprise. "I didn't know I would act like that," she said. "That's really scary."

"It's only natural," Rachel answered. "You were really disciplined, I've heard, but you're still a teenage girl, like me. You don't want to take torment, and that's the natural response. And I don't think that you can't be disciplined when it matters and just a normal person every other time."

That seemed to provoke some thoughts in Caitlin. To keep disciplined, but only when it actually matters, and be willing to be a more normal person when the discipline was not called for… it was an idea that intrigued her. She was finding all of her new emotions fascinating and a little addictive, but if what Rachel suggested was possible, that she could walk a line between her discipline and her emotions, then she was minimizing the risks in her mind. She could still be susceptible when she was not protecting herself, but she could also embrace the benefits of being open. It surprised Caitlin just how grounded Rachel was, determined and cool-headed when she needed to be, but capable of fun and emotion. She was an exhibit to Caitlin, in some ways, on how she could act in this way.

"Speaking of which, that reminds me," continued Rachel. "I was going to ask you about being emotionally suppressed and what that was like for you, since you say that was you. What was that like?"

Caitlin frowned, a little disappointed in the question. "I just kept very disciplined and kept a block on my emotions so I would not feel them."

“Okay, my apologies,” said Rachel, picking up that that may have been an offensive question she asked. “I didn’t mean to oversimplify. I just wanted to know about your experiences. I’m curious.”

For a moment, Caitlin thought about it, then nodded. “If you would have asked me that about a month or two ago, I would have told you that I thought it was the best way to live. You become very self-dependent and come under a false sense of strength. Realism and bluntness in observation does come with that, since you don’t feel any emotion in your decision-making whatsoever. No love, no hate, no shame…”

“No shame?” interrupted Rachel.

“Yes, no shame,” responded Caitlin.

“I guess I don’t get what you mean by that.”

“Well, let me make an example, then,” said Caitlin, her mind thinking about how best to explain it. “Did you know that many upper-level wielders of magic will practice the art while in the nude when they’re by themselves?”

“No, not at all,” said Rachel. “What benefit does it do?”

“It helps to channel energy,” answered Caitlin. “Open skin does so because it is easier to absorb more element to channel into magic through skin that is not covered or restricted tightly. Of course, it’s not practical or ethical to practice magic in the nude publicly, but it’s a common practice when in privacy. Now let’s say, for example, that Kevin caught me in the act of practicing magic in the nude. I’m sure that both of us would be very embarrassed and I would be rushing to cover myself up quickly. But, when I had no personality, I would have felt none of the natural shame from that. It’s likely that I wouldn’t have bothered to cover up and would have told Kevin that it was just the human body and there was nothing to be ashamed of.” She paused for a second. “Isn’t that funny? It makes so much more logical sense, but it doesn’t make you human.”

“And what makes you human makes you stronger,” answered Rachel. “I believe we’re truly a package deal in that we have the most strength embracing ourselves for who we are.”

“And the happiest for it,” added Caitlin. “That’s a lesson I’ve had to learn the hard way. I've actually really loved the feelings of happiness I've had lately. I understand now the upsides of having emotions."

"Maybe you need a psychologist," responded Rachel lightheartedly, joking.

"I'm sure I do," laughed Caitlin. "Some friend you turned out to be, huh?"

"Careful, I'm the only one you've got, other than Kevin," joked Rachel. "You intrigue me so much, Caitlin. You might be the most unique person I've ever met before."

"And you may be the most understanding," chuckled Caitlin.

Rachel laughed. "I'm sure, I'm sure," she said. Then, she decided to try and get to know Caitlin a bit more. "Do you do anything for fun?"

Caitlin thought for a second. "Not a lot, other than magic," she answered. "But in my spare time, reading is my one guilty pleasure. Kevin and I actually bonded over our shared adoration of *Tale of the Valkyrie*."

"Oh, so you like fantasy adventure stories?"

"Like I said, it's my guilty pleasure. I especially like *Tale of the Valkyrie* because it's so different. Not many of those kind of stories have a female hero, after all."

Rachel nodded, thinking in that moment that Caitlin having a "guilty pleasure" before gaining emotions meant that she was not totally emotionless or suppressed, or else she would not have such a hobby. "True," she said. "I'm not a fan of fantasy stories, but I have heard of *Tale of the Valkyrie*, and I know Kevin likes it. Honestly, I think more stories in general could use female heroes."

"Agreed," smiled Caitlin. "Do you do any reading?"

"Oh, tons," Rachel said.

"So what do you read?"

"A little bit of everything," answered Rachel. "I'm in a book club… or at least I was until I got kidnapped. Anyway, I tend to like some horror stories, some history and historical fiction, and a little bit of romance. I also write my own stories, though I haven't written anything like a novel."

Caitlin became excited. "You write your own stories? That's so awesome!"

Aside, Rachel laughed a bit. Caitlin was adorable when she was excited, she thought to herself. She did not seem to have a lot of restraint when excited.

Together, Rachel and Caitlin shared a laugh before they talked into the night, in turn building a close friendship between them. As the night grew later, though, Caitlin napped for a while before waking up again.

Back in the tavern, Kevin sat awake with Kron, unable to sleep. Kron was seated at a table near the fireplace, reading over the papers from *Immortality is a Truth* that were sitting on the table. Professor Magnon had entrusted it to Kron overnight under the condition that it was not to be damaged. Nearby, Kevin was in a chair in front of the fire, trying to rest in front of its warm glow.

"Kron, what are you looking for in there?" Kevin asked, out of tired curiosity.

Flipping a couple of pages, Kron said, "My way home. There is much in these pages, but the translation is very rough and incomplete, and five thousand-year-old *rengan* is very different than the *rengan* I know how to speak. I do not know if there is an answer here, though. I cannot say with any certainty that I know anything of importance to the here and now is written in this book. I do know, though, that this is the foundational text of my society."

"It is?" questioned Kevin. "And you don't have a copy in the Realm of the Angels?"

"At least not one I know of," answered Kron. "Most of the lessons Setaeus Demota wanted his followers to have, he taught them personally. Then, those original gods taught them to later ones like myself who were adopted into immortality, or to those who were children of the original immortals. I have known that Setaeus Demota wrote his fundamental principles into a text, and that it was called *Immortality is a Truth*, but I have never seen the book itself."

"Unusual," remarked Kevin. "I wonder what Professor Magnon thinks he'll find in it, then."

At this, Kron closed the book. He stayed seated at his table, but turned toward Kevin. "I should advise you that I have some strong suspicions about the professor, Kevin. I am now convinced that his knowledge is transcendent, nearly impossible."

Kevin shot a look at Kron. "Are you suggesting the professor is an immortal of some kind?"

Kron shook his head. "No," he answered firmly. "Though it is not something I could detect, that I do not believe. However, he has some dangerous, ancient knowledge, including of powerful spells that have not been used in centuries. He may be, and likely is, the most powerful wizard in the mortal realm, but I cannot help but feel as though he has access to some very rare, very old knowledge to do so."

With that, Kevin breathed a small sigh of relief. "So… he's too smart?"

"I mean it more seriously that you credit," answered Kron, standing up and walking toward Kevin. "Someone like that carries a lot of influence. He has already directed you where to go, and so far you have followed his advice. While I do not see that as a bad decision so far, I want you to be wary. He has to have some reason for his intentions."

Kevin nodded. "I'm taking you seriously, Kron, please understand that. I just don't know what has you so riled up about him."

Kron looked around for a second to make sure no one else was near, then knelt down by Kevin's chair. "Let us simply say that some of the discussions the professor has had with me were very odd. At one point, he went on a polemic about the crimes of Setaeus Demota, the author of the very same *Immortality is a Truth* that sits on that table and which he is planning to read. It is true that Setaeus Demota did do a number of horrible things, yes, but to hear a mortal speak of it in such a manner… I would almost wonder what kind of books he has read to give himself such a strong impression."

"The professor is a scholar and an educator," Kevin pointed out. "I bet he has access to lots of books, old and new."

"Perhaps," acknowledged Kron, "and I do know there have been books written about Setaeus before; he did not keep his life a secret. More unusually, though, he oddly tried to make me question whether or not Tyrinion was responsible for the Alliance-Daritel War and if he's responsible for Desolunar today."

Kevin was confused. "And you told him what?"

"That he is, because there can be no other," Kron answered. "Tyrinion attacked us and fled. He is the only immortal, barring myself being stuck here the last twenty years, who still lives and is not in the Realm of the Angels. Only he could be pulling the strings to make such powerful moves and turn small uprisings into invasions. He is the true conqueror."

Tired, Kevin turned his head. "I suppose," he said.

"Kevin, you do not seem to be understanding," Kron stressed. "Something about Professor Magnon is not right. And if I were you, I would be wary of him and his daughter. I understand you and her now have some kind of relationship, but I want you to be mindful and careful."

Hearing this, Kevin was upset. "Are you really trying to imply that there's something suspicious about Caitlin?"

Immediately, Kron backed off. "No, not at all," he said, "but if Professor Magnon is up to something, she would be the easiest piece for him to manipulate. She has already shown she is loyal to him because he is her father, which is only fair."

Reluctantly, Kevin sighed. It was a good point, though he truthfully thought of Caitlin as one of the strongest people he knew and not susceptible to something like that. Still, her father did seem to command that kind of powerful presence.

Seeing as he did not want to frustrate or upset Kevin any further tonight, Kron bade him a good night and walked down the hall, leaving Kevin alone in the tavern. At night, alone in front of a stone fireplace in an otherwise wooden building, The Old Ball and Chain felt more like a cozy lodge than a tavern. It was comfortable, peaceful, a relaxing place for him to be.

As Kevin sat and waited for the fire to burn itself out, he heard more steps coming down the hallway. He looked in the dim glow of the fire to see Caitlin approaching him.

"Couldn't sleep?" Kevin asked her as she approached.

"I couldn't sleep knowing you couldn't," Caitlin answered, as she pulled up a chair next to him. "What's on your mind?"

There was a momentary pause. Then, Kevin let out a sigh. "Stress," he said. "I haven't had much trouble with it at all for the last couple of weeks or so, but now it's all on me again. I can't focus and I can't sleep. All I can tell is that what seems to be causing my stress is uncertainty about the future."

"Sounds like your thoughts have built up over the past few days, and they've finally blown over the top," said Caitlin. "Uncertainty about the future is perhaps the biggest strain any one person can have in a normal situation, much less someone in one as abstract as yours."

"That doesn't make me feel any better," responded Kevin.

Caitlin put her face in the palm of his hand. "I'm sorry, Kevin. I'm not very good at this just yet, but I'm trying to get better at being uplifting."

Hearing that, Kevin slid out of his chair and knelt next to Caitlin and held her hand. "You do just fine. You're here, and that's all I need. I wish I could do better for you so you don't have to carry me all of the time."

"Oh, don't be silly," joked Caitlin as she slid off her chair and placed an arm around Kevin. "Naturally, you're not perfect, but you're just right for me."

Kevin started to blush a bit. Together, Kevin and Caitlin spent a few moments together snuggled up, enjoying their short time alone as the fire slowly burned out.

Chapter 36

A Heartwarming Reunion

The next morning, everyone was getting ready for the day to come. The first ones in the tavern were Professor Magnon and Kron, who spent the early morning discussing *Immortality is a Truth.* Then, they consequently woke up Arthur, Caitlin, and Rachel. Kevin was still not awake, but after Kron had told everyone about Kevin being awake late into the night, the group decided to let Kevin have some extra time to sleep in. The Lord Dragon showed up about an hour later, seeing that everyone else was enjoying some water at the tavern. He was dressed in his full battle outfit, with the full suit of brown leather, the leather headpiece, and the silver and iron breastplate with the red dragon etched into the back. Furthermore, the Lord Dragon was also carrying a weapon in his hands this morning: a two-handed pike with a particularly large jagged blade on the tip.

As the day warmed up, it seemed that temperatures on the plateau of Scurnia were not as high as they had been before, and that the record high temperatures would not be breached again on this day. Even so, it would be a warm day nonetheless. A couple of hours later, Caitlin finally walked into Kevin's room to wake him up. Slowly, he began his day while very groggy, needing Caitlin's assistance to find his jacket, get his sword strapped to his belt, and straighten himself up before heading to the tavern. After Kevin was awake and united with the rest of the group, Professor Magnon had an announcement. He would not be going with everyone else on today's day trip, citing a desire to begin reviewing the papers from *Immortality is a Truth* while everyone else took to their trip into the Cliffs of Vallia. He declared that it would take days to analyze fully and fill in the gaps, that he wanted to start right away, and that he trusted Kevin and company to explore the lead to Vincent Stryker.

As the sun was up in the eastern sky, about halfway between the horizon and high noon, Kevin and company set off to the south. Lord Dragon was leading the way along the road to the south, which seemed to close in on the nearby mountains to the west the further south it went. The further south they went from Vallia, the more the road began to degrade and become little more than a torn-up section of the plateau. It was not a very well kept road by any means, although enough was still traced out in the ground to identify it as a road that continued to the south. Occasionally, the ground became so undistinguishable that corners might sometimes be obscured.

Further down the road, the mountains had become so close on the west side and the plateau had receded so much on the east that a pathway about as wide as six people standing next to each other an arm's length apart was the width of the road. While it was wider than the road had previously been, only a high cliffside sat on the west and a sheer drop on the east. It was a dangerous area. Lord Dragon was quick to explain that this was the beginning of the Cliffs of Vallia, and that the town was actually named for these cliffs and not the other way around. Despite its danger, the region had some visual appeal. The large split rock that was the cliffside exposed a reddish brown color, which seemed almost vivid and artistic when combined with the texture of the chiseled cliffside.

In the front, Kronius walked next to Lord Dragon, striking up a conversation with him. Behind them were Kevin, Caitlin, Arthur, and Rachel, walking in a horizontal line. Kevin and Caitlin were holding hands as they walked.

"Ugh," said Arthur spontaneously, "do the two of you have to do that now?"

Kevin and Caitlin looked over at him. "What are you talking about?" asked Caitlin.

"The two of you holding hands," answered Arthur. "I swear I'm never going to get used to this mushy stuff between the two of you."

"What's your problem?" asked Kevin, jokingly. He knew Arthur well enough to know that Arthur was picking on him just for the sake of picking on him.

"I have to agree with Kevin," interjected Rachel, on the other side of Kevin and Caitlin as Arthur was. "It's their right to hold hands if they want to. They are together, after all. Besides, I think it promotes the spirit of love around here in these barren cliffs."

Getting sarcastic, Arthur responded, "Well, if that's the case, Rachel, then why don't you come over here and start holding my hand?"

Rachel rolled her eyes. "Smartass," she said.

At this, Kevin, Caitlin, and Arthur started laughing at Rachel's comment. Arthur had created quite a laugh by using Rachel's comments against her. "I don't see what's so funny about it. Why are the three of you laughing?" asked Rachel.

"Oh, come on," said Caitlin, still laughing as she swung her free arm around Rachel. "Even I thought it was funny."

"Whatever," said Rachel, rolling her head in the other direction.

"Hey! I thought it was funny!" responded Arthur. "That's why I said it. If you're really that insulted, then lighten up. I was joking about the whole thing."

Rachel turned her head back toward Arthur, looking across Kevin and Caitlin. "Oh, I'm not insulted," she said. "I just don't see what's so funny about it."

"Sounds like Rachel doesn't have much of a sense of humor," joked Kevin.

"I do too!" exclaimed Rachel.

At this point, Kron turned around, scowling. "Are the four of you going to argue all day like little children, or are you actually going to act like civilized young adults and stop?"

Kron's words instantly stopped the four teenagers, making all of them feel a little childish for their arguing. Not one of them had a word to say in response, too dumbfounded for comment. Kevin had never seen Kron react so harshly, and he felt like he and his friends did not deserve it.

Suddenly, the Lord Dragon made an observation before Kevin could say anything to Kron. "Hey, there's something up here," he said. "It may just be my eyes, but it almost looks to be a small shack house set up a little bit ahead."

"So is it in the middle of the road?" asked Kevin, curious by the perplexing situation of a small house sitting on a cliffside. "How does it even fit on this cliff road?"

"I can't exactly tell from this distance yet, but it looks like the road widens just a bit," responded the Lord Dragon. "And it looks like the house is up against the side of the rock, maybe even built into it some."

"Maybe it's just a façade," suggested Arthur. "Maybe a cave is used as the main living space."

"It's the only real explanation, but that still leaves the question as to who would be living out here," said Rachel. "Better yet, how can someone live here? There's not any water around here, and this road is too dangerous and deserted to be a road for traders to exchange goods."

Lord Dragon pointed toward the top of the cliffs. "Actually, there is water nearby," he said. "Beyond those cliffs, and the mountain behind it, is the source for the Grandiose River. The right caverns through here lead out to the river's source deeper in the mountains."

Caitlin's eyes widened as the Lord Dragon was talking. She pulled Kevin over and said, "Something's here. The sensation of earth, the rocky movements just like the cold sensation when we found the Stripe of Ice. It's there, in that house."

"You're sure?" asked Kevin, surprised.

"Absolutely," responded Caitlin. "I can sense it within myself, almost like it's a tugging of the earth. It must be a stripe."

This caught Rachel's attention. "A what?" she asked.

"I'm lost," interrupted Arthur, confused. "What are you talking about? What can you feel?"

Kevin raised his right arm and pulled back his jacket sleeve, revealing the Stripe of Air; simultaneously, Caitlin pulled back her dress sleeve to reveal the Stripe of Ice. "There's another one of these around," Caitlin said. "Even if we can't find Vincent Stryker, our day trip will be worth it after all if we can get it."

All the discussion about stripes caught Kron's attention. He stopped for a second and turned around to see what Kevin and Caitlin were talking about. "What exactly are those?"

"Not really sure," shrugged Caitlin. "Supposedly they're pieces of a weapon of some kind?"

Kron frowned, not knowing what these were. "Does the professor know you have these? I did not notice these on your skin until now. The two of you have kept them under your sleeves."

Kevin and Caitlin looked at each other for a moment. "To tell you the truth, I don't know if he knows or not," Kevin said.

At that, Kron shrugged and turned back around. By now, everyone was stopped in front of the house front.

Arthur asked, confused, "So, if we need this 'stripe', how are we going to do this? Walk up to the front door and say 'Hi, we think you have a magic stripe; can we have it?'."

Lord Dragon elbowed Kevin in his side to get his attention, and said to him quietly, with a bit of a chuckle, "Your boy has no patience, I see."

"He's just a little hazy on it," answered Kevin jokingly while also speaking quietly. Louder, he continued, "So, do you know who lives in here?"

"Nope. Never seen this before," answered the Lord Dragon as he and everyone else stared at the wooden walls built into the side of the rock. It was almost like a house front, with a two-piece door split about midway across, dividing the door into an upper and a lower section.

"Such a different style of architecture," said Caitlin, staring at it alongside everyone else. "Simple, but unusual. I'm almost a little scared to see who's inside."

"Well, let's not even do anything if we don't have to," suggested the Lord Dragon. "Are you guys sure this is where you need to be, if you're not sure who lives inside?"

"Completely," affirmed Kevin, displaying confidence. He was well-travelled by now, and not nervous. "Just stand back and let me handle it. I'll talk to whoever's inside. There's no need to argue about it."

Quietly, everyone acknowledged this and took a step back to allow Kevin to step up to the door. He was showing his leadership by taking up that which had to be done. Walking up to the door, Kevin observed the hinges on the door and noticed that they swung the door outside instead of inside when they were opened, another irregularity in the façade's door. He knocked three times on the top door, and then stepped back so as to avoid being hit by the door when it swung open.

After a brief moment of tension among the group, the upper door opened outward, and in the new opening appeared a man who appeared to be in his forties. His hair was dark, and his face was clean-shaven. However, his body, or at least the upper half of his body, appeared to be in excellent shape for his age, with his muscles showing their size within his skin. He wore no shirt at all. This man seemed pleasantly surprised to see people at his door. "Ay, what do we have here?" he asked in an unusual accent. "Welcome, welcome indeed! How can I help all of you today?"

Straightening out his jacket for a second, Kevin took a step forward and reached out to shake the man's hand. "Hello to you too," he said as he shook hands. "This might seem to be a little unusual that all of us are here, but we are looking for something and we think it might be here."

Kevin's comment made the man raise an eyebrow. "And what are you looking for, chap?" he questioned, in a serious tone of voice.

Kevin was unsure how to proceed. Obviously this man was either one of two things: a protective owner who did not want people in his home on a chase for nothing, or he had something valuable and did not want anyone to find out or take it from him. Either way, Kevin did not want to infuriate the man if he could. It was not what he was here to do. Thinking that a visual would be the best way to talk about the stripe that he was looking for, Kevin pulled up his right sleeve, revealing the three stripes he was currently carrying, displayed on his arm. "We're looking for one of these," he said pointing to the stripes. "It's not a tattoo. What it is is a magical energy, and we believe that one is somewhere within your house, whether it is behind it or in your possession."

"And now you and your posse come to me," answered the man. As he did, Kevin's eyes widened, realizing that the man knew full and well about what the young Auranian was looking for. "Only earth could be what you are looking for in a dry, jagged place such as this. What would you do if I told you that I have it but do not wish to give it to you?"

Stopping for a moment, Kevin felt as though he was forced to consider this question. If he tried to force it out of this man, then he was certain he could retrieve the stripe, presuming he did have it. However, doing so also meant that Kevin was defying all that he was working for: the good and honest people of the world. Kevin had to be truthful in answering the question. He was not one who was much for lying and trying to sustain one. "I would walk away," he said. "I can't take anything unwillingly from anyone who means no harm to myself or anyone else."

The man inside the façade nodded, and started to smile. "Ay, you are an honest chap with good intent. I can tell by your voice and your words." He reached out to shake Kevin's hand again, this time revealing the Stripe of Earth across his right wrist. "I would be Samuel," he continued. "Sammy for short, if you prefer, chap."

Kevin shook Sammy's hand, also smiling. "Kevin Trent Stryker, Vanguard of Aurana," he said. Caitlin, Arthur, and Rachel all caught that he seemed to be getting comfortable using his full name, with the Stryker surname.

"Related to Vincent Stryker?" asked Sammy, curiously. "The one who we in Scurnia referred to as the 'Pure One' back around twenty years ago?"

"The very same," answered Kevin. "He is my father."

"Is that so?" questioned Sammy, surprised but in a pleasant way. "He is also a well-known man in Scurnia, as you know. I can see where you get your honesty." Sammy then gestured with his arm in as he reached with his other arm for the lock on the lower door. "Please, feel free to come in, chap. Your fellow travelers are welcome as well." He then opened the lower door.

As Sammy opened the bottom door, everyone else gasped at the sight of the unexpected. Sammy was not completely human all across his body.

He had the lower body of a horse, attached to him at the bottom of his abdomen. His appearance was very similar to the mythical figure of the centaur, a creature known not to exist in actuality.

Seeing that everyone was looking at him surprised, Sammy tried to be reassuring. "Oh, all of you noticed my lower body. Don't worry about that, chaps. I'll be willing to explain all of that to you chaps after you step inside."

Shakily, Kevin nodded, and proceeded to walk inside, unwavering. Kevin's lead proved to be inspiring for the others, however, and all of them were more willing to enter the façade after seeing Kevin walk in first. Inside, the group's suspicions were confirmed: the wood front was a façade and the majority of the interior space was a large cavern opening, cleared out of any stalactites and animals. The façade's windows allowed in some natural sunlight, although not enough to light the cave very far. A larger table was situated a little further back into the mouth of the cave, and a bed of hay was set against a cave wall. Otherwise, there was nothing else in the cave opening other than some storage space.

Sammy picked up two pieces of flint and scraped them to create sparks and light the candles on his table. "It's not much," he said, "but it's home. So, then, Kevin Trent Stryker, would you like to introduce me to the members of your group here?"

"Certainly," said Kevin, gesturing with his hands to each person he introduced. "Over there on the left are Arthur Falchor and Rachel Reinhart, two of my very closest friends. To their left is Caitlin Magnon, sorceress and very close friend."

"As in, girlfriend?" interrupted Sammy.

This made Arthur start laughing, as much as he tried to hold it back. Caitlin giggled a little bit, catching Kevin's little blunder. Kevin was on the spot, but he responded casually, "Yeah, I suppose you could put it that way. How did you figure that one out?"

"By the way you set her apart from your other two friends, chap," answered Sammy. "Please, do go on."

"Very well," said Kevin. "In the gold and white robes right there is Kron Kalavere, faithful man of many arts. And next to him in the leather and metal is Christoph Dewellus, the Lord Dragon, the leader of the Knights of the Dragon."

Lord Dragon leaned forward to shake Sammy's hand. "Pleasure to meet you indeed," he said. "Strange that we have not met before."

"It is strange that I have not seen you before, chap," responded Sammy as he shook the Lord Dragon's hand. "I know what kind of things your Knights of the Dragon do. I have seen your practices outside of this cavern. Very amazing work you do, indeed."

"Why thank you," said the Lord Dragon. "I'm surprised that I didn't notice you, given the condition of your body. I apologize for my reaction to seeing it, but it is unusual, as you know. What ever happened to bring this to you?"

The others nodded in agreement, very curious as to this situation.

Sammy took a breath. "As you wish. Now, if you chaps couldn't tell from my accent, I'm from southwestern Gardolk. Twenty years ago, I was a soldier representing Gardolk in the great war in the west. True, Gardolk was not a major force in the war at the time, but they did send some troops for relief units. I served on one of these units. After the war was over, I returned to Gardolk only to find that tensions were starting to rise with Scurnia over the city of Tron. I couldn't believe it; just how much Gardolk seemed more concerned over its own territory than peace and the safety of its people." He paused for a moment. "So I did what nobody, not even my family, expected. I defected to Scurnia, hoping to find my answer here. Unfortunately, on my way here while I was passing through Tron, I was caught by several Gardolkians who worked in the intelligence offices. They knew what I was up to, so they left me for dead by cutting me in half at the abdomen. They're quite brutal, as you chaps can tell."

"No kidding," said Kevin, stunned by this revelation. "Go on."

"I was fortunate that a Scurnian army general had found me and had me sent to a hospital in northern Tron as soon as possible. Without my lower body, though, my chances of survival, even with magic as part of my treatment, were slim. A surgeon there had a brilliant idea, though. He happened to have the body of a horse given to him the day before. In a fit of brilliance, he cut off the horse's head and stitched my body to the horse body. A couple of brilliant sorcerers working for the Scurnian military, aided in making this impossible task possible. And that's how I became the centaur," he paused. "I decided after that incident that all I wanted was a life of peace, and knowing that I would be treated as a freak by everyone I met, I came here and built this façade and made a life here in the Cliffs of Vallia. Other than that, there's not much more I think I have to tell you chaps."

"Quite an interesting story," answered the Lord Dragon. "Must be difficult having to live so far away from civilization in order to find some peace."

"Oh no, I don't quite think that way at all, chap," chuckled Sammy. "I have everything that I need here. Through these caverns is the Grandiose River, where I retrieve my daily food and water, and as for socialization I talk occasionally with the man who I help to take care of in these cliffs."

"So you've got your basic needs taken care of," said Caitlin, with a sense of curiosity in her voice. "Who is it that you're taking care of?"

Sammy chuckled again. "Why, but surely Kevin has told you already! Kevin, has your father not told you anything about me?"

Kevin looked confused. "Why would my father tell me anything about you, Sammy?" he asked. "I've never even met my father."

A sudden state of realization hit Sammy. "Oh, my, well this is awkward, chap," he said. Then, his voice turned serious. "Kevin, your father, the great Vincent Stryker, was the man who saved my life that day in Tron by taking me to that hospital. Today, he lives in a cave just south of here, and I'm his caretaker."

Eyes widening, Kevin was in disbelief. The truth about his father, and getting to meet the man who was a world hero, was just around the corner. Kevin almost locked up in his amazement, unable to react from the sheer impact of these words. Kron was more excited about the prospect of meeting the previous pure one before and finding out more about his life and what became of him after the war. In one way or another, this revelation had impacted everyone in the small cave room. The long pause in between these previous words and the next signified their power.

"I can take you to him if you'd like, chap," said Sammy, breaking the silence.

Looking to the ground and sheltering his eyes, Kevin had to

take a moment to recover from his emotions and gather himself. Meanwhile, Arthur took note of how Kevin was standing and said to Caitlin and Rachel, "Would you look at that? He looks so overcome by all of this. What do you think we're going to do?"

"I would suppose we have to see Vincent Stryker," answered Caitlin. "One way or another, he is a key to this whole puzzle. It's his history that contains more than we could ever want to know, I'm sure."

"Plus I'm sure that Kevin wants to finally meet his father," added Rachel. "I know that if I didn't have two parents that were still married and in love, then I'd want to know both of them as well."

"But I don't think it's quite that simple," interjected Arthur. "Vincent Stryker may not even know that he has a son."

"He does," mumbled Kevin, his head still down. Then, he raised it. "He signed my birth certificate in Aurana. That means he was there when I was born. King Andrew II showed me the certificate itself, and I saw it with my own eyes." Kevin stopped to take a deep breath, fearful yet anxious about the prospect of meeting his father. "I suppose that only good can come out of this," he said, uncertain with himself. "We should go there as soon as we can."

"Is that your decision?" asked Sammy, questioning for certainty. "You don't have to go if you don't want, chap. You could always stay here and have everyone else go for you."

Shaking his head, Kevin said, still in a meek tone of voice, "No. I have to go along. There's no answers for me if I don't."

Sammy nodded reassuringly. "A smart decision, I'm sure, chap," he said as he placed his arm around Kevin to help make him more confident. "Let me warn you, though, that what you see may not be what you expect to see. Vincent is in poor health, and has been for the longest time."

Kevin sighed. "Thanks for the warning," he said. "We had better be going." As everyone else looked on at Kevin, and heard the distress in his voice, they realized that distress was not the true emotion he held. He was simply so overcome by everything that this reaction was all he could muster.

"Very well, chaps," acknowledged Sammy. "Mr. Kalavere, would you be so kind as to get the door for everyone? And be mindful of the cliff outside, chap, as I have nearly fallen off of it a couple of times with my horse legs myself."

Kron nodded, and proceeded to the doorway to open it up. Lord Dragon was the first to follow him out the door, followed by Arthur and Rachel, who proceeded to talk about Kevin and the pleasant surprise of Vincent Stryker being nearby.

Inside the cave opening, Caitlin put her arm around Kevin and tried to encourage the overwhelmed boy as gently as possible. "Come on, Kevin," she said. "We can do this."

"I know we can," responded Kevin, still very uncertain in his voice. "I just don't know how I'm supposed to feel. I think I'd always been hopeful we would be able to find my father. And now that we're so close, I don't know what to think."

"No one expects you to be certain, chap," said Sammy. "But I think you'll find it easier once you meet Vincent. He's a good man, and one who is very understanding."

Kevin took another moment to pause, struggling to find any response in how overwhelmed he was.

Taking a brief look at the door, Caitlin turned to Sammy and said, "Bring him on outside once he's ready. In the meantime, I'll go outside and tell everyone out there that it will be a few more minutes, and talk to them about it."

Sammy nodded. "All right," he said. "Anything else I can do for you?"

Caitlin took a second to think. "Make sure Kevin gets that magical energy from you before you bring him out," she said. "I don't think we want to forget that if that's what we originally knocked on your door for."

"Fair enough," said Sammy. "I'll have him outside when he's ready."

Acknowledging this, Caitlin nodded, and then proceeded toward the door and exited through it. Outside, Arthur and Rachel were talking with Kronius and the Lord Dragon about Kevin's mental state and the prospects of meeting Vincent Stryker. "He'll be out in a few minutes," she said as she quietly closed the door behind her. "I think Kevin's going to be fine. He's just a little overawed at the moment."

Everyone else nodded, in understanding. "He'll be fine," said Arthur. "Kevin's actually a pretty tough guy. I'm sure that he's actually more than overjoyed to get to meet his father for the first time in his life."

"I know I would be if I ever had the opportunity to meet my mother," added Caitlin. "Still, I guess that none of us really know what that is like right now. Only he does. We'll have to see what he's like when he comes out of there."

A few minutes had passed before Kevin and Sammy had finally stepped out of the façade. Kevin looked much more confident, having regained his composure. He flipped up his right arm, revealing a green stripe lined up with the orange stripe wrapped around his wrist.

"Feeling any better?" asked Kron.

"Much," said Kevin. "Just needed some time, I guess."

Hearing this, Caitlin walked up to Kevin and grabbed him by the hand, interlocking hers with his. "Glad to have you back," she told him.

Arthur rolled his eyes, and then turned about. "Oh gosh, you two," he said, almost mockingly. "I swear I'm never going to get used to the two of you doing stuff together like that."

Then, Rachel turned to Arthur and asked, "What's wrong with you? All they did was grab each other's hand."

Before Rachel could go any further, however, Kevin stopped her. "Rachel, you might not want to get into this," he interrupted. "Arthur's trying to harass me some, that's all."

Rachel rolled her eyes. "Whatever," she said. "Can we just get going now? I'd rather not get involved in these petty arguments."

Lord Dragon chuckled at this. "She's got a point," he said. "Especially if we're going to get back to Vallia before nightfall, we do have to go as soon as possible."

Sammy nodded in acknowledgment, his horse hooves kicking up a bit of dust as he stretched his legs. "I'll lead the way," he said, as he started to direct himself to the south. "Everyone follow me. It's not far to where we are headed."

The group proceeded south along the cliffside road through the Cliffs of Vallia, following Sammy as far as they went. As they traveled, they talked about a variety of things, looking to pass the time together. About a ten minute walk down the path, the group came upon another cave opening, this time without a façade in front of it. The opening was very plain otherwise, but upon first glance it seemed like no life inhabited this cavern entrance.

"This is it," said Sammy, halting the group behind him. "Stand back and be quiet. Vincent is in relatively poor health and does not come out much." Sammy then stepped into the cave entrance and said, into the darkness, "Vincent! Are you in here?"

After a slight pause, the sound of steps echoed out the cavern entrance, audible to everyone outside the cave. The steps then stopped, and a grizzled voice said, "What is it that brings you here, Samuel?"

"Ay, Vincent, cheer up," said Samuel with a bit of a chuckle into the cave. "You have a visitor today. Or, should I say, several visitors, but one stands out as one you will be particularly interested in." Sammy then signaled over to Kevin to step over, which he did.

"Curious indeed," stumbled the man in poor health as he reached the edge of light reaching into the cavern. "Who have you brought today, Samuel?"

Sammy took a step to the side, and began to say in a slow yet stately way, "May I present to you, Mr. Kevin Trent Stryker."

The man's eyes widened in the darkness. "Kevin… Trent… Stryker…" He clutched his chest in shock and struggled to sit down on the cave floor. "My gosh, Sammy, you have brought me my son!"

Kevin stepped forward and took the next words. "Hello, father," he said.

Vincent Stryker nudged himself along the ground forward into the light, and to the shock of Kevin and everyone else, all of them saw in just how bad of shape the old war hero was. He was hunched over, and his hair was white and fragile. Many of his bones appeared bowed from years of abuse and lack of proper nutrition. He wore old, worn tan clothes. Altogether, he looked almost twenty years older than his actual age and gave people the impression that he was about to fall apart like an old rag doll.

He looked up at Kevin, as if the sunlight was sensitive on his eyes. "Please," he said, "would you kneel down here?"

Nodding gently, Kevin kneeled down next to his father as everyone else looked on in wonder. Kevin leaned in and looked into his father's eyes as his father placed his hands on Kevin's face, feeling all around his face, getting familiar in ways his vision-deficient eyes could not. "You have your mother's face," said Vincent, letting his hands off of Kevin.

"Yeah, I get that a lot," said Kevin, quietly, trying to restrain the feelings of finally seeing his father. This was it. Years of wonder, and all of it had come down to this. No matter what his condition was, Kevin felt like the happiest person in the world. "I can see the similarity between you and me."

"You are more of your mother than you are of me," said Vincent. "Lavinia, your mother, was a great person. I was very saddened to hear about her death."

"It was a rough time," said Kevin as he took a deep breath. "Mother was the best, indeed. She really meant that much to you, too?"

Vincent nodded. "Of course she did, my son. Lavinia was my everything, but after you were born, I knew I was making a mistake being in Aurana." Vincent stopped to let out a sigh. "To tell you the truth, Kevin, I knew that my presence was endangering you and your mother. Even if you think I am lying to you, you must understand that I am being serious."

"I know you are," said Kevin. Behind him, a cloud passed over the sun, reducing the light in the cave. To add some light, Kevin reached over and drew his Sword of Purity, lighting it up in its bright blue light as he drew it.

Staring at the sword, Vincent said, "Is that what I think it is? What are you doing with it?" Then, Vincent shook his head. "No, no, no, you cannot be doing that! How did you get that sword?"

"From War Commander Eukert, via a god," he said, not naming Kron.

Vincent started to shake his head in disbelief, with his hand over his face. "No, no, no!" he exclaimed. "Curse that damn Vinz Larinion and his gods drawing you into this!"

Before Kevin could say anything in response, Kron stormed into the cave and said with force, "How dare you curse the name of he who sacrificed himself in the name of all that is good? How ungrateful must you be?"

Rolling his eyes up, Vincent looked at Kronius, straight into his eyes. "You must be a god," he said. "A younger one at that, since your naivety shows. You don't know what that was like, to think you were the one who had to make a difference."

"Sounds like you should talk about it," said Kevin, as he sheathed the Sword of Purity again. "Tell me, tell us all, what happened to make you think so."

A short pause occurred before Vincent said, "Very well. Bring everyone in here who is still standing outside, and I will explain all to you, my son."

Kevin nodded, and then signaled toward the cavern opening for Caitlin, Arthur, Rachel, and the Lord Dragon to come inside.

Vincent began, "It was twenty years ago when I was invited by Vinz Larinion to come to the Realm of the Angels. There, I was told that I was selected to become the 'pure one' and that I would have a task to defeat one by the name of Tyrinion and an army powered by him. I was told that I was the only one with such potential, and that I was some type of beacon of light in a dark world, and Vinz Larinion made sure I knew he was sacrificing himself to create the sword I would need."

Everyone was listening intently.

"With the united forces of the Triple Alliance and a weakness I discovered, I led a strike into Seta Archa. By the day's end, the city was in flames, and many innocent lives were lost. It was then that I found the access to my true goal: the defeat of Tyrinion. I went with the Sword of Purity in hand, determined that what I was doing was right. But, as I was about to find out, that was about as far from reality as I could ever get."

There was a momentary pause. No one said a word.

"I stood no chance and I lost handily. To my surprise, he made a deal with me: he would spare my life and walk away in exchange for me putting down the sword and never picking it up again."

"And you accepted that?" asked Kevin.

Letting out a breath, Vincent responded, "I did."

"And in doing so you sentenced all of us to death," interjected Kronius, very upset at this realization. "Tyrinion then disappeared, and sealed off the Realm of the Angels. The gods thought you saved us, but you did not. He simply walked away for a while."

"The facts you have stated are true," responded Vincent. "So much, I am made out to be a hero around the world for the strike on Seta Archa. But I am no hero. And the truth is that no one ever will be who dares to challenge him."

"So you just gave up," said Kevin in realization. "You didn't even try to keep fighting."

"Because to fight on would have been futile," responded Vincent. "Have I not made that clear already? To do so is suicide, even with that piece of metal strapped to your belt. There is no need for sacrifice if you are going to willingly throw your life away for nothing."

Kevin shook his head. "You don't know that," he said. "I understand that you want the best for me and my friends behind me, but I won't back down from what I am doing."

"You haven't been there and seen what I have seen," answered the broken Vincent. "I fled from Aurana and you and your mother because he would have found and killed us all. I heard his threats, and I knew he would make good on them. I fled to protect you. Now please, I am begging you, do not throw away your life. For your own safety, please, just stop whatever you're doing with that cursed object."

Looking down, Kevin stood up and kept his head lowered. No one could see his eyes. Without another word, he turned toward the sunlight and walked to the exit. Seeing this, Vincent called out, "Son, wait!"

Kevin continued to walk on, pulling out the Sword of Purity with his right hand. As he walked on, he took the sword, with its blade pointing down, and spiked it into the ground, stepping outside and out to the left.

After Kevin had left and disappeared from sight, Caitlin stormed over to Vincent, reached down, and slapped him hard across the face, creating a whack sound that echoed all throughout the cave. "You jackass!" she exclaimed. "Your son made his way all the way out here because he hasn't given up yet! He didn't even give up on you! And now you, his father, tell him that everything he is doing is wrong. What kind of heartless person are you?"

Vincent took a breath as he closed his eyes in a pause. "One who knows what the consequences of such actions are," he said. "I am only looking out for his safety."

"And still you're so careless for his feelings!" exclaimed Caitlin. "I don't care what you say. I'm going out there and I'm going to help Kevin to remember who he is!" With this, Caitlin turned and stormed off toward the exit.

A moment passed, and no one said anything as Caitlin left the cave.

Back inside the cavern, Kron, the Lord Dragon, Arthur, Rachel, and Sammy all knelt down next to Vincent. "You know, Vincent, maybe you were too hard on him," said Sammy. "He's an honest chap who believes he can do what you think is impossible. Why don't you?"

Vincent took a breath. "He thinks, but I know," he said. "That may have been the hardest thing for me to do in my life."

"No one's going to blame you for doing what you think is right," remarked Rachel. "I think we can all agree on that. What you did, though, was crossing the line between telling and demanding."

"And you're his father," added Arthur, in frustration. "I've known Kevin for much of my life, and let me tell you, he's dreamed for years of getting the chance to know you. He's made it clear he doesn't want your 'legacy', but he wants to know you as a person. He finally finds you, and the first impression you give him is that you think everything that brought him to this point is futile."

Vincent shook his head.

"The young ones here have a great point," said Sammy at last. "As a man of logic and as a general, you did not treat Kevin too harshly. However, as a father to his son, you did treat him poorly. There's a difference."

All that Vincent could do was close his eyes and let out a sigh, unable to get things through his head.

"Your only chance to have any shot with your son is if he decides to give you a second chance," added Sammy. "Let's hope that he won't be too upset with you that he won't want to talk with you ever again, and maybe you'll have a second shot at a heartwarming reunion with him."

Chapter 37

The Reconciliation, Part I

Caitlin managed to find Kevin sitting along the cliffside road, staring up into the sky. He was thinking, deep into thought, and Caitlin recognized this. Instead of saying anything to him directly, she slowed herself down, and then sat down next to him and proceeded to look up into the sky as well.

After a couple of minutes, Kevin was the first to break the silence. "You know, maybe I don't deserve a father," he said. "I didn't care if he was a great person or not, but I didn't expect the first thing he would do would be to tear me down."

"What really matters is what you think of yourself, not what others do," responded Caitlin. "Likewise, if you think you're doing the right thing, you have to do it no matter what others say." She paused for a second. "You know, you always told me you're not a hero. Now you know who you're really related to, and that you're not following in his footsteps."

Kevin rolled his eyes. "I know," he said. "Still, it frustrates me more that I have to be related to such a pessimistic man than it does what he actually said. It kind of killed my dreams of meeting my father, you know?"

"Oh, but parents are sometimes like that," said Caitlin, attempting to lighten up the atmosphere. "Trust me, my father's quite the pessimist sometimes." Then, she paused before redirecting the topic back to Vincent Stryker. "He may be a jackass now, but he's still your father, Kevin. If you're willing to give him another chance, you may find yourself thinking differently of him. It doesn't have to be now, and there's nothing wrong with giving it time."

Taking a breath, Kevin replied, "I know, and I really don't think too badly of the man," he said. "I had to stop and take a moment, at least. I just couldn't take anymore of what he was saying." He paused. "I guess I just have to try and stay positive."

Caitlin nodded with a smile. "That's the Kevin I know," she said. "Though, to be honest, I think both of us had to have some optimism to make it as far as we have today."

Kevin nodded. "We did," he said. "It means a lot to me that you came out here to help me out."

Standing up, Caitlin said, "Always." Then, she extended her arm down to Kevin. "Here, I'll help you up. We can go back for the Sword of Purity that you left behind, and then you can decide what you'd like to do next. Is that fair enough?"

Taking her hand, Kevin stood up with Caitlin's help, appreciative of everything that Caitlin had told him. "You know, it's times like this that I'm glad I have you, Caitlin. You believe in me in ways I sometimes don't even believe in myself."

Caitlin nodded as she clutched Kevin's hand tighter. She and Kevin proceeded to walk down the cliffside road, back to Vincent Stryker's cave. Kevin had not walked too far from the cave when he walked off, and the entrance was still within sight.

Suddenly, Kevin heard a mysterious sound. It was almost a whistling sound through the air, coming from the cliffside above. Instinctively, he reached his free arm in front of Caitlin as he pulled her back with his other one that was still clinched in hers. His instincts were proven correct. Right in front of Kevin and Caitlin in the road, a spear had landed, wedged in the dirt. A black cloth was tied around its neck, right below the spearhead. From the angle, Kevin could tell it came from the cliffside above. He looked up there to see a frightening sight.

"Hello, Kevin Trent," said a dark, yet eerily familiar voice, standing on the cliff above. "What a wonder, indeed, that we should meet here today. It is just as Demonicus told me: you would be here on this exact day."

Kevin and Caitlin looked up. It was Kevin.

Or, at least someone who looked a lot like him. Sounded like him, too. He was dressed like Kevin, in a military uniform, except his was black in color and kept buttoned up. He also had a large scar across his eye that was very prominent, a clear physical deformity. Otherwise, he looked identical to Kevin

"What a wonder indeed," called Kevin up the cliff, recognizing only that this was clearly trouble if this person knew his name. "I guess it's a small world after all."

"You didn't need my presence here to tell you that one," responded the person. "You've known that one for a while now, I presume."

He was right, and Kevin knew it. He knew that an attack by Demonicus had to be coming. It was long overdue since the first attacks in Kevin's first couple of days after retrieving the Sword of Purity.

Caitlin tugged on Kevin's sleeve. "I admire your confidence, but be very careful," she warned. "Whoever he is, he's not human."

"Very intuitive of you," said the man, as he jumped down the cliff onto the road. As the cliffside above was nowhere near as tall as the one below the road, the man landed with force but without injury. "Do you like the work of the immortal father? Demonicus was certainly proud to see his completed project."

As the Kevin lookalike finished his statement, Arthur, Rachel, Kronius, and the Lord Dragon had walked out of the cliff and were looking in the direction that Kevin and Caitlin were in. Immediately, Arthur recognized who it was. "Pseudo! Have you come to kill us?" he yelled.

Pseudo turned to see Arthur and the group down the road. "I see you have the heir of Desolunar with you. I will deal with him soon enough," he said as he took the spear and threw it off the side of the cliff, "as I will deal with you first." He withdrew a sword from his scabbard.

It was at this point that Kevin remembered he left his sword behind. If he could not see it, he could not call it to him. Caitlin charged ice magic in her hands, ready for a fight.

"I hope you are prepared to die," said Pseudo as he pointed his sword to Kevin regardless, "but if you would like to prolong your life a few more minutes, then tell me where I can find Vincent Stryker. I know he is here."

Caitlin put a hand to Pseudo's neck with her magic charged, threatening him.

"I'm not telling you anything," said Kevin. He knew his friends were behind him and on their way. "Even so, you're outnumbered!"

Raising his right arm, Pseudo snapped his fingers. Like a call to arms, almost fifty Desolunar soldiers emerged from beyond the cliff's edge and leapt down to the road below. Some held swords, others held spears or bows, but all were dressed in the black Desolunar uniform, and all were pointing their weapons at Kevin and Caitlin.

Kevin raised his hands just below the level of his eyes in surrender. Caitlin de-powered her magic and followed suit for the moment. At least in this moment, they were beaten. "So, was this your plan, Pseudo?" asked Kevin. "To bring enough men here to force us to surrender and take us as prisoners?"

"Now, why would I do such a thing like that?" said Pseudo as he brought the tip of his blade closer to Kevin. "If it were up to me, of course I would take you prisoner. And then, I would see that you were tortured until you gave me the information I want, in a long and slow process. But my ruler's business policy is not to take prisoners unless he makes an exemption. For you, he made no such exemption. You should count yourself lucky that your death will be quick."

Approaching the men, Arthur drew his Sword of Corruption, Rachel set up an arrow in her bow, the Lord Dragon clutched his pike tighter with both hands, and Kron began charging energy for an attack. They were not backing down. Noticing their presence, Pseudo called out loud so that the somewhat distant Arthur and Rachel could hear, "If you come any closer, I will kill the pure one and the sorceress. This is your only warning!"

"Why should we listen to you?" called back the Lord Dragon. "We have no guarantee that you won't take their lives anyway if we back down."

"Are you really looking for these two to die?" responded Pseudo. "Or perhaps it's your own life you value more." Then, he barked an order. "Men! All but two of you, approach them cautiously and defensively. Take no prisoners!"

Responding to the order, the men started to march down the cliffside road. All that the Lord Dragon and company could do was to take position in a line across the road and prepare to brace for an attack.

Sammy then stepped out of the cavern. He observed the situation and was shocked to see what he did. Sammy did not have any armament, but knowing that he had a horse's body for his lower body, he stepped behind the other four and prepared to use his hooves if necessary. As a former man of the military himself, retreat was simply unacceptable.

"Keep your line straight and strong, and mind the cliff edge!" commanded the Lord Dragon. "Along this narrow road, numbers will not mean much since they will have to file in narrow rows. They cannot swarm us unless anyone leaks through the line." Arthur, Rachel, and Kron all nodded, keeping the simple battle tactic in mind and being prepared to follow through on it as the Desolunar troops approached their line. The Lord Dragon was clearly an experienced military person, and knew what he was doing.

Further down the road, Kevin and Caitlin were still stuck. Pseudo stood in front of them with his sword drawn and pointing at them. Behind them, two Desolunar soldiers were pointing weapons at them as well. Blast, Kevin thought to himself. Of all the times for him to leave his sword somewhere, even in frustration, this was by far the worst possible one.

"Now, then," continued Pseudo, "where were we? Oh yes, we were just now at the part where I take your lives. Anyone here have anything they want to say?"

Not a second after Pseudo finished his sentence, another blade lined up on the side of his neck, causing him to freeze up.

"How does this sound for something to say? Release them, and I will let you live."

Behind Pseudo, Vincent Stryker was standing with the lit-up Sword of Purity, pointing it at Pseudo's neck from behind him. He had completely caught Pseudo by surprise. Kevin was pleasantly surprised to see this, and also to see Vincent Stryker wearing his old Scurnian war jacket, which was faded from years of wear.

A smirk came across Pseudo's face. "Well, so you must be the legendary Vincent Stryker himself, as that is the Sword of Purity you have pointed at my neck. Tell me, Vincent, how is that deal with my boss's father working for you? You stay away and he stays away?"

"He broke that first, and you know it," responded Vincent, not finding the situation funny like Pseudo did. "Now, I am not here to argue about the past. Leave my son alone, or you die."

"Heh," scoffed Pseudo. "Good luck making that one work. In the meantime, I think I'll start with the sorceress over here." He angled his sword to Caitlin's neck.

In a fit of rage and instinct, Kevin caught the sword before it could make it to Caitlin's neck by using the stealth bracer on his left arm that he had received from Raijin Shane. Then, he threw a punch at Pseudo.

The punch was hard enough that it knocked Pseudo backwards, and when his head hit the hard rock of the cliffside road, he was temporarily knocked out of the fight. Vincent Stryker then seized the opportunity to jump in front of Kevin and start to deal with the two other Desolunar soldiers. These soldiers showed fear in facing Vincent Stryker, however, and Vincent took advantage of this to defeat both of them quickly by exploiting their defensive weaknesses from their fears, along with some ice magic support from Caitlin.

As the soldiers retreated, Kevin looked at his father. "Glad to see you could make it out here. I thought you were supposed to be in poor health."

Vincent started clutching his back with his free hand. "I shouldn't have done that on account of my back," he grimaced in pain. "But nothing is more encouraging and more inspiring than the prospect of a good fight, especially when it's for family."

"I know what you mean," nodded Kevin. "I do have to ask, how did you get around the backside, away from all the troops?"

"These caverns run all through this cliffside," answered Vincent. "And when you spend as long as I have here, you get to know the caverns quite well. One of them happens to exit just behind where he was standing."

Kevin and Caitlin nodded, understanding what Vincent meant.

After a short pause, Vincent flipped the Sword of Purity over to Kevin and said, "You had better take this. You're going to need it."

Catching the sword in the air, Kevin said, "Then what will you use?"

"I have my own," said Vincent as he pulled out the other sword on his belt. Kevin noticed that this blade's scabbard was curved slightly, although the scabbard was regular length. He recognized this sword as a rare variation of the longsword, called a katana. Vincent then drew this katana and pointed it toward the unit of Desolunar troops currently fighting against Arthur, Rachel, the Lord Dragon, and Kronius, who were struggling to fend off so many troops. "Looks like our friends need some help over there with that amount of soldiers. You two deal with this one while I go to help them out."

"Are you sure about this?" asked Caitlin.

"Absolutely," answered Vincent, as he pointed over to Pseudo standing again. "Let's do this," he said before he dashed off down the road to help out the others.

Before anything else happened, Kevin and Caitlin looked at each other, and nodded in acknowledgment of what had to be done next. Kevin raised his sword, and Caitlin began to charge ice magic in her hands. "I won't let you threaten us, Pseudo," called out Kevin.

"You will die today, pure one," said Pseudo, gripping his sword tightly. "I will make sure of that." He then lunged straight for Kevin.

Kevin pulled his sword up to block, and started to swing his sword and catch Pseudo's attacks in each direction. Left and right, Pseudo and Kevin battled. First, they fought into the cliff, including a couple of sword smashes into the side of the rock. As they continued exchanging slashes and blocks, they started edging toward the other side of the road, where the edge was, along with the precipitous drop off of the cliff.

Caitlin could only stand back and watch for the moment. Even if her magic could get past Pseudo's sword, Kevin's back was toward Caitlin, which put him in the way between her and Pseudo. She would hit him if she attacked.

Fiercely focused, Kevin focused his Sword of Purity on fighting very defensively, hoping to give Caitlin an opening to attack Pseudo.

He was using every ounce of confidence he had and every bit of sword tactics he did know from school—he refused to be caught off guard again as he had with Demonicus over a month ago. This defensive fighting started to get to Pseudo, who was annoyed that Kevin was not as easy to defeat as he wanted.

Needing to make a strong move, Pseudo pulled another leaping move with his sword angled downward. Kevin attempted to avoid it by trying to crouch and roll underneath Pseudo, putting Pseudo behind him. But Kevin was unable to make the roll work as far as he was hoping, which ended up with Pseudo landing on Kevin with his body. The sword strike had missed, but by accident Pseudo was not able to clear Kevin with his leap.

Now, Kevin was caught. He was stuck underneath Pseudo, and even worse, he was very close to the edge of the cliff. Desperate, he tried to pull himself up using the Sword of Purity as a pole to drag himself out from under the body of Pseudo. Kevin was hurt badly, but he had to try and pull himself up as best as he could if he was to continue on.

Pseudo, however, managed to stand up easily on his own power. As he lifted off, Kevin popped up onto his hands and knees, still struggling to stand up. Seizing the opportunity that was now in front of him, with the edge of the cliff as close as it was, Pseudo kicked Kevin hard in his side, forcing him off of the cliff and down a shear drop.

And in that instant, Kevin was gone.

Chapter 38

The Reconciliation, Part II

From a couple of steps away, Caitlin shrieked in horror.

She had almost lost Kevin once before, and now he was lost for good.

Then, she started to cry, unable to hold herself back. She had never felt such sadness in her life. Kevin was dead, killed by Pseudo. In that moment, she was inconsolable.

Stepping back from the edge after kicking Kevin off the side, Pseudo said, "All too easy." Then, he turned toward Caitlin and began walking toward her, positioning himself between her and the cliff as he spoke, "And now it is your turn. Do not cry, for you will be joining the pure one in death soon enough."

In a sad fury, Caitlin took the ice magic energy she had been charging and threw it as hard as she could at Pseudo. She threw more and more orbs of ice energy, desiring only death to Pseudo in revenge for him killing Kevin. All of it proved to be futile, however, as Pseudo blocked every single orb with his sword, merely deflecting the magic energy. Caitlin's fury meant that she was not aiming with her magic to try and get around Pseudo's sword, making his defense easy.

Even more furious with this failure, Caitlin began to charge darkness energy, which she felt was a more powerful weapon. With a scream, she unleashed a beam of darkness, pushing every bit of energy she had into this blast. Fury was driving her on; the sadness in her heart was all that she had for fuel.

Caitlin let up after a moment, too tired and drained to continue on. As her blast ended, she saw an even more frightening sight than she thought she would. Pseudo was still standing with his sword pointed at

Caitlin. "Is it my turn now?" asked Pseudo.

With her eyes widening, Caitlin was in disbelief.

Then, Pseudo unleashed darkness energy through his sword, into a blast. Caitlin had no time to defend it as it broadsided her with a great amount of force, launching her off the side of the cliff.

A loud scream ripped through the air.

Caitlin was plummeting, and fast. What lasted only a few seconds seemed to last an eternity as she fell.

No one else saw her fall, with her being so far separated from her friends. There was no rescue, no saving to be had.

It was all over for her. Just as it had been for Kevin a moment earlier. Caitlin closed her eyes, afraid to see her fate in front of her.

"Caitlin!"

That voice…

Suddenly, she slowed down. She felt her angelic power activate, and she began to decelerate and float down slowly. And then, there was a soft landing.

Puzzled, Caitlin opened her eyes to see how she had landed softly. To her surprise, as she opened her eyes, she saw Kevin holding her horizontally. He had caught her.

Overjoyed but confused, Caitlin gently stroked Kevin's face, trying to tell if he was really there, still in disbelief. "Kevin, are you really…"

"I'm not a ghost," answered Kevin, chuckling a little bit. "A little beat up, yes, but it's still me."

"But, but…" stammered Caitlin, "how did you… how did you…"

"Survive the fall?" asked Kevin, as he set Caitlin back on her feet. He then pointed up at the rock side, at a sight that made the young sorceress stare in amazement. Down the side of the rock, all along what was a steep precipitous drop, was a gigantic cut, almost like a slash mark in the cliffside. "It was all about the right amount of energy," continued Kevin. "I stuck the Sword of Purity into the rock face, and slid right on down…"

Interrupting, Caitlin reached over and kissed Kevin and hugged him with all of the strength that she could. She was incredibly happy just to see that she had not lost Kevin after all. As she did, her translucent angel wings became visible, and she started to float off of the ground. "I'm just so glad you're safe," she said gently as she held onto Kevin.

"I'm glad you're safe, too," responded Kevin.

For a moment, the two embraced.

Then, Caitlin looked up. "But we're not done yet." She pointed toward a nearby pile of a couple of fallen Desolunar soldiers that Arthur, Rachel, Vincent, the Lord Dragon, and Sammy had knocked off of the cliff. She pointed up the cliffside, then clutched Kevin tightly and started to lift higher and higher,. Her ascent was slow, at a rate that would take a couple of minutes for them to reach the top.

Kevin was lifted off the ground, but not in a dragging motion. He was floating upward with Caitlin, rising by the ability of Caitlin's angelic power. "This is amazing!" said Kevin in wonder as he and Caitlin floated up the cliff. "I knew you could fly, but this is just beyond description!"

"It's thanks to you that I can do this," answered Caitlin delicately.

"You don't have to make me the cause of everything," chuckled Kevin, in good spirits despite what he had to look forward to back on the cliffside road above. "You were what you are now all along."

Caitlin responded, "But I'm being serious. I asked my father about it last night, and he said that somehow you're the trigger that made it show up." And then, the hesitation hit again. No, Caitlin thought. She suppressed it again, with as much effort as she could, without giving Kevin a sign of it.

The road was coming up once again, and Kevin was certain that he would not get another chance at Pseudo again. Either he would kill Pseudo, or Pseudo would kill him. One way or another, somehow Kevin knew that one of them would die today. As they floated over the cliff edge and above the cliffside road, Caitlin gently set Kevin down. He drew the Sword of Purity, pointed it at Pseudo, and commanded, "Turn around, Pseudo! This isn't over!"

Pseudo, who was standing near where he was before, watching everyone else battle his Desolunar soldiers, turned back in surprise to see Kevin standing on the ground and Caitlin floating in the air. Despised, Pseudo picked up his sword again, started walking toward Kevin with heavy, forced steps of fury, and said, "Don't you two ever die?" He then took a swing toward Kevin.

Kevin blocked the ill-planned strike easily. "Not as long as I have people to fight for," he said.

"Or maybe you can just die now!" yelled out Pseudo as he swung his sword away and at a different angle again in another forceful strike.

With a little effort, Kevin blocked this strike as well. But, as Pseudo pressed harder and harder, Kevin had to press harder as well to keep the Sword of Purity blocking Pseudo's attack. If he kept this up, Kevin would not be able to hold the block longer and he would likely take a devastating strike. Something had to be done. What could Kevin do to avoid a repeat of the same scenario that happened last time? Breaking off his guard to disengage would put Pseudo in a strong advantage and let him take the offensive very quickly. Kevin was not sure he could recover from that.

Then it came to him. Kevin turned his head carefully toward his back and said, "Caitlin, I need your help. Fire some magic at Pseudo, but stay where you are."

In line with Caitlin, Kevin was standing directly in the way of Pseudo. "But why?" asked Caitlin, confused with this request. "I'll just hit you with it!"

"Just do it," responded Kevin, as the strain of pushing his sword was starting to take a serious toll on his muscles. "Please, Caitlin, you need to trust me, even if you never do it again, I need your trust now. Trust me."

Caitlin paused for a second. If she did not trust him, then why was she following him in the first place? Trying to reassure herself that it was what she needed to do, Caitlin began charging darkness magic in her arms again, creating various charging noises as she did. After a second, she unleashed it toward Kevin, who was standing in front of Pseudo.

Hearing the unleashing magic, Kevin reacted by instinct and spun around Pseudo's side at the last instant, releasing his block as he did. The blasting beam of continuous darkness energy struck Pseudo straight in his sword, allowing him to block the blast.

Just like Kevin wanted.

Spinning around Pseudo's side, Kevin managed to get right behind Pseudo. With Pseudo preoccupied with his forward side, he had no guard whatsoever on his backside. Seizing the opportunity, although feeling a bit guilty for pulling such a cheap move, Kevin took his Sword of Purity and stabbed Pseudo through the back with it.

Pseudo stopped cold, unable to believe what had just happened. Also surprised, Caitlin cut off her beam of darkness that she was using. Just down the road, the remaining Desolunar soldiers stopped at the stabbing of their commander, only standing to observe. Arthur, Rachel, the Lord Dragon, Kronius, Sammy, and Vincent were also watching on, surprised to see what they were witnessing.

He was a dead man. Pseudo was not actually dead yet, but he would be. He looked down at his chest in surprise from the pain, to see the Sword of Purity wedged all the way through his chest. He was defeated by a two-on-one tactic.

Kevin, however, was in a state of cold, commanding strength. He had no sympathy at the moment; only business was on his mind. "Now I want an answer," commanded Kevin. "Why does Demonicus want me dead?"

"And why should I tell you?" Pseudo struggled to say, having severe difficulties breathing. "Demonicus will kill you yet, whether it's the sisters or his Enlighteners, or himself personally. You've already ended my life. You can't make it any worse for me than that, denying me that glory."

Angry, Kevin turned his Sword of Purity a quarter turn, putting Pseudo in greater pain. "You're not dead until I withdraw this sword from your chest. Answer the question, or it gets worse."

"Why do you ask questions for which you have the answers?" asked Pseudo, still struggling to talk as he grimaced in pain. "You know why he wants you dead. You, as the pure one, are a threat to his conquest of the realms." He looked down at Kevin's wrist, where his sleeve had fallen back. "And now he knows, through my eyes, that you're collecting the 'stripes'. You are looking to topple his kingdom.

You are his greatest challenge."

"And how many of the stripes does he have?" asked Kevin, seeing that Pseudo knew about the stripes.

"That, you will not know," said Pseudo.

Kevin twisted the blade again. "I will know. I won't end this until I do."

Pseudo yelped in pain. "Three!" he exclaimed. "Fire, light, and darkness!"

Letting out a breath, Kevin responded, "Very well. I suppose I should relieved you of this burden." He started preparing his grip to withdraw his sword.

"Mark my words, pure one," sniped Pseudo, "that your days are numbered. If it is not me, it will be the sisters. If not them, it will be the wizard. Or maybe our lord himself will dirty his hands with you. One way or another, the immortal conqueror will see to your end, as he eclipses the world in darkness."

"I don't think so," quipped Kevin. Then, he gave a quick tug to his sword, withdrawing it. As he did so, he gave Pseudo a hard kick in the back, forcing him off the cliff.

All looked on in disbelief. Never before had Kevin performed such a violent move as he had just done. It was a move of a coldhearted warrior, not one who was as loving and caring for his friends as Kevin was. In disbelief at himself after such a move, Kevin sheathed his Sword of Purity and looked at the ground. He was overwhelmed and needed a minute to gather his thoughts.

Back down the road, the remaining Desolunar soldiers were quick to surrender after the loss of their commander. They immediately retreated, and Arthur and company let them retreat on their own. As the soldiers began to march southward on their own, looking only to return to Desolunar, Arthur and company returned toward Kevin and Caitlin. Kevin was kneeling on the ground as he tried to regain his composure, and Caitlin was kneeling next to him.

"I knew it was coming," said Kevin after a long pause. "I knew we were going to be attacked. It was long overdue. Yet I didn't know that it would end like this."

"You did what you had to," responded Vincent, sheathing his

sword. "Oftentimes I have found myself in such a situation before where you have no choice but to deliver a fatal blow. It is a part of being a warrior."

Kevin sighed. "I know it is," he said. "I knew it had to happen. I guess that I wasn't as prepared for the moment as I thought I would be, though. I just need a minute, that's all."

Everyone nodded in acknowledgment, and gave Kevin a few brief seconds to help recollect himself. What he had just done had impacted him so profoundly as to give Kevin the feeling of concussion shockwaves resounding after the initial impact.

Then, Arthur reached his hand down. "You did great out there today," he said. "Here, take my hand and I'll help you up."

Extending his arm, Kevin pulled himself upward with the help of Arthur. "Thanks, Arthur," he said. "I'm glad that you've been my best friend for years, but I do have to ask, where's your sarcasm?" Kevin was chuckling a little bit, apparently in a lighter mood.

"It's taking the rest of the day off," joked Arthur. "Not to worry, though, as it'll return tomorrow."

Laughter was in the air as everyone got a kick out of Arthur's humor. Furthermore, it had helped Kevin to forget his stresses and strains, if only for a moment.

"We had better not stay out here much longer," said the Lord Dragon as he watched the sun, interrupting the good moment of everyone. "If we want to make it back to Vallia by nightfall, we have to leave as soon as possible."

Looking up at the sky, Kron added, "He is right, you know. We have time to catch up on the way, but if we do not leave now, we will not make it back to Vallia before nightfall. We should get there as soon as possible to obtain shelter again and to rendezvous with Professor Magnon."

Kevin looked up to the sky himself to check the position of the sun and get an idea of the time. After a short pause, he said, "You're right. It is starting to get late. We had better say goodbye to Sammy and Vincent, and prepare to roll out."

"Correction," interrupted Vincent Stryker. "My son, as long as my back will hold up, I will be coming with you."

Everyone was surprised. "You really mean that?" asked Kevin, excited.

Vincent nodded. "Of course I do. Sammy made me realize that as your father, I have to trust that you know what you are doing, and that you can do what you believe you can. And if that is the case, then I must help you so long as my health will allow it. I do not want you to fail, so I will help. Please, consider it my reconciliation with you for the cruel comments I made before."

Kevin could only smile. "Thanks, dad," he said, using the three letter word for the first time ever to refer to his father. "It'll be great having you along."

Then, everyone turned to Sammy to hear what he had to say about the potential of coming along if Vincent Stryker was going. Sammy saw everyone looking at him, and knew what it was about. "I can't go, chaps," he said, depressed. "Much as I would love to, I still can't bring myself to come back to society with these horse legs."

There was a momentary pause, somewhat in disappointment. "We can't make you go," said Rachel, finally breaking the silence. "I'm sure I speak for all of us when I say that if you don't want to go, you don't have to."

"It's going to be fine, Sammy," stepped up Vincent Stryker to reassure his longtime friend. "Take care of yourself, and I promise you that I will be back at some point."

Sammy nodded, glad to know that he would not be forced into an uncomfortable position.

Everyone took a moment to say their goodbyes to Sammy before leaving to the north, back along the cliffside road that they had come down earlier. In the front were the Lord Dragon and Kronius, with Vincent, Kevin, Arthur, Caitlin, and Rachel following behind. It would be another couple of hours back along the treacherous Cliffs of Vallia back to the town.

As they traveled, Kevin still kept looking down, unable to get his thoughts of Pseudo out of his head. Concerned, Caitlin gripped Kevin's hand tighter to get his attention and show him that she was still there. "What is it, Kevin?" she asked as Kevin raised his head. "Are you still wound up about the incident with Pseudo?"

"Sort of," answered Kevin, not in the best of spirits. "He's a part of it, and I did what I had to do in that instance. That part I realize. But what bothers me is how he nearly killed me." He paused for a second. "Caitlin, I should have lost my life several times over by now. By all rights, several of us here should not be alive today. We've all saved each others' lives several times over, and we've nearly lost everything. I've been squarely defeated before, and it's only a matter of time, I fear, until that defeat is permanent."

"Oh, Kevin, don't be so pessimistic," said Rachel from the other side of Kevin. "You've always been an optimist. Leave the realism to me."

Kevin chuckled. "Maybe I should," he joked. "You're good enough at that already."

"You can say that again," said Arthur, rolling his eyes while walking next to Rachel.

"Are you four always like this?" interrupted Vincent Stryker. "Kevin, you and your friends may be the most unusual collection of personalities of young people that I have ever seen together."

"You bet," nodded Caitlin, with a smile. "Still, I do understand that Kevin does make a good point. We can't be so lucky all of the time."

"Or can we?" asked Vincent jovially. "Trust me, over the years I have learned how much better it is to be lucky than it is to be skillful at something. The longer you survive, the luckier you can get. However, if you have really survived at least three narrow escapes as you indicated, then to use an old expression, you must really have an angel watching over you, Kevin."

Kevin and Caitlin looked at each other and chuckled awkwardly. Though she felt strongly connected to Kevin at this moment, Caitlin felt the hesitation stopping her yet again. She hated it so much. Something was wrong, and she knew it. Every time she was in her closest moments with Kevin, it seemed to create an uneasiness within her.

It would be a trip back to Vallia, but one that everyone would find enjoyable with a sense of a moderate victory today. They were all tired and exhausted, but perhaps none were as exhausted as Vincent Stryker himself, who had to deal with the overwhelming emotions of meeting his son for the very first time and having to deal with his own health problems as he came out of retirement and decided to travel great distances by going with his son.

Yet, for Kevin, victory today came with the sickening feeling of his most violent action in his young life, as well as the fright of almost losing his life again. Somewhere, in the back of his mind, he was afraid that someday he would not be so lucky as to come out of such a situation alive again.

Chapter 39

Race to the City of Dreams

By the time Kevin and company arrived in Vallia, the sun had already set below the mountains, casting a shadow across the entire town with the exception of the north edge where the Northern Pass ran in the same line as the town. Night was quickly approaching, and the day was much later already than when the group had checked into The Old Ball and Chain's inn the night before. There was no sun, no sky cascading with the colors of the sunset. There was only a dim blue sky, with the sunset now low enough to be blocked by the mountains from sight. In less than an hour, it would be completely dark.

The dusk was cool and crisp. A slight wind winding around the mountains crossed over the town, giving off a relaxing feeling in the highland town, much in contrast to the record high days shortly before. Lanterns lit around The Old Ball and Chain provided a slight orange glow, providing what was currently the only light in the town aside from what was left in the sky.

"Looks like we made it just in time," said the Lord Dragon as the group entered the south end of the town. "Dusk is setting in perfectly. It'll be nightfall in a few minutes."

"Are our rooms on you again, Lord Dragon?" asked Arthur.

Everyone else became nervous in an instant, thinking Arthur was being cocky and assuming. But the Lord Dragon merely responded, "Naturally, but tomorrow, I must be headed back to my faction. The Knights of the Dragon do need a leader and to hear the good news, after all. Just like the egotistical jerk always cutting in front of you at the bar, we always have to get it all." He started laughing a bit at the joke he cracked.

It was an awkward chuckle for everyone else. "Well, it's been great to have you along this far, at least," said Kevin.

From beside the group, a voice said, "And along for the ride in the future."

The voice was that of Professor Magnon. Everyone stopped when they heard the voice, and turned to see him leaning up against a building, simply waiting. It was a surprise to all of them.

"Father, how long have you been waiting here?" asked Caitlin in surprise.

"Oh, not long," answered the professor. "I hope all of you enjoyed your day trip to the Cliffs of Vallia. Did it turn up rewarding?"

"In more ways than one," said Kevin. "It also turned out to be damaging as well, however."

Professor Magnon nodded. "So I can see," he said. "You look a little scuffed up, Kevin. Rough day out there?"

"Very," responded Kevin. "An unexpected attack straight out of Desolunar caught us off guard. We survived, at least."

"I suppose that all is fine as long as you are alive," said Professor Magnon. "I hope you kept in mind the promise I made you take about protecting my daughter and kept her out of danger as well."

Caitlin stepped up next to Kevin. "He protects me as well as I protect him," she said. "Don't worry, we both came back in one piece."

Again, Professor Magnon nodded. Then, he looked through the crowd for a brief second and said, "Well, I am surprised indeed. Long time no see, Mr. Vincent Stryker."

Vincent stepped forward. "Professor James Magnon, it has been quite a long time indeed."

Kevin turned toward his father, stunned at what he had just heard. "You actually know the professor?"

"I do," nodded Vincent. "I am actually surprised that you know him, my son."

"It is true," added the professor. "I worked to help out your father for a few weeks under the same sense of obligation which makes me work to help you as well."

Obligation indeed, Kevin thought to himself. Kron may have been right after all. Something was not adding up here, and Kevin was not sure what it was. It seemed apparent to him that Professor Magnon had something more to gain than just world security and a slap in the face of someone he despised from this whole mess. Still, Kevin had no evidence of this at the moment, much less an idea of what the professor did have to gain. "I see," Kevin finally responded after a moment's pause. "That does explain some things."

After another short pause, Professor Magnon changed the subject. "So, tell me, Vincent, what brings you out of retirement? I thought you had said that you were never going to try again and that you were headed into exile."

"Still don't have plans to try again," said Vincent. "I am much too old for that sort of thing, and my health would not allow it even if I was younger and had more stamina. The reason I am here is to support my son and what he is doing."

"Good to hear," replied the professor. "I would say it is the right decision. Have you and your son decided where you are headed next?"

Kevin had not really given this much thought, simply assuming it had to be Scurniapolis, the capital city of Scurnia. He figured that, although it was out of the way of almost everywhere else in the world, Scurniapolis had to be his next destination, and the answer the professor expected. It was the only capital of the Triple Alliance that he had not yet visited. "Scurniapolis," he finally said after a moment. "It's all that is left to go to at the moment, if we want to keep going on."

The professor merely bowed his head and said, "Very well, as it should be, to complete our reunification of the Triple Alliance. We are leaving tomorrow, then?"

"Yes we are," nodded Kevin.

Nodding in acknowledgment, the professor then continued, "Now, then, may I invite everyone to The Old Ball and Chain for the night?"

Accepting the invite, everyone followed the professor to the tavern. Lord Dragon made good on his word, and purchased another night of rooms before saying goodbye to everyone and taking his leave. He gave his assurance to Kevin that if Scurnia did authorize military action, he would lead the Knights of the Dragon into battle.

Several hours later as the night fell, everyone was in their respective room for the night. Caitlin once again roomed with Rachel, while Kevin roomed with Arthur. Kevin was receiving one of the first relaxing rests that he had had since arriving in Vallia. He found his stress stiffening up as well, although his was focused on his tasks ahead. Slowly, he managed to push these thoughts from his mind and relax. The rest was slowly recovering his mental clarity and relieving his stress, if only temporarily. Still, the thought of what he was going to do in Scurniapolis did get to him, as he had almost made that decision on impulse. Truthfully, Kevin did not want to go to the Scurnian capital. It was a long distance away across harsh terrain, and Kevin was not really sure what good it would be if Scurnia was in favor of the alliance already. A simple letter would be quicker and easier, and not cost Kevin weeks of time traveling there and back. And in that time, Demonicus would surely discover of Pseudo's defeat and seek another means of killing him. He was sure that Demonicus would become more furious with his attacks after the fall of Pseudo and the loss of his tracking of Arthur.

The night was peaceful, yet a little chilly. All night long, the skies remained clear, and the only light in the town not from the sky came from a pair of torches outside The Old Ball and Chain's main entrance. The moon was not quite to a full moon position, but still shone brightly in the sky.

Then, all of that peace broke down.

Early in the morning, before the light of dawn, Kron burst into Kevin's room, walked over to him, and shook him some. "Kevin, come quickly," he said. "There is someone here to see you, and it is an emergency."

Kevin's eyes cracked open from the shaking, only to be unable to believe what he was hearing. He rolled back over and mumbled, "Can't they wait until after the sun is up? I'm trying to get some sleep."

"I wish it could, but it cannot," answered Kron. "There is a phoenix here to see you."

Those words made Kevin's eyes pop open all of the way. What was a phoenix doing this far east? Kevin had encountered the phoenixes earlier on his quest, while he was retrieving the Stripe of Air, and as far as he knew, the phoenixes kept themselves to the west of Aurana, in a land they called Avalon. Quickly, Kevin pulled himself up out of bed, trying not to wake Arthur. He put on his clothing, threw his jacket around his shoulders, strapped his sword to his belt, and left his bedroom.

Kron started walking with Kevin after he left his bedroom and headed for the exit. "Do you have any idea what this is about?" he asked.

"I was hoping you could answer that for me," responded Kevin. "You were the one who woke me up. What happened?"

"All I know is that I was outside for a few moments, taking a break from my nightly reading, when suddenly this phoenix lands by The Old Ball and Chain," began Kron. "I asked who and what he was, then he asked me if I knew who you were, and when I said yes, he told me that he had to speak with you urgently."

"Hmmm," said Kevin, as he rubbed his eyes, trying to wake up further. "I guess we'll see what this is about after we get outside, then." He and Kron then passed through the tavern's main doors to the outside. Two torches, one on each side of the door, were the only lights in the town. In front of Kevin and Kron as they exited was a tall phoenix, with the distinctive red, orange, and yellow feathers in a gradient from top to bottom.

"Kevin, it is a great pleasure to see you again," said a familiar voice, coming from the phoenix.

Recognizing the voice instantly, Kevin extended his arm in a handshake. Excited, he said, "Wheldon, how have you been? Good to see you again."

Wheldon extended a wingtip to meet Kevin's handshake. "It is good to see you too, Kevin. Sacred Avalon has graced us with this meeting tonight. I am sorry to trouble you so late at night, but I bring you a message that is urgent. The Red Phoenix himself asked me to rush this to you."

"Then how did you find me?" asked Kevin. "Scurnia is a long way away from Avalon, you know."

Wheldon nodded. "Just as the sky is connected to the earth, we phoenixes are connected by our spirits. And if you remember from that day in Avalon, the Red Phoenix made you an honorary phoenix on that day. Those were not just words, Kevin. Those words had meaning, and it connected you to us in the same way. Because you are an honorary phoenix, and because you spent an extended time with me, I am bonded to you in this way, and can sense where you are, no matter where you are, if I put effort in to finding you."

A little confused by this, Kevin nodded in acknowledgment anyway. "So how long did it take you to get here from Avalon?"

"About a week," responded Wheldon. "This message is a week old, so you had better keep that in mind when you read it." Wheldon then reached over with his wingtip and pulled a piece of paper out of his back feathers. He then passed it to Kevin.

Carefully, Kevin began to open the paper. He then started to read the letter to himself:

Dearest Kevin, honorary phoenix,

Once again, the phoenixes wish to thank you for your service to us. Since your visit to Avalon, the phoenixes and ravens have had the chance to re-associate and become a part of one another once again. Uruson, the Grand Raven, has been most helpful in helping to bring together our clans, but ultimately we have you to thank for everything.

However, it is for other reasons that I have sent you this message today. As a part of our payment to you for the help you gave us, we decided that one of the best things we could do for you was to provide some aerial reconnaissance on your land of Aurana. It seemed like an honest idea at the time, so we apologize if this offends you. Little activity was occurring for much of the time, until we noticed some strange happenings coming from a city called Atwals, far to the south beyond Aurana's southern border. What we noticed was an army regrouping and forming up, preparing to go on an offensive. This did not at all appear to be a regular battling army; from its size and its ranks, we guessed it to be an invasion army.

These forces were lined up along a road leading north, directly toward a city called Rikleifer. We believe that city to be in extreme danger from invasion, as the force we saw appeared to be capable of breaking through defensive lines with little effort. Therefore, as soon as we found out, we wrote you this message, with the intent of sending it to you via Wheldon, my lieutenant.

I hope this information has been helpful to you. Sincerely, Sairon, Red Phoenix.

"Kron," began Kevin as he finished the letter, "wake everybody up and bring them down here. I don't care what time it is, just do it."

Silently, Kron nodded and then proceeded to head into the inn. Within a few minutes, everyone was awake and outside, although a little upset at having been woken up so early. Once they were outside and saw Wheldon, however, all could see some reason to be woken up, at least. Although none of them had ever seen a phoenix before, Kevin and Caitlin introduced Wheldon to their group and gave a brief explanation sharing that they had met before. Kevin then passed his letter to Professor Magnon and said, "Take a look at this." Vincent, Arthur, Rachel, and Caitlin all crowded around him, also trying to read the letter at the same time.

As they collectively finished at about the same time, Professor Magnon looked up at Kevin and said, "Oh my. Sounds as though there are lots of innocent lives in danger right now."

"Exactly," nodded Kevin. "Rikleifer is my hometown; I know exactly what's at stake here. I'm going to go back there."

"You cannot be serious!" exclaimed the professor. "What justification do you have for risking your life on the intention of backtracking for your homeland?"

Kevin glared at the professor. "I don't care for your argument," he said, with no doubt in his voice. "Professor Magnon, I am the Vanguard of Aurana. While that title means nothing to you, it means something to the people of Aurana. My hometown and thousands of innocent lives are in danger. How can I just sit idly by while I lose what I stand for?"

"Because you have to," responded the professor, raising his voice some. "You have already unified the lands, save for Scurnia, which is already behind the idea. Now, you need to get Scurnia on board. Aurana will survive without Rikleifer; its troops will fall back and be ready to counterattack when the alliance is set. You have no need to go about risking your life for no absolute gain!"

"Now, wait a moment here," interrupted Vincent as he put his arm in front of Professor Magnon. "What Kevin is saying does have merit, Professor. One cannot be ignorant to those who helped to create him, to those he swore to protect." Professor Magnon looked to be ready to exclaim another response, but Vincent Stryker interrupted him again. "Save your breath, Professor," he said. "That is not the only reason Kevin needs to go back. There is legitimate military strategy behind safeguarding Rikleifer as well. Does anyone have a map?"

Nodding, Kron pulled out a map and gave it to Vincent. Although he wanted to argue, the professor decided to listen to Vincent's military logic.

Vincent unrolled the map in front of everyone and began speaking, "This point right here is Rikleifer. Now, as you can see, several major roads run through it. One leads to Aurana City, another to Wyntrail and the Aurana Protection Forces Supply Acquisition Center, yet another south to Haventown and eventually into Desolunar by way of Atwals, and even more to various points, such as Cornelia in Nuve and along to other towns. It's a key hub. By capturing Rikleifer, one would have access to all of these roads. In other words, in merely a couple of weeks' time after the fall of Rikleifer, Aurana City would be likely to fall as well, and the enemy would likely be able to raid the Supply Acquisition Center for all sorts of raw materials." He paused, as he moved his finger. "Furthermore, take a look to the east. Capturing Rikleifer gives the enemy excellent position to start a two-sided conflict with Nuve, and the enemy's position gives them the advantage to outflank the Nuve forces. Then, Professor Magnon, you have lost two of your three Triple Alliance nations, just on the basis of one city falling."

Professor Magnon looked on in disbelief. Kevin looked at him, frustrated that the professor was still so set on his way. Steadily, it started to come to Kevin that it was possible Professor Magnon had his own agenda, and for whatever reason that was, Kevin could not be sure. So far, he had done everything as the professor had dictated. Now, he really needed the professor's support, and he was not getting that.

Maybe there was another solution.

"Look, if it means that much to you, Professor Magnon, we'll split up," Kevin finally said. "I'll go to Rikleifer and try to help out the best I can there. You, on the other hand, can go to Scurniapolis. You're associated with the government of Aurana, in a way, and can claim yourself as an ambassador. Now, does that sound fair to you?"

Reluctantly, the professor sighed. "I can see that I will not sway your mind on this instance, Kevin, and I cannot stop you. Be warned that I still do not consider this a good idea, and I hope not to hear of your death in Rikleifer. If this is how it is to be, however, then I will carry the message to Scurniapolis on your behalf, and I will bring the papers from *Immortality is a Truth* with me and continue to study them."

Kevin nodded. "Now, then," he said, "it seems we will be splitting up for now. Who wants to go with who?"

Wheldon was the first to step up. "I can probably take three or four people with me to Rikleifer," he said. "It is the fastest way that we can get there."

Immediately, Kron glared at the professor, who was not mentioning that he could teleport the group with his ancient magical technique. It seemed apparent that since he did not support Kevin doing this, he would not help in any way.

"Then I will go to Rikleifer," stepped up Vincent Stryker. "My son, you can probably find some use for my knowledge of military there."

"Good to have you on board, father," said Kevin, very proud in his father's turn around from just the day before.

Arthur turned to Rachel. "I think we had better go to Scurniapolis with the professor," he said. "We'll just be taking up space if we go home to Rikleifer."

Rachel sighed as she pulled up her bow and spun it around a bit. "Do as you will, Arthur," she said. "Unlike you, I actually have respect for my hometown. I'm going with Kevin."

Surprised, Arthur said, "Really?"

Kevin then picked up, "Are you sure, Rachel? This isn't a fight; it's a battle. This isn't going to be an arena; it's going to be a warzone. Of course I'll be risking my life out there, but I don't want to needlessly risk yours, or anyone else's."

Before he could say anymore, however, Rachel started speaking. "I understand that you're looking out for our safety, Kevin," she began. "I can see why you want to keep us out of danger, and as a friend, it shows us all that you care. But the fact remains that just like you, we're human as well, and sometimes we need to get things done, regardless of the danger. You do that everyday with this little journey you've been on, so please understand me when I tell you that we need to be able to do it too."

Rachel had an excellent point, and Kevin could not deny that it made a lot of sense. There was a balance to be reached between protection and freedom, and the more he thought about it, the more Kevin knew that he should not try to impede the freedom of anyone when trying to protect them, no matter how emotional he was about any of them.

He knew what had to be done. "All right, then," Kevin said. "Rachel, you're coming with us."

Rachel nodded with pride.

A smile came to Caitlin's face. "And I'm coming along too," she proclaimed. "You and I are a team. We stick together wherever we have to go."

Kevin smiled and gave Caitlin a nod. That was four. He then said, "Kron, I suppose you have to go with Professor Magnon, then."

"That is fine," nodded Kron. "Best I not get involved in mortal affairs. It should not be public knowledge that I am a god. Whether or not I flew with you four, I would not be any help. "

Kevin acknowledged Kron's comments with a nod.

"Wait a moment," questioned Caitlin. "With us four? Are you suggesting you can fly, too?" She was consciously connecting Kron's comments with the levitation of which she was capable in her angelic form.

"Indeed," acknowledged Kron, "but it is not something I have done in years. Since being trapped in this realm, I have not done so."

"Are you sure you don't want to come?" asked Rachel. "We could probably use someone with that kind of power and ability."

Before Kron could answer, Kevin shook his head. "I won't

make Kron give up his convictions unless it's really necessary. We could use all the help we can get, but I won't ask that of him yet."

Kron nodded. "Thank you," he acknowledged.

"Excuse me," interjected Wheldon, "but how soon can we leave? I really do not mean to be a disturbance here and break you all apart again so quickly, but I would like it if I was not seen by any more humans than all of you. The phoenixes currently live outside of human domains for a reason, and as far away from Avalon as I am now, I wish to observe that unwritten law of our society."

Putting his face in the palm of his hand, Kevin shook his head. That was why he was up at this time of night: Wheldon would not show up in the daylight around human territories. There would be too much risk of being spotted. The best move, and the one that would make Wheldon the most comfortable, would be to leave immediately. However, Kevin knew it would mean a night he and his friends would be deprived of all of the sleep they needed. He looked to Vincent, Caitlin, and Rachel, gesturing to ask if they should leave now. Much to Kevin's surprise, however, all of them agreed.

"I guess we can go right away," Kevin said to Wheldon. "We'll have to make sure we have everything we need before we go, however." Rachel was the only one who took Kevin up on this, going inside to retrieve her bow, quiver, and arrows.

"We will leave in the morning," said the professor, "and we will catch up later. Don't worry about finding us; we'll find you."

Kevin nodded, confident that the professor had this ability. Then, he turned to Arthur. "Good luck, Arthur. It'll be hard not having you out there on the battlefield."

"Meh, don't sweat it," joked Arthur. "Look at it this way: you get to have a little fun while I do your dirty work. Besides, Rikleifer has always meant more to you than it did to me. Go take it back, come back in one piece, and we'll meet up later about it." Arthur reached out his fist.

Bumping his fist with Arthur's, Kevin said. "Thanks. I'll make sure I will."

At this point in time, Rachel walked out of the inn. Wheldon saw this and leaned down, preparing to carry the humans on top of him.

After he indicated that he was ready to go, Kevin, Caitlin, Rachel, and Vincent hopped aboard Wheldon, being forced to crunch up a bit in order to fit on the back of the phoenix. It made for little space on his back if he was to be able to fly.

Kevin, his father, and the ladies all said their final goodbyes as Wheldon began to beat his large wings, slowly beginning to gain altitude. As he made a high amount of altitude, he started to take off to the west, being mindful of his speed and cautious enough not to knock anyone off by mistake. And as he started to disappear from the sight of Vallia, the tall range of the Peaked Mountains quickly obscured the little town. It was now as though it was the horizon of the past, and that the horizon of the future lay to the southwest.

Once they had disappeared from sight, Arthur looked up to where they had disappeared from and said, "Goodbye, my friends, and good luck." It was a serious moment for Arthur, to be parted from his friends again because of his decision.

Professor Magnon then said, "Get some sleep, Arthur. Tomorrow morning, we'll be in Scurniapolis. We still have a job to do ourselves."

"Right," said Arthur. Then, he realized what the professor said. "Wait a moment. What do you mean, tomorrow? There's no way Scurniapolis is that close to here."

"It is not if you walk," responded the professor, "but by teleportation, it is instantaneous, just like anywhere else in the world. I have that power to teleport by creating my own gates, and I can take anyone with me at will."

Arthur scowled. "Then why didn't you take Kevin to Rikleifer?" he said, pointing to the sky in the direction where Wheldon had just flown.

"I have good reason," responded the professor.

Chapter 40

When War Comes Home

As the days and nights passed, Wheldon flew with quickness and stability, having to be extremely cautious as not to knock anyone off. Save for during times to rest, he flew mainly at night under the moonlight, and around as many cities and villages as possible during the day. Wheldon flew for many hours each day, straining himself to make sure that he, along with Kevin and company, arrived in a timely fashion to Rikleifer.

One very long week had passed. Kevin Trent Stryker, ever eager as always to defend his hometown and his homeland of Aurana, simply lacked the patience to remain calm on the long way back to Aurana. It was true that traveling on Wheldon made the trip more than three times shorter in duration, but even so, the wait seemed like an eternity.

Still, there were some pleasant subtleties to this trip. The time had allowed Kevin and his father to reunite better and to learn a little bit more about the histories of one another. Kevin also seized the opportunity to explain the story behind his friends, their histories or at least as much as he knew about them, including Caitlin being an angel. There still was not too much time for Kevin and Caitlin to relax together, since they spent most of their time either in flight or preparing and taking shelter on the ground in order to sleep or escape a thunderstorm. It also meant that with Kevin rushing around with his father and Rachel to help set up these shelters, Caitlin still did not have time to talk with Kevin about the internal issues and hesitations that were still bugging her. They had a few minutes together every now and then during the trip, but not enough for Caitlin to be able to express herself.

On the seventh day after the midday hour, Kevin spotted Rikleifer from the sky. To him, it was home and it would always be home. It had been several weeks since he had been home, but what he saw horrified him. He pointed it out to Caitlin, Rachel, Vincent, and Wheldon. All of them looked out to see a sight that almost appeared to be nightmarish. The City of Dreams, as Rikleifer was sometimes called based on its literal translation of its name from *rengan*, looked like an abandoned metropolis. There was no liveliness to the city, no movement, nothing.

"Looks like the citizens must have fled north," said Kevin, in awe as he looked upon the city. "Let's hope we're not too late."

"We're not," stated Caitlin. "Take a look over there, in the castle in the center of the city. The flag hanging from the pole at the top is a green field with three red triangles all in line horizontally. That's the standard of Aurana still flying, which means that the castle hasn't been taken yet. Even Desolunar is not so cruel as to set a trap by stealing someone else's flag."

"And you're sure of that?" asked Kevin. "We're about two weeks behind the day that message was sent out. We could have missed the entire battle by now."

"Trust me, I know," nodded Caitlin. "If you had an invasion army rip through here, even if it were two weeks ago, there'd probably still be some units outside of the castle. We would see someone from the air."

"Caitlin has a point," added Vincent Stryker. "What makes more sense is that Rikleifer was evacuated and that the remaining forces are inside the castle, preparing for its defense."

Rachel seemed to stare at the walls carefully. "At least the castle has good fortifications," she commented. "Multi-layered, the walls outside the grounds and the secure doors of the inner castle."

Caitlin took note of this comment. "So Rachel, have you been thinking about defending Rikleifer for a time, then?"

"I have," acknowledged Rachel. "Rikleifer has an unofficial civilian all-female defense force here, to defend the city by volunteering a few hours a week, and I was planning on joining soon."

That caught Kevin's attention. "I didn't know you were planning to join," he said. "What kind thing would you be doing with them?"

"Oh, stuff like castle defense," Rachel said. "There's a lot of things the volunteer force does, but one is to stand guard with arrows ready on top of the outer wall. There was one time I remember, in fact, when a criminal gang was in the courtyard and they secured the castle and closed the outer and inner gates. Those guys had nowhere to run and were basically sitting ducks for the volunteers to pick them off, trapped between the outer and inner layers." She paused for a second, realizing she had gone off on a tangent. "I would guess, though, that with this battle being as big as it will be, they were probably evacuated, too."

"That would be my guess," added Kevin. He paused for a moment, thinking. "Very well, then. Wheldon, can you bring us in toward the main gate on the south side of the castle?"

"Certainly," responded Wheldon. "Hang on tight, because you will feel yourself lighten as I descend." As Wheldon finished his sentence, he started to curve downward carefully, still trying not to knock anyone off. Gently and slowly Wheldon descended, going down and down using his wings to control his descent. Kevin and company watched on as he first approached the castle walls, and then floated down to where the castle walls almost appeared to be rising above them.

Carefully, Wheldon then touched the ground and landed softly. He then bent down, allowing Kevin and company to slide off and stand up on their own. After everyone was off safely, Wheldon said, "Good luck to all of you. I must be headed back to Avalon to inform them of my return."

"Very well," said Kevin. "Thank you for your help."

Wheldon nodded, and then began to beat his wings hard, taking off. Once he achieved a standing liftoff above where he had started, he started to fly off to the northwest, in the direction of Avalon. Kevin, Caitlin, Rachel, and Vincent all waved goodbye to the phoenix as he continued to fly. As Wheldon disappeared out of sight, Kevin said, "I don't think there's quite as majestic of a sight as a phoenix flying off into the distance."

"It's certainly a lovely sight," added Rachel. "Suppose that we don't have too much time to think about that, though."

Kevin nodded in acknowledgment, knowing that to wait around would not be a smart move. Turning to the wooden gate in front of the castle in front of him, Kevin looked up toward the garrison above him, not completely sure what to do next. He let out a sigh and said, "So, is it as easy as just knocking on the door?"

"Certainly couldn't hurt," said Vincent in response. "If I remember right, three knocks is usually the Auranian signal for friendly forces. If you're going to knock, Kevin, then knock precisely three times. No more, no less."

Turning to his father, Kevin nodded. Then, he turned back, took a breath, and knocked on the large wooden doors three times. Awkward silence loaded the air for a moment, making Kevin more and more nervous as he had to wait. Caitlin, seeing Kevin nervous, walked up closer to him in an attempt to help reassure him that he was doing the right thing. A moment later, three men called down from the top of the garrison above, "Who is it down there?" shouted one of them. "Rikleifer is under a mandatory evacuation, and all civilians should depart for Aurana City. There is no shelter here."

"I'm not looking for shelter," called back Kevin. "I'm here to contribute to the defense of Rikleifer, and as such, I must speak with whoever is in charge here."

"And who wants to see our commander?" asked back the man who shouted before.

"The name would be Kevin Trent Stryker, Vanguard of Aurana," responded Kevin loudly so the man could hear it.

Surprisingly, there was no response to this from the men. Instead, they turned around and walked off. Kevin was not quite sure what this response meant, only that he was worried it was not good. Another minute later, the large wooden doors of the castle started to swing open, making a loud creaking sound as they swung. Kevin took a step back so as not to be directly in the entrance of the door after it opened up. The door finished opening to reveal an Auranian soldier, dressed in the uniform of the rank of Knight in the Auranian military.

"Honorable Vanguard, what a pleasant surprise for you to show up in Rikleifer today," said the man at attention. "Please, follow me. I will escort you inside to the command center right away."

"Thank you," responded Kevin politely, as he approached the soldier. They started to walk together inward toward the castle, with Caitlin, Rachel, and Vincent.

Within a few seconds, the soldier asked, "Before we continue much further, I must ask you a question of security. Can you personally vouch for all three of the people that you have brought here with you?"

"Indeed, I can," said Kevin. "The two ladies are Auranian citizens, and both have some skill in the arts of battle: one in magic, and one in archery. They are both civilians, however."

The soldier nodded. "Of course. And what of the other man?"

"That's my father," responded Kevin, "and a great war hero, formerly enlisted with Scurnia. His name is Vincent Stryker."

Suddenly, at the sound of that name, the soldier's eyes widened. "You mean, as in *the* Vincent Stryker?"

Vincent stepped up next to the soldier. "As far as I know, I am the only Vincent Stryker there is."

While the soldier had not ever seen Vincent Stryker before, or knew what he looked like, one look at Vincent Stryker's military uniform told everyone before him that he was Vincent Stryker. His faded uniform was colored red, in the same color as the flag of Scurnia, with gold trim all around. No medals were present on his jacket, as Vincent was typically a general in battle and medals usually were difficult to keep on a uniform of someone who battled with his troops, but a large wealth of patches ran across the chest piece and down the sleeves. For every medal Vincent earned, a corresponding ribbon was stitched into the jacket, adding up to almost fifty. By now, the jacket was old and tattered, but it was still a real Scurnian uniform nonetheless.

"Oh my," said the soldier. "I am certain the commanders will be most pleased to hear you are here, Vincent Stryker. Your presence here will be a huge morale boost to the men."

"We will see about that," responded Vincent.

"And speaking of commanders," interrupted Kevin, addressing

the soldier as they together entered the castle building itself, "I have a question for you as well. Who is in charge here today?"

The soldier responded, "The royal leader Edmund Cleary, also known as the Duke of Rikleifer and King Andrew II's uncle, evacuated the city northward when he heard of an incoming invasion. It was confirmed by some of our spies that Desolunar will advance through the front lines to Rikleifer shortly, so King Andrew II called in a large amount of the Auranian military. The head commander here is War Commander 'Ironman' Eukert."

"Eukert's here?" jumped Vincent Stryker. "Gosh, I have not seen my old buddy Eukert in a long, long time. It must have been almost twenty years from now. Who else is here?"

"Well," continued the soldier, "several other officers, including commanders and paladins by rank, make up the rest of the command staff. If you are looking for friends of yours, Vincent Stryker, then I presume that you are looking for the oldest officers, in which case the only other commanding veteran of the previous war here is Knight of Archery John Bryant."

"Bryant's here too," said Vincent. "That is simply amazing. They were my two best friends back in the war twenty years ago, when I was commanding a mixed unit of Auranian and Scurnian forces. Perhaps we will have time to catch up after the battle. We will see what happens."

Nothing more was said for the next minute. The rest of the walk into the castle was silent for the most part. As they walked by, Kevin saw many of the offices that were normally housed in Rikleifer, such as that of the city council, the Duke of Rikleifer's personal office, and other rooms used for the purpose of government. All of them were somewhat familiar, as Kevin had been in the city's central castle before, although only a couple of times.

Then, Kevin and company stopped in front of the door to a large conference room. "This is it," said the soldier as he stopped everyone here. "Wait outside here for a minute, while I clear your visit with the commanders inside."

The soldier opened and walked in the door, closing it behind him. For nearly a minute, all there was, was silence. The door was soundproof, leaking absolutely no sound at all through its cracks. What was going on behind that door was unknown to everyone standing outside of it. Within a minute, the soldier had opened the door again from the other side, leaning out toward Kevin and company. "The Vanguard and the general may enter," he said, holding the door open. "Access is otherwise to be restricted to authorized military personnel."

Disappointed, Caitlin agreed to wait outside. She said a short goodbye to Kevin, and walked down the hallway with Rachel.

Vincent and Kevin then walked through the door. As Kevin walked into the conference room, however, he was overwhelmed by what he saw. Various maps of Rikleifer, of Aurana, and of the world were posted up across the gray stone walls. Several maps of the city were also laid down on the table, with figures representing military units standing up on top of the maps. Behind the table, seven other men wearing Auranian uniforms were discussing procedures at various charts around the room, although most discussion centered on the table maps. When Vincent Stryker stepped into the room, however, everyone suddenly stopped discussing matters. As was usually the case for the old war hero when he entered a room full of generals, Vincent received a large amount of respect. It was one of the chronic events that had driven the regretful Stryker to withdraw from society years before.

Almost as immediately as the silence had begun, War Commander Eukert stepped up and around the table to Vincent, and extended his arm. "Vincent Stryker, old friend, it is really you." Then, Eukert turned to wave over John Bryant, who was standing in the corner of the room. "Where have you been all these years?" he chuckled.

"In a simpler place," laughed Vincent Stryker, as he shook Eukert's hand. He then turned to Bryant. "John, good to see you too."

"The same to you," nodded John Bryant, excited but with a calm demeanor. "So what brings you to Rikleifer today? This isn't exactly the best of times for a reunion."

Vincent stepped aside, and gestured toward Kevin. "He does," said Vincent.

John Bryant looked at Kevin, and saw the Vanguard patches on his jacket. "I know of him, the new Vanguard. Kevin Trent Stryker, was it?"

Kevin nodded. "Yes, it is. Kevin Trent Stryker."

Eukert walked up to Kevin and shook his hand. "I understand from Kron Kalavere that I owe you my life."

"You don't owe me anything," Kevin answered. "Just glad you're alive."

"As am I," nodded Eukert. "How does that sword on your belt work for you?"

"Works well," he said, giving a short answer. "We'll see how much I get to use it tomorrow."

Eukert nodded. "That we will." Then, he turned and yelled out, "Everyone! Let's cut the chatter. We've got to discuss our defense plans for tomorrow."

No one dared to defy the order of the War Commander. At this call, everyone in the room silenced themselves and proceeded to stand around the table, where the map of Rikleifer was sitting. Eukert stood at the table's head, while everyone else wrapped around the sides. After everyone was silent and at the table, Eukert continued, "Now, let's try this again from the top. We have approximately three thousand troops currently here to defend Rikleifer. It was all that we could get together with two weeks' warning, and it does constitute a decent portion of the Auranian military. However, our foes have at least nine thousand on the march toward Rikleifer. Not only are there nine thousand troops, but they are nine thousand well-trained, strong, powerful troops. Because of this disadvantage, our strategy in this battle is paramount. We have the castle, which will be where the battle is centered. We must use its fortifications to our advantage, and at the same time keep it protected. If we lose the castle, men, we lose the battle, and we lose Rikleifer."

Silence filled the air.

"Of course, we also believe that the castle will be of the utmost importance to the Desolunar troops as well, and they will likely advance directly for the castle. Based on what we know of their tactics, their weapon of choice for breaking into the castle would likely involve aligning their troops in a 'diamond' formation. What this formation does is advances a major front unit directly toward the middle of the castle, and after its arrival, slings units that had been holding back behind the front units, around the flanks of the castle in an attempt to provide a surprise flank pincer attack. Lastly, they'll force a final chunk of their troops up the middle to reinforce the front unit. It's a deadly three-pronged tactic, and one that can be used in combination with siege weapons to outmaneuver and surround an enemy in a castle offense situation. Given this tactic, the best option is to engage the troops outside of the castle, on the roads leading in to the city's center across the concentric circles, and to extend our lines out to the edges of the city and keep the flanks there for the inevitable second wave."

That wouldn't work, Kevin thought to himself. He knew the troops here were outnumbered. Simply spreading out would not do if they were outnumbered three to one. A battle scene like this played out in an adventure book he had read once, and even though it was fiction, Kevin felt the author had a good point. Worrying too much about the flanks without a numbers advantage makes the center too weak to hold.

All in that instant, the thought of fighting with a disadvantage had reminded Kevin of his travels so far. Against the foes he was facing, he was fairly certain that nobody would have given him much of a chance, yet he had succeeded. Even when he lost, he and his friends had managed to overcome in each of the little battles that put him as far as he did.

Winning the little battles. Now that was a thought. Rachel had talked about a little battle on the flight into the city, where a volunteer defense force of women soundly defeated a criminal gang that made it into the castle walls, but were locked out of the castle building and from exiting the courtyard. They turned the courtyard into a trap. What if that were done on a larger scale?

Before Eukert could say anymore, Kevin raised his hand and interrupted, "Excuse me, but why would do that? We're outnumbered; playing defense alone won't save us."

Kevin's comment attracted the attention of everyone in the room, who proceeded to stare at the young vanguard. "So, then, Vanguard of Aurana, do you have an idea?" asked Eukert, warily and a little annoyed. "I am sure that all of us would like to hear it."

Vincent Stryker was certainly intrigued to hear what his son had to say. He saw it too.

Immediately, though, Kevin became nervous. "I do," he said with hesitation, realizing he might be in over his head. He began carefully, "All right, so this diamond formation that you described relies on a three-pronged attack, correct?"

"That is correct," nodded Eukert. "It's hard to beat, even when one is aware that that formation is in use."

"So let's not even try to beat it," answered Kevin. "Let's completely throw it off. Tomorrow morning, let us open the castle gates, as if to invite the Desolunar troops in. Their first troop should take this as a sign that we've abandoned the castle, and they will enter themselves. And then, that's when we slam the gates to the castle and ambush them from every angle right there in the castle yard. We'll take the advantage in that 'little battle', and consequently destroy the entire Desolunar strategy."

Chatter started to erupt throughout the command center, bursting from Kevin's comments. It became so loud that War Commander Eukert had to call for silence from the other generals before he could comment himself. While Eukert was still a bit annoyed by Kevin's audacious comment, a confident look from Vincent Stryker changed his annoyance to intrigue. "An interesting idea that our Vanguard presents. Surely it would help to annihilate the front unit of a diamond formation. However, should they win that 'little battle', Vanguard, they will have the castle. Are you willing to bet our castle on this chance?"

Straining, Kevin gripped his hand against his forehead in a moment, trying to be sure of what he was about to say. "I am not a military expert," he said, "but if we don't do something drastic, if things are as desperate as you say, then we won't survive until the next morning. I'm here to defend my hometown, and I'll take chances if it does the job. The question is, will all of you?"

A moment of silence was present in the room. No one said anything.

Kevin was worried. He spoke boldly in the moment, but he knew the dangers of what he said, knowing he did not fully understand them. He had just come up with a radical idea on the fly, but he was sure it was the only idea that would work in the battle ahead. And for him, just like for any other loyal person, when war comes home, keeping home safe instantly becomes the top priority. Whether or not someone is opposed to war, and hates it when their land invades a foreign territory, suddenly those men and women become passionate about protecting their homes and their lives when war comes home.

After the moment of awkward silence, Vincent Stryker spoke out. "I believe that my son is right in this case," he said with strength, making his image all the more respectable. "While it is unlikely, in my opinion, that such a move will win the battle for us by itself, it will provide a swing that we need to push momentum in our direction, should it work. I say, let us try it."

And just that simply, all of the generals and other officers were on board. Hearing this from a highly respected general such as Vincent Stryker, one who was revered worldwide, left little for any general in that room to doubt. Nods came from everyone, displaying their sense of agreement with the elder Vincent Stryker. Looking on at this, Kevin was amazed to see just what kind of respect the Auranian generals had for the long-retired Scurnian war legend. For the first time, he was seeing what his father truly brought him as a partner on his journey, and not just as his estranged father alone. Seeing the agreement in the room, War Commander Eukert nodded and said, "Then it is what shall be done. Now, shall we continue?"

As the generals, including Vincent Stryker, began to discuss matters further on the specifics of troop placement and how to conduct the battle, Kevin pulled up a chair. He then took a seat at the table, struggling to listen attentively. True, it was an important discussion to hear, but as someone with no military experience and little understanding of professional tactics, he found it hard to listen. Shortly, however, Kevin found himself zoning out, simply unable to maintain focus while the many details of strategy were being talked about. His attentiveness had only been able to last so long for him to get out his one idea before the endless complexity and lack of understanding the subject had drained him of his focus. Before Kevin knew it, however, the meeting was over. Unsure of the entirety of what was discussed, Kevin assured himself that he knew as much as he needed to know, and as much as he cared to know, about the battle ahead. Much as Kevin liked having an idea and a plan to follow, he was not here for the purpose of directing a war. He was there to defend his hometown and nothing more.

As Kevin realized that War Commander Eukert was dismissing the generals and advisors, he perked up, realizing the discussion was over. He stood from his chair along with everyone else for the formal dismissal, and then rubbed his eyes, realizing that he had missed most of the talk. Other generals and advisors started to leave, but Vincent Stryker walked up to Kevin and said, "So, my son, was it an interesting discussion for you?"

"For as much of it as I was here for," joked Kevin as he finished rubbing his eyes.

Vincent Stryker chuckled. "Well, I suppose it is something you have to get used to. There are those of us who find military tactics interesting, and those of us who do not. Just because you do not does not make you any less appropriate to be here."

"Never said it did," responded Kevin. "I suppose we'll find out tomorrow just how well this whole thing works."

"Just be advised," strongly interrupted War Commander Eukert, before Vincent Stryker could respond, "nothing in a battle ever works according to plan. I hope you're right about this."

Vincent nodded, knowing well the implications of a battle. "He is. I trust him."

In that brief moment, Kevin truly felt like he had earned the respect of his long-lost father.

He opened the door to the conference room, and exited with Eukert and Kevin following him. By now, Caitlin and Rachel were sitting on the floor against the wall of the room. They both stood up when Kevin and Vincent emerged.

"Now, then," continued Eukert, "I'm sure that all of you would like a place to be put up for the night. All we have left are beds of hay, but you'll do as well as the soldiers with them. Vincent, if you'd like, I can room you with myself and John."

"That will do fine," acknowledged Vincent Stryker.

"Very well," said Eukert. "We only have one room left for you and the two civilians with you to share, in a storage room. It's not much, but it's all we have left after trying to provide rooms to as many of our soldiers as possible for the evening. If you'll all follow me, I can lead you there."

Kevin, Caitlin, and Rachel all acknowledged, knowing that they would need a place to sleep if the battle were to take place the next day.

Eukert nodded in acknowledgment as well, and started to lead everyone else out and down the hallways again. As familiar as Kevin was with the building, he had never been above the first floor before, and that was precisely where he was being led. Still, there was a sense of familiarity among the gray stone walls that Kevin had come to know so well, having lived in Rikleifer for years and seeing the castle every day. The lights were dim in the hallways, as Kevin was surprised to see that nightfall had set in, and that several hours had passed while he had zoned out in the command center.

As he walked through the hallways, Kevin felt more and more passionate about protecting his hometown in the battle ahead. While he had never been to war before, and did have his fears about rushing to the city to do what he was doing, Rikleifer meant enough to him to be worth risking his life. Yet it also made Kevin stop and think for a moment. How much was Rikleifer really worth to him when compared to everything else in his life? Was it worth more than his best friends, including Arthur, Rachel, and even more so, Caitlin, the love of his life? He had forgotten to consider this. Instead, he was so fixated on protecting his hometown and his homeland of Aurana that he had placed it at the forefront of his mind. What kind of friend was he for not placing them first?

Now standing in front of a plain door, War Commander Eukert stopped everyone. "The young Stryker and the two girls, this shall be your room." He opened the door to reveal a small storage area that was emptied out. Two mounds of hay sat on each end of the small room, which was barely large enough for each person to lie down without bumping their heads against the wall in either direction. The tiny room was also on the inside of the building, meaning there was no window and no light source, as the room also contained no candles. "It is late, so I do recommend that all of you get some sleep. We never know how early the enemy will arrive in the morning."

The first to respond, Rachel nodded and said, "Good, I'll take the right side. I haven't had a good night's sleep in over a week, at least." She took her bow and chucked it to the back of the right corner, then took the quiver off of her shoulders and carried it in her hands as she walked in.

Caitlin then walked in as well, without so much as a word.

Then, Kevin turned to Eukert and said, "You will wake us up should we be asleep when the Desolunar forces arrive, correct?"

"Naturally," nodded Eukert. "I hope this stunt of yours works, or else it's going to be a short and bloody skirmish."

Kevin nodded in acknowledgment while taking a deep breath, knowing that if his ambush strategy failed, it would be on him for the loss of Rikleifer, as the one who suggested such a brazen strategy. He then stepped into the room himself, removing his Auranian military jacket and sword as he stepped in.

"Good night to all of you," said the voice of Vincent Stryker into the dark room, as he closed the door, and then proceeded to walk off with Eukert further down the hall.

In the darkness, Kevin settled himself down on the left side of the room. There was absolutely no light to see, but the darkness and the hay made it at least bearable to sleep. "Caitlin?" he called, trying to locate her.

"Right here," said Caitlin, who was lying next to Kevin in the middle of the room, in between the two piles of hay.

"And Rachel?" continued Kevin.

"Over here," echoed Rachel's voice from the other side of the small room, lying on the other stack of hay. She paused for a moment before she continued. "Eukert seemed a bit irritated, didn't he?"

"That's my fault," Kevin answered. "I didn't mean to make him mad, but I may have said something that was out of my place."

"What did you do?" laughed Caitlin.

Reluctant, Kevin answered, "I may have told him how to defend his city."

"And he listened?" asked Rachel. "You didn't say he didn't."

"He did, but I think only because my father agreed with me."

Kevin paused for a second. "Hey, Rachel, I have to give you some credit. You told me about the volunteer defense force fighting off that criminal gang, and it gave me an idea for the city's defense that I pitched to our forces. I think they're going to do it, and try and ambush the Desolunar forces between the castle walls and the castle building."

"Wow, that's awesome!" Rachel said excitedly. "Maybe I'm a military strategist and I never even knew it!"

Kevin and Caitlin laughed with her for a second. Then, Kevin turned serious. "Listen," he continued. "Tomorrow, if we get drawn into the battle, I want us to stay together. The three of us each have a better chance to stay alive if we stick together."

Rachel chuckled a little bit. "Still concerned for our safety as always, huh?"

"Yours and mine," chuckled Kevin back. "Don't think I'm not out there to save my own skin as long as the two of you are safe as well."

"Come to think of it, that would make us quite an interesting team," added Caitlin. "A swordsman, an archer, and a sorceress… I can see a lot of potential in the three of us taking care of business in this battle. We could do a lot of damage if we wanted to, since we can each cover for most of the weaknesses of the other two."

"Except that I'd rather not do that much damage," said Kevin, staring up to the dark ceiling, unable to see it. "I know that I came here to protect Rikleifer, and that can't be done without some loss of life. But when you think about it, the Desolunar forces are no different than us. Yes, they're being ordered to do something heinous, but at their core they're simply people like us who were either ordered to fight or found a reason to fight for their country. Only the commanders and leaders are the really bad people."

Rachel considered this for a moment. "You're right," she said. "Sounds like something back from school in our literature classes, but it does seem to make a lot of sense. So, Kevin, does that mean you have sympathy for those you are going up against tomorrow?"

Kevin nodded, although nobody could see him nod. "Yes, I do," he responded. "Pseudo hurt me to kill anyway despite the fact that he isn't one of these people. But compared to killing someone who is only doing as they are ordered, like the Desolunar troops, I feel sorry for those people. And they do what they do because their leader orders it, and maybe in some cases, because they feel strongly about it themselves."

"That's pretty deep," commented Caitlin. "But it's passion that lets us fight for Aurana, and dragged us over here today. It's got to be even more difficult for the two of you to fight here in your hometown."

"Ah, but that's the beauty of it," Rachel said. "When you fight in your hometown, you're familiar with every part and every area around you. Furthermore, though, you're fighting for a town or a city that, unless you despise it, is greater than any other city of your dreams."

"Which in itself makes this awkward, since Rikleifer is the 'City of Dreams'," chuckled Kevin, making a play off of the city's nickname.

Caitlin chuckled as well. "Interesting," she said.

"Sure doesn't seem that way now, though," commented Rachel. "As frightening as it is to see a ghost town, or even a ghost city, it's much worse when that town or city is your hometown. When we flew over, I had to reach down and secure myself to Wheldon tighter just to keep myself from falling off in stun from the sight."

"I see," said Caitlin, reaffirming her curiosity. "I don't really have a hometown, as much as Aurana is my homeland, but I guess I would say if I saw such a thing happen to Wyntrail, where I was born and where my father lives, I think I might react the same way. It does seem like a scary sight for anyone."

Rachel tossed and turned a bit in her bed of hay. "You don't know it until you see it, though, Caitlin," she said. "And Kevin and I saw that today. And as much as Arthur Falchor is not as big into Rikleifer as Kevin and I are, I'm sure he would sense that amount of shock as well if he saw that sight."

"He must be the lucky one tonight," added Kevin. "He gets to do some boring work in Scurniapolis while we get to play the 'try not to die' game tomorrow."

"Yeah, whatever," said Rachel as she tossed over again, turning toward the wall. "We'll all listen to him complain about it later. In the meantime, I'm going to sleep. Goodnight, you two."

Though neither Kevin nor Caitlin could see Rachel in the small dark room, after a few minutes of silence and some heavier breathing coming from Rachel's side of the room, both had assumed that she did actually fall asleep. It was very quiet in the room, as the conversation had stopped. Kevin was still looking up at the ceiling, in thought. Then, as he listened, he heard Caitlin moving around some hay next to him. She was still lying in between the two bunches of hay, with no soft bed, and was trying to gather some hay in between Kevin and Rachel's stacks for a pillow.

What was he doing? Kevin could not believe he had not even thought about being nice to Caitlin and sharing his stack of hay with her. Had he really become that ignorant of Caitlin while his mind was off with the thoughts of his duties preoccupied him?

Well, he was not about to allow that to continue. Seizing the opportunity, Kevin reached over while Caitlin was scooping hay and grabbed her by the hand in the dark. Then, he pulled gently on her arm, signaling for her to move toward him.

As she pulled herself up a bit, Kevin pulled Caitlin closer to him, helping her to find a space next to him on the pile of hay. Caitlin settled into the hay, and then felt around with her own hands until she found Kevin's face, trying not to hurt him while doing so. Then, she leaned over close to where his ear was, and whispered, "What is it, Kevin?"

"Nothing," whispered Kevin. "I just thought that it would be awful cruel of me not to offer you a spot on the pile of hay, that's all."

"Well, you didn't have to mind if you didn't want to," responded Caitlin. "I'm all right with sleeping over there if you'd prefer."

"Don't be ridiculous," whispered back Kevin. "It's cold on the floor, and it's not comfortable at all. We can share some space, or if you're not comfortable with that, I'll move to the thin space on the floor."

Before Caitlin could respond, however, the divisions and hesitations within herself were happening again. She could feel them trying to part her away from Kevin, in the worst way possible, exactly the way she feared. Mentally, she could feel herself being torn apart. Something felt like it was tearing her away, as much as she only wanted to press herself closer to Kevin. Trying to say something after the short pause caused by her splitting, Caitlin began, “That’s sweet of you, Kevin. I… I…”

And she could not say it. Caitlin just could not bring to Kevin her troubles within her mind. As much as she tried, she was afraid to. She nearly broke out in tears, unable to talk about it.

“You what?” asked Kevin.

Caitlin shrugged, restored her smile, and held Kevin tightly. “It’s nothing,” she said delicately. “Never mind.” While Caitlin could not bring herself to tell Kevin just yet about her parting personality, she still felt comfort in being close to Kevin.

Together, Kevin and Caitlin fell asleep, finding a great amount of comfort from each other’s presence. And on a night before what would be for certain an eventful and deadly day, nothing could be better to prepare both of them for it.

Yet there was also a great amount of anxiety about the day to come. By all statistical likeliness, at least one, and possibly all three of them, would likely die in the middle of the bloodshed, especially since none of the three had ever fought in a large-scale conflict before. And against a merciless foe, with numbers, with strategy, and with a strong desire by its leader to seek their death, such a fate seemed imminent, if only as an afterthought.

Chapter 41

The Sound of Drums

The skies were lit up in apocalyptic thunder, spreading light across a darkened sky. The world was tearing itself apart in the wake of the chaos that had just ensued… an aftermath foreshadowing the end of a long journey that would change the world forever. The end was coming.

It was an ominous sight among the skies of lightning and the ruined city surrounding, but it was a sign of the final battle to come. Fires burned all around, some from the burning buildings of the city and some from the troops, relaxing in victory. In front of a tall white temple, larger than any building around within the ruined city, the angel Caitlin Magnon stood watching the temple, dressed in her white traveling dress with the red trim.

By now, it was an all too familiar sight.

Before any of the events could progress, Caitlin called out, "Show yourself, Amelia! I know you're here, and I know what you're trying to tell me."

"Very good," said an emotionless voice from behind her. "You remember this nightmare well. I am glad to see that you have retained this memory for the past two and a half weeks."

Responding to this voice, Caitlin flipped around to see the ever-familiar sight of herself, dressed in her old black dress that she had worn before she and Kevin had reached Nuvenia. The face was her own, and so was the long and straight red hair, but it showed no emotion whatsoever. It was the identity of the personality that had identified herself as "Amelia", which was Caitlin's middle name.

Amelia raised her hand and snapped her fingers, blanking out the scenery. "Now, then, you have a good memory of what I wanted you to remember, so my part of this dream is done. Now, it's your turn. I sense that you have something that you want to ask me."

"More than one thing," Caitlin rolled her eyes. "What part do you have in this internal conflict that I've been feeling?"

"So you are bothered by it?" asked Amelia, emotionless.

"Yes!" answered Caitlin, very frustrated. "It hurts me every day. I love Kevin, but now I am finding myself being nagged and pulled back inside. And every day, it feels like it's more and more difficult to push through it."

Nodding, Amelia said, "I see. I wish I could tell you that I know everything and that I can fix it, but I cannot."

Caitlin shook her head in frustration, her face in her hands. "That doesn't make any sense," she said. "Is it because you are responsible for it that you can't fix it?"

"Indirectly, yes," nodded Amelia. "I represent the side of you that believes in your strength and your accomplishments. You fear that by having emotions, and the life that will follow, you will lose what made you strong, and your mind is struggling to reconcile that."

"I still don't think I get what you meant by that," interrupted Caitlin, confused. "Nor do I get why you know all of this while I don't. In fact, I'm still a little unsure who you even are."

Amelia lowered her head. "A mind is complex, but it's only natural that uncertainty about the future creates hesitation." Then, Amelia bolted her head up. "You see me because you struggle to see both the strong side and the sensitive side of yourself as the same person. You are at a crossroads, and a deep conversation with the person responsible is inevitable."

Sighing, Caitlin said, "I hope that's not really the case. It shouldn't need to be. It should be so much simpler than that."

"Yet it never is." Then, Amelia looked up and observed the lighting above for a moment. She raised her right hand, and said, "We're out of time. Just remember what I told you last time; in a dangerous situation, don't get separated from Kevin if you want him to live." Then, she snapped her fingers.

At once, Caitlin's eyes popped open, into the darkness of the room with no light. Once again, her encounter with Amelia had all been a dream. She rolled over and fell asleep again, not thinking about the battle to come.

Several hours later, a furious knocking on the door blasted a loud sound throughout the tiny room. From the other side of the door, the voice of Vincent Stryker was screaming, "Kevin! Caitlin! Rachel! It's time to get up! The Desolunar forces are marching toward Rikleifer and will be here within the matter of an hour!"

The first to sit up, Rachel rubbed her eyes, and reached behind herself in the dark to grab her bow and quiver full of arrows. Then, she said aloud, still tired, "Hey, Kevin, Caitlin, are the two of you up yet?"

From the other side of the room, the voice of Caitlin said, still very tired and lacking energy, "I woke up as soon as I heard the knocking. I don't think Kevin is, though."

"Well, you had better wake him," responded Rachel. "It sounds like it's time for action. We don't have any time to spare."

Nodding, although also knowing that Rachel could not see her nod in the dark, Caitlin turned and tapped Kevin on the side of his face. "Kevin," she said, "you have to wake up now. It's time for us to go."

In response, Kevin's eyes struggled to crack open. He started to shuffle around a bit, reaching for his jacket, his sword, and his Nuve stealth bracer that he had removed the night before in order to sleep more comfortably. "Figures it would be so early that we'd have to start this off," he said, as he tried to gather himself together. "Anyone know what time it is?"

"No clue," answered Caitlin, "but it's time for the battle. Your father came by and knocked, saying they'd be here in less than an hour."

"Guess we'll find out here shortly enough," said Kevin, as he strapped his sword to his belt and opened the door, letting in some light. "Is one of you two ready enough to head out there ahead of us and secure us a spot on the garrison over the south gate? I think it's our safest place to watch that isn't inside the castle building."

"I'll do it," answered Rachel immediately, as she slung her quiver around her shoulder. I'll get you guys up to speed about how the ambush is being set up once you guys are up there with me."

"Great," responded Kevin. "But before you go, hold on for a second."

Rachel looked up at Kevin, curious by the request. Kevin then signaled to Caitlin as he took a couple of steps closer to Rachel. Caitlin followed suit as well, stepping close to Rachel.

"Rachel," began Kevin, starting to get a little soft but holding strong, "be safe out there. If at any point we get separated, I want you to know how much I appreciate your friendship and your help."

Closing her eyes with a slight smile, Rachel responded, "And thank you, Kevin, for being a real friend," she said. Then, Rachel detached and reached over to hug Caitlin. "Thank you for being a real friend, too."

Caitlin reached back and hugged Rachel. "I hope we'll always be friends, for a long time to come."

"We will," said Rachel, still holding on to Caitlin. "I promise you, we will." Then, wanting to hurry, Rachel let go of Caitlin, grabbed her bow tighter, and ran out of the room and down the hall toward the south side of the castle.

After a few seconds, Caitlin turned back to Kevin as he fastened up his Nuve stealth bracer. "You've just got a way with words, don't you?" she asked.

Kevin pulled the last strap tight on his bracer when he started stepping closer to Caitlin. "You could say that," he joked, "but I didn't forget you, either." He gently put his arms around Caitlin, causing her to start hugging him tightly. "One, or maybe both of us could die out there today." Kevin started to tear up a little bit, saddened by the thought. "And if that happens to be the case, I just want you to know that…"

Before Kevin could finish his statement, Caitlin interrupted him by grabbing him lightly by the side of the head, pulled him in, and kissed him. It lasted for a few seconds before they both released, and Kevin finished his sentence, "I love you."

"I love you too," smiled Caitlin.

As she said the words, the hesitations kicked in again. She had thought she had rid herself of them by talking to her Amelia personality. She believed that talking to Amelia would have relieved her resistances, if Amelia's theories were correct.

No. Amelia was wrong.

Suddenly, throughout the castle echoed a large thumping sound.

It was very rhythmic and bounced around the gray stone walls of the hallways. Both Kevin and Caitlin knew exactly what it was.

"War drums," said Kevin. "They're within sight of the castle. The battle is set to begin within a few minutes."

Caitlin sighed, and had to forget about it for now. Now was the time for more important affairs. The sound of drums was an indicator of events to come, and both Kevin and Caitlin knew it. Almost as if responding to the call, they instantly started rushing down the hallways toward the southern gate, making no waste of time as they hustled down the straights and slid around the corners.

"Tell me again, Kevin," began Caitlin as they kept running down the hall, "why would they sound the war drums if they're planning an ambush? Wouldn't that alert the approaching Desolunar troops as well?"

"It would if they sounded the drums outside," answered Kevin, "but I doubt they did since they have so many people outside and could easily tell them without the drums. They probably sounded one inside the building here to let everyone inside know it's time, and let it bounce around."

"Oh," said Caitlin. "That's a pretty unique idea. Still means we have to be in a hurry to get out of here."

Kevin nodded. "Yes it does." He flipped up the end of his stealth bracer, checking to see that there was indeed at least one dart in there, like Raijin Shane had told him there would be. He had not yet used the bracer for the purpose of shooting a dart from its hidden compartment, but in battle, Kevin was not sure if he would have to use it or not. "After we round the next corner to the left, we'll be outside, so get ready," said Kevin, panting. He drew his sword. They rounded the corner and bolted straight for the door, still hurrying as quickly as they could.

Quickly, they burst out of the wooden doors into the castle, arriving in the yard on the south end, with the main gate in front of them. Once in the yard, neither Kevin nor Caitlin stopped as they continued to hurry to the stairs around the sides of the gate, leading to the garrison above. At the top, they finally stopped to catch their breath, and as neither was very athletic, both were winded and breathing heavily. Waiting for them on the garrison were Rachel, War Commander Eukert, Knight of Archery John Bryant, Vincent Stryker, and a couple of other commanders of the Aurana military.

The sun was just cracking over the edge of the eastern sky, creating a cascade of blues, purples and reds across the sky while an orange light glowed to the east. "You made it just in time," said Vincent Stryker as the two young adults tried to catch their breath. "Rachel told us in advance that you were on your way, but we did not honestly expect the attack to come this early. We are fortunate that we are already set."

Still breathing heavily, Kevin struggled to say, "They're here, then?"

Nodding, War Commander Eukert answered by extending his arm in the south direction, across the garrison's battlements. "Take a look," he said.

Bent over and still trying to catch his breath, Kevin took a couple of awkward steps over toward the battlements, and leaned out toward the south. At the edge of Rikleifer, Kevin could make out the shapes of marching men in rank and file, dressed in the black uniforms of Desolunar soldiers. Some light gold trim on the uniforms of the officers highlighted them from the remaining soldiers.

"That's just their first units," continued War Commander Eukert. "Approximately three thousand of their troops are armed in that first set of units alone, or a third of their estimated force. Now, while you cannot see them yet, there are two more groups of units, totaling another third, to the southwest and to the southeast. Those are the flanking units, or the second wave of the diamond formation we talked about yesterday. Beyond the first units, still out of sight, are the third units, comprised of the last third, who will reinforce the center after the flanks have entered and caused distraction."

Kevin took another heavy breath. "Tough tactic, huh?"

"Very," nodded Eukert. "We hope your strategy works to make it less difficult, but if it doesn't, and we end up undermined by the unit we're trying to ambush, then we've already lost the battle."

"Is that even possible?" asked Caitlin as she stepped closer to the battlements. "I don't know much about war either, but I would think that ambushing someone would provide you a gigantic advantage."

"Oh, it does," acknowledged War Commander Eukert, "but until you have seen the sight of these troops in action that we are facing, you won't think any differently. A couple of months ago, I had a unit of five hundred men south of Aurana Protection Forces Post 3, on what was at the time the unofficial border with Desolunar. We had an ambush set up, but they saw through it before we could spring it. We were demolished. I suffered a nearly fatal injury myself in that fight."

Suddenly, Kevin and Caitlin's eyes widened as they looked at one another. They realized that the defeat Eukert had just described was the exact same one that they had seen the aftermath of around the time they had first met. What both of them had seen was an absolute massacre of the Auranian forces. These thoughts were a hard dose of reality that the upcoming ambush would not be a guaranteed success, especially with the memory of the men who had sacrificed their lives for Aurana in that area, and seeing them with their own eyes.

"We do have a good setup," added John Bryant. "Take a look around. We have troops placed around the other end of the circular castle yard, ready to bolt around the other side in a full-on charge as soon as the Desolunar troops have entered. We have archers placed at all of the battlements around the castle, and at first they will face inside toward the castle yard before shifting to the outside after the ambush is done. And," he said as he pointed downward to a trap door in the bottom of the garrison, "we have two men in the gate room that will close the doors as soon as the Desolunar forces enter, isolating them from retreat."

Bryant was silenced, however, by the sound of war drums and rhythmic footsteps a short distance to the south. The Desolunar units were advancing closer and closer. At the sound of this, War Commander Eukert gestured down with his hands, signaling for everyone on the garrison and along the walls to duck below the battlements. Kevin, Caitlin, and Rachel snapped down against the same wall, as Eukert and Vincent Stryker ducked next to them, and John Bryant ducked next to the trap door in the garrison floor.

"We're about to see if your strategy works, my son," said

Vincent quietly, trying not to make much noise. "Let's see what happens."

Chapter 42

The Battle of Middle Aurana

Kevin nodded, and then proceeded to peek out between a couple of the battlements facing in to the castle yard. Closely and carefully he was watching, waiting for the inevitable. Next to him, Caitlin held his hand tightly, hoping to reassure the young Vanguard of Aurana that his decision was the right one.

Was it the right move to come back to Rikleifer, endangering his life as well as that of his friends and family to try and make a difference in his hometown? Was it a good decision to suggest a risky ambush to try and reduce the massive three to one advantage the Desolunar forces had? Those answers, Kevin was soon to find out. What was to come was a battle for Rikleifer, for the province of Middle Aurana, for the great nation of Aurana, and ultimately one for the entire mortal realm. At this sunrise, the battle of Middle Aurana was about to begin.

Listening closely, all in the castle heard the thundering footsteps of Desolunar troops as they passed through the doors and into the castle yard. It was almost as if they had not stopped at all to question why the doors to a foe's castle were open. Patiently, Kevin peeked out over the edge of the battlement, watching as the Desolunar forces marched in. This was the worst part of the ambush: waiting and watching as he let them enter the castle. Slowly, the Desolunar forces marched in rank by rank, flooding the inner yard of the castle. Rhythmically, they continued to march, still unfazed by the open castle door. Kevin started to bite his fingernails, worried that if the Desolunar troops were not asking questions about the opening, they would not be bitten by the ambush.

As the last of the front units moved in, Vincent Stryker gave a hand signal to John Bryant, who knocked twice on the trap door below. A second after he did, the workmen inside the gate control room below tugged hard on the pulleys inside, slamming the doors behind the Desolunar troops. Several troops at the rear turned around in surprise when the door slammed, giving Kevin a glimmer of hope that maybe the Desolunar forces would be disrupted heavily after all.

It was a chance, at least.

After the doors had closed, War Commander Eukert snapped his fingers, which was the command for a bugler to blow out a command to war from the garrison. The sound of the horn caught the attention of all of the Desolunar forces in the castle, just before they were taken by surprise.

At the sound of the bugle, archers stood up from behind the battlements of the castle walls. Thousands of Auranian troops, numbering all three thousand between the ground forces and the archers, quickly struck hard into the Desolunar front units. The ground forces attacked from both the east and west sides of the castle, charging with a sound similar to the thunder from the heavens.

Kevin drew his sword, preparing for battle. He was set to start running down to assist the ambushing forces, when Vincent Stryker extended his arm in front of Kevin. "Not yet, son," he said. "The men are doing their job. Be patient so we can do ours."

Frustrated that there was nothing he could do at the moment, but also knowing that Vincent Stryker was right, Kevin sheathed his sword. There was no point in jumping into the fight so early when the ambush forces were engaging with the advantage already.

Several minutes later of watching the battle inside, the Desolunar forces began to show weakness as their unit was pressed together without room to move at the south gate. Many of them were starting to back down, and the Auranian forces were holding their own. Surprisingly, it looked like Kevin's strategy of an ambush attack was working. The Auranian forces had the advantage of the castle fortifications and the ambush, which was proving more and more to be very effective.

Within an hour, much of the Desolunar forces had been stripped away by the ambush offensive. Outnumbered and low on morale, the officers were beginning to surrender to the Auranians.

It was an overrun. An absolute rout.

Aurana had won its first ever victory over Desolunar, although it was not yet a victory of the entire battle.

Seeing the most decorated officer surrender his men, Kevin turned to War Commander Eukert, who said, "It looks like it's worked out after all. You were right, Kevin. We won the small battle with your strategy."

Eukert nodded, and started speaking before Kevin could. "Indeed, but the true battle is yet to come." Then, without skipping a beat, he leaned out over the battlements of the garrison and shouted inward toward his own officers, "Disarm their men, and lead them inside the castle. Post guards all around to make sure they do not revolt inside the castle. We will discuss their surrender later after the battle is done."

Abiding by these instructions, the men on the ground began to pull the weapons of the Desolunar soldiers from them. Non-soldier workmen, people who were unable to perform military duty, proceeded to remove the dead bodies from the castle yard and move them inside to be buried after the battle. The whole process of arresting the enemy combatants and processing the yard took at least an hour, during which Kevin and Rachel watched from the wall at the military precision of the operation. It was almost heartbreaking in itself to watch, with Kevin fully believing the conquering darkness of Demonicus was not fully in the hearts of the people of Desolunar, nor all of its soldiers.

As the cleanup was being finished up, War Commander Eukert redirected himself to look out upon the southern horizon, toward where the Desolunar forces were advancing. He was scoping out the sight with binoculars. Curious about what was up, Kevin, Caitlin, Rachel, Vincent Stryker, and John Bryant all followed suit, curious as to what the war commander was thinking. "What's on your mind, Eukert?" asked John Bryant after a moment of silence from all.

"They have a backup plan," Eukert said after a pause, staring off toward the massing splotches of black in the distance. "They always do. We took away a third of their force, but now they have twice what we captured forming up outside the wall, and our numbers are lower as well."

Vincent looked over at Eukert. "Think they know about the loss of the front units?" he asked.

Taking a breath, Eukert said, "I do," as he passed the binoculars to Vincent. "Look out there. Their units are reforming from the two flank units and the rear reinforcements into a V formation, probably to wrap all the way around. They are cycling out of the diamond formation into something different."

Confused, Rachel looked over at Eukert. "How can you tell?" she asked.

"Those black spots you can see out there are from the uniforms of the Desolunar troops," responded Eukert as he pointed to the south. "Earlier, they were divided and thicker in their spots. Now, the black coloring is not as thick, but more spread along the south. They have us fairly well surrounded by now, from the south, all the way over between due southeast and due southwest."

"So how do they know?" asked Kevin. "I didn't see a messenger run out, or any birds or anything like that. How would a message from here get carried that far out? You can't exactly shout that difference."

"Yeah, that's something, isn't it?' responded John Bryant, pushing himself up from the edge. "I'll admit, I haven't been back with the Aurana military for very long, just since a couple of days after you and your traveling companion left Haventown. But let me tell you, in that short amount of time I've seen these soldiers of Desolunar have frightening abilities. Who knows, maybe some of them can send messages to each other using their minds, or something like that. Could be anything they've developed, for all we know."

Caitlin looked over at Kevin, and said mentally as she had done before, *You don't think there are spellcasters here who have the strength in mind magic to do this, do you?*

Well, you're the expert on magic here, and not me. But I wouldn't be surprised if Demonicus's forces contain several spellcasters, since he is that crafty.

That's what I was afraid of. Someone's got to be sending mental signals to the forces outside, telling them of their surrender.

If that's the case, then we're going to have to be extremely cautious. They're strong in magic as well as in the physical forces. When the next wave comes in, chances are we'll be down there to help, so stay close to me, okay? I'll especially need your help if we run into one of these people.

All right. I'll keep my eyes open. Get ready; it probably won't be long until we're up again.

"Looks like they want to press their way in," said Vincent Stryker, as he passed the binoculars back to Eukert. Naturally, as he had been unable to hear Kevin and Caitlin's discussion between their minds, he continued on after a slight pause. "But with what?"

"With whatever they have," stated John Bryant.

Nodding, Eukert took the binoculars and looked through them toward the south. "They look to be pretty well organized already," he said. Then, he found what he was looking for. "Ah, there they are," he said. "A couple of rams. The perfect, yet expensive, pieces of weaponry for besieging and breaking into a castle."

"It's still not much though," began Vincent Stryker, "without at least one…"

"Catapult!" exclaimed Eukert, suddenly. "Bearing due south! It's launching right now!" Eukert then pulled the binoculars away from his eyes, turned into the castle, and screamed, "Incoming!"

Quickly, everyone on the garrison crouched below the battlements. Caitlin pulled hard down on Kevin to make sure he was low enough. In less than a couple of seconds, the boulder fired from the catapult soared over their heads, into the top of the castle building, and down the side of the castle as it did not have the momentum to break through. On the floor of the garrison, Vincent Stryker looked up past the battlements, examined the damage, and said, "That was a warning shot. It was too far away, and its ammunition too light, to cause any real damage."

Still crouching, Eukert started barking, "If that catapult gets any closer to the castle, it will knock pieces off of it with a heavier payload, and I guarantee they have one. If it gets too close, it could destroy part of the wall. We have to engage them outside of the castle. There's no choice now."

Everyone stared blankly in awe, knowing that this was true but dumbfounded by the action that had to be taken. Leaving the fortifications of the castle would increase their chances of death.

"Can you hit that, Caitlin?" asked Rachel. "Maybe light the catapult on fire or something?"

"No, it's too far away," Caitlin shrugged. "Even if it gets closer, it'll probably be in range with its heavier payload before I'm close enough to light it up."

Sighing, Kevin had an idea. He tried to sound confident. "Then I'll go," he said. "Send me out there with the men. We'll go for the catapult, and I can cut it apart with the Sword of Purity. It cut through a solid rock cliff face a little over a week ago. I'm sure it can cut through a catapult."

Vincent said nothing, but simply listened.

"Are you sure you want to do this?" asked War Commander Eukert.

"Absolutely," nodded Kevin. "Me standing around here does nothing for Rikleifer. That's not what I came here to do. Even if it means risking my life, I'd rather do that than see my hometown crumble."

Silently, Eukert nodded. "Very well," he said. "As long as you're sure, then it shall be, and there shall be no complaints."

The other officers acknowledged this. Then, Caitlin walked over to Kevin and said to everyone, "Trust me, he's sure."

Seeing this, Eukert stepped forward to the end of the garrison facing in to the castle. "Form up!" he called. "Organize in rank and file under your senior officers! The Vanguard will be leading a charge!" And at the call of Eukert, his orders were carried out in quick speed.

Ready to take his part in the battle as well, Kevin gripped the handle of his sword tightly, drew it, and started racing down the stairs. Without skipping a beat, Caitlin immediately followed suit. Seeing them both run down the stairs, surprised, Rachel picked up her bow and started following them, saying, "Hey! Wait up!" Kevin did not stop, however, until he was standing in front of the wooden doors underneath the garrison. He stopped there, breathing heavily as he stood waiting for the doors to open. Then, for the very first time since he received it,

Kevin fastened up his green Auranian vanguard jacket, securing it around his body and covering up his red shirt completely. He wanted to make sure that if he was wounded, he would be spotted by Caitlin and she would be able to heal him if necessary.

Caitlin and Rachel took positions behind Kevin, putting the three of them in the shape of a triangle where they stood. After a second of catching his breath, Kevin said, "Stay close to me, girls. Make sure we don't get separated."

"I understand, Kevin," nodded Rachel, "although you've said it several times over by now. Are you really that afraid for us?"

Shaking his head while still breathing heavily, Kevin responded, "I'm afraid for your safety. I'm afraid for Caitlin's safety. And I'm afraid for my life, too. What will happen today once we get out there, no one knows. I guess we'll find out soon enough." Standing there in front of the door, Kevin was scared out of his mind. As much as he wanted to do this, and fight for his country like what he came for, there was much to fear in the upcoming battle. Death, the loss of Caitlin or Rachel, the failure of his efforts to stop the conquest of the realms… all of these potential consequences put pressure on his mind.

Caitlin saw this within Kevin as she saw him standing and breathing heavily, almost as if he was in panic. She felt a little sorry for the young Vanguard of Aurana, knowing that his mind was constantly weighted with his decisions and difficulties, but now was unfortunately not the time for her to be able to help console him. She would have to focus on using her magic to support him in combat. And she knew she had to stay close to him, to protect him. Messages from Amelia resonated in her mind.

Contrary to what Caitlin was focused on, however, Rachel felt frustrated and scared within herself with what was coming forward. In many ways like Kevin, Rachel started to become concerned that she had made the wrong decision to come along as well. Furthermore, as an archer, she was not accustomed to being a "melee archer", or someone who fights with a bow and arrows in close-range combat, which involves quicker shots with more arrows. She was used to the traditional role of an archer: long distance shots from a safe place where she could take more time to aim. Something new, perhaps more dangerous than anything ever experienced before, lied just beyond those wooden doors.

Within a few minutes, the Auranian military units had formed up behind Kevin, and were ready to attack. The troops that remained were formed up at three gates of the castle: the south, the west, and the east. They were as ready as they could be to deal with the Desolunar V formation with their siege weapons. The doors slowly began to open as the men in the control rooms opened the doors. As the doors slowly cracked open, however, Eukert called down, "Remember to target their siege weapons. If the catapult gets closer, it can damage the castle and its walls, and getting the rams against the walls will allow their forces direct entrance into the castle. The catapult is by far the most dangerous target and should be your first priority."

In response, the soldiers below raised their swords, pikes, spears, and other weapons, a common symbol of command acknowledgment among large military units.

Then, the large doors started to open wider. "Good luck to all of you, and stay safe out there," called down Vincent. He then turned toward the castle walls, and turning in between them as he issued the next command, he ordered, "Archers, cover our men and protect the gates of the castle. Take precise and careful aim if our men are nearby."

At last, the doors opened with a thud, and the objective was clear. Visible straight down the road was a large splotch of black, colors of the large amount of Desolunar black military uniforms. Now, it did not matter who they were to Kevin. They were the enemy, the ones that threatened his hometown of Rikleifer, and the ones that had to be stopped at any cost.

With a thunderous scream of "Charge!", Kevin raised his sword and led the Auranian troops in a rush toward the Desolunar troops in the middle of their V formation, where most of their siege weapons were centered. The Auranian military thundered loudly as they plunged hard and fearlessly into the Desolunar forces.

Quickly, Kevin made his first couple of strikes in fury at anything wearing black. He moved nimbly and accurately, making use of that swordsman skill to pick on the weaknesses of each enemy in front of him. Covering his sides and rear were Caitlin and Rachel, sticking closely to him as Kevin had asked. Caitlin was fighting hard with darkness magic, using its manipulating abilities to strike several enemies at once, while Rachel had to pick up on using her arrows quickly and conservatively. Struggling to execute melee archery, however, she often found herself being covered by Caitlin.

Furiously, Kevin swung right, then left, then right again, keeping his awareness high and making sure he did not end up surrounded. All of the shame he had for defeating Desolunar soldiers did not matter now. All that did matter was keeping his friends alive, keeping himself alive, and keeping his hometown safe. Behind him, Kevin's unit of Auranian forces was making little progress against the Desolunar front lines, but were holding their own as they pushed back.

A few minutes into the battle, a glimmer of reflected light off of the metal pieces of a nearby siege ramp caught Kevin's eye amongst the battling troops. He had to get over there and destroy it as soon as possible, lest it be used against the castle. Moving quickly, Kevin started working his way there, being cautious as to not let himself be struck on his way over. He threw up a couple of defensive blocks, trying not to get too tangled into a fight. When he made it about halfway toward the ram, he yelled out, "Cover me!" to Caitlin and Rachel, directing them to help him cut his way over there.

Rachel kept Caitlin from being harmed by using her bow while Caitlin took careful aim and shot blasts of ice, making sure not to hit Kevin with any shot. While she did, Kevin ran straight for the ram, his sword raised and fully energized, lit up in its bright blue magic. This was no time to be shy about the sword's divine power. Just as he reached the ram itself, the men rolling the ramp along the ground leaped away in fear as Kevin smashed his sword into the wooden ram's front wheel.

The sword's energy sliced off the wheel, causing it to collapse and be rendered useless. Kevin did not have a second to relax, however, as he had to go straight back on the defensive, making sure he did not get himself into trouble. He then worked his way back to regroup with Caitlin and Rachel, being cautious again not to get himself too caught up.

Desolunar's officers were not difficult to spot, as all of them wore gold trim on their black uniforms. But, after almost a half hour of fighting on, Kevin could not manage to achieve his goal of working his way to one of them and slaying them. He had hoped that he could work his way over to any one of them with his sword, but it seemed as though the red and black Vanguard triangle patch on his sleeves made him a target to all of the troops around him as someone to go after. This fight was exhausting, and already Kevin was feeling worn out.

In a clearing for a brief second, Kevin took a look around and saw that the Desolunar forces in the center where he was were starting to wrap around the outnumbered Auranian forces. Though Kevin was no military expert, he did know that where his forces were was now a dangerous spot. They were close to being surrounded on all sides.

"Pull back!" commanded Kevin, taking the reins of leadership. "Move back to the next ring and set up defenses there!"

Fortunately, Aurana's officers had recognized the same situation and were already working their men back. Slowly, the Auranian forces began to fall back one ring along the roads that ran across Rikleifer to attempt to escape being surrounded. They kept fighting the whole way back, being cautious as not to be outflanked in the middle.

The fight kept pressing on, and as much as Kevin wanted to make a press toward the officers, he could not advance because of all of the troops he had to worry about, and having to protect Caitlin and Rachel out on the battlefield as well. So far, he had had to cover Caitlin a couple of times, and Rachel several more times, but in return they had made sure he was not blindsided as well. Caitlin covered for him multiple times, more than he had covered for her.

Unfortunately for Kevin, he had his objectives all wrong. The strategic step back protected Auranian lives for now, but lost sight of the reason they were there to begin with. And he did not realize it until it was too late. Seeing it for herself before Kevin even had a faint memory of it, Caitlin exclaimed, "Kevin! The catapult!"

That was what Kevin had forgotten, and he knew it. Eukert had said that if the catapult had moved any closer, with a heavier payload it could destroy a portion of the castle. And retreating back one ring to prevent being surrounded had allowed the catapult to advance as well, placing it closer to the castle walls. It now sat just behind the

Desolunar front units, in their control.

In furious realization, Kevin started charging through the crowd of Desolunar troops, desperate to reach the catapult before it fired again. With less care he ran, resulting in him getting very close to taking a couple of slashes. Caitlin and Rachel took shots trying to cover for him as much as possible. He was focused solely on the catapult, knowing it had to be stopped.

Kevin made it a few steps from the catapult, but then the catapult released, releasing a boulder almost twice the size of the first one. He turned around to see the boulder flying through the air toward the castle. Caitlin, a short distance away, shot a couple of shots of ice magic into the air, hoping to intercept the boulder. She missed both shots.

The boulder came down exactly where Desolunar wanted it to: right into the castle walls beside the southern gate, taking down a segment of the wall as it crumbled on impact. Now, there was a gaping hole in the wall, big enough to allow Desolunar's forces in. With the hole opened in the castle's wall, the Desolunar forces started advancing, pushing through the Auranian lines. Clearly, they had accomplished what they wanted, and were going for the kill.

A call of "Retreat to the castle!" came from several of the officers of the Auranian military on the ground, who wanted to prevent the castle from being taken. Abiding by this, Kevin turned, grabbed Caitlin and Rachel, and started retreating to the castle. Neither Caitlin nor Rachel were surprised by Kevin's actions, knowing that he wanted to make sure they all stuck together in the chaotic retreat.

Together, with the Auranian military, they pulled back several rings to the edge of the castle, where Auranian troops started to flood into the castle in desperation. On his way into the hole, however, Kevin stumbled, falling to the ground with both Caitlin and Rachel hanging on to him.

He lost physical contact with both of them in that stampede of men.

A large amount of dust was stirred up as the Auranian soldiers rushed through the hole in the castle wall, making breathing difficult for Kevin as he tried to push himself up off of the ground. He started coughing and hacking, and his eyes strained to see anything but a brown cloud and a storm of green uniforms. The dust cloud had made things very difficult to see.

As he finally managed to push himself up, Kevin started to panic, realizing that Caitlin and Rachel were nowhere near him. However, he could not see where they were in the dust. He tried to wipe his eyes to see if he could see clearer to find the girls. Little cleared up, however. Kevin could not see, and he could barely speak because of all the coughing in the dust cloud. The only way he was going to be able to locate the girls was to get out of the dust.

Skinned up from hitting the ground and struggling to see and breathe, Kevin struggled to his feet and started to step forward. He kept his arms out, hoping to find the wall and get himself inside the castle, just around the corner and into the clear. Carefully, Kevin used the little amount of sight he had in the dust, being careful not to walk into a soldier running into the hole, to find the castle wall. Within a few seconds, he found the edge with his left arm. Kevin used it as a guide to make sure that he was past the wall, turned parallel to it, and started running along the wall. A short distance later, he was out of the dust cloud.

Finally, there was fresh air to breathe. Kevin started coughing out the dust and wiping his eyes to clear them. His eyes were still squinting to see, but at least he had his vision back to a much better level than he did in the cloud of dust. Kevin's Auranian uniform was covered in dust, save for the spots of red below his knees where he was bleeding from skinning his knees in the fall. Altogether, he looked like a wreck, tired from the fighting and covered in dust.

As soon as he was able to take a few breathes and clear the dust out of his lungs, Kevin called out, "Caitlin! Rachel! Where are you?"

There was no response, only the silence of the dust and a cloud that was impossible to see through. As was common for Auranian units without directional orders, they chose to start staging their defense to the right as opposed to the left, as they were trained, and as such all of the troops headed to the right side of the hole opening. Kevin had stumbled to the left.

He called again, "Caitlin! Rachel!"

Again, there was no response. Kevin was starting to panic. He had promised them he would help keep them safe, and now he had lost both of them. Where were they? Kevin feared the worst.

Then, a few seconds later, Rachel stepped out of the dust, coughing and rubbing her eyes in an attempt to see. She was covered in dirt as well, from the bottom of her skirt to her long dirty blonde hair. After a couple of coughs, she asked, "Kevin? Is that you?"

Kevin stepped up to Rachel and put his hands on her shoulders, letting the girl struggling with her vision know where he was. "Rachel, where's Caitlin?" he asked firmly, desperate to find the one he loved.

Still rubbing her eyes, Rachel said, "I don't know. She's not with you?"

"No" responded Kevin as he shook his head. "We got separated after I tripped over and fell at the hole's entrance. I tried to find both of you in the dust cloud, but I couldn't."

Rachel finally had her eyes cleared. "After you fell, I was knocked around a bit by the troops moving in, and it shuffled me away from the two of you. I didn't see what happened to Caitlin."

For a second, Kevin nodded. Then, he gently pushed Rachel aside for a second and called out, "Caitlin!"

"Kevin, get up here!" called a voice from behind.

It was not Caitlin. It was a male voice. Vincent Stryker's, to be exact.

Turning around, Kevin looked to find that the main gate was just behind him, and his father and the Auranian commanders were still on the garrison above it. Deciding that maybe he could get a better view from the garrison of where Caitlin was, he decided to head up there and listen to his father. Rachel followed suit right behind him.

Together, Kevin and Rachel ran up the stairs to the garrison, and each began to brush themselves off, attempting to remove the dust from their clothes and hair. "Thank goodness you're alive," said Vincent Stryker as they did. "Are you both all right?"

Catching his breath, Kevin shook his head. "No," he said. "I can't find Caitlin."

Vincent let out a sigh. "I can't tell where she could be from up here," he said. "Our forces are preparing to plug the hole. They'll probably manage to hold out, but things don't look good."

"We're holed up here," added Eukert. "Rikleifer is lost, but we'll retreat through the north gate. Presuming that the hole's defense doesn't completely topple and let in a swarm of Desolunar forces, we'll be able to escape, albeit with quite a few casualties."

Kevin did not care. All he could think about was Caitlin. He missed her. He needed her, and he was sure that she needed him as well. But where was she? Kevin was afraid for her safety, worried to death that he had let her down, and that she might be gone forever.

And then, everything changed for the worse in an instant.

A loud crash came from the west side of the castle, catching everyone's attention. The sight of what had caused the crash caused everyone to panic. One of the commanders on the garrison started to shout hysterically, "The west gate has been breached by a ram! Enemy troops are pouring in!"

Eukert's arms fell to his sides. "We're done for," he said, horrified.

Almost instinctively, Rachel leapt toward Kevin, grabbed him around his body in a hug, put her head on his shoulder, and started crying. For a second, Kevin was confused until he heard Rachel say as she was crying, "Kevin, I'm scared."

Suddenly, Kevin had a deeper understanding of Rachel, his friend, just in that moment. Beyond the critical, realist exterior, and the devoted and trustworthy middle that made her a great friend, was an inner core of an innocent. In a moment like this, it was exposed. Gently, Kevin placed his arms around Rachel as well, stroking one hand along Rachel's hair. "It's going to be all right," he said. "Everything's going to be all right."

And yet, Kevin knew it was not going to be all right. Desolunar troops did not take prisoners, except in rare circumstances. They killed on the spot. And such a fate, Kevin knew, was what was going to happen next.

Chapter 43

The "Try Not to Die" Game

The thunder of marching men erupted as nearly two thousand Desolunar soldiers, those that had composed one flank of their V formation, began to flood the castle with soldiers. The smaller Auranian unit that had been engaging them outside of the castle was nowhere in sight. To the south end of the castle, the Auranian unit there, or what was left of it, was trying to defend the opening in the castle created by a Desolunar catapult. It was a futile effort, however, as the breached gate in the west had already allowed what the defense to the south was trying to prevent.

Standing on the garrison above the southern main gate, Kevin could only look on in horror, resisting an instinctual quaking of his nerves. Rachel, a close friend of his, stayed clung to him in fear. All around, various commanders and advisors to the Auranian military, such as War Commander Eukert, Knight of Archery John Bryant, former Scurnian general Vincent Stryker, and several others also watched on, knowing that they had lost.

Kevin had made the biggest mistake he could have. He allowed himself to be taken off by his own admiration for his hometown into a battle that was an imminent loss from the start, if only by sheer force. Then, he could not prevent the holes in the castle from being punctured, allowing in the Desolunar troops and pinning himself in between both of their units. Lastly, he lost contact with Caitlin, and her fate and location were unknown to him.

It was his worst nightmare come true. Nothing could have prepared him for it. "Too late to call for retreat. We'll be cut off from our only escape route before we can even get the gate open." Eukert stood back to watch. “Nothing more left to do,” he said, breaking a moment of silence. “Gentlemen, it’s been a great honor to serve with you all of these years. The two of you have been the best friends and allies anyone could ever ask for.”

“As with you,” nodded John Bryant. “And as with Stryker as well.”

Vincent also nodded in response. “For us, our time probably should have ended long ago.”

Before any of those three could continue, however, they recognized a sound that made them all look over. On the garrison, they could hear Rachel crying, clung to Kevin, who was himself showing difficulties in trying not to shake from how scared he was. It was a sobering visual for the three war veterans. “But not for them,” observed Eukert. “What we’re seeing with our eyes by itself is a sight that would dry out the most drunken war veteran. They don’t deserve this fate.”

All three of the veterans had been brought down by this. As warriors, they fully expected to die someday, with Eukert being the closest to that so far, and knew that to die in battle was the most honorable way to die. But seeing Kevin and Rachel so afraid as they were reminded them harshly of the defeat this battle truly meant. Chaos surrounded the castle. Chaos had infected the castle. But chaos did nothing for letting in death, the true enemy of war. Victory in war meant surviving to die from old age, not from death on the battlefield.

Subtly, John Bryant thought he heard something different as he looked on in distress. Amidst the meshing of the stampeding forces on the west side, the clashing weapons near the hole opening, and Rachel’s crying, it almost seemed like there was something more that had not been there before. Perking up his ears, he tried to tell from which direction it was coming. His eyes widened as he recognized the familiar sound. “Do you guys hear that?” he asked to Vincent and Eukert. “Eukert, pass me your binoculars.”

The war commander reluctantly passed over the bronze-plated binoculars he had used earlier. John then carefully brought them up to his eyes, and looked to the north side of the city. After a few seconds, a smile came to his face. “Take a look at this,” he said, passing the binoculars to Vincent Stryker, who took a look through. "Horses. It's an Auranian cavalry unit, and it must be so big that they had to have used every horse in Aurana to fill it. Must be at least two thousand soldiers there."

Vincent passed the binoculars over to Eukert. "We're saved!" he exclaimed. Then, he rushed over to Kevin. "Kevin! Rachel! We're going to be all right!"

"Seriously?" asked Kevin.

"I mean it!" exclaimed Vincent in response.

Both the eyes of Kevin and Rachel widened. As they let go of each other, both of them were curious as to what was going to happen.

Immediately, Eukert gave direction to Bryant, who picked up a bugle and blew out three notes repeatedly, in succession, to the north. It was a command, specifically directing advancing Auranian forces to the west, an audio command recognized by Auranian troops as a part of their training.

"Now, quickly!" snapped Vincent to Kevin and Rachel. "Follow me, but don't stop for anything!" He took off, along with Eukert and Bryant, along the top of the the west side of the wall.

Kevin and Rachel followed, but Kevin had one focus on his mind. "Wait!" he called out. "I can't leave without Caitlin!"

"Just follow!" Eukert yelled back. "There's time for that later!"

Frustrated with a lack of an answer, Kevin did as he was told. He looked down inside the castle as he ran, looking for any sign of her. The Auranian forces, along the south wall where he was, were still trying to defend the gap created by the catapult. It was a massive cluster of humanity, but no visible sign of Caitlin.

As Kevin hesitated, Rachel kept a hold of Kevin's wrist and dragged him on to make sure he kept up. She too was worried about Caitlin, but understood the importance of what they were doing. Fortunately it was not too difficult to keep up with the older men who were running around the wall. Kevin kept his focus on trying to find Caitlin inside the castle as they ran, knowing he probably had little chance of saving her if she were stuck outside the walls. As they approached the west gate, however, Rachel tugged him and pointed him over to the outside.

It was not for Caitlin. Rachel was showing Kevin what Eukert had meant when he said they were saved.

The cavalry had charged toward the west side of town, and within a few minutes they were slamming into the Desolunar ranks, which had stopped trying to encircle the castle because of the breached gate. The west gate was still blown open, but the Desolunar forces were forced to turn their attention back outside to the Auranian reinforcements.

With the west side now verified to be secure for the moment, and the east side not yet encircled, Eukert called out, "Full retreat! Open the north gate! Fall back to Wyntrail!" John Bryant stopped for a moment to belt out five notes on his bugle, which he repeated three times, commanding a retreat to the north. Hearing the tone, a war drummer on top of the castle itself sounded a large gong, also a sound telling Auranian soldiers to retreat.

At the sound of the retreat command, the north gates opened. The besieged Auranian forces inside the castle now had access and direction to retreat. "All right, kids," Vincent Stryker turned and said to Kevin and Rachel, "once you get over the north gate, go down using the stairs and follow the retreating forces. Head northwest, toward Wyntrail, and don't stop running until you're well clear of the city. We'll make sure as many of our men get out as we can, and then we will catch up with you in Wyntrail. It's imperative you don't stop, okay?"

Rachel nodded.

"I'm not going yet," Kevin said firmly. "I'm not leaving Caitlin behind."

Eukert turned. "Kevin, with all due respect, I'm ordering you out of Rikleifer. I can't risk you going back. As everyone retreats, you would quickly be enveloped by enemy forces."

Pulling out his sword, Kevin responded, "You can't order me to do that. I'm the Vanguard of Aurana. I'm not subject to your orders."

Quickly, Eukert's face turned to one of rage, but John Bryant put an arm up in front of him. "I'm afraid the Vanguard is right," he observed to the war commander. "As the Vanguard, his position exempts him from any commands if he wishes, other than from the king himself."

"Are you sure you want to do this, Kevin?" asked Vincent Stryker, putting his hands on Kevin's arms. "I can't stop you, and neither can Eukert, but I'm with him in that I strongly advise you not to go back. You have to fall back. I… I mean, Aurana, all of us, we can't afford to lose you."

Kevin stood firm. Calmly, he lit up his sword in its bright blue magic, proving to Vincent Stryker that he was not acting rashly. "And I can't afford to lose Caitlin," he said. "We're responsible for each other. I made a promise to Professor Magnon I wouldn't let any harm come to her, but more than that, we have a promise to each other to look out for one another. I won't betray her by leaving her behind."

Inspired by the confidence, Rachel felt the pull not to leave her new friend behind, either. Terrified as she had been, she grabbed her bow firmly. She was still extremely scared, but willing to carry on. "If you're heading back into the castle, I'll cover you from the wall. I'm a better archer from a safer point than in the fray, anyway."

Stepping back, Vincent Stryker then nodded. "Both of you must do what you must. I firmly believe this won't be the last time we see each other."

Eukert stepped forward, not angered. "If you must go, then when you return, flee through the north gate and fall back to Wyntrail. Don't get lost and head toward Aurana City; King Andrew II has made headquarters in Wyntrail because our supply base is there. I am sure he would like to speak with you after all of this is done."

"Understood," acknowledged Kevin. He flashed his sword and began running south along the wall, leaving the generals behind. He had to go, and go now, if he had any chance of saving Caitlin.

Rachel kept pace with Kevin, running next to him as she grabbed an arrow out of her quiver. Quickly, they ran along the top of the wall, looking out across Rikleifer to see men in black uniforms swarming all over the city. "Are we heading to the south gate again?" Rachel asked.

Kevin nodded. "That's where we last saw Caitlin, before the retreat into the castle. If she's anywhere, she has to be down by the hole in the wall."

"Got it," nodded Rachel. "I guess we really are playing the 'try not to die' game. I'll give you as much cover fire as I can, but if you get surrounded, I can't shoot a bunch of men at once."

"Then I won't get surrounded," acknowledged Kevin. "The same goes for you. Don't let yourself get pinned on both sides, and if you do, scream for help so I can cover you." He took a breath while he ran, as the adrenaline and determination kept him going. "We're still a team, and I'm not going to let anything bad happen to you."

Confidently, Rachel responded, "And I won't let it happen to you either."

As Rachel finished her sentence, she and Kevin arrived at the stairs above the south gate. Down below was the hole in the wall, where dust had been kicked up in a great amount. Kevin could see plenty of Auranian soldiers still holding the line, using the hole in the wall as a narrow point to keep Desolunar's numbers advantage from pushing into the castle. Their unit leaders knew that the soldiers at the south end were the rear guard, holding long enough to allow the units in the castle to retreat through the north gate, and they would follow once they had bought those units opportunity to escape.

From above, Kevin leaned over the wall, searching desperately for Caitlin. He was hoping that her white dress would stay visible amongst a sea of green and black uniforms. Rachel looked over the other side, in case Caitlin were stranded outside of the wall.

No luck. Caitlin was nowhere to be seen.

"I can't see her at all," Rachel called out to Kevin. She turned back to him. "I don't see her on that side."

Where could she be? Kevin knew he had to find her. Every second, the Desolunar soldiers would keep advancing on their position and they risked being overcome.

An idea came to mind, as Kevin considered what to do. He held his sword straight in front of him, vertically so the blade extended in front of his eyes. He remembered the night in Venarose, while imprisoned by The Syndicate, how the Sword of Purity had guided him to Caitlin. Now, he needed it to do so again. He closed his eyes, kept the sword lit brightly, and said, "Show me the way to her."

For a brief moment, Kevin kept his eyes closed, as nothing

seemed to happen. This was not something he was sure his sword would do. Hesitant, Rachel kept her bow up, wanting Kevin to do what he was doing but not wanting him to simply waste time if this kept up too long. As time passed, Kevin loosened his grip on the sword, allowing it to pull him if it chose.

The sword swung with the new slack in Kevin's arms, and it pulled him in a direction down the stairs inside the wall. Caitlin was inside the castle walls, at least.

Without hesitation, Kevin ran down the stairs and into the castle courtyard. A cluster of Auranian soldiers were around the hole in the wall next to the gate, trying to hold off the Desolunar soldiers still trying to push their way inside the walls. They were slowly failing; while they were not at risk of being surrounded at the moment thanks to the cavalry charge to the west, the Desolunar forces were slowly forcing them back. More black uniforms were entering the castle, threatening any Auranian in the courtyard.

Immediately, Kevin held out his sword and relied on it to guide him through the crowd. He had to be extremely careful to avoid running into anyone amidst the chaos of mass sword fighting, especially as black uniforms leaked into the courtyard.

Thirty seconds in, he ran into a Desolunar soldier. Kevin pulled his sword up to defend, and blocked a couple of strikes. Before the bout could continue, an Auranian soldier turned and struck down the Desolunar soldier. Another Desolunar soldier snuck up behind Kevin, almost unnoticed. At the last second Kevin turned around to see him holding a short sword over his head, then to see him fall over dead, an arrow sticking from his neck. Kevin looked up to the wall, to see Rachel had another arrow in her quiver and ready for another shot. He gave her a quick thumbs up in appreciation.

On the ground, Kevin raced past the hole in the wall and into the east side of the castle yard. All around on this side, there were Auranian soldiers moving the injured out of the area, trying to get them away to evacuate them. It was a mess of people, one that forced Kevin to slow down and walk through. Many of the injuries looked bad, which accelerated Kevin's fear that Caitlin had been seriously injured, or possibly worse. Behind him, the battle for the hole was raging, as the rear guard were holding onto the hole as long as they could.

Where could she be? Amidst so much destruction, how could she possibly be okay?

Kevin walked too far to the east. The sword began pulling him back toward the hole, back into the fracas. He worried even greater as he worked his way into the crowd once again. The air was full of dust from all the movement and debris, almost creating a cloud over the area. Where in here could Caitlin be? Could she have even survived without being trampled?

Lost in the crowd for a moment, Kevin closed his eyes. He wanted to feel the sword guide him, trusting it to tell him where to go. He knew it made him vulnerable for a moment, but he would risk everything for her. The sword felt like it was pulling Kevin to the wall, so he opened his eyes and turned to face the bricks.

Then, a voice from near the wall weakly said, "Kevin," catching Kevin's attention. He turned to see what he was looking for.

It was Caitlin, sitting against the wall with her legs out. She was covered in dust and looked very beaten up. In one hand, she was clutching an arrow over an open wound on her palm. Quickly, Kevin rushed to her side and knelt down next to her, so ecstatic that she had not been killed after all. "Caitlin, are you okay?" he asked, his heart racing.

Still a little weak in her voice, she said. "I'm fine. Now that I have you next to me, I'm fine." She smiled just a little bit.

Kevin smiled at her. "And I'm just so glad to see you're safe," responded Kevin, with a great sense of relief as he sat down next to her. "Are you injured anywhere?"

Caitlin took a breath, her face dropping to a more serious look. "Yes," she said meekly. "I can't stand up."

As instantly as that, Kevin immediately worried "Where are you hurt?"

"Lower right leg," answered Caitlin, in a worrisome tone of voice. "It's in the middle of the leg." Then, her voice became more desperate. "I can't put any weight on it. Kevin, I think it's broken."

"Can you heal it yourself?" asked Kevin, optimistically.

Shaking her head, Caitlin said in a more depressed tone, "No.

I've tried, and I've tried again, and I just can't make it work. I can't make any of my magic work at all."

Kevin let out a sigh, taking a brief look out on the triage in front of him, still moving around in a chaotic organization. He then knelt down next to Caitlin, seeing that she was crying.

"I don't have any magic," she said. Then, she started to sob. "I don't have any magic at all. I've never been without it before, Kevin. I have no magic, and I can't walk." She started to break down in tears, crying. "I feel so helpless and weak, Kevin."

"Hey, everything's going to be all right," responded Kevin reassuringly. He still had no idea how he could get her out of here now, but this was no time to give up. "Let's start with this one thing at a time, okay? There's no need to panic. Can you trust me enough to show you how we'll make this work?"

Still tearing up some, Caitlin nodded.

Seeing this, Kevin thought about what he could do. He took off his jacket, and, using the Sword of Purity, cut off the sleeves and cut the back into three strips. The energized sword made this a much easier feat, making Kevin able to destroy his Vanguard jacket in a few seconds. Then, he took the two sleeves and the three strips from the back and tied them end to end, creating a crude bandage. Kevin then moved over to Caitlin's right side, and sat down beside her right leg. "First off, I'm going to wrap your leg so it doesn't get inflamed if you're certain it is a broken bone. Okay?"

Caitlin nodded.

With her permission in hand, Kevin carefully reached for the end of Caitlin's dress, and pulled the skirt piece of it up to Caitlin's knees. Then, Kevin unrolled the bandage and proceeded to carefully and slowly wrap up Caitlin's right lower leg, all the way down to her ankle and around her foot to secure it. As he was wrapping her leg, Kevin said, "Once we catch back up with your father, if you haven't already recovered your magic, we'll have him heal your leg for you. If you get it back before then, you can hopefully take care of it yourself."

"And if it doesn't come back?"

Tough question, Kevin thought to himself. "Let's get you out of here for now, and we'll figure that one out when we don't have a war at our backsides."

Silently, Caitlin closed her eyes and looked away. She was resigned to accept her fate with her magic, for whatever reason it may be.

Suddenly, there was a loud banging sound, disrupting the whole fight for the wall. The Desolunar forces had advanced a ram to the south gate, looking to blow open a bigger access into the castle. Time was up; they had to flee before that south gate was breached, or there likely would be no retreat.

Carefully, Kevin reached forward and put his arms underneath Caitlin. Then, he gently lifted her up. Kevin was not particularly strong, especially while so worn out from battling and the frantic search, but he found the strength within himself to get Caitlin to safety. The trouble was, he did not have the strength to run with Caitlin in his arms, and the ram was audibly starting to crack the southern gate open.

The crowd at the hole was starting to get more chaotic. Desolunar troops were starting to seep in at an even quicker rate. Then, a great amount of whipping sounds swished through the air.

It was a volley of arrows.

"Kevin! Back up!" Caitlin yelled at him, seeing it coming.

Instinctively, Kevin stepped backwards, against the wall. The arrows spread in front of him and into the crowd, striking down a number of both Auranian and Desolunar soldiers. Desolunar's units were firing with no regard for their own troops. After all of the sounds had ended, Kevin was greatly worried if Rachel was okay. He stepped out across the courtyard to the castle and looked up to the gate, and had just enough view to see that Rachel was okay. She was now facing outside the castle, returning fire presumably at the archers who had shot up and over the wall.

Kevin needed a plan, and he needed one fast. If he were to save Caitlin, he had to get her out quickly. He was not going to be able to run her out on his own, nor did he figure he could with Rachel's help. If he had a good cart, he could put her in it and try to run her out. That was the best idea he had, but where would he find a cart in the castle courtyard?

The sound of a bugle resonated through the air, toning out a five note sequence over and over. It was the call for retreat. Kevin was out of time. The rear guard was being ordered to fall back. As they retreated, Desolunar soldiers would start to pour in, and there would be no escape.

The bugle sound was getting closer. So were the familiar clopping sounds of a horse.

Turning his head to the west, Kevin saw John Bryant riding a horse, holding a repeating crossbow in one hand and the bugle in the other. Bryant was sounding the bugle over and over. "Full retreat north!" he would stop to yell.

"I have an idea," Kevin told Caitlin in that moment. Seeing his only opportunity he thought he would have, Kevin leaned out and stepped in front of the horse, enough distance ahead that it would have plenty of time to stop. Bryant saw Caitlin's white dress first and immediately stopped, as Kevin held her in front of himself.

"What are you doing?" Caitlin asked.

With the horse stopped, Kevin walked up to Bryant's left, and spoke to him. "Please take her and get her out of here."

Silently, John Bryant nodded. He reached over and pulled Caitlin onto his horse, in front of him.

"Kevin, please don't…" Caitlin said weakly. "I can't be without you…"

"Don't worry, Caitlin, I'll catch up," he said, as he lowered his head and allowed Bryant to ride on. Knowing his mission, Bryant tapped his horse with his heels, heading off with Caitlin slumped in front of him, bugling the retreat command as he drove the horse to the east around the castle.

Please come back to me alive. I don't know what I'd do without you.

Caitlin spoke the words into Kevin's head.

Suddenly, the south gate shattered. The noise it made as it broke open shattered through the air. Immediately, the remaining Auranian forces began to retreat, knowing they would be overwhelmed unless they did. Time was up. Kevin had to grab Rachel and get out of here.

Although he was quite tired, Kevin ran with what energy he had left to the stairs by the south gate. Navigating the soldiers around the hole was difficult, but Kevin's absence of his Vanguard jacket made him less of a known target for the Desolunar forces. Once he made it to the stairs, Kevin hustled up them as quickly as he could.

Then he saw with what Rachel had been contending. A number of siege ladders had popped up, and Rachel was actively trying to shove them down as they connected at the battlements. Enough were now starting to come up that she was not able to force all of them down. When Kevin made it up the stairs, he was a sight for her sore eyes. Desolunar soldiers were starting to reach the top on the standing ladders, and now with the south gate busted open, they would have easier access to the stairs inside as well.

"Thank goodness, Kevin," Rachel exclaimed, grabbing her bow and pulling an arrow from her quiver. "Let's get out of here before it's too late!"

Kevin could only nod. He was very weary.

As quick as they could, Kevin and Rachel ran to the west along the top of the wall. They were going to follow the directions Vincent Stryker had given; around to the north, down the stairs at the north gate, and out and northwest toward Wyntrail.

Running with all of the energy they had left, Kevin and Rachel rushed along the western wall, determined to make it to freedom. Their lives were at stake; if they did not reach the road to Wyntrail, they would surely be captured and face execution.

Nearing the halfway point between the south and west gates, they ran into disaster.

At least ten siege ladders had been erected at the southwest corner of the castle walls. Five Desolunar soldiers were now standing in front of them, blocking their progress forward, with more ascending the ladders. Knowing they had to fight through, Kevin held up his sword and lit it up. This was life or death.

Quickly, though, Kevin pulled back and let Rachel step in front. She already had an arrow nocked, and was ready to fire. Without a moment's hesitation, Rachel pointed the arrow at the first enemy and fired, hitting the soldier in the right eye. The other soldiers around him hesitated.

Then came the sound of clattering from behind Kevin and

Rachel. More Desolunar soldiers were climbing the ladders behind them. Several were now on the wall, approaching them.

They were surrounded. This was the one situation they had both agreed from which they could not rescue the other. And now they were both pinned. Surrounded on both sides, Kevin and Rachel were now both trapped. There was no escape to be seen.

Immediately, Rachel dropped her bow. She was now more scared than she had ever been. It was not hard to understand that they were doomed.

Chapter 44

Final Gambit

A tired Kevin raised his arms, without letting go of his sword. Although he too was scared, he was too exhausted to show the emotion. Rachel stood next to him, as frightened as he was. As far as he could tell, he had one shot to get him and Rachel to safety, and he was going to take it. He had to do it for her. He had to do it for Caitlin, too.

"Rachel, close your eyes," Kevin said out loud.

"What does it matter?" Rachel asked.

"Trust me," Kevin responded, shaking. He was not sure of what he was about to do, but he needed Rachel to close her eyes.

Reluctantly, Rachel did so and put her hands over them to show Kevin they were closed.

The Desolunar soldiers began to advance toward them. Kevin was ready to try his final gambit. Holding the fully lit Sword of Purity high, he did the unthinkable. He looked at his sword, remembered the name Kron told him of whose sacrifice it was that created this sword, and said, "Great Vinz Larinion, please clear the way for us. I beg for your help in this moment."

For a moment, nothing happened. Kevin looked visibly disappointed. He had had no idea if that would help or not, but he had no options.

The Desolunar soldiers continued to advance. Rachel stood next to Kevin with her eyes still closed, hoping beyond hope he had a plan that would work.

"Please! Help us!" Kevin yelled as he held out his sword in front of him, pointing to the sky.

Suddenly, it happened.

Kevin held onto his sword tight as a brilliant flash of energy emitted from the blade. Brilliant blue energy dispersed in every direction, slowly pushing out in all directions, although Rachel was unaffected because of how close she was standing to Kevin; she was almost enveloped in a bubble with him. The energy shone outward, pushing the Desolunar soldiers back or off the wall entirely. Those that were shoved back were knocked down.

The light was visible from all around Rikleifer because it was so bright. As soon as the troops ahead of him were incapacitated or removed, Kevin loosened his grip on the sword, and the flash disappeared as quickly as it began.

Hearing all the noises, Rachel opened her eyes. Relieved but completely surprised, she asked, "What the hell was that?"

"No idea, and no time to explain," Kevin answered, as he tugged Rachel's dress. "We have to go before more come back!"

Without hesitation, Rachel reached down to pick up her bow and started running with Kevin. As they ran, with so little energy left between them, they passed the west gate. Over the side of the wall, they could see that the cavalry was starting to fall back. With the call to retreat being issued, and the rear guard evacuating from the north gate while everyone else was out, the cavalry was dropping back to support the retreat.

There was no time to stop, however. They had to reach the north gate, and then get out of town. Kevin looked over at Rachel as they ran, and though she looked very tired, she nodded to him confidently. The pathway down the wall was clear all the way to the north gate. Kevin felt like he could fall over and collapse at any moment, before he made it to safety.

As the path ahead remained clear, more and more Desolunar soldiers were mounting the wall behind them. They were being pursued.

Before anyone could come close, Kevin and Rachel finally made it to the north gate. Below, the gate was open, and inside the gate a fresh group of Auranian cavalry had formed lines on either side of the castle courtyard. They were protecting the retreat and trying to be the last ones out.

From below, Vincent Stryker and Milton "Ironman" Eukert were watching from their horse mounts they had been given when the cavalry arrived. Both had seen the flash and worried about Kevin and Rachel.

Eukert was watching through his binoculars, when he first caught a glimpse of the two young adults approaching the gate. He pointed them out to Vincent Stryker.

Quickly, Kevin and Rachel made it down the stairs, within the Auranian pocket at the gate. Worried, Vincent Stryker asked, "Kevin, are you all right?"

Kevin was too exhausted to say anything. With the relief that he was safe, he passed out and fell to the dirt.

Shocked, Vincent Stryker pointed to two men standing nearby. "Pass him up to me immediately! I will get him out of here."

Rachel was out of breath, but was similarly relieved, She worried for Kevin, but after Vincent Stryker volunteered to take him, she turned to Eukert.

"Hop on," Eukert said to her. "You must be as tired as he is. I'll get you to Wyntrail."

It would be a couple of hours before Kevin regained consciousness. When he finally awoke, his father told him where he was and where they were going, that everyone was safe and that John Bryant had Caitlin further up the road. The retreat march to Wyntrail would take at least a day or so. Sadly, Kevin looked back in the direction of Rikleifer, long out of view. Tears came to his eyes as he fully felt the realization that his hometown was lost.

Defending Wyntrail would at least be easier than Rikleifer. Nestled in a projection of the Auranian Wilderness, Wyntrail was normally a quiet forest town built among the trees that also sat nearby a geographical anomaly—the Forked Mountain, a twin peak, nowhere near any other mountains. This unique combination of forest and mountain, along with its relative proximity to Aurana's western meadows and farmland, made Wyntrail's outskirts an ideal place for supply acquisition for Aurana's military. As such, its largest supply base was here, but the town itself was relatively isolated from military activity.

Until today. The mass retreat from Rikleifer was coming this way, in large part because heading directly north would result in a retreat to Aurana City and surrender of Aurana's most critical resources it needed to continue the battle.

A night passed and camp was set, and the next day the Auranian soldiers packed up and carried on to Wyntrail, as per their orders. A reluctant Kevin, now feeling a little more energized after a night's sleep, carried on aboard Vincent Stryker's horse with his father, while Eukert continued to take Rachel on his own. Neither one had seen John Bryant or Caitlin, to which Vincent Stryker assured them he had rushed Caitlin straight to Wyntrail at a full gallop rather than wait to keep pace with the army, as Eukert had to do. Vincent, not wanting to abandon the men, stayed with Eukert as well and told Kevin to be patient.

"You'll see her soon enough," he reassured Kevin.

Kevin sighed. He looked depressed.

"Aw, what's wrong, Kevin?" Rachel asked him. "I know Caitlin is important to you just like she is to me, but she's fine. You got her out of Rikleifer safely. I'm sure she'll be happy to see you when we get to Wyntrail. That's where she's from, isn't it?"

"It is," sighed Kevin. "It's where her father lives, too."

There was a moment's pause. Kevin's mind was clearly elsewhere. He seemed distracted.

Picking up on this, Vincent Stryker asked, "It's not just about the girl, is it?"

Kevin gave no answer.

"What could it be?" asked Rachel, aloud.

That made Kevin look at Rachel, not in disgust but just to answer what he did not want to discuss. "I'm responsible for them," he said. "All of them. It was my idea to let in enemy soldiers and entrap them. It was my fighting that allowed the catapult to get close enough to the wall to knock a hole in it…"

"*Our* fighting," emphasized Rachel. "You, and me, and Caitlin, we all fought as one unit. And for a group of three who don't normally fight, we got extremely close."

"Not close enough," shrugged Kevin. "How many men did we lose at Rikleifer? How many didn't make it out in the retreat?"

"That's not your fault, Kevin," answered Vincent Stryker. "You did the best you could to put together a winning strategy and execution, but we were up against very long odds."

Kevin shrugged, as he turned away. "It wasn't enough."

"But it was," commented Rachel. "You're no hero, right? That's what you always say, at least. You're responsible for helping to maintain Aurana's diplomacy as its Vanguard. You're not responsible for single-handedly leading its armies to victory."

Still looking down, Kevin said nothing.

Eukert then chimed in. "For what it's worth, it was probably your idea that let us hold Rikleifer long enough for the cavalry to come and secure our retreat. Had we not had your suggestion, it's likely we would have engaged the bulk of the Desolunar forces sooner and been surrounded much quicker, before the king's cavalry could arrive to protect our retreat."

"Surely not what you intended," added Vincent Stryker, "but an accidental success is a success nonetheless. Your suggestion was honestly a good one and it did give us our best chance at success."

Kevin looked at Eukert. "I'm sorry I was so bold in suggesting it. And I'm sorry I argued with you during the retreat. If I would have realized…"

"Don't," interrupted Eukert firmly. "Perhaps it was I who was out of line not to give you the respect that you actually deserve."

Starting to look up, Kevin listened intently.

"Maybe what you said in the planning room was bold, and the audacity of hearing you say it was shocking, but it was the right thing to do. What you did, has ultimately saved more lives than it claimed. More of the men will see their families again because you did what you did. You can't pick and choose which lives to save when the burden of command is on you; you can only save as many as you can."

"But I did pick Caitlin," said Kevin. "I risked my life and Rachel's to save hers."

This time, Rachel looked at Kevin and, while she still looked scuffed up and dirty from the battle, smiled. "We did that as her friends, not as leaders," she said. "Eukert and your father were filling the leadership parts there. We had the flexibility that we could do an action for a friend."

"Exactly right," added Vincent Stryker, giving a nod to Rachel. "The order to retreat and its execution were not your responsibility."

A humble Eukert looked at Kevin. "And I apologize that I gave you so much grief about it. I'm not used to having my orders questioned or defied, but you were right that your position grants you leeway from the king to do as you need. It was wrong of me to argue it with you."

Still appearing a bit somber, Kevin nodded. "Thank you," he said.

It was becoming increasingly clear to the three that cheering Kevin up was not going to be so easy. He was feeling a sense of responsibility greater than any he had ever felt in his life. That accountability, Vincent Stryker felt, would actually serve him well in the future as he learned to make decisions and the consequences of doing so.

The ride to Wyntrail took into the late afternoon, as the horses kept with the marching speed of the retreating Auranian soldiers. Although morale was low because of the defeat, the thought of restocking and refreshing in Wyntrail, where supplies were aplenty, kept the army's morale high enough to motivate the march.

Initially, Kevin could not see Wyntrail as they approached because it was nestled in the forest. It eventually became more clear as the meadows through which the road passed transitioned into forest, and the Auranian Wilderness edges enveloped the route. Only a few minutes after the terrain had changed, the town came into view. Tiny clearings gave way for the largest buildings of the town, including the town hall, government buildings, and shops. The houses of the small town were built in even smaller spaces, surrounded by trees. The pathways in town wound in various curved shapes, conforming to the flora around them. Vincent Stryker explained to his son that the supply base was further on past the town, much closer to the Forked Mountain in the distance. That was where the military would set up camp, not in the town itself.

As the army came into town, John Bryant emerged on his horse to welcome them. He explained to Kevin that Caitlin had requested to be taken to a specific house in town. Kevin reasoned that was her father's house, and perhaps where she had been in her childhood. He asked his father if he could hop off and see her, to which Vincent agreed. Rachel also decided to hop off, but told Kevin she would explore the town for a bit first. She knew that although she missed Caitlin as her friend, Kevin and Caitlin had a special relationship and wanted to give them time to reunite, especially in light of what happened.

Reaching the door of the house, Kevin took a quick look around. It was a simple house, not unlike his in Rikleifer, albeit a bit different in style featuring wooden siding. Clearly, Professor Magnon had no desires for riches and lived quite modestly, Kevin thought to himself. He would otherwise have a larger house with more extravagance.

Kevin knocked on the door. He stood there for a moment, but heard no response. Realizing that if Caitlin were in there she still had a broken leg, he decided to open the door and call for her.

"Come in, Kevin," Caitlin called back. Her voice sounded stronger than it did yesterday.

Opening the door, Kevin walked in and closed the door behind him. Much like Kevin's house, there was one common room with two small bedrooms attached. The common room was empty, not even including a stove or anything for cooking. Ignoring this for now, Kevin proceeded to the bedroom from where he'd heard Caitlin's voice. The door was open, so he walked in.

Inside, Caitlin was sitting up on her bed, wearing her thoroughly dirtied white and red dress. She had the skirt pulled up to the bed, exposing her legs at the knee and below. Her broken leg was wrapped in a proper bandage, not Kevin's uniform jacket. She looked up at Kevin, and smiled. "Thank goodness you're safe. I was really worried about you."

As Kevin sat down on the bed next to her, Caitlin reached over and hugged him and gave him a kiss on the cheek. "You seem to be in really good spirits," Kevin answered.

"Well, about as good as I can be, I guess," Caitlin answered. She looked down at her leg and swung it a bit. "I don't think the leg is broken, but the ankle may be. It's still nearly impossible to walk on." She pointed to a stick at the corner of her bed. "I've had to use my father's old spell casting staff to support myself getting around here."

Kevin nodded. "Why don't you tell me about what happened, then?" he asked her. "Start from where we got separated."

"Okay," began Caitlin, taking a breath. She looked a little reluctant to bring up the subject and admit her weakness, but she knew Kevin needed to hear it. "After you fell over and the dust cloud was stirred up by all of the soldiers running through there, I was pushed away and shuffled out of the cloud. But when I was shuffled out, I ended up on the outside of the wall, not the inside. A Desolunar soldier then saw me and shot at me with an arrow. The arrow scraped me across my hand, narrowly missing. Afraid, I tried to rush back into the cloud, hoping to just cut around the edge of the wall and get inside quickly. But as I tried to flip around the corner, I was broadsided by one of the soldiers rushing in. I felt my leg twist hard, and I hit it against the edge of the broken wall. I fell hard to the ground in pain, but I had been nudged hard enough to be just past the wall. I couldn't stand up and walk, so I dragged myself as far as I could and propped myself up as much as I could." She paused. "As much as it hurt, though, the whole time I was worried about you."

Gently, Kevin put his arm around Caitlin. "That must have been a lot to go through. As long as you're okay, I'll always be fine," he said.

"I know you will," smiled Caitlin back. Kevin's support made her happy, as did knowing he was okay. He was starting to get strong. Then, remembering something, Caitlin said, "Oh! I have something for Rachel, speaking of which. She's all right, right?"

Kevin nodded. "She's fine. She actually helped me get back to you."

"Like a true friend," responded Caitlin, still happy. "The arrow that barely scraped my hand landed next to me, so when I dragged myself away from the hole, I took it with me." She pulled the arrow up from beside her with her other hand. "Rachel told me the day we met that you're not supposed to waste good arrows. I thought she could use it."

"Probably," nodded Kevin as he took the arrow. As he grabbed it, however, he looked carefully at the arrowhead and noticed something odd. "Caitlin, did you see these black splotches on the arrowhead?" he asked. "What is it?"

Surprised because she had not seen that, Caitlin said, "Let me see that arrow again."

Kevin put the arrow in Caitlin's hand, arrow tip pointing across her body so she could examine it closer. "What is it?" he asked.

Caitlin took a brief second to examine the tip, placing the arrow on the bed as she made her determination. "Antite. Damn it." She then showed the palm of her left hand to Kevin, noting the slight scratch across it that barely broke the skin. "Well, that explains why I have no magic."

Confused, Kevin asked, "How so?"

In response, Caitlin showed Kevin the scratch on her hand from the arrow. "That's all it takes," she said. "Antite is a type of metal that, if it cuts open a spellcaster, disables their magic. It can be so potent that just a single scratch will disable your magic for hours or days. This is part of why users of magic were taught to fear the arrow for many years, because antite arrows were relatively common. It's a lot rarer nowadays with so few magic users around."

"So what does that mean?" asked Kevin.

"It means it may be a day or two until I'm back in action," Caitlin said, "so no getting into fights or serious situations until I have it back, you hear?"

Kevin chuckled. "Yeah, I get what you're saying," he said. "I wouldn't do either without you being somewhere I could call you for help."

"You better not," laughed Caitlin. She then changed her tone to a more serious one. "Truth is, I'm not sure how much longer I can keep telling you I'm stronger than you. What you did at the battle showed me just how strong you've become as a person. You weren't like this at all when we first met."

"And I have you to thank for that," Kevin said. "You can blame the situation or the constant backing into accomplishments all you want. If I didn't have you here to guide me, or save my life like you did in our first fight with Demonicus or in the Abyss of the Royal Sovereign, I don't think I would've made it."

Caitlin started counting. "You saved my life in Venarose, on the Cliffs of Vallia, and in Rikleifer. By my math, that makes us three to two on the life-saving, so let's just say I owe you one."

“If you say so,” chuckled Kevin. “Hopefully I won’t have to cash in that favor until at least the winter or so.”

Smiling, Caitlin said humorously, “Yeah, for as often as it’s happened, I think I could wait until winter to return the favor.” She then made her tone more serious again. “In all reality, though, thank you for coming back for me.” She paused for a second. “Just please don’t tell my father, okay?”

Kevin nodded. “I won’t tell your father anything you don’t want me to tell him.”

“Good,” acknowledged Caitlin. She leaned in to give Kevin a kiss.

Before they could share one, there was a knock at the door.

Chapter 45

Weight of the World

The knock on the door happened to be Rachel, who was all too eager to catch up with Caitlin herself and see her friend. All three of the friends spent the day and the evening together, checking on each other and recounting what had happened after they were separated at the battle. Kevin also gave Rachel the arrow that scraped Caitlin's hand and explained what it was. Fairly sure that her father would not mind, Caitlin treated her friends to dinner from the provisions in her father's house. She also had some tea, which she offered to Kevin and Rachel.

Politely, Kevin declined the tea and asked Caitlin if she would mind if he took a walk. Having seen him in such a mood before and knowing he clearly had thoughts weighing on him, she expressed it would be okay with her if he went alone. She felt that he would talk about it when he was ready.

Rachel, however, accepted. She helped to make the tea, given that Caitlin was still limping on an injured ankle and leg. For a moment, though, Caitlin forgot that there was no stove in the house, and she did not have her magic to light a fire. Fortunately, Rachel had a small tinderbox with flint tucked in her quiver to light a fire. She had to tell Rachel that there was a fire pit outside with a hook and a tea kettle, and ask her to make the tea. Rachel did not mind, however, being a willing friend.

As the sun set, Caitlin and Rachel were sitting on Caitlin's bed. The two were sipping the hot tea together as the sun set. A moment or so later, Rachel shook her head. "Beyond belief," she said. "I'm still pretty tired. I think I can safely say that this is the last time I will consider myself as being of sane mind and ready to jump into a battle at the same time."

Caitlin started giggling a little bit. "I'm not sure I'm not thinking the same thing myself," she laughed. "That was as awful as it gets. I don't think I ever want to do that again. It's a miracle we survived as well as we did."

Rachel nodded, as she glanced out the window in Caitlin's room. "I have to wonder if we'll ever get Rikleifer back again."

Silently, Caitlin looked out the window as well. "Good question," she began. "At least, compared to the carnage I saw outside my own house a few weeks ago, Aurana appears to be getting its act together in war. Surely they know this and will regroup to mobilize and retake Rikleifer. People will want to return home. Surely no one likes that Aurana City is so crammed with the civilian evacuees right now."

"Heh, no kidding," said Rachel, as she took another sip of her tea. "I can't imagine what it must be like for my parents right now, being stuck up there. I imagine they're probably staying with a few of my relatives. If they are, they're actually lucky. I'd hate to be up there with no one to shelter me."

Caitlin shrugged. "If there was nowhere I could stay by myself or with you or Kevin, I think I'd take the battlefield over that."

Rachel laughed. "I bet you would," she said. "I've always had the impression from what you've told me about yourself that you don't mind being away from the general public."

"Being different than others can do that," observed Caitlin. "Especially when one doesn't have the emotional tools to overcome."

"Do you think you have those now?" asked Rachel.

After thinking about it for a moment, Caitlin answered, "No. This is still a strange world to me in a number of ways, but I'm striving to do better everyday." Much like how she strove to perfect her magic techniques when she had a barrier around her emotions, Caitlin now strove to learn and master how to handle herself with emotions. She had never lost her determination, only channeled it a little differently.

"A good place to be," nodded Rachel. "You seem to do just fine with me, but I digress." She then changed the subject back. "As for me, I don't think I'd mind having to stay with a bunch of strangers if I had no choice. I'm pretty well trained in archery, but nothing like being in the fray like that, and I don't want to do it again if I can avoid it. I have to admit that I was terrified out there."

“So was I,” said Caitlin. “And I hate to admit that.” She sighed for a moment. “For what it’s worth, we all survived.” She glanced down at her leg, which was still wrapped up in a bandage.

Taking note of this, Rachel asked, “Any sign of your magic coming back?”

“Not yet,” nodded Caitlin. “Antite is pretty awful stuff, but its effects are temporary. They’ve never been known to be permanent. I’m expecting my magic will be back by the morning, at the latest.”

For a moment, Rachel pondered what this meant. She looked over at her bow and quiver, sitting in a corner of the kitchen. She now had one of these antite arrows, the one that had hit Caitlin and caused the disruption in her magic. It could be a powerful weapon in the right circumstance, she hoped.

Before Rachel could ponder further, Caitlin saw where she was looking and said, “I hope you kept that arrow I gave you. Someday it could be the difference between a good outcome and a bad one.”

“Oh, I’m not letting go of it,” smiled Rachel. “As long as no one runs away with it wedged in them, I’ll keep reusing that arrow until the shaft warps.”

Caitlin smiled and nodded. “I’m sure you’ll have the chance to use it. We’re pretty far from being done.” Then, she stopped and looked out the window.

Knowing why Caitlin looked that way, Rachel thought about it a minute. It was very clear that Caitlin cared deeply about Kevin and thought about him when she talked about more to do even after such a significant battle. Another thought came to her mind. “You don’t suppose he has post-traumatic stress, do you?”

Caitlin looked somberly at the door for a moment. “I’m really afraid he might,” she said. “He tends to let a lot more weigh on him than he needs.”

“For what it’s worth, I agree,” noted Rachel. “On the way in, he seemed to be feeling personally responsible for the loss of Rikleifer. We only came to help, and that’s what we did. That does not make us responsible for Aurana’s failure.”

“Except I’m getting the feeling that Kevin thinks the weight of the world is on his shoulders,” Caitlin answered. “He told me, when we first started out, that he wasn't a hero or anything like that. He was just the person who was asked to help a god get home, and said he would." She thought about it a moment longer. "He's grown a lot since then."

"I get that," nodded Rachel, breaking a short pause. "I've known Kevin for a bit. He was always kind of quiet in school, and kept to himself a lot. Pretty socially awkward. He never really seemed like he wanted to stand out. Now he does stand out in a lot of ways."

As she looked at Kevin's door again, Caitlin nodded. "I'm pretty sure my father's to blame for a lot of that," she said. "My father put him on this path when he sent Kevin to Aurana City to help put Andrew into power. Add to that Demonicus wants him dead because he happened to be one of two people who can hold onto a magic sword blessed by the sacrifice of a god, and what you get is that Kevin had to grow up fast. Throughout our travels we united two human kingdoms and a society of phoenixes, fought off an abyssal monster and an assassination squad from Desolunar, and now we survived a battle for his hometown by the skin of our teeth. I'm pretty mentally tough other than my newfound emotions, and even I find so much of this overwhelming and a bit traumatizing. I can't imagine what it would be like for someone who hasn't spent a long time training their mental discipline."

An idea came to Rachel. "Have you ever thought about taking a bit more charge, Caitlin? You talked about being mentally tougher, even if you're not emotionally tougher right now. I mean, you seem to me like you have a handle on all of this kind of stuff better than he does."

"What, you mean like going to war?" asked Caitlin, sarcastically.

Rachel laughed. "Haha, no," she said. "But you know what I mean."

"I do," chuckled Caitlin. She then became more serious. "When we first met, I did take charge a lot. Kevin was scared, and he needed to lean on me, so I did everything I could to help keep him moving forward." She took a sip of tea. "You know, I told him I'd follow him where he went, even if I led a bit more than I followed."

"I believe it," said Rachel, as she also took a sip of tea. "What changed?"

"Kevin's confidence," Caitlin acknowledged. "He's developed this sense of what needs to be done and the guts to get it done no matter the risks, and I don't want to undermine it. Nowadays I do let him lead more because he just does it. I'm okay with supporting him because I see how he's growing." She paused for a second. "I actually kind of hope he doesn't forget about me in the process."

"Oh please, you're the only real girlfriend Kevin's had," said Rachel. "If you like him, I don't think he's going anywhere. I bet he'll want to build a life with you, given enough time."

Caitlin stopped and thought about it for a moment. That hesitation was kicking in again. It was tearing her apart, making her second-guess every decision and every thought.

Rachel took notice that something seemed wrong with Caitlin. "Are you okay?" she asked. "This has all been a lot on me, and a lot on Kevin. I can't imagine that it's not a lot on you, too."

Shrugging, Caitlin looked down for a moment. She felt awkward talking about her feelings after years of suppressing them, but she felt that she could trust Rachel. "It is, but it shouldn't be," she said. "I know I'm stronger than this. I know, it sounds dumb for me to say that."

Rachel took a second to process all of this through her head. "It doesn't sound dumb to me," she said. "Maybe you're just having a little bit of a crisis because so many things in your life have changed in a relatively short amount of time, and that includes Kevin, too."

"I thought about that," responded Caitlin. "It seems like it would make sense, but… well… I don't know. I guess I don't know myself the way I thought I did before."

Taking a breath, Rachel answered, "Are you worried that you want something different than Kevin?"

Caitlin rolled her head, appearing to be conflicted. She was trying not to say much. This was part of the emotional weakness she had described before. To Rachel, it seemed she was struggling to come to terms with her relationship with Kevin in some way. Rachel did not know why, and she was certainly quite curious. However, Caitlin was her friend, so she did not want to probe. "No one says you have to go with him, not even me," she began, "but at the very least, you should tell him what you decide to do, when you make that decision. It's only the right thing to do."

Caitlin sighed. "I've been too scared to talk to Kevin about it. The worst part about it is, what would he think?"

"Caitlin, I don't know what you need to get off your chest, but Kevin's an optimist," responded Rachel quickly. "Why would you think he would think something bad about you if you told him you don't want to go with him? And if you want to leave, you should tell him that, too. You just have to trust yourself."

Shaking her head, Caitlin stuttered, "I don't think I want to leave. I just… I just don't know."

Rachel let out a sigh, and took a second. This was getting frustratingly difficult, but she was not mad at Caitlin. She understood that whatever Caitlin was facing were new emotions to her. "Is there something wrong with him? Kevin's far from a perfect person, as we all are."

Again, Caitlin shook her head. "No. He's perfect for me," she said. "No one has ever been so kind to me, who tried to find common ground with me, who was willing to open up to me."

"Just like you, he's different, too," smiled Rachel. "That's why you two find so much in common when you come from totally different backgrounds."

Quietly, Caitlin nodded. "I've never been able to open up to him in the same way." She paused for a second to gather her thoughts. "I've told him more than I've told anyone, maybe even more than I've told my father. But to tell him these feelings… I don't think I really can."

Rachel thought about it for a moment, but then smiled. "Telling anyone you're with how you feel can be difficult," she said. "But I'm guessing in your case, being so new to having feelings, it's hard for you to tell anyone how you truly feel inside."

Caitlin sighed.

"For what it's worth, you're doing a good job with me telling me you have them," said Rachel.

Reluctantly, Caitlin said, "I guess."

There was another momentary pause. "Take some time and think about it," Rachel said. "Whatever it is that's on your mind, you'll have to tell him someday. Who knows? Maybe it'll be something that won't bother him at all."

Caitlin only let out another sigh. In her mind, it was not. She was starting to understand her hesitation.

Seeing no need to press further, Rachel changed the subject. "I wonder what his intentions are," she said as she looked at the door again. "From what you've told me, he's already done what your father asked in getting the Triple Alliance back together, as long as your father, Arthur, and Kron make good on getting them on board. You've told me Kevin was doing all of that to rescue Arthur, but he's safe now, as am I. What more do we have to do?"

Briefly, Caitlin looked out the window. Dusk was starting to set in. "There's still the matter of getting Kron home, which Kevin swears he's going to do and has never forgotten." She took a sip of her tea, as she thought for a second. "But the truth be told, I can't imagine that he won't want to rescue Rikleifer. Demonicus still wants him dead and just captured his hometown. Kevin was so passionate about coming back here to defend his home that he had us come here from Scurnia. He won't feel like this is over just because we survived."

"Arthur told me he does care about this city, a lot," Rachel added, recalling talks she had with Arthur on their travels. "Kevin lost his mother three years ago. I wonder if his house is what he has left to remember her, and if that's why he cares so much."

"Could be," commented Caitlin. "He was lucky to have a mother that long; I never had the chance." She paused for a moment, pulling herself together from the painful reminder that her mother died before she could formulate memories of her. She then told Rachel, "Regardless, I have no intention of trying to stop Kevin. I agree that we can't leave things like this."

"And what do you want to do?" asked Rachel.

For a moment, Caitlin thought about her answer. She was still quite emotionally conflicted, but in the end, she came up with a simple answer.

"Whatever I need to," she said.

Chapter 46

Helpless

As nightfall arrived, Kevin was still walking through the forest. A hiking trail extended out from Wyntrail's north side deeper into the Auranian Wilderness. Under the light of shining stars on a clear night, and the distant glow of fires from the military campsite, Kevin was not worried about getting lost. He always had his sword if it became too dark to see.

He just wanted time to think, to process his thoughts. It was true that he was starting to feel the pressure of his actions. Kevin reminded himself that he was not the person on whom the battle hinged, but he still could not shake the feeling. He was not a general, but he had injected himself into the battle for Rikleifer like he was one.

And he had failed. Had he done the right thing by speaking up, or by charging at the approaching catapult, or by going back for Caitlin? The answer was yes to all of them. Had he done the right thing by coming in the first place? Perhaps Professor Magnon was right, and that answer was no. He did leave the bigger mission of reuniting the Triple Alliance undone by choosing to go back to Rikleifer. He had invested all of that time to cross eastern Nuve and the Northern Pass, only to take a day trip in Vallia to find his father and defeat an assassination attempt before turning back to come to Rikleifer. And in the end, he had failed to save his hometown from invasion. That his input in the battle unintentionally delayed actions long enough for the arrival of reinforcements no one knew were coming, and that a number of live were saved as a result of the successful retreat, gave him no comfort.

It was hard for Kevin to figure out what he could do next. As long as Professor Magnon was successful in getting Scurnia on board, then everything the professor had asked of him was complete. But what good would that do now? Rikleifer was a critical loss, one that even

Kevin knew would be nearly impossible to take back.

What was he supposed to do now? He still had a promise to Kron to fulfill, with no idea how to do it. Demonicus still wanted him dead, but he could not exactly run in to Desolunar and negotiate for his life or fight. He could not simply go home, either, since he had no home in Aurana where to go.

He could certainly spend time with Caitlin. That was something he wanted to do, but it seemed so difficult knowing the situation was bad and there was no solution in sight. It was frustrating and a firm distraction, feeling that he had to atone for the loss of Rikleifer and that action was required, even if he could pretend it was not, simply because he felt helpless.

Still, however, Kevin tried to push those thoughts out of his mind. As he walked on, he realized just how dark it was getting as he made it further away from the town. Kevin pulled his sword out, just in case. He stopped, pondering whether to keep walking or to turn back, when he heard a voice.

It said, "You cannot defeat me, for I am nothing."

You cannot defeat me, for I am nothing. The words were echoing in Kevin's head. Still he slept on, trapped listening to these words.

"You cannot defeat me, for I am nothing. I will take it all away from you. I will take your power. I will take your homeland. I will take your realm. And you will be helpless, for I am nothing."

Kevin lit up his sword and turned around. "Show yourself!" he demanded.

Nothing happened. Kevin kept turning and looking around the dark forest, as the voice kept speaking. "You do not see how the game is played. You will see that for which you have worked stripped away before your eyes. Then, you will see your friends murdered before you, one by one. You will watch as I torture them all, including the love of your life. And you will be helpless, for I am nothing."

The voice was somewhat familiar; Kevin thought he had heard it before. "Demonicus! Show yourself!" he demanded.

Further in the dark, there he was! The robe of the Enlighteners from the Shadows was plain as day.

Kevin charged the figure of Demonicus with all his might, and went in for the slash.

The figure did not move. As Kevin ran, it said, "Then, only then when you have lost all that you have, and you have seen them die because of you, will I take mercy on you and allow you to die from the lack of a will to live. And you will suffer until your last breath, because you cannot defeat me, for I am nothing."

Slash! Kevin cut through the figure of Demonicus.

His sword went too clean through it. It was only air.

Kevin tried again. The same result.

Slowly the figure started to disappear, as it changed form as well. As it faded out, it said, "This fate is yours, Kevin Trent Stryker."

This fate is yours, Kevin Trent Stryker.

And as it faded, the shape of Demonicus changed. Briefly, it looked like a man in golden robes, before it faded into nothing.

That man it changed into was Professor Magnon. Kevin was sure of it. He stared at the spot the figure stood for over a minute, hoping it would come back so he could confirm it. Had it all been just a horrendous nightmare? It almost seemed too real to be.

Then, he heard another voice behind him. "Kevin, is that you?"

Immediately, Kevin flipped around and pointed his sword at the voice. As soon as he saw, though, he dropped his sword. This time, it was Wheldon.

"I am sorry, Kevin," said the voice of Wheldon, as the phoenix stood in front of Kevin. "I did not mean to startle you. Is Catie with you?"

Catie. That was not a word anyone but Wheldon would use in reference to Caitlin. Taking several breaths as he was still trying to regain his composure, Kevin stepped up to Wheldon, and reached out to shake his wingtip. Wheldon offered his, and they shook. The corporeal feeling of Wheldon's wingtip was real; he was not an illusion, "That's all right, Wheldon, but no, Caitlin's in the town right now. I'm on my own." Kevin finally said. "It's good to see you again."

"Indeed, the same for me, my friend," Wheldon answered. "Sacred Avalon has graced us with our meeting tonight."

Kevin nodded, acknowledging the common phoenix greeting.

"How did you find me out here?"

"I came down to look for you after the battle, to see if you were okay. As you know, we only travel to human-inhabited areas at night, and when I saw your sword lit up as it was in the City of Phoenixes, I knew you were here. I did not even need to use the connection of our bond."

"Oh," chuckled Kevin awkwardly. He was still trying to rid himself of the paranoid feeling he had from whatever illusion that was. Wheldon, though, was a sight for sore eyes. "I'm very grateful to see you."

Wheldon nodded, before he continued. "Avalon wishes to express its gratitude to you for coming to fight in the Battle of Middle Aurana," responded Wheldon. "It had come to the attention of the Red Phoenix that a loss in this battle could be a precursor to Avalon being threatened. While that is the case, we respect that one of our own fought hard to protect Avalon in the fight, and that is you, honorary phoenix. In order to express their gratitude, the Red Phoenix and the Grand Raven have come here personally to meet you, under the cover of darkness as always."

Surprised, Kevin asked, "They're here now?"

Wheldon nodded. "Yes, they are. They want to see you."

It was almost too good to be true. "Excellent!" exclaimed Kevin, having to catch himself as the word left his lips to keep it from getting too loud. "That saves me a trip to the City of Phoenixes. I have to talk to them about something very important."

"Then please, follow me," said Wheldon. "You are anxiously awaited."

Kevin took a quick look around for any more illusions, then followed Wheldon a bit deeper into the wilderness, off the trail. After a couple of minutes, he saw the all-red feathers and the black and gray feathers of the Red Phoenix and the Grand Raven, respectively.

Bowing before them, Kevin said, "It is a pleasure to make your acquaintances again, Red Phoenix and Grand Raven."

The Red Phoenix and Grand Raven looked at each other for a second, and then turned back to Kevin. In an upbeat tone, the Red Phoenix responded, "And a pleasure to meet you again too, Kevin, honorary phoenix. Sacred Avalon has graced us with this reunion tonight. Please, if you feel more comfortable, you may call me by my given name, Sairon."

"And you may call me Uruson if you would like," added the Grand Raven.

"I'll remember that," responded Kevin. "Thank you. And while you are here, I also want to thank you for allowing me to have your treasured Stripe of Air."

"Still collecting those things?" asked the Red Phoenix, with a little bit of a chuckle. "I am glad that you could make use of ours. How many do you have now?"

Kevin pulled up the right sleeve of his unfastened vanguard jacket, and raised his right arm. "Two," he said, "and Caitlin has one as well. Each one represents an achievement, in a sort of way."

"Good to hear," responded the Red Phoenix. "And while we are on the subject of giving thanks, Uruson and I wish to thank you personally for your defense of this region today."

Frowning, Kevin said, "As nice as it is to hear, I didn't win the battle."

"Ah, but you carried with you the spirit of the phoenix onto the battle," interjected the Grand Raven. "Though it may not have been on the top of your mind at the time, you fought for us, as one of us. You represented us in battle. There is nothing more noble than that, and for that we thank you, even in defeat."

Shaking his head, Kevin responded, "It was nothing, really, but I thank you both for your kindness. With all due respect, I hope you can share the same kindness with each other."

"Oh, yes, on that subject," interrupted the Red Phoenix, "since your departure from Avalon, and the events that took place on that day, the phoenixes and ravens have come to become one again. United we stand, and we no longer acknowledge such a separation, nor are we likely to ever again."

"We are no longer phoenix and raven," added the Grand Raven. "We are now phoenixes, one and all. We live together, we grow together, and we join together in strength, no longer set apart from our brothers and sisters."

A smile came to Kevin's face. "Just as it should be," he said. "How have things gone since I left?"

The Red Phoenix took a step forward and started to explain. "The sacred land of Avalon has never seen a greater time in its history, I believe. After you took action in the battle between phoenixes and ravens that day, Uruson and I left on our own to talk about the situation. He and I had never felt any ill will toward one another, as his was directed at my father and not me, and my efforts were on the matter of defending my people from an aggressor, not at my adopted brother Uruson."

Then, the Grand Raven stepped forward to continue, "Sairon and I spoke for several hours, almost ecstatic to have seen each other again after so long. Had I known that Sairon was the Red Phoenix, it is likely that I would not have continued my campaign against the phoenixes."

"As it turns out," continued the Red Phoenix, "while we left to talk, so too did our people. Uruson's wife, Ravena, led the reconnection of the phoenixes and ravens herself. We reconnected, our people did, and we each found that we were not so different after all. Because we were not different. We were the same, in every way save for feather colors. And once we realized that, things became better almost instantly. We are building our society together again."

Kevin nodded. An idea came to him in this moment. "It is great to hear that you're doing very well. In fact, I am more than glad to hear it, because I must ask for your help."

"Our help?" asked the Grand Raven. "Enlighten me, human with the phoenix spirit. How can we be of assistance to you?"

The realization was that Kevin was still thinking about Demonicus after the illusory encounter. He recalled how the first time he encountered Demonicus, the dictator had a gryphon with him, and Caitlin mentioned that Desolunar was experimenting with gryphon-flying troops. Whether or not they could do it on a larger scale, having phoenixes on board could be a huge help if Aurana was going to reclaim its territory and take the fight to Desolunar.

Taking a deep breath, Kevin's thoughts were focused on what he was about to ask for. He was nervous, knowing that this was much more than just one small favor he was going to ask for, but he also knew that it was a necessary request. "I long had a desire not to ask anyone to abandon their convictions, but now, with this significant loss, I feel I must. This war, the one that sparked the battle today, must come to an end soon lest all nations of the world, human and phoenix alike, be destroyed. At the center of this 'conquest of the realms' is Demonicus, who controls ancient magics through a cult known as the Enlighteners from the Shadows, and rules from the capital city of Desolunar, a city called Seta Archa."

"Ah, yes, I have been there before," interrupted the Grand Raven. "It is quite an old city, but mixes with the new nonetheless in its design. Still, nothing seems 'right' around there. There is almost a rather dark, ominous sensation experienced when flying over that city."

"Appropriate indeed," responded Kevin. "Seta Archa is the capital of an expanding dictatorship under Demonicus. His conquest seeks to rule everything and everyone. And if we're going to try and end the war before it's too late, we need all of the help that we can get."

"So you want our help," interrupted the Red Phoenix. "I see where this is going. You want us to reveal ourselves in front of the humans and join them in the fights ahead."

Nervously, Kevin acknowledged the Red Phoenix's comment. "Yes," he said. "For the human nations, and for Avalon as well. We need your help, and if we lose this war, you and the rest of the phoenixes are likely to find yourselves in mortal danger before too long. So, for your people, and for mine, and those of the world, I ask of you to join in on the fight. Will you?"

The Red Phoenix turned to look at the Grand Raven, and then turned back to Kevin. "Such a decision cannot be made instantly," he said. "We must have some time to talk with our people and listen to their opinions, as well as consider the consequences of either possibility."

"Fair enough", said Kevin, with a sigh of relief. At least it was not an outright rejection, which he deeply feared. "I can understand that. But I thank you anyway for at least making some consideration."

"Your words will be deeply heeded, fellow phoenix," responded the Red Phoenix. "We will not take lightly what you have to say."

At this, however, Wheldon interjected. "Red Phoenix, with all due respect, can we not do something to help Kevin now?"

"You wish to help, Wheldon? Even personally?" asked Uruson.

Wheldon nodded. "Kevin and Catie have proved to be great friends. I would not turn my back on a fellow phoenix in need, especially not someone who has proven to me they are worthy of friendship and loyalty."

Then, the Red Phoenix turned toward Wheldon. "Then so it shall be. Wheldon, you are to remain with Kevin," ordered the Red Phoenix. "Attend to whatever he needs you for. Provide transport, combat aid, and any other needs. Attempt to stay out of view of as many humans as possible, at least for the moment, but proceed with your orders. Is that clear?"

Trying to hold back his excitement at getting to work with Kevin, Wheldon responded again with, "Yes sir!" While Wheldon was very military in how he took care of things, he had grown to become friends with Kevin, and was proud to be serving his home nation of Avalon while working with his only human friend.

"I leave Wheldon as a sign of appreciation for you," continued the Red Phoenix to Kevin. "Protect him, and he will protect you."

"Thank you," nodded Kevin, glad to have Wheldon permanently on board. Wheldon was a friend, too. Now, Kevin had another friend along for the journey.

With that, the Red Phoenix and Grand Raven said their goodbyes to Kevin and Wheldon, as they sought to return to Avalon under the cover of darkness to discuss his request. For now, this was the way it had to be until the phoenixes were willing to be visible to humans. They then took off to the northwest, headed back to Avalon. Although they were difficult to see under the moonlight, Kevin squinted to watch them fly off into the dark northwestern sky.

After they had left, Wheldon was willing to fly Kevin back toward Caitlin's house, although he would land short of town to protect his cover. Wheldon decided to stay where he was to stay out of sight, but encouraged Kevin to catch up with him in the morning. Kevin then had to walk for a couple of minutes to the house, where Caitlin and Rachel were likely sleeping by now. He had huge news to share with them.

Walking down the rest of the trail, Kevin arrived back at the house that belonged to the professor and around to the front door. Before he could make it to the door, however, a twisting sound was heard through the air, and in front of Kevin appeared a spinning magic of yellow and purple. It was light and darkness, twisted together.

What was it? Something seemed suspicious, like this was a gate of some kind. Was Professor Magnon here? And what was his connection to the illusions earlier this evening?

Then, out from the gate, emerged Arthur, Professor Magnon, and Kron. The first comment of those three came from Arthur, who said, "See? I told you he would be here, if this is where they were heading from Rikleifer."

"Never let it be said that I doubted you," responded the professor, "although I would have anticipated the same."

"Precisely," said Arthur. "But it still should be said that I'm taking credit for it…"

As Professor Magnon and Arthur continued to argue a little bit while the professor closed the teleportation gate behind him, Kron stepped up to Kevin and said, "Do not mind them. They have been at it all day today."

"I believe it," responded Kevin. To get their attention, Kevin let out a loud whistle. Professor Magnon and Arthur instantly stopped arguing upon hearing the whistle. "Hey, don't make me get out the sword and put it between you two."

Arthur's eyes widened, seemingly surprised. "Hey Kevin, when did you get here?"

"Earlier today," responded Kevin with a laugh, as he extended his fist to bump Arthur's in a friendly gesture. "You missed the whole battle."

Briefly, Arthur looked around to see he was in Rikleifer, having forgotten for a moment that he walked through a teleportation gate. "Oh, damn," chuckled Arthur as he bumped Kevin's fist. "For what it's worth, I don't regret skipping out and letting you have this one."

"Whatever you say; I'm glad to see you too," laughed Kevin. "And Professor Magnon, too, how are you doing tonight?"

"Very good," nodded the professor. "Arthur and I were just having a discussion on magic and its capabilities, that is all. Your friend here has quite a loud mouth. He could be a heck of a politician if he wanted." He paused for a second to refocus his attention. "My daughter?"

"She's well. She's inside, sleeping," Kevin answered.

"May I see her?"

"Let her sleep. We had a long day getting here."

"I see," acknowledged the professor. He appeared frustrated, but dropped his point for a moment. He turned to Arthur. "Share with him the news we have found, if you would, please."

Arthur nodded. "Of course, how could I not? Kevin, I've got a heck of a story to tell you about our trip to Scurniapolis. I think we know where to go next."

"Go on," said Kevin, interested. A smile came to his face with his pride in knowing there was something coming that would be important.

"Well," began Arthur, "there wasn't too much in Scurniapolis, really. It took a few days before we could get an appointment with King Warren of Scurnia, but we got him on our side pretty quickly. Professor Magnon is a sharp talker and that really helped. Although, I will tell you the king expresses that he would have preferred to see you in person, when he heard Aurana had a new Vanguard."

Kevin shrugged, but hoped the king understood the situation. He had to do what he had to do, and hearing that did not make him second-guess his decision, much as he had lingering feelings about the battle.

"We didn't have much to do after that, so I basically let Professor Magnon and Kron do what they wanted to do," continued Arthur.

Immediately, Kevin shot a look at Kron.

"Do not give Kron any grief," Professor Magnon interjected, in a rare example of giving Kron a break. "It was my idea to stay in Scurniapolis for some time longer. We needed time to look over the papers Arthur and Rachel brought; from *Immortality is a Truth* by Setaeus Demota."

And he didn't even bother to come and help, Kevin thought to himself. While it seemed initially like Professor Magnon had rejected Kevin for opting out of the plan to go to Scurniapolis and instead to join the battle in Rikleifer, why would he then, having time to come to Kevin's aid, still elect not to do so? Why would he not come to the rescue of his daughter?

Something was starting to bother Kevin about the professor, and that was without considering the illusions he had seen earlier. Kron had been right to warn him to be careful around Caitlin's father.

"Setaeus Demota's writing was highly detailed and lengthy, and the translated papers were incomplete and poorly interpreted, so we had to be quite slow and meticulous in our review. Fortunately, I can speak and read *rengan*, and translated the missing parts myself. We found part of a chapter on a 'weak point' in the fabric of our realm, and it was at that point where the original gods crossed into the Realm of the Angels five thousand years ago. It was said, according to Setaeus Demota, that this weak point was the most viable point anywhere for a breach to be made to the Realm of the Angels, and that 'even something as strong as a seal would stand no chance of holding up at this point'. Then, the book goes on to give us the spot of this point: north of 'the pass between the mountains', at a site known as the 'Ancient City'."

Kron interjected, "Kevin, I think we have found my way home."

Eyes widening, Kevin was in disbelief and amazement. To him, it had been quite a long time since Kron found him and asked him to find a way to take the god home. It was a promise that Kevin had always been intent on keeping. Now, he could finally fulfill that promise.

"That's fantastic news, Kron!" Kevin said excitedly. "But are we really okay to leave here to do that?"

Kron thought about it a moment. "Think of it as an opportunity to recruit more help to your cause, Kevin. Not only are you fulfilling a promise you made to me, but you'll have the chance to recruit the gods themselves to your cause to save Aurana and overthrow Demonicus. They will want to be rid of the threat to their existence that is Tyrinion, his immortal father."

Excited, Kevin nodded. That was the best news he could hear.

Gods on his side could totally reverse the course of the war and make Kevin's home a safe place again in the hands of Aurana.

"I doubt you will have an easy time finding such a city, though," interrupted the professor. "Five thousand years is an awful long time, and given the nature of the world, things are bound to change in that amount of time. There are methods of the land changing via natural forces; earthquakes, volcanoes, wind, water, and so on. After five thousand years, such forces add up. And when you consider the fact that this city talked about in the literature was referred to as 'ancient' even by their standards, the chances of finding this city, especially in such a broad and rugged area like the Peaked Mountains, are pretty slim. Please do not misunderstand, as I am not trying to be a pessimist and demoralize everyone, but I do ask that you keep your expectations low."

Kevin took a moment to gather his thoughts. "I understand your point, professor, but this time I have an idea. I can get us a flight over the area. We'll search by air."

"Your phoenix friend?" inquired the professor.

"The very same," nodded the professor. "I can guarantee his help."

The professor considered this for a moment. "Very well," he responded. Then, he took a good long look around. "I can only presume that Aurana has lost the battle. I hope you had the kind of effect you wanted when you ran back here."

That was a shot across the bow, Kevin realized. He answered straightforward, "The smallest of differences is still a difference."

"Indeed," acknowledged the professor, not flinching. "But did you accomplish anything?"

Kevin hesitated, not expecting to be pressured. Then, he pressed forward, deciding not to tell Professor Magnon about how his suggestion defeated part of the Desolunar offensive and likely bought the time needed for the Aurana cavalry to arrive in Rikleifer and support the retreat. If he was going to have such an attitude toward the situation, then it was not information he needed to know, as far as Kevin was concerned. "I think we did play our part in helping."

There was a momentary pause. "Very well," he then said, as he made for the door. "I will now check in with my daughter."

Knowing Caitlin still had a broken ankle or leg, Kevin stepped in front of the professor. "Now, hang on. Don't you think she should get a full night's rest?"

Immediately, the professor reached out and pushed Kevin's side. "Step aside, Kevin. I must see my daughter this instant!"

"Hey, wait a moment!" Kevin tugged on the professor's sleeve, as Arthur and Kron stood back and watched.

"No, Kevin. I will see my daughter. What are you hiding from me?"

Then, the door swung open. And out marched Caitlin, in her dress and walking like normal, no sign of an injury. "He's not hiding anything," she asserted, as she looked directly at her father. "He was pretty clearly trying to do something nice for me. I'm glad to know you have such concern for me, but you could've simply come back tomorrow, and given Kevin a bit of slack."

Aside, Kevin breathed a sigh of relief. Caitlin must have had her magic return. He was surprised, however, that she was so fiery this evening. She did not seem fully in control of her emotions in this moment, struggling to control her anger.

"I was only concerned for your safety," Professor Magnon told his daughter. "You were in a dangerous situation."

"And you placed your trust in Kevin to keep me safe, as he did in me to keep him safe," Caitlin retorted. "Yet for all of the trust you placed in him for the security of the world, you still did not trust him with me."

Professor Magnon smiled a bit, for just a second. He had been concerned about how much his daughter would change since her emotional shell fractured, but she was showing that she was still a strong person. "My apologies. I did not mean to offend you, my daughter."

"Don't apologize to me," Caitlin answered. "It's Kevin to whom you should apologize."

"And when I feel the time is right, I shall," said the professor.

What the hell did the professor mean by that? Kevin thought to himself.

There was an awkward silence for a moment. Then, Kron broke it. "Interesting place for the army to retreat," he observed. "I am surprised they did not head back for Aurana City, to defend the capital. Getting there from here without going through Rikleifer would require a walk through the wilderness."

"They are here because Aurana's supply line is here. They could not afford to lose the supply base if they wish to keep the army fighting," answered the professor. He then thought for a second, looking like an idea was coming to him.

Arthur rolled his eyes and stood next to Kevin. "There he goes again," he said. "A little bit like your constant daydreaming, this guy gets lost in thought."

"Quiet, Arthur," answered the professor. He then pondered aloud what he was thinking. "There is a road, not a wide one, that leads to the south from Wyntrail. It runs west of Rikleifer through some small villages and down to Haventown, south of the city. Desolunar would not have stored their supplies for the attack further south due to the distance in crossing the southern forest. If they moved fast and swept into Haventown…" There, he stopped and asked Kevin, "Were there any Auranian cavalry at the battle?"

"They came in at the very end to support our retreat," said Kevin. "They're here too."

"Excellent," answered the professor. "Then perhaps this retreat might work to Aurana's advantage. If we can move with the cavalry and strike at their supply line, we can isolate the Desolunar troops in Rikleifer, cut them off from their supplies, and cut off their retreat all at the same time."

"It sounds like you ought to be advising the Triple Alliance," quipped Arthur to the professor. Immediately, Kevin cringed. He knew of Professor Magnon's distaste for the military. He glanced at Arthur for making the suggestion.

Surprisingly, however, Professor Magnon did not seem upset. "I suppose you may be right, Arthur," he answered. "We have not heard personally from Demonicus in a while, but between the attack on the Cliffs of Vallia and the battles with Desolunar, his message is still loud and clear. He seeks to conquer us all." He paused for a second.

"Perhaps if I wish to see Demonicus meet his end, advising his opponent on how to seize the initiative will be worth putting aside my feelings about militaries."

Kevin sighed, recalling that the professor had an unknown vendetta against Demonicus. This unexpected result also meant something slightly disappointing. "So, I suppose you won't be coming along with us to take Kron home, then."

"No," answered the professor, "but you are quite capable, Kevin. Take Kron home, and we can meet again after that." He paused for a second. "Get some rest, all of you. I will stop by in the morning to say goodbye to my daughter before I depart." He then turned and started walking away.

Everyone else, other than Caitlin, stood a little bewildered as they watched the professor walk on down the pathway into Wyntrail. "Is he always like that?" inquired Arthur to Caitlin.

Kron turned away, shaking his head.

Frowning a bit, Kevin commented for Caitlin, "Sort of. I think he's more about the business than the formalities."

"Huh," expressed Arthur, jokingly. "It's no wonder his daughter wanted to be like that."

"Hey!" exclaimed Caitlin. "Save it for the morning when people actually have had enough sleep to argue!"

It occurred to Kevin in that moment that Arthur was right. Certainly, Caitlin was not like her father now, but what she had disciplined herself to be, with the assistance of a shell of some kind of mind magic, was in many ways a version of her father. Was that why she wanted to be protected from her emotions, to be more like him? And was all of this anger in her voice a part of what happened when she was unprotected, or just because she was inexperienced in emotion?

Before Kevin could respond, Arthur started walking past him and towards the door of his house. "Whatever, I'm too tired," he said sarcastically. "I'll find some space inside to sleep. Come along now, Kevin, so that I can have someone to talk to while I'm hitting the sack." He was intentionally adding a false sense of pompousness to his voice at the end.

Briefly, Kevin looked to Kron. "I suppose I will see you in the morning, then," Kron said as he gave Kevin a nod and walked away the opposite direction of the professor to wander.

Silently, Kevin looked up at the stars. Everyone was going to bed, and he had to do the same. But as he took a brief second to look up, he pondered everything he had seen. So much had happened the last couple of days, and now to add to it, the illusion he had seen troubled him. Something seemed very off about Professor Magnon, and Kevin was starting to fear who he might truly be.

"Come on, Kevin!" yelled Arthur. "Are you dreaming *again*?"

Ignoring the call of his friend, Kevin kept his eyes fixed on the sky. He swore he could hear the voice in his mind. *You cannot defeat me, for I am nothing.*

Chapter 47

The Nearest Place to the Heavens

The night had seemed shorter than it actually was, as morning came very quickly. Even operating on a full night's sleep plus a couple of hours in the afternoon still made Kevin tired in the morning from the fatigue of the previous day. As usual, he was the last one to wake up, with Caitlin having to wake him to make sure he did not sleep in. She was surprised a bit that he was the last to sleep in, but knowing he had a lot on his mind, she did not ask about it.

As the morning went on, Caitlin treated her friends to breakfast with preserved provisions. She and Rachel caught up Arthur on what had gone on in the battle. As they talked, Professor Magnon knocked on the door for his promised morning visit. Caitlin hugged her father tightly, and the professor spent an hour catching up and discussing what he would be doing—linking up with Vincent Stryker and the planning groups to encourage a swift counterattack. He did not, however, offer Kevin an apology.

That did not bother him, but Kevin found it frustrating that the professor was someone who could teleport but was not offering one to him and his friends. In fact, the professor seemed to want nothing to do with taking Kron home or being anywhere remotely near there. The location that Arthur had for the "Ancient City" was all the way back by Vallia and the Northern Pass, meaning it was a long way back to explore this lead. Fortunately Kevin and his friends did have Wheldon, so the trip would probably take about a week of flying as opposed to a month or more of walking.

More and more, Kevin was becoming suspicious about the professor. Some of these actions he was taking and his recent abandonment of Kevin's group made him wonder if at this point Professor Magnon was more concerned with what benefited him. Maybe it was this personal score with Demonicus that was motivating him and Kevin had all but served his usefulness at this point in his eyes. Maybe it was something more nefarious and he was protecting his daughter and Kevin from it. Maybe, he was actually the enemy in disguise. The illusions that appeared last night supported the latter.

Regardless, he could not tell Caitlin. She would never understand these suspicions he was having. If he did tell her that he thought her father were up to something bad, he could end up ruining his whole friendship and relationship with her. Kevin really did love her and worried about losing her. All of his friends were special to him, but she was the most special thing in his life right now.

A little later that morning, Kevin and company headed down to the town center to briefly meet up with Kevin's father. Vincent Stryker explained to Kevin how Professor Magnon had offered the counterattack suggestion overnight and personally wished to offer support. Accordingly, King Andrew II was so enthralled by this idea that he ordered the army restock and immediately move for the road to Haventown, and even Eukert agreed this was the right move. The king, upon meeting Vincent Stryker for the first time this morning, had also requested the retired Scurnian general and Auranian legend come along to consult with these actions. Vincent told Kevin he felt he had no choice but to accept, knowing how badly Aurana had struggled in war and feeling that he could help in this war against Desolunar.

Sadly, Kevin agreed without any arguing. They had not long been reunited as father and son, already gone through trials and tribulations, and now they had to be separated again to accomplish what needed to be done. Much as Kevin felt responsible and wanted to help as well, his oldest promise was to take Kron home. He had the opportunity to do that now. And if Kron really were a god, as he had said, then perhaps Kevin could rally gods to his cause by taking Kron home.

Still, he would miss his father. Vincent Stryker reassured Kevin that he was doing the right thing by taking Kron home rather than joining the battle to come, and that it would not be another sixteen years before they saw each other again. Kevin was more than certain his father would be safe despite his ailing health, but naturally, like any good son, he worried for his father's safety nonetheless. He was also a little disappointed that he would not have the time to catch up with King Andrew II, who was enough of a believer in him to bestow the title of Vanguard to him. Kevin hoped they may have that opportunity to meet again in the future.

In town, the foursome also ran into Kron, who had been trying to remain inconspicuous. He explained how he had spent much of the night exploring Wyntrail, and was ready to go. He also explained how he had caught up with Wheldon already to talk about the flight. The plan was set in place, and early that afternoon, they were ready to go.

Although it was the middle of the day, Wheldon was willing to take off as long as they did so from a clearing in the wilderness, off the path behind the professor's house. With everybody packed and ready to go, they met in the forest clearing, ready for an afternoon of flight. Kevin expressed concern about overburdening Wheldon with carrying five people at once, but it was there that Kron demonstrated his hidden ability to fly, to which he had referred in Vallia. Kevin and Caitlin looked at each other briefly at this revelation, knowing Caitlin could fly as well if she were in her angel form, and realizing it must be some kind of divine effect.

As the sun passed its high noon point, Wheldon took off from the clearing with Kevin, Caitlin, Arthur, and Rachel aboard. Kron followed, levitating himself before eventually keeping pace. Wheldon took off away from Wyntrail and over the wilderness before banking to the east to begin the week-long trip back to the Northern Pass and to this "Ancient City" that had been described. He had stayed over the Wilderness until nightfall, when it was safe to traverse over human-occupied areas.

Over the course of the seven-day trip, Kevin and Arthur had a chance to catch up about everything that had happened while they were separated. They were close friends, and even though their experiences had been mostly separate since they first met Kron, they remained as tight-knit as ever. After all, Kevin had gone to the lengths he had because he wanted to rescue Arthur from Demonicus. Now, he was going to those extents to rescue his home from the same conqueror. And Arthur, while wanting no part of being in battle, wanted to avoid being killed by his father while doing what he could to help his friend.

There was a little time during their rest periods for Kevin, Caitlin, Arthur, and Rachel to all spend a little time with each other. As they sat together, with Wheldon as well, all five of them talked about where they had been and what they wanted to do in their lives. Kron chatted a bit with the group as well, but worked to take care of their basic needs such as food and shelter while they spent time resting together. It was the least he could do, he felt, for the favor they were doing for him.

As Caitlin realized over the course of the days, Kevin seemed to have less and less tension on him the further he was from Aurana. Spending days with his friends far from the war gave him a bit of a departure from the things that were troubling him. He would still talk about the battle in Rikleifer and how he cared for his homeland and the people for whom he was responsible for their lives, but the stress of it did not seem to be affecting him nearly as bad.

Unfortunately for Caitlin, her hesitations still affected her. Long nights of flying meant that she had time to think about her feelings and process them. It gave her more of an idea of what she was feeling and why she was hesitant. Talking to Rachel alone helped quite a bit as well, as Rachel was supportive and also realistic. Rachel was glad to spend parts of their rest time talking with Caitlin as she was happy to be building a friendship with a new friend, and also to avoid Arthur calling her a cynic.

Seven days in, Wheldon brought Kevin and company in overnight to the town of Rugger, at the mouth of the Northern Pass on Nuve's side. Kevin and Caitlin had been through here before, but took a little more time to look at the town from above. Rugger was not very large, little more than a trading post with a few shops and stone buildings in the same style as those in Nuvenia. Despite this, it was the capital of Nuvenia's northeastern province of Katalina, so there were a couple of small government buildings as well. Much of eastern Nuve was less populous than its west, as the Aurun and Rhonean rivers supplied water to the west, which was harder to find in the mountainous east.

Kron scouted ahead and led Wheldon to a perfect point on Rugger's north side and out of sight of anyone. It was perfect for Wheldon especially, not wanting to be spotted by any other humans. Since they had flown at night, and that would make searching for the Ancient City difficult, Kron suggested that the group take a day and night of rest, walk into Rugger for a hot meal and to resupply as needed, and adjust their sleep schedules back to normal. Kron paid for the hot meal, the first for Kevin and company since they were in Vallia. Together, they spent one more night together before what would be a busy day of searching the mountains.

The next morning, Wheldon took off with his human passengers and Kron accompanying him. North of the pass, the Peaked Mountains were especially jagged, rugged, and pinched together close enough to make civilization impossible to exist here, much less an entire city. This would be a difficult search.

Over the course of the day, Wheldon flew between mountains as Kevin and company looked in all directions. No one, even Kron, quite knew what they were looking for, only that it was some kind of city that was likely in ruins. Several hours had passed, and the search had still been futile. The group was sweeping the mountains back and forth, and still found nothing. To make matters worse, the day was already becoming late. The sun was going past the horizon, and several storm clouds were also moving in from the west. It was going to be a very hairy twilight, one way or another.

Things had progressed to the point where Kevin was sick of searching. "Guys, I think we had better pack it in for today," he called out. "The weather's getting bad, and we're getting low on daylight."

Next to Wheldon, Kron nodded.

Then, Caitlin tapped Kevin on the shoulder. "Can we stay five more minutes?" she asked. "Something's been bothering me for the last couple of minutes. I want to see if I can figure it out before we go back."

Kevin nodded. "Fair enough, if everyone's okay with it," he called back.

Arthur and Rachel exclaimed their agreement, trusting Caitlin.

Kron hung around close to Wheldon, wanting to see what Caitlin was doing. She had her eyes closed, holding on to Kevin so as not to fall off, but she was clearly focused on something.

She found it, and tapped Kevin's shoulder. "I sense a stripe."

"Out here?" asked Kevin in surprise.

Caitlin tapped Kevin's shoulder. "I'm sure of it" she said. "It's really subtle, but I can almost swear it feels like another stripe."

"Maybe this stripe is in the city," called out Arthur up to Kevin, letting him know of his theory.

It was a good idea considering there was so little else in the treacherous northern range of the Peaked Mountains. Kevin came up with an idea since he was the one sitting nearest to Wheldon's neck, and called it out. "Caitlin, tap me on the left or right and I'll tap Wheldon to tell him where to go."

Although he could not see it, Caitlin nodded. She then almost immediately tapped Kevin on his right side, and in turn Kevin tapped on the right side of Wheldon's neck.

Confidently, Wheldon carefully made the turn to head due east, with Kron following close behind. The next peak seemed unfamiliar, like it was one they had not passed yet. Caitlin gave Kevin a couple more taps, and Kevin relayed them, directing Wheldon around the mountains and between the peaks.

Ten minutes later, Kron pointed it out. Behind the next peak was something that was definitely not natural-made. What was behind there was a spire, a tall one. It was difficult to tell how tall it was, but it appeared to be older than the mountains themselves. A closer look from above showed a bunch of smaller buildings clustered around the spire, tucked into a space surrounded by mountains on all sides. All of the buildings were carved out of rock, and it appeared that the spire sat directly in the middle of the city. It was hidden from sight, camouflaged by the rock's color being nearly identical to that of the nearby Peaked Mountains. No roads appeared to be anywhere near this ancient site, much less even possible to reach it around or over all of these mountains. Truly, it was a grand sight in the setting sun. So old, and so ruined, yet so antique in its appearance nonetheless.

"That has to be it," called out Rachel as she saw it. "Isn't that amazing? Just look at it. It must be older than the mountains themselves!"

"Certainly looks that way," responded Kevin, too impressed with what he was seeing to form a more elaborate response. It was almost too grand of a sight for him to believe. Then, there was a mighty thunder crash. The sky was getting darker as clouds were starting to cover from above, and the sun was setting below the mountains. Immediately, Kevin tapped Wheldon in the center of his neck and said, "Set us down on the city's edge! Be very careful not to hit yourself on the rock as you land."

Wheldon nodded and proceeded to enter a slow spiraling descent to get down to the ground without hitting the mountainsides. As Kron was able to land straight, he landed on the ground first and helped guide Wheldon to the best spot to land.

From the ground, the ruins looked even more pristine. As craggy and as deserted as the barren land of the city was, in a gap between several mountains, the old structures of the ruins stood out in their beauty. There was simply something about them, possibly their age, that made them prominent. Amid the darkening sky, there was something even more majestic about these ruins than one could imagine. Their plain structures seemed to possess a very unique style about them, one that struck all that viewed it with awe.

Kevin, Caitlin, Rachel, and Arthur stepped off Wheldon as soon as he had landed, still staring at the ruins. Only a small bit of the city's ruins were visible, but they were all around the spire in the center. Taking a moment to survey the city, Caitlin declared, "It truly is the nearest place to the heavens. It's like there's something you don't see from its outward appearance that makes it special." She was captivated by the sights.

There was a pause, before Kron explained, "These are First Era structures. Probably some kind of sacred site."

Kevin looked at Kron, puzzled.

"Oh," said Kron in realization. "Well, I am not as old as most of the gods above, but this city is older that even them. We are in the Fourth Era at the moment, and the oldest gods come from the Second Era. We know very little about the First Era that preceded them, but I do know enough to recognize their structures."

After about a moment, though, Caitlin took note of the darkening sky. "We had better hurry," she said. "There won't be any lights for miles from here once the sun completely sets and the storm front moves in."

"Right," responded Kevin. "Now let's get moving."

Before they could go anywhere, however, a loud bang rang through the air. It was so loud as to shake the whole spire in front of them, and it was different than anything they had heard. "Is that thunder?" asked Arthur.

Kron shook his head. "No," he said, pointing to a fire burning on the side of the spire. "Something exploded."

The sight of the burning fire and the column of smoke that was forming a pillar up from that point created a sense of injustice within Kevin. Such an explosion, Kevin was sure, must have been intentional. And to damage a city that seemed so sacred as the Ancient City did was almost like a spike to the heart. It hurt, and it hurt badly. Immediately, Kevin made a hand gesture for everyone to move in the direction of the explosion to check it out. He was running as quickly as he could, and so was everyone else behind him. Whatever had caused this explosion, Kevin was desperate to find out.

Within less than a minute, they were at the spire's edge. And what they saw was very unexpected. It was a man, dressed in dark red wizard's robes, blasting some kind of magic energy into the side of the spire. He seemed intent on destroying it.

Kevin stepped up to him in haste, reacting to what he was seeing, and screamed, "What are you doing? How dare you!"

Before Kevin had any opportunity to get another word in, though, the man turned around, and in that instant, Kevin was blasted by a wave of fire, beyond the power of any magic. He was thrown back a great distance, and ended up against the ground back at the edge of the city.

Caitlin ran towards Kevin, screaming his name and rushing to his aid. Arthur, meanwhile, drew his Sword of Corruption while Rachel placed an arrow in her bow and pulled the bowstring taut. The man in wizard's robes raised his hands, and started speaking in *rengan*.

Quickly, Kron extended his arm in front of Arthur and Rachel. "Wait!" he commanded. "That blast that hit Kevin, that was not magic. Magic does not let you expand a blast of fire to that size and power. It had to be divine power."

"Then how would he have it?" asked Rachel. "Unless…"

"Unless he not only has the Stripe of Fire, but he knows how to use it too," interrupted Arthur, in realization.

Chapter 48

The Spire

Kron nodded, acknowledging that what Arthur said was correct, and then proceeded to say, in *rengan*, "*What are you doing, and why are you destroying these ruins?*"

A cold response was what was returned. "*Stay out of my way*," said the man in wizard's robes, in *rengan*. He then turned back and continued to blast away at the spire.

"*You will cease and desist, by order of the gods, or you will suffer the consequences. I will give you a few seconds to comply.*" Kron made his ultimatum strong and with force, as he was not one to allow such senseless destruction to continue.

The man in wizard's robes responded in *rengan*, and swore at Kron without turning away.

That was the last straw. Kron had given this man a chance to surrender and he had refused. Kron took a look behind him to Kevin, who was now sitting up where he had stopped. Caitlin was treating him for his wounds, her angel wings now visible and her power rising from the shock across her heart at seeing Kevin hit so hard. But it appeared that Kevin was all right for the moment. Rain began to fall from the skies, and crashes of thunder started to erupt through the air. It was very dark now with such black clouds blanketing the sky overhead. With all of that in mind, Kron signaled over to Arthur and Rachel. "Let us go for him," he said. "Be mindful of his fire, as it is not normal magic fire, but in all likelihood a flame wave from his stripe. Fight to kill, not to injure."

A little stunned, Arthur looked over at Kron. "What did he say?" he asked.

"Trust me, you do not want to know," responded Kronius, "but let me tell you it was not kind. If we do nothing, these ruins are going to be destroyed."

Rachel pulled her bowstring tighter, and asked as she took aim, "But who is he? I'm still a little edgy on the 'shoot first, ask questions later' concept, even if he just attacked Kevin."

"Worry about it later," responded Kron. "Kevin will be fine. Caitlin is treating him. But now we have a job to do." He began to charge energy in his hands.

Arthur pulled up his sword to a battle stance, not really knowing how to use it. Nervous as he was, he was steeled by a desire to avenge that shot to Kevin. "In that case, would you mind letting me take the first shot?"

"Suit yourself," said Kron, gesturing almost in a way as to invite Arthur to make the first attack.

Acknowledging this, Arthur nodded over to Rachel, placed his sword in an attack stance, and began a forward charge on the man in wizard's robes. But as he struck, Arthur felt his strike blocked. As he looked, though, it was not just a block. The man had blocked it with one finger, and just one finger. In sharp surprise, Arthur hastily tried to make another swing, only to have it blocked as well.

And then, the man grabbed Arthur by the arm and with his other hand blasted at Arthur. With only a split second to spare, Arthur pulled up his Sword of Corruption to defend the blast. The heat from the sea of fire was nearly unbearable, but Arthur was managing not to be thrown back by it in the same manner that Kevin just had been.

Ready to rescue Arthur, Rachel let loose her arrow towards the man in wizard's robes. Responding to it, the man let go of Arthur with his one hand, still blasting the sea of fire at him, as he blew wind magic at the other arrow to throw it off course and make it miss.

Within a moment, however, the man stopped firing his sea of flames, allowing Arthur, Rachel, and Kron to form up again. Kevin and Caitlin were actually behind him by a short distance, but the man seemed not to be concerned. Strong and clear in his mission, the man in wizard's robes lowered his arms and began to make a lengthy statement in *rengan*.

"You who dare to interfere shall die," translated Kron, so that Arthur and Rachel could understand what he was saying as well. "No one, not ever, shall interfere with the missions of those who stand superior to you. As such, you will either stand aside, or you will be bathed in a sea of fire. This is my ultimatum."

Arthur shook his head. "No way," he responded. "Kron, you better tell him that."

"*Under what right do you have to make such a claim?*" asked Kronius in *rengan* to the man in wizard's robes. "*Who are you, and why do you seek the destruction of such ruins? We cannot allow you to destroy these ruins, not here in the Ancient City.*"

The man continued to speak in response, as Kronius continued to translate, "Then you will die. Who I am and what my purpose is have no concern to anyone but myself. I warn you not to push the issues or try to retaliate any further, or you all will suffer the consequences of interfering with the…"

Suddenly, the man yelped in pain. He looked downward, almost in shock more that he had been hit with something more than the sudden pain of being injured. In his ankle, sticking out from under his sock, was a small dart, the likes of which none of them had seen before.

Behind them, Kevin was finally being helped to his feet by Caitlin. His Nuve stealth bracer was open at the front, and it had just been fired for the very first time while he was lying on the ground. "Hit him when he's not looking!" called out Kevin. "It may be a cheap shot, but then his defense is useless."

The rain began to fall harder outside, and the thunder was getting louder and louder. Nearby lightning strikes seemed very frequent. It seemed to inspire Arthur to an extent, for he took up his sword again fearlessly and said, "Enough is enough. Talk is cheap. Let's finish this on our own."

Rachel stepped forward, arrow drawn. She kept her knees loose, ready to start moving around, as her black Desolunar prototype bow was fixated on the man in front of her. "Such acts cannot be tolerated. You must be stopped."

Then, Kron began charging energy. "*Very well, you were warned,*" he said in *rengan* straight to the man. "*If you will not abide by the order of the gods, then you will have your life terminated for your crimes.*"

As they stood together, and the rain began falling harder, Kevin and Caitlin were still several steps behind them. Caitlin was now floating, as her angel wings were now visible. She looked on at everyone in front of her and said, “We had better focus on making sure that spire doesn’t sustain any more damage.”

“You took the words right out of my mouth,” responded Kevin.

Arthur, Rachel, and Kron started circling the man in wizard’s robes. As much as the rain would be a distraction to them as they fought, together they had a collective determination to save these ruins and see to the defeat of this man. But would it be enough?

Tensely waiting to see who would make the first move, it would end up being Rachel losing control of her bowstring in the rain, accidentally unleashing the first attack. Almost in a split second, the man in wizard’s robes blew away the arrow with wind magic. Then, throwing it away, he turned to blast Kron with a sea of flames from the Stripe of Fire, recognizing the god as his greatest threat. Kron did not have much time to mount his energy into a shield, but he managed it anyway.

Then, from behind, Arthur made another charge, sword in front of him. Fearlessly he charged, knowing full and well what the result would be. The powerful, forceful sword strike was blocked by the man’s free arm, perfectly holding back Arthur’s sword without flinching.

Just as Arthur had intended.

With both arms being used to fend off his attackers, and his focus divided between the two of them, the man’s efforts left himself open to an attack from Rachel. She nocked the antite arrow in her bowstring, intent on depowering this wizard. She took a second to take aim, and fired.

The arrow struck the wizard hard in the shoulder, causing him to flinch heavily and call out in pain. Both his sea of fire and his block on Arthur fell as he immediately started clutching his shoulder in pain. The wizard fell to his knees. Taking advantage of this, Arthur seized the opportunity to strike the wizard.

But almost instantly, he was gone, just as the sword reached the cloth of the man’s wizard robes. The clothes sunk to the ground with no figure inside to give it structure. And from the robes below, a band of red floated into the sky, almost as if fire, in a pure elemental form and not flames, was emanating into the air. It was almost certainly the Stripe of Fire.

"What the hell just happened?" asked Arthur, more or less stunned at what his sword strike had just done. He kept staring at the Sword of Corruption. "It's almost like he disintegrated!"

Kron stepped forward and put his foot down on the mass of cloth left below. "I doubt he disintegrated or we would find some remains," he responded. "I would reason, however, that he is either dead or safely somewhere else."

"You don't know?" asked Rachel.

"No," shrugged Kronius. "It is something beyond anything I have ever seen, although I suppose that anything is possible. He has left us a lot of questions to attempt to answer. Namely, who was he and why did he want to destroy the ruins including this spire? It just seems like a senseless crime."

Arthur sheathed his sword as the heavy rainwater glistened down the blade's side. "Maybe there's something in his clothes that may give us a clue. If not, then we really don't have anything else we can go off of."

"It is possible," said Kron. He then had a thought. "Rachel, would you mind going around the spire to get Kevin? I thought I heard him and Caitlin heading for the spire. He will definitely want this stripe."

Rachel nodded, and rushed off to fetch Kevin and Caitlin. As she did, Arthur and Kron bent down to the wet ground and started shuffling through the man's wizard robes. They observed that there was nothing particularly special about these dark robes, and they just appeared to be fairly generic robes. No special identifiers, color patterns, patches, or anything else could be found on the robe.

Then, Kronius reached his hand down into the robe, and felt something hard. He pulled it out through the top and started to inspect it, showing it to Arthur as he did. It was a gold pendant, printed with red ink smashed into two letters stamped in the pendant. The two letters read *WN*. "Great," said Kron sarcastically as he saw this. "It only seems justified that the Enlighteners from the Shadows are involved."

Before Arthur could respond, however, Rachel came running back around the spire again with Kevin and Caitlin with her. As they came around, Caitlin said loud enough for everyone to hear, "It looks like the spire hasn't suffered severe damage. It should be fine."

"Great to hear," responded Kron. "Our attacker was an Enlightener." Standing up, Kron began to pass around the golden pennant. "*WN* stands for *Wondamer Notuerew*, a pair of *rengan* words that translate to 'Negation of Glory'. It happens to be the motto of the Enlighteners from the Shadows."

Kevin shook his head. "What the hell are they doing here?" He looked at the spire again. "What would Demonicus want with such a place?"

"Maybe the same thing we do," Caitlin said to Kevin. "If what my father read about the Ancient City and the 'weak spot' is true, then getting rid of these ruins could also rid the world of the last possible access to the gods, or at least how to find it."

Immediately, Kevin looked back at Caitlin. That made a lot of sense, and she came up with that answer very quickly. She established a motive for Demonicus, and the method was the power of that stripe. The opportunity was that Demonicus had a powerful wizard of some kind in his ranks who could capably use it, something Kevin had never done with the two he held, nor Caitlin with her one. Kevin could not say he was impressed, however, because Caitlin had amazed him with her logic many times before, and this was no different.

"It does seem quite possible when you put it that way," acknowledged Kron. "Tyrinion might know about this place; he was one of the twenty original gods."

Might, Kevin thought to himself. "Are you sure about that?" he asked aloud.

"Reasonably," Kron answered. "I do not know much precise knowledge, but I know that Setadev's original gods followed him through the weak point to the Realm of the Angels, and that Tyrinion would have been one of them."

"Well, thank goodness we got here when we did," commented Arthur.

"No kidding," commented Kevin. He reached out to fist-bump Arthur. "And nice fighting. That was awesome."

Arthur returned the fist bump. "You too, man," he said. "And really, everyone. That was a heck of a team effort."

Kron signaled over the the energy floating in the air. "Indeed, but before we spend much time expounding on things, Kevin may want to collect the Stripe of Fire here before we forget about it."

He was right; that was important to handle right away. "Indeed," nodded Kevin. He stepped forward and extended his arm, ready to absorb the still free-floating stripe in the rainy night. By now, it did not seem like something out of the ordinary to take a stripe within his body, and Kevin showed no fear in approaching it. The stripe was conducted very easily into Kevin's body, as by now Kevin knew exactly how to do it properly. It came to him very naturally, and flowed into his body, lighting up a stripe of red on Kevin's forearm alongside his four other ones.

Suddenly, though, Kevin doubled over, coughing and hacking.

Quickly, Caitlin and Arthur grabbed him by both arms, trying to keep him from completely falling over. "Are you all right, Kevin?" asked Caitlin as she held tightly onto Kevin.

He coughed a few more times before catching his breath and straightening himself back up. "Yeah, I'm all right," he said. "I don't know what that was about."

"You haven't been sick or anything like that," responded Caitlin. "Unless you're hiding something from us?

Kevin shook his head. "No," he said. "I'm not hiding an illness that I know of, at least." He was telling the truth. "But whatever that was, for that moment, it was horrible. It kind of felt like my insides wanted to rip themselves out."

"It was really that painful?" asked Arthur.

"Very much so," nodded Kevin. "It was nearly impossible to breathe for that minute."

There was a slight pause as Kron considered all of this in the falling rain. "Take him inside the spire," he then instructed, pointing to an opening in the side of the spire. "Kevin, I would like to take a look over you and make sure you are fine before we go on, and I would rather do so in a dry place."

Kevin nodded, wiped his head to brush off the rainwater on his forehead, and proceeded to head for the opening in the spire. Caitlin, Arthur, Rachel, Kronius, and Wheldon followed him in carefully, with Wheldon having to duck his head underneath to fit inside the small doorway-type entrance.

Inside the spire, though, was a sight itself. An old tile and stone altar sat in the middle of the spire's core, placed precisely an equal distance from the walls in all directions. The decorations on it were very elegant, and depicted creatures such as dragons, serpents, phoenixes, gryphons, chimeras, and so on. Furthermore, all of these creatures were depicted as serving one man, who stood above the rest of them.

Around the spire was a set of murals painted all across the inside walls. Their style was fairly crude, and the paint had worn away after so many years. Despite this, faint images of men and various creatures were visible when one looked closely upon its walls. They appeared to be standing on clouds, a unique site.

It was the Realm of the Angels, Kevin realized.

Were the gods truly not the first to be visitors to the Realm of the Angels? It was exactly what the paint on the walls appeared to depict. And, just like the altar in front of him, all of the men and creatures pictured on the walls appeared to be worshipping one figure. It was shaped like a man, but looked like a complete shadow. Whether or not that was a result of the faded paint or how it was actually pictured, Kevin could not be sure.

Caitlin proceeded to light the four torches attached to the altar, somewhat surprised that the altar's torches did light at all considering their age. "Pretty amazing place," she said aloud as she lit the torches. "Just look at some of these images in here. They're almost divine."

"Correction," said Wheldon as he took a closer look at the murals and at the altar. "They are divine. See this man pictured here?" he said as he pointed to the figure the creatures and men on the walls were worshipping. "This is the Great One, the one we phoenixes worship. He is the master of all organisms, no matter what type or kind. And he is not a man or a phoenix, but rather he can take any form he wants. This altar, and these murals, all show every type of creature, including man, basking in the glory of the Great One."

"Some believe that the Great One was really Setadev, the first king of gods and the man you all know through the facts you've uncovered as Setaeus Demota," commented Kron. "Setadev's time was after that of this site or the belief of the Great One, yet those who believed that believed he had always been there. Regardless of who the Great One is or was, however, it seems obvious that what we have here is a worshipping center to the Great One. If this were believed to be a holy site, I can understand why such a city was built here. Such a magnificent worshipping site for the Great One does not spring up on a shear whim."

"No, it does not," added Wheldon. "We have such sites in the City of Phoenixes, with quite eloquent decorations in our Great Temple. Although we are quite familiar with the history of our land of Avalon, we do not know how this, or even our entire city, came about. We merely moved in to a vacant city. It has led us to believe that the City of Phoenixes might have had a civilization that also worshipped the Great One, before we ever arrived."

Kron carefully considered this. "Interesting, Wheldon," he said. "We should ask some of the oldest gods about what they know of the people that built both cities. If I know Chatka, he will likely know more about it than I do."

"One of your friends?" asked Kevin.

"Very much so," acknowledged Kron. "Chatka, the god representing peace and war, has been a friend of mine for many years. He is over five thousand years old, and he has gained a great amount of knowledge over all of his years."

Across the room, Rachel said, "One way or another, this place does intrigue me so much that I want to learn more about it."

Arthur rolled his eyes from across the room. "You're not the only one," he said. "Given what we see here, though, would this be reason for the Enlighteners from the Shadows to attack this place?"

"It's such a treasure trove of a history that it would make sense," responded Rachel, putting together the pieces she saw. "Still doesn't answer why he had the Stripe of Fire or how he disappeared, but it lends reason to the argument that he acted on behalf of the group he supposedly represents."

On the backside of the room, Caitlin spotted something in the mural and said, "Look at this!" She pulled Kevin over, who was standing just a couple of steps away anyway. Then, she pointed to a winged figure on the mural. "Is that what I think it is?" she said.

It took Kevin less than a second to have an answer. "Sure does," he said. "It looks like an angel. Just like you do." Kevin was taking note of the fact that Caitlin still had her visible angel wings and was still floating lightly off the ground. "I wonder what it's doing on the mural."

"I'm not sure," responded Caitlin. "The angel is a mythical figure that has been around for millennia, but as far as we know, I'm the first real one. Is that correct, Kron?"

By now, everyone else had been drawn over to Kevin and Caitlin. "That is correct," answered Kron. "It is most certainly the case, although the Realm of the Angels takes its name from the mythical figure."

"Then why is one on here?" asked Caitlin, curiously. "It doesn't really seem to have any meaning in the context of the image we see around us, and the faded paint might have removed something that would have given us a better hint of what it did mean at the time."

Kron looked around for a second. "There is really not much that would give any hints of what any of these murals mean. All we can infer was that this spire was a worshipping center to the Great One."

"It was," said Kevin, as he looked up to the ceiling of the spire, which was hollow all the way to its top. He then noticed something, and he grabbed Caitlin's attention as he told the group, "And, it's our ticket to the Realm of the Angels."

Everyone else started looking to the ceiling as Kevin drew his Sword of Purity. At every angle he then moved it around in, the sword started glowing in the direction of the ceiling. Then, the Sword of Purity started tugging on Kevin's arm again, like it had done before in Aurana City and in the battle at Rikleifer. This time, though, it was pulling upward.

"There it is," said Caitlin in realization of what Kevin was showing her. "I'm sure of it. That's the weak point up there, in the top of the ceiling. It's directly above the altar!"

"Are you sure?" asked Arthur, looking up confusedly. "I can't really see anything up there. It just looks like the spire's ceiling."

Kevin shook his head, still looking up. "No, I'm absolutely sure Caitlin's right," he said. "I know exactly what that is, because we fell into one in Nuve before. There's a hole in the realm, in the top of that spire. That's probably how the original gods actually made it up into the Realm of the Angels."

Kron stared into the ceiling in disbelief. "Heh," he said, still shaking his head. "So it is as simple as that. How unbelievable."

"But it's not that simple," noted Caitlin, also looking into the hole above. "If you're right, Kron, there's still the seal to deal with. Somehow there has to be a way to break it."

"How do we do that?" asked Kevin.

Caitlin shook her head. "No idea," she said. "I think we'd have to see it first."

"And I think I know just the way to do that," said Kevin, staring at his sword for a brief second as it continued to tug upwards at him. He was not sure of what he was wanting to do, but he was confident that he had to try. "I've got an idea."

"Now, hold on a moment," interrupted Kron, looking directly at Kevin. "Like I told you, it is best that we make sure you are fine first. No one folds over coughing like that unless there are some serious issues with their health."

Caitlin stepped up to Kron. "Take a look at him," she said. "Of course, *I'm* going to worry about Kevin for every little detail. But when you look at him now, he's more than fine. There hasn't even been a sign of weakness out of him since then."

Kevin nodded. "Thanks, Caitlin," he said. "And I do feel fine, so if we can, I'd like to get started right away. The gods have waited for twenty years for that seal above us to be undone. It would be better if they didn't have to wait a second more."

Seeing that he was losing the argument, Kron sighed. "Very well, then, let us go on. If you are going to be stubborn about this, then there is no point in holding you up any longer."

"Mhmm," said Kevin. He then took a few steps forward, and climbed up onto the altar. "Everyone step aside except for Caitlin," he said. "I want you to come with me on this."

Acknowledging the request, Arthur, Rachel, Kron, and Wheldon all backed away from the altar. Caitlin, still floating and her angel wings still visible, climbed onto the altar and stood directly behind Kevin.

"Kron," continued Kevin, "in five minutes, I want you and Wheldon to follow me. Bring everyone on up."

"A point of order," Kron retorted. "Humans are not allowed in the Realm of the Angels." He looked at Wheldon. "I would presume that applies to phoenixes as well."

Reluctantly, Kevin sighed as he lowered his sword. "You're my friend, Kron, but if you don't, I won't do this. Everyone here worked to bring you this far. They deserve to be a part of this."

For a moment, Kron looked around the room at the faces of Kevin and his friends. He then looked at Kevin. "As you wish," he said. "It is deserved." He gave a small salute to show he did acknowledge and respect Kevin. "Are Caitlin and you going through the hole, then?"

"Absolutely," Kevin declared. "I hope this works."

From behind Kevin, Caitlin laughed a little bit "It will," she chuckled. "As long as you believe it will, I know it will." She wrapped her arms around Kevin from behind, ready to be tugged up on the ride to come.

"If you say so," laughed back Kevin. "Now, hold on tight." He then pulled up his Sword of Purity with both arms, allowing its tugging force to gently lift him and Caitlin off the ground. It caught both of them by surprise at first, but then its speed of levitation became very consistent as it carried them to the top of the spire.

On the spire floor, Arthur looked up to Kevin and Caitlin, and joked, "Hey, don't forget to write to us when you get there!"

"I hear you, Arthur," called back Kevin as he laughed. "We'll see you guys on the other side."

Kevin and Caitlin finished wishing everyone else their goodbyes as the Sword of Purity's ascent reached the edge of the hole. Then, it continued to move without hesitation through the hole. Kevin clung tighter to the blade's crossguard, and Caitlin clung tightly to Kevin, seeking not to fall. Crossing the hole was an unusual and somewhat uncomfortable experience, as it created a pulling sensation that was very strong. It almost felt to Kevin and Caitlin like they were being sucked through the hole in the building's ceiling. And although it was a somewhat frightening experience, it was nothing new to either one, having traveled through the hole at the bottom of the Abyss of the Royal Sovereign several weeks before. Because of this, some of what happened was to be expected.

Still, the experience was a little terrifying. Then, as Kevin's eyes passed through the hole, and he looked out upon the surroundings, his eyes widened at what they saw. A short moment later, when Caitlin came past the hole and was able to see as well, her eyes also widened, stunned by the sight in front of her.

It was a clear sky, one without flaws. Nothing was below, and nothing appeared to be above. All around, not a sight was to be seen other than clear blue sky. Almost immediately in response to this sight, Caitlin nearly jumped, clinging to Kevin tighter and pulling herself up higher to him. Once she regained control of herself, she then proceeded to use her angelic powers and apply some floating herself to make sure neither she nor Kevin fell.

But the Sword of Purity was still pulling them higher.

"This one seems so different than the one we saw before," Caitlin observed. "Spacious and flawless, and almost without imperfection."

Kevin responded, his voice full of wonder at what he was seeing, "It's the passageway of the gods. And the Sword of Purity is leading us through it."

Caitlin paused for a second to look around again and think. Her eyes were full of realization, and her mechanical mind of magic was solving the puzzle. After a moment, she finally had it. "I've got it!" she exclaimed, almost with enough force to break her loose from Kevin.

"Got what?" asked Kevin, curious.

"The answer!" responded Caitlin in excitement. "I think I know how this seal works. My father taught me something about a theory called ‘phantasmal space theory’, where all of the realms lie on planes, one on top of the other with spaces in between these realms, kind of like this one.”

Kevin was confused. “Okay, so what does that mean?"

“It means I bet I know why the gods haven’t broken this seal.” explained Caitlin. “They haven’t figured out that this seal isn’t placed in the Realm of the Angels. It’s right here, in this space between realms. It extends out in a plane, as a layer between the realms, and only can really ‘exist’ in this space. Kron didn’t know about this place, so it’s obvious the gods haven’t crossed here in some time, but since the seal exists here and in the respective gap between the realms, it keeps them from crossing anywhere.”

For a moment, Kevin was in disbelief and amazement. Caitlin truly had an amazing sense of logic when it came to magical things. Whatever it all meant, this ‘phantasmal space theory’ provided an explanation that was at least possible. Was it another fact that only Professor Magnon knew of, though? Every time he heard of a story like this, slowly and surely Kevin became more convinced of a hypothesis of his own that he had of the professor, but still did not have enough evidence to make a statement.

“That’s amazing, Caitlin,” Kevin finally responded. “I hope you’re right.” He was interrupted, however, by a crash of thunder.

Kevin took a brief look above him to see a mass of clouds that looked very dark above him. The clouds were black and there were streaks of lighting coursing all through it. As he and Caitlin continued to ascend, the sky around them started to turn blacker and blacker, like the entrance of a nightmare. It was as if the skies were lit up in apocalyptic thunder, spreading light across a darkened sky.

That thought frightened Caitlin. Almost instantly reminded of her nightmare as she looked up into the dark cloud, she quickly wrapped herself around Kevin, needing to be sure that he was still there. “Please don’t let me go,” she said as she clutched Kevin tighter. “Please don’t leave my side.”

A little confused, Kevin let go of the sword with one hand and wrapped his free arm around Caitlin. He was not quite sure why it was that Caitlin was afraid, or what was bothering her, but he was not about to let her be afraid if she was legitimately scared. "I'm right here," he said in a comforting tone. "And the seal is above. Get ready, because we're going to smash right through it."

Caitlin looked up again and braced herself for what was coming.

As they approached the clouds, the intense darkness, and the thundering clouds, Kevin's sword started to shake. It became very violent in its quivering, making Kevin sure that this was the seal, indeed.

Fearlessly, as the Sword of Purity came into contact with the clouds, Kevin lit up the sword in its bright blue magic and gave it one large slash.

And then, it all went blank.

A flash of light coursed through the space between realms, accompanied by a loud explosion noise. It blinded and deafened both Kevin and Caitlin for over a second, and in that course of time, they were separated from the force of the blast. As the light faded, Kevin found himself still holding his sword, but Caitlin was nowhere to be seen. Where was she? Kevin called out desperately for her, looking all around frantically. But she was still nowhere to be seen.

Then, the most frightening thing possible happened. The Sword of Purity stopped pulling upward, its mission apparently done for now and not needing to take Kevin anywhere. It was highly unfortunate for Kevin, however, because gravity was still in effect in the space between realms.

Now he needed Caitlin, and he needed her fast. Still he looked around, and still he could not find her.

Then, he started falling. He started falling fast.

In a last moment of desperation, he called out, "Caitlin! Help!"

All of it seemed to be ending. A falling death. Kevin had never pictured it. And then, there was a snag, and a force pulling on his hand.

"I've got you!" responded the desperate voice of Caitlin, her hand as firmly gripped to Kevin's as she could make it. She then reached down to grab the other one, which meant that Kevin had to sheathe his sword first before he could grab her other hand. Then, once she had a hold of both hands, Caitlin pulled up Kevin to her level, where they both began levitating, hands locked into one another's.

Kevin took a second to catch his breath before he stared directly into Caitlin's eyes, hands locked into hers, and said, "Thank you, Caitlin. Thank you so much again for saving my life. Are you okay?"

Caitlin stared directly back into his eyes. "I'm fine, as long as you are okay." She held on even tighter. "I don't ever want to lose you."

Smiling, Kevin said, "I never want to lose you, either."

No past resistances, no fears or hesitations, could shake her for this one moment.

And as they both levitated together, eyes locked with each other in passion, the thoughts of their futures together danced around a bit in their minds. Their futures were just ahead of them. Almost simultaneously, both of them looked to the sky. "It's almost time," Kevin said, seeing that they were floating up to another hole in the realm. "I guess you don't owe me one life saving anymore."

"Oh, who's keeping score?" responded Caitlin as she watched the above hole in the realm approaching ever closer. "Our future lies above us. To the Realm of the Angels!"

Chapter 49

To Stand With the Gods

And so it was, in the Realm of the Angels, that the god Chatka, a deity of peace and war, looked out upon the soft landscape of his home. In his typical garb of robes split precisely down the middle with half being black and the other half white, Chatka represented the concept of balance.

At the moment, there was nothing for Chatka to do but stare off into space. While he did, he thought about how he had become what he was. About how he joined a party of powerful men and women to find his new home. About how he wanted to help the mortals and protect them. About how he was sealed where he was, physically unable to leave the Realm of the Angels. He sat on the steps of Angel Tower, a cylindrical sandstone building that seemed to extend upward into infinity. Out he looked into the Realm of the Angels, where the ground was made of golden clouds and the skies were bright and completely clear. It had been his home as an immortal for the past five thousand years.

With him, the king of gods Ralios Larion—a god with an older appearance in royal red robes—sat staring out into the golden-cloud landscape and crystal clear skies of the Realm of the Angels, along with Necnea, the goddess of time, with long black hair and a darker skin tone adorned in purple robes. There was a fairly serious case of boredom going around. Sighing, all that Chatka could do was stare out into the distance. In particular, his focus was on what he and his fellow gods had been dwelling on week after week, the "corrosion" in the realm that they saw in front of them. It was still a point of confusion for all of them, as it was something unseen to everyone's eyes, but had been visible since they were locked in their realm.

Larion stared out into the emanating darkness coming from the corrosion, shaking his head. His face was in the palm of his hands. Depressed, he asked, “Where are Skanj, Jarnis, Taurin, and Zoron? I thought I asked them to come by with the latest news they have from the research they have been doing in the library.”

“They should be on their way,” responded Necnea. “I spoke with Skanj earlier today, and he said they thought they might be on to something, but they could not be sure.”

Chatka wiped his eyes. “That is about the last time I want to hear that we are ‘on to something’. Every time, it turns out to be a bust. I know I am usually one of the greater optimists we have here, but in this instance I think that I am about sick of hearing it. It is starting to be more and more that I doubt we will ever find anything.”

Necnea let out a sigh. “I think I know what you mean, Chatka. It does kind of get to be that way as the days, the weeks, the months, and the years pass.”

“It does,” responded Chatka. “I think of Kronius in a time like this. We are stranded here, but he we can only presume to be stranded on the other side.”

“You always did care for everyone,” commented Necnea, “a quality I always appreciated about you."

Before Chatka could answer, Larion corrected, “As he should, as we all should,” as he stood up. “Some gods are here because they came here five thousand years ago, like Chatka. Some were born here, such as myself. And some were brought here later, like Kronius. Yet we are all immortals of the same society. We should care for everyone equally.”

Necnea rolled her eyes. “I would like to respect your words, Larion, but you know better than us that other gods do not always see it that way. My husband Vinz Larinion’s decision to sacrifice himself to form the Sword of Purity and pass leadership to you, a god born here, was quite controversial. Should it have been? Absolutely not. Yet it was. We are not so great a society that we will dismiss these things, unfortunately.”

“Yes, yes, I know,” swatted away Larion. He just shook his

head as he sat back down. "I do respect your words, Necnea. If there is any god whom I see as wise beyond their years, I believe it to be you, especially after you endured the loss of your husband for our sakes," he said.

Saying nothing, Necnea only gave a silent nod of acknowledgment.

Larion then put his head down into his hands again, staring harder out into the distance. "I miss him," he said after a momentary pause.

"Miss who?" asked Chatka.

"The pure one," answered Larion. "Vincent Stryker was a shining light in a world full of darkness, our chosen one. I fear the worst has happened to him, and what the world below looks like now. What could Tyrinion have done to the mortal realm?"

Sighing again, Necnea responded, "All we really can do, though, is wait."

Larion nodded.

A few seconds later, Larion started to think he was zoning out a bit. The dark-colored hole in the distance appeared to be shifting around a bit chaotically, but at the same time it also looked like it was reducing in size. Larion could not believe his eyes. He rubbed them once just to make sure that what he was seeing was what he was actually seeing, and not an illusion. "Am I seeing what I think I am seeing?" he then asked. "Chatka, Necnea, do the two of you also see what is going on with that corrosion?"

"It is not just you," responded Chatka, restoring Larion's feeling of his own sanity for a moment. "What is it doing? It really is shrinking, like the corrosion is disappearing."

Necnea's eyes widened. "It is shrinking," she said, almost as if she were realizing it to be true. "The seal! Do you suppose someone destroyed it?"

Then, a large flash of light came from out of the hole, and all semblance of what was the corrosion was gone. Although there was no proof yet, Larion ecstatically made the claim, "The seal is gone! But who or what could have done it?"

"Now, Larion," rose Necnea, "it is probably very premature to make that declaration as of yet. How do we know that is what happened?"

Larion continued to stare out at the empty space left by the disappearance of the corrosion. "I just do," he said. "I know it is done. Somehow, I feel almost certain of it." Before Larion could continue much further, though, another strange sight came from where the corrosion had once been. It was almost like the sight of a god coming up through the floor.

And up from the floor of the Realm of the Angels emerged a sight that made Larion rise to his feet and start running toward it. Initially, Chatka and Necnea were confused as to what this was, but upon a closer look, they followed suit. Touching ground with a firm, familiar feeling, Kevin Trent Stryker and Caitlin Amelia Magnon looked all around to see an amazing sight. It was the Realm of the Angels in all its splendor and glory, an all-new sight that truly defied belief, even more so than the Ancient City had done before.

As Caitlin set Kevin down on the golden-cloud ground, the Sword of Purity flashed briefly before the color ran away from it. They were facing away from Angel Tower, and saw no one behind them. Sheathing his sword, Kevin looked around at all of the empty space and the ground of golden clouds, he turned and asked, "What is this place?"

Before Caitlin could say a word, the gods were all around them, near them.

A little weirded out by the gods staring at them, Kevin said, "Uhh… can I help you?"

"I believe you already have," nodded Larion. "Perhaps the prophecy was correct after all. Are you the second pure one?"

Aside, Caitlin rolled her eyes. She knew how much disdain Kevin had for being called that.

"No," answered Kevin, "I'm just someone here to help a god get home."

"So you are with Kronius?" asked Chatka. "Where is he?"

Caitlin answered the question, "He'll be up in a couple of minutes. We wanted a little time to make it up here on our own first."

It was at this moment that Larion saw Caitlin and realized from her translucent wings at whom he was looking. "Well, I will be!"

exclaimed Larion. "How… how… how in the realms? An angel! An actual angel!" He extended his hand to Caitlin. "Angel, it is a great pleasure to meet you. I am Ralios Larion, deity of light and king of the gods. Beside me is Chatka, deity of peace and war, and Necnea, goddess of time."

Caitlin giggled a little bit at how much the king of gods seemed to marvel her. "Pleasure to meet you too," she said as she shook Larion's hand. "I'm Caitlin."

Larion just shook his head, almost in disbelief and amazement at what he was seeing. "The pleasure is all ours, I am sure," he said. "If our lore is to be believed, you must be half immortal. Who, may I ask, are your parents?"

Somewhat scowling a bit, Caitlin said, "My father is a wizard, and I never knew my mother, but I know she died a long time ago. Certainly neither of them are gods, if that's what you're implying."

Kevin thought about that comment for a moment.

Bowing, Larion said, "I see. I apologize if I am being rude in my curiosity, but you must understand that to see an actual angel, which has never existed before you, is outstanding."

"No, I understand," responded Caitlin, lightening up her mood. "You should have seen Kevin when he and I found out together."

Nodding, Larion acknowledged, "I can understand that." He then turned back to Kevin. "Please forgive our odd behavior; we are simply not used to having visitors. You must be Kevin, then?" Larion reached out to shake hands.

"Indeed," said Kevin, as he shook hands with Larion. "Kevin Trent."

Observant as ever, Caitlin noticed that Kevin did not use his full name. It was apparent to her that he did not want the gods to know he was Vincent Stryker's son.

"A pleasure to meet you as well, Kevin Trent," acknowledged Larion. "I see you are the bearer of the Sword of Purity?"

"I would be."

From next to Larion, Chatka commented "Amazing. How someone else can wield that sword astounds me. You must be one special person."

Kevin shook his head. “Please, I’m no one special,” he said.

At that moment, Kron emerged from behind. He ascended through the golden clouds, grabbing the attention of everyone around. Kevin and Caitlin each stood back, allowing the gods to meet their fellow member. Recognizing Kron Kalavere almost immediately, Chatka was the first one to greet him. “Welcome home, Kronius,” he said as he bowed.

As he came up, Kron smiled. “Hello, Chatka,” he said. “It is so good to be home after so long.” He paused for a second to see Kevin and Caitlin around with him, and then said to the gods, “I see you have met Kevin Trent Stryker and Miss Caitlin Magnon already.”

“Stryker?” Larion inquired immediately. He looked at Kevin. “You did not mention that you were a Stryker.”

Frowning, Kevin said, “It wasn’t relevant.”

“But it must be!” exclaimed Larion. “Your abilities are rooted in your blood! You carry the legacy of the pure one. It is as the conquest prophecy foretold.” He then recited, “*A hero will arise and end the conqueror’s rampage, but his wrath will only be delayed. The conqueror’s evil shall seep through the realms and his influence will spread. He will cause great pain and suffering, unless the purest of heroes can stop him. The reign of evil can be defeated, but victory will be difficult. The first one will fail no matter what, but the second might succeed, should he be able to stand out against the evil flow and survive. The odds are against the light, and darkness will expand. Beware, all who know this prophecy, for the conquest of the realms has already begun.*”

Kevin felt extremely awkward.

Kron stepped in. Remembering what Professor Magnon told him about prophecy, and despite his qualms about the professor, he was finding himself more of a doubter now than he had been the last time he was in this realm. “I don’t think prophecy has anything to do with it,” he insisted. “Kevin grew up not knowing who his father was, and happened to run into me with a shard of the sword in his hometown. I had no idea until quite a bit later. Everything that has followed since that day has been only because he wanted to fulfill a promise to me to take me home.” He paused, as he looked at both Kevin and Caitlin.

"These two have been perhaps the kindest people I have ever known, for no other reason than they were willing to help me, and yet I have also identified talent in both of them."

There was a pause for a moment. Then, Necnea stepped forward. "And I will choose to believe you." She looked at Kevin. "I trust my husband well enough that his sacrifice would be entrusted to the most pure, not simply the one with the family legacy." Then, she knelt in front of Kevin, and reached out to put her hands around his. "His soul lives on within that sword, I have always believed. He must have seen purity within you, paired with the talent and the desire to do better. Please do right by him, and I know he will do right by you."

Kevin nodded. "Thank you," he said.

As Necnea stood back up, Larion smiled. "I trust Necnea implicitly. When she speaks, I know it to be the truth." He then took a step back and took in both Kevin and Caitlin together, as Caitlin floated just off of the ground, her translucent angel wings starting to fade as she fell back to the ground. Then, he looked over at Kron. "Do you know anything of Vincent Stryker?"

Kron nodded. "Yes, he is alive. Apparently he fought Tyrinion and made a deal to keep himself alive. Vincent would admit it was not his finest hour, but he has since reunited with Kevin, who is his son. Right now, he is helping in the war efforts against Tyrinion's 'chosen one' Demonicus, his organization the Enlighteners from the Shadows, and his Kingdom of Desolunar which rose up in place of the Daritel's territory."

Chatka's eyes widened as he looked at Larion. "So Tyrinion is trying this again, just as he did twenty years ago?"

"It appears that way," acknowledged Kronius, "and Demonicus is a much crueler and more effective foe than the Daritel ever were." He then paused for a second. "I'm afraid Demonicus is after the conquest of the realms, and he plans to do so by gathering the Seven Stripes."

Immediately, Larion leaned over to Chatka and tapped him. He then pointed to Angel Tower and said. "Book of Magic Energies. Bring it to the meeting room."

As Chatka turned and departed as he was instructed, there was a flash behind Kevin and Caitlin. Everyone turned to see a phoenix rise up through the clouds, with two humans on its back. Arthur, Rachel, and Wheldon had made their arrival.

Kron looked directly at Larion as he said, "I promise, these are the last ones. May I present Arthur Falchor, Rachel Reinhart, and the phoenix Wheldon, Kevin and Caitlin's traveling companions."

Wheldon settled down on the ground, allowing Arthur and Rachel to disembark. "Where the hell are we?" quipped Arthur. "Is this meant to be heaven?"

"Er, not exactly," answered Larion, as he approached Arthur, "but I am sure that descriptions of this place inspired humans to believe it is." He paused as he extended his hand. "Welcome to the Realm of the Angels. I am Ralios Larion, king of gods."

Arthur nodded, knocking off the sarcasm, and shook Larion's hand and introduced himself.

Larion then turned to acknowledge Rachel, only to see her offering a deep curtsey. "Rachel Reinhart, I presume. You need not show such formality here; we welcome you to our realm."

Rachel looked up and stood up. "My apologies," she said. "It's just such an honor to stand with the gods who are worshipped by many."

Necnea walked up. "Erroneously so, I am afraid," she began. "We actually try not to intervene in the lives of the mortal. We are a society, not a ruling class. Those that have heard of us may call us nameless ones, and fantasize about great deeds we can do, but that is more the imagination of mortals than the actual us."

"Interesting," commented Wheldon, "so no one here is the Great One."

Looking over at Wheldon, Necnea acknowledged, "No. Tales of the Great One predate our existence." She walked over and bowed to him. "It is excellent to see your race still survives. We are pleased to make your acquaintance, Wheldon."

"And I, yours," bowed Wheldon.

Chapter 50

Underneath the Luster

With the introductions out of the way, Larion then invited everyone to join him in the meeting room of Angel Tower. As a group, led by Larion and Necnea, everyone walked to the stairs as Kron brought up the rear. It was a short walk to the stairs. Angel Tower, made of what appeared to be sandstone, was perfectly cylindrical in shape. There were about twenty stairs up to the tower's entrance, and above that the tower appeared to extend upward into infinity.

On the way up the stairs, Arthur leaned in to Kevin and asked if he should tell the gods about his father being Demonicus. Kevin told him not to worry, as that had little to do with anything at the moment and that Kron would surely tell them when the time was right, if it ever actually mattered. He felt the same way about his own parentage, although Kron had innocently let that slip simply by calling Kevin by his full name.

Inside the entrance to Angel Tower was a long hallway. Larion led everyone into a side room, and they filed inside. This room was solid white, all around, and appeared to extend into infinity in every direction save for the doorway through which they had entered. Larion extended an arm, and a large round table with chairs popped up out of nowhere. He invited everyone to sit down. A brief moment later, with everyone seated, Chatka walked in with a large tome in his hands. This was the Book of Magic Energies.

As Larion began to flip through the book, he said, "It is good to have everyone here today, and I thank each and every one of you for the role you have played in breaking the seal on our realm and bringing Kronius home to us. Words cannot express the gratitude we have for you and your accomplishments." He then stopped at a page on the Seven Stripes of the Elements. "Do any of you know how many stripes this son of Tyrinion has?"

Kron shook his head, "No, but I know he has less than half of them."

As he said that, Kevin and Caitlin placed their right arms on the table and pulled up their sleeves, revealing the long stripes that appeared in their skin wrapping around their arms. Kevin revealed he was carrying stripes in orange, red, and green; representing the elements of air, fire, and earth. Caitlin's blue stripe was that of the element of ice.

Necnea's eyes widened. "Amazing," she said. "You have already accomplished more of Tyrinion's own goal than he has."

"What do these things do, anyway?" asked Kevin.

Larion pointed to the open page in his book. "Separately, in very powerful hands, each has a power associated with it, although no one with enough power to wield them has been around in a long time. Aside from the Stripe of Life, no one here ever had one."

Caitlin was intrigued. "So you have one of these?"

"Tyrinion did," responded Larion. "He should still have it now."

So much for getting one more, Kevin thought to himself.

Larion continued, "We did have that one, yes, and we passed it around to allow gods to try and activate its power. Tyrinion was the god with it when he attacked us and tried to take over our society. So we know he has at least one."

Kevin was listening intently, concerned about what Larion was saying. He looked at Caitlin, who looked like she had concern in her eyes as well. "Demonicus has two more," she stated. "One of his Enlighteners from the Shadows had the Stripe of Fire that we claimed, and an assassin of his told us he also has light and darkness."

"Then we are in a bad place," stated Necnea, stepping forward. "The two of you have four. Between Demonicus and Tyrinion, they have three. That's all seven, and if you have had entanglements with his people before, then he likely knows you have the other four. That will make you two his targets."

Before either Kevin or Caitlin could say anything, Rachel asked, "Would it be smarter to hide?"

"He already knows who we are and that we have them,"

commented Kevin. "We can only hide for so long, even if we ran to Avalon or something."

"Phoenixes do not run and hide. We stand up for ourselves and for our kin," added Wheldon. "Kevin is an honorary phoenix, and he exemplifies our values."

Always so noble, Kevin chuckled to himself. Wheldon was a good friend, if a bit stilted with the poetic language at times. That came from his culture, and Kevin embraced it.

"Yeah, I'm with Kevin on this one," commented Arthur to Rachel. "I know you guys have been in some fights already, but there's only one real way to settle this. Kevin needs to run his sword through Demonicus like he did that clone," referencing Pseudo.

"As powerful as Demonicus is, he does not match the strength of his immortal father Tyrinion, I am afraid," said Larion. "Only twice have we ever had an immortal exit our society, and both times have been the result of an attempted coup. Setadev at least had the decency to accept being stripped of his immortality for it." He paused for a second. "Tyrinion, though, clearly will not. With his gathering of the Seven Stripes of the Elements, it is clear he is assembling what the book calls the 'ultimate weapon', although it does not say what that is. He is among the most educated of gods, a very dedicated scholar and a man of focus. Without a doubt, he would know about these."

Thoughts ran through Kevin's head as Larion said these words.

"Have we ever speculated on what this 'weapon' might be?" asked Kron.

Chatka stepped in. "No one has ever put forth any solid research or reasoning, but I can recall some of our most scholarly members suggesting it could mean the destruction of an entire realm."

There was a long pause. Everyone seemed speechless for a moment.

"Were that to be true, Tyrinion could hold whole realms hostage and threaten to destroy them unless he were allowed to conquer them," commented Necnea. "That includes ours as well as the mortal realm."

Larion turned to look at Kevin and Caitlin, as he closed the book. "Keep those stripes safe," he said. "I hope you now understand the severity of the situation we are in. Ever since Tyrinion attacked us, his eyes glowing red, he has had one goal in mind. He wants to conquer the realms and rule all of existence, perhaps leaving the mortal realm to Demonicus while he schemes to take ours. Under no circumstances can he be allowed to capture all seven of these stripes."

Kevin was listening closely. He had much to consider from what Larion told him. "I know. I've lost my home already because Demonicus invaded and captured my hometown."

"Mine too," chimed in Arthur. Rachel nodded her head as well.

"And he will not stop until all of the realms are in his grasp," commented Chatka. "His conquest of the realms cannot be allowed to further progress."

Larion rose to his feet. "We need to make sure you are ready for the fight ahead. To that end, we would like to offer all of you combat training with the greatest experts that have ever lived. All of you have accomplished something great in getting here and breaking the seal that kept us in place. Let us help you to accomplish something even greater—guarding the world from a conqueror. We want to prepare you "

Kevin looked over at Caitlin, then at each of his friends. Everyone gave him a confident look, that that was a great idea. For the situations they had survived, some training on how to actually defend themselves felt like a necessity at this point. "That sounds great!" Kevin exclaimed. "Then after training we can take the fight straight to Demonicus with the gods by our sides."

Suddenly, the gods appeared quite sullen.

What did he do wrong? Kevin was lost, but he was afraid of what he was about to hear.

"Kevin, no," Larion said as he lowered his head a bit. "We have a policy of not interfering in affairs in the mortal realm. This is for good reason; we are not going to influence the mortal into believing we are to be worshipped any more than they believe us to be. It is dangerous to humans to believe they wage wars for us, or decide their actions on whether or not we would be pleased."

"But this is your mess!" Frustration was starting to leak heavily into Kevin's voice. "Take a minute and weigh the odds, Larion," he said, not being kind about what he was saying. "Demonicus and his immortal 'father' are in position to conquer the realms because you and your gods failed to stop him. Instead of dealing with him, you chose my father to deal with your issues for you."

"My husband did what he did because he knew what was right," interjected Necnea. "The Sword of Purity is stronger than any god, even than he was. And he chose the sword's bearer carefully. Now, he has chosen you, and you are tasked by him to finish the job and end Tyrinion's conquest. Doesn't that mean anything to you?"

Kevin withdrew his sword. "With all due respect to your husband, I'm not 'chosen' by anyone. I chose to help as I could." He turned to Larion. "Now I have my homeland to rescue, and a world to protect from a conqueror who threatens my world as well as yours, and despite all that I've done for you already, you still refuse to help?"

"Hold!" commanded Larion, raising his hand to Kevin. "Our decision is final, pure one. Unless Tyrinion presents himself, we will not intervene, and even so, we will only work against him, not Demonicus."

Kevin looked to Kron. "Can you help me out here? You told me that coming here was an opportunity to find help!"

The humans and Wheldon looked over at Kron.

Instead of answering, Kron turned his head away.

At that, Kevin jumped out of his seat. "You lied!" he exclaimed.

"I needed you to free my society and take me home," Kron answered. "It could not wait any longer than it already had."

"Kronius did what he thought was right," commented Chatka. "As you should. Accept the training so we can prepare you for the fight ahead."

Kevin's fury was starting to boil over. It was getting to the point where he could not control it. Fist clenched tight and shaking, he looked like he was ready to burst. Every muscle in his body appeared to be tense in rage. He was holding back a screaming desire to call the gods cowards.

Seeing this, Caitlin quickly approached Kevin and latched her right arm around his left. "Don't do anything, Kevin," she said, looking him directly in the eye. "Step outside with me. We'll make a decision together."

As frustrated as Kevin was, he could not feel so furious when Caitlin was there to get him to stop. It simply was not in him to continue on like that. Still fuming, though, he set down his arm and turned away dejectedly, following Caitlin's advice. Caitlin followed him out of the meeting room. The gods did nothing to stop them from exiting.

Still seated at the table, Rachel shook her head. Then, she addressed Larion, "Isn't that a testament to how much Kevin puts into what he does? You can see why it frustrates him to hear this."

"I do," nodded Larion, "but there is nothing more that I or any of the rest of us can do. We are grateful to all of you for what you have done, but even as gods, we have limits to what we can and cannot do."

"Except you're making the choice not to help," commented Wheldon. He rose and spread his wings.

Chatka crossed his arms, as if slightly defensive. "And what would you know about that, phoenix?"

"Much, human immortal," Wheldon snapped back. "I too live in an isolated society, where phoenixes have long since isolated themselves from humans and the rest of the world. Kevin and Caitlin found us in a civil war on the edge of disaster, and though they were outsiders with no responsibility for our situation, they brought us to the table to negotiate, and in the end we found out the two sides were not so different and our war was based on a misunderstanding. Initially we were hesitant to be much help, yet we ultimately decided that giving Kevin some help was the right thing to do, whether or not it resulted in the exposure of our society."

"I'm afraid it's not that simple," responded Larion. "I understand what you are trying to say, but humans understanding the presence of another sentient species in their world is only a minor consequence. Humans worshipping gods and allowing all of their decisions to be guided by that misconception is extremely dangerous. Our actions have already given them false impressions of existing and needing worshipped. Leading them to believe we are powerful or that they must appease us, through any further level of involvement incidental or accidental, is a risk we simply cannot take."

Then, Arthur said it. "You do understand you're all coming off as massive cowards, right?"

Chatka raised an eyebrow. "Discretion is the better part of valor."

"Everyone, just stop," Rachel said as she threw her arms out over the table, gesturing. "We're getting nowhere with this."

Reluctantly, Larion nodded. "Agreed." He sat back down in his chair. "Let us wait for the pure one to return. We will have our decision then."

Arthur looked over at Rachel. "Should we go check on him?"

Without hesitation, as she stood up, Rachel nodded in the affirmative. She turned to Wheldon, who also gave a nod.

Outside, Kevin had sat down on the steps of Angel Tower. Caitlin sat next to him, as they sat alone. Kevin took a moment to stare out among the golden clouds of the Realm of the Angels, wondering if what he saw was real. He was not sure what hurt worse: that the "gods" were still pushing their problems onto his family, or that Kron had knowingly lied to him. Somehow this whole situation seemed familiar, like when his father had admitted to cowering out. How could they just expect him to do this on his own?

Well, he was not on his own, Kevin reasoned to himself. He still had his friends who remained by his side, and he was thankful for that. Arthur and Rachel really had no reason to stay other than because they were friends with Kevin, Wheldon was duty-bound by the Red Phoenix and his own loyalty, and Caitlin… maybe she was a little of both.

"I get it," were the first words out of Caitlin's mouth, after they sat down.

"Are you saying I was wrong?" asked Kevin, his face in his arms, which were perched on his knees as he sat.

Caitlin shook her head. "No. I didn't disagree with you for walking out on your father a couple of weeks ago, and I don't disagree with you now for this." She pulled herself next to Kevin on the steps. "I'll admit I slapped your father after you walked out on him, though, and I didn't slap any gods."

Kevin smiled a bit, finding that a little funny. "Is that why he came around?"

"Maybe," shrugged Caitlin, herself smirking. "I'm still not entirely sure how to control these new emotions. Sometimes things will make me feel sad, or frustrated, and other times I can still act with a little bit of discipline."

Nodding, Kevin said, "That's just a normal part of being a teenager. Trust me when I say I've been there, and that's nothing new just to you."

"I see," acknowledged Caitlin. As much as she knew many things that she had taught Kevin, some of these things were things he was teaching her, whether he knew it or not. "So what hurt you more: that the gods aren't helping as they should, or that Kron lied to you?"

Sighing, Kevin said, "A lot of both. Kron intentionally deceiving me, though, hurts the worst. I'm actually surprised you aren't more upset with him."

"Oh, I'm bothered by what he did," acknowledged Caitlin, "but I always knew that Kron was a bit craven and somewhat weak. I'm sure your first impression of him was one of strength because he is the first experience you ever had with a god, and you didn't have a good idea of what was underneath the luster of that image in your head. I, having been told of this society by my father, and having watched his behavior, thought he might not be the most strong-willed person. His behavior today and in the last week has proven me right."

Kevin was reminded in that moment of a fact he had known for a while but had nearly forgotten: that Caitlin knew of this society even if she did not know them, through her father. How Professor Magnon knew anything of this society was a good question. "I suppose you're right," Kevin said, shaking his head. "I guess I just don't want to believe it's true. Everything I've done, and all of the consequences of that, are because I picked up a shard of metal that he dropped, and he came to my house afterward to ask me to take him home. Then I met you, and Arthur was kidnapped by his father, we did a lot of diplomacy at your father's suggestion, we were nearly killed over and over…"

"I know," Caitlin gently interrupted. "I lived it with you." She reached down to hold Kevin's hand.

That made Kevin feel better. He interlocked his fingers with hers. He looked at her, and saw her smiling. It made him smile. "So, speaking of you living it with me, you first decided to help me as my guide. I trust your advice. What do you think I should do now?"

"Yeah, what would we do now?" came a voice from behind. It was Arthur, with Rachel and Wheldon in tow. They sat next to Kevin and Caitlin on the stairs.

After briefly acknowledging her friends with a tip of her head, Caitlin looked thoughtful for a second. Her smile dropped some, although she did not appear upset. "Honestly, if you ask me, I would take the gods up on their offer."

Suddenly, Kevin looked very confused. "Really?"

"That's not at all what I would've expected you to say," commented Rachel.

"Really, though," affirmed Caitlin. She stood up and turned to face the group. "I'm looking at this strategically. If we can't get the gods to help us, we could at least better ourselves. Make them train all of us on combat. That way, we won't find ourselves in a situation like we did in Rikleifer. If you want to make an impact in turning the tide on Demonicus, and there's no other help to be found, then that's the next best thing you can do."

Kevin considered this for a moment. Why did Caitlin have to be so reasonable? He still wanted to be angry, but she made a good point. "Then how do we know when to go back? The war still goes on, with or without us. What if Aurana ends up in trouble again, if the operation has failed and the Alliance is in danger?"

"Make Kron keep tabs on it for you," remarked Caitlin in response. "He should be able to cross into the mortal realm at any point he wants, now that the seal is broken."

"Okay…" Kevin was skeptical. "Why would he do that for me?"

"He's not strong enough to be okay with manipulating you into placing his return home so high on your priorities," Caitlin observed. "He'll want to apologize, I assure you. Make that a condition of his apology."

Kevin smirked as he looked down again. "I can do that, I guess," he said. "Remind me never to cross paths the wrong way with you."

"Whatever," laughed Caitlin. "So, are you in?"

Looking around for a second, Kevin then said, "I think I know what I would do now, but shouldn't that be a question for everyone?"

There was a slight pause. "I won't do it unless you do," said Rachel. "I won't split up from any of you this time."

"It's your call, Kevin," Caitlin acknowledged. "Everyone who is here is only so because they believe in you. We all do." She took a brief look at the group to see Arthur, Rachel, and Wheldon appearing to be in agreement. "I've seen you grow and mature into a great leader since the day I met you. I think we all agree you should make this decision for us."

Wheldon bowed to Kevin. "My friend, my fellow phoenix, Catie does speak for me. Where you choose to lead, I will follow."

"Thanks, Wheldon," acknowledged Kevin. "I think you're a great friend, too."

Arthur had to wisecrack. "So does this mean we can cue the montage?"

Rachel looked at Arthur in disbelief over what he just said.

Seeing this, Arthur turned to her. "What?" he asked.

"Cue the montage? Really?" she asked.

Shrugging her off, Arthur said, "You know what I mean." He then turned to Kevin. "Are we doing this?"

Briefly, Kevin looked at the faces of his friends. They were placing their trust in him to make the right call. And honestly, Caitlin had a very good point.

"Absolutely," he acknowledged. He then said, "I guess it's time to cue the montage."

"Oh, come on!" exclaimed Arthur. "That's my line!"

Chapter 51

Enveloping Darkness

Day after day had passed by as Kevin and Arthur trained with the gods on swordplay, and Rachel was taught how to survive as an archer in a melee. Kevin and Arthur trained with Taurin, the god of swordplay and Chatka's son, and perhaps the greatest sword fighter Kevin had ever seen in person, while Rachel was working alongside Skanj, the god of earth. Taurin worked with Kevin and Arthur day and night, and although Arthur appeared to become bored at times, Kevin was always interested and focused on what he was learning. Taurin noted how motivation had made Kevin a good student. He also noted that Kevin was quite capable of learning technical skills with his sword, including identifying and figuring out the optimal swing or stab for his sword based on the defense his opponent presented. He was also quite the defensive fighter, which would be important for him to stay alive.

As Caitlin had suggested, Kron made regular trips to Aurana to monitor the situation. He absolutely did feel guilty for what he had done to Kevin, and wanted to make amends in any way he could. As the god Kronius, his normal job as a messenger was to carry messages from the Realm of the Angels to gods on assignment in the mortal realm, but now he was communicating battlefield reports to Kevin on a regular basis.

And from the sounds of it, within a month, something amazing was happening down below.

Professor Magnon's suggestion had paid off. The Desolunar forces' supply line was cut off by the circle attack on Haventown, leaving the Desolunar forces in Rikleifer cut off. Imperiled for the first time, many of them surrendered rapidly as Auranian forces pushed back toward the city. It had turned out as well, Kronius explained, that Nuve had also seen the city of Cornelia conquered briefly in a violent fight, but the combined Nuve forces had maintained a line north of the city and, with news of Aurana's victory, were seizing the momentum to recapture the city. Kevin reasoned that although this was good news, it certainly would not please Arsuf Maxwell, leader of the Cornelia Chimeras, that his main city had fallen to Desolunar even if only briefly.

Kevin and Caitlin spent plenty of time together during the training, with Caitlin joining in to assist Taurin with the effort. During their downtime, Kevin and Caitlin would spend the days talking and spending time with their friends, and even rereading their favorite book, *The Tale of the Valkyrie*, together. As Larion explained, their library in Angel Tower had as many published works as the gods could acquire. When they were not training or spending time together, they were spending time with Arthur, Rachel, and Wheldon. Kron would pop in periodically as well, but was usually so busy with assignments from other gods that he would have only a few minutes at most.

Another month had passed. Sixty days in total. In that time, it had become apparent that Desolunar had nearly lost all of their momentum, as if they simply could not recover from the defeat and were now in a tailspin. The resurgent Auranian forces, now joined by reinforcements from Scurnia and the dragon troops of the Knights of the Dragon, were now advancing on the city of Atwals, in the province of Southern Aurana. This was territory Aurana had not occupied in a long time. Nuve had also just finished recapturing Cornelia and was advancing southward as well.

Professor Magnon had also touched base with Kronius as the battle for Atwals was beginning. Much of the defense of Atwals had been abandoned before the Auranian forces had arrived, and to the professor, it suggested that Desolunar was going to pool its remaining forces for a defense of Seta Archa. This was where he was requesting Kevin's assistance, as they would be advancing on Demonicus and his Enlighteners from the Shadows, and perhaps the true conqueror. The fall of his empire seemed astounding.

Then came a bad day. Professor Magnon told Kron to gather Kevin and his friends immediately, that there was an emergency. When that day came, Kevin, Caitlin, Arthur, Rachel, and Wheldon all discussed their options and decided it would be best to end training here and head back. Larion, knowing this day would come, acknowledged the request and agreed to have them taken wherever they needed to go. Based on the professor's instructions, Kron, while still hesitant to fully trust him, was willing to send them where he wanted them. Caitlin, always trusting her father, agreed that it was a good idea.

On that fateful day, Kevin was walking out of Angel Tower with Kron after having a long period of rest. He and his friends had just slept for the imperceptible night, and were ready to go for the next day. While they were gathering, Kevin was making sure to say goodbye to Kron while he had the opportunity. He had asked his friends to allow him a few minutes.

"I hope you can forgive what I did," Kron told Kevin rather suddenly, as they walked out of the tower and stood at the top of the stairs.

Kevin looked at him and frowned. "It's been two months. Why would you ask for forgiveness now?"

Kron sighed. "It still weighs on me."

"Well, don't let it," Kevin answered. "I forgave you a long time ago. I know you didn't mean any harm. You know I wanted to help you get home all along, and you didn't need to lie to me to get me to take you sooner."

Lowering his head, Kron said, "I am sorry. I became desperate after we found out how it was possible. Twenty years is a long time to be away, and the threat of war meant there may not be another opportunity."

Kevin shrugged. "I get it. I don't agree with it, but I get it." He looked out upon the landscape. "My father made that decision, too, in a way. I don't know if I will have to do the same, but…" He stopped.

"But?" asked Kron.

After a pause, Kevin continued, "But I hope that I will make the right decision in that moment, whatever it may be."

Silently, Kron nodded. "It is harder than it looks, is it not? I know that you and Caitlin have each nearly been killed multiple times. Making the right decision is not always making the most noble one, yet it is more often than not."

"I wish your society understood that, Kronius." Kevin used

Kron's god name.

Kron sighed. "Perhaps someday we will come around. It is difficult knowing our intervention can do more harm than good in the long run, yet it has become clear to me in our travels that sometimes action is required."

"And you?" asked Kevin. "I know Larion won't let you leave again, but have you come around?"

Thinking about it for a moment, Kron said, "Yes. I understand our commitment to non-intervention, yet I now understand one must do what they must when they need." He paused for a second. "I learned that from you."

Ever humble, Kevin said, "It was nothing, Kron. I don't really have anything to teach."

"But you do," insisted Kron. "I have long believed you to be a young man of talent, and I see that again today." He turned and looked down at Kevin's friends, who were amassed with Larion and Necnea a short distance away on the ground. "Do not get me wrong; I do not believe you could do this alone. Caitlin is intelligence and strength, Rachel is determination and courage in the face of fear, Arthur is friendship and a reminder not to take life too seriously even in the darkest of circumstances, and Wheldon is loyalty and dedication to those who were not born to his society. All of them have important traits that support you."

Kevin nodded, as he looked upon his friends waiting below. For someone who had previously thought of himself as not capable of making good friends other than Arthur, he had certainly amassed them quite well. He also thought of King Andrew II of Aurana as a friend, as well as Raijin Shane, the Vanguard of Nuve, and perhaps his father's old cohorts War Commander Eukert and Knight Bryant, as well. It was somewhat amazing how the circumstances into which he fell gave Kevin so many friends.

He would need many, if not all of them, to save Aurana and stop the conquest of the realms. Even if Desolunar's momentum had faded out, Demonicus had already tried to have Kevin killed at least twice. This battle was not over until Demonicus and his Enlighteners were removed, the people of Seta Archa were liberated, and Aurana was forever free from his grasp. It was important to see this through.

A quick look down as his right arm gave Kevin some pause as well. He had three stripes around this arm, and he knew Caitlin had one as well. Demonicus could not be allowed to have these, and though Pseudo had refused to tell him how many the dictator and his cult held, Kevin feared he had at least one, if not more. It seemed strange he would allow a member of his organization like the one destroying the ruins of the Ancient City to have one if he did not have at least one himself. Though he did not know what these stripes did, he saw enough from the ruins destroying Enlightener to know they were extremely dangerous. Who knew what they could do if all of them were assembled in the wrong hands? For this reason, Kevin refused to allow the gods to take them for safekeeping. He and Caitlin would be their protectors, for now.

From all the way over where his friends were grouped, Kevin heard Arthur yell, "Hey, slowpoke! You're going to miss the magic transit thing!"

Rolling his eyes, Kevin then looked at Kron. "I guess that's my call to go."

Kron nodded. "Indeed. Please do not allow me to hold you up any longer." He paused, before he said, "Goodbye, Kevin Trent Stryker. I hope that someday our paths may cross again."

Silently, Kevin nodded. "As do I," he said, as he turned and walked down the stairs. He would miss Kron, but now he had to do what Kron's society had asked him to do.

As they stood together, Larion wished well of the five friends and the best of luck to them in going after Demonicus and Tyrinion. He briefed them of what they knew of the situation with Tyrinion again, to refresh their memories, and warned them of the powerful danger that Tyrinion posed, even without Demonicus. Then, he thanked them for what they were to do, and raised his hand. From it emitted a bright flash of light, enough to temporarily blind everyone around.

The light eventually dimmed, and suddenly Kevin, Caitlin, Arthur, Rachel, and Wheldon were regaining their vision. At first, only some simple colors started to appear, such as orange and dark green, until their sight was fully restored. And then, they saw where they were.

All around was a thick coniferous forest. Above, the sun was currently setting, leaving an orange glow across the horizon and the skies above. The entire group was standing on a road, one that seemed oddly familiar. Kevin was amazed at what he saw. He knew exactly where he was.

As his vision returned, Arthur looked around at the setting all around him, and said, "Hey, I think I recognize this place."

Rachel and Wheldon looked confused. They had never seen this place before.

"This is where I met you and Kevin for the very first time," commented Caitlin. "My house is near here."

Arthur nodded. "I can see that the remains of the soldiers that were here when we were months ago are finally gone. Hopefully they've finally been given a proper burial."

"Probably," answered Caitlin as she looked at the ground around. "No remains around to signify this was a battlefield. This cleanup is not something typical of Desolunar, according to my father, which suggests Auranian troops have been through here recently."

Rachel sighed. "Well, that's a relief, at least. I didn't get to see what it looked like to start, but I can only imagine. The dead deserve a ceremony and honor for what they died fighting for."

"Let us hope they received it, then," added Wheldon. "We will have to ask the military about the battleground when we catch up with them."

"Indeed," nodded Kevin, thoughtfully. A question was running through his head at the moment, and he was trying to answer it. "If this is Aurana territory, though, then the forces are further south of us. The question is, how far?"

As everyone turned to the south to look, it was apparent that something was very wrong.

"Hey, what's that?" Arthur asked.

They were staring into darkness. It was about sunset overhead and the sky was turning shades of oranges and purples. To the south, however, everything looked like it was pitch black nightfall already. That was not a normal phenomenon. Something felt eerie about it.

Wheldon took to the sky and flew up to get a better look over the trees of the southern forest. There was absolutely no reason why it should be so dark to the south, and its presence created a sense of dread within the group.

Caitlin looked up and asked, "Do you see anything, Wheldon?"

"It is completely dark, Catie," he answered. "It is hard to say for sure because of the sunlight around us, but I cannot see any stars in that night sky, either. Mysteriously, they have vanished."

A curious Rachel asked Caitlin, thinking it was magic, "Is it some kind of spell?"

For a second, Caitlin remained silent. She was stunned. "I've never seen anything like it. I couldn't tell you whether that's a spell or not."

Then, from behind them, a voice said, "I can."

Everyone turned around, in surprise, to see Professor James Magnon standing behind them.

Caitlin ran up and hugged her father for a moment, while the others stood back, still wondering where the professor had come from. After the momentary hug, the professor disengaged his daughter and continued, "Two months and a week is a long time for all of you to be gone. I hope you used that time well?"

Kevin and company stared at Professor Magnon. "I would say so," Kevin said.

"Hmmm, I see," acknowledged the professor, knowing Kevin had been taking Kron home, and that Kron was not with him now. "I am aware, and concur it was a good idea. That being said, you can see why I recalled you."

Descending back to the ground, Wheldon said, "I presume you must know what is causing the southern nightfall?"

"It is not night," answered the professor. "The sky is being blackened out, and it appears to be centered over Desolunar. And every day, it reaches further north."

An enveloping darkness that was rapidly expanding. Pseudo had made a comment about Demonicus eclipsing the world in darkness. This was what he meant, Kevin realized. He meant it literally.

Tyrinion was the god of darkness. Was this the inspiration for

Demonicus' plan?

Rachel looked confused. "What the hell could that be? Is it some kind of magic?"

"No," the professor retorted. "No one, not even I, could conjure that much magic. The amount of energy needed to sustain and grow such darkness would be beyond the limits of the mortal, or the immortal, I would imagine."

"It must be Demonicus," Kevin said as he stared, saying what he feared was true.

"How would you know that?" asked Arthur. "He's my father and I've met the man, and I know he's strong, but I don't think he's that strong."

In that moment, Caitlin realized what was going on. "He's not, Arthur. He has to be channeling the energy of those two stripes he has." She glanced down at the blue stripe concealed under the sleeve of her dress, and glanced over at Kevin, who was holding three more.

Professor Magnon did not flinch. "You are correct, my daughter. He must somehow know how to channel the powers of these stripes to use them to his advantage. He absorbs the light and releases the darkness."

Kevin kept staring south in shock. "You said it's spreading?"

"Every day," nodded the professor. "The further it expands, the more the darkness will incite mass panic among people. Armies will be demoralized from constantly fighting in the dark, and civilians will act erratically in fright. Then, as time goes on, those areas in darkness will be unable to grow or harvest crops because no sunlight is getting to them." He looked north for a second. "Summer is nearly ended and autumn is beginning. The plants need more time to be ready for harvest."

"We're in danger of a famine," Rachel stated aloud, in realization.

"Not just any famine," commented Caitlin. "One humanity would never recover from, presuming the darkness never lifts."

Arthur shook his head. "No, I don't think so." He paused for a second, as his friends looked at him for the contradiction. "When Demonicus had me as his prisoner, he made it clear he wants to conquer, not destroy. If you kill everyone, then who do you rule?"

"Exactly," Professor Magnon pointed out, "which is why I believe he will use the darkness to take the world hostage. He's pulled all of his forces back to Seta Archa to protect this strategy."

Kevin realized what Demonicus was contemplating. "Either he rules, or no one lives. That's absolutely sadistic."

"I fear this was his ultimate plan for conquest all along, his ace up his sleeve," said the professor. He then looked to the south. "The allied forces are gathering in Atwals. Our only chance to prevent this catastrophe is to defeat Demonicus."

"You have four stripes to his two," noted Wheldon to Kevin and Caitlin. "Surely these treasures will give you the power to overcome him.

Looking down at his arm, Kevin frowned. "I don't know about that," he said. "We don't know how to use these. He does."

Caitlin shrugged. "We have no choice but to try, stripes or not."

Kevin smiled at her and nodded. She was absolutely right.

At this, Wheldon extended his wings. "I can take four at most to Atwals." He looked to Professor Magnon. "I am afraid I cannot take five. I would have to make a second trip."

The professor was about to answer, but Kevin interrupted him. "Actually, Wheldon, would you be okay taking Arthur, Rachel, and the professor? I'd like to take Caitlin to her house for a moment."

A bit surprised, Caitlin stepped next to Kevin and held his hand. She was not sure why Kevin wanted to take her to her house, but the thought excited her a bit. Truthfully, even though she loved all of her new friends, she still was happy at having a bit of time alone with Kevin.

"Very well," nodded the professor. He did not offer to transport the group through his techniques, nor did it seem to matter much in this moment. A flight would give everyone a chance to survey the darkness as an added bonus.

Arthur approached Kevin and gave him a fist bump. "Try not to get lost on your way there."

Kevin rolled his eyes. He knew Arthur knew the house was only a short distance away.

Rachel gave Caitlin a hug, promising to catch up with her soon, while Wheldon offered a bow and promised he would be back as quickly as he could. Then, Arthur, Rachel, and the professor hopped aboard Wheldon, and the phoenix took off into the skies.

Heading for the darkness, Wheldon made sure to stay above the path through the forest below him. Professor Magnon, who was sitting in the front, offered to use a bit of light magic to keep the way illuminated for him. Behind the professor, Arthur and Rachel were hanging on tight, making sure not to fall off on the ride to Atwals.

"I wonder what that was all about?" Rachel asked to Arthur. "What's Kevin up to?"

"Oh, he probably just wants smoochy time with Caitlin," Arthur commented.

At that, Rachel hit him in the side of the arm. "Come on, Arthur! Be serious!"

"Don't be such a cynic!" Arthur yelled back at her.

Soured by that comment, Rachel scoffed. She looked back at the setting sun in the distance, feeling a little anxiety that they were separating again. Kevin and Caitlin had been her security blanket at the battle in Rikleifer, and for the first time since then, she did not have them with her. At least she had Arthur and Wheldon, and even though Arthur was a sarcastic clown as he always was, he was growing on her. They had been through a lot together, too, including a desperate escape from Seta Archa. Their bonds of friendship as a group were becoming ironclad, hopefully never to be broken.

Chapter 52

The Key of Hearts

Kevin and Caitlin were now left on the road, alone. As their friends disappeared from sight, they turned to walk to Caitlin's house. While they were walking, they held hands and enjoyed the sunset.

"I remember this so well," said Caitlin, as she looked around. "It didn't mean much to see it then, but it means so much more now. We walked this exact route on our way from your arrival point to my house the first time we met."

A smile came to Kevin's face. "I remember it vividly. You weren't exactly the nicest at the time, but the more that I see you, the more that I think of this road as one of the best places I've ever been. And it's all because this is where I met you."

Hearing this, Caitlin clung to Kevin by his arm. "That's so kind of you," she said. "I wish I had been more like I am now than I was at that time. It just has such a special feeling now."

"You can't blame yourself for that," said Kevin. "It was the way you were at the time. You're still the same person, you're just better able to express yourself."

"Thanks," smiled Caitlin. "But I don't know if I'm doing it better. I'm just actually doing it, thanks to you."

Kevin rolled his eyes a little bit. "Life does act in weird ways sometimes," he said. "I never meant to break you out of your emotional barriers, you know. I just needed to tell you how I felt about you."

"It's okay," smiled Caitlin. "Maybe it was that, or maybe it was saving your life from the Existence, or maybe it had just been happening since I met you. It doesn't matter how it happened. You were my friend and I liked you since we got to know each other."

Smiling, Kevin said, "I'd like to say the same thing about you. I didn't think when I first met you that that would happen, but I was surprised how much we really had in common. Even with a few frustrations about dealing with your lack of emotion, I couldn't believe how quickly we became friends."

"Feels like we've been through a lot, hasn't it?"

"A lot doesn't even begin to describe it."

Caitlin giggled. "No kidding," she said. "I'm a heavily-trained sorceress, and even I think this has been a lot to go through." She smiled at Kevin. "And you've changed as well, you know. You went from being a nervous young man to someone who has the confidence to handle anything that comes in front of you."

Kevin considered this for a moment. "Yeah, I guess you could say that," he said. "I never really felt that change, though. I just did what I thought I had to do."

"And that's really all it takes, in the end," said Caitlin.

They had arrived in front of Caitlin's house. Just as it always had been, it was a small little house sitting alongside the road, with barely anything to make it stand out. "Here we are," Kevin pointed out as they stopped in front of the door. "Out of curiosity, why do you live here and not in Wyntrail with your father?"

Shrugging, Caitlin said, "I wanted to train away from him."

"Why so?" asked Kevin.

"Well," she paused, "some things you're better off learning on your own, and that's the case in magic, too. You've met my father. He's a great teacher, but he can be pretty controlling with how he wants things to go. And I needed more freedom to learn what I wanted to learn."

Thinking for a moment, Kevin said, "Okay, I get that. Why here, though?"

Briefly before beginning, Caitlin waved Kevin around the house, leading him to follow her into the woods behind her house. They went beyond the house and into the woods as she continued. "I needed to be somewhere alone, so no one would be bothered that I was practicing magic near them, and this fit the bill. Magic can be scary for people because so few people learn the arts anymore, so it's safer to practice where no one is nearby. And this happened to be my mother's house, so it was a perfect place."

"Your mother's house, really?"

"That's what my father tells me. She lived here with my father until she died. He moved to Wyntrail after that. He always said it was her house because she picked where she wanted to live and he made sure to have the house built for her. After she died, he says it was too painful for him to stay here. He won't ever tell me much about my mother, but he did share this place with me, and it's the most connection I have with her."

Kevin now understood why she lived here.

Ahead, there was a fallen tree log in the forest. There was a small clearing as well, from which there was a beautiful view of the surrounding trees. "I was hoping I could show you this one day," Caitlin said, as she stepped over the log and sat down, inviting Kevin to sit as well. "I accidentally knocked this tree over with a spell one day. Since then, I've promised I will come out here periodically to meditate, so I can make use of the resource of this tree that I wasted with my mistake. It's sort of my special place now."

Taking a seat next to Caitlin, Kevin said, "I'm honored you would share this with me. It's a lovely place."

Caitlin smiled. "I thought you might like it," she said. "Whenever I was frustrated with something, or just needed a few minutes of peace, I would come out here and sit and think. Something about the serene nature of this place just puts me in the right mind, but…" She looked around, "but now I feel like I see it differently. The beauty of this place is captivating."

"It is," said Kevin, as he looked around. Then, he remembered that he had something for her. "Speaking of which," he said, as he reached into his pocket, "the reason I asked to take you to your house is because I have something beautiful to share with you, too."

Kevin slid off the log in front of Caitlin and showed her what was in his hand. It was a little pink key, cylindrical in shape with the head bent into a heart. It was painted a light pink with some tiny red accents, with a small leather string long enough to be hung around the neck. Though it contained no gems and was little more than a painted piece of metal, it was a small and inexpensive piece of jewelry.

Surprised, Caitlin's jaw dropped and she put her hands over her mouth. "Kevin, it's beautiful!" she exclaimed. "Where did you get that?"

"Remember the key we saw in Aurana City?" Kevin explained. "I couldn't afford it at the time, but I happened to mention it to Kron while we were training in the Realm of the Angels, and he volunteered to go to Aurana City and purchase it for me to give to you. Kron said the shopkeeper told him it represents the Key of Hearts, just like you said it did."

"I remember," said Caitlin, a tear of happiness forming in her eye. She smiled, as the tear fell.

Kevin nodded. "We've been busy a lot lately, and I'll admit I feel like I struggle a bit to tell you how much I love you. But I do love you, Caitlin. Every day I'm amazed that I get to spend my life with you, and I want to remind you every day that I love you."

Another tear of happiness fell from Caitlin's eye. Then, the hesitation hit again.

This was such a sweet gesture. Kevin did not deserve to be heartbroken by her accepting this meaningful gift if she was so hesitant. She needed to tell Kevin.

Her tears turned sad. "Kevin, I want to accept this, but I… we need to talk."

Stunned by this response, Kevin kept a hold of the necklace and sat back up on the log next to Caitlin. "What's up?" he asked.

Caitlin took a deep breath. She had not wanted to talk about this, because she enjoyed the time she was spending with Kevin. However, she owed it to Kevin to tell him about her feelings.

Nervously, Kevin sat looking at Caitlin, with his knees spread and his hands knotted between them. He was worried that Caitlin would break his heart.

"Kevin, you're wonderful," she began, struggling to find the words and switching to telepathy, *but I really worry if we have a future together*.

Sitting there, a tear to Kevin's eye. No words of thought went through his mind. He allowed Caitlin to continue to explain.

I know you know I'm not your typical woman, but if we keep going like we are, someday we'll want to be married. I love you so much that there is no one else I would rather be with, for the rest of my life. Even atypical me would love nothing more than to be married to you someday.

A smile cracked through Kevin's tears. "So what's the problem?" he asked aloud.

Nervously, Caitlin took a breath. Again, she could only express herself through telepathy. *I'd be a terrible wife. And the truth is, I don't want to be a normal wife. I never really learned how to cook and I don't want to cook every day. I don't want to worry about maintaining a house or waiting for you while I sit at home all day. I want to continue my studies, to become a wizardess and be known for what I've done for humanity. And...*

Kevin looked at her intensely. Another tear fell from Caitlin's eye as she hesitated. She reached up to wipe her tear before she looked at Kevin and continued.

And I don't know if I want to be a mother to children. I don't even know if I can, since we know now that I'm an angel for some reason, but even if it were possible, I don't think I would want to stay home and take care of children all day. That's just not me, Kevin. I'm not wife material. And why would you want to stay with me knowing all of that?

"Caitlin, I love you for you," Kevin said confidently, wiping a tear from his eye. "I know who you are and I support everything you want to be. Why would I ever want to leave you? Because our relationship wouldn't be traditional?"

"But you will leave," interrupted Caitlin, her tears turning into sobs. Again she stopped to wipe her eyes, but she continued to cry. "You will be upset, and then you'll leave." Her crying increased in volume again as she paused to cry more. "What kind of man would want a wife who can't or won't have children?"

You will be upset, and then you'll leave.

No. It could not be that way. It was a shot of passion directly into Kevin's veins.

Passionately, Kevin scooted off the log, stepped in front of Caitlin, and kneeled down in front of her. He grabbed her hand, put his other hand on her cheek, and said, "The kind of man who loves a woman regardless of her individual flaws."

Almost instantly, Caitlin's eyes lit up.

"Caitlin, when I told you that I loved you, that night in Nuvenia," continued Kevin after a pause, "I didn't tell you that because I thought you were perfect, or because you were an angel, or anything like that. I told you I loved you because it was the truth, and because I knew that there was something special about you that made you the one I believed was for me. And to this day, Caitlin, I still believe the same thing. Why would that ever change? I don't need a traditional life the way society expects it. I need you, however I can have you."

Suddenly, Caitlin's free hand came over her heart, as her teary eyes and soggy cheeks started to smile in surprise.

"I love you for who you are, not what you are," added Kevin, as he presented the necklace. "That's what this Key of Hearts represents. Love is stronger than just boy and girl meet, boy and girl marry, and boy and girl have children. It means something more than that, and I know that you know it too. So, let me ask you," he said, as he brushed Caitlin's face gently, and then took her hand and placed it on his heart, "what do you feel here? Is it just a thumping pulse, or is it something more?"

Is it something more?

It was.

Immediately, Caitlin sprung off the log down to Kevin's level, hugging him tightly. She closed her eyes and said, "It's everything. I can feel it, stronger than I ever have before." Another tear fell from her eyes, this one from happiness rather than sadness. "After all of that," Caitlin continued, still holding tight to Kevin, "I was so worried about not being typical that I forgot you're special, too."

"And I promise, I will always support your life the way you want to live it," said Kevin, holding Caitlin gently as he reached around her neck and tied on the key necklace. "I love you, Caitlin."

Then, there was only silence for over a minute. But the messages continued on.

I love you so much, Kevin Trent Stryker echoed Caitlin's voice in Kevin's head, as she kissed him. *I promise you, I'll never doubt you again.* She felt herself starting to lift involuntarily, and she started to glow. The translucent white wings appeared from her back.

They held each other for a few moments before Caitlin released her arms. She looked up at the sunset quickly turning dusky and said, "We should probably head back before Wheldon wonders where we are."

Kevin nodded. "Good point," he said. He held a floating Caitlin's hand as they traveled back to her house. The walk took a couple of minutes, but all the while Kevin and Caitlin could not help but glance at each other smiling and feeling like their relationship was as strong as ever.

Caitlin had taken the weight off of her chest and told Kevin what she needed to tell him. She bared her feelings and revealed her fears, and in turn Kevin alleviated those fears. Maybe they did have a future together after all.

As they approached the house together, however, Kevin felt a different hesitation. Stopping for a moment, he pulled out his sword. It felt like it was trying to tug him away from the house, although not so hard as to drag him. "Huh, that's odd," Kevin pointed out to Caitlin. "I don't think the Sword of Purity wants me to return to the house."

Confused, Caitlin said, "We were just there a few minutes ago. Why would it not want us to be here?"

Kevin shook his head. "Not sure," he said, "but we need to be where Wheldon can see us." He continued around the house and to the middle of the pathway. Caitlin followed him, her suspicions raised but not concerned yet.

The Sword of Purity had only tugged at Kevin before to take him somewhere, usually if he asked it to do so. Now it was pulling him away. Kevin walked around the pathway a bit to study this resistance, and found one spot near the house where it seemed to push back the hardest. The blade started vibrating with the high amount of force with which it was trying to push Kevin, although not acting in such force as to tug him.

"What could this be?" asked Caitlin. "Is it warning you of danger?"

"I don't know," said Kevin, as he waved his sword around a bit. "But I've got a very bad feeling about this…"

"Look out!" screamed Caitlin. She shoved Kevin to the ground, as she fell herself. A suspicious warped sound rang out through the air.

There was a sound of an explosion.

"Magic exploding shot!" called out Caitlin, as the blast rang out over their heads. "Advanced technique when fire is combined with light magic in an unstable way!"

Another shot then rang out, this one closer to their side, hitting the road. The force of the blast recoiled along the ground, shaking them again. It also stirred up dust alongside the road, making it difficult to see in that direction.

That was the last thing Kevin needed. He recalled from the battle at Rikleifer how much dust had played havoc with him before. It was blinding and made it much more difficult to breathe. Fearing the results of walking into this dust cloud, Kevin stood up but then took a couple of steps backwards. His sword was drawn, and he was awaiting the next shot.

Seizing the opportunity of the pause, Caitlin also stood up, staring into the dust and preparing to defend from another shot. "Well, what a way to spring a trap," commented Caitlin. "Be careful, the next attack could come from any side."

Nervous, Kevin was looking around while still in a combat stance. "But from which one?" he asked. "It'll be awful hard to catch the next one at this rate. Whatever shot this is likely changing its angle as we stand here."

"And it could be mobile," added Caitlin. "Just stay sharp."

Patiently, Kevin took a brief observation of his surroundings before he said, "Taurin taught me there are two rules to maintaining awareness as a warrior. The first is to always watch your rear, and make sure you're not taken from behind."

"And the second?" asked Caitlin.

"It's metaphorical," said Kevin, "but also appropriate. "That saying would be…"

Kevin's words were cut off as he was knocked off his feet and slid against the ground.

Not sure what happened, Caitlin urned to see him, in a sight that she could not believe she were seeing.

From the dust, someone had emerged and tackled Kevin to the

ground. It was a young woman wearing a yellow top that covered only the upper half of her torso, and a very short pair of shorts. Her hair was tied up on both sides into large puffs, and she had a tan complexion. She was now on top of Kevin, with a knife pointed at his throat.

"Never trust a cloud of dust," she said, as she intended to stab Kevin.

Chapter 53

The Sisters

Instinctively, Caitlin unleashed a blast of darkness magic at the woman, coming to Kevin's defense. The blast was right on target, knocking off the woman and throwing her a short distance away from him.

Then, another exploding blast erupted from behind Caitlin, knocking her to the ground. It was a hard hit, one that threw her with a significant amount of force. The violent blast was between her and Kevin.

The young woman with a knife then stood up, and brushed herself off a bit. She appeared to be in her early twenties and in excellent physical shape. Kevin was still on the ground, but he was using his senses to make observations of his surroundings.

As the young woman flipped around her knife a little bit, another one stepped out from behind the dust. This one was slightly younger but still older than Kevin, dressed in a yellow and green dress, with the skirt section cut off at the knees. It was a female spellcaster's dress, cut up, stained, and discolored.

"That was pretty well done, Rouge," said the younger girl in the dress. "You totally caught him by surprise."

"Sure did," answered the older girl, "but we're not done yet, Resa. Now, we have to finish the job."

"But Rouge," whined Resa, in a seemingly immature tone, "why do we? We pretty clearly finished the job with my magic. What more reason do we have to make a big mess? It's disgusting every time you decide that you have to make sure their blood is spilled."

Rouge flipped her knife around again. "Hey! That's what we do, Resa," she said. "We're assassin sisters. We don't leave our marks with the appearance of being live." Then, she approached Kevin and pointed her knife at him. "Besides, your magic shots never got close to this one. He's still alive."

Kevin's hand was still on his sword, which was lying across his body. Without opening his eyes, or moving another muscle, he tightened his grip on it.

"Are you sure you didn't get him hard enough?" asked Resa. "I mean, you did plow him pretty hard when you leapt at him. You don't think you hit him hard enough to kill him?"

Shaking her head, Rouge responded, "Of course not. It's pretty hard to kill someone like that. You'd have to get a hit just right to the neck to kill someone with a tackle, and you'd have to do it with a lot of force." She then flipped her knife again as she approached Kevin, and pointed the blade to his neck. "And I know for a fact, I didn't hit him that hard." Then, Rouge brought the blade down closer and closer to Kevin.

The knife lowered and lowered, until it was just above Kevin's neck. Right where he wanted it to be.

The second Rouge had the knife placed there, Kevin flipped his sword upward, knocking it away. His eyes popped open as he smashed Rouge with the flat side of his blade, throwing her off her balance and over to the side.

As Kevin then stood up, a frightened Resa started charging up energy, with the intent of counter-striking at Kevin. Before she had enough energy to unleash another exploding shot, however, Kevin pointed his sword downward at Rouge, placing the point precisely in the side of her neck. Rouge was sitting up with her legs underneath her, putting her at the perfect height for the tip of Kevin's sword to push just a slight bit into the side of her neck, right at the vein.

It was so well placed and so close as to make even the most skilled warrior freeze up with the fear of death.

Immediately, Resa stopped charging energy, and placed her hands in front of her, shaking them nervously. "Please, don't!" she screamed. "I'll surrender, and I'll do whatever you want, but please, spare my sister!"

Rouge took a cautious breath, sword still pointed at her neck. "Do it, Resa," she said. "Blast him to kingdom come. Don't worry about me, just do it to save your own life."

"I can't live without you, Rouge," responded Resa. "I can't do it."

At this point, Caitlin started to stand up from where she was, catching everyone's attention. She was not in angel form as she stood, but she pointed her right hand at Resa, charging a bit of darkness magic. Resa's eyes widened as she looked at Caitlin. "How… how… how are you still alive? Those exploding shots should have killed you!"

Caitlin started brushing herself off, appearing to still be in a little bit of pain. "Obviously you missed your shot. It takes more precision than that to pull off a fatal exploding shot."

"But I swear… I swear that my shots were right on!" exclaimed Resa.

"Then you thought wrong," commented Caitlin. "The results speak for themselves."

"Hey! You don't challenge my sister!" screamed Rouge, pointing at Caitlin.

Kevin stuck his sword a little closer into Rouge's neck, still not enough to stab her but enough to make her feel the sharpness of the blade. "Enough of that," he demanded. "The two of you just took a shot at assassinating us, and I want to know why." He paused for a second. "Now, there are some things I want to know here. Let's start with something basic. What are your names?"

Seeing no need to resist anymore, with the feeling that she was beaten, Resa said, "My name is Resa Kirkwood. My counterpart over there is my older sister, Rouge Kirkwood."

"And how old are you two?" asked Kevin.

Rouge answered this one, with the expression on her face of being let down. "I'm twenty-one," she said, "and my sister is nineteen."

Kevin took a second to consider this. "Awful young for a pair of assassins. Then again, I suppose I'm in no position to comment about someone's age myself. And what do you two know about me?"

"Presuming you're our mark," responded Resa, "your name is Kevin Trent Stryker. You're the Vanguard of Aurana, and you're also some kind of 'pure one', or at least that's what our boss told us. Other than that, we really don't know much about you."

Nodding, Kevin pointed his sword at the reluctant Rouge, who still seemed much more disappointed and less willing to cooperate. "And you, Rouge, does she tell the truth?"

"She does," said Rouge.

"Very well," answered Kevin, willing to accept that as an answer for now. "Are the two of you from Desolunar?"

There was a pause for a second. "We are," said Resa. "We're both from Seta Archa."

An assassination attempt from Demonicus. How did Kevin figure that one before he even knew where Rouge and Resa were from?

"Way to go telling him everything," scoffed Rouge.

In response, Kevin immediately placed his blade at Rouge's neck again. "Hey! Nobody asked you!" said Kevin with force. "I'll come back to you when you're more willing to cooperate. Until then, I want only your sister to say anything."

"It's okay, Rouge," added Resa. "We lost this one. The more we tell him, the less we have to worry about."

Puzzled, Kevin asked, "Worry about? What do the two of you have to worry about?"

Resa sighed. "Death," she said. "Our boss, our leader, doesn't take failure too well. He kills everyone who fails at the missions he assigns for them."

"Demonicus, I presume?" asked Kevin, curious.

"That's him," answered Resa, starting to sound more down in her tone of voice. "He gets very angry at those who fail at the tasks he assigned for them. Our father… he learned that the hard way." A tear came to Resa's eye.

Kevin sighed. He let the pressure off of Rouge's neck. While he knew he had to stay intimidating in this moment, he felt bad for these sisters and the losses they had already faced at the hands of their boss.

Sisters. These were the sisters that Pseudo referenced months ago on the Cliffs of Vallia. "Tell me more," asked Kevin, directly but removing any anger from his voice. "How did you get to be assassins in the care of Demonicus?"

Although Kevin was expecting Resa to answer, Rouge did

instead. "We're technically only half sisters with the same father; my mother's a former Toronaga tribe member from the Wastes, and Resa's mother is from Nuve. We were both taken by our father when we were very little and trained to be warriors in Seta Archa. We were both taught magic, but I was never any good at it. So, instead, they let me learn some Toronaga-style martial arts and ways of fighting to disable opponents quickly. Resa, my younger sister, learned magic very well, though, and so we kind of became a team like that."

Resa then took over again. "We've been on a number of missions before, but we were told by Demonicus to wait here for you." Resa then teared up more. "He said that one of us would have to watch the other sister be brutally killed if we failed. If we run, he will hunt us down and make sure our fates are even worse. Of course we waited here for months, because that's what we were told to do, and we dared not defy him."

Kevin's hand came over his mouth. How cruel was Demonicus, really? This was beyond description in terms of the cruelty of Demonicus and the iron fist with which he ruled his land. More and more, Kevin was seeing the invasion of Seta Archa to come as a justified attempt to overthrow a cruel tyrant. Something in his heart told the young hero that Rouge and Resa were telling the truth about this, from the bottom of their hearts. Normally, Kevin would be wary of such a story from people who had held bad intent for him before, but Kevin felt a deep sense of sympathy for the assassin sisters.

Carefully, Kevin let down his sword from Rouge, as Caitlin kept her eyes open. Then, he approached Resa, and said, in a tone of optimism, "It's going to be all right. I won't let such a fate befall either of you."

"But you can't," said Rouge with a serious tone, still on her knees on the ground. "The second we return to Seta Archa, that's exactly what will happen. Unless, of course, you decide to kill us first for trying to assassinate you."

"Now, now, no one's going to die today," responded Kevin. He looked to Caitlin. "How would you feel about taking them with us?"

Caitlin scowled at Kevin. "After they tried to kill us?"

"You tried to kill me the first time we met. Wheldon met us by kidnapping us. Arthur and Rachel tried to kill us once by shooting at us in the Northern Pass. Isn't this kind of how we meet our friends?"

Rolling her eyes, Caitlin shook her head. She had not contemplated that before. "Fair point. I guess you're right," she said. "It's okay with me if it's okay with you."

"You mean to take us prisoner?" inquired Rouge.

Kevin shook his head. "Not at all. There is one more option for the two of you. We are headed to Seta Archa, with the intent of storming the city and overthrowing Demonicus. Would the two of you be interested in joining this cause and saving Desolunar from its ruler?"

There was a slight pause as Resa looked over at Rouge. Then, she looked back at Kevin, and said, "We're Seta Archa natives. We can't just turn on our own country even if we fear our leader. What are we to do?"

"Nobody's asking you to turn on your own country," responded Kevin, recalling on his own experience in overthrowing the former king of Aurana, Arnold IX, in order to put his son into power. "But sometimes, it's a greater treason not to do anything at all as opposed to standing up against your leader. If it helps you, though, I can take you to see his son."

This caught Rouge's attention. "The heir? You mean the heir to Desolunar, the son of Demonicus? He is here?"

"Not here," responded Kevin, "but near here. He should be in Atwals by now, and he's my best friend. He stands by my side, and we fight together for the same purpose."

"You do?" exclaimed Rouge, surprised. "Okay, this one I've got to see. And you're sure the heir won't try to tear us apart or anything like that?"

Kevin nodded. "Absolutely. He's a jokester, but otherwise he's a pretty docile guy who wouldn't hurt any innocent person. I think that if the two of you had the chance to meet him, you'd be willing to come along with us and help make Desolunar and the world a much better place to live."

Resa looked over at her sister. "I like this boy," she said. "The least we could do is check out the person he says is the heir. If it is him, maybe we could save ourselves and our country after all."

There was a pause as Rouge took a breath. "We couldn't end up any worse off than we are now."

"You're skeptical," said Caitlin to Rouge. "That's very smart of you. It is good not to trust anyone who promises you the world upon meeting you. We can't promise that we can keep you safe through this whole experience we have coming before us."

Rouge let out an awkward chuckle. "Oh good, I thought it was going to be boring there for a moment," she said. "Resa, I say we go for it. It might be the only way we can both stay alive together, given what awaits us if we return."

"I agree," nodded Resa. Then, she turned to Kevin. "Mr. Stryker… uhm…"

"Call me Kevin," chuckled Kevin. "I understand what you're going to say. You two seem to really depend on one another, which makes you perfect sisters. But if you're going to go with me to meet him and continue to Seta Archa, then you have to understand that I have to have some trust in you as well. Today, both of you tried to take my life, and I can't be sure that you won't try it again, at least not yet. Do you understand?"

"We do," nodded Resa. "If it lets me stay with my sister, then it's worth it to me."

Kevin took a breath. "Very well, then," he said, as Caitlin stepped up next to him. "As far as I'm concerned, you're with us now. Okay?"

"Sounds great," responded Rouge as she walked over to Kevin, and reached out to shake his hand. "I promise you, we won't let you down."

In return, Kevin exchanged a handshake with Rouge, and then also with Resa. Caitlin did the same, and for the next few minutes, Kevin and Caitlin shared their story, and who they really were. It would be about another hour until Wheldon arrived.

Chapter 54

Great Survivors

Atwals was a city that lay in ruin, having been burned to the ground by Desolunar back during the initial invasion some fifteen years before. Most of the buildings, including several tall spires, were made of stone, however, which meant that the city's buildings all still stood and had not burned down. On the negative side of that, though, was that the buildings' interiors had all been destroyed, and the structures compromised, making many of them unsafe to enter on the fear of collapse.

At one point, Atwals had been the second largest population center in Aurana, being the capital of Aurana's southernmost province, an area rich in its local forest resources. The logging and carpentry businesses were very important in Atwals because of the forest, and oftentimes companies in the area were unable to find enough people to harvest the trees, carve them down, and ship them out all around the world. It was partially because of Atwals that Rikleifer had become such a successful city, as Rikleifer's location served it well as a ground transportation hub for most goods coming out of Atwals or going into it.

Ethnically, much of Atwals' population before the invasion of Desolunar was a mix of Auranians and Seta Archans, with many of the cultural traits of people who had emigrated from the city-state over centuries. Under Aurana's care, the city was a melting pot of the two ethnicities, and while there would periodically be some tension between the two ethnic groups, the two were mostly blended without issue.

Until recently, though, both Atwals and the entire province of Southern Aurana lay in Desolunar territory. One massive battle had been lost in Atwals, and in that one battle, the entire province had been lost. Since then, a fierce resistance in Atwals had continued to try and claw back the city from its occupiers, yet it never seemed to grasp a foothold until now.

Desolunar had held the city for years, but with the recent full retreat back to Seta Archa, the city was now in the control of the coalition Auranian, Nuvenian, and Scurnian forces. Alongside them were the factions of the Demons, the Cornelia Chimeras, and the Knights of the Dragon. That said, it was now a city enveloped in darkness by Demonicus's plan

Kevin, Caitlin, Rouge, and Resa were flying in aboard Wheldon. Caitlin sat in front, helping to light the way in the heavy darkness that pervaded the sky. As they arrived over Atwals, they saw many torches burning to keep the town lit for the moment. Though it was difficult to see, the military presence was quite clear.

Kevin let out a sigh as he saw the buildings. "If this isn't an example of the destruction Desolunar can cause, I don't know what is. This place looks awful."

Caitlin pulled up next to Kevin. "It does, but it'll reflect what we do. If we can defeat Demonicus, Aurana will rebuild this city. I'm sure Andrew will see to it."

Nodding but appearing to still be hesitant, Kevin took a breath. "Indeed. But that makes me worry. If the gods are to be believed, Demonicus may be a despot and a threat, but he is just the marionette, not the puppeteer."

"What are you talking about?" asked Resa, curiously, not questioning the 'gods' comment. "My sister and I have met Demonicus before, and trust me, that guy pulls all of the strings. All of his advisors are frightened beyond belief to serve him, as he usually kills most of them if they don't understand him or if they recommend something he doesn't like."

"But that doesn't mean there isn't a bigger fish," responded Caitlin. "The best puppeteers hide the fact that they exist and make the marionettes the focus of the show, almost as if they are alive and in control."

For a moment, Kevin had to stop and think about what Caitlin had just said. She was right: there was a distinction to make between the puppeteer and the marionette. As the gods had said, Tyrinion, god of darkness, was the real puppeteer behind this whole mess.

Rouge nodded. "Very deceptive, indeed. Resa, Caitlin does

have some good logic here. Just because something doesn't seem likely doesn't mean it isn't there. Thus, if you think about it, everything good or bad could have something or someone pulling the strings, if you think about it."

"My thoughts exactly. Now it'll be our job, if we find the strings, to cut them," said Caitlin, as Wheldon began to descend toward a clearing just outside of town. Near that clearing, Professor Magnon had lit up a bit of light magic at the tip of his fingers, to guide Wheldon to a safe spot to land in the darkness.

As they landed, Professor Magnon greeted the group and noted the two additional individuals with them. Kevin and Caitlin recounted the meeting to her father and how the sisters had tried to kill them, with Caitlin recalling that she met Kevin in much the same way. The professor politely advised caution, but appeared to sympathize with the story.

Together, the group walked into town. Wheldon was advised by Professor Magnon that the phoenixes were here as well, having decided to join in the fight, and therefore he did not need to hide. He would be welcome here. As they walked toward the city center together, Professor Magnon decided to point out everyone in Atwals. "Take a look around at all of these groups," he said. "So many diverse troops from all around, all here with one purpose. Over to the left are some Auranian troops in the green uniforms, while there's some Nuvenians and Scurnians to the right, in blue and red, respectively. And in front of us, a member of the Demons in a half crimson, half black uniform, alongside a Cornelia Chimera in light blue. Over behind us," the professor paused for a moment, "they are the underground. They have kept the fight going for Atwals long after the city was lost."

Rouge lowered her head. "We've probably killed a few of them, I'm afraid. Resa and I were here on assignment previously."

"I am sure all will be forgiven for those who band together now to fight Desolunar, as we cannot afford not to have all the help we can get," the professor responded. "It turns out my thoughts were correct, and the ultimatum was received by the leadership council a few moments ago. Either we surrender to Desolunar, or Demonicus will cloak this realm in darkness."

Sighing, Kevin knew the professor was correct often enough that this was to be expected. Feeling a bit distant as he listened, he looked over closely at the underground members they were passing, and saw that their clothing was much less clothing and more of rags. Then, Kevin saw a more surprising sight: Arthur was standing there with them, talking with them.

Quietly, Kevin leaned over to Professor Magnon and asked, "What's Arthur doing over there with them?"

"He's the heir of Desolunar, Kevin," responded the professor. "Many members of the underground include Desolunar deserters and refugees. To all who hail from Desolunar, even if they have never met him before, he is an influential figure to all of them, especially since he is on the side of the alliance."

Kevin shook his head, absolutely confused. "I still don't get that," he said. "Why would he be treated like that? He's never lived in Desolunar and hasn't lived as a crown prince or something like that. He can't be that important to them."

"You want to bet?" Rouge looked over and gave an odd glance at Kevin. "The heir is the crown prince, or at least he is intended to be, and he is legitimate in Desolunar. The story in Desolunar goes that Demonicus found a specific woman to bear his child because she could provide him a strong child. It was a case of selective breeding, if you will. He would live away from Desolunar until he was ready to learn how to lead as Demonicus entered his final years of life. He is so respected because he is the heir to the Desolunar ruling position."

Stunned for a second, Kevin responded, "Wow, that's actually more well thought through that I would have given Demonicus credit for. Disturbing as that story is, it's strange that he would plan that so well."

Professor Magnon shook his head. "Absolutely not," he said. "Believe it or not, every action taken by Demonicus is usually calculated and precise. It is true, his anger makes him very impulsive and causes him to make rash decisions, but he has the genius of the world's greatest strategists and the know-how and resources to use them. You may wish to keep that in mind."

Kevin nodded, thinking it smart not to forget that. He looked over to Caitlin, who also seemed confused that Arthur was so respected.

"May we meet him?" Resa asked.

Looking at Arthur interact, Kevin said, "I think you should, in due time. Let's let him have his moment with the underground first."

Rouge nodded. She looked at Resa to signal to her that was the right thing to do.

From there, the professor pointed out a tall spire in the center of the city, used as the capital building both of Atwals and of the province of Southern Aurana. "The commanders are all in there, and have set it up to be a temporary headquarters. That is where we are heading now, as they are about to present the war council's strategy for the advance on Seta Archa."

"Oh? Who's all there?" asked Caitlin.

The professor thought for a moment. "When I came from here, there were quite a few people. I saw King Andrew II, Head Commander Forkman, and War Commander Eukert representing Aurana; King Raijin Lester and his brother Raijin Shane, Vanguard of Nuve, representing the official Nuve government; King Warren, your father Vincent Stryker, and Gilbert Griffith, Vanguard of Scurnia, representing Scurnia; Steffen Robert representing the Demons faction of Nuve; Arsuf Maxwell representing the Cornelia Chimeras; the Lord Dragon representing the Knights of the Dragon; the Red Phoenix and Grand Raven representing Avalon, and some of the underground leaders. No leaders or soldiers from Gardolk have come, though, as expected."

"That's a shame," responded Kevin. Disappointed, he said, "As much as we don't like their decision, we have to respect it."

"Yes, we do," said the professor. "You have done well in your diplomacy, Kevin, but the whole world will never change despite your efforts. And to be frank, I did not send you to Gardolk because I was certain they would never willingly join. They have never been threatened by Desolunar in the ways the Triple Alliance has."

"That's reality for you," commented Rouge. "I didn't know you were a diplomat, Kevin."

Kevin shrugged. "The professor started that, but it sort of comes with being the Vanguard of Aurana, as I've found out."

At this point, Kevin and his group reached the security checkpoint in front of the spire. Professor Magnon presented Kevin as the Vanguard of Aurana, which was necessary since Kevin had no military jacket since tearing it apart to bandage Caitlin during the battle in Rikleifer. Unfortunately, Rouge and Resa were not allowed to enter, so Professor Magnon pointed them to where they could get fresh water and a decent meal, and a chance to clean themselves up after months of having to stake out Caitlin's house. Because the professor introduced Caitlin as his daughter, she was allowed to enter. Wheldon, being the Red Phoenix's second-in-command, was also allowed to enter.

Once inside, the professor led Kevin and his friends down several hallways and to a central room. He quietly said to them, as they stopped at the door, "The most powerful people in the world are behind this door. Remember that today, you stand with them."

Kevin nodded, and then proceeded to carefully open this door. He pushed it in slowly, seeking not to create a large amount of noise. As the door widened, the lights of candles reflected through the opening, indicating to both Kevin and Caitlin that this was the right room. Inside the large room was a giant round table, with nearly thirty chairs seated around it,. Several tables were set up in the room's corners, completely stacked up with maps. It was truly a command center at this point. The rulers of their respective countries were all seated around at the head end of the tables together, with their generals.

The instant they walked in, Kevin and Caitlin realized how many people here they had met in person. The closest people upon their entrance were King Andrew II and Head Commander Travis Forkman, along with War Commander Eukert and John Bryant, who for his actions in Rikleifer had been promoted from Knight to Paladin. Immediately, though, Kevin's eyes lit up when he saw his father, Vincent Stryker, seated between the Auranian and Scurnian representatives. All five of them stood up to greet Kevin personally, although the generals made sure that the king had the opportunity to speak personally with him first.

King Andrew II was wearing a military uniform of green, with small sidearm capes of red and blue draped behind his shoulders, and a crown atop his head. "Kevin Trent Stryker, my loyal retainer, I was hoping to see you in Wyntrail."

Kevin bowed his head, but reached out to shake Andrew's hand as well. "My apologies that I could not make that happen," he said.

"I understand," acknowledged the king. "I have heard much of your endeavors from the people in this room. It seems we have much for which to thank you, from temporarily reuniting Nuve to reuniting this entire alliance, and also for holding the line in the Battle of Middle Aurana long enough to ensure a successful retreat, which led to a highly successful counterattack."

Kevin seemed shy about it. "Well, you're welcome, I guess," he said. "I just did what I had to do."

Smiling a bit at Kevin's humility, Andrew said, "And that is all you needed to do. You represent Aurana well, Kevin. We are proud to have you as our Vanguard." He then looked aside at the red-haired girl in the white dress with red trim, as if he recognized her, but something seemed different about her. "Would you be Professor Magnon's daughter, then?"

Caitlin smiled as she offered a curtsey. "A pleasure to meet you, your majesty. I am Caitlin Amelia Magnon, and Kevin's traveling companion."

Andrew's eyes widened, remembering the professor's daughter as being quite different before. He then thought of how Kevin had told him about his feelings for the professor's daughter. Then, he smiled at Kevin, as if proud of him, before looking to Head Commander Forkman.

From under the table, Head Commander Forkman presented a new Aurana military jacket. Its rank representation from the triangular insignia on the arm near the shoulders was Vanguard. "Of course," began Head Commander Forkman, "we cannot have our Vanguard running around not appearing as a representative of Aurana. It took us a bit to recreate this; as we understand from their insistence, we had to acquire a couple of small flag patches from the Demons in Nuve in order to make it complete."

Kevin smiled as he accepted the new jacket. It looked just like his old one. He chuckled a bit about the Demons flags, too, but was grateful that the fact they had been on his jacket previously was important enough to ensure they were on his new jacket.

Invited to take a seat, Kevin and his friends sat down with the Auranian representatives, with Kevin sitting with Caitlin on one side of him and his father on the other. Kevin made sure to give his father a hug before he sat down, grateful that they were indeed reunited today.

Everyone was here, it appeared. Vincent Stryker pointed out to Kevin some of those he had not met; in the Scurnian delegation further down from him were King Warren of Scurnia, as well as the elder Gilbert Griffith, Vanguard of Scurnia. They were seated next to Christoph Dewellus, the Lord Dragon. Sure enough, the Knights of the Dragon were keeping their promise to join if permitted. Further away were King Raijin Lester and his brother, Raijin Shane, along with Arsuf Maxwell and Steffen Robert, although they were each seated as far apart as three parties could sit at such a table. Nuve's internal issues would not be so easily resolved, Kevin reasoned to himself. There were also representatives from the underground, as well as the Red Phoenix and Grand Raven, who had come out of hiding for this. Barring Gardolk, the world was truly united for this cause.

Standing near a map was Raijin Shane, Vanguard of Nuve, who was chosen to open the briefing. He began, with a strong voice of confidence, "Lords and generals of our nations and independent groups of the world: of Aurana, Nuve, and Scurnia; of Avalon and the entire phoenix race; of the Demonstrative Organization of Northern Nuve and the Cornelia Chimeras; of the Knights of the Dragon; and of the underground resistance to the occupation of Desolunar; truly, a great battle that will change the course of history is in thy hands."

Kevin was listening intently. He had heard Raijin Shane speak before and knew why this was his task. He was a great speaker.

"A great terror has, for almost twenty years now, loomed with a mindset of destruction as it has built itself up from the remains of a previous threat. In the time span of twenty years, Desolunar has taken a large former city-state as its capital, conquered lands belonging to Aurana and Nuve, taken the lives of many of our soldiers and innocent civilians alike, and continued to ravage crimes against its people. Now comes a new threat—an eternal darkness that will never end, unless we surrender our nations to Desolunar. Of course, we cannot allow this darkness to spread, and we will not surrender ourselves to a foreign invader who will not honor our sovereignty as kingdoms. Therefore, it is thy decision that we strike at Desolunar and their capital at Seta Archa before they can follow through on their threat. Such massive losses such as at the Battles of Atwals, Cardol, the Aurun River Delta, Middle Aurana, and Cornelia have shown the aggression of Desolunar and the threat it places on all of us. It was not until recently, at the Battle of Haventown, that we were able to turn the tide of the war, and now it seems apparent that Desolunar would rather retreat to protect this destructive strategy with a blatant disregard for life, rather than face us in a fair fight. A fight, however, is what we will give them. For that task, the council at Nuvenia has appointed Sir Vincent Stryker, retired Scurnian general, as the head consultant for strategizing this battle. Mr. Stryker has years of military experience and also served as the head commander and strategist during the savage wars twenty years ago for the Scurnian forces, including orchestrating a surgical strike on Seta Archa that to this day is the only known successful invasion and capture of Seta Archa in history. For that, I ask that all of thee show thy respect." Upon finishing this sentence, Raijin Shane began walking toward Vincent's seat.

Vincent stood up, allowing Shane to have his seat. Then, the old war hero walked to where Shane had been standing, picked up a long wooden stick, and pointed it to a large map of Seta Archa in detail that was laying on the table. "This is an overlay of the city. As you can see, there is one wall surrounding the whole city, and no gate in or out, which makes invasion difficult. No roads lead to the city, so we will have to march over terrain and set up in narrow areas as the forest serves as a natural barrier before we reach the walls. It is unlikely because of these defenses that the Desolunar forces will set up outside of the walls, so we will easily be able to surround the city, but we also project that Demonicus's strategy relies on having a great amount of food stock and grain reserves in the city itself, and therefore starving them out is not an option given the expanding situation with the darkness. Taking in siege weapons and ramps to such an area is difficult because of the lack of roads; but ramps, at least, are paramount without a gate in the wall. It will be a difficult advance, but one that is completely possible. May I ask, to any one of you who knows, how many siege ramps we have?"

King Andrew II took to answer. "Amongst all of our armies, we brought about twenty to thirty," he said.

"Excellent," responded Vincent Stryker. "We will have to leave all other siege weapons here because we will not have any place to set them up and we will be encumbered by them." He paused for a second. "If we have any advantage in this battle, it is that Desolunar soldiers are used to fighting on offense, and not on defense. Setting up the first stage of our assault will be difficult, as archers will rain arrows from the top of the walls and Desolunar soldiers will set up spontaneous ambushes using the trees and the top of the wall as cover. They may use fire as a tactic to destroy our ramps, so it will be important to keep that in mind."

Fire was a frightening tactic, Kevin thought to himself. Hopefully it would never come to that.

Vincent Stryker continued, "Our goal will be to establish ramp 'bridgeheads' that we can defend. Capture a portion of the wall around a ramp, and defend it well, and our troops can pour into the city. Should a bridgehead be recaptured, however, then the men inside will be surrounded. It will be nearly impossible to capture the whole wall, so we must pour into the city to strike at the core. As we get into the city, our target is a pyramid covered in black stone. It is the capital building of Desolunar, and most likely where Demonicus will be. However this darkness is being generated, this will either be the source of it or will lead us to the source."

"Is there another way?" interjected a question from Arsuf Maxwell. "This seems very dangerous."

"It is very dangerous," acknowledged Vincent Stryker. "Seta Archa is a well fortified city. And we're sure they will have gryphon soldiers to harass us, but we will counter with phoenixes and dragon troops from the Knights of the Dragon. For those soldiers, we estimate we will not have enough to penetrate those defenses, but should the tide turn, a flight directly to the pyramid could be possible. And… there is one other way." He pointed to the north side wall. "Twenty years ago, we found a pathway under the wall, which we called 'the main thoroughfare' because it links to Seta Archa's most central street. We don't know where the entrance to it is, but we know of its existence. We also know it to be booby trapped. Should you be able to find it and evade its trap, however, it could be a safer path into the city."

Beside Vincent, seated in a chair, Gilbert Griffith, Vanguard of Scurnia, was shaking his head. "It sounds awfully difficult, Vincent. Are you absolutely, completely sure we have a better chance at this wall assault than we do versus a focus on this underground passageway?"

Without even a second's hesitation, Vincent nodded. "I am absolutely certain and sure." He paused for a moment

From there, Vincent explained the battle setup. He assigned select forces by country to attack the city from certain sides. Scurnia was given the east, Nuve and its factions were asked to ally together to the south, and Aurana was given the west. Nuve's unit only came together after King Lester assigned Steffen Robert and Arsuf Maxwell to be his top two generals in the fight, giving them leadership power. A fourth unit for the north was constructed from the underground soldiers, along with some of each of the other units. Kings Andrew II and Warren assigned War Commander Eukert, Paladin Bryant, and Vincent Stryker to this unit as well. Kevin and his friends would be a part of this unit, too.

In all, the meeting took two hours. Every contingency that could be conceived was explained, and plans were made and explained to foresee any potential issues. Then, to finish, Vincent Stryker made a bold statement. "Before we finish," he began, "I want everyone to understand the severity of what we are facing. Should the world be enveloped in darkness, our nations will fall. Whether that is all at once or one by one is irrelevant. People will die. Those that do not will be conquered. The fate of our world is in your hands, and those of our soldiers. We cannot retreat. We cannot fail. To fail is to submit our kingdoms to eternal darkness. Our kingdoms, however, have long been great survivors. Each survived the feudal Third Era to become the superstates we know today. Each has survived attempts at conquest in its history. Today, we must show the tyrant Demonicus that we will survive."

Chapter 55

Calm Before the Storm

As Vincent Stryker finished his sentence, everyone stood up and started to shake hands with others, thanking them for the pleasure of fighting on the battlefield together and talking about the battle ahead. Kevin took this opportunity to approach his father, gratefully and with purpose. "You do a great job with strategy. I hope your plan works."

"It will give us the best chance," Vincent Stryker told his son. "That is all we can ask for. The rest is in our hands to determine." He paused for a second. "And when the time comes, I hope that you will step up to lead your unit."

Kevin was puzzled. "What do you mean? I'm not a military leader!"

"Take a look around you," responded Vincent, confidently, as he extended his arm. "These people need a good leader, an inspiring one. They don't need an old man whose body is slowly falling apart, no matter how successful he is as a strategist and what experience he has."

For a second, Kevin rolled his eyes. "You're not that old, dad."

"Even so," responded Vincent, with an encouraging look in his eyes, "he or she who inspires will be the one able to keep his troops behind him or her, and those troops will be more prepared to fight on through the difficulties of battle. You have the confidence and the personality to do just that, and you do know it. It's your time to shine, Kevin."

Shaking his head, Kevin said, "Battle's really not my thing, though. I kind of realized that back in Rikleifer."

"Then why did you go to Rikleifer in the first place?" asked Vincent.

Kevin sighed. His father had him on that one. "Because they needed me," he said.

"Precisely," responded Vincent. "You were willing to step up in the name of others. That is what makes an inspiring leader. And that's all you need to be for now, because you'll have myself, other generals, and your friends with you."

"And I appreciate that," nodded Kevin, feeling a little pressured. "I have a feeling I'll need it."

"Well, we'll just have to see," said Vincent, gripping his son's shoulder a little tighter. "Now, then, there's still a lot of organization of troops to do, especially amongst the leaders of all of the units. I know you're having a rough time dealing with things due to the added complications, I'm sure, but I think you should get the opportunity to take a night off before everything starts unfolding tomorrow."

Kevin was thankful for that. He knew how much Caitlin, and probably Arthur and Rachel as well, were looking forward to having a night off and spending time with friends. And honestly, so was he as well. He did hold a high value on his friends, and he did not want any of them to feel alienated by how much he was focused on what he was doing. There was a persistent feel to Kevin that he was perhaps too focused on defeating Demonicus, but now more than ever the stakes were so high that it had to be the priority.

At about that time that the thought passed through Kevin's head, Caitlin stood up, stepped up next to Kevin, and grabbed him by the arm. It made him stop thinking and put him into action. "Thanks, dad," he said, "I'd be glad to take you up on that offer. It has been a little rough lately."

"I'm sure it has," nodded Vincent. "And it's best that you not be overloaded with a whole lot of stress just before we go out there to battle."

Kevin rolled his eyes. That was easy for Vincent to say, but Kevin knew he would still be filled with stress anyway. There simply was not a way around it. As people all around the room were starting to file out, Kevin said, "We'd better get going then, while the fires are still burning around the city. Thanks again, dad. I promise you, we'll catch up on the way to Seta Archa."

"I'm sure we will," responded Vincent. He then gave his son a hug and turned to talk with the generals in charge of the main units in the battle ahead. Professor Magnon mentioned to his daughter that he too would be staying, and encouraged Caitlin to spend time with her friends before the battle. “Enjoy the calm before the storm,” he advised her.

With that, Kevin and Caitlin looked for Wheldon briefly before seeing he was still catching up with the Red Phoenix. Expecting that he would catch up later, they turned for the door and exited through it. They followed the twisting pathways out through the spire and to the exit. It was a long walk of a few minutes, but Kevin and Caitlin did not say anything to each other. They just held hands together as they made for the exit, not wanting to think about all the strategy that had been discussed.

Just outside the spire, Arthur and Rachel were waiting for them. “That took you guys long enough,” joked Arthur, as Kevin and Caitlin walked up to them. “We heard all about what went on in there. I hope we at least have the rest of the night off?”

“We do,” responded Kevin, starting to walk down the hall with his friends in tow. “We’re leaving tomorrow, though, so we’d better make use of the time while we have it.”

Rachel became excited. “That’s great to hear,” she said. “It’ll be fun, just the four of us and Wheldon, if he wants to hang with us…”

“Uhm, actually, that won’t be all,” interrupted Caitlin. “We have two more people we just met to hang out with us as well. We just met them a little while ago back where we were by my house.”

Arthur’s eyes widened. “Oh? And how did you meet them up there?” he asked.

“They tried to kill us,” responded Kevin in a joking manner. “But they’re not bad people; they were just misled and afraid. I thought it might be fun if we hung out with them tonight and let them know they do have friends.”

In response, Arthur gave Kevin the weirdest look. “You’re crazy, you know that?” he said.

Kevin laughed. “If I’m crazy, then you’re certifiably insane,” he said. “But I think I like things that way. When we first started this whole journey, Arthur, you were my best friend, Rachel was just a friend, and I didn’t even know Caitlin. Now, though, I think we’re all a lot closer to each other because of what’s happened.” Kevin reached down to grab Caitlin's hand again, which she more than willingly let him have.

Both Arthur and Rachel had seen this move. "Figures," said Arthur sarcastically. "You two both make me sick."

"We only do it to leave you out of the group," joked Caitlin.

"Yeah, whatever," responded Arthur, still being sarcastic. Then, he decided to pull on Rachel a little bit. He turned to her and said in a mocking tone, "Hey Rachel, maybe we should join in with what they're starting."

Rachel rolled her eyes uncomfortably. "Smartass," she said.

Almost as instantly as Rachel said that, Kevin, Caitlin, and Arthur broke into laughter.

"Yeah, yeah, whatever," she said, passing it all off. "Don't get all uppity on me just because my sense of humor isn't quite the same at taking a joke."

"You and your realism," laughed Caitlin. "Come on, Rachel, live a little!"

"Says the girl who had no emotion whatsoever for years," mentioned Arthur. This made Arthur and Rachel start laughing at the irony, and made Kevin resist the urge to laugh.

"Hey!" exclaimed Caitlin, now with a shocked look on her face. "You take that back! That was different, and you know it."

Placing her hand over her mouth as she laughed, Rachel said, "Take a look now who doesn't think it's so funny."

Caitlin couldn't help but chuckle at this. What a way to turn the tables; she found the irony quite humorous. "At least I'm not hiding anything anymore," she responded as she gripped Kevin's hand tighter. "Unlike one of us who makes jokes on the girl he traveled with because he can't find the guts to just tell her the truth already."

"Now wait just a minute here…" exclaimed Arthur, interrupting. "I don't have anything for Rachel. Where in the world are you getting that notion?"

From beside the group, a voice said, "Because you're joking about it."

Everyone turned to see it was Rouge Kirkwood. Her sister Resa was right beside her, laughing. "And who the hell are you supposed to be?" asked Arthur.

Almost as immediately as Arthur said that, Rouge and Resa curtseyed, with Resa grabbing the ends of her skirt as she did so. "Forgive my intrusion, our lord. My name is Rouge Kirkwood, and this is my sister Resa. It is a great honor to make your acquaintance."

Arthur shrugged. "Honor? What honor?"

Gently, Kevin hit Arthur in the side. "They're sisters from Desolunar, Arthur. You're still the 'heir', remember? They practically worship the ground you stand on."

It took Arthur a second to process that word 'heir' through his brain again. It was still something he was getting used to, being called the 'heir of Desolunar' and being hailed by at least quite a few citizens of Desolunar, including Chief Aspectra and the Metoi tribe of the Wastes. The underground's Desolunar deserters, after finding out that Arthur was the heir and wanted to fight against his father, had all but tried to make Arthur their leader. Now was the time for Arthur to get serious, and he knew it. There were times for joking around, but this was not one. "I see," he finally said aloud. "It is a pleasure to meet some of our fellow friends. So, then, I would like you to meet Rachel Reinhart, and over here is…"

Resa raised her hand to interrupt. "That won't be necessary," she said. "We know the other two already." She giggled a little bit.

In response, Arthur's eyes rolled over to Kevin, in a manner of questioning. However, Caitlin was the one who took to answering. "They're assassin sisters, Arthur," she said. "They tried to kill us. And now, we'll be hanging out with them tonight."

"Oh, you've got to be kidding me!" exclaimed Rachel in surprise. "You mean you're now friends with them after they nearly killed you both?"

"Uhm, yeah, that was kind of an accident," responded Resa quickly.

Kevin gave an odd glance at Resa. "Accident my foot," he said. Then he looked back over at Arthur. "But there is an alternate explanation. Perhaps we'll explain it while we're having some fun tonight."

Arthur sighed. "Whatever you say," he said. "We met Caitlin

the same way, so I guess I'm beyond the point of asking questions."

"As am I," shrugged Rachel. "Tell you what. I'm going to go and get Wheldon so we can all hang out together. Why don't you guys get started without me?"

Nodding, Caitlin said, "Sure. He's in the spire here, so if you want to wait for him, that would be great." She thought for a moment. "Say, maybe, we meet in that clearing over there just past the trees?" She was pointing to an area just on the edge of Atwals, where enough fires were burning around by the troops to light the area up, but there were no troops sitting in the clearing.

"That'll do great," responded Rachel. "See you guys there," she said as she stepped closer to the spire and allowed her friends to walk away.

Together, Kevin and Caitlin walked with Arthur, Rouge, and Resa as they headed for the clearing. Behind Kevin, Arthur was listening to Rouge and Resa pepper him with questions, excited to meet the fabled heir of Desolunar. Kevin, however, had his eyes fixed to the sky. He was hearing strong telepathic words in his mind, and they were not coming from Caitlin.

I will take it all away from you. Come to my city, I dare you. I do not fear you and your pathetic minuscule power. Come to the city of my creation. It will be the city of your entrapment and destruction. You cannot defeat me, for I am nothing. And there, I will take everything that you value away from you. This fate is yours, Kevin Trent Stryker.

"Kevin," said Caitlin, as she tugged gently on his arm, "are you okay?"

It took Kevin a second to snap out of it. "I'm all right," he said. Then, he said to his friends as a group, "Anyone got a ball? We could play a game of dangerball in that field if we've got one."

"I bet we could find one pretty easily," responded Rouge, knowing they were walking around a large city. "Once we do, how do you want to decide teams?"

"Well, we can figure all of that out on the field," said Caitlin. "You guys will have to show me how to play, because I've never even seen a dangerball game before."

Resa chuckled. "We can do that, but let me warn you it's not an easy game to play in a long dress like the one you're wearing. You can't run that fast in one."

"Oh yeah?" responded Caitlin. She grabbed her ankle for a second, and then started running toward the field. "Race you there, Resa!" she called back.

As Resa started running to chase her, Rouge waited just a moment before deciding to follow her sister. Arthur hung back with Kevin for a moment. "Would you look at them go?" he laughed. "There must be something wrong with us, that these are the friends we made."

Kevin laughed. "I used to think that when you were my only real friend."

"Oh, come now," Arthur joked. "I was your best friend, remember?"

"You still are," chuckled Kevin. "What's all this 'was' stuff?"

"Please, Kevin, you've got a girlfriend now. What do you need me for?"

"For plenty," Kevin responded confidently. "Who else is supposed to keep me sane in all this chaos and remind me the world can be fun?"

Arthur stared at Kevin. "If *I'm* keeping *you* sane, then you have issues."

"Only the ones you caused," Kevin joked.

"Whatever," Arthur said. He then was quiet for a moment. "You know, Caitlin told me the other day about how you set off to do everything we're now doing because you wanted to rescue me after I was possessed and kidnapped, and it's led to all of this. I remember you explaining that to me before, but I guess it didn't really hit me until recently that you went to these lengths for me. And I've never said until now, but I guess I should tell you thank you."

Kevin shrugged it off. "Oh, it's nothing, Arthur. You and I are best friends; you would've done the same for me."

"The hell I would!" interjected Arthur. "Rachel and I only ran into you and Caitlin in the Northern Pass because we were running like cowards. Do you honestly think I would've tried to put three kingdoms together in an alliance to storm a city, all so you could rescue me?"

"Honestly, I wouldn't have been able to do it if we hadn't run into Caitlin," Kevin answered.

"But you still did it," Arthur said. He thought about it for a moment. "You know what, never mind. I was wrong; a sane person would've written me off as a loss and went home. Therefore, I'm clearly the more sane of the two of us."

"Whatever you say," chuckled Kevin. "If it makes you feel any better about my sanity, I don't lay around and daydream anymore."

Arthur rolled his eyes. "That's because your whole life is a daydream now," he said. "You always wanted to be an adventurer, and now you're living it for real. You're just lucky you have friends like me around to pick you up when you fall." He ran ahead toward the field.

Kevin thought about it for a minute. He was lucky to have Arthur, and to have all of his friends with him. He was living a dream, in a way, as long as he could avoid being killed. But for a moment longer, Kevin looked to the sky and to its ominous sight as the dark voice paralyzed him, made him listen with intent. It was his reminder that this was no dream.

In ten days' time, you will be in my city. And when you arrive, I will have a nice little surprise waiting for you. I await your arrival, for then the time will be right to tear you to shreds on all levels. You cannot defeat me, for I am nothing.

This fate is yours, Kevin Trent Stryker.

Chapter 56

The Confrontation

The time had come.

Ten days had passed since the meeting of the war council in Atwals. Months of preparation were finally coming together into effects. Allied forces were converging on the city of Seta Archa, the capital of Desolunar, and the site of one last desperate attempt to prevent the conquest of the realms from the eternal darkness of Demonicus. The final battle was just about to begin.

For Kevin Trent Stryker, it was also time. Time to put this all to rest, to protect Aurana and his homeland once and for all. He did not see himself as a 'chosen one'. All he had was a tool that only he could use, and that alone did not make him anything special. What made him special to others, at least in his eyes, was that he had the desire and drive to keep pushing on and to stand up to whatever tragedy struck him.

In some ways, Kevin thought he was living a dream by doing what he was doing. Before he had met Kron, he had dreamed of being an adventurer who traveled the lands to do some good. Already he had met so many new friends by traveling, and he was glad to have been given the opportunity. Among them, however, Caitlin had to be the most special person he had met, and ever since the first day he had met her, there was never a doubt in his mind of how special she was.

In more ways than there were positives, however, there were negatives. Kevin could only begin to count all of the things that happened to him: he accidentally killed an innocent man in Aurana City, he had nearly lost his life several times over, he had put Caitlin in danger, he had nearly lost Arthur and Rachel, and he was walking into a battle that was sure to be a maelstrom. It was a horrible set of conditions, and had it not been for Kevin's optimism and sense of responsibility carrying him through, he would not have made it this far.

Kevin was grateful to have so many good friends with him, and he gave them all the credit in the world for his success. It gave him a greater amount of encouragement to know that he would be sharing the battlefield with all of them on this day.

Under the darkened sky, no stars or moon gleamed any light whatsoever, although torches within the walls of Seta Archa lit the sky up in a faint red glow. There was something even more terrifying about the look of this sky than the one in Atwals ten nights before. Getting this far from Atwals had been a rough journey for everyone. No roads led into Seta Archa, few maps pinpointed exactly where the city was, and a highly dense portion of the southern forest, filled in by occasional patches of wasteland, surrounded the entire city. As Vincent Stryker had explained, there was barely any room to set up troops around the city, and all were tired from a long trip across uneven ground and rough terrain with limited supplies.

By now, however, the troops were all finally set. Aurana had its forces anchored in the west, Scurnia in the east, Nuve in the south, and the mixed unit in the north. Everything was organized according to plan. Standing a short distance from the wall, Kevin stood facing it, with Caitlin standing next to him. On his other side were his best friends Arthur Falchor and Rachel Reinhart. Behind him were Rouge and Resa Kirkwood, along with the phoenix lieutenant Wheldon, who decided to stick with Kevin's unit and did so with permission from the Red Phoenix. Professor Magnon, however, was with other units as he was serving as a coordinator between the different armies. Why he would not be with them, Kevin did not know, but he was disappointed.

He wondered if the professor knew that he suspected something.

All of the work they had done to this point, and all that they had accomplished, was all in preparation for this. All they needed to do was breach the wall, make their way into the city, and capture Demonicus. It seemed so simple when put into words, but as Kevin and everyone else knew, it would be anything but simple.

Also staring at the walls, Vanguard of Nuve Raijin Shane and Vanguard of Scurnia Gilbert Griffith approached Kevin. Having volunteered to join the mixed unit, they were seeing much the same thing that he was. Noticing their presence, Kevin asked, without turning his head, "Think they know that we're here and we're about to try and get into there?"

Raijin Shane nodded. "They most certainly do know, and they are prepared for it. They have known since their defeat at Haventown, I am sure. Otherwise, we would have seen resistance of some kind when we walked into Atwals."

"For certain, they've retreated into their shell," added Gilbert Griffith. "They're waiting for us in there, stalking us as does a chimera who lives in a cave or a burrow. If it has faced a stiff defense, it will retreat into its shelter and make the one it has attacked curious. And once its prey approaches, it leaps out from its retreat and strikes hard, often killing its prey in one shot."

Kevin rolled his eyes. "That's very encouraging," he said with some sarcasm. "We'll have to be very careful, then. They're ready for us, both on top of that wall and behind it."

"Precisely," nodded Shane. "These are not ideal conditions, but given the circumstances, they are the only ones we have. As soon as we get the signal, thou and I and all of us will begin our attack."

"Right," acknowledged Kevin. "The signal should be coming soon. In the mean time, we should get the siege ramps into position."

Gilbert Griffith looked at Kevin confused. "Is that an order?" he asked. "You need to be more commanding and less suggestive."

"Oh, is that so?" Kevin asked with a tone of being slightly irate with Gilbert Griffith about his last criticizing comment. He knew he was not a military leader, but if they were trying to get him to act like one, they could have it. "Very well then, if that's the way you want to play it, then we will." Then, Kevin turned around and pointed at Raijin Shane and Gilbert Griffith. "You two, go and have the men ready the siege ramps and get them into position for the advance."

Almost immediately in response, Raijin Shane and Gilbert Griffith came to a salute and said, "Yes, sir!" Then, they each turned in opposite directions and proceeded to the men behind them.

Then, Vincent Stryker approached Kevin, along with War Commander Eukert. "The men are all prepared for battle," the old war hero said. "Eukert and I have seen to that personally."

"They will be ready on your command," added Eukert.

Kevin nodded. "Good," he said. "Then all there is left is to wait for the signal."

There was a fairly long pause. Then, briefly, Arthur sighed. "How much longer is it going to be?"

"Patience, now," responded Eukert. "Wars are not won in a day, you know."

A gust of wind blew across the wall, brushing across all of the trees. "No, they are not," said Kevin. "But that does remind me, War Commander Eukert, there is something that I want to say to you before we begin."

Eukert became curious. "What is it, Vanguard?" he asked.

Pausing for just a second, Kevin took a breath, looked to the top of the wall of Seta Archa, and said, "Eukert, of all of the men and women that I have met, of all of those who fought alongside me, of everyone that has helped me in some way, shape, or form, you are the unsung hero of all of them."

An eyebrow of Eukert's lifted. "How do you figure that?" asked the war commander.

"As I understand it, after my father left Seta Archa the first time, he left this sword in your care." Kevin then proceeded to draw his Sword of Purity as he continued to speak, "Therefore, you must have carried it for twenty years, and held it until you found someone who could use it. And even if you didn't know it at the time, that's exactly what you were doing. But since then, you've done more too. You've defended Aurana and fought alongside me at Rikleifer. You've come back from what should have been a mortal injury and walked right back into the role you were in before. And for that, I appreciate what you've done."

Eukert was a little stunned and found it difficult to respond. "Well, thanks… erm…" He turned to Vincent Stryker. "Vince, buddy, help me out here?"

"Oh, just take the damn compliment," interrupted Paladin of Archery John Bryant before Vincent could respond. Bryant had been standing just behind the others. "It's just like old times, Mr. 'Ironman'. Someone respects you, and you can't own up to it."

"Yes, all right," responded Eukert. "You are probably right, and

Kevin, I do appreciate your kindness in your comments."

Kevin nodded in acknowledgment.

Eukert took a step back and said something to Bryant. "But now that you mention old times, John, doesn't this look familiar? Battle at Seta Archa, the two of us standing alongside our friend Vincent Stryker, and waiting for our chance. It is just like old times."

"Sure is," said Vincent Stryker, placing his hands on the shoulders of his two old friends. "Twenty years later, even if my back isn't what it used to be, we're going together once again for one last battle."

"You really think it'll be the last?" asked John Bryant. "Are we really that old?"

Vincent shook his head. "It's not that," he chuckled, "but if we presume that war is the pathway to peace, which it is, then I'm hopeful, at least, that this battle will be the last one before there is peace for a while."

Still staring at the wall, Kevin picked up the response. "You and everyone else hope so," he said. "I can only imagine what it would be like if we somehow managed to end the tyranny of Demonicus. And then, what lies beyond…" Kevin stopped.

Seeing that Kevin had stopped, Caitlin grabbed Kevin by the arm as Arthur and Rachel put their hands on his shoulders. "Whatever it is, we'll take it on together," said Caitlin. As she said this, Rouge, Resa, and Wheldon each extended a hand – or in Wheldon's case, a wingtip – to Kevin and touched his shoulder, as a sign of confidence.

Kevin nodded. "I know we will," he said. "And wherever we go as long as we're in battle, I'd like all of you to stick by me so we can protect each other, okay?" His voice sounded a little shaky, as his worry for the safety of his friends, like it had been in Rikleifer, was weighing very heavy on his mind as it had done so before.

No one had any complaints. "You are smart to be so wary," said Rouge after a short pause. "And for that, we all have our trust in you."

"Friendships that are made in a day can last a lifetime," added Resa, "and we'll be by your side all the way as long as you'll have us."

"You truly are a phoenix on the inside, and I am very proud to call you my friend, Kevin," said Wheldon. "And a phoenix never backs down when a friend is in need, like you are right now."

Then, Rachel took a breath, before saying with all of the idealistic sweetness in her realistic heart, "Kevin, in the months since we started traveling together, I'm proud to say that we've gone from just friends to being the best of friends. I promise you, that as long as there's something that you need to do, I'll stand by you no matter how ridiculous it sounds to start."

Arthur turned his head and nodded. "Best friends live forever," he said, "and if you can take my jokes, you're resilient enough to walk your way through that wall. We'll cut the path through it together, if we need to."

Caitlin gripped Kevin's hand even tighter, as she looked directly into the eyes of Kevin's turned head. "We share as strong of a bond as there can be. I will never leave your side, and if we ever get separated again, the bond between our hearts will always lead me back to you."

There was a long pause, as Kevin took a breath. "Thanks, guys," he said. "It means a lot to me that you're all right here for me."

A thunder crash lit up the sky in light and sound at that instant. There was no rain falling, but the sky was dark, lit up by lightning and thunder that seemed almost apocalyptic. It was almost like an omen, a force trying to tell Kevin that whatever he was talking about was futile. No, shrugged Kevin, he was not going to let any omen stand in his way this time.

Then, another sight came across the sky. It was the Red Phoenix, his all-red feathers standing out against the background. He started flying above the city, eventually making a circle around the center of the city. It was visible from all around the city over the walls.

"The signal!" exclaimed Kevin. He then started using his commanding voice, and called out to the troops behind him, "Advance to the walls! Bring forward the siege ramps!"

As soon as Kevin made the command, the men began pushing the siege ramps forward from the forest. Troops started to march out from the dense forest into the clearing where Seta Archa sat, advancing in the direction of the wall.

"Showtime, guys," said Arthur as the troops started to march past them. "Let's go and show Demonicus what crimes against nations at peace will earn you."

The second that the troops came out from behind the tree lines heading toward the wall, a rain of arrows came down from the top of the wall. Just as strategist Vincent Stryker had expected, the Desolunar troops were waiting for the advancing troops to clear the trees before making the first strike.

Even with planning, the northern unit was caught by surprise, yet it continued to press on forward. Some men tried to stop and use their weapons to defend themselves, while others chose instead to press to the wall. Casualties instantly started to rack up from the arrow volley coming from the wall.

In response, the men still behind the tree line stood in wait. Vincent looked to Kevin, wanting him to give the direction. Now was not the time for hesitation. It was the time to be a leader and make confident commands. And Kevin was ready, having studied the strategy extensively on the trip to Seta Archa.

"Archers to the ready!" he commanded, which made a line of archers form up around the tree line. "Take aim for the archers on top of the wall!"

As the men continued to rush out of the forest, the line of archers formed up and took aim carefully. Bowstrings were drawn all across the tree line, waiting for the command. "Fire!" commanded Kevin.

A return volley traveled over the ledge of the wall, taking down several archers at the top of the wall. However, it was much less effective than the volley from the wall due to the difference in height. "Continue to fire at will!" commanded Kevin. "Keep their archers off balance!"

Responding to the command, the archers of all nations that were part of the northern unit began to draw arrows as quickly as each man could, took aim, and fired. Having the archers fire at will created a sort of continuous fire, although not as powerful as one large volley. As the continuous fire began to erupt, the men of the northern unit started pushing the siege ramps forward to the wall. Five ramps, spaced out by a moderate amount of distance, were rolled out toward the large walls. The large wooden structures took most arrow hits without penetrating, as they were made to be very sturdy siege weapons. Arbitrarily, before the battle the ramps allocated to the northern unit were numbered from one to five, one being the most eastern ramp and five being the most western. Since his forces were attacking from the north and were facing south, this meant that the ramps were numbered from left to right from their perspective.

The ineffectiveness of arrows against these siege ramps caused the Desolunar forces on the wall to shift to attacking the men pushing the ramps forward. Still, because of the size of the massive siege ramps providing moderate shelter from the arrows, this attack also proved to be ineffective, as the siege ramps closed in tightly on the wall.

A loud thump from ramp number five signaled that it was against the wall and ready to be used on the far western side of the north wall. Quickly, Kevin took a look around from the safety of the tree line and saw the fifth ramp latch into place and men of the northern unit starting to ascend the ramp. Over on the other side, ramp number one at the far east was almost up to the wall, while four was the next closest to the wall. Ramps number two and three were a little further back.

Then, for a second, something moving through the air caught Kevin's eye. The sky battle had begun above him, with large dragons and phoenixes engaging Desolunar troops on gryphons. The power and strength of the allied forces seemed to be locked in a struggle with the large numbers of gryphon flight troops that were flying about with Desolunar soldiers aboard them.

An explosion then was heard from the far left side, quickly grabbing Kevin and company's attention. They turned to see ramp number one now on fire, burning as the troops that were pushing it were now trying to run from it.

"What the hell caused that?" exclaimed Kevin in surprise.

No one had any response for a second. Then, Resa tapped Kevin's shoulder and grabbed his attention. She then pointed up to the top of the wall on the far east side, and said, "That's a sorcerer."

Kevin looked and saw who it was. "That's an Enlightener. Then we'd better take care of him quickly." He then turned to Rachel, and said, "Rachel, if I can get you close enough on that wall, can you take him out with your antite arrow?"

"Probably only if we're on the top of the wall," shrugged Rachel. "I don't think I'd get a shot with half a chance otherwise. But why does it have to be me?"

"Because you are the only one I know that has the weapon that can disable him, with that one arrow," said Kevin. "Can you do it?"

Nervously, Rachel nodded. Never before had she felt so pressured to make a power move before, or to be the one whose success everyone was riding on. "I can do it," she said shaking. Secretly, she was also afraid to rush into the gauntlet of battle again, especially after what had almost happened at Rikleifer and the fear of battle that had been instilled in her since then.

Seeing Rachel's nerves, Caitlin reached her arm around Rachel as to be comforting. "Hey, don't worry about it," she said. "We can do this together, and we'll cut your way open to it. Are you ready?"

Rachel nodded again, still nervous about the situation. Clearly she was afraid to go on, but it did appear to help her that she had the support of her friends with her.

Kevin took a brief glance at the sky battle, judging its progress for just a second. "We'd better move quickly if we're going to do this." Then, Kevin reached over and put his hand on Rachel's shoulder. "Rachel, are you sure you're up for this? I'm not going to make you do this if you're too afraid to go."

There was a second's pause as Rachel took a breath. Then, she reached out to Kevin and Caitlin, and grabbed each of their hands tightly. "No, I have to do this," she said. "I want to do this, for you guys. For all of you." She then let go as she stood up straighter, trying to be more confident.

"Then we're going," nodded Arthur, as he drew his Sword of Corruption. He then extended his right hand to Rachel, and latched it to her left hand. As Arthur was left-handed himself, it meant his sword arm was still free to use his sword. "Whatever you do, Rachel," he then continued, staring directly into Rachel's eyes, "don't let go of my hand until you've got a shot. I can promise you we'll keep you safe all the way there. Have I let you down yet?"

An awkward chuckle came to Rachel's lips. "Every day," she

joked, grabbing her bow and clutching it tightly with her free hand.

Together, everyone seemed ready to go, prepared to assault the top of that wall despite their odds of success. But, as Kevin noticed, one of them appeared to be deep in thought. It was Wheldon the phoenix. Deciding that it would not be smart to ignore this, Kevin tapped Wheldon and asked, "What's up?"

Wheldon shrugged. "Nothing," he said. "Just an idea that might make it easier to get that sorcerer."

"Then tell me what it is," responded Kevin, curious and wanting to hear ideas.

Wheldon took a brief look up at the sky battle. Then he turned back to Kevin and said, "There is no way I am going to be able to hover and give Rachel a straight shot with that battle going on above. But I can clear the path along the wall with your help so we can get Rachel within range of that shot."

Kevin nodded. "Then let's do it," he said. He turned toward the rest of his friends. "Wheldon and I will cut the path forward. When ramp number four latches to the wall, I want you guys to be the first ones on it. Get just close enough so Rachel gets a clean shot."

Caitlin nodded in confidence.

Answering for the rest of the group, Rouge nodded and said, "Right. But where are you going, then?"

As Rouge asked this question, Wheldon was crouching to the ground, to a level where Kevin could climb on his back. Kevin did so, and then drew his Sword of Purity. "To clear your path," he finally responded. "Rachel, whenever you're comfortable with the shot, take it. Don't get any closer than you have to, but don't stand too far back as to not be able to make the shot at all."

Rachel nodded, and it appeared that everyone else was acknowledging the command as well. Noticing that ramp number four was very close to the wall, Kevin glanced to it, and gave a brief head movement to signal to his friends where the ramp was. Then, he double-tapped Wheldon on the side of the neck, signaling for him to take off.

Chapter 57

Fallen

While Kevin and Wheldon took off, the others made a break for the ramp, seeing it fall into place. Kevin and Wheldon ascended higher, which gave them a view of what was on top of the wall and what was behind it.

It was quite an astounding sight.

Thousands and thousands of homes and small business buildings stood clustered behind the walls of Seta Archa, all in close proximity with one another. That much made sense to Kevin, considering there were so many people packed into Seta Archa. Although the city was large, all of its homes were inside the city walls. Given that Seta Archa was one of the largest cities in the world, surpassing even the massive Aurana City and containing most of the non-tribal population of Desolunar, civilians were packed into the city in very small spaces despite the large amount of area within the walls. Houses were packed tightly in all directions, with little to no yard space in between.

For a brief second, this made Kevin consider biting his fingernails. He did not want to cause any civilian casualties, and the tight fit of civilians in Seta Archa would make that very difficult. There was no honor in killing the innocent, no greatness in killing those who wanted only to live in peace. War would be a complete disgrace if even one innocent were harmed.

Kevin managed to get a good look at the troops atop the wall. Archer units lined the outside, but then there were more basic troops behind them, almost as if lying in wait for advancing troops. Many more Desolunar troops, all dressed in black, appeared to be stationed all across the city. With so many lines of defense, Kevin started to become gravely concerned; was this assault completely futile? Could such a defense ever be penetrated?

It had to be, Kevin tried to make himself believe. Nothing was impenetrable. But it seemed so hard to believe with such a sight.

Then, Kevin had an idea. A brilliant idea. If the Desolunar forces would use magic against him, then he would use divine power against them. As long as he was careful not to hit any houses, a plan came into his mind.

"Hold here!" commanded Kevin to Wheldon, hovering just above the wall edge a moderate distance away from the wall. Wheldon was unable to maintain a very level, still height, however, making him bobble around while hovering. Now, Kevin could see another reason why Wheldon had not wanted to carry Rachel. It was not only the shots from above or from the archers on the wall. Wheldon could not maintain still enough in a hovering position for Rachel to get an accurate shot from a bow.

Carefully, Kevin flipped up his sword and pointed it toward the wall. His thoughts were clear, and he focused hard on precisely the target in front of him: the troops on the wall. Despite the power he was wielding, he was still not going to try it on the sorcerer for fear of having it deflected back at him or something else that he did not have the knowledge to avoid. Then, he cleared his mind.

His sword lit up in blue. The power of the Sword of Purity was visible.

"Take us in!" Kevin then commanded.

With confidence, Wheldon descended and gained speed, taking Kevin along the length of the wall. Kevin extended his sword in front of Wheldon's right wing, impacting enemy soldiers or scaring them backwards as he sliced along the wall with his divine blade. The speedy swipe cleared out space in front of the fourth ramp. Standing on its edge, Caitlin, Arthur, Rachel, Rouge, and Resa all had to shield their eyes as the bright flash from the sword sliced through the air.

Not wanting to waste this opening while it was there, Caitlin led the way racing down the length of the wall, shooting blasts of air magic at anyone who tried to get in the way. Following behind were Arthur and Rachel, with Arthur still tightly clutching Rachel's hand to guide her there. Rouge and Resa were bringing up the rear, making sure that no one came up from behind to surprise them.

Kevin and Wheldon continued to watch on from the air as the group below pressed down the wall. About halfway between ramp number four and where the sorcerer was, Caitlin stopped short, consequently bringing Arthur, Rachel, Rouge, and Resa to a stop as well. Further down the wall, Desolunar soldiers were running about in chaos to figure out how to fill in the opening carved in the defense on top of the wall, inadvertently leaving the Enlightener as the only one focused on his job. He had just torched the second of the five siege ramps, and was completely exposed despite the troops behind him.

Perfectly vulnerable.

As everyone stopped short, Caitlin flipped around to let Rachel up to the front. It was at that point that Arthur let go of Rachel's hand to allow her to use her bow. Quickly, Rachel drew the antite arrow from her quiver, nocked it, and pulled up her bow in the direction of the sorcerer. It took just a second for her to get her aim on target. Then, she pulled back hard on the bowstring and let the arrow fly.

Rachel's accuracy was truer than ever. The sorcerer was hit dead on, and he appeared to be calling out in pain. It was a perfect strike.

Success. From above, Kevin let out a sigh of relief. The plan had worked after all, and that sorcerer had been disarmed. All was not going well, however. It did not take long for the troops to realize the opening in the wall defense was still not filled, and the Desolunar soldiers soon began advancing from both ends to fill in the gap.

Everyone down below had no choice to retreat down the third ramp, which had since latched into place. While they ran down, troops of the northern unit were advancing up ramps three, four, and five. They would try to seize the gap and make some headway on the north wall, as was planned.

Kevin was relieved as well to see his friends escape safely from the wall. However, before he and Wheldon could settle to the ground themselves, Wheldon took off, taking Kevin by surprise. Kevin had just a second to grab a tight hold of Wheldon as he said, "What the hell's going on? Are you trying to knock me off?"

"No," responded Wheldon frantically, still flying quickly and taking sharp corners that caused Kevin to have to hold on tighter. "Look behind you."

Carefully, Kevin turned his head amidst Wheldon's jackknifing and twisting to see a gryphon with a Desolunar soldier aboard in pursuit of him. Wheldon had been picked up after all.

In battle, gryphons had the potential to be more deadly than phoenixes. Phoenixes had their sharp talons and their greater burst speed in the air, but gryphons each had four claws as part of the chimera-like body structure they had. They also held greater stamina than the phoenix, allowing them to continue to fly fast for longer amounts of time. Though they were smaller than the phoenixes, they were ferocious with their claws and their four legs allowed them to tear apart opponents in midair. Consequently as well, against the dragons that the Knights of the Dragon were using in the battle, gryphons held a speed advantage despite their lack of power in comparison.

Great, Kevin thought to himself. That was the last thing he needed. Confident in what had to be done, however, he tapped Wheldon on the neck and commanded, "Full right, one quarter turn! Head straight into the sky battle."

Regardless of his own doubts, Wheldon did as he was told and turned at a right angle into the sky battle. "Why are we doing this?" he then asked after completing the turn.

"We've got to escape this pursuit," responded Kevin. "Sometimes, going into danger is the way out of it. And what's the best way to keep him off our backs while we try to escape?"

Reluctantly, Wheldon did as he was asked. "I trust you, my friend." He suddenly made another set of quick turns as he entered the sky battle zone, making Kevin have to grip Wheldon tighter to keep from falling off.

The turns into the battle were working. Kevin could see that the gryphon following him was having trouble keeping up, just as Kevin had intended to happen. "I see how this works," responded Wheldon, realizing that the gryphon behind him was being shaken off. "There is enough chaos in the battle zone that it is difficult for anyone to follow."

"Bingo," responded Kevin. Then, he noticed another set of gryphons, this one flying in a formation of three, coming onto

Wheldon's tail. "Better keep moving," he then told Wheldon, "because we're dead if you don't."

Acting in quick response, Wheldon started making some quicker moves, this time including ascents and descents. He had to be careful how sharp of an angle he took, however, so Kevin would not be knocked off. Still, the fleet of three gryphon troops stayed tight on Wheldon's tail, not losing any ground.

When Wheldon made his next turn to try and evade, a couple more gryphons were in place waiting for him in the midst of the chaos. For a second, Kevin was in panic. Wheldon was not going to back down, however, and he continued to charge fearlessly, taking up a more streamlined position to gain extra momentum.

Before Wheldon could reach the gryphons he was approaching, a dragon struck down on the gryphons, knocking them out of the sky. Immediately, Kevin breathed a sigh of relief, glad to know he was safe for the moment. Still, Kevin knew staying out here in the sky battle zone would be certain suicide.

Kevin looked over to the dragon that flew by, and saw that the rider was wearing an iron and silver breastplate. It was Christoph Dewellus, the Lord Dragon, aboard his partner dragon, Patch. As soon as Kevin recognized him, though, the Lord Dragon started cutting the other direction, back toward Kevin and Wheldon. "Are you all right?" called up the Lord Dragon to Kevin. "It's not safe here. You need to get back to your men."

"I know!" called back Kevin, hoping he was loud enough for the Lord Dragon to hear amidst the chaos. "We're going to need some help cutting through the ground forces. Can your dragons help us to cut a pathway?"

There was no response as the Lord Dragon flew by. Kevin could only hope that he was heard, but he had no time to wait. The Lord Dragon was right. Kevin and Wheldon were going to be killed if they didn't escape the sky battle zone. Knowing this, Kevin tapped Wheldon's neck again and said, "Turn north! Head back to the north wall, but take as many twists and turns as you have to!"

As quickly as he could, Wheldon acknowledged and made a sharp turn to the north, seeking to get out of the chaos zone as quickly as possible. Behind him, the three Desolunar flight soldiers regrouped and resumed their pursuit. Seeing this, Kevin came to the sudden realization that he was a marked man out here. These soldiers had likely been instructed to target specifically him. He could not escape them.

"Bolt forward!" commanded Kevin to Wheldon. "Use as much speed as you have! We have to shake them!"

Immediately, Wheldon pushed as hard as he could, streamlining himself as much as he could in order to gain momentum. He was flying so fast that Kevin was struggling to keep a hold onto the fleeing phoenix. Within a couple of seconds they had crossed the north city wall below them and had safely exited the sky battle zone, but the gryphon formation stayed anchored on Wheldon's tail.

They were gaining ground on the tired phoenix quickly. Wheldon's repeated bursts and turns were starting to wear him out. Then, one of the gryphons clawed at Wheldon's tail. Wheldon started grimacing in pain immediately, as the gryphon's claws were sharp and had torn through Wheldon's tail feathers into his skin. It forced Wheldon to slow down significantly in order to maintain his balance in the air.

Just enough for the gryphon formation to catch up. Wheldon was pinned now, and there was nowhere for him to retreat to.

From the right side, a gryphon weaved out of formation, and then back in with the intent of smashing into Wheldon's side. As he approached Wheldon, however, Kevin took his sword and started fighting off the gryphon's claws. If there was anything he could do to protect Wheldon in midair, he would.

Suddenly, all three then converged from three different sides. Kevin could not fight them all off.

Smash!

A hard hit slammed Wheldon in the head, as a gryphon's front claws slashed into his neck. Immediately, Wheldon started falling to the ground. Kevin was thrown off, ejected by the gryphon's sudden strike.

There was nowhere to run. There was nowhere to hide. There was nowhere to fly to. There was only the ground below. Kevin was falling fast, and he knew the ground was not too far below him.

Was this really how it was all to end? After he had come so far? After all that his friends had done for him, and he had done for them? After what he had made himself to be, was he to fall short before he did what he set out to accomplish?

No. Somehow, he had to keep fighting. For Rouge and Resa, his newest friends. For Wheldon, whatever was becoming of him. For Rachel, his endeared friend. For Arthur, his best friend. For Caitlin, his guardian angel…

Kevin closed his eyes and swore he would continue fighting. Then, he let the darkness take over and awaited his next move.

The ground was coming up fast, and there was nothing Kevin could do to stop it.

He blacked out as he fell.

Then, there was the oddest sensation he had ever felt.

He was slowing down, decelerating. There was no landing, no hard impact to be felt. Even stranger, he then began to feel his direction reverse, as though he was ascending again, although slower than he had been falling.

Was this how it felt to die? Kevin had to ask himself this as he kept his eyes closed. And for a second, he almost thought he heard Caitlin's voice calling to him. It called, "Kevin! Kevin, are you all right? Please wake up, please tell me that you're all right!"

Suddenly, Kevin realized something. He was not dreaming. And he was not dead either. As he opened his eyes, he knew exactly where he was, even if he could not believe it.

Caitlin, in her angelic state, had somehow managed to catch Kevin and keep him from hitting the ground. She was now carrying Kevin back toward the north wall, with her translucent glowing wings lighting the way.

Kevin was still in a great amount of pain from being knocked off of Wheldon. He was still wincing as he opened his eyes, but he was so glad to see Caitlin carrying him from what would have been the site of his death. Struggling to speak a little bit from the pain, he managed to say, "Caitlin, thank you so much. You've saved my life again."

A tear came to Caitlin's eye in happiness as she floated down to the ground and stood Kevin back up. Then, she gave him as big of a hug as she could. "I was so scared I'd lost you," she said.

Kevin breathed a sigh of relief. "I can't tell you how much I'm grateful to you for saving my life again."

Caitlin giggled a little bit. "Don't think anything of it," she said, still laughing. "Like I said, who's counting?"

This made Kevin chuckle a little bit. "Well, I suppose you have a point there," he said. Then, he slowed down, and asked, "Wait a minute, where's Wheldon?"

A worried look came to Caitlin's face. "Somewhere over there," she said, pointing away from the city and deeper into the forest. "I couldn't save you both, and I was hoping he would recover after you were knocked off and manage to keep himself off the ground. But that didn't happen, Kevin. I think he hit the ground hard."

Instantly, a look of shock came over Kevin's face. He grabbed Caitlin by the hand and started sprinting off in the direction she had been pointing. For a brief second, Caitlin was caught in surprise by this, but then she started trying to stay alongside Kevin when she realized how much Kevin's friendship with Wheldon meant to him. Wheldon was a trusted friend. Kevin could not afford to lose him, just as he could not afford to lose any of his friends.

As she started trying to run alongside Kevin, he asked her, "Do you think you can heal him if he's badly wounded?"

Caitlin shook her head. "I won't know until I see him," she said. "Healing magic depends on so many factors as to if it will work or not, and I can't tell you for sure what will happen."

It made Kevin worry about Wheldon. What kind of injury had the phoenix suffered? Kevin knew Wheldon was hurt badly, especially if he had hit the ground. And Kevin felt very guilty for his friend, knowing that he was the one who had issued the commands to put Wheldon in such danger.

Kevin and Caitlin made a sudden stop once they hit a clearing. In the clearing, Wheldon was flat on the ground as the three gryphons circled him on the ground. All were walking around, their heads angled toward the injured phoenix. They were getting ready to make a finishing blow.

Immediately, Kevin picked up his sword almost over his head, preparing to charge in there. But before he could, Caitlin extended her arm in front of him, telling him not to. She then held up one finger to tell him to be patient for a moment. As hard as it was for Kevin to be patient at a moment like this, he held back as hard as he could, fairly certain that Caitlin had a plan.

After a brief pause, Caitlin was ready. Still with one arm in front of Kevin, she extended her other out toward the gryphons and fired a powerful shot of ice at the one in front of her.

The gryphon hit by the ice shot was frozen in place, and so was the soldier riding on top. Both were frozen solid by the sheer cold of the ice shot. The consequence of this, however, was that both of the other gryphons quickly caught attention of this. Immediately, they turned toward Kevin and Caitlin. Then, despite commands from their Desolunar handlers not to attack, they did so anyway, in a full body-up position.

One of them Kevin repelled using his Sword of Purity, executing a perfectly timed stab straight into the gryphon's heart. Precise and accurate, Kevin had picked on his opponent's weakness and made an excellent strike. The other one, Caitlin unleashed a blast of darkness straight into its chest, blowing it back hard into the forest. Frightened by this, the gryphon handlers started running off into the forest.

Almost as immediately as the gryphons were thwarted, Kevin rushed up to Wheldon, seeing that the phoenix was in trouble. When Kevin saw what had happened, however, he found his worst fears were not even close to what he was actually seeing.

Wheldon had been cut up all across his body, from tail to head. He appeared to be in great pain all over, and Kevin was afraid that he had several broken bones from the hard impact to the ground. The phoenix was barely moving on the ground, wings spread but only wiggling a little bit.

Kevin rushed up to Wheldon's head, put his hand on top of it, knelt down, and said, "Are you all right, Wheldon?"

Grimacing in pain, Wheldon was only barely able to turn his head. "Under… the… feathers…" he struggled to say. "At the neck…

under the feathers…"

Nodding in acknowledgment, Kevin moved over to Wheldon's neck and brushed along his red feathers at his neck. As Kevin did, he felt his fingers become wet. Kevin pulled back his hand to look at it, and saw red liquid across his fingertips.

It was blood.

Seeing this, Kevin signaled over to Caitlin for her to come over. Then, he reached his hand back down to Wheldon's neck and brushed Wheldon's blood-soaked red feathers aside. Underneath those feathers was a deep, deep gash. A great amount of blood was coming from that open wound.

Caitlin arrived at this point, and also hit the ground to take a close look at the wound. Carefully, she examined it, albeit with a horrified look from all the blood that had soaked into Wheldon's thick red feathers. She shook her head with the saddest face Kevin had ever seen. "This is too much blood, Kevin," she said, whispering. "The gash inflicted by the gryphons must have slashed through the veins in his neck. He's lost so much blood that…" Caitlin paused, starting to choke on her words as her voice saddened, "…that even if I try to heal him, he won't survive."

Kevin nearly choked. Tears instantly started flooding his eyes, although he tried to hide them as he stroked Wheldon's neck and said, "It's going to be okay. Everything's going to be all right." He was trying to hide the fatal injury to Wheldon.

But Wheldon already knew of it. Somehow he knew that his wound would be fatal. "It will be," he said, with a very shallow voice, "because I've managed to protect you and save you."

Almost immediately, Kevin's eyes widened.

"Come around so I can see both of you," asked Wheldon, his voice fading.

Reacting quickly, Kevin and Caitlin did as they were asked. They did not want to miss anything that Wheldon was going to say.

Wheldon took a hard-pressed breath, struggling to breathe. "The two of you, I think, are the best friends I have ever had. I could not be more blessed than I am now to have the opportunity to know both of you. Without you two, humans and phoenixes would never have reconnected with one another, and I… I… I would continue to lead a selfish life of serving the Red Phoenix and otherwise only thinking of myself. Meeting you showed me there was so much more, and to see your friends made me envious of you, until I became one of you. And for that, I am forever indebted to you."

Still tearing, Kevin shook his head. "No," he said. "May your debts be forgiven if you feel you have them."

Trying to move, Wheldon managed an awkward nod. Then, he turned his head to Caitlin. "Catie, you are an angel in more than just a physical way. It's hard not to see your kindness and innocence, and at the same time your determination and passion, and not be inspired by it. My only wish was that someday I could see the two of you marry when you were ready, but it appears this was not how things were meant to be."

Crying heavily, Caitlin responded while she hugged Wheldon around the neck.

Then, Wheldon turned his head between Kevin and Caitlin to talk to both of them. "But even that is fine, not to be able to see the two of you grow up together. Today, I get to pass on with honor, knowing that I gave it my all for a cause I believed in. You both taught me there are more important things, sometimes, than the life of one. I am proud to have fallen if it means we can succeed."

Wheldon had given it all to protect Kevin. He had surrendered his own existence just so Kevin, and the cause, could live on. This, in particular, struck Kevin hard. Once again, it caused Kevin's mind to ring with a very specific set of words. These were words that Kronius had told him one day, and words that continued to press on his mind:

If you truly believe in something, then you will give up everything you have for it. All of your worldly possessions: your wealth, your memories, your friendships, and even your love, must be forsaken for your cause. You must even be willing to give up your existence for what you fight for. Do not fear it, for if the cause is good, others will follow your example and fight for your cause. So be willing to forsake everything and follow your heart to a better future.

Already, Wheldon had done that for Kevin. Now, Kevin felt even more obligated to finish what he had started: to overthrow

Demonicus and his father, to rescue the world from eternal darkness, and to honor the memories of everyone who had fallen in his defense. Still in tears over the fatal injury to Wheldon, Kevin clinched his fist tight, determined and carrying a more fiery passion than he had before.

"And now it is time for me to leave," continued Wheldon, his voice becoming more faint. "Time to move on to other things, I am sure. I am scared, but… strangely at peace. The Great One will know what to do with me." Then, Wheldon's eyes closed as he relaxed.

"But Wheldon, how will you find your way?" asked Kevin tearfully.

There was no response. For a minute, Kevin and Caitlin held onto each other, waiting. But still, no response came.

Together, Kevin and Caitlin each broke down, clinging onto each other for support. Wheldon's death was very hard to bear. It was the loss of one of their best friends and their closest ally, a true friend until the end. Whether or not Wheldon had felt that he had died for a good cause, his loss would still cause sadness to all who knew him. How would they break the news? To their friends Arthur, Rachel, Rouge, and Resa? To Vincent Stryker and to Professor Magnon? To the Red Phoenix and Grand Raven, long Wheldon's noble leaders? It was only a minor thought in the great surge of sadness from Wheldon's death. The phoenix had been another victim to this great maelstrom of a battlefield, another life taken far too early.

Then, there was the oddest sensation: one of heat coming from where Wheldon's body was. It took Kevin and Caitlin each a moment to realize that what they were feeling was not actually a symptom of their loss, but an actual source of heat. They turned and saw, in surprise, that Wheldon's body was burning. It was encased in flames.

The bright flames lasted only for a moment before they subsided, and then faded out as a large pile of ashes were left behind where Wheldon's body had once been. But as surprising as the flames had been, what was left in the ashes was even more surprising than the spontaneous combustion.

Sitting in the middle of the ashes, coated very lightly in soot, was a large egg with an orange shell. It stood out prominently in the ash pile, even as dark as the sky was and how little light was around.

Almost simultaneously, Kevin and Caitlin each put a hand over their mouths. "Is that… is that what I think it is?" gasped Kevin.

"I think it is," responded Caitlin, also in surprise. "Phoenixes used to reincarnate, they say, and would rise from their ashes. But Wheldon told us they haven't in years now…"

Suddenly, Kevin grabbed Caitlin by the hand and started running straight for the egg. "But it happened again!" exclaimed Kevin. As he reached the egg, he crouched and put his arms around it, gently lifting it off the ground. "Take a look, Caitlin!"

Having to use all the effort she had to slow down, Caitlin stopped and then gently put her own arms around the egg as well. Like Kevin, tears were still falling from her eyes, but in a more grateful feeling. "There's hope for him," she said. Then, she looked straight into Kevin's eyes, her angel wings glowing even slightly brighter than before. "Do you think we could take care of him together?"

Kevin had to bring up one of his hands to wipe the tears out of his eyes. He was not crying anymore, but his eyes were still wet and puffy. "Maybe if the phoenixes will let us," he said, overjoyed. "They probably won't, and we really don't know how to take care of him anyway, but for now we had better make sure he stays safe."

"Right," nodded Caitlin, wiping away a tear.

Before either of them could say another word, however, there was calling from the south. A few seconds later, it was clear who was calling. Just a little bit later than that, the figures of Arthur, Rachel, Rouge, and Resa appeared. All of them looked beat from running through the forest.

"There they are," gasped Arthur, out of breath. He and the three young women all stopped together at the edge of the clearing where Kevin and Caitlin were. Together, the four of them had to stop and take several breaths from having run so far. The fact that all of them were out of breath led Kevin to the conclusion that he was much farther out of Seta Archa than he had thought he was, for his friends to run so far.

"Thank goodness you guys are all right," huffed Rachel, trying to catch her breath. "We were worried after Caitlin saw what happened and went after you, Kevin. Is everyone okay?"

Kevin and Caitlin started walking toward their friends, not

wanting to exhaust them any further. "We're fine, but I wish we could say the same for Wheldon," responded Caitlin. She then started to spend the next couple of minutes explaining to everyone how Wheldon had been fatally wounded and then reincarnated.

While she did this, Kevin's attention was directed by something that had caught his eye. In the middle of the ash pile left from Wheldon's remains, something else was reflecting the light from Caitlin's angel wings. It was right behind where the orange egg had been sitting. Deciding to check it out, Kevin drifted over to it, practically unnoticed because of the detail Caitlin was going into for her explanation.

As Kevin approached it, he started to see the shape of what was reflecting light. It appeared to be a metal handle, sticking out of the ground. What was one of those doing in an empty clearing a distance away from the city?

Kevin knew. His father, Vincent Stryker, had spoken of the "main thoroughfare", an underground passage on the north side of the city that led underneath the wall. And Wheldon, with his larger size and positioned with his wings spread, had accidentally and unintentionally covered the door that led into the tunnel. For as wide as Vincent Stryker had said the tunnel was, it certainly could not have a very large door into it if this were it, but Kevin reasoned that it made sense for an entrance that was supposed to be hidden to have a smaller, less noticeable entrance.

Standing by the handle, Kevin looked back over to check on everyone else. It appeared, at least from this short distance, that Arthur, Rachel, Rouge, and Resa were in a state of surprise, although Caitlin was still explaining things. Then, being as gentle as possible, Kevin carefully lifted up on the handle. Ashes on the ground started shifting, moving, and shaking as Kevin lifted on the handle. Within a second, Kevin had the door up enough to peer inside. All he saw was darkness, but somehow Kevin knew that this was right. This was the thoroughfare entrance.

Gently, Kevin let the door back to the ground, and placed a hand over his heart. To himself quietly, he said, "Thank you for showing us the way, Wheldon." When the door shut, however, it made a loud thud as the tunnel below served to resonate the sound of the door contacting its frame again.

That sound grabbed everyone's attention. From the pile of ashes, Kevin stood up and started to walk back toward everyone as he said, "It looks like Wheldon gave us one more gift as well. He led us to the main thoroughfare entrance."

Arthur was still shaking his head, still in shock from what had happened to Wheldon and the fate he suffered. "Bless him for everything," he said. "Even in falling, he gives us more."

"Are you suggesting we make use of this?" Rachel then asked.

Kevin nodded. "Absolutely," he said. "Things aren't going so well at the wall, correct?"

"Not really," answered Rouge, pulling out one of her daggers and flipping it around.

"Then it's settled," commanded Kevin. Now was the time to be a real leader, to show no fear, to make the calls that no one wanted to make. "Rouge, Resa, take the egg and go get my father and the other two vanguards. Tell them to order the men to fall back to this point and prepare to make a push through the main thoroughfare. Make sure they know I said that."

Rouge and Resa, almost as if by perfect synchronization, acknowledged the command and started running back toward Seta Archa. As sisters of Desolunar with the disciplined training to be assassins, they knew when it was time to act and when they had time to have fun. And now was a time to act.

Once the sisters had raced off, Kevin addressed Caitlin, Arthur, and Rachel, trying to lighten his tone a little bit. "I can't make you guys follow me down into that tunnel, through traps, and straight into a gauntlet of Desolunar troops. But I'm going down there anyway, regardless. So, let me ask, any of you want to back out after we've come this far?"

Caitlin, Arthur, and Rachel all shook their heads. It was too late to back out now. They had come too far with Kevin now just to give up. "We're definitely coming along," proclaimed Arthur, raising his fist to tap Kevin's in a sign of confidence. "But what's your strategy here?"

Kevin returned the fist bump. "Same as in a typical game of

dangerball, Arthur. When plan A doesn't work, and all your elaborate stuff is not working, you push through the middle and blitz into where you need to go."

"Ooh, I like the sound of that!" commented Rachel, herself being a fan of dangerball and knowing what Kevin meant by what he said. "Force your way behind them and you're in the clear."

"As long as you remember that this isn't dangerball," nodded Kevin. "It's very real. That being said, let's do this. For Wheldon."

"For Wheldon," said Caitlin, extending her hand into the middle of the "circle" they were standing in. Kevin followed suit as well, and so did Arthur and Rachel.

Kevin then walked over and pulled open the door, opening the entrance to the narrow tunnel entrance. The campaign for Seta Archa was not yet over, and the next part of the battle was coming ahead.

Looking upward at the dark sky, Kevin paused as he saw shapes moving around. They were circling, stalking, and preparing. "Gryphons," he said aloud. "We'd better get moving, even without the troops."

Things were becoming more dangerous by the second. And Kevin was fearing that despite having the good fortune of finding the entrance to the main thoroughfare, he was leading his friends into a trap.

Chapter 58

Maelstrom

Along the walls of Seta Archa, the troops of Desolunar were repelling the allied forces with ease. Although the allies had, for the first time ever, far superior numbers in a battle, once again the force of Desolunar blasted away at the allied troops and shredded through their lines.

In the skies, an allied force of phoenixes from Avalon and the Knights of the Dragon were engaged against Desolunar's flight troops, an army of soldiers riding gryphons. On three sides of the city walls, the three countries of the Triple Alliance were locked in a death struggle with the heavy Desolunar defenses to penetrate the walls. Over on the north side, the combined unit of troops from all three kingdoms was starting to see its tactics fall short.

On that north side, several of the siege ramps that were planned to be used to scale the massive walls of Seta Archa were being torched and destroyed as the Desolunar forces focused on these ramps in their defense. With Kevin and his company seemingly gone, and with the vanguards Raijin Shane of Nuve and Gilbert Griffith of Scurnia working with their troops on the attack, the legendary Vincent Stryker stood back in command, trying to come up with some sort of strategy. Though he technically represented no specific land anymore, he still wore his old Scurnian general uniform. Next to him were his old friends, Paladin John Bryant and War Commander "Ironman" Eukert.

Watching his forces being pushed back, Vincent Stryker shook his head and said, "This is bad. I'm thinking we will have to pull back and regroup."

John Bryant sighed. "You won't get another chance at this, Vincent. If we pull back, the other three sides of the offensive instantly suffer as well."

"If they're not already suffering," added Eukert. "We just

received a report from the messengers. To the south, east, and west of the city, all but a couple of their siege ramps have been destroyed. Furthermore, the Desolunar troops are starting a counteroffensive toward the Scurnians."

Vincent Stryker shook his head. "Great," he said with some sarcasm. "I suppose that we had better hold on for now." He then started looking around. "Where's Kevin and his company, anyway?"

Eukert shrugged. "Beats me," he said. "Perhaps they're working on that answer we need on what to do. Funny how such young minds like that can have the brilliance to top even our great amounts of experience."

"Indeed," nodded Vincent, "but take a look around. Unfortunately, I don't know what kind of strategy would work here."

Vincent then paused as he and his two old war buddies saw a siege ramp come around the east corner of the city. It looked like the Auranian forces, who were on that side, were attempting to redirect at least a portion of their offensive for some more leverage. Quickly, it was being snapped into place just around the corner. Immediately, however, it was already under fire. Waves of Desolunar soldiers were beginning to bombard it, and although for the moment there were no sorcerers trying to set fire to it, the Desolunar troops were already swarming it. Vincent Stryker merely shook his head at what he saw, knowing that it was going to happen.

Then, he saw a stunning sight, and he pulled Eukert and Bryant close to him to point it out to them. Standing at the corner of the city's wall, on top of it directing the traffic of Desolunar soldiers, was General Sayo.

Sayo was an old friend of the three of them, a traitor to his homeland of Aurana, and Demonicus's most trusted general. He stood like a stone statue on the top of the wall. He never really said much when he was friends with Stryker, Eukert, and Bryant, but now he was absolutely silent most of the time.

The sight of Sayo especially infuriated Eukert, who had been attacked by Sayo, kicked by his horse, and left to die.

"Sayo," grunted Eukert, trying to keep his fury down. "Now there's one man I would like to personally take down."

Vincent Stryker shook his head. He had been gone from Aurana so long, much less society in general, that he did not know what had become of Sayo. "What in the world?" he asked. Then, he turned to his two friends standing next to him. "Why did Sayo defect to Desolunar?"

Before Eukert could respond in some sort of rage, John Bryant interrupted him. "No one really knows for sure, but if you and I remember right, Sayo was from Atwals, in the province of Southern Aurana. Perhaps Sayo felt such a loyalty specifically to the people of his home city more than his homeland."

"I doubt that," added Eukert as he gripped his sword tighter. "Being Demonicus's lapdog shows that's not the case. John, he tried to kill me once already, and he almost succeeded, too. Now, I want some revenge on him."

"Milton, you had better not get any delusions into your head," interrupted Vincent Stryker. "Revenge is not the reason to fight here."

"No, Vincent, it is not," interrupted Eukert. "Ignore the facts that we have something to pick with Sayo for what he did to us. Ignore the fact that he was our friend once, and betrayed Aurana and us. Take a look at what he is doing. He's commanding the defense against us. If we can take him out, we heavily demoralize the troops on this end. We take an all-or-nothing risk, or we lose it all anyway playing the safe route. I say, let's do this!"

As Vincent Stryker listened to these words, his eyes glared at General Sayo. Fury started to run, especially at the thought of the treason one of his closest friends had committed. Finally, what had happened had started to set in. Memories of the past began to run through Vincent's head.

Back in the days of the Alliance-Daritel War, the spectacular Vincent the Pure One was a Scurnian general, considered to be one of the most brilliant military minds as well as an excellent individual combatant, all at the age of thirty. He was fifty today. After gaining his role as the hero the gods needed and proclaiming himself a "pure one" in that sense as well, he became the chief mind behind the Triple Alliance offensive on Seta Archa against the Daritel armies.

On his way leading his unit through the Northern Pass and then south through Nuve, Vincent Stryker ran into an Auranian unit heading the same way. That unit was led by Commander "Ironman" Eukert and Commander Sayo, with Knight of Archery John Bryant being Eukert and Sayo's friend and a part of the unit. Together, the four became fast friends. They decided together to establish a joint unit and follow Vincent's brilliant plan: to execute a strike on the city of Seta Archa, behind the enemy's lines.

After the war was over, and Vincent Stryker had disappeared, the group split up. Sayo took to his home city of Atwals, while John Bryant retired to his home in Haventown, Aurana, and Eukert remained with the Auranian military.

Now, Sayo was a traitor to all of that.

"Let's go for it," said Vincent confidently as he drew his sword, a katana he had named after Kevin's mother, Lavinia. He heard Eukert unsheathe his sword and Bryant pick up his bow. There was no hesitation in any of their voices, in any of their actions.

The newly placed ramp at the corner of the city was their best shot at Sayo.

"Charge!" commanded Vincent to his friends, as he, Eukert, and Bryant rushed toward the siege ramp. Though it was swarmed in Desolunar troops already, nothing was going to stand in their way.

Immediately, the surrounding Desolunar troops were awestricken with what they were seeing: three older gentlemen rushing into combat. The allied vanguard unit troops took advantage right away at this sense of awe to create some leverage on the Desolunar forces, beginning to create a perimeter around the ramp. It was a weak perimeter, however, after the Desolunar troops regained their composure and began to fight back again. Vincent Stryker, "Ironman" Eukert, and John Bryant charged directly into this, fearless as long as they had a mission to complete.

Still, the Desolunar troops surrounding the ramp were great in number. They had a large amount of force, and three men added to the vanguard unit's defense could not break the attack on the ramp. The three men fought on, however, unwilling to give up.

As they fought on, a rush of troops attacked around the ramp. This time, however, it was a set of allies. Vanguard troops led by one of the vanguards, Raijin Shane of Nuve. Shane's troops pummeled at the Desolunar defense, trying hard to shake them loose. As they pushed toward the ramp and managed to take positions for defending it, Shane screamed to Vincent Stryker, "Go! We'll cover thou!"

It was an opportunity not to be wasted. Vincent signaled down to Eukert and Bryant to continue up the ramp. As they did, more of the allied troops under Raijin Shane followed them up, continuing to force back the Desolunar troops.

Then, there was silence.

Fighting continued down below, but on the wall, everything was silent. At the top of the ramp stood General Sayo with his hand raised, and all of his troops at least several steps back. Vincent Stryker stood with Eukert and Bryant, unnerved by this.

"So, we meet again," said Vincent Stryker as he flipped his sword around a bit. "Commander Sayo, or should I say, General Sayo of Desolunar. Did you expect me to be here on this day?"

Sayo crossed his arms and lowered his head. Typical Sayo, Vincent thought to himself. He never talked much when he was on the battlefield.

Vincent raised his sword and pointed it at Sayo, as Eukert and John Bryant took to his side with weapons at the ready. "This is the end, Martin," said Eukert, from beside Vincent.

Immediately, Sayo turned around and pointed to two of his soldiers, directing them forward to take his side. He then turned around and raised his hand again, commanding his soldiers to hold.

So, the framework was set. Sayo wanted a three-on-three duel.

If that was the way he wanted to play it, then the three old warriors of the Alliance-Daritel War were more than glad to oblige. For a moment, neither side flinched. Everyone was waiting for the other side to strike. Troops were gathered a distance away from the corner, creating a circle for the duel as they watched on.

There was only silence as they all stood still. Loud sounds were still coming from all around, but no one in the circle made a sound. No one dared move. He who moved would be the first cut down, and the duel would begin. Everyone stood like walls of stone.

Flinch. The Desolunar soldier on Vincent's right flinched.

Almost instinctively, Eukert charged out and struck this soldier in his flank, knocking him to the ground.

Sayo reached over to lash back at Eukert, but Vincent Stryker placed his sword in a position to block Eukert. Bryant then drew an arrow and strung it in his bow, pointing it directly at Sayo's neck.

The soldier on Sayo's other side pointed his sword at John Bryant. For a moment, no one moved, no one flinched.

Now what?

Relaxing his tension, Sayo let go of his sword. Then, he stood directly up, took a step back, and said, "Well done."

Vincent, Eukert, and Bryant all widened their eyes.

In that second of stun, Sayo pointed two fingers in the direction away from the city, making his command. Then, he leapt over the wall and down to the ground, with many of his troops on the wall following him down. It was a full retreat.

As the last troops leapt over the wall, John Bryant approached the battlements with an arrow drawn in his bow, pointed toward Sayo on the ground.

His aim was true. His eyes, keen. The wind, minimal. But his heart was not in it.

Vincent and Eukert approached and looked on, as Bryant loosened the tension in his bow, keeping the arrow strung in it as he lowered his weapon. "I can't do it," he said. "I can't kill an old friend like that, even if he did betray his country."

Eukert shrugged. "In all honesty, though he nearly killed me, I think I would do the same as you, old friend," he said as he patted John's shoulder. "However, I believe that tactically what we failed to do today may come back to bite us should Sayo decide he wants revenge."

"Let's hope that day never comes," added Vincent Stryker, sheathing his katana, the *Lavinia*.

Sounds of chaos started coming from the other side of the wall. Vincent and company rushed over to look down into Seta Archa from the wall, and saw a victorious, if not horrifying, sight.

Dragons were torching the ground, scaring thousands of Desolunar soldiers into retreat away from the city's main thoroughfare.

Quickly, Vincent Stryker looked above to see that the gryphon troops that had belonged to Desolunar were all but gone. The phoenixes, led by the Red Phoenix and Grand Raven, were maintaining the sky and ensuring the safety of the dragons, which were attacking the ground.

"Victory in the sky!" exclaimed Eukert. "I love it when a plan comes together like that!"

"No," interrupted Vincent Stryker. "Something's wrong here. That was far too easy, considering the difficulty they were having up there earlier. Something's making the gryphons flee, but I don't know what."

There was a slight pause, as Eukert prepared to try and tell Vincent to take it easy, that a victory was a victory. However, before he could do so, Rouge and Resa Kirkwood came rushing up the ramp from behind them.

"Sir Vincent Stryker!" exclaimed Resa, trying to catch her breath as she made it to the top of the ramp, clutching an orange egg. "We bring a message from Kevin. It is an order."

That made Vincent turn his head. "An order?" he asked.

"Yes," acknowledged Rouge. "We found the main thoroughfare. Kevin has asked that you direct your forces through the thoroughfare tunnel. He is proceeding on ahead, and asks that you do the same."

Now, what was Vincent to do? He had a corner of the wall, an entry point for his troops to leap over and enter Seta Archa. However, his son needed help in the tunnel. What was the best course of action?

Why not have the best of both worlds?

Thinking quickly, Vincent turned to Eukert and Bryant. "Divide the men!" he commanded. "Send half with me, and we will go back and through the tunnel. You two, take the other half and continue over the wall. We'll meet on the inside."

Eukert and Bryant both nodded. "Yes, sir!" they responded simultaneously. Veterans of war, together, they knew what was needed of them.

"You heard him!" commanded Eukert. "Advance over the wall!"

Quickly, Vincent started descending the ramp, with Rouge and

Resa Kirkwood in tow. As they reached the bottom, however, he turned to them and said, “Ladies, can I trust you with a favor?”

Almost instantly, Rouge nodded. “Sure,” she said. “Name it.”

“Very well,” said Vincent. “Go with War Commander Eukert and John Bryant. Make sure that any civilians and innocents inside the city are not hurt by them entering. The fewest number of innocent casualties we can cause in this maelstrom, the better. Got it?”

“Absolutely,” nodded Rouge. She turned right away and started walking back up the ramp. As the younger sister and more of a follower, Resa then followed suit and pursued her sister up the ramp as well.

Back on the ground, Vincent gathered up some of his men of the vanguard unit and ordered them to follow him to the tunnel. Despite this, his part in this battle was over. What was left would have to be handled by his son.

Chapter 59

Through the Middle

Sliding into the tunnel may not have been the best idea.

Had Caitlin's angel wings not been giving off light, the tunnel would have been absolutely pitch black. There were no torches or other sources of light in the main thoroughfare, which confused Kevin.

He shook his head. "It looks like my dad was right," he said. "It's definitely not a preferred way to enter the city, if you can avoid it."

"Definitely not," shrugged Arthur. "So tell me, Kevin. We're going on ahead without the troops. What's the plan here?"

Kevin took a breath. "We're going straight for Demonicus," he said. "All of us, together. We're going to ignore the enemy troops and rush for his palace. Our soldiers will come in behind us and fill in the space and take the enemy's attention."

In response, Arthur chuckled. "Aggressive as ever, huh? Can't argue with that, since it's just the way I like it."

"You're still insane," said Rachel as she rolled her eyes. "The only reason I'll agree with this is that Kevin's using an aggressive tactic when it's appropriate. It's not something to like."

"Yeah, whatever," responded Arthur as he rolled his eyes.

Rachel shrugged. "Well, that takes care of Arthur being rational," she said. "What about you, Kevin? Why are you doing this?"

"Hey, I'm just making this up as I go along, okay?" answered Kevin.

"Oh, you've got to be kidding me!" exclaimed Rachel. "Why in the world would you do this? It's absolutely ridiculous!"

Kevin put his face in the palm of his hand. "Look, Rachel, if I had a choice I wouldn't be doing this," he said. "But we didn't have a choice. We had to move down here before more gryphons attacked, and now that they know we're down here, we have to move quickly through this tunnel before they pin us in."

“Or we could just wait for our troops,” interrupted Rachel. “Your unit will be along shortly, and we can plow through this tunnel with their help. Why do you have to insist on the aggressive and quick route that has very little chance of us even reaching Demonicus’s capital without being killed, much less defeating him at all?”

It did not take Kevin long to have a response. “Because if we don’t go now, they’ll be on to us and we’ll never get through here. The troops already have little chance of actually breaking through, and if we wait we may never get through.”

“And we won’t get through if we’re killed on the way there,” said Rachel. She turned and said, “Caitlin, you’ve got to agree with me, right?”

There was no response from Caitlin. She was just staring into the tunnel. So, Rachel prompted her again. “Caitlin?” she asked.

“Something’s wrong,” responded Caitlin.

Arthur shook his head. “What’s wrong?”

Caitlin took a breath. “Look around, guys. This is supposed to be the only way in or out of Seta Archa, but there’s not a single light or torch around. Even if they’re airlifting things in, don’t you think that’s a little suspicious?”

Everyone else took a moment to consider this. It was a good point. “Even so, if they don’t use this tunnel much, why would they keep it lit?” asked Kevin. “Just a waste of effort to do that.”

Shaking her head, Caitlin responded, “Then why are there fresh boot prints on the tunnel floor? Take a close look. At least someone has been here in the last week or so.”

“So what?” said Arthur, walking around. “So someone’s been through here. Simple as that. It doesn’t take a genius to figure this one…”

Arthur was interrupted by a grumbling sound underneath his foot. “Out?” he said, confused as he finished his sentence.

Following the grumbling, several switching sounds were heard. Lots of clicks and clunking sounds were heard. For a moment, these sounds did not register with anyone as being recognizable.

Then, the thought finally clicked with Rachel. “Oh, shoot, Arthur, did you just step on a trap switch?”

"A what?" asked Arthur, not sure what Rachel meant.

Suddenly, there was a quick, repeating whistling sound through the air. "Arrows! Run!" called out Kevin. No one hesitated to act.

From the sides of the walls, arrows were launching out in waves from the trap weapons hidden in the walls. As Kevin, Caitlin, Arthur, and Rachel sprinted down the tunnel, more arrow waves started firing, making everyone run faster in order to stay ahead of the arrows. Clearly, this was a trap designed to take out a whole army.

Then, waves of arrows just in front of Kevin and company were illuminated. The waves were advancing forward from the rear and in towards Kevin from the front. Arrows were closing in on both sides from the trap.

"Duck!" called Arthur, being the first to make a move.

Everyone had only a fraction of a second to react. As they did, arrows flew at rapid speeds from the trap shooters in the tunnel walls.

After what seemed to be a long moment of arrows continuously firing, there was only silence. "Everyone all right?" asked Kevin as he stood up.

From beside him, Kevin heard heavy breathing coming from one of his friends. Someone was hit, and he could tell.

"I…I…I'm hurt," said Rachel as she struggled to make the words come out.

Almost immediately in response, the other three, all having escaped any injury, circled around Rachel. They were stunned to see what they were seeing. Rachel had been struck three times by the arrows: once in the side of her arm, another into her abdomen, and a third straight into her chest, very near her heart. She was bleeding profusely, but unlike the fate that had befallen Wheldon just a few moments earlier, she was not bleeding extremely rapidly and her injuries had been identified before she could bleed out.

Rachel was looking down at herself, seeing the three arrow shafts wedged into her body. Carefully, she tried to stand up.

"Whoa, stay down," responded Kevin as he knelt down to help her. Then, he turned his head up to Caitlin. "Can you help her?"

With confidence, Caitlin nodded. "Sure thing," she responded as she knelt down and began to work her magic. She looked quickly and evaluated Rachel's injuries, and despite what they had just seen with Wheldon, she had confidence that she could fix this.

Meanwhile, Rachel kept staring at the ceiling of the tunnel. "I'm scared," she said. "I'm scared to die."

Caitlin shrugged, but still she had compassion for Rachel. "You're not going to die," she said, as the light magic of healing began to course through her hands. "You'll be fine, but it's going to take some time to work all of these arrows out and patch up your wounds."

"Really?" asked Rachel.

"Really," nodded Caitlin. "Kevin, Arthur, go on without us. I'll stay here and help Rachel, and we'll wait for the troops. It's up to you guys to go for Demonicus."

Kevin's eyes widened in response. "Are you sure?" he asked.

"Just go!" Caitlin interjected. "Get going! Time is of the essence here!"

She was right, and Kevin knew it. He knew his strategy to rush through Seta Archa to Demonicus was all dependent on beating the gryphons that saw him enter the tunnel, getting to Demonicus before they could warn the troops in the city of the tunnel being used. Regardless of the fact that the tunnel had been booby trapped, Kevin knew things could be much worse.

Before he could leave, though, Kevin said, "Once you're done here, head back and alert the troops of the trap. Get them through the tunnel safely."

Caitlin acknowledged. "Will do."

Then, Kevin turned with haste toward Arthur and down the tunnel. "Let's go, Arthur," he said, as he started running off down the tunnel.

He had to stop after a few seconds, though, because he realized that Arthur was not following him. Kevin turned around and called back, "Arthur!"

From back down the dark tunnel, Kevin could hear footsteps begin just as he had called. It was Arthur approaching. Thinking quickly while he had a few seconds about the fact that he did not have a light source, Kevin drew his Sword of Purity and lit it up in its bright blue magic, using it is a source of light.

As Arthur caught up with Kevin, both of them continued to run down the tunnel. "What the hell was that all about? Did you just freeze up back there or something?" asked Kevin.

Arthur shrugged as he drew his Sword of Corruption with his left hand. "I don't know," he said. "I just stood there staring at Rachel, and maybe it was just because she was injured badly, but I couldn't stop. You yelling at me snapped me out of it."

"Are you just that bugged by seeing such drastic injuries to a friend, or is there something else you want to talk about?" asked Kevin.

Again, there was some hesitation from Arthur as they continued running. "I guess I'm just that bugged," he said. "I stepped on the switch that caused that. What's to keep Rachel from dying just like Wheldon did? A shot to the stomach and near the heart are bound to be serious, if not fatal almost all of the time."

Kevin nodded in acknowledgment. "You just have to have trust in Caitlin's ability to heal. If Caitlin believes she can heal Rachel, you need to let her." Optimism was leaking through Kevin's words, visible as ever.

"I sure hope so," said Arthur.

Something was intriguing about the way Arthur was talking of Rachel, and Kevin was catching on to this. "You want to talk about it some more?" he asked.

Arthur shook his head after a moment's pause. "Not now. As I recall, we have some business to attend to, don't we?" Arthur's last words were in a more upbeat tone.

Taking this as a good, positive sign, Kevin said, "We sure do. We've come a long way for this moment, Arthur. Are you ready for it?"

"Absolutely," nodded Arthur. "I'm ready to face my father again. I don't care how he's related to me. In fact, I don't think there's anything better I can think of right now than to see him fall by us together."

"That's good," acknowledged Kevin.

Only a minute or so into the run, there was a flash of light ahead, as if it were coming from the sky. The ground also seemed to be rising a bit along the tunnel. Ahead was the exit, and the light was coming from fires inside the city of Seta Archa.

The future was just ahead.

"Keep running!" called out Kevin, starting to wear down. "No matter how many troops we see on the other side, you have to keep going!"

The tunnel exit was closing forward, and Kevin could hear more arrow traps being set off behind them. The arrows were severely late, almost as if they were malfunctioning. Mistake number one from Demonicus. Somehow, it also seemed suspiciously too easy. As the tunnel floor rose in elevation, Kevin and Arthur both gripped their swords tighter. What was on the other side of the open threshold ahead? They were about to find out.

Together, Kevin and Arthur burst through the exit of the tunnel and straight into a road running straight down the middle of Seta Archa. They were just inside the wall, with a good distance still left until they reached the capital.

Inside the wall, the troops of Desolunar were completely swarming the grounds and roads.

Where was there to run? Nowhere.

The second Kevin and Arthur ran out of the threshold, they were instantly surrounded. "Keep running!" called Kevin, knowing it was their only chance.

Still a wall of troops stood in front and all around. Kevin and Arthur raised their swords in defense, and prepared for the worst. There was nowhere to go but forward, and if it meant running into a wall, that was the fate that would befall both of them. Of course, neither of them hoped it would come to that.

The troop walls were closing in as the Desolunar soldiers took notice of Kevin and Arthur. Would this be the end? Was there no way through? Kevin was afraid to try any one of his stripes, both those he had used and those he had not, knowing that he would be forced to stop and take some time to channel energy through his sword to do it.

Every path was blocked in. Therefore, the only way to go was forward, straight into a wall of troops.

It was suicide.

Then, almost as if the wrath of a god had descended, hundreds of Desolunar soldiers in front of Kevin and Arthur started to scatter.

Fire was torching down from the sky over their heads, causing them to flee from the road.

Kevin could not believe his eyes. Then, he looked up at the sky, and indicated to Arthur to do the same.

Above them, there was a dragon circling around, focused on the road. Riding it was the Lord Dragon, commanding his dragon Patch to clear the road. Flames were now forcing the troops below to move aside or be torched.

Unable to resist the urge, Kevin called out, "Way to go, Lord Dragon!"

Still, Kevin and Arthur had to be careful themselves not to be torched. They couldn't be sure how well Patch and the Lord Dragon could see them from above. Nonetheless, they kept running to the capital.

A good distance into the city, Arthur pointed to the tip of a building colored black and in the shape of a triangular pyramid. "Kevin, that's it," he said over to Kevin, short of breath from running so far. "I'm almost sure of it."

"You're sure that's the capital?" asked Kevin.

Arthur shook his head. "No, that's it," he said. "He's up there at the top. I know it. I just do, okay?"

Kevin nodded, confident in Arthur. "Then that's where we're headed," he said.

Pretty shortly, Kevin and Arthur were beside the building, and they quickly tucked in to an entrance in the side of the pyramid. As they did, both stopped immediately after getting in, so short of breath from the forced run and the panic ensuing behind them. It took them minutes to catch their breath.

"That was a close one," huffed Kevin, very exhausted. "Between the arrow trap in the tunnel, the soldiers on the road, and having fire breathing down over our heads, it was like running through a gauntlet."

"A very long one," responded Arthur, trying to catch as much breath as he could. "I swear I don't ever want to do that again. I think I just remembered why I didn't try out for sports back at the academy."

Kevin rolled his eyes. "You and me both," he said. Then,

finally getting ahold of his breath, Kevin looked around the building and deeper into it.

Darkness consumed the hallways, and even dim torches did not seem to be enough to keep them lit. There was hardly any visibility at all. "I don't like this," commented Kevin, as he stared down the hallway. "Why would a capital building be this dark inside?"

"Because it belongs to Demonicus?" asked Arthur, with a pointy attitude. "I've met the guy, Kevin. He does have that kind of attitude about him, you know. Basically, he's pure evil."

From down the hallway, a voice echoed, "Good and evil are human concepts."

In surprise, Kevin and Arthur both glanced down the hallway, wondering where the voice was come. Kevin then looked over at Arthur, and Arthur nodded. "That's him," said Arthur.

"If you want to know the definitions of good and evil," continued the echoing voice, "then you will come to me."

"Where are you?" called out Arthur firmly.

Arthur had his answer almost instantly as torchlights came up over a wooden platform with rails on it just down the hallway. It was a cargo lift, resting in the middle of the pyramid. Somehow, it seemed all too conveniently placed.

Still, Kevin and Arthur both knew that they had come too far to back down now. Nervously, they gave each other a glance of reassurance and started walking down the hallway together. Though Kevin was wary of the fact that this could be a trap within the capital building itself, he also knew that, just like the arrowed tunnel and the wall of soldiers he had just cut through, that the only way forward had to be the way that was taken. If it was a trap, it had to be sprung.

Carefully, Kevin and Arthur stepped onto the lift together, and just after they did, the lift began to rise. Slowly and awkwardly, the lift bobbled as it rose, increasing the nerves the two teenagers were experiencing. A creaking noise was heard as the pulleys lifted the lift, which did not serve to help their nerves.

Three floors up, the lift locked into place as wood beams slid below the lift. On this floor, the hallways were still dim and there was still little to be seen. There was a little bit of relief for Kevin and

Arthur, though, in that the lift had not been a trap after all.

Breathing a sigh of relief, Kevin asked Arthur, "Where do we go now?"

Arthur shrugged. "I'm not sure," he said. "We're not at the top, though, or else we'd see those glass sides."

"Hmmm," said Kevin, deep in thought. He looked around again, squinting in the dark hallway. The light was so dim that seeing very far was nearly impossible. Then, however, he spotted a spiral staircase near the lift. The stairs went one direction: up. Kevin tapped Arthur on the shoulder and pointed it out to him. "Nowhere to go but up," said Kevin, as he unsheathed his sword. "Shall we?"

Unsheathing his own sword, Arthur nodded. "It is time," he said. "With all due respect, Kevin, if you're kind you'll let me take the first shot at Demonicus."

Kevin chuckled. "Naturally," he said. "He's all yours."

With this, Arthur gave Kevin a slight nod and a gesture of tipping a hat he was not actually wearing. Then, he rushed up the stairs, with Kevin right behind him. Winding around, the spiral staircase took more than one floor's worth of height to climb, and were quite steep. Fatigue wore on Kevin and Arthur somewhat from rushing up these stairs, and they had to slow down a little bit.

At the top of the stairs was a trap door with a handle. Arthur was the first to get there and was caught by surprise by the door, hitting his head on it by accident. Regaining his bearings, he looked back to see Kevin just a couple of steps behind him. As Kevin finally caught up, Arthur gripped his sword tighter in his left hand and, with a thunderous force of readiness, slammed the door open above him.

He stepped up the last couple of stairs, suddenly hit by his nerves somewhat at seeing the throne room. Kevin then caught up with him and stepped up next to him. Ahead of them at the other end of the room was a desk, and a chair turned facing away from the two.

The voice of Demonicus was there as well. From the other end of the room, it echoed, "Welcome, welcome one and all. I have been awaiting your arrival."

Quickly, Kevin looked over at Arthur and rolled his eyes. Then, he gripped his sword tighter. Arthur then followed suit, raising the

Sword of Corruption in an attack stance.

Demonicus's voice continued as the chair behind the desk stayed with its back facing toward the two young men. "Kevin Trent Stryker, I have never forgotten your name since I first heard it. Every trap I have set for you, you have overcome. Every person who has confronted you, you have bowled over. I placed thousands of men in your way of getting to this very room, and you and your friends found a way to penetrate my defenses. And from the start, I saw all of this coming."

Kevin was confused. Was Demonicus being cocky or did he really have foresight?

"And Arthur Falchor, my son," continued Demonicus, with intermittent pauses, "your return to Seta Archa is quite admirable. How, may I ask, did you work up the courage for that?"

Arthur's eyes were glaring with fury. "Sheerly by the thought of ending your life," he responded.

"Ah yes, that thought does intrigue me so," responded the voice of Demonicus, as a man in a dark red robe stood up from the chair, still facing away from Kevin and Arthur. The hood was pulled up on the robe, completely masking his appearance from all sides, but it was apparent this was an Enlighteners from the Shadows robe. "Upon my fair city I watch as it falls from grace. I see dragons blowing fire upon my troops below, as my gryphons stay locked with your phoenixes. I see troops crossing the walls from the east and west by siege ramps, and coming in through the tunnel in the north, aided by the assault from the air. A perfect defense has been blown wide open, for whatever reason. Hmmph…"

"This is your own undoing, Demonicus," said Kevin, raising his Sword of Purity and pointing it. "You caused all of this, and because of it, your kingdom is falling around you. The eternal darkness will end."

Demonicus raised his hand, still not turning to face Kevin. "Being self-righteous and claiming there is a good and an evil does not give you reason to pin my failure on me. There is no good. There is no evil. There is only action and reaction."

Picking up the response, Arthur shook his head. "No," he said. "Whatever you believe is true, what do your actions say for you? I promise you, I will have no remorse for cutting your head off."

"Oh, really?" asked Demonicus with a pointy tone, as he turned around to face Kevin and Arthur at last. His eyes looked to be those of demons, and his appearance, similar to Arthur's but with more age, radiated darkness. "You would have no remorse for killing an unarmed man?"

Kevin's eyes widened, the thoughts of the drunken man in Aurana City he had accidentally killed filling his head. Arthur, though, stayed focus on Demonicus, hatred pouring through his soul. "Unarmed?" asked Kevin.

"Why, yes," responded Demonicus. "Take a look around you, pure one. There are no guards, no soldiers, and no one else anywhere in this capital building. I have no weapons here: no swords, no bows, no canes, nothing that can injure anyone and all. I have no magic either. All of the magic I conduct is all set up for myself to use with the assistance of wizards."

Gripping his sword tighter, Kevin responded. "I don't believe that last one. You would not have such adept control of Arthur when you took him over several months ago if you had no experience with magic whatsoever."

"I can manipulate, but I cannot create," answered Demonicus. "If you must know, that is the case. Unless, of course, you count this little number." Swiftly, Demonicus raised his right hand and a wave of black came out from it. A small dark orb of energy appeared in that hand.

Kevin had never seen it before. However, it was all too familiar to Arthur.

Recognizing it almost instantly with eyes wide open, Arthur leapt over and tackled Kevin. They both hit the ground with a large thud.

"What the hell was that all about?" asked Kevin, trying to push Arthur off of him and keep a grip on his sword.

"Don't let yourself get hit by that!" scrambled Arthur as he stood up, taking to his stance again. "If you get hit by that wave, you're going to fall unconscious. He's done it before."

Demonicus took a second and let out a dark laugh. "Or you

could die, Arthur," he said as Kevin stood up and took to a stance as well. "So, I see you remember this power. I would advise you to be on your guard, as I will not be limiting how much energy I put into it this time."

To Kevin, it was frightening. He did not want to find out what kind of killing power it had.

Arthur, however, showed no fear. He approached his father with sword drawn and placed the Sword of Corruption at his father's neck. "Game over, Demonicus," he said, more confidence in his voice than ever before. Arthur's determination in this matter surmounted any he had ever had before. "If it were completely up to me, this would be your life right now. Lucky for you, Kevin has another pressing matter, so I will leave your fate to you. Surrender the stripes to him willingly, or suffer the consequences and we will take them forcefully."

Back a few steps, Kevin stayed in a ready stance in case things turned ugly.

Demonicus closed his eyes. "Have it your way," he said. He swiftly turned and punched Arthur in the gut.

Arthur buckled over like the core of his body was jelly. Kevin reacted to this and started charging toward Demonicus, without fear and without anguish.

In response, Demonicus raised his hand again and produced the cascading blackout of magic. Kevin had only a split second to hit the ground and attempt to avoid it.

As Demonicus unleashed the wave, Arthur stood up straight again and swung his sword at Demonicus's chest. Split-second decision time for Demonicus. It should have been an easy one for him: focus his stripe energy on Arthur and kill him.

It was not so easy. Something pulled Demonicus back. Something told him not to do something so horrible to his son. At the same time, something else told him not to interfere with Kevin and Arthur.

The Sword of Corruption lit up as it hit Demonicus square in the chest. The sword's "bloodline", its venation, glowed exceptionally bright as a shot of force unleashed from the sword.

No resistance. No shame. All energy.

In that instant, Demonicus was thrown back with such force that he was launched through the glass of his throne room, shattering the pane. The Stripes of Light and Darkness also came free, as well as a necklace that Demonicus was wearing.

Neither Kevin nor Arthur could believe their eyes at what they had just witnessed.

Quickly, Arthur looked out the broken pane of glass, looking for the result of what he had just done. However, his father was not to be found on the ground or the side of the building. "He's gone," said Arthur, looking out in amazement. "Where did he go?"

So many thoughts were surging through Arthur's head. Had he just done the right thing? To where had his father disappeared? And why was he starting to feel bad over what he had just done? Was it because Demonicus was his father and he had just thrown him out a window? All of that was made worse by the fact that Demonicus had seemingly disappeared, and even his fate, alive or dead, was unknown.

"I don't know," responded Kevin, standing up from the ground where he had fallen. He walked over to fist bump Arthur. "Good job."

Arthur returned the fist bump, but he did not turn his head. His mind was still lost in the thoughts of Demonicus.

Uncertainty was also cycling through Kevin's mind. He started walking over to the open hole in the window, only to have his foot tap the necklace that flew off Demonicus. Curious, Kevin picked it up and examined it closely. Kevin's eyes grazed over it, and in reaction he dropped his hand. There was a "*WN*" printed on the tag on the necklace. "Arthur, it's an Enlighteners from the Shadows tag. The '*WN*' letters are printed on it. *Wondamer Notuerew.* Negation of glory."

Sheathing the Sword of Corruption at last, Arthur said, "No surprise there, I guess. So he disappeared like the one we fought in the Ancient City."

Kevin nodded. "It certainly connects Demonicus with someone who did not want the gods to be free from the imprisonment of their realm." His eyes then diverted to the stripes, which was still floating around the room in energy form. "I'll be honest with you, though. I feel like that was too easy."

Arthur sighed, and took a breath in relief. "It's better to be lucky than good. I'm just glad this whole thing is over," he said. "We did it, even thought it was a tough road getting here."

A tough road getting here. Yet, all things considered, it should have been tougher to get into Seta Archa and take a capital building.

"No," shrugged Kevin with a serious tone. "I don't think it was luck. It was far too easy. Something's not right here."

"Oh, will you just be glad it's over?" exclaimed Arthur. "Just grab the stripes already and let's get out of here. This place gives me the creeps, the more that I look at it."

Shaking his head with the palm of his face in his hands, Kevin responded, "Fine. We'll talk more about it later." Then, Kevin straightened up and extended his arm, intending to channel the stripes into his body. After so many collections, Kevin was quite good at it now.

Focusing, forcing, directing, Kevin controlled the Stripes of Light and Darkness, absorbing them into his body seamlessly. For a brief moment afterward, he merely stood in place, motionless. Curious, Arthur asked, "Kevin, what are you doing just standing there?"

Kevin's eyes were locked in place, widened. His gaze was vacant, not even focused on any particular object or person.

Then, collapse.

Suddenly, Kevin fell to the ground. He was coughing badly and looked several times like he was going to vomit. He could not lift himself off the ground. Arthur had to go into response, and he had to do so immediately. "Kevin, are you all right?" he asked with a desperate tone of voice as he ran over to help his best friend.

Unable to respond from the coughing, Kevin struggled to stand up again, only to fall over onto his hands and knees. Not wanting to give up, Kevin attempted to stand up yet again. This time, however, Arthur positioned himself under Kevin's shoulder before Kevin could fall over again, and said, "Don't worry, buddy. We'll get you down to the ground and fix you up, all right?"

Struggling to breathe, Kevin could only give a very slight nod.

Carefully, Arthur led Kevin to the trap door, and opened it with his foot. Then, step by step, he and Kevin climbed down the stairs to the floor below. It felt to Arthur as if it were taking ages to move Kevin to the ground safely.

Hitting the bottom of the staircase, Arthur led Kevin over to the lift where they had just ascended the building from a few minutes before. He looked around after entering the lift to find the operation cables that attached to the pulleys and allowed the lift to move controllably. Keeping one hand around Kevin, Arthur used his other hand to grip the cord and push it upward, moving the lift downward slowly.

There was no time to lock the lift into place at the bottom floor, but at least this lift did not descend to the basement. With caution, Arthur let go of the lift cables and escorted Kevin out of the lift and down the long hallway. The dim lights seemed a little brighter the further they went, until at last they were outside the capital building.

At the exit, Arthur sat Kevin down on the ground again and immediately went after help. It was not more than a few steps away, however, that he ran into Caitlin and Rachel. They had made it through into the city just fine, and had also met up with Professor Magnon and Vincent Stryker. As immediately as he had found them, Arthur directed all of them to Kevin, pleading for help as he did. There was no hesitation from any of them.

Instantly, Caitlin was on the ground, trying to use her magic to help Kevin. The effects were fairly minimal from an initial glance, but Kevin's coughing did appear to be slowing down.

Concerned, Vincent Stryker turned to Arthur and asked, "What happened to my son?"

"I don't know," responded Arthur frantically. "One second we were knocking Demonicus from his high perch on top of that capital building, another Kevin was retrieving the stripes that Demonicus held, and in the third he was on the ground like this."

"So, Demonicus is finally deposed," interrupted Professor Magnon, maintaining his cool. "Did you kill him?"

Arthur was almost too frustrated to answer the professor's question, wishing that the professor would just think about Kevin's safety for once rather than the quest's completion. "I really don't know," he responded. "Demonicus disappeared after we threw him out the window. Just… why can't you help Kevin, Professor Magnon?"

Professor Magnon placed his hand over Arthur. "I can help him," he said, "but he will not need it. In just a moment, he will be fine and he will be able to stand up. Already from what you have told me, I can tell you why he is sick."

This caught the attention of Arthur, Rachel, Vincent, and Caitlin all at once. "You can?" asked Vincent Stryker, still with concern in his voice.

"Yes, I can," said the professor. "Tell me, Arthur, Rachel, or Caitlin, has Kevin felt sick after taking in a stripe before?"

The first to respond, Arthur started thinking out loud, "Not that I can recall…"

"He did, Arthur!" interrupted Rachel. "The stripe in the Ancient City, remember? Kevin was really sick for just a moment, and we weren't sure why. Kron wanted to hold him back for a minute and check on him, remember?"

"Right!" said Arthur, coming to the realization after Rachel's comment. "Come to think of it, he did get sick after that for just a brief moment."

"And that is exactly what you are seeing right now," answered the professor, "only in a more severe form, for reasons logic can explain. In order to collect the stripes and keep them, Kevin has to use his body as a container for all of that energy. As he collected more stripes, more energy stacked up inside his body, making the reactions even more violent each time. What you are seeing is a reaction to him trying to hold in all of that energy within his body, until his body adjusts to it."

Vincent Stryker then turned to the professor and asked, "Now, wait just a minute here. He and Caitlin have six of these things, but there are seven of them in existence. If each reaction has been getting worse and worse, then what will happen if he is given all seven?"

Eyes were locked on the professor as Kevin continued to cough and seize up from the reaction. Arthur, Caitlin, Rachel, and Vincent Stryker were staring at Professor Magnon, wanting to hear his answer. The professor sighed, and then said, "It is likely that seven stripes would kill him." He paused for a moment. "That is, of course, if we can find the seventh stripe," continued Professor Magnon. "It is still missing, and we do not know anything of its location."

From the ground, a voice said, "Yes we do."

Everyone looked over to see Kevin, still shaking off the coughs, trying to stand up again. He did so successfully this time, using the Sword of Purity as an aid to put pressure against the ground to support himself.

Almost instantly, Caitlin stepped up to his side. "Are you okay, Kevin?" she asked. "Are you sure you should be standing up right now?"

Kevin nodded. "Absolutely. Besides, there are more pressing matters right now that we must discuss."

"Oh really?" asked the professor. "And what is it that we have to discuss?"

"Kevin, there's nothing to discuss," added Vincent Stryker. "We've won the battle here, and the Desolunar forces are being driven out or made to surrender. You and Arthur defeated their leader already, as well."

Coughing, Kevin struggled to take a breath. "No, we haven't," he said. He looked to the black sky, where lighting was crossing in sporadic bolts. Even if it were actually night now, no stars were visible. "The fall of Demonicus has not made the darkness recede. It wasn't coming from him. He was just the marionette." Kevin paused to take another breath. "This power must be that of the puppeteer. The true conqueror."

"You mean Tyrinion," chirped Vincent Stryker. "I've fought him before. This darkness is his doing?"

Arthur rolled his eyes. "So that's who's enabling my father. Where did Demonicus go after we knocked him out the window?"

"And how do we end this darkness?" asked Rachel.

Struggling to stand and walk toward the professor, Kevin shook his head and said, "No. None of that matters right now. All of that is secondary to what we should be talking about."

"And that would be?" asked Caitlin, seeing Kevin walk to her father.

Kevin paused to take a breath. "Something more dangerous

than the darkness is here. It's all of the Seven Stripes."

"I think you lost count, Kevin," Caitlin said. "We only have six stripes between us."

"Between you and me, yes. But someone here isn't telling the truth." Straightening up, without fear and with air in his lungs, Kevin walked up with courage to Professor Magnon. He took the Sword of Purity and placed it at Professor Magnon's neck. "Give up the Stripe of Life, Professor Magnon."

Professor Magnon did not budge. Caitlin, however, immediately panicked. "Kevin! What are you doing?" She started running toward Kevin, appearing to be more shocked than ever before.

"Stand down, Caitlin!" Kevin yelled. "I don't want to have to point this sword at you, too!"

Everyone else was absolutely stunned. Immediately, Caitlin stopped, dead in her tracks. This was not the Kevin with whom she fell in love.

"Stand back, everyone!" commanded Kevin, pointing his sword around to everyone before returning it to Professor Magnon's neck. Everyone was in disbelief except for Kevin and the professor.

There was no fear in Kevin's voice, as Professor Magnon waited to hear what he had been waiting months to hear. And Kevin was ready to unveil a theory that he had been building for months. One that Kevin was now sure was more than true.

He continued, "Now, give it up, Tyrinion."

Chapter 60

Prelude to an Ending

Silence filled the air.

Everyone standing around Kevin and Professor Magnon were speechless. Such an accusation was completely unexpected. Was Professor Magnon really Tyrinion, the god who had chosen Demonicus and was seeking to complete the conquest of the realms?

Professor Magnon, however, merely crossed his arms and closed his eyes. "Very well played, Kevin Trent Stryker. Very well played, indeed. The gods could not figure me out, but you, I could not pull the wool over your eyes."

Vincent Stryker started rolling up his sleeves. He began, "Why, you evil son of a…"

"Hold!" commanded Kevin to his father. "Let him speak."

Continuing, the professor started speaking a little louder, making sure that Arthur, Rachel, Caitlin, and Vincent Stryker could hear as well. "I am Tyrin Amtensen, also known as the god Tyrinion. I am the former god of darkness, one of the elite from the Realm of the Angels, those who dare to call themselves gods."

Stunned reactions came from everyone there. For Kevin, though, he had finally proven what he had believed for a long time. Tyrinion then continued, "Allow me to ask you something, Kevin. How did you figure it out?"

"There were several things that alerted me," responded Kevin, sword still pointed at Tyrinion's neck. "Kron told me that he thought he recognized you from somewhere, although he couldn't tell me where. And where else would he know you than from the Realm of the Angels? How else would you know so much about the gods unless you were one yourself? Your techniques are very unique, and Kron identified them as ancient." He paused for a second, as he looked at Caitlin. "And if Kron was right that Caitlin is an angel because she's half-immortal, she must have an immortal parent. Her mother is no longer alive, so that leaves you, the fallen god who has been here one hundred and fifty years."

Caitlin's eyes widened greatly in surprise. It all made sense now, including why her greatest strength in magic was in darkness. Her father was the god of darkness.

"Absolutely brilliant," responded Tyrinion. "All of that is true. You know a great deal of logic, Kevin. And, as I am sure the gods have told you, I am the one who has caused havoc to this land for many years. I am the conqueror in the great conquest of the realms." He paused. "So, Kevin Trent Stryker, the choice is yours. Will you kill me with the Sword of Purity? Will you try to end my life?"

Everyone surrounding Kevin and Tyrinion could only watch on in anxiety.

In an even greater twist, however, Kevin flipped his sword around and down into its scabbard. "No," he said with confidence. "Why should I end the life of an innocent man? You never did any of that. You're not the one behind Demonicus, and you're not the conqueror."

A sense of shock and ease came over everyone there. At least Kevin was sure that Tyrinion was innocent. "You are so confident in your opinion," responded Tyrinion. "How can you be so certain that you are correct?"

Kevin stood with confidence. "The gods told me a story of your attack on the Realm of the Angels, which you did," he stated. "They observed your red glowing eyes during the attack. Just like how Arthur was when Demonicus possessed him and kidnapped him, just after I found this sword and met Caitlin. You weren't responsible;" he paused to take a breath, "you were possessed. You've had something to prove, more so than just trying to help, and that's why you had such disdain for Demonicus, who is playing up the narrative. You want me to prove that Tyrinion, the former god of darkness and the only god to flee from the Realm of the Angels, is an innocent man."

"Father, is this true?" Caitlin asked in desperation.

There was a long pause.

"It is true," nodded Tyrinion, as he lowered his head. "For the longest time, I have been a seeker of redemption within the eyes of everyone. That does not, however, form the entire purpose of what I have done."

Caitlin had no response. What could one say to that?

"Keep going," said Kevin, stiffly. "Tell us what happened to you. What put you in this sort of predicament where you've been framed for years?"

Tyrinion paused, and then said, "Very well, then." He stopped, struggling to recount this story. "It was many years ago that I became suspicious of some happenings in the Realm of the Angels. Odd things were starting to happen, such as the sensation of a mysterious presence around and sounds no one actually heard. Before I could report this to at-the-time king of gods Vinz Larinion, however, something very wrong happened. I felt as though I was losing control of my body. Pain started surging through my eyes, and I lost consciousness."

These descriptions were quickly stirring up dark reminders in Arthur's head. "That sounds all too familiar," he interrupted, with a tone as if he were deep in thought. "If that's what happened to you, and it happened to me exactly the same way, then that must mean…"

"That they were caused the same way," picked up Kevin. "Kron called it 'tracer magic'."

Tyrinion lowered his head. "Alas, that I believe is what came to be. It takes an individual with far superior magic than his or her victim to use tracer magic, and yet I, an immortal of the original gods to ascend to the Realm of the Angels, fell victim to its powers. In this case, I suspect the tracer may have been attached to the Stripe of Life, as I was given it shortly before the chaos began. I was forced to attack the Realm of the Angels, my home, without control of my body or my mind. As my attack ended, I was horrified at what I saw, and when I saw the gods finally mobilizing to come after me, I fled in fear of the backlash that would come for what I had been forced to do. Where else could I flee, but the mortal realm, where I could blend in with the people and hide myself?"

Caitlin appeared somber. "Father…" she said meekly.

The professor continued. "To hide here, though, I had to form an entirely new identity. I settled myself down in what is now modern day Aurana, and I established myself as a teacher and educated wizard, so I would not have to hide my power as much. I changed my looks a bit; I took a more upper-middle aged appearance, with a different hairstyle than I had ever had as god of darkness. I traded in my purple and black robes for red and black. As the final touch, I took the name of James Magnon, an alias that, as the years went on, I started to believe was my real name. As a teacher, I became an esteemed professor with tenure, making me 'Professor James Magnon'."

Kevin crossed his arms. "How did you know about the Sword of Purity?"

"It was a creation that I knew Vinz Larinion believed could destroy even the strongest of gods, to concentrate the divine power of one into such an object. It was his planned final gambit, when he felt he was out of options for an emergency situation, but it had to be keyed to a mortal because immortals would be incompatible with wielding it," Tyrinion answered. "That is a long story of fascinating magic and divine principles to explain, and how Arthur's Sword of Corruption is exactly the opposite where every immortal could, but I digress."

Aside, Arthur commented to Kevin, "That explains how he could pick up my sword and remove the tracer when we were in Vallia, if he's telling the truth."

Kevin nodded in response.

The professor continued. "Knowing Vinz Larinion as I did, I thought it very possible that might happen, especially as the Alliance-Daritel War broke out. I knew seeking out the 'pure one' might help me to establish my innocence, but by the time I found him, it was too late."

Vincent Stryker lowered his head, feeling his shame.

"While on a trip to Scurnia, I met Vincent Stryker years after the first battle at Seta Archa that ended the Alliance-Daritel War. I imagine it was shortly after you were born, Kevin. Nonetheless, I had the chance to become acquainted with him and help him survive the mental trauma he had suffered, although the events had still left a great mental scar that I could not work out." Tyrinion then turned to Vincent. "Is that not correct?"

Vincent Stryker nodded. "It is," he said.

"And yet," continued Tyrinion, "I still had hope. So, I

continued to study and I continued to teach, awaiting another opportunity with hope. Only this time, as I waited, something unexpected and miraculous happened."

Everyone knew exactly what Tyrinion was about to talk about next. Some slight tears of happiness came from Tyrinion's eyes from the thought of it. Caitlin walked up next to her father, and gently said, "Father, what can you say about my mother?"

Tyrinion shook his head, tears in his eyes. "Very little," he said, "because so much of her cannot be expressed through words. She was… well… everything to me, more than I had ever had in five thousand years of life. When I had met Caitlin's mother, she had been hurt, and hurt badly. To make matters worse, I had not met her until after she had already had a baby, and the baby's father took the child and kept it away from her. Seeking only to help this poor soul out, I took her in and tried to show her the good still left in life, that there was still very much to live for. And during that time, she fell in love with me and I with her. We were together for quite some time. As her emotional scars healed, something else amazing happened, too."

"She became pregnant with Caitlin," added in Rachel, having figured it out like everyone else had.

"Yes," said Tyrinion. "More months had passed, the whole time during which I spent studying about angels and whether or not this was even possible. It had never been documented before, and all we knew about them was from lore that predated even the gods. It never became a serious thought, although I did have to wonder how such a thing had happened in the first place. After all, it was generally believed that mortals and immortals could not interbreed." The professor paused for a moment. "Nonetheless, those months were the best of my life. Every day I spent with Caitlin's mother was like a present that was waiting for me. At the time, I was completely consumed by it, yet blackened by the fact that I was living a lie to her. I was not really James Magnon; I was the god Tyrinion, in exile.

"At the end of the nine months, however, several officers from an Auranian military patrol broke away from the ranks to come to my house, looking for Caitlin's mother. She was from Desolunar and had been considered a danger to Aurana for her skillset as a warrior herself, but I did not learn until later they were actually Desolunar spies in disguise. I did not lie to them when they showed up, but I tried to convince them that she was now very much a reformed person and was fully devoted to Aurana from the heart. They instead chose to walk into our house and arrest her, at full term of pregnancy. It enraged me beyond my normal thresholds that anyone, much less a group of military officers, could show so little compassion to their own people. Caitlin's mother was the one love I had ever had in my life, and I had to protect her. I struck back, with no resistance, with all of the divine power I had.

"Within a couple of minutes, I had driven them off. When I went to untie her, however, I found an arrow straight through her heart. And no matter the power of magic used, no matter if one has divine power or not, such a wound is always fatal if the heart is pierced. For the first time in my long life, I felt great emotional pain, knowing what was coming. And yet she held on as I kept her alive as long as I could for one reason, and for one reason only: to make sure Caitlin would be born and have a chance at life. Caitlin was born an hour later, in a very quick delivery, and almost as soon as that happened, her mother started fading fast. She lasted long enough to hold Caitlin for a few minutes, then pass her to me and ask me to take good care of our daughter." He paused briefly. "No one ever reported the incident. Yet to this day, I still cannot shake the thought that it was my decisions that resulted in her death. What I had done had created chaos, and it was in that chaos that… that…" Enough tears were coming to Tyrinion's eyes that he had to pull out a handkerchief to wipe them away.

"And now I understand," interrupted Caitlin, finally in realization. "That's why you never told me about my mother. You've taken all the responsibility for her death this whole time."

Tyrinion shook his head. "Not entirely, but yes, that is the case. Caitlin, I am sorry that I would not tell you the truth, but the memories haunt me day by day, and to talk about it even now is still painful."

With a sense of understanding at last, Caitlin walked up to her father and hugged him tightly, her angel wings being a source of light amidst a darkened city. "It's okay, father," she said. "I'm sorry for harassing you for so long about it."

"You have nothing to be sorry about," responded Tyrinion.

Standing a few steps away, Kevin was deep in thought. A few seconds later, after a brief pause, he said to Tyrinion, "You mentioned that Caitlin's mother had a baby before you met her. Does that mean she has a half-sibling?"

Carefully, Tyrinion let go of his daughter. "It does," he said. "She has a half-brother, actually."

"And by the years you mentioned, he must be around Kevin's age, perhaps slightly older," added Vincent Stryker, also trying to piece things together. "What do you know about him, Tyrinion?"

"A great deal," acknowledged Tyrinion, "but just as I did not want to tell Kevin and Caitlin the emotions they had for each other before they each discovered them, I did not want to say anything earlier about this, to protect both Caitlin and her half-brother."

"But everything's settled now," interrupted Arthur, "and you're telling us all of this now. So where is this guy?"

"He is closer than you realize," said Tyrinion.

"And what do you mean by that?" asked Arthur. "He's somewhere here in the city or something?"

Swiftly, Tyrinion turned and established eye contact with Arthur. "That he is." Then, Tyrinion turned back to address everyone. "When the baby was taken away from Caitlin's mother, he was given to his mother's sister, an abusive sort of woman. The father had set it up this way to raise his son away from Desolunar and out of the hands of a loving parent who would grow too attached. Still, the child believed this person was his mother, and continues to do so to this day." Then, Tyrinion took a breath. "Caitlin's mother's name was Christine. Her sister was Rita. Rita Falchor."

Immediately, Arthur turned away and walked off.

"Rita Falchor claimed to be Arthur's mother," said Kevin, in realization, "but she really wasn't. It was actually her sister Christine, who is also Caitlin's mother."

Rachel turned to Caitlin. "Oh my gosh, Caitlin, Arthur is your half-brother?"

A surprised look came across Caitlin's face. Before she could respond, however, Tyrinion did. "That is true," he said. "Demonicus is his father, and Christine Falchor was his mother. Likewise, Christine and I became parents with Caitlin."

That brought another wave of stun to everyone. Not even Kevin had figured out this particular detail in advance. Now that Tyrinion was identified, he seemed to be more than willing to share all that he had been hiding.

All of it was spilling out.

"Oh dear! Arthur!" Kevin finally said in realization, noticing Arthur had turned and walked away. He started running toward where Arthur had gone. Caitlin and Rachel, also hitting that same point of realization, started to follow Kevin.

As they ran off, Vincent Stryker stepped closer to Tyrinion. "So all is finally explained," he said. "Darkness meets truth for the first time in years. Long-standing lies are brought to light. Makes me feel bad for thinking that for twenty years, you were the cause of this hell in some shape or form."

Tyrinion shook his head. "Ah, do not feel bad about it, Vincent," he responded. "You could not have known. It took Kevin to figure it out."

Meanwhile, Kevin was finally catching up to Arthur. He was standing on the other side of the capital building, looking up into the dark cloudy night sky. Immediately, Kevin slowed down, and walked up to Arthur.

"You know, it's not that it bugs me," said Arthur, acknowledging the fact that Kevin was there, although he did not turn his head. "It's just that… for so long I didn't know how my own mother could hate me so much. For so long, I was afraid of Caitlin and thought you were crazy for falling in love with her. And now, everything's just turned so upside down that I needed a minute to think."

Kevin took a breath and paused, as Caitlin and Rachel took to Arthur's side as well. "Are you sure you're going to be okay?" asked Kevin.

Arthur nodded. "I'm sure," he said. Then, he looked over at Caitlin. "Somehow, I always knew that that was not my real mother. I don't think, though, that it matters to me anymore that I don't actually have a mother. And that's because I have a sister."

"That's great," said Caitlin. "I'm glad to have a brother too." She and Arthur shared a brief hug, followed by Kevin and Rachel joining in to make it a large group hug.

It was about a couple of seconds later that Vincent Stryker and Tyrinion finally caught up. "Well, I am glad to see that did not cause a lot of controversy," interrupted Tyrinion, causing the four young adults to break their group hug. "As you can tell, for the longest time there have been the most shrouded secrets surrounding all of you. Slowly, over the course of the time you have spent together, all of them have been revealed, and the connections you have with each other have come to light."

"So it seems," nodded Kevin. "Still, a couple of things remain unsolved, Tyrinion. Why was Arthur raised so close to me, if I was the pure one?"

Tyrinion shook his head. "An oversight of a young Demonicus, I would presume," he answered. "Demonicus is still a person, and as such has all of the human characteristics. This includes conscience, oversight, and fear. Though he is a somewhat older man now and is very wise in many aspects, even today he is capable of making severe mistakes."

"Then it was just a coincidence?" asked Arthur.

"Not at all," said Tyrinion as he shook his head. "Christine, your mother, had told me that you had been left with her sister Rita, and sent away from Desolunar. She had also told me that there was a woman, currently in late term pregnancy at the time, with whom both Rita and herself were friends. This woman, as Kevin and Vincent will recognize, was Lavinia Trent, Kevin's mother. Your mother, Arthur, was close friends with Vincent Stryker and Lavinia Trent long before either of you were born. So too was her sister Rita, who raised you as if she were your actual mother. As such, when Rita was entrusted with you and told to move, she moved close to friends, in Rikleifer just down the street from her friends, Vincent and Lavinia."

Next to the professor, Vincent Stryker nodded. "The Falchor sisters were our friends for some time before Kevin or Arthur were born. We weren't close friends, but they knew us well enough."

Skeptically, Rachel asked, "Then why was Rita abusive to

Arthur, if he really was a true relative?"

"Because Rita's always been that way," answered Vincent Stryker. He then paused before he continued, "Unfortunately, people have a tendency to do that, and for as long as I've known Rita, when I've seen her, she's had a drinking problem and some temper issues. She did the best she could, I'm sure, but some people just can't control the problems they have, even though she never should have taken any of that out on Arthur."

Arthur shook his head. He would need to have a long talk with his 'mother' when he returned home.

Tyrinion then added, "Such is the case with Demonicus, as well. All he has done has been to please the one he calls his father, to play the role of the marionette. But to the puppeteer, to his true immortal 'father', none of that matters. It has left Demonicus empty."

"His true immortal 'father'?" Caitlin asked.

"That is correct," nodded Tyrinion. "Not really his actual father, but who he serves."

"It must be," added Vincent Stryker. "I fought *someone* twenty years ago…"

"Then who is it?" Caitlin asked, drawing the silence of everyone around him. "Tell me for certain, father. Who is the real puppeteer? Who had the power to possess you that day in the Realm of the Angels, and who created Demonicus and is the true mastermind behind the conquest of the realms?"

Silence filled the air again. Then, Kevin said. "I think I know."

"You do?" exclaimed Caitlin in surprise.

"Not for certain," Kevin said, "but I think I do. There's another god who was banished from the Realm of the Angels."

Caitlin's eyes widened. She knew it now.

Tyrinion let out a sigh, to explain to everyone else. "There is another," he confirmed. "There is but one who is powerful enough to do so." Tyrinion allowed a brief pause before continuing. "There is one more powerful than me, who could use tracer magic to control me. One man is stronger than each and every immortal there is. He defeated the gods, and placed a seal over their realm so strong it took a weapon blessed by the second strongest god's sacrifice to break."

Second strongest. Vinz Larinion, who sacrificed himself to create the Sword of Purity, was only the second strongest. Now, Kevin knew for sure who Tyrinion would say.

"He is the only one who has a reason for revenge on the gods, for kicking him out of the society he founded," continued Tyrinion. "The one stronger than every god in the Realm of the Angels…" he stated as he looked to Kevin.

"Is the one that brought them there in the first place." said Kevin, having made the connection.

A wave of surprise filled the eyes of everyone there.

"Very good, Kevin," answered Tyrinion. "He is the god Setadev, and his real name, before he took his name in the Realm of the Angels, was Setaeus Demota."

"That's the man who wrote that *Immortality is a Truth* book!" exclaimed Rachel. She looked over at Arthur. "Remember?"

Arthur nodded.

"That's also who the Existence said was his eternal immortal rival," said Caitlin, turning toward Kevin to remind him. "The Existence lost and was cursed to live in that space between realms where we found the Stripe of Ice."

"And he was also the first king of gods," added Tyrinion. "Setadev was the one we followed before being ousted by Vinz Larinion and almost the entirety of the gods at the time. Kronius spoke highly of him, but he was naïve to the truths behind Setadev's true motives."

Caitlin turned her head to Kevin. "How long have you known that Setadev is the conqueror?" she asked.

"I didn't for sure until now," answered Kevin. "However, I knew that Setaeus Demota carried a reputation from the story of his expulsion and from what the Existence told us. Kron mentioned recognizing your father, though he was not sure from where, and though Kronius is a god, he is a newer god and wouldn't have ever seen or met Setadev. He also mentioned how the professor had unpleasant knowledge of Setadev, just as Tyrinion might have had being the voice advocating Setadev's removal. If Setadev and Tyrinion are the only two fallen gods, then it makes sense as to who is who."

"Again, very well thought out, Kevin," said Tyrinion. With this, everyone started listening closely to Tyrinion again. "Kron spoke highly of Setadev being the founder of the gods, but he did not know the Setaeus Demota I knew. Setadev never had any desire to merely create a body in a realm above to oversee the mortals and do an eternity of studying. He sought conquest and total rule of the universe." Tyrinion paused for a moment. "Vinz Larinion and the rest of us who came to the realm would have none of that. And so, we decided that we had to remove Setadev immediately, a few weeks after we arrived and discovered his true intentions. Setadev was sentenced to be stripped of his immortality by the powers of the gods and left in the mortal realm to live out his days, a sentence he took voluntarily."

Arthur threw his hands up in the air. "That clearly didn't work, did it?"

"Unfortunately not," answered Tyrinion. "We thought we did, but we did not really know what we were doing. Not like Setadev did, at least." He paused. "Still, he feigned being depowered, and came to the mortal realm for a short time. While here, he founded this city of Seta Archa, and a few years later, he disappeared. We presumed he died."

"But instead he's been planning his vision ever since?" inquired Rachel.

"Exactly," remarked the professor. "I was singled out because I advocated strongly for his removal, and his move to frame me was to mislead the gods and settle a score while at it. The Daritel, twenty years ago, were manipulated by him because he was able to possess many of their leadership the same way that he possessed me. When that failed because of the brilliant military moves of Vincent Stryker, he switched to his backup plan: a cult that worships a figure known as the 'conqueror', and selected his new representative from them."

"You mean the Enlighteners from the Shadows, and Demonicus," identified Arthur.

"I have to believe the war was the first strategy, but Setadev is not one to take it slow and play defense. He takes long times to plan, but quick action to get his results. Once that failed because the Desolunar forces were overextended, this eternal darkness was his next plan. It was always in his plans."

Caitlin looked confused. "So is it not the Stripe of Darkness doing this?"

Professor Magnon considered this for a moment, as he looked up at a lightning crash across the blackened sky. "I actually thought it was," he began, as he hesitated, "but I must have been wrong."

From around the corner, a voice struggled to say, "I can explain that…"

Chapter 61

Apocalyptic Thunder

Everyone turned to see Demonicus, supporting himself by the side of his capital building, struggling to stand up. Almost instantly, Arthur took out his Sword of Corruption and pointed it straight at Demonicus.

"Do so if you must, my son," Demonicus struggled to say, "but what you need, I can give you. If you end me now, you may never find out."

"Then why are you helping us now?" asked Arthur strongly.

Demonicus took a couple of very heavy breaths. "The voice… the voice… it is angry. It is pleased. It is…"

No one really had a grasp on what Demonicus was saying. Not only was he mumbling somewhat, but also what he was saying were a series of contradictions. What was clear, however, was that something serious was changing in Demonicus's mental state. Then, it cleared. "You are still my son…"

Reluctantly, Arthur rolled his eyes as he stepped away. "Someone else talk to him, please. I don't want anything to do with him."

Kevin pointed his sword at Demonicus, taking over for Arthur's desire not to be there. "Spill it," he said.

Demonicus coughed as he pulled down his hood. He had short blonde hair and blue eyes, and looked remarkably similar to Arthur. "I did start the darkness, with the stripe. My father gave me the knowledge of how to use it. But now that it is begun, it is out of my control. He told me the Stripe of Light would reverse it, but I tried that when the blackening over Seta Archa grew out of control. It did not work. My father lied to me. He is pouring energy into the eternal darkness as we speak."

Professor Magnon stepped up next to Kevin. "That settles it.

You have to take this fight to Setadev. It is the only way to undo the darkness and save the world from panic and famine."

Silently, Kevin took a deep breath. "Fine. You're coming with us this time."

Next to him, Caitlin nodded confidently to her father.

"Absolutely, I will," the professor acknowledged. "This is not the time to run. It is the time to act. But I would suggest if we act, that we need all seven stripes. Setadev is stronger than us. We will need every tool we can get."

Kevin pulled up his sleeve, revealing the five Stripes of Air, Earth, Fire, Light, and Darkness he was carrying. Caitlin also revealed the Stripe of Ice she was holding. Then, Kevin stared at the professor.

"Then what of the seventh?" asked Vincent Stryker to Tyrinion. "Kevin accused you of holding it. Is that true?"

"Oh, he has it," Kevin interrupted before Tyrinion could answer, "You said it yourself; that's why Setadev possessed you when he did. You've known where the Stripe of Life has been all along, haven't you? You're the holder."

Silently, Tyrinion nodded. "It is true," he said as he pulled up the right sleeves of his robes. Underneath his robes, on the back of his arm, was a white stripe. "Seven powers, yes they are, of stronger powers than the stars," he then recited from the poem on the stripes. "Setadev knew how to activate this stripe, and then Vinz Larinion. Since then, it has been passed around to various gods to attempt to figure out its activation, to no avail."

"Then what does it do?" asked Caitlin.

"What no mortal can do," responded Tyrinion. "It is that which makes people immortal, that grants them the gift of divine power. Those that were made into gods, both the original few who ascended to the Realm of the Angels and the ones found later, such as Kronius, were given their power by this stripe. Although Setadev was the original one to know how to work it, Vinz Larinion later figured out how to do it himself. He then decided that, should he have to pass on his throne of leadership someday, he wanted other gods that were well trusted to try and activate the Stripe of Life, which to this day no other god has been able to figure out."

Kevin nodded. "No wonder it's so prized."

"Father, I'm confused," Caitlin said. "Along my travels with Kevin, I found out I'm sensitive to the stripes and can feel them. Why can't I feel the Stripe of Life?"

"Life is not an element that can be sensed," the professor said. He then took a step back. "Yet you have found the Stripe of Life nonetheless. Well done, you have found all of the pieces to the ultimate power… if you can figure out how to use them." He looked to his daughter. "I do not wish for Kevin to have this stripe because his body is at critical mass for the energy it is containing. However, I think it best that you carry this. Setadev will want me, and I do not want to give him the chance to take it from me." He looked to Kevin as well. "Is that agreeable to both of you?"

It was a good idea, Kevin thought to himself. As far as he was aware, based on the history, Setadev knew Tyrinion had that Stripe of Life. Moving it meant that was no longer the case. Caitlin also felt entrusted by her father, and was willing to help him.

"I believe when the moment is right, you will know how to use the stripes," Professor Magnon said. "I trust the two of you to make that happen."

Kevin looked at Caitlin, and nodded. He was showing his confidence. Caitlin, still in her angel form, nodded as well. They would have one chance to end this darkness before more people died of famine. Before the darkness could spread to Rikleifer, or to Aurana City, Nuvenia, or Scurniapolis. Before it reached any further than it already had. Before the world would be plunged into absolute panic.

"Great," commented Arthur, near the group. "Now what do we have to do to find Setadev? It's not like he's anywhere near here, I'm guessing."

Rachel scowled at him. "Arthur! You don't know that!"

A weak voice spoke up. "I do…"

Everyone looked over to see Demonicus, slumped against the pyramid side. He was still weak, but chirping like a bird.

"My father lives in another realm."

Arthur walked over, still not interested in talking to his father, but knowing Demonicus would tell him. "Is there a way there? A portal or a pathway, or something?"

Weakly, Demonicus turned his head toward a temple across the street from the pyramid. He then spoke up, "The portal you are looking for, it is here in Seta Archa. Hidden inside the Temple of Setaeus, you will find the Well of Souls, an ancient praying artifact. In the bottom of the well is the passage you need."

The temple Demonicus was indicating was old, and made of white stone. It was also a pyramid, but composed of three white square blocks in descending sizes with the base being the largest part. The sides were ornately carved, and were clearly done much older than the new pyramid construction that formed Desolunar's capital building.

As Caitlin saw the temple, she nearly screamed.

It was the same temple that had been a vivid image in her nightmares. Kevin had walked in there, and at the time that he did, the temple had exploded and killed everyone inside. Amelia, the mental rendering of what Caitlin had been that lived on inside her head, had shown it to her. Frightened by what she was seeing, Caitlin looked up to the sky to see what it looked like.

The skies were lit up in apocalyptic thunder, spreading light across a darkened sky. The world was tearing itself apart in the wake of the chaos that had just ensued… an aftermath foreshadowing the end of a long journey that would change the world forever. The end was coming. It was an ominous sight among the skies of lightning and the ruined city surrounding, but it was a sign of the final battle to come. Fires burned all around, some from the burning buildings of the city and some from the troops, relaxing in victory.

This was it. This was exactly it. It was the vision from the nightmare.

Suddenly, the lightning became even more intense. It started flashing across the sky every second, creating numerous loud booms of thunder. Something was happening, something that was about to tear the city apart.

"What in the world?" asked Vincent Stryker, as thunder boomed.

Although most lost their balance and were struggling to question what was going on, Kevin stood straight and tall. In his head, the dark voice was speaking to him:

You cannot defeat me, for I am nothing. However, if you wish to find your own defeat, you may come to me. Demonicus has told you where you will find me: you need only to go there.

Kevin tried to shake it off. "Get out of my head!" he yelled aloud.

Come to me, Kevin Trent Stryker. Come to me, oh pure one. Show me the futility of the gods. Come, only you.

The thunder was finally coming to a stop. "Are you okay, Kevin?" asked Arthur. "That was kind of weird for you to exclaim."

"You didn't hear that?" asked Kevin.

Arthur shrugged. Next to him, Rachel and Caitlin shook their heads.

Professor Magnon looked to Kevin. "I did," he said. "It would appear that he is trying to send a message," responded Tyrinion, as he regained his balance. "If this keeps up and any of that lighting hits the ground, the wooden buildings of Seta Archa may catch fire and kill a lot of people here."

That definitely could not be allowed to happen. It was a signal if there ever was one. Kevin had to go now.

I will only allow you. No one else will be able to pass through my portal. If they jump, they die.

Kevin immediately took to pulling the straps on his Nuve stealth bracer tighter and straightening out his jacket. It remained unbuttoned as usual, showing the red shirt he was wearing underneath the green uniform of the Auranian military. He drew his Sword of Purity, and with a confident air started marching toward the temple. "Stay here, everyone," he immediately said. "I'm going on alone."

"Kevin, don't do this," Caitlin instantly responded, clinging close to Kevin.

"He may have to," Professor Magnon pointed out to his daughter. "I did hear the voice that Kevin did. Setadev's voice stated that anyone other than him who jumps into his portal will die."

"I don't buy it," Caitlin snapped back. She looked at Kevin. "Even so, no one said that you have to go right this instant, and why do you have to go by yourself?"

A glare of determination rang through Kevin's eyes as he was fixated on the temple. "This has gone on far too long," said Kevin. "He has brought nothing but pain to innocent lives and seeks to rule them all. He will bring more if he isn't stopped, and he may kill thousands in this city if that lightning keeps going. I can't let this go on a second more."

"But really, by yourself, Kevin?" interrupted Rachel. "After all that we've done to help bring you here, you're really going to go it alone?"

"Yes," nodded Kevin. "It's not my choice, but I'm not going to let any of you come to harm."

"Oh, don't feed us that load of dragon manure!" exclaimed Arthur. "Kevin, we wouldn't be here right now if we weren't ready to go to the ends of the earth to do the same thing you're about to do."

"I know what you're trying to say," responded Kevin, "but on this one, I'm drawing the line. I can't risk Setadev's threat being right. And even if you do go down there, what is down there is going to be far worse than anything we've ever faced before, and I'm going to face him alone. Please, just stay back. I don't want to have to force you guys to stay back." Kevin started running forward.

Professor Magnon stepped forward. "Regardless of this threat, I will not fear Setadev. I will go with you, as promised."

"No," Kevin firmly answered. "If I don't come back, someone has to be here to take care of Caitlin."

"Excuse me?" Caitlin exclaimed. "Who says someone has to take care of me? It's I who need to take care of *you*."

Sighing, Kevin knew he was caught. That was totally the wrong thing to say of Caitlin, who had saved his life many times. Before he could respond, though, Kevin was interrupted by a wave of rolling thunder, stunning everyone again for a few seconds. It was evident now that Setadev was definitely beckoning for Kevin to confront him. And now, it was Kevin's time to oblige.

As the booms subsided, Kevin continued, "All of you have to stay back, and let me do this alone." Then, Kevin continued on.

Arthur and Rachel almost lunged out to try and catch Kevin and keep him from going alone, but Vincent Stryker raised his arm in front of both of them. They looked over to see Vincent shaking his head, telling them no. "Let him go," said Vincent Stryker, knowing what was coming. "Kevin knows what he wants here. If he feels it, he needs to do this one alone."

Beside him, Tyrinion nodded. "Even if he doesn't have all seven stripes with him he's still our best chance."

As she watched Kevin walk off toward the temple, visions of her recurring nightmare started cycling through Caitlin's head, faster and more frantically than ever before. Would the temple explode? What would happen next?

The message of Amelia came to her mind: don't let Kevin go in there alone. She wanted to believe that Setadev was bluffing. Even if Kevin wanted this, she couldn't let him go like this. Not alone. Not without the seven stripes. Not now. Never.

Just as Kevin was reaching the temple entrance, Caitlin shot forward, letting her angel wings carry her with all the speed she could to the temple entrance. Nothing was going to stop her. She reached Kevin's side and joined him as he walked through the temple entrance. "I'm going with you," she said, as though she were making a declaration.

Kevin shook his head. "Caitlin, I told you to stay back. Please, just do this for me. I can't risk you."

"Absolutely not!" exclaimed Caitlin, still walking alongside Kevin undeterred. "I have two of these stripes, remember?" she asked pointedly with her right hand up. "If you go there alone, you won't have all of them!"

Shaking his head, Kevin responded, "I would rather go in there myself with only five stripes than take you in there with me and risk your life needlessly."

"But you don't need to protect me. I'm here to protect you," responded Caitlin, with more emotion in her voice than she had ever had before. "Did you forget about the promise I made to you the night we met? I promised I would be there to support you."

Nodding, Kevin responded, "I know, Caitlin. I really do, and it has meant so much to me to have you standing with me all the time." Kevin had to pause, though, as he and Caitlin saw the inside of the

Temple of Setaeus.

All around on the white stone, paintings of a man ruling the land, the people, and the animals created one giant mural that continued in an unending circle around the room. They appeared to be somewhat similar to the paintings inside the spire at the Ancient City, in which the Great One was depicted guiding everyone else. At the very center was the Well of Souls, a simple brick raised opening into the floor, with a couple of stairs leading up to it.

Was this Setadev's inspiration?

It was of no matter. One way or another, this evil deity who had been pursuing the conquest of the realms, who had killed Kevin's mother while searching for him in the mortal realm, who had torn apart his family and those of his friends, who had caused wars that had decimated the nations of the world, had to be stopped.

"This is what I have to do, and I have to do it alone," continued Kevin. "Please try to understand." Then, without reservation, Kevin started stepping up the stairs on the side of the Well of Souls.

"No!" called out Caitlin as Kevin reached the top stair. She leapt out and grabbed Kevin by the ankle, accidentally tripping him on the last ledge up to the edge of the well. Kevin called out in pain as he fell over the well opening.

Sure enough, there was a hole in the realm at the bottom of the well. As Kevin fell over it, a large tug of gravity from the well pulled hard on Kevin, forcing him and Caitlin downward into the well and through the hole.

Chapter 62

Conquest of the Realms

"Damn it, Caitlin!" exclaimed Kevin, absolutely upset. "Why'd you have to go and do that? I told you I wanted you to stay behind!"

"And I told you I'm not letting you go alone!" yelled back Caitlin. "Can't you trust me, Kevin? After all we've been through, don't you see that I know what I'm doing by coming along?"

Together, Kevin and Caitlin were falling through another space between realms, through an endless vertical tunnel. Nothing was along the sides except for a dark glow of flowing energy.

When Caitlin had grabbed Kevin's ankle and tripped him, Kevin had fallen directly over the Well of Souls, the opening into the space between realms. As it had turned out as well, the hole into the space also exerted a greater amount of gravity than normal, pulling Kevin in with a great amount of force. Since Caitlin had not managed to let go of Kevin's ankle, given how quickly the force had pulled Kevin in, she too was dragged down into the hole. She had since let go of Kevin's ankle, but was now falling with Kevin.

"Caitlin, I don't want to put you in danger again," responded Kevin as he shook his head. "Why can't you understand that?"

"Because I can't let you put yourself in danger," said Caitlin, not even needing a second to think about the answer to that question. "I know you're scared of losing me, Kevin, but I know what that feels like. I almost lost you once too, remember?"

Kevin eased up, knowing that Caitlin had a point. She was absolutely right. "You're crazy, you know that?"

"So are you," responded Caitlin as she reached her arms around Kevin. "You're really willing to throw yourself at this alone?"

"If that's what would have happened, then yes," responded Kevin. Then, he began to recite, "If you truly believe in something, then you will give up everything you have for it. All of your worldly possessions: your wealth, your memories, your friendships, and even your love, must be forsaken for your cause. You must even be willing to give up your existence for what you fight for. Do not fear it, for if the cause is good, others will follow your example and fight for your cause. So be willing to forsake everything and follow your heart to a better future."

Caitlin had never heard these words before. "What's that supposed to mean?"

"They're words that former king of gods Vinz Larinion gave to Kron, and then he gave them to me," explained Kevin. "That was a long time ago. Ever since then, though, the words have resonated in my head. What it means is that you have to be willing to give up all that you have, even your life if you must, to protect what you truly believe in."

Shaking her head in disbelief, Caitlin responded, "You better not have been thinking that you were going to come down here on some kind of suicidal rampage. Aren't you scared to die, Kevin?"

"A little," responded Kevin, reaching his own arms around Caitlin now, "but there are things worse than death. Seeing you die, seeing any of our friends fall like what happened to Wheldon, seeing the world die, all of these are those things. I would rather fall myself than see any of that."

Tears came to Caitlin's eyes a little bit. Finally, she saw the determination and drive in Kevin's eyes, and the reason he was continuing to press on to whatever was coming next. So much he wanted to protect everything he loved, and that included Caitlin, too. A little bit of time had passed on the fall, and the situation was cooling down between them. "You really think seeing me die would be worse than dying yourself?" Caitlin asked. "No wonder you resisted me coming along so hard."

Kevin looked around for a moment. "Seems to have been a moot point, I guess. I don't know if that's because you fell while holding my ankle, or if Setadev was lying."

“For someone who did what he did to my father, I won’t trust a single word he says,” Caitlin stated defiantly.

Quietly, Kevin gave her a nod.

Before anything more could happen, though, another hole opened up, and Kevin and Caitlin fell through it. They were forced to let go of each other by the force exerted from the hole.

When all the chaos of falling had stopped, Kevin and Caitlin found themselves standing next to each other on a windswept plain. Looking around, they saw some miraculous sights. Columns stood all around in a circle, making a sort of ritualistic altar. The skies above were dark red and full of black clouds, and the land all around was barren. It was dead land.

“What kind of place is this?” exclaimed Caitlin.

“It is my nightmare!” echoed a voice from above.

Kevin and Caitlin looked up to see someone flipping through the air. Then, that person landed on the ground in front of them, perfectly and precisely. His robes were made of gold and were as elegant as any Kevin or Caitlin had ever seen before. He gleamed a brilliant light that seemed to emanate from him. The man’s skin was pale and white, and his hair was a very dark brown, very much like the picture Kevin and Caitlin had just seen inside the Temple of Setaeus. Very quickly, they realized who they were seeing.

“Of course, nightmares and dreams of power are not always well expressed,” said Setadev as he approached Kevin and Caitlin. “Pure one, I have been expecting your arrival for some time now, as you are the only one who challenges my dream.”

Immediately, Kevin drew his Sword of Purity, not wanting to take any chances. He ignored Setadev referring to him as “pure one”, knowing this was not someone with whom he could argue.

This made Setadev laugh. “I find it quite amusing,” he said, taking steps closer to Kevin, “that you do not trust me in the least. Yet, you are wise to be on your guard,” he continued, as he grabbed Kevin’s shoulder.

As Setadev touched Kevin’s shoulder, Kevin shrieked in pain and collapsed to the ground, clutching his shoulder. In response, Caitlin immediately tried to charge some magic but found herself knocked back and to the ground by Setadev before she could get anywhere close to firing any.

Setadev looked over at Caitlin. "Pity," he said. "The first angel in over five thousand years is in my presence, fighting on the side of the pure one, and yet she is pitifully weak. You are not worthy to be alive. Still, as you are such a unique creation, I believe I will let you live for now." Then, Setadev turned to Kevin. "And you," he said. "Are you so reliant on your sword as to think it can defeat me? I find it sad that Vinz Larinion decided to give his life so that you would have that sword. He was my assistant, you know, and he was always inferior to me. I never feared him. Nor do I fear his sword, nor will I ever fear his sword."

Kevin struggled to stand, still in pain.

"Get up!" demanded Setadev, quickly changing his demeanor. "Get up! Get up!"

Slowly, Kevin managed to regain his balance and regain his position. "You ever touch Caitlin again, and that'll be the end of you," he said.

A smirk came to Setadev's face. "Ah, I see now," he said. "What an interesting situation, indeed. "The pure one and the angel are in love? Who would have guessed?"

Looking over at Caitlin, Kevin saw that she was starting to stand up again as well. "The game is over, Setadev," he said. "It all ends here. The conquest of the realms is over. Your son has been defeated, and his kingdom is crumbling."

There was a pause of silence.

Then, to the surprise of Kevin and Caitlin, Setadev began to laugh again. "You fools!" exclaimed Setadev. "Do you really not see how the game is played?" he asked. "Or should I explain it to you?"

Kevin and Caitlin did not respond with any words. They merely took back to battle stances, in preparation for an attack anytime from Setadev.

Setadev shook his head, still chuckling a little bit. "Very well, then, I will explain something to you. Pure one, did you not see the dragons dominating Demonicus's gryphon troops after engaging them for so long first? Better yet, do you not remember how the arrow traps in the tunnel fired on a delayed switch that could not manage to catch you?"

Suddenly, Kevin's eyes widened. So did Caitlin's.

"It was I who sabotaged the defense of Seta Archa," continued Setadev. "Yes, and now you see how the game is played. I allowed Aurana to win at Haventown. I let your forces cut a pathway through the defense of Seta Archa. I allowed you to defeat Demonicus. He was expendable."

What? The thought just shot across Kevin and Caitlin's thoughts. Caitlin started speaking to Kevin using mental magic again; *did he just say his chosen one was expendable?*

"Do not try to hide your words by speaking them mentally," interrupted Setadev. "I can intercept all of your messages. And yes, I did say he was expendable. He has been all along."

"Then why even choose him?" asked Kevin. "What was the point in Desolunar, in Demonicus?"

Setadev chuckled, as if he wanted to gloat. "It served two purposes, really. Just as in what you mortals term the 'savage war', Alliance-Daritel War, whatever, twenty years ago, I created a kingdom from Seta Archa to search for the Seven Stripes of the Elements, all seven of which I see the two of you carrying now. The Daritel were not successful at this, so when your father arrived, pure one, I decided to let him tear through the ranks and approach me. I looked forward to the challenge of this 'pure one' that the gods had sent to destroy me, even if they did not know it was me."

Kevin grunted. His father had been lured here as well. It was never the end goal. It was a trap.

"As you just figured out before you came here, for a couple hundred years or so by now, I had been baiting the gods into thinking it was Tyrinion, and not me, who sought to destroy them all. Vincent Stryker, however did not know that. He was more than willing to surrender when he saw how weak he truly was. Still, I let him live as long as he would abandon his sword, making the sacrifice of Vinz Larinion pointless and reaping revenge on my old apprentice. As I found his incursion quite annoying, I decided to place a stumbling block in front of my adversaries in the form of a seal on the Realm of the Angels, keeping their meddling out of my affairs for some time. Such a measure I knew would only be temporary, but it allowed me to continue working toward my goals without their interference, and the timing only worked the best to continue to frame Tyrinion."

Caitlin felt anger. How much was this god trying to inflict pain on her father? It never seemed to end.

"Still, all of this brought me no closer to collecting all seven stripes. Demonicus, after twenty years, had only managed to collect one stripe for me, the Stripe of Darkness. Had it not been for his second purpose, to distract the mortals from the game I was playing, I would have deemed him a failure right then and there."

"Man, do you ever stop monologuing? You sure seem to love doing it," interrupted Kevin.

"Silence!" commanded Setadev. "This is my moment! When you surfaced, Kevin, I left Demonicus to finish you off. In fact, I even gave him a weapon of my own creation: an exact duplicate of yourself that you are familiar with as Pseudo. Even so, Demonicus could not manage to kill you, because you were ever persistent. And then, I found the most interesting secret of all. You, the pure one, were collecting the stripes at a much faster rate than Demonicus ever could. In a matter of a day, you had discovered two of them, and then you went in pursuit of the other five. With that in mind, I stopped providing my voice to Demonicus, and that is how he began to crumble. The darkness was a nice final touch, a tip of the cap to Tyrinion for being my patsy for so long."

Caitlin then interrupted, "Are you saying you let Kevin collect all of the stripes intentionally? Why would you do that?"

"Foolish angel," responded Setadev. "I let him collect the stripes for me, and I let him get all of the way here so you two would bring all seven. As a matter of fact, I find it humorous that neither of you appreciate all that I have done for you. It was I who set you two free that day in Venarose, kept the superior Pseudo from killing both of you, and let the pure one through Seta Archa to Demonicus's throne room. I figured that you would follow the pure one even though you were warned it would kill you. Now, you have delivered to me the greatest known power in the realms, that which will allow me to complete my conquest, and you carried two of them yourself."

Kevin gasped. How could he have been so foolish? Not only had he just collected all of the stripes, he had delivered them for Setadev on a silver platter. The distance he had traveled had all been because Setadev wanted him to get this far.

"Now, I am not normally one for mercy," continued Setadev, "but in this case I will make an exception, as you both have been good servants. Surrender all seven of the stripes to me now, and I will allow both of you to live out the rest of your days. The choice is yours, but I would not recommend that you make this any harder than it has to be."

Turning their heads together, Kevin and Caitlin looked at each other and nodded. Then, they both charged at Setadev.

As Kevin reached over with his Sword of Purity to slash downward, Setadev grabbed the sword precisely by the blade and threw it, Kevin and all, behind his back. Caitlin then hammered him with a blast of magic, which Setadev reflected and threw back in her face.

Kevin then lunged up again and started swiping at Setadev. Being cocky, Setadev raised one finger and moved his arm to block every sword strike with that one finger. Kevin was searching hard, trying to find a weakness in Setadev's defense that he could exploit.

Up, down, left, right, straightforward, parry around to the back, nothing was working. Setadev was managing to block everything.

That did it. Kevin had to try a new tactic. Taking a step back, Kevin threw the Sword of Purity over Setadev's body. Then, he called it to himself while it was in midair, hoping it would penetrate the god.

In a flash, the energy of the sword passed through Setadev to reform in Kevin's hand. As the power ran its course, the flash dissipated and Kevin carefully looked at the results.

He was shocked. No effect.

"Very funny, indeed," said Setadev, brushing a hand across his face.

Kevin's eyes widened as Caitlin finally managed to stand up again and return to Kevin's side.

"You are not worthy to be the bearer of the Seven Stripes of the Elements," continued Setadev. "Only he who can activate them all has such worth. Now, why do you not stand aside?"

Kevin stood there in silence.

Suddenly, Setadev unleashed a great amount of force, shoving Kevin and Caitlin into two separate columns with enough force to crack the rock. Both of them screamed in pain, as Setadev shot them with a great amount of energy.

Then, Kevin fell off the side of the rock and to the ground. For a minute, he just stayed on the ground, unable to stand up. Caitlin managed to pull herself off the side of the rock consciously, and immediately flew down to Kevin's side to help him.

"Now you see how the game is played, pure one," said Setadev as he approached them both. "I will give you one last chance for mercy. Give me all seven stripes right now, or I will end your life, right here and right now. I will not give you any more chances."

Caitlin tried to help Kevin stand, and it finally worked. Kevin was able to keep his weight underneath his legs for the moment. He coughed a few times as he took a moment to think. The right decision, it was in his grasp one way or another. What was wrong and what was right? Could Setadev be injured, much less defeated? It was clear now that Setadev was more powerful than any god had ever been before. He was not playing games; he was dominating.

If you truly believe in something, then you will give up everything you have for it. All of your worldly possessions: your wealth, your memories, your friendships, and even your love, must be forsaken for your cause. You must even be willing to give up your existence for what you fight for. Do not fear it, for if the cause is good, others will follow your example and fight for your cause. So be willing to forsake everything and follow your heart to a better future.

If you truly believe…

A memory of the poem from the Stripe of Air's chamber in the temple in the City of Phoenixes suddenly flashed through Kevin's mind:

But when all is said and done,
You must merge them into one.
And should you survive all blasphemy,
You have a small chance at victory.

The last part of the poem was incomplete. What was he forgetting? Maybe, just maybe, the answer was a little more clear than the words implied. He remembered what the gods had suggested the "weapon" was, as well.

Kevin took a deep breath. "I'll do it," he said. "I'll give you them all."

"Are you insane?" exclaimed Caitlin almost instantly. "Kevin, don't give up now! You're not your father! You can still beat this joker!"

Setadev scoffed. "I would not say such things if I were you, angel," he said, "unless you wish to join him in death."

"Please trust me," responded Kevin. "Caitlin, if you've ever trusted me before, please trust me now, and give your two stripes to Setadev while I surrender my five."

Caitlin shook her head. "I can't do that, Kevin. You can't do that either. After we've come all this way, you're really going to surrender? Just like your father?"

"Just trust me," responded Kevin weakly as he struggled to stand. "Please do it, Caitlin," he said. "It's what has to happen."

That caused so much conflict in Caitlin's head. What could she do? It definitely felt like the wrong decision to just surrender everything over to Setadev like that. Still, she wanted to trust him. And she did trust him with all the heart she had. Love is sometimes more powerful than doubt.

"Okay," she finally said. "I trust you."

"Thank you," said Kevin in response, as he raised his arm up to channel the stripes out.

Caitlin put her arm on top of Kevin's as a sign of trust, allowing her stripes to channel out with Kevin's. She clutched Kevin tightly with her other hand to show how much she took what Kevin was saying to heart.

None of that mattered to Setadev. All that mattered to him was taking all seven stripes, all at once. He channeled them all into his own body so quickly that there would have hardly been any time to take a breath. Then, Setadev extended his right hand and saw it. His glow began to surge with even greater energy before as his laugh became more and more evil. "And now it is complete," he proclaimed. "Seven powers combined, and now the conquest of the realms will be done!"

"Or so you think!" called back Kevin, confidently.

Caitlin and Setadev were both confused.

Then, suddenly, it happened.

A hole ripped straight through Setadev's body, glowing white. "What in the realms?" he asked, surprised and frightened. "What is going on with me?"

"That's the price you pay for your greed!" claimed Kevin strongly. "You wanted all seven stripes, Setadev? Well, they have given you your reward!"

Setadev kept looking at himself as his body began to disintegrate. "But… But… why?" Then, he stared directly at Kevin. "You… what have you done?"

"I did exactly what you wanted," responded Kevin. "I gave you the Seven Stripes. But you never stopped to ask why I was only carrying five myself, did you? Tyrinion had told me that if I were to take in the last stripes, I would likely die from trying to contain so much energy within my body."

After a moment's pause, a dark chuckle came to Setadev, as his body began to disintegrate from his feet upward. "So, you took a wild guess this might happen. You were lucky."

Kevin shook his head. "No, it was not luck. It was your overconfidence." Closing his eyes, Kevin maintained his cool. "I merged my stripes with Caitlin's by having us both give them all to you at the same time, and by doing so created the weapon I needed to defeat you: your own greed."

"This cannot be!" screamed Setadev as more of his body disintegrated. "What are you? Are you a hero?"

Silence filled the air for a brief second. Caitlin looked at Kevin, wondering what he would say, or if his answer had changed.

"No," responded Kevin. "I am the one who sought your downfall. Nothing more. Nothing less."

There was a moment of only silence as Setadev continued to disintegrate. Then, there was another evil laugh.

Kevin and Caitlin were unsure why.

"You may think this is the end," laughed Setadev, "but I promise you, it is not. What did I tell you, pure one? You cannot defeat me, for I am nothing. And so shall it be. Revenge I promise upon you, upon your angel, and upon your friends. The gods will see their end soon, the mortals will tremble in fear, and all will bow to the true destined ruler of the realms, the ultimate deity. This is only a delay, nothing more. The conquest of the realms will never end until it is done, I swear it!" As the last bits of Setadev began to disintegrate, he said one more time, "You cannot defeat me, for I am nothing."

Then, he was all gone. Nothing was left behind.

Silence filled the air.

Caitlin looked at the empty space that was Setadev, puzzled. "So, what just happened?" she said. Then, she turned directly to Kevin. "How did you know that giving Setadev all seven stripes would kill him? I mean, other than the fact that father said it might kill you if you took them all, or that the gods thought it could destroy a realm?"

"I didn't really know for sure," responded Kevin, shaking the dust off his clothes. "I had to take a chance that it would, because we were out of options. If there's one thing I did know, though, it was that if that was going to work, I needed you to be there with me and help me with it."

"Well, thanks, Kevin," nodded Caitlin. "Now see? It looks like you needed me after all," she joked.

Kevin chuckled a little bit, still brushing himself off. He was beat, tired, and very worn down, but still he was able to muster the energy to stay standing. "I guess so," he said.

Then, a rumble rang through the air.

Above, the dark skies of this realm were starting to flash light.

Kevin and Caitlin instinctively looked behind them to see the scariest sight of all. Behind them, the entire realm was beginning to disintegrate.

Crumbling away into nothingness, the realm was falling into pieces, and only white was left behind. Things were starting to tear themselves apart, and the wave of disintegration was fast approaching.

"Oh no," said Kevin in disbelief, worried about what happened.

"Looks like the gods were right. We have to get out of here now!"

Instantly, Caitlin grabbed Kevin and took off into the sky with her angelic ability. There was no time for hesitation. They had to fly higher and higher, and they had to do it now. Somewhere above was the escape route where they had entered.

Below them, the realm was tearing apart faster from the ground up. Caitlin kept flying higher, looking for the hole, their only way to escape from death.

"Where's the hole in the realm?" she asked frantically. "It has to be in the sky somewhere, right? We fell in!"

Kevin was turning his head continuously, looking around for that hole. "It has to be!" he screamed back. "Hurry, Caitlin! The boundary below us is starting to rise!"

Which way was it?

Both Kevin and Caitlin were frantically looking around while Caitlin continued to shoot herself higher and higher, clutching Kevin by his arms to keep him from falling.

Suddenly, Caitlin saw it. "There!" she called out, pointing to it in the distance. It was just a small opening, a tear above that looked just like all of the holes that Kevin and Caitlin had seen before.

As quickly as she could, Caitlin started ascending in the direction of the hole. She had to keep going, keep moving.

Looking down, Kevin realized something horrific.

The realm below was eating itself away quickly. Caitlin still had a great distance to climb, greater than the distance between the angel and the boundary where the disintegration was happening.

And the boundary was advancing fast. Caitlin could not fly fast when she was carrying Kevin with her. At this rate, both of them would die before reaching the hole.

Kevin looked up at Caitlin. He knew that no matter what he said or did, Caitlin would not let go of him. Even as much as Caitlin and Kevin trusted each other, Caitlin would never knowingly give up Kevin.

Still, Kevin knew he was a dead man. But Caitlin did not need to die.

An idea came to Kevin's head. He had to save Caitlin if he

could, even if it meant surrendering his own life.

The words started to echo in Kevin's head again. If you truly believe in something, then you will give up everything you have for it. All of your worldly possessions: your wealth, your memories, your friendships, and even your love, must be forsaken for your cause. You must even be willing to give up your existence for what you fight for. Do not fear it, for if the cause is good, others will follow your example and fight for your cause. So be willing to forsake everything and follow your heart to a better future.

If you truly believe…

In Caitlin, in his angel, in his love, he truly did believe.

He wanted Caitlin to be safe, no matter the costs.

Quickly, he looked down again. It would be only a few seconds until the boundary impacted them, and they would both be disintegrated.

Caitlin looked down as well and saw this.

"We're not going to make it!" she exclaimed. "I can't go any faster, and the boundary's closing in!"

Kevin shook his head, then looked up at Caitlin. "No, we're not," he said. "But you will."

Eyes widening in surprise, Caitlin had no time to express any other reaction to what was about to happen next.

As quickly as he could, Kevin drew the Sword of Purity again. Rapidly, Kevin broke Caitlin's grip around him. The flip he pulled to break Caitlin's grip resulted in her necklace ripping and being knocked off, which he caught. Almost as instantly as it happened, Caitlin tried to turn back and pick him up quickly, but Kevin had other plans.

Holding the sword in front of him as he fell, Kevin said, "Great Vinz Larinion, help me save her!" and unleashed the flash of light energy as he had done in the battle at Rikleifer. Caitlin shrieked as the light made impact with her and forced her upward at an angle. It was such a powerful force that it threw her completely through the hole.

Seeing what he had done, Kevin closed his eyes and relaxed, glad to know that he had just saved the life of his angel, of his one true love. And now, with his mind at peace, he continued to fall, with a sense of serenity, into the disintegrating boundary.

Chapter 63

If You Truly Believe

Crash!

A loud explosion destroyed the Temple of Setaeus, exerting a force far beyond what had ever been seen in the mortal realm before.

At the very top of the explosion was Caitlin Amelia Magnon, having been thrown out with such enough force in time. Her body was shot through several layers of rock, as she went completely through the building as the explosion tore it apart.

Many eyes widened as they saw the rubble flying into the sky.

"Whoa!" exclaimed Resa Kirkwood, caught by surprise by the exploding temple much like everyone around her. "What in the world caused that?"

Outside the ruined Temple of Setaeus, Arthur and Rachel were still waiting alongside Vincent Stryker and Tyrinion, wondering what the result would be. Rouge and Resa Kirkwood had managed to catch up to them by this point, and it was up to Arthur to tell them about what had happened with Kevin and Caitlin.

Fortunately, they were all a safe distance away from the temple by now. The troops in town did not have much reason to linger around the temple either, so the area around it was mostly clear.

In stunned silence, Tyrinion shook his head. "Oh no," he said, staring in disbelief.

Before he could continue, Arthur interrupted him. "Look!" he exclaimed, pointing Tyrinion in the direction of something that had been launched through the air from the temple.

It was not a piece of rubble. It was a falling angel.

Immediately, Tyrinion launched himself skyward, higher and higher, to catch his daughter. He had to be very careful to avoid any of the flying rubble, but being as methodical as they come, he was able to navigate the rubble with very precise motion.

Down on the ground, as everyone else observed, Rouge asked, "How does he fly like that? As far as I know, magic doesn't let you do that."

"It doesn't," nodded Vincent Stryker, "but Tyrinion is a god. What he does have is divine power, which is what allows him to fly. We haven't seen him fly before only because he was keeping his identity secret until now."

After Vincent said this, everyone looked up to see Tyrinion with his daughter in his hands, lying across his arms. A great sense of worry spread across all of them, fearing that Caitlin might be unconscious, or worse.

As Tyrinion brought her down to the ground, it became clear that Caitlin was not unconscious or dead.

She was crying. She was hurt.

Only the damage was not physical.

Quickly seeking to help their friend and find out what happened, Arthur, Rachel, Rouge, Resa, and Vincent Stryker all clustered around the landing Tyrinion. When he landed, though, Caitlin rolled out of his hands onto the ground, and straight to her knees. Her tears would not stop falling, and the sounds she made would not be silenced.

"Setadev is gone," she cried, having to stop to cry some more, "but the price was too high!"

Rachel kneeled down to Caitlin's height and stroked her back to comfort her. "What happened?" she asked.

It took another minute of Caitlin crying before she could choke out the words. "Kevin… the realm started to tear itself apart… he knew we couldn't make it out of there together…" Caitlin's crying became louder, "…he sacrificed himself so I would get out alive…" At this point, Caitlin was crying too hard to make any more words.

It struck everyone like a thunderbolt.

Surprise and disbelief took hold of everyone. The thoughts of losing their best friend, the fears that they had all had for so long, had finally come to fruition. Whether or not the conquest of the realms were really over now, was it really worth the cost?

Not to Arthur. Not to Rachel. Not to Rouge or Resa. And certainly not to Vincent Stryker.

And for Caitlin, her nightmare had happened despite the fact that she had heeded Amelia's warning and stayed close to Kevin. The temple exploded with the force of the disintegrating realm below it and Kevin had been killed in the blast, trying to save her from having the same fate.

All of them began to join together with Caitlin to share their sadness and tears. The crying lasted for several minutes as everyone was huddled together. No one cried as hard as Caitlin did, however, who lost her love, the one who had set her heart free, the one who was her "Key of Hearts", the one who she truly loved from the very bottom of her heart.

And it was all so she could live.

Standing by himself, Tyrinion contemplated what had happened. "Maybe it was the stripes that caused it. Maybe Setadev's existence was been critical to the stability of the realm below, and eliminating him caused a chain reaction that destroyed the entire realm. We will never know for sure." Then, Tyrinion started shaking his head. "I should not have thought it was the best idea to let him go by himself," he said. "I should have gone in there with them."

"And what good would that have done?" asked Vincent Stryker. "Caitlin surviving the trip doesn't mean that you would have. Setadev's threat may have been legitimate. I know what Setadev was like, and so do you."

"I know," nodded Tyrinion, crossing his arms and lowering his head. He looked up briefly to see the stars starting to show in the sky as the darkness receded rapidly, proving that Kevin had accomplished the reversal. "Even so, I am still very bothered by this. He fell for something he believed in, but things did not need to happen that way."

"Yes they did," echoed a voice behind Tyrinion.

The voice caught everyone by surprise.

Suddenly, Arthur took a look around and noticed something very strange. "Hey, look around!" he exclaimed.

As everyone else took to what he said, they realized that time had stopped all around them. No one was moving. Dragons and phoenixes were stuck in midair. Only Arthur, Rachel, Rouge, Resa, Vincent Stryker, Caitlin, and Tyrinion had any awareness of what was happening, and what was about to happened as time had stopped.

Then, all of them turned to the voice that had come from behind Tyrinion. Descending from the air, across the starry sky, was the king of gods himself, Ralios Larion. Behind him and to his left and right sides, respectively, were Kronius and Chatka, and beside Kronius was Necnea, the goddess of time.

Larion touched the ground and bowed. "My apologies for catching you all at a time like this," he said, "but now had to be the time I had to speak with all of you. Pardon me for my intrusion to those of you who do not know who I am, but I am Lord Ralios Larion, king of gods and protector of the realms."

"Ralios Larion…" interrupted Tyrinion, his thought cycle brought to life, "I had not anticipated that Vinz Larinion would have selected you to be the next king of gods."

"It was a decision that had stunned most of the gods, Tyrinion," responded Larion, knowing full and well who Tyrinion was. "I am not here to discuss the semantics of deity affairs, however. I have come to deliver you all a message, personally."

Everyone else stood up and had to wipe their eyes. Though there was still a great deal of sadness in their eyes, listening to the words of the king of the gods was bound to be an important task. Never before had the king of gods come down to speak to mortals personally.

Chatka stepped forward in front of Larion, just as planned. "A great war has ended here in the mortal realm, ceasing things far beyond my own powers as the god of peace and war. For that, I am grateful to all of you. A dark kingdom has been laid to rest, and hope can return to the kingdoms of the mortal realm."

"Still, peace in the mortal realm was not enough," said Necnea as she stepped forward. "All of you have rescued the gods and allowed us to experience a greater freedom than we have had in a long time. Since you broke the seal on the Realm of the Angels, we have been able to observe what has happened, although we chose not to intervene."

"And Tyrinion, we are sorry to you," continued Kronius, picking up the speech. "We understand now that you are innocent of any crime against the gods. Hopefully, however, this will be the last time we will ever hear of Setadev. Now that we know the truth of his elaborate plan, we will not be fooled again."

Tyrinion nodded. "I am glad that the truth has finally come upon you all," he said.

Larion then continued, responding to what Tyrinion said, "You are more than welcome to return to the Realm of the Angels at any time that you want, Tyrinion. I am more than sure that most of the gods miss you and would love to see you take the reins as god of darkness again."

"Thank you for the offer, but for now I must respectfully decline," answered Tyrinion, very sure of himself. "Despite the fact that the situation that drove me away turned out to be an odd case of mistaken identity because of Setadev, I am still affected by the stigma of returning to where I was exiled."

"It is your home," responded Larion, "and you should never forget that. Still, your invitation to return is open-ended. Whenever you want to return, if only for a visit, you will be welcomed."

Tyrinion nodded. "I will remember that. Thank you, my lord."

"You are welcome," said Larion. Then, he turned to Arthur. "Arthur Falchor, heir of Desolunar and carrier of the Sword of Corruption, would you step forward?"

Arthur did as he was asked. His mind was not completely in focus given the fate that had happened to Kevin, but he knew it was important to listen to whatever the king of gods had to say to him.

"Though I am sure much of the land of Desolunar will be given back to Aurana and Nuve," continued Larion after Arthur had stepped forward, "there will still be thousands of people in Seta Archa that need a leader. They will be looking to you, since Demonicus has been removed. Will you take the mantle of command here, and make this land yours?"

That made Arthur freeze up. It was the last thing he was thinking about, to have the keys to a kingdom simply handed over to him, much less the one whose ruler had cursed his mind and created such a sense of injustice. A kingdom that was his? Even if it was his father's, that did not mean he had to rule like his father had. He could set things in Desolunar the right way, and see to it that his people were well cared for. Still, it was an awful lot of responsibility. But what would Kevin say? Arthur had to think about that one, but he came to the conclusion that Kevin would tell Arthur to do the right thing, regardless of the burden that would be placed on his shoulders. After all, Kevin himself had bore such a burden for so long.

And he would have help if he really wanted it. The assassin sisters Rouge and Resa would help, and though Arthur was a little unsure, he was hopeful that Rachel might be willing to help as well. Maybe even his half-sister Caitlin would, although for the moment Arthur figured it would take some time until she was over Kevin's death enough to even consider it. Finally, after a long moment of thought, Arthur nodded. "For the people," he said. "I'm sure it's what Kevin would have wanted."

Larion nodded again. "Very well," he said. He then turned to Vincent Stryker and continued, "With respect, Vincent Stryker, we owe you a great deal of gratitude for being the first to take the position of the pure one, and though you failed to defeat Setadev yourself, you set forth the groundwork that would lead to his eventual defeat. And for that, we thank you."

Vincent shook his head. "I'm not a hero," he said. "I never did anything worthy of your respect, Ralios Larion."

"Kevin never thought of himself as a hero, either," added Larion, somewhat interrupting Vincent Stryker. "Still, he continued on because he knew that he was the one who was willing to do it. You do not need to be a hero, though, to be deserving of our gratitude. You need only be the one who steps up. By being willing to accept the sacrifice of a god, making the attempt to do the impossible, and sticking through it to help your son despite your initial failure, you deserve all of the gratitude we have."

This time, Vincent nodded. He could accept that.

Larion then turned to Rachel, Rouge, Resa, Arthur, and Caitlin, who were all standing together. Tears were still dripping heavily from Caitlin's eyes, much less so from everyone else. "The same goes for all of you," continued Larion. "You five, along with the fallen phoenix Wheldon, must be the best friends in the world. It is astounding that despite the burden Kevin had to carry, all of you stuck by him and helped him through it. It is unlikely that he would have survived for so long without all of his friends. We thank you so much for everything, and in return, we are very hopeful to see what kind of futures all of you will have."

In response, Rachel took a step forward and gave a nice little curtsey. "We're honored," she said. "Thank you, Larion."

Shaking his head, Larion responded, "No, thank *you*, Rachel Reinhart."

Rachel had to resist the urge to smile from that. Though it was still a depressing time, how often does the king of gods remember your name?

Still, though, there was one more thing on Larion's mind as he looked past Rachel and the others to see Caitlin, with tears still falling from her eyes. Gently, Larion walked up to Caitlin and wrapped his arms around her. "Angel," he began, "for you, we have the greatest gift we can bestow. We have been observing you and Kevin since your departure from the Realm of the Angels. The truth be told, we feel it is necessary to tell you that we violated our policies."

Caitlin rolled her head up to look into Larion's eyes. "What are you saying?" she asked.

Larion raised his head from looking down into Caitlin's eyes to looking toward everyone. "Now, we are fully well aware that we must be wary of the consequences of our actions," he continued, "but we will do our best to deal with that should it come around to bite us. That being said, we feel strongly that Kevin Trent Stryker's fate to be was not warranted, and his mortal life, as we came to realize, meant more to us than any other mortal life that we had ever observed before."

Caitlin gasped at what she realized he was saying. "You mean…"

"Yes, young angel," nodded Larion. "We intervened. Kevin Trent Stryker is alive, and he is waiting for you."

A glimmer of hope came across everyone's face. Caitlin's face in particular lit up like crazy as she started to float uncontrollably off the ground and her angel wings became even brighter. "Really?" she asked in a very hopeful tone.

"Really," responded Larion.

Almost simultaneously, a wave of celebration came from Arthur, Rachel, Rouge, Resa, and Vincent Stryker. Tears of happiness were in the eyes of everyone. Then, Vincent Stryker asked, "So where is he?"

"Above," answered Larion, ever serious, "in the Realm of the Angels. Before he returns, however, he has asked to speak with Caitlin personally, and then he will be back to see everyone again." Larion extended his hand to Caitlin. "Please come with me," he continued, looking directly into Caitlin's eyes. "I will take you to him myself."

Caitlin's eyes were still full of tears, although now they were tears of happiness. For her, the answer was obvious. "Take me to him!" she nearly exclaimed, so happy as she stared at Larion. She was so excited that she jumped over toward Rachel, looking for someone to hug because of how glad she was she was.

Rachel raised her arms, almost laughing a little bit at how excited Caitlin was. "Hey, easy now," she said, happiness in her voice as well, "we're all excited to see Kevin again, but leap at him like this and you just might break him."

Gently, Caitlin let go, laughing a little bit at her own folly. Rachel could see in Caitlin's eyes the tears of happiness that were continuing to fall.

Then, Arthur walked up and extended his arms as well, allowing Caitlin to hug him too, letting them share a special moment. "Bring him back in one piece, okay, sis?"

"Of course!" said Caitlin, as she pulled back and nodded. "I'll bring him home for all of you guys." Caitlin then parted away from Arthur and Rachel. "Thank you all… for everything."

There was a nod from Arthur, Rachel, Rouge, Resa, and Vincent. They were together united, and knew Caitlin would bring back Kevin with her to make them whole once again. And had Wheldon still been around, he would have been proud as well.

"Very well, then," nodded Larion. He then raised his head again. "To the rest of you, I am sure we will be back shortly, with Kevin and Caitlin. In the mean time, the time flow here will restart."

Nodding, Caitlin grabbed onto Larion's robes to follow him. Then, Larion began lifting off the ground, with the gods behind him following him. "We will see you soon," he said.

As Larion, Caitlin, and the gods floated higher, everyone below was waving goodbye to them, knowing that they would be back soon.

The time flow was restored by Necnea as the gods continued to ascend out of sight. Perhaps, maybe the future would not be so bleak after all.

The future was just around the corner.

Larion and the gods continued to fly higher and higher, eventually passing through the boundary into the Realm of the Angels. As they did, Caitlin looked around in amazement at the realm's golden-cloud landscape. She had seen it before, but even so, it was still such a striking sight.

Then, Larion brought Caitlin down to the ground. He let go of her and took a few steps back. "Where is he?" asked Caitlin.

Suddenly, Caitlin felt herself being hugged from behind. "Right behind you," said the voice of Kevin.

It caught her by surprise, in the most pleasant way possible.

"I'm really sorry, Caitlin," Kevin said as he held onto Caitlin tightly, "but I had to save you even if it meant dying myself. I'm sorry that I made you so sad, that I hurt you so badly. Can you ever forgive me?"

Caitlin turned in Kevin's arms so that she would face Kevin. Then, she wrapped her own arms around him. "I'd do the same for you if it ever came to that," she said. "It's all going to be okay now, just because I have you here with me."

"I know," Kevin said as he held her tightly. "I love you, Caitlin."

"And I love you too, Kevin." Caitlin hugged him even tighter and kissed him

They held onto each other for over a minute, sharing a kiss the whole time. Then, for a second, Kevin let go of Caitlin. He reached into his pocket, and pulled something out. He laid the necklace over her neck, and retied it. "I didn't mean to accidentally remove your Key of Hearts. I hope you can forgive me for that."

Caitlin looked down to see her Key of Hearts, and with her right hand she clutched it. More tears of happiness started to come to Caitlin's eyes as she looked at the key on a necklace. "It's okay, Kevin," she said as she kissed him and went back to hugging him tightly. "I'll never take it off. Every time I see it, I'm going to think of you, and I'll be happy."

Silently, Kevin nodded.

Caitlin was happy.

There was peace in the realms for the first time in over twenty years.

Yet the words of Setadev still stuck in Kevin's head. They were the darkest words that Kevin had ever heard, and still they echoed through his head, even as the sensations of relief and happiness were in his head. It was that sense of doubt that perhaps Setadev had not been truly defeated after all.

The words rang out.

You cannot defeat me, for I am nothing.

Nothing. How could one with a physical form be nothing? What was Setadev's true intention?

It did not matter. Setadev was gone, and now only the best of life remained. Love, friendship, and fulfillment. Kevin needed only look into what was wrapped around him, hugging him, to see the best of life. Somewhere in the eyes of an angel was the brightest light he had ever seen.

Kevin reached back around and held Caitlin again. He kept himself in her arms, and together, for just a moment, it felt like they were one.

Epilogue

To: The Reinhart Family
Rikleifer, Aurana: Office of Postage and Messages
Please Deliver Personally

If letter cannot be delivered, return to:
Rachel Reinhart
Seta Archa, Solunar Empire: Capital Building

Dear Mom and Dad,

How have you been? I know, I have a lot to explain for since I left on my own a few months ago. I wish I could have told you more when I had the opportunity, but it seems like things just didn't work out the way I was hoping they would.

It's been a few weeks now since the end of the battle at Seta Archa, and life has certainly been different, that's for sure. I understand, though, that you heard what happened from some of the Auranian troops returning home, and that Vincent Stryker himself came to talk to you guys and told you the whole story of where I've been and the people I've been with, so I thought I might try and catch you guys up on how things have been going since then from my own perspectives.

After Arthur Falchor was given rule of Desolunar following the fall of Seta Archa, he made several decisions to try and help the people here. So much of it is going to change the world as we know it, and I'm excited to see what will happen. The first thing he decided to do was to change the system of government: although Desolunar was always called a "kingdom", Arthur recognized it as more of a dictatorship even though just like a monarchy, leadership was passed to him. He came to the realization that he was a leader over several domains: over the city-state of Seta Archa and of all of the tribes of the Wastes, which were their own separate nations yet part of the state of the kingdom of Desolunar. So, Arthur brought together all of the leaders of the tribes, with the help of Chief Aspectra of the Metoi, and forged an empire from it. He is now Emperor Arthur I of the Solunar Empire, and the tribal chiefs who follow him are all his council and advisors.

Speaking of which, Arthur did change his nation's name from "Desolunar" to "Solunar", claiming it to be a symbolism of the good he would do for his people. He's added orange to the flag's color, and created a sort of sunburst of orange from a black horizon as the empire's flag. He still uses his father's capital as the empire's capital building, and he flies the flag of the Solunar Empire plus the standards of any tribe that has them, as well as some of the old standards of the city of Seta Archa.

Still, it didn't leave very many people to control his empire, so Arthur asked some of his closest friends to help. He asked Kevin at first if he would do anything to help, but Kevin declined, saying that it wasn't really his thing to be a world leader. So, Arthur made some other decisions. I think he really took some things to heart, like how women had not been treated well in Desolunar before. Arthur decided to counter this in some unique ways, and it all started with his new Vanguards: Rouge and Resa Kirkwood. Not only are they the first female Vanguards the world has ever seen, they're also the first to represent this new nation.

Then, Arthur gave me the shock of my life: he asked me to be his Prime Minister! I was so excited! I guess it means you'll have to expect me to be wearing black and orange when I come back. It's so neat to be the Prime Minister of a new country, and the idea was so awesome that I just couldn't say no, whether or not I realistically thought I could do it yet. Hmmm, guess maybe my friends are starting to influence me! That also means, of course, that I might not be coming back to Aurana for a while. Maybe you guys would like to come and visit me, then. I know, it isn't exactly a happy situation, because I will miss you guys, but it's not every day your daughter gets to be the Prime Minister, you know. Recently, I've been very busy with it, dealing with recalling all the former Desolunar troops back to Seta Archa, starting new relations, and all that. I think you'll be glad to know, though, that I'm still not going to give up on my dreams and what I do best. I'm still practicing archery and I'm still writing. In fact, I'm writing a book about the events of the last few months. I'm sure you guys would love to have it once it's done.

Things are a little weird, though, since Arthur put his first prisoner in the dungeon. After a long amount of thought, Arthur finally put his father down there as a sign of giving the sorrowful dictator a second chance at being a father. Demonicus hasn't taken this harshly, fully well aware that his decisions in life have consequences that must be served. Arthur goes down to visit him quite a bit, although he never goes behind the locked door. What their relationship is, I'm not really sure, since Arthur only goes down there by himself, no exceptions.

As for the others, well, let's just say things have been interesting. Professor Magnon was finally allowed back home after so many years of banishment, when it was realized that after all these years he was innocent of the crimes he was accused of. Even so, though, he still lives in Aurana to do the one thing he has passion in his life for: teaching. He comes to visit his daughter and Kevin quite a bit, too.

Kron Kalavere managed to get much more respect from his peers for his role in this whole incident. We haven't heard from Kron in a little while, but we hear that everything's going all right with him in the time that's passed.

Scurnia and the Lord Dragon's Knights of the Dragon are still on their return to Scurnia. The trip takes an awful long time for them, but it sounds like with the issues with Gardolk settled and this battle at Seta Archa finally over, peace is finally headed to Scurnia for the first time in a long time.

As for Nuve, though, things don't look so bright over there. Though Nuve's capital city of Cardol was returned to them by Arthur, and all of their lands returned to them as they originally were, the factions of Nuve still have yet to settle their differences. It appears now that they are headed toward becoming three separate countries; according to Arthur, the expectation is for Cornelia to become its own state in the southwest by the Cornelia Chimeras, and for a new state to be formed in northern Nuve by the Demons, with its capital in Edenbrook. Whether or not that will actually happen is yet to be determined, but only time will really tell.

King Andrew II hasn't been happier since this war ended, I hear.

He should just be making it back to Aurana City by now after he stayed here for a while as a guest. Lucky for him, Arthur arranged for a gryphon flight to take him home after the stay.

Hey, you know, the more that I think about it, Mom and Dad, I think it's kind of odd that so many of the world leaders right now are so young. Aurana's King Andrew II is eighteen, and Arthur is sixteen here. Though it's pretty odd, I've got a strange confidence in both of them. Andrew is very bright and well taught in diplomacy and all the important stuff, and Arthur, well, as much of a jokester as he is, he's got the spirit and the right ideas. Importantly, they both listen to the opinions of others. Don't worry, Mom and Dad, I'll make sure he gets it right.

I'm sure you guys heard of the phoenixes of Avalon, too. They've been doing well, although Kevin and the Red Phoenix had to have a serious talk about the egg reborn from Wheldon's ashes, as it was something that had not happened in a long time and there was no real reason for why there was a resurrection in that case. Nonetheless, the Red Phoenix decided to keep the egg himself, but promised to allow all of us to visit depending on what became of it.

I doubt Vincent Stryker told you of what's going on with himself, so I might as well share it with you. The great war hero's going to be moving into the castle at Rikleifer, to be taken care of by the Duke of Rikleifer. The Duke has already sworn to try and help him get back into good health, since Vincent has actually injured himself more by taking part in the war activities. He didn't take a specific injury, just a history of repetitive damage. It's uncertain if he'll ever be back in shape again, but we can only hope so.

The longest story, though, has to be of Kevin. After victory at the battle, Kevin was offered a lot of money from a lot of nations for what he did in bringing the nations together, leading the Vanguard unit in the battle, and overthrowing Demonicus alongside Arthur. He declined all of them. The one thing he did accept, though, was a stipend from King Andrew II to serve as the Vanguard of Aurana and continue to serve in that position. It came with some perks: a moderate middle-class salary, a private room in the Royal Palace in Aurana City to be reserved at all times for the Vanguard, and respect from the officials of Aurana. The amount of money itself that Kevin will receive monthly won't make him rich, or even upper-middle class, but it'll be enough that he won't need to worry about money again.

For the most part, though, Kevin still lives in Rikleifer, in his mother's old home. Unlike a few months ago, however, there's someone living with Kevin too, and that's Caitlin. She's still practicing magic, but has been mixing in the new powers she's developed into her repertoire, and is still exploring and learning a lot about life. So much has changed for her since her heart opened up, and it has been almost like she still has to learn everything about life all over again. Still, she's got a good start with Kevin by her side all of the time. Around the time they got back to Rikleifer together, Kevin promised her that he would show her everything she was missing from life. I doubt that Kevin knows the whole world, but you know, they'll be fine together.

It's really hard being so far away from Kevin and Caitlin. Somehow, I don't think I'd be quite the same without them. Things will be all right with Arthur, though, and I'm looking forward to working a lot with him. No, Mom and Dad, I'm not in any relationship with Arthur, and you can't expect any grandchildren soon. I'm sure you're breathing a sigh of relief right about now!

It's been hard being away from the two of you as well, you know. I didn't really feel ready to leave home yet, but I guess you guys have heard the story by now and hopefully you can agree with me that it just seemed to work out that way. I promise I'll make it up to you guys, though, and I'll find a way to come and visit you soon.

Keep in touch, Mom and Dad, and don't forget to write. I'm sure I could use the letters for my own sanity. If I forget to answer one, then don't worry about it. It just means that I'm either really busy or I'm being dragged along on another journey doing who-knows-what. If that's the case, well, I guess I'm just a lost cause then, aren't I?

Your daughter, Rachel Reinhart

www.ingramcontent.com/pod-product-compliance
Lightning Source LLC
LaVergne TN
LVHW050908080826
845145LV00001B/5

* 9 7 8 0 9 8 9 7 9 6 6 0 6 *